TRANSGRESSIONS

TRANSGRESSIONS

Edited by Ed McBain

A TOM DOHERTY ASSOCIATES BOOK
NEW YORK

TRANSGRESSIONS

This book is printed on acid-free paper.

Book design by Mary A. Wirth

A Forge Book
Published by Tom Doherty Associates, LLC
175 Fifth Avenue
New York, NY 10010

www.tor.com

Forge® is a registered trademark of Tom Doherty Associates, LLC.

ISBN 0-765-30851-7
EAN 978-0765-30851-1
ISBN 0-765-31443-6 (Limited Edition)
EAN 978-0765-31443-7 (Limited Edition)

First Edition: May 2005
Printed in the United States of America

0 9 8 7 6 5 4 3 2 1

28

Contents

INTRODUCTION *by Ed McBain* 7

WALKING AROUND MONEY *by Donald E. Westlake* 11

HOSTAGES *by Anne Perry* 75

THE CORN MAIDEN: A LOVE STORY *by Joyce Carol Oates* 131

ARCHIBALD LAWLESS, ANARCHIST AT LARGE: WALKING THE LINE *by Walter Mosley* 223

THE RESURRECTION MAN *by Sharyn McCrumb* 311

MERELY HATE *by Ed McBain* 375

THE THINGS THEY LEFT BEHIND *by Stephen King* 451

THE RANSOME WOMEN *by John Farris* 481

FOREVER *by Jeffery Deaver* 603

KELLER'S ADJUSTMENT *by Lawrence Block* 725

Introduction

When I was writing novellas for the pulp magazines back in the 1950s, we still called them "novelettes," and all I knew about the form was that it was long and it paid half a cent a word. This meant that if I wrote 10,000 words, the average length of a novelette back then, I would sooner or later get a check for five hundred dollars. This was not bad pay for a struggling young writer.

A novella today can run anywhere from 10,000 to 40,000 words. Longer than a short story (5,000 words) but much shorter than a novel (at least 60,000 words) it combines the immediacy of the former with the depth of the latter, and it ain't easy to write. In fact, given the difficulty of the form, and the scarcity of markets for novellas, it is surprising that any writers today are writing them at all.

But here was the brilliant idea.

Round up the best writers of mystery, crime, and suspense novels, and ask them to write a brand-new novella for a collection of similarly superb novellas to be published anywhere in the world for the very first time. Does that sound keen, or what? In a perfect world, *yes*, it *is* a wonderful idea, and here is your novella, sir, thank you very much for asking me to contribute.

But many of the bestselling novelists I approached had never written a novella in their lives. (Some of them had never even written a short story!) Up went the hands in mock horror. "What! A novella? I wouldn't even know how to *begin* one." Others thought that writing a novella ("*How* long did you say it had to be?") would constitute a wonderful challenge, but bestselling novelists are busy people with publishing contracts to fulfill and deadlines to meet, and however intriguing the invitation may have seemed at first, stark reality reared its ugly head, and so . . .

"Gee, thanks for thinking of me, but I'm already three months behind deadline," or . . .

"My publisher would *kill* me if I even dreamed of writing something for another house," or . . .

"Try me again a year from now," or . . .

"Have you asked X? Or Y? Or Z?"

What it got down to in the end was a matter of timing and luck. In some cases, a writer I desperately wanted was happily between novels and just happened to have some free time on his/her hands. In other cases, a writer had an idea that was too short for a novel but too long for a short story, so yes, what a wonderful opportunity! In yet other cases, a writer wanted to introduce a new character he or she had been thinking about for some time. In each and every case, the formidable task of writing fiction that fell somewhere between 10,000 and 40,000 words seemed an exciting challenge, and the response was enthusiastic.

Except for length and a loose adherence to crime, mystery, or suspense, I placed no restrictions upon the writers who agreed to contribute. The results are as astonishing as they are brilliant. The ten novellas that follow are as varied as the men and women who concocted them, but they all exhibit the same devoted passion and the same extraordinary writing. More than that, there is an underlying sense here that the writer is attempting something new and unexpected, and willing to share his or her own surprises with us. Just as their names are in alphabetical order on the book jacket, so do their stories follow in reverse alphabetical order: I have no favorites among them. I love them all equally.

Enjoy!

ED MCBAIN
Weston, Connecticut
August 2004

TRANSGRESSIONS

Donald E. Westlake

It's an accepted fact that **Donald E. Westlake** has excelled at every single subgenre the mystery field has to offer. Humorous books such as *Sacred Monster* and the John Dortmunder series; terrifying books like *The Ax*, about a man who wants vengeance on the company that downsized him out of a job, and probably Westlake's most accomplished novel; and hard-boiled books that include the Parker series, a benchmark in the noir world of professional thieves and to which he recently returned to great acclaim; and insider books like *The Hook*, a twisty thriller about the perils and pitfalls of being a writer. One learns from his novels and short stories that he is possessed of a remarkable intelligence, and that he can translate that intelligence into plot, character, and realistic prose with what appears to be astonishing ease. He is the sort of writer other writers study endlessly; every Westlake novel has something to teach authors, no matter how long they've been at the word processor. And he seems to have been discovered—at last and long overdue—by a mass audience. His recent books include *The Road to Ruin*, the latest novel chronicling the misadventures of inept thief John Dortmunder, and *Thieves' Dozen*, a long-awaited collection of the Dortmunder short stories.

WALKING AROUND MONEY

Donald E. Westlake

1

"Ever since I reformed," the man called Querk said, "I been havin' trouble to sleep at night."

This was a symptom Dortmunder had never heard of before; on the other hand, he didn't know that many people who'd reformed. "Huh," he said. He really didn't know this man called Querk, so he didn't have a lot to say so far.

But Querk did. "It's my nerves," he explained, and he looked as though it was his nerves. A skinny little guy, maybe fifty, with a long face, heavy black eyebrows over banana nose over thin-lipped mouth over long bony chin, he fidgeted constantly on that wire-mesh chair in Paley Park, a vest-pocket park on East 53rd Street in Manhattan, between Fifth and Madison Avenues.

It's a very nice park, Paley Park, right in the middle of midtown, just forty-two feet wide and not quite a block deep, up several steps from the level of 53rd Street. The building walls on both sides are covered in ivy, and tall honey locust trees form a kind of leafy roof in the summer, which is what at this moment it was.

But the best thing about Paley Park is the wall of water at the back, a constant flow down the rear wall, splashing into a trough to be recycled, making a very nice kind of *shooshing* sound that almost completely covers the roar of the traffic, which makes for a peaceful retreat right there in the middle of everything and also makes it possible for two or three people—John Dortmunder, say, and his friend Andy Kelp, and the man called Querk, for instance—to sit near the wall of water and have a nice conversation that nobody, no matter what kind of microphone they've got, is going to record. It's amazing, really, that every criminal enterprise in the city of New York isn't plotted in Paley Park; or maybe they are.

"You see how it is," the man called Querk said, and lifted both hands out of his lap to hold them in front of himself, where they trembled like a paint-mixing machine. "It's a good thing," he said, "I wasn't a pickpocket before I reformed."

"Huh," Dortmunder commented.

"Or a safecracker," Kelp said.

"Well, I was," Querk told him. "But I was one of your liquid nitro persuasion, you know. Drill your hole next to the combination, pour in your jelly, stuff the detonator in there, stand back. No nerves involved at all."

"Huh," Dortmunder said.

Querk frowned at him. "You got asthma?"

"No," Dortmunder said. "I was just agreeing with you."

"If you say so." Querk frowned at the curtain of water, which just kept *shooshing* down that wall in front of them, splashing in the trough, never stopping for a second. You wouldn't want to stay in Paley Park *too* long.

"The point is," Querk said, "before I reformed, I'd always get a good night's sleep, because I knew I was careful and everything was in its place, so I could relax. But then, the last time I went up, I decided I was too old for jail. You know, there comes a point, you say, jail is a job for the young." He gave a sidelong look at Dortmunder. "You gonna do that *huh* thing again?"

"Only if you want me to."

"We'll skip it, then," Querk said, and said, "This last time in, I learned another trade, you know how you always learn these trades on the inside. Air-conditioner repair, dry cleaning. This last time, I learned to be a printer."

"Huh," Dortmunder said. "I mean, that's good, you're a printer."

"Except," Querk said, "I'm not. I get out, I go to this printing plant upstate, up near where my cousin lives, I figure I'll stay with him, he's always been your straight arrow, I can get a look at an honest person up close, see how it's done, but when I go to the printer to say look at this skill the State of New York gave me, they said, we don't do it like that any more, we use computers now." Querk shook his head. "Is that the criminal justice system for you, right there?" he wanted to know. "They spend all this time and money, they teach me an obsolete trade."

Kelp said, "What you wanted to learn was computers."

"Well, what I got," Querk said, "I got a job at the printing plant, only not a printer. I'm a loader, when the different papers come in, I drive around in this forklift, put the papers where they go, different papers for different jobs. But because I'm reformed," Querk went on, "and this isn't the trade I learned, this is just going back and forth on a forklift truck, I don't ever feel like I *done* anything. No planning, no preparation, nothing to be careful about. I get uneasy, I got no structure in my life, and the result is, I sleep lousy. Then, no sleep, I'm on the forklift, half the time I almost drive it into a wall."

Dortmunder could see how that might happen. People are creatures of habit, and if you lose a habit that's important to you—being on the run, for instance—it could throw off your whatayacallit. Biorhythm. Can't sleep. Could happen.

Dortmunder and Andy Kelp and the man called Querk sat in silence (*shoosh*) a while, contemplating the position Querk found himself in, sitting here together on these nice wire-mesh chairs in the middle of New York in August, which of course meant it wasn't New York at all, not the real New York, but the other New York, the August New York.

In August, the shrinks are all out of town, so the rest of the city population looks calmer, less stressed. Also, a lot of *those* are out of town, as well, replaced by American tourists in pastel polyester and foreign tourists in vinyl and corduroy. August among the tourists is like all at once living in a big herd of cows; slow, fat, dumb, and no idea where they're going.

What Dortmunder had no idea was where *Querk* was going. All he knew was, Kelp had phoned him this morning to say there was a guy they might talk to who might have something to say and the name the guy was using as a password was Harry Matlock. Well, Harry Matlock was a guy Dortmunder had worked with in the past, with Matlock's partner Ralph Demrovsky, but it seemed to him the last time he'd seen Ralph, during a little exercise in Las Vegas, Harry wasn't there. So how good a passport *was* that, after all this time? That's why Dortmunder's part of the conversation so far, and on into the unforeseeable future, consisted primarily of *huh*.

"So finally," the man called Querk said, breaking a long *shoosh*, "I couldn't take it any more. I'm imitating my cousin, walkin the straight and narrow, and that's what it feels like, I'm *imitating* my cousin. Once a month I drive up to this town called Hudson, see my lady parole officer, I *got nothin to hide*. How can you talk to a parole officer in a circumstance like that? She keeps giving me these suspicious looks, and I know why. I got nothin' to tell her but the truth."

"Jeez, that's tough," Kelp said.

"You know it." Querk shook his head. "And all along," he said, "I've got a caper right there, right at the printing plant, staring me in the face, I don't want to see it, I don't want to know about it, I gotta act like I'm deaf and dumb and blind."

Dortmunder couldn't help himself; he said, "At the printing plant?"

"Oh, sure, I know," Querk said. "Your inside job, I'm first in line to get my old cell back. But that isn't the way it works." Querk seemed very earnest about this. "The only way this scheme works," he said, "is if the plant never knows it happened. If they find out, we don't make a thing."

Dortmunder said, "It's a heist."

"A *quiet* heist," Querk told him. "No hostages, no explosions, no standoffs. In, out, nobody ever knows it happened. Believe me, the only way this scores for us is if nobody ever knows anything went missing."

"Huh," Dortmunder said.

"You oughta try cough drops," Querk suggested. "But the point here is, this is a beautiful job, and I'm sick of getting no sleep, so maybe I'll leave reform alone for a while. But."

"Sure," Kelp said, because there was always a "but."

"I can't do it alone," Querk told them. "This is not a one-man job. So I was on the inside for six and a half years, and I'm both reformed *and* upstate for almost eighteen months, so I'm well and truly out of the picture. I try calling around, everybody's inside or dead or disappeared, and finally I reach Harry Matlock, that I knew years ago, when he first partnered up with Ralph Demrovsky, and now *Harry's* retired."

"I thought he maybe was," Dortmunder said.

Querk nodded. "He told me," he said, "*he's* not reformed, he's retired. It's a different thing. 'I didn't reform,' he told me, 'I just lost my nerve. So I retired.' "

"Pretty much the same thing," Kelp suggested.

"But with more dignity," Querk told him. "So he gave me your name, Andy Kelp, and now here we are, and we look each other over."

"Right," Kelp said. "So what next?"

"Well," Querk said, "I check you guys out, and if you seem—"

Dortmunder said, "What? *You* check *us* out?" He'd thought the interview was supposed to go in the other direction.

"Naturally," Querk said. "I don't want us goin' along and goin' along, everything's fine, and all of a sudden you yell *surprise* and pull out a badge."

"That would surprise the hell out of *me*," Dortmunder told him.

"We're strangers to each other," Querk pointed out. "I gave Kelp a few names, he could check on me, and he gave me a few names, I could check on him and you both—"

"Huh," Dortmunder said.

"So after we all meet here now," Querk said, "and we check each other out, and we think it's gonna be okay, I'll call Andy here, same as this time, and if you two are satisfied, we can make another meet."

Dortmunder said, "You didn't tell us what the heist is."

"That's right," Querk said. Looking around, he said, "Okay with you guys if I go first? You'll wanna talk about me behind my back anyway."

"Sure," Kelp agreed. "Nice to meet you, Kirby," because, Querk had said, that was his first name.

"You, too," Querk said, and nodded at Dortmunder. "I like the way you keep your own counsel."

"Uh huh," Dortmunder said.

2

If you walk far enough into the west side, even in August, you can find a bar without tourists, ferns, or menus, and where the lights won't offend your eyes. In such a place, a little later that afternoon,

Dortmunder and Kelp hunched over beers in a black Formica booth and muttered together, while the bartender behind his bar some distance away leaned his elbows on the *Daily News*, and the three other customers, here and there around the place, muttered to themselves in lieu of company.

"I'm not sure what I think about this guy," Dortmunder muttered.

"He *seems* okay." Kelp shrugged. "I mean, I could buy his story. Reforming and all."

"But he's pretty cagy," Dortmunder muttered.

"Well, sure. He don't know us."

"He doesn't tell us the caper."

"That's sensible, John."

"He's living upstate." Dortmunder spread his hands. "*Where* upstate? Where's this printing plant? All he says is he goes to some place called Hudson to see his parole officer."

Kelp nodded, being open-minded. "Look at it from his point of view," he muttered. "If things don't work out between him and us, and he's gonna go ahead with some other guys, why does he wanna have to worry we're somewhere in the background, lookin to cut in?"

"I mean, what kind of heist is this?" Dortmunder complained. "You steal something from this plant, and the plant isn't supposed to *notice*? 'Hey, didn't we use to have a whatchacallit over here?' You take something, especially you take something with some value on it, people notice."

"Well, that's an intriguing part of it," Kelp muttered.

"Intriguing."

"Also," Kelp muttered, leaning closer, "August is a good time to get out of town. Go upstate, up into the mountains, a little cool air, how bad could it be?"

"I've been upstate," Dortmunder reminded him. "I *know* how bad it could be."

"Not that bad, John. And you were up there in the winter."

"*And* the fall," Dortmunder muttered. "Two different times."

"They both worked out okay."

"Okay? Every time I leave the five boroughs," Dortmunder insisted, "I regret it."

"Still," Kelp muttered, "we shouldn't just say no to this, without giving it a chance."

Dortmunder made an irritable shrug. He'd had his say.

"I don't know about *your* finances, John," Kelp went on (although he did), "but mine are pretty shaky. A nice little upstate heist might be just the ticket."

Dortmunder frowned at his beer.

"I tell you what we should do," Kelp said. "We should find old Harry Matlock, get the skinny on this guy Querk, *then* make up our minds. Whadaya say?"

"Mutter," Dortmunder muttered.

3

Where do you find a retired guy, sometime in August? Try a golf course; a municipal golf course.

"There he is, over there," Kelp said, pointing. "Tossing the ball out of that sand trap."

Dortmunder said, "Is that in the rules?"

"Well, remember," Kelp said. "He's retired, not reformed."

This particular municipal golf course was in Brooklyn, not far enough from the Atlantic to keep you from smelling what the ocean offers for sea air these days. Duffers speckled the greensward as Dortmunder and Kelp strolled over the fairway toward where Harry Matlock, who was fatter than he used to be and who'd always been thought of by everybody who knew him as fat, was struggling out of the sand trap, looking as though he needed an assistant to toss *him* up onto the grass. He was also probably as bald as ever, but you couldn't tell because he was wearing a big pillowy maroon tam-o'-shanter with a woolly black ball on top and a little paisley spitcurl coming out the back. The rest of his garb was a pale blue polo shirt under an open white cashmere cardigan, red plaid pants very wide in the seat and leg, and bright toad-green golf shoes with little cleats like chipmunk teeth. This was a man in retirement.

"Hey, Harry!" Kelp shouted, and a guy off to his left sliced his shot then glared at Kelp, who didn't notice.

Harry looked over, recognized them, and waved with a big smile, but didn't shout. When they got closer, he said, "Hi, Andy, hi, John, you're here about Kirby Querk."

"Sure," Kelp said.

Harry waved his golf club in a direction, saying, "Walk with me, my foursome's up there somewhere, we can talk." Then, pausing to kick his golf ball toward the far-distant flag, he picked up his big bulky leather golf bag by its strap, and started to stroll, dragging the pretty full golf bag behind him, leaving a crease in the fairway.

As they walked, Dortmunder said, "These your own rules?"

"When only God can see you, John," Harry told him, "there are no rules. And when it comes to Querk, I wouldn't say I know what the rules are."

Sounding alarmed, Kelp said, "You mean, you wouldn't recommend him? But you sent him to me."

"No, that's not exactly what I— Hold on." Harry kicked the ball again, then said, "Andy, would you do me a favor? Drag this bag around for a while? This arm's gettin longer than that arm."

Kelp said, "I think you're supposed to carry it on your shoulder."

"I tried that," Harry said, "and it winds up, one shoulder lower than the other." He extended the strap toward Kelp, with a little pleading gesture. "Just till we get to the green," he said.

Kelp had not known his visit to the golf course today would end with his being a caddy, but he shrugged and said, "Okay. Till the green."

"Thanks, Andy."

Kelp hefted the bag up onto his shoulder, and he *looked* like a caddy. All he needed was the big-billed cloth cap and the tee stuck behind his ear. He did have the right put-upon expression.

Harry ambled on, in the direction he'd kicked the ball, and said, "About Querk, I don't know anything bad about the guy, it's only I don't know that much good about him either."

Dortmunder said, "You worked with him?"

"A few times. Me and Ralph— He didn't retire when I did." Harry Matlock and Ralph Demrovsky had been a burglary team so quick and so greedy they used to travel in a van, just in case they came across anything large.

Kelp said, "Ralph's still working?"

"No, he's in Sing Sing," Harry said. "He should of retired when I did. Hold on." He stopped, just behind his ball, and squinted toward the green, where three guys dressed from the same grab bag stood around waiting, all of them looking this way.

"I think I gotta hit it now," Harry said. "Stand back a ways, I'm still kinda wild at this."

They stood well back, and Harry addressed the ball. Then he addressed the ball some more. When he'd addressed the ball long enough for an entire post office, he took a whack at it and it went somewhere. Not toward the flag down there, exactly, but at least not behind them.

"Well, the point of it is the walk," Harry said. As he sauntered off in the direction the ball had gone, trailed by Dortmunder and Kelp, he said, "Ralph and me used to team up with Querk, maybe four, five times over the years. He's never the first choice, you know."

"No?"

"No. He's competent," Harry allowed, "he'll get you in where you want to get in, but there are guys that are better. Wally Whistler. Herman Jones."

"They're good," Kelp agreed.

"They are," Harry said. "But if some time the guy we wanted was sick or on the lam or put away, there was nothing wrong with Querk."

Kelp said, "Harry, you sent him to me, but you don't sound enthusiastic."

"I'm not *not* enthusiastic," Harry said. He stopped to look at his ball, sitting there in the middle of an ocean of fairway, with the green like an island some way off, ahead and to the right. Two of the guys waiting over there were now sitting down, on the ground. "I don't know about this thing," Harry said. "Let me see those other clubs."

Kelp unshouldered the bag and put it on the ground, so Harry could make his selection. While Harry frowned over his holdings in clubs, Kelp said, "What is it keeps you from being one hundred percent enthusiastic?"

Harry nodded, still looking at the clubs in the bag. Then he looked at Kelp. "I'll tell you," he said. "This is *his* heist. I never been around him when it's his own thing. Ralph and me, we'd bring him in, point to a door, a gate, a safe, whatever, say, 'Open that, Kirby,' and he'd do it. Competent. Not an artist, but competent. How is he when it's his own piece of work? I can't give you a recommendation."

"Okay," Kelp said.

Harry pointed at one of the clubs in the bag, one of the big-headed ones. "That one, you think?"

Kelp, the judicious caddy, considered the possibilities, then pointed at a different one, with an even bigger head. "That one, I think."

It didn't help.

4

New York City made Kirby Querk nervous. Well, in fact, everything made him nervous, especially the need to never let it show, never let anybody guess, that he was scared.

He'd been away too long, is what it was, away from New York and also away from the entire world, That last six and a half years inside had broken him, had made him lose the habit of running his own life to his own plans. Jail was so seductive that way, so comfortable once you gave up and stopped fighting the system. Live by the clock, their clock, their rules, their rhythms, just go along and go along. Six and a half years, and then all at once they give you a smile and a pep talk and a handshake and an open door, and there you are, you're on your own.

On his own? His two previous periods of incarceration had both been shorter, and he'd been younger, and the rhythms and routines of stir hadn't engraved themselves so deeply into his brain. This time, when he was suddenly free, loose, on his own, he'd lost his own, didn't have any own to be any more.

Which was the main reason, as soon as those prison doors had clanged shut behind him, that he'd headed for Darbyville and Cousin Claude, even though he and Cousin Claude had never been close and didn't really have that much use for one another, Claude having been a straight arrow his entire life while Querk had from the beginning been rather seriously bent.

But it was to Darbyville that Querk had gone, on a beeline, with a warning phone call ahead of time to ask Claude where he would recommend Querk find housing. The excuse was that Querk had learned the printing trade while inside (or so he'd thought), and he'd known the Sycamore Creek Printery was in the town of Sycamore, not far from Darbyville, one hundred miles north of New York City. Claude was a decent guy, married, with four kids, two out of the nest and two still in, so he'd invited Querk to move into the bedroom now vacated by the oldest, until he found a more permanent place for himself, and now, a year and a half later, Querk was still there.

He hadn't known it then, and he still didn't know it now, but the reason he'd gone to Cousin Claude in the first place was that he'd felt the need for a warden; someone to tell him when it's exercise time, when it's lights out. It hadn't worked that way exactly, since Claude and his wife Eugenia were both too gentle and amiable to play warden, and the printing trade skills that were supposed to have given him a grounding had turned out to be just one more bubble blown into the air, but that was all right. He had the job at the printery, riding the forklift truck, which put some structure into his life, and he'd found somebody else to play warden.

And it was time to phone her.

One of the many things that made Querk nervous about New York City these days was the pay phones. He was afraid to use a phone on the street, to be talking into a phone while all these hulking people went by, many of them behind him, all of them unknowable in their intentions. You had to *stop* to make a call from a pay phone, but Querk didn't want to stop on the street in New York City; he couldn't get over the feeling that, if he stopped, a whole bunch of them would jump on him, rob him, hurt him, do who knew what to him. So if he was out and about in New York City, he wanted to keep moving. But he still had to make that phone call.

Grand Central Station was not exactly a solution, but it was a compromise. It was indoors and, even though there were just as many people hurtling by as out on the street, maybe more, it was possible to talk on the phone in Grand Central with his back to a wall, all those strangers safely out in front.

So that's what he did. First he got a bunch of quarters and dimes, and then he chose a pay phone from a line of them not far from the Metro North ticket windows, where he could stand with his back mostly turned to the phone as he watched the streams of people hustle among all the entrances and all the exits, this way, that way, like protons in a cyclotron. He could watch the buttons over his shoulder when he made the call, then drop coins into the slot when the machine-voice told him how much it was.

One ring: "Seven Leagues."

"Is Frank there?"

"Wrong number," she said, and hung up, and he looked toward

the big clock in the middle of the station. Five minutes to two in the afternoon, not a particularly hot time at Grand Central but still pretty crowded. He now had five minutes to wait, while she walked down to the phone booth outside the Hess station, the number for which he had in his pocket.

He didn't like standing next to the phone when he wasn't making a call; he thought it made him conspicuous. He thought there might be people in among all these people who would notice him and think about him and maybe even make notes on his appearance and actions. So he walked purposefully across the terminal and out a door onto Lexington Avenue and around to an entrance on 42nd Street, then down to the lower level and back up to the upper level, where at last the clock said two, straight up.

Querk dialed the pay phone number up in Sycamore, and it was answered immediately: "Hello."

"It's me."

"I know. How's it going?"

"Well, I got a couple guys," Querk said. "I think they're gonna be okay."

"You tell them what we're doing?"

"Not yet. We all hadda check each other out. I'm seeing them today at four o'clock. If they say yes, if they think *I* check out, I'll tell them the story."

"Not the whole story, Kirby."

Querk laughed, feeling less nervous, because he was talking to the warden. "No, not the whole story," he said. "Just the part they'll like."

5

For this meet they would be in a car, which Kelp would promote. He picked up Querk first, at the corner of Eleventh Avenue and 57th Street, steering the very nice black Infiniti to a stop at the curb, where Querk was rubbernecking up 57th Street, eastward. Kelp thought he'd have to honk, but then Querk got in on the passenger side next to him and said, "I just saw Lesley Stahl get out of a cab up there."

"Ah," said Kelp, and drove back into traffic, uptown.

"I used to watch *60 Minutes* regular as clockwork," Querk said, "every Sunday. Even the summer reruns."

"Ah," said Kelp.

"When I was inside," Querk explained. "It was kind of a highlight."

"Ah," said Kelp.

"I don't watch it so much any more, I don't know why."

Kelp didn't say anything. Querk looked around the interior of the car and said, "I happened to notice, you got MD plates."

"I do," Kelp agreed.

"You aren't a doctor."

"I'm not even a car owner," Kelp told him.

Querk was surprised. "You boosted this?"

"From Roosevelt Hospital, just down the street. I give all my automotive trade to doctors. They're very good on the difference between pleasure and pain. Also, I believe they have a clear understanding of infinity."

"But you're driving around— You're still in the neighborhood, with a very hot car."

"The hours they make those doctors work?" Kelp shrugged. "The owner's not gonna miss this thing until Thursday. In the private lot there, I picked one without dust on it. There's John."

They were on West End Avenue now, stopped at the light at 72nd Street, and Dortmunder was visible catty-corner across the street, standing on the corner in the sunlight as though a mistake had been made here. Anybody who was that slumped and bedraggled should not be standing on a street corner in the summer in the sunlight. He had looked much more at home in the bar where he and Kelp had conferred. Out here, he looked mostly like he was waiting for the police sweep.

The green arrow lit up, and Kelp swept around to stop next to Dortmunder who, per original plan, slid into the back seat, saying, "Hello."

Querk said, "Andy boosted this car."

"He always does," Dortmunder said, and to Kelp's face in the rearview mirror as they turned northward on the West Side Highway, he said, "My compliments to the doctor."

Traffic on the highway was light; Kelp drove moderately in the right lane, and nobody said anything until Dortmunder leaned forward, rested his forearms on the seatback, and said to Querk, "Jump in any time."

"Oh." Querk looked out ahead of them and said, "I thought we were headed somewhere."

"We are," Kelp told him. "But you can *start*."

"Okay, fine."

As Dortmunder leaned back, seated behind Kelp, Querk half-turned in his seat so he could see both of them, and said, "One of the things the printery prints, where I work, is money."

That surprised them both. Kelp said, "I thought the mint printed the money."

"*Our* money, yes," Querk said. "But the thing is, your smaller countries, they don't have the technology and the skills and all, they farm out the money. The printing. Most of the money in Europe and Africa is printed in London. Most of the money in South America is printed in Philadelphia."

"You're not in Philadelphia," Kelp pointed out.

"No, this outfit I'm with, Sycamore, about ten years ago they decided to get some of that action. They had a big Canadian investor, they put in the machinery, hired the people, started to undercut the price of the Philadelphia people."

"Free enterprise," Kelp commented.

"Sure." Querk shrugged. "Nobody says the money they do is as up to date as the Philadelphia money, with all the holograms and anti-counterfeiting things, but you get a small enough country, poor enough, nobody *wants* to counterfeit that money, so Sycamore's got four of the most draggly-assed countries in Central and South America, and Sycamore makes their money."

Dortmunder said, "You're talking about stealing money you say isn't worth anything."

"Well, it's worth *something*," Querk said. "And I'm not talking about stealing it."

"Counterfeiting," Dortmunder suggested, as though he didn't like that idea either.

But Querk shook his head. "I'm the guy," he said, "keeps track of the paper coming in, signs off with the truck drivers, forklifts it here and there, depending what kinda paper, what's it for. Each of these countries got their own special paper, with watermarks and hidden messages and all. Not high tech, you know, pretty sophomore, but not something you could imitate on your copier."

"You've got the paper," Dortmunder said. He still sounded skeptical.

"And I look around," Querk said. "You know, I thought I was gonna be a printer, not a forklift jockey, so I'm looking to improve myself. Get enough ahead so I can choose my own life for myself, not to have to answer every whistle. You know what I mean."

"Huh," Dortmunder said.

"That's back," Querk pointed out. "That throat thing." He looked forward as Kelp steered them off the highway at the 125th Street exit. "Isn't this Harlem?" He didn't sound as though he liked the idea.

"Not exactly," Kelp said.

Dortmunder said, "Go on with your story."

"I don't think I can yet," Querk said. He was frowning out the windshield as though rethinking some earlier decisions in his life.

"Be there in a couple minutes," Kelp assured him.

Nobody talked while Kelp stopped at the stop sign, made the left around the huge steel pillars holding up the West Side Highway, drove a block past scruffy warehouses, turned left at the light, stopped at a stop sign, then drove across, through the wide opening in a chain-link fence, and turned left into a narrow long parking lot just above the Hudson River.

Querk said, "What is this?"

"Fairway," Kelp told him, as he found a parking space on the left and drove into it, front bumper against fence. It was hot outside, so he kept the engine on and the windows shut.

Querk said, "I don't get it."

"What it is," Kelp told him, putting the Infiniti in park, "Harlem never had a big supermarket, save money on your groceries, they only had these little corner stores, not much selection on the shelves. So this Fairway comes in, that used to be a warehouse over there, see it?"

Querk nodded at the big warehouse with the supermarket entrance. "I see it."

Kelp said, "So they put in a huge supermarket, great selections, everything cheap, the locals love it. But also the commuters, it's easy on, easy off, see, there's your northbound ramp back up to the highway, so they can come here, drop in, buy everything for the weekend, then head off to their country retreat."

Querk said, "But why us? What are *we* doin' here?"

Dortmunder told him, "You look around, you'll see one, two people, even three, sitting in the cars around here. The wife—usually, it's the wife—goes in and shops, the husband and the houseguests, they stay out here, keep outa the way, sit in the car, tell each other stories."

Kelp said, "Tell us a story, Kirby."

Querk shook his head. "I been away too long," he said. "I hate to have to admit it. I don't know how to maneuver any more. That's why I need a cushion."

Dortmunder said, "Made out of South American money."

"Exactly." Querk said, "I'm pretty much on my own at the plant, and I've always been handy around machinery—starting with locks, you know, that was my specialty—and also including now the printing presses they don't use any more, and so I finally figured out the numbers."

Kelp said, "Numbers?"

"Every bill in your pocket," Querk told him, "has a number on it, and no two bills in this country have the same number. That's the same for every country's money. Everything's identical on every bill except the number changes every time, and it never goes back. That's part of the special machinery they bought, when they went into this business."

Kelp said, "Kirby, am I all of a sudden ahead of you here? You figured out how to make the numbers go back."

Querk was pleased with himself. "I know," he said, "how to tell the machine, 'That last run was a test. *This* is the real run.'" Grinning at Dortmunder, he said, "I also am the guy puts the paper here and there inside the plant, and checks it in when it's delivered, and maybe makes it disappear off the books. So you see what I got."

Kelp said, "It's the real paper, on the real machine, doing the real numbers."

"There's no record of it anywhere," Querk said. "It isn't counterfeit, it's real, and it isn't stolen because it was never there."

As they drove back down the West Side Highway toward midtown, each of them drinking a St. Pauli Girl beer Kelp had actually paid for in Fairway, Dortmunder said, "You know, it seems to me, there's gotta be more than one chapter to this story."

"You mean," Querk said, "what do we do with it, once we got it."

"We can't take it to a bank a hundred dollars a time to change it back," Dortmunder said.

"No, I know that."

Kelp said, "I suppose we could go to the country and buy a hotel or something . . ."

Dortmunder said, "With cash?"

"There's that. And then sell it again for dollars." He shook his head. "Too complicated."

"I got a guy," Querk said. His shoulders twitched.

They gave him their full attention.

"He's from that country, it's called Guerrera," Querk said. "He's a kind of a hustler down there."

Dortmunder said, "What is he up here?"

"Well, he isn't up here," Querk said. "Basically, he's down there."

Dortmunder said, "And how do you know this guy?"

"I got a friend," Querk said, "a travel agent, she goes all over, she knows the guy."

Dortmunder and Kelp exchanged a glance in the rearview mirror at that pronoun, which Querk didn't appear to see. "We run off the money," he went on, "and it comes out in cardboard boxes, already packed by the machinery, with black metal straps around it. We get it out of the plant, and I got a way to do that, too, and we turn it over to this guy, and he gives us fifty cents on the dollar."

"Half," Kelp said. "What are we talking about here?"

"The most useful currency for Rodrigo—that's my guy—is the twenty million siapa note."

Kelp said, "Twenty *million*?"

Dortmunder said, "How much is that in money?"

"A hundred dollars." Querk shrugged. "They been havin a little inflation problem down there. They think they got it under control now."

Kelp said, "So how much is this run?"

"What we'll print? A hundred billion."

Dortmunder said, "Not dollars."

"No, siapas. That's five thousand bills, all the twenty million siapa note."

Dortmunder, pretending patience, said, "And what's *that* in money?"

"Five hundred grand," Querk said.

Kelp said, "Now *I'm* getting confused. Five hundred. This is in dollars?"

"Five hundred thousand dollars," Querk said.

Dortmunder said, "And we get half. Two hundred fifty thousand. And Kelp and me?"

"Half of the half," Querk said promptly.

They were now back down in a realm where Dortmunder could do calculations in his head. "Sixty-two thousand, five hundred apiece," he said.

"And a little vacation in the mountains," Kelp said.

"Next week," Querk said.

They looked at him. Dortmunder said, "Next week?"

"Or maybe the week after that," Querk said. "Anyway, when the plant's shut down."

"We," Dortmunder decided, "are gonna have to talk more."

6

"May?" Dortmunder called, and stood in the doorway to listen. Nothing. "Not home yet," he said, and went on into the apartment, followed by Kelp and Querk.

"Nice place," Querk said.

"Thanks," Dortmunder said. "Living room's in here, on the left."

"I used to have a place in New York," Querk said. "Years ago. I don't think I'd like the pace now."

They trooped into the living room, here on East 19th Street, and Dortmunder looked around at the sagging sofa and his easy chair with the maroon hassock in front of it and May's easy chair with the cigarette burns on the arms (good thing she quit when she did) and the television set where the colors never would come right and the window with its view of a brick wall just a little too far away to touch and the coffee table with all the rings and scars on it, and he said, "I dunno, the pace don't seem to bother me that much. Take a seat. Anybody want a beer?"

Everybody wanted a beer, so Dortmunder went away to the kitchen to play host. When he was coming back down the hall toward the living room, spilling beer on his wrists because three was one more can than he could carry all at once, the apartment door at the other end of the hall opened and May came in, struggling with the key in the door and the big sack of groceries in her arm. A tall thin woman with slightly graying black hair, May worked as a cashier at Safeway until Dortmunder should score one of these times, and she felt the sack of groceries a day was a perk that went with the position, whether management thought so or not.

"*Damn*, May!" Dortmunder said, spilling more beer on his wrists. "I can't help you with that."

"That's okay, I got it," she said, letting the door close behind her as she counted his beer cans. "We've got company."

"Andy and a guy. Come in and say hello."

"Let me put this stuff away."

As May passed the living room doorway, Kelp could be heard to cry, "Hey, May!" She nodded at the doorway, she and Dortmunder slid by each other in the hall, and he went on into the living room, where the other two were both standing, like early guests at a party.

Distributing the beers, wiping his wrists on his shirt, Dortmunder said, "May'll come in in a minute, say hello."

Kelp lifted his beer. "To crime."

"Good," said Querk, and they all drank.

May came in, with a beer of her own. "Hi, Andy," she said.

Dortmunder said, "May, this is Kirby Querk." They both said hello, and he said, "Whyn't we all sit down? You two take the sofa."

Sounding surprised, Querk said, "You want me to tell this in front of, uh, the lady?"

"Aw, that's nice," May said, smiling at Querk as she settled into her chair.

Dortmunder said, "I'll just tell her anyway, after you go, so you can save me some time."

"Well, all right."

They all seated themselves, and Dortmunder said to May, "Querk has a job upstate at a printery, where one of the things they print is South American money, and he's got a way to run off a batch nobody knows about."

"Well, that's pretty good," May said.

"Only now, it turns out," Dortmunder said, "there's some kind of deadline here, so we come over to talk about it."

Kelp explained, "Up till now, we weren't sure we were all gonna team up, so we met in other places."

"Sure," May said.

"So now," Dortmunder said, "Querk's gonna explain the deadline."

They all looked at Querk, who put his beer can on the coffee table, making another mark, and said, "The plant's called Sycamore Creek, and there's this creek runs through town, with a dam where it goes under the road, and that's where the electricity comes from to run the plant. But every year in August there's two weeks when they gotta open the dam and just let the water go, because there's always a drought up there in the summer and it could get too low downstream for the fish. So the plant closes, two weeks, everybody gets a vacation, they do their annual maintenance and all, but there's no electricity to run the plant, so that's why they have to close."

Dortmunder said, "Your idea is, you do this when there's no electricity."

"We bring in our own," Querk said.

Dortmunder visualized himself walking with a double handful of electricity, lots of little blue sparks. *Zit-zit*; worse than beer cans. He said, "How do we do that?"

"With a generator," Querk told him. "See, up there, it's all volunteer fire departments and rescue squads, and my cousin, where I've been living temporarily until I find a place, he's the captain of the Combined Darby County Fire Department and Rescue Squad, and what they got, besides the ambulance and the fire engine, is a big truck with a generator on it, for emergencies."

Dortmunder said, "So first you boost this truck—"

"Which I could do with my eyes closed," Querk said. "The locks up there are a joke, believe me. And the keys to the emergency vehicles are kept right in them."

Kelp said, "Do we do it day or night?"

"Oh, night," Querk said. "I figure, we go pick up the generator truck around one in the morning, there's *nobody* awake up there at one in the morning, we take it over to the plant, hook up the stuff we need, the run'll take just about three hours for the whole thing, we take the boxes with the money, we put the generator truck back, we're done before daylight."

Dortmunder said, "You're gonna have to have some light in there. And some noise."

"Not a problem," Querk said.

Dortmunder said, "Why, is this plant out in the woods all by itself or something?"

"Not really," Querk said. "But nobody can see it."

Kelp said, "How come?"

"High walls, low buildings." Querk spread his hands. "The way I understand it, in the old days the plant used to dump all its waste straight into the creek, the people downstream used to make bets, what color's the water gonna be tomorrow. Every time the state did an inspection, somehow the plant got tipped off ahead of time, and that day the water's clean and clear, good enough to drink. But finally, about thirty years ago, they got caught. People'd been complaining about noise and stink outa the plant, in addition to this water even an irreligious person could walk on, so they did a consent. The plant upgraded its waste treatment, and did a sound-baffle wall all around, and planted trees so people wouldn't have to look at the wall, and now those trees are all big, you'd think it's a forest there, except the two drives in, with the gates, one for the workers and one for deliveries, and they're both around on the stream side, no houses across the way."

Dortmunder said, "We'd have to go up there, ahead of time, take a look at this place."

"Definitely," Kelp said.

"That's a good idea," Querk said, "you can help me refine the details. I could drive you up there tomorrow, I've got my cousin's van, I've been sleeping in it down in Greenwich Village."

"Nice neighborhood," May commented.

"Yeah, it is."

Dortmunder said, "We oughta have our own wheels, we'll drive up, meet you there."

Grinning, Querk said, "Another doctor gonna be on his feet?"

"Possibly," Kelp said. "You say this place is a hundred miles upstate? About two hours?"

"Yeah, no more. You go up the Taconic."

Dortmunder said, "If this is a plant, with workers, there's probably a place to eat around it."

"Yeah, just up from the bridge, you know, where the dam is, there's a place called Sycamore House. It's mostly a bar, but you can get lunch."

Dortmunder nodded. "You got a problem, up there, being seen with us?"

"No, it's not *that* small a town. You're just people I happen to know, passing through."

"So before you leave here," Dortmunder said, "do a little map, how we find this town, we'll get some lunch there, come out at one o'clock, there you are."

"Fine," Querk said.

Kelp said, "What if there's an emergency around there, the night we go, and we've got the generator truck?"

"For three hours in the middle of the night in August?" Querk shrugged. "There isn't gonna be a blizzard. The three vehicles in the garage are in separate bays, so even if they come for the fire engine or the ambulance, which would almost never happen, middle of the summer, they still won't see the generator truck's gone."

"But what if," Kelp said.

"Then we're screwed," Querk said. "Me more than you guys, because there won't be any question who put the generator truck in the printery, and there goes my quiet life not being on the run."

Kelp said, "So you'll take the chance."

"The odds are so extreme," Querk said. "I mean, unless one of you guys is a Jonah, I don't see I've got anything to worry about. I'll risk it."

Nobody said anything.

7

First Querk split, and then Kelp, and then Dortmunder filled May in on the rest of the setup; Rodrigo, and the half of a half of a half, and the barely mentioned female travel agent.

"Well, she's the one behind it all," May said.

"Yeah, I got that part," Dortmunder said. "So what was your reading on the guy?"

"Rabbity."

"Yeah."

"Something's bothering you," May said.

Dortmunder shook his head. "I don't even know what it is. The thing is, this job *seems* to be doing everything you shouldn't do, and yet somehow it doesn't. You should never rip off the place where you work or you used to work, because you're who they look at, but that's what Querk's doing, but this time it's supposed to be okay, because, like Querk says, nobody's supposed to know any rip-off happened. If they know there's a hundred billion siapas gone missing, then the job's no good."

"I can't imagine money like that," May said. "But how do you get *your* money, that's the question. The dollars."

"We gotta work on that," Dortmunder said. "So far, Querk hasn't made any suggestions. And the other thing, I keep thinking about what Harry Matlock said, how he knew Querk was all right, not a star, when he was just a sideman in somebody else's scheme, but he couldn't say how Querk would be when the scheme was his own. And this is a weird scheme."

"In parts," May agreed.

"In all the parts. You got a factory closed because they open the dam to help out the fish downstream, you like that part?"

"Well, if that's what they do," May said.

"I guess." Dortmunder frowned, massively. "It's the country, see, I don't know what makes sense in the country. So that's what's got me geechy. Querk talks about how he isn't comfortable in the city any more, but you know, I *never* been comfortable in the country. Why can't they print these siapas in the city? In Brooklyn somewhere."

"Well," May said, "there isn't any fish downstream in the city."

"Oh, yes, there is," Dortmunder said. "I just hope I'm not one of them."

8

As Querk walked toward Cousin Claude's van, he thought what a pity it was he couldn't phone now, give this progress report. But it was after five, so Seven Leagues was closed, and he couldn't call her at home, even if she'd got home so soon. Well, he'd see her in the morning, when he drove up to Sycamore, so he'd tell her then.

And what he'd tell her was that it was all coming together. Yes, it was. The two guys he'd wound up with were sharp enough to do the job without lousing anything up, but not so sharp as to be trouble later. He had a good feeling about them.

Walking along, he kept his hands in his pockets, even though it was a very hot August afternoon, because otherwise they'd shake like buckskin fringe at the ends of his arms. Well, when this was over, when at last they'd be safe—and rich—he wouldn't tremble at *all.* Hold a glass of wine, not a single wave in it.

Traveling from Dortmunder's place on East 19th Street to where he'd parked the van in the West Village seemed to just naturally lead Querk along West 14th Street, the closest thing Manhattan has to a casbah. Open-fronted stores with huge signs, selling stuff you never knew you wanted, but cheap. Gnomish customers draped with gnomish children and lugging shopping bags half their size roamed the broad littered sidewalk and oozed in and out of the storefronts, adding more and more *things* to their bags.

What got to Querk in this spectacle, though, was the guard on duty in front of every one of those stores. Not in a uniform or anything, usually in just jeans and a T-shirt, bulky stern-looking guys positioned halfway between the storefront and curb, some of them sitting on top of a low ladder, some of them just standing there in the middle of the sidewalk, but all of them doing nothing but glaring into their store. Usually, they had their arms folded, to emphasize their muscles, and a beetle-browed angry look on their faces to emphasize their willingness to dismember shoplifters.

Walking this gauntlet, Querk was sorry his hands were in his pockets, because those guys could see that as a provocation, particularly in this August heat, but he figured, if they saw him trembling all over instead that would not be an improvement in his image.

Finally, he got off 14th Street and plodded on down to 12th, which was much more comforting to walk along, being mostly old nineteenth-century townhouses well-maintained, intermixed with more recent bigger apartment buildings that weren't as offensive as they might be. The pedestrians here were less frightening, too, being mostly people either from the townhouses or who had things to do with the New School for Social Research, and therefore less likely to be homicidal maniacs than the people on 14th Street or up in Midtown.

When Greenwich Village becomes the West Village, the numbered grid of streets common to Manhattan acts all at once as though it's been smoking dope, at the very least. Names start mingling with the numbers—Jane, Perry, Horatio, who *are* these people?—and the numbers themselves turn a little weird. You don't, for instance, expect West 4th Street to *cross* West 10th Street, but it does . . . on its way to cross West 11th Street.

Cousin Claude's van was parked a little beyond that example of street-design as funhouse mirror, on something called Greenwich Street, lined with low dark apartment buildings and low dark warehouses, some of those being converted into low dark apartment buildings. The van was still there—it always surprised him, in New York City, when something was still there after he'd left it—and Querk unlocked his way in.

This was a dirty white Ford Econoline van that Claude used mostly for fishing trips or other excursions, so behind the bucket front seats he had installed a bunk bed and a small metal cabinet with drawers that was bolted to the side wall. Querk could plug his electric razor into the cigarette lighter, and could wash and brush teeth and do other things in restaurant bathrooms.

It was too early for dinner now, not yet six, so he settled himself behind the wheel, looked at the books and magazines lying on the passenger seat, and tried to decide what he wanted to read next. But then, all at once, he thought: Why wait? I'm done here. I don't have to wait here all night and drive up there in the morning. It's still daylight, I'm home before eight o'clock.

Home.

Janet.

Key in ignition. Seatbelt on. Querk drove north to West 11th Street, seeming none the worse for wear after its encounter with West 4th Street, turned left, turned right on the West Side Highway, and joined rush hour north. Didn't even mind that it was rush hour; just to be going home.

After a while he passed the big Fairway billboard on top of the Fairway supermarket. Those two guys sure know the city, don't they?

Well, Querk knew Sycamore.

9

In the end, Kelp decided to leave the medical profession alone this morning and rent a car for the trip upstate, which would mean fewer nervous looks in the rearview mirror for a hundred miles up and a hundred miles back. Less eyestrain, even though this decision meant he would have to go promote a credit card, which in turn meant a visit to Arnie Albright, a fence, which was the least of the things wrong with him.

Kelp truly didn't want to have to visit with Arnie Albright, but when he dropped by at John's apartment at eight-thirty in the morning, just in time to wish May bon voyage on her journey to Safeway, to suggest that *John* might be the one to go promote the credit card, John turned mulish. "I've done my time with Arnie Albright," he said. "Step right up to the plate."

Kelp sighed. He knew, when John turned mulish, there was no arguing with him. Still, "You could wait out front," he suggested.

"He could look out the window and see me."

"His apartment's at the back."

"He could *sense* me. You gonna use O'Malley's?"

"Sure," Kelp said. O'Malley's was a single-location car rental agency that operated out of a parking garage way down on the Bowery near the Manhattan Bridge. Most of the clientele were Asians, so O'Malley mostly had compact cars, but more important, O'Malley did *not* have a world-wide interconnected web of computers that could pick up every little nitpick in a customer's credit card and driver's license, so whenever Kelp decided to go elsewhere than doctors for his wheels it was O'Malley got the business.

"I'll meet you at O'Malley's," John demanded, "at nine-thirty."

So that was that. Kelp walked a bit and took a subway a bit and walked a bit and pretty soon there he was on 89th Street between Broadway and West End Avenue, entering the tiny vestibule of Arnie's building. He pushed the button next to *Albright*, waited a pretty long time, and suddenly the intercom snarled, "Who the hell is that?"

"Well, Andy Kelp," Kelp said, wishing it weren't so.

"What the hell do *you* want?"

He wants me to tell him *here*? Leaning confidentially closer to the intercom—he'd been leaning fastidiously away from it before this—Kelp said, "Well, I wanna come upstairs and tell you *there*, Arnie."

Rather than argue any more, Arnie made the awful squawk happen that let Kelp push the door open and go inside to a narrow hall that smelled of cooking from some ethnicity that made you look around for shrunken heads. Seeing none, Kelp went up the long flight of stairs to where the unlovely Arnie stood at his open door, glaring out. A grizzled gnarly guy with a tree-root nose, he had chosen to welcome summer in a pair of stained British Army shorts, very wide, a much-too-big bilious green polo shirt, and black sandals that permitted views of toes like rotting tree stumps; not a wise decision.

"It's buy or sell," this gargoyle snarled as Kelp neared the top of the stairs, "buy or sell, that's the only reason anybody comes to see Arnie Albright. It's not my lovable *personality* is gonna bring anybody here."

"Well, people know you're busy," Kelp said, and went past Arnie into the apartment.

"Busy?" Arnie snarled, and slammed the door. "Do I look *busy*? I look like somebody where the undertaker said, 'Don't do the open coffin, it would be a mistake,' and the family went ahead anyway, and now they're sorry. That's what *I* look like."

"Not that bad, Arnie," Kelp assured him, looking around at the apartment as a relief from looking at Arnie, who, in truth, would look much better with the lid down.

The apartment was strange in its own way. Small underfurnished rooms with big dirty viewless windows, it was decorated mostly with samples from Arnie's calendar collection, Januarys down the ages, girls with their skirts blowing, Boy Scouts saluting, antique cars, your ever-popular kittens in baskets with balls of wool. Among the Januarys starting on every possible day of the week, there were what Arnie called his "incompletes," calendars hailing June or September.

Following Kelp into the living room, Arnie snarled, "I see John Dortmunder isn't with you. Even *he* can't stand to be around me any more. Wha'd you do, toss a coin, the loser comes to see Arnie?"

"He wouldn't toss," Kelp said. "Arnie, the last time I saw you, you were taking some medicine to make you pleasant."

"Yeah, I was still obnoxious, but I wasn't angry about it any more."

"You're not taking it?"

"You noticed," Arnie said. "No, it made me give money away."

Kelp said, "What?"

"I couldn't believe it myself, I thought I had holes in my pockets, the super was coming in to lift cash—not that he could *find* the upstairs in this place, the useless putz—but it turned out, my new pleasant personality, learning to live with my inner scumbag, every time I'd smile at somebody, like out in the street, and they'd smile back, I'd give them money."

"That's terrible," Kelp said.

"You know it is," Arnie said. "I'd rather be frowning and obnoxious and *have* money than smiling and obnoxious and throwing it away. I suppose you're sorry you didn't get some of it."

"That's okay, Arnie," Kelp said, "I already got a way to make a living. Which by the way—"

"Get it over with, I know," Arnie said. "You want outa here, and so do I. You think I *enjoy* being in here with me? Okay, I know, tell me, we'll get it over with, I won't say a word."

"I need a credit card," Kelp said.

Arnie nodded. As an aid to thought, he sucked at his teeth. Kelp looked at Januarys.

Arnie said, "How long must this card live?"

"Two days."

"That's easy," Arnie said. "That won't even cost you much. Lemme try to match you with a signature. Siddown."

Kelp sat at a table with incompletes shellacked on the top—aircraft carrier with airplanes flying, two bears and a honeypot—while Arnie went away to rummage and shuffle in some other room, soon returning with three credit cards, a ballpoint pen, and an empty tissue box.

"Hold on," he said, and ripped the tissue box open so Kelp could write on its inside. "I'll incinerate it later."

Kelp looked at his choice of cards. "Howard Joostine looks pretty good."

"Give it a whack."

Kelp wrote *Howard Joostine* four times on the tissue box, then compared them with the one on the credit card. "Good enough for O'Malley," he said.

10

Dortmunder's only objection to the car was the legroom, but that was objection enough. "This is a *sub*-compact," he complained.

"Well, no," Kelp told him. "With the sub-compact, you gotta straddle the engine block."

They were not the only people fleeing the city northbound on this bright hot morning in August, but it is true that most of the other people around them, even the Asians, were in cars with more legroom. (O'Malley's bent toward Oriental customers was because his operation was on the fringe of Chinatown. However, he was also on the fringe of Little Italy, but did he offer bulletproof limos? No.)

In almost every state in the Union, the state capital is not in the largest city, and the reason for that is, the states were all founded by farmers, not businessmen or academics, and farmers don't trust cities. In Maryland, for instance, the city is Baltimore and the capital is Annapolis. In California, the city is Los Angeles and the capital is Sacramento. And in New York, the capital is Albany, a hundred fifty miles up the Hudson.

When the twentieth century introduced the automobile, and then the paved road, and then the highway, the first highway in every state was built for the state legislators; it connected the capital with the largest city, and let the rest of the state go fend for itself. In New York State, that road is called the Taconic Parkway, and it's *still* underutilized, nearly a century later. That's planning.

But it also made for a pleasant drive. Let others swelter in bumper-to-bumper traffic on purpose-built roads, the Taconic was a joy, almost as empty as a road in a car commercial. The farther north of the city you drove, the fewer cars you drove among (and no trucks!), while the more beautiful became the mountain scenery through which this empty road swooped and soared. It was almost enough to make you believe there was an upside to the internal combustion engine.

After a while, the congeniality of the road and the landscape soothed Dortmunder's put-upon feelings about legroom. He figured out a way to disport his legs that did not lead immediately to cramps, his upper body settled comfortably into the curve of the seat, and he spent his time, more fruitfully than fretting about legroom, thinking about what could go wrong.

An emergency in town while they were in possession of the generator truck, that could go wrong. The woman travel agent who was running Querk, and whose bona fides and motives were unknown, she could go wrong. (Harry Matlock's instincts had been right, when he'd said he could recommend Querk as a follower but not as a leader. He was still a follower. The question was, who vouched for the leader?)

Other things that could go wrong. Rodrigo, for one. No, Rodrigo for four or five. Described as mostly a hustler down on his home turf, he could run foul of the law himself at just the wrong moment, and have neither the cash nor the leisure to take delivery on the print job. Or, as unknown as the travel agent, he could be planning a double-cross from the get-go. Or, he could be reasonably trustworthy himself, but unaware of untrustworthy friends waiting just out of sight. Or, he could get one of those South American illnesses that people get when they leave the five boroughs, and die.

All in all, it was a pleasant drive.

Querk's instructions had said to exit the Taconic at Darby Corners and turn east and then north, following the signs past Darbyville, where Querk lived temporarily with his cousin, and on to Sycamore, where the Sycamore Creek Printery stood in woodland disguise beside Sycamore Creek.

They approached Sycamore from the south, while the creek approached the town from the north, so for the last few miles they were aware of the stream in the woods and fields off to their right, spritzing in the sun as it rushed and tumbled the other way.

There were farmhouses all along the route here, some of them still connected to farms, and there were fields of ripe corn and orchards of almost-ripe apples. The collapse of the local dairy farming industry due to the tender loving care of the state politicians meant several of the farms they passed were growing things that would have left the original settlers scratching their heads: llamas, goats, anemones, ostriches, Christmas trees, Icelandic horses, long-horn cattle.

The town was commercial right from the city line: lumberyard on the left, tractor dealership on the right. Far ahead was the only traffic light. As they drove toward it, private housing was mixed with shops on the left, but after the tractor man it was all forested on the right almost all the way to the intersection, where an Italian restaurant on that side signaled the return of civilization.

"That'll be it in there," Kelp said, taking a hand off the steering wheel to point at the dubious woodland.

"Right."

"And all evergreens, so people don't have to look at it in winter, either."

"Very tasteful," Dortmunder agreed.

It wasn't quite eleven-thirty. The traffic light was with them, so Kelp drove through the intersection, and just a little farther, on the right, they passed Sycamore House, where they would eat lunch. It was a very old building, two stories high, the upper story extending out over and sagging down toward an open front porch. The windows were decorated with neon beer logos.

A little beyond Sycamore House a storefront window proclaimed SEVEN LEAGUES TRAVEL. This time, Kelp only pointed his nose: "And there *she* is."

"Got it."

Kelp drove to the northern end of town—cemetery on left, church on right, "Go and Sin no More" the suggestion on the announcement board out front—where he made a U-turn through the church's empty parking lot and headed south again. "We'll see what we see from the bridge," he said.

Here came the traffic light, this time red. Moderate traffic poked along, locals and summer folk. Kelp turned left when he could, and now the pocket forest was on their right, and the creek up ahead. Just before the creek, where the bosk ended, a two-lane road ran off to the right, between the evergreens and creek, marked at the entrance by a large black-on-white sign:

PRIVATE
SYCAMORE CREEK PRINTERY
NO TRESPASSING

Right after that, there was what seemed to be a lake on their left, and a steep drop to a stream on their right, so the road must be the dam. Dortmunder craned around, banging his legs into car parts, trying to see something other than pine trees along the streamside back there, and just caught a glimpse of something or other where the private road turned in. "Pretty hid," he said.

There were no intersections on the far side of the creek, and in fact no more town over here. All the development was behind them, along the west side of the creek. On this side the land climbed steeply through a more diversified woods, the road twisting back and forth, and when they finally did come to a turnoff, seven miles later, it was beyond the crest, and the turnoff was to a parking area where you could enjoy the view of the Berkshire Mountains in Massachusetts, farther east.

They didn't spend a lot of time contemplating the Berkshires, but drove back to Sycamore, ignoring the traffic that piled up behind them because they insisted on going so slowly down the twisty road, trying to see signs of the printing plant inside the wall of trees. Here and there a hint, nothing more.

"So if he's careful," Kelp said, "with the light and the noise, it should be okay."

"I'd like to get in there," Dortmunder said, "just give it the double-o."

"We'll discuss it with him," Kelp said.

11

It was still too early for lunch. Kelp parked the little car in the parking lot next to Sycamore House, in among several cars owned by people who didn't know it was too early for lunch, and they got out to stretch, Dortmunder doing overly elaborate knee-bends and massaging of his thighs that Kelp chose not to notice, saying, "I think I'll take a look at the League."

"I'll walk around a little," Dortmunder said, sounding pained. "Work the kinks out."

They separated, and Kelp walked up the block to Seven Leagues Travel, the middle shop in a brief row of storefronts, a white clapboard one-story building, with an entrance and a plate glass display window for each of the three shops. The one on the right was video rental and the one on the left was a frame shop.

Kelp pushed open the door for Seven Leagues, and a bell sounded. He entered and shut the door, and it sounded again, and a female voice called, "Just a minute! I got a bite!"

A bite? Kelp looked around an empty room, not much deeper than it was wide. Filing cabinets were along the left wall and two desks, one behind the other, faced forward on the right. Every otherwise empty vertical space was covered with travel posters, including the side of the nearest filing cabinet and the front of both desks. The forward desk was as messy as a Texas trailer camp after a tornado, but the desk behind it was so neat and empty as to be obviously unused. At the rear, a door with a travel poster on it was partly open, showing just a bit of the lake formed by the dam and the steep wooded slope beyond.

Kelp, wondering if assistance was needed here—if a person was being bitten, that was possible—walked down the length of the room past the desks, pulled the rear door open the rest of the way, and leaned out to see a narrow roofless porch and a woman on it fighting with a fishing pole. She was middle-aged, which meant impossible to tell exactly, and not too overweight, dressed in full tan slacks, a blue man's dress shirt open at the collar and with the sleeves cut off above the elbow, huge dark sunglasses, and a narrow-brimmed cloth cap with a lot of fishing lures and things stuck in it.

"Oh!" he said. "A *bite*!"

"Don't break my concentration!"

So he stood there and watched. A person, man or woman, fighting a fish can look a little odd, if the light is just so and the fishing line can't be seen. There she was with the bent rod, and nothing else visible, so that she looked as though she were doing one of those really esoteric Oriental exercise routines, bobbing and weaving, hunching her shoulders, kicking left and right, spinning the reel first one way, then the other, and muttering and grumbling and swearing beneath her breath the entire time, until all at once a *fish* jumped out of the water and flew over the white wood porch railing to start its own energetic exercise program on the porch floor. The fish was about a foot long, and was a number of colors Kelp didn't know the names of.

She was gasping, the woman (so was the fish), but she was grinning as well (the fish wasn't). "Isn't he a beauty?" she demanded, as she leaned the pole against the rear wall.

"Sure," Kelp said. "What is it? I mean, I know it's a fish, but what's his name?"

"Trout," she said. "I can tell already, I give you one more word, it's gonna get too technical."

"Trout is good enough," he agreed. "They're good to eat, aren't they?"

"They're wonderful to eat," she said. "But not this one." Going to one knee beside the flopping fish, she said, "We do catch and release around here."

Kelp watched her stick a finger into the fish's mouth to start working the hook out of its lower lip. He imagined a hook in his own lower lip, then was sorry he'd imagined it, and said, "Catch and *release*? You let it go again?"

"Sure," she said. Standing, she scooped the fish up with both hands and, before it could shimmy away from her, tossed it well out into the lake. "See you again, fella!" she called, then said to Kelp, "Just let me wash my hands, I'll be right with you."

They both went back into the office and she headed for the bathroom, a separate wedge in the rear corner of the room. Opening its door, she looked back at him and waved her free hand toward her desk. "Take a seat, I'll be right with you."

He nodded, and she went inside, shutting the door. He walked over to the diorama of tornado damage and noticed, half-hidden under a cataract of various forms and brochures, one of those three-sided brass plaques with a name on it, this one JANET TWILLEY.

He wandered around the room, looking at the various travel posters, noting there was none to tout Guerrera, and that in fact the only South American poster showed some amazing naked bodies in Rio, and then the toilet flushed and a minute later Janet Twilley came out, shut the bathroom door, frowned at Kelp, and said, "I told you, take a seat."

"I was admiring the posters."

"Okay." Coming briskly forward, she gestured at the chair beside the front desk. "So *now* you can take a seat."

Bossy woman. They both sat, and she said, "So where did you want to go?"

"That's why I was looking at the posters," he said. He noticed she kept her sunglasses on. Then he noticed a little discoloration visible around her left eye.

She peered at him through the dark glasses. "You don't know where you want to *go*?"

"Well, not exactly," he said.

She disapproved. "That's not the usual way," she said.

"See," he told her, "I have this problem with time zones."

"Problem?"

"I change time zones, it throws me off," he explained, "louses up my sleep, I don't enjoy the trip."

"Jet lag," she said.

"Oh, good, you know about that."

"Everybody knows about jet lag," she said.

"They do? Well, then, you know what I mean. Me and the wife, we'd like to go somewhere that we don't change a lot of time zones."

"Canada," she said.

"We been to Canada. Very nice. We were thinking of somewhere else, some other direction."

She shook her head. "You mean Florida?"

"No, a different country, you know, different language, different people, different cuisine."

"There's Rio," she said, nodding at the poster he'd been admiring.

"But that's so far away," he said. "I mean, really far away. Maybe somewhere not quite that far."

"Mexico has many—"

"Oh, Mexico," he said. "Isn't that full of Americans? We'd like maybe somewhere a little off the beaten path."

Over the next ten minutes, she suggested Argentina, Belize, Peru, Ecuador, all of the Caribbean, even Colombia, but not once did she mention the name Guerrera. Finally, he said, "Well, I better discuss this with the missus. Thank you for the suggestions."

"It would be better," she told him, a little severely, "if you made your mind up *before* you saw a travel agent."

"Yeah, but I'm closing with it now," he assured her. "You got a card?"

"Certainly," she said, and dumped half the crap from her desk onto the floor before she found it.

12

The less said about lunch, the better. After it, Dortmunder and Kelp came out to find Querk perched on the porch rail out front. Dortmunder burped and said, "Well, look who's here."

"Fancy meeting you two," Querk said.

Kelp said, "We should all shake hands now, surprised to see each other."

So they did a round of handshakes, and then Dortmunder said, "I feel like I gotta see the plant."

"I could show you a little," Querk said. "Not inside the buildings, though, around the machines, the management gets all geechy about insurance."

"Just for the idea," Dortmunder said.

So they walked to the corner, crossed with the light, and turned left, first past the Italian restaurant (not open for lunch, unfortunately), and then the abrupt stand of pines. Looking into those dense branches, Dortmunder could occasionally make out a blank grayness back in there that would be the sound-baffle wall.

At the no-trespassing sign, they turned right and trespassed, walking down the two-lane blacktop entrance drive with the creek down to their left, natural woods on the hillside across the way, and the "forest" on their right.

A big truck came slowly toward them from the plant entrance, wheezing and moving as though it had rheumatism. The black guy driving—moustache, cigar stub, dark blue Yankees cap—waved at Querk, who waved back, then said, "He delivers paper. That's what I'll be doing this afternoon, move that stuff around." With a look at his watch, he said, "I should of started three minutes ago."

"Stay late," Dortmunder suggested.

At the entrance, the shallowness of the tree-screen became apparent. The trees were barely more than two deep, in complicated diagonal patterns, not quite random, and behind them loomed the neutral gray wall, probably ten feet high.

Passing through the entrance, Dortmunder saw tall gray metal gates opened to both sides, and said, "They close those when the plant is shut?"

"And lock them," Querk said. "Which is my specialty, remember. I could deal with them before we get the truck, leave them shut but unlocked."

And the closed gates, Dortmunder realized, would also help keep light in here from being seen anywhere outside.

They walked through the entrance, and inside was a series of low cream-colored corrugated metal buildings, or maybe all one building, in sections that stretched to left and right and were surrounded by blacktop right up to the sound-baffle wall, which on the inside looked mostly like an infinitude of egg cartons. The only tall item was a gray metal water tower in the middle of the complex, built on a roof. The roofs were low A shapes, so snow wouldn't pile too thick in the winter.

Directly in front of them was a wide loading bay, the overhead doors all open showing a deep, dark, high-ceilinged interior. One truck, smaller than the paper deliverer, was backed up to the loading bay and cartons were being unloaded by three workmen while the driver leaned against his truck and watched. Beyond, huge rolls of paper, like paper towels in Brobdingnag, were strewn around the concrete floor.

"My work for this afternoon," Querk said, nodding at the paper rolls.

"That driver's doing okay," Dortmunder said.

Querk grinned. "What did Jesus Christ say to the Teamsters? 'Do nothing till I get back.' "

Dortmunder said, "Where's the presses?"

"All over," Querk said, gesturing generally at the complex of buildings. "The one we'll use is down to the right. We'll be able to park down there, snake the wires in through the window."

Kelp said, "Alarm systems?"

"I've got keys to everything," Querk said. "I studied this place, I could parade elephants through here, nobody the wiser." Here on his own turf he seemed more sure of himself, less, as May had said, rabbity.

Kelp said, "Well, to me it looks doable."

Querk raised an eyebrow at Dortmunder. "And to you?"

"Could be," Dortmunder said.

"I like your enthusiasm," Querk said. "Shall we figure to do it one night next week?"

"I got a question," Dortmunder said, "about payout."

Querk looked alert, ready to help. "Yeah?"

"When do we get it?"

"I don't follow," Querk said.

Dortmunder pointed at the building in front of them. "When we leave there," he said, "what we got is siapas. *Money* we get from Rodrigo."

"Sure," Querk said.

"How? When?"

"Well, first the siapas gotta go to Guerrera," Querk said, "and then Rodrigo has stuff he's gonna do, and then the dollars come up here."

"What if they don't?" Dortmunder said.

"Listen," Querk said, "I trust Rodrigo, he'll come through."

"I dunno about this," Dortmunder said.

Querk looked at his watch again. He was antsy to get to work. "Lemme get a message to him," he said, "work out a guarantee. What if I come back to the city this Saturday? We'll meet. Maybe your place again?"

"Three in the afternoon," Dortmunder said, because he didn't want to have to give everybody lunch.

"We'll work it out then," Querk said. "Listen, I better get on my forklift, I wouldn't want to get fired before vacation time."

He nodded a farewell and walked toward the loading bay, while Dortmunder and Kelp turned around and headed out. As they walked toward the public street, Kelp said, "Maybe the dollars should come up *before* the siapas go down."

"I was thinking that," Dortmunder said. "Or maybe one of us rides shotgun."

"You mean, *go* to this place?" Kelp was astonished. "Would you wanna do that?"

"No," Dortmunder said. "I said, 'one of us.' "

"We'll see how it plays," Kelp said. They turned toward the intersection, and he said, "I talked to Seven Leagues."

"Yeah?"

"Her name is Janet Twilley. She's bossy, and she's got a black eye."

"Oh, yeah?" Dortmunder was surprised. "Querk doesn't seem the type."

"No, he doesn't. I think we oughta see is there a Mr. Twilley."

13

Roger Twilley's shift as a repairman for Darby Telephone & Electronics (slogan: "The 5th Largest Phone Co. in New York State!") ended every day at four, an hour before Janet would close her travel agency, which was good. It gave him an hour by himself to listen to the day's tapes.

Twilley, a leathery, bony, loose-jointed fellow who wore his hair too long because he didn't like barbers, was known to his co-workers as an okay guy who didn't have much to say for himself. If he ever *were* to put his thoughts into words (which he wouldn't), their opinion would change, because in fact Twilley despised and mistrusted them all. He despised and mistrusted everybody he knew, and believed he would despise and mistrust everybody else in the world if he got to know them. Thus the tapes.

Being a phone company repairman, often alone on the job with his own cherry picker, and having a knack with phone gadgets he'd developed over the years on the job, Twilley had found it easy to bug the phones of everybody he knew that he cared the slightest bit about eavesdropping on. His mother, certainly, and Janet, naturally, and half a dozen other relatives and friends scattered around the general Sycamore area. The bugs were voice-activated, and the tapes were in his "den" in the basement, a room Janet knew damn well to keep out of, or she knew what she'd get.

Every afternoon, once he'd shucked out of his dark blue Darby Telephone jumpsuit and opened himself a can of beer, Twilley would go down to the den to listen to what these people had to say for themselves. He knew at least a few of them were scheming against him—mom, for instance, and Janet—but he hadn't caught any of them yet. It was, he knew, only a matter of time. Sooner or later, they'd condemn themselves out of their own mouths.

There are a lot of factors that might help explain how Twilley had turned out this way. There was his father's abrupt abandonment of the family when Twilley was six, for instance, a betrayal he'd never gotten over. There was his mother's catting around for a good ten years or more after that first trauma, well into Twilley's sexually agonized teens. There was the so-called girlfriend, Renee, who had publicly humiliated him in seventh grade. But the fact is, what it came down to, Twilley was a jerk.

The jerk now sat for thirty-five minutes at the table in his den, earphones on as he listened to the day the town had lived through, starting with Janet. Her phone calls today were all strictly business, talking to airlines, hotels, clients. There was nothing like the other day's "wrong number," somebody supposedly asking for somebody named Frank, that Twilley had immediately leaped on as code. A signal, some kind of signal. He'd played that fragment of tape over and over— "Is Frank there?" "Is Frank there?" "Is Frank there?"—and he would recognize that voice if it ever called again, no matter what it had to say.

On to the rest of the tapes. His mother and her friend Helen yakked the whole goddam day away, as usual—they told each other recipes, bird sightings, funny newspaper items, plots of television shows—and as usual Twilley fast-forwarded through it all, just dropping in for spot checks here and there— ". . . and she said Emmaline looked pregnant to *her* . . ."—or he'd be down here in the den half the night, listening to two women who had raised boringness to a kind of holy art form. Stained glass for the ear.

The rest of the tapes contained nothing useful. Twilley reset them for tomorrow and went upstairs. He sat on the sofa in the living room, opened the drawer in the end table beside him, and his tarot deck had been moved. He frowned at it. He always kept it lined up in a neat row between the coasters and the notepad, and now all three were out of alignment, the tarot deck most noticeably.

He looked around the room. *Janet* wouldn't move it. She wouldn't open this drawer. Had somebody been in the house?

He walked through the place, a small two-bedroom Cape Cod, and saw nothing else disturbed. Nothing was missing. He must have jostled the table one time, walking by.

He did a run of the cards on the living room coffee table, a little more hastily than usual, to be done before Janet got home. He wasn't embarrassed by the cards and his daily consultation of them, he could certainly do anything he damn well pleased in his own home, but it just felt a little awkward somehow to shuffle the deck and deal out the cards if he knew Janet could see him.

Nothing much in the cards today. A few strangers hovered here and there, but they always did. Life, according to the tarot deck, was normal.

He put the deck away, neatly aligned in the drawer, and when Janet came home a quarter hour later he was sprawled on the sofa, watching the early news. She took the sunglasses off right away, as soon as she walked in the door, to spite him. He squinted at her, and that shouldn't look that bruised, not four, five days later. She must be poking her thumb in her eye to make it look worse, so he'd feel bad.

You want somebody to poke a thumb in your eye, is that it? Is that what you want? "How was your day?" he said.

"I caught a fish." She'd been speaking to him in a monotone for so long he thought it was normal. "I'll see about dinner," she said, and went on through toward the kitchen.

Watching antacid commercials on television, Twilley told himself he *knew* she was up to something, and the reason he knew, she didn't fight back any more. She didn't get mad at him any more, and she almost never tried to boss him around any more.

Back at the beginning of the marriage, years ago, she had been an improver and he had been her most important project. Not her only project, she bossed everybody around, but the most important one. She'd married him, and they both knew it, because she'd believed he needed improving, and further believed he'd be somebody she'd be happy to live with once the improvement was complete.

No. Nobody pushes Roger Twilley. Roger Twilley pushes back.

But she wasn't pushing any more, hardly at all, only in an automatic unguarded way every once in a while. Like a few days ago. So that's how he knew she was up to something. Up to something.

"Is Frank there?"

14

Since he didn't plan to stay overnight in the city this time, Querk didn't borrow Claude's van but drove his own old clunker of a Honda with the resale value of a brick. But it would take him to New York and back, and last as long as he'd need it, which wouldn't be very long at all.

Three o'clock. He walked from his parked heap to the entrance to Dortmunder's building and would have rung the bell but Kelp was just ahead of him, standing in front of the door as he pulled his wallet out. "Whadaya say, Kirby?" he said, and withdrew a credit card from the wallet.

A credit card? To enter an apartment building? Querk said, "What are you doing?" but then he saw what he was doing, as Kelp slid the credit card down the gap between door and frame, like slicing off a wedge of soft cheese, and the door sagged open with a little forlorn *creak*.

"Come on in," Kelp said, and led the way.

Following, Querk said, "Why don't you ring the doorbell?"

"Why disturb them? This is just as easy. And practice."

Querk was not pleased, but not surprised either, when Kelp treated the apartment door upstairs the same way, going through it like a movie ghost, then pausing to call down the hallway, "Hello! Anybody there?" He turned his head to explain over his shoulder, "May doesn't like me to just barge in."

"No," agreed Querk, while down the hall Dortmunder appeared from the living room, racing form in one hand, red pencil in the other and scowl on face.

"God damn it, Andy," he said. "The building spent a lot of money on those doorbells."

"People spend money on anything," Kelp said, as he and Querk entered the apartment, Querk closing the door, yet wondering why he bothered.

Dortmunder shook his head, giving up the fight, and led the way into the living room as Kelp said, "May here?"

"She's doing a matinee." Dortmunder explained to Querk, "She likes movies, so if I got something to do she goes to them."

"You don't? Like movies?"

Dortmunder shrugged. "They're okay. Siddown."

Querk took the sofa, Dortmunder and Kelp the chairs. Kelp said, "So here we all are, Kirby, and now you're going to ease our minds."

"Well, I'll try." This was going to be tricky now, as Querk well knew. He said, "Maybe I should first tell you about the other person in this."

"Rodrigo, you mean," Kelp said.

"No, the travel agent."

"*That's* right," Kelp said, "you said there was a travel agent, he's the one gonna ship the siapas south."

"She," Querk corrected him. "Janet Twilley, her name is. She's got a travel agency, up there in Sycamore."

"Oh, ho," said Kelp. He looked roguish. "A little something happening there, Kirby?"

"No no," Querk said, because he certainly didn't want them to think *that.* "It's strictly business. She and I are gonna split our share, the same as you two."

"Half of a half," Kelp said.

"Right."

Dortmunder said, "You trust this person."

"Oh, absolutely," Querk said.

Dortmunder said, "Without anything special between you, just a business thing, you trust her."

Treading with extreme caution, Querk said, "To tell you the truth, I think she's got an unhappy marriage. I think she wants money so she can get away from there."

"But not with you," Kelp said.

"No, not with an ex-con." Querk figured if he put himself down it would sound more believable. "She just wants to use me," he explained, "to make it so she can get out of that marriage."

Dortmunder shrugged. "Okay. So she's the one takes the siapas to Rodrigo. *You* trust her to come back with the dollars. But we still got the same question, why do *we* trust her?"

"We talked about that," Querk said, "Janet and me, and the only thing we could come up with is, one of you has to travel with her."

Kelp nodded at Dortmunder. "Told you so."

"See," Querk said, hurrying through the story now that they'd reached it, "she's putting together this travel package, I dunno, fifteen or twenty people on this South American bus tour. Plane down, then bus. And she'll have the boxes in with the whole container load of everybody's luggage. So what she can do, she can slip in one more person, and she'll get the ticket for free, but you'll have to tell me which one so she'll know what name to put on the ticket."

Dortmunder and Kelp looked at each other. Kelp sighed. "I knew this was gonna happen," he said.

Querk said, "It won't be bad. A few days' vacation, and you come back."

Kelp said, "Can she promote two tickets?"

"You mean, both of you go down?"

"No," Kelp said. "I mean my lady friend. I could see myself doing this, I mean it would be easier, if she could come along."

"Sure," Querk said, because why not, and also because this was turning out to be easier than he'd feared. "Just give me her name. Write it down on something."

Dortmunder, rising, said, "I got a pad in the kitchen. Anybody want a beer?"

Everybody wanted a beer. Dortmunder went away, and Kelp said to Querk, "Her name is Anne Marie Carpinaw. Your friend—Janet?—they'll like each other."

"I'm sure they will," Querk said. Then, because he was nervous, he repeated himself, saying, "It won't be bad. A few days' vacation, that's all. You'll have a good time."

"Sure," Kelp said.

Dortmunder came back with a notepad and three unopened beer cans. "Here, everybody can open their own," he said.

Kelp took the pad and wrote his lady friend's name on it, while the other two opened their beer cans, Dortmunder slopping beer onto his pants leg. "Damn!"

"Here it is," Kelp said, and handed the slip of paper to Querk.

"Thanks." Querk pocketed the paper and lifted his beer. "What was that toast of yours? To crime."

Kelp offered the world's blandest smile. "To crime, with good friends," he said.

"Hear, hear," Dortmunder and Querk said.

15

Wednesday. The last thing Janet did before shutting Seven Leagues for the day was cut the two tickets, in the names of Anne Marie Carpinaw and Andrew Octavian Kelp, JFK to San Cristobal, Guerrera, change in Miami, intermediate stop in Tegucigalpa, Honduras, departure 10 P.M. tomorrow night, arrival 6:47 A.M., first leg Delta, second leg the charter carrier InterAir. She tucked these two tickets into her shoulder bag, put on her sunglasses, locked up the shop, took a last long look at it through the front plate glass window, and drove home to the rat.

At almost the exact same instant Janet was opening the door of her hated home, Kelp was opening the driver's door of another O'Malley special (small but spunky) rented with another short-life-expectancy credit card. Dortmunder tossed his bag in the back and slid in beside Kelp.

Kirby Querk, being on vacation along with the entire workforce of Sycamore Creek Printery, spent the afternoon fishing with a couple of friends from the plant, well downstream from town. (It was while fishing this part of this stream, almost a year ago, that he'd first met Janet, beautiful in her fishing hat and waders.) The unusually high water made for a rather interesting day, with a few spills, nothing serious. The influx of water from the opened dam starting last Saturday had roiled the streambed for a while, making turbid water in which the fishing would have been bad to useless, but by Wednesday Sycamore Creek was its normal sparkling self and Querk spent a happy day playing catch and release with the fish. There were times he almost forgot his nervousness about tonight.

Roger Twilley watched television news every chance he got, a sneer on his face. He despised and mistrusted them all, and watched mainly so he could catch the lies. A lot of the lies got past him, he knew that, but some of them he caught, the blatant obvious untruths the powers that be tell to keep the shmos in line. Well, Roger Twilley was no shmo; he was on to them, there in their 6:30 network news.

Meanwhile Janet, allegedly in the kitchen working on dinner, was actually in the bedroom, packing a small bag. Toiletries, cosmetics, a week's worth of clothing. She left much more than she took, but still the bag was crammed full when she was finished, and surprisingly heavy. She lugged it from the bedroom through the kitchen, out the back door, and around to the side of the house where a band of blacktop had been added, for her to keep her car. (*His* car got the attached garage, of course, which was all right in the summer, less so in the winter.) She heaved the bag into the trunk, which already contained her fishing gear, and went back into the house to actually make dinner, asking herself yet again, as she did every evening at this time, why she didn't just go ahead and poison the rat. But she answered the question, too, as she always did, with the knowledge that she'd simply never get away with it. A battered wife and a poisoned husband; even a Darby County cop could draw that connector.

Using the same credit card that had promoted the rental car, outside which now Dortmunder was stretching and groaning and wailing, "Why me?" Kelp took two adjoining rooms in the Taconic Lakes Motel, just about twenty miles north of Sycamore. It was not quite 7:30; even leaving the city in the middle of rush hour, they'd made good time.

Querk ate a bland dinner (meat loaf, mashed potatoes, green beans, water) with Cousin Claude and Eugenia and the two kids, then went into "his" room and packed his own bag. His years of being in and out of various jails had left him a man of very few possessions, all of which either fit into the bag or he wouldn't mind leaving behind. He put the bag on the floor next to the bed, on the side away from the door, and went out to watch television with the family.

Dortmunder and Kelp, after resting a little while in the motel, drove down to Sycamore and had dinner in the Italian restaurant by the traffic light there, the printery's forest crowding in on it from two sides. Dinner wasn't bad, and the same credit card still had some life in it. After dinner, they strolled around town a while, seeing how absolutely dense and black that forest was. There was some traffic, not much, and by evening the other joint in town, Sycamore House, where they'd had that lunch they were trying to forget, turned out to be where the rowdies hung out, the kind of place where the usual greeting is, "Wanna fight?" Their bark was presumably worse than their bite, though, because there was absolutely no police presence in town, neither around Sycamore House nor anywhere else, nor did it appear to be needed. Maybe on weekends.

When Janet washed her hair, which she usually did about three evenings a week, she was in the bathroom absolutely *forever*. This was a one-bathroom house, so Roger complained bitterly about the time she hogged in the bathroom, forcing him to go outside to piss on the lawn, but secretly this was the time he would take to search her possessions. Sooner or later, she would slip, leave something incriminating where he could find it.

And tonight, by God, was it! His hand shook, holding the airline tickets, and something gnawed at his heart, as though in reality he'd never wanted to find the proof of her perfidy after all, which was of course nonsense. Because here it was. *She* was Anne Marie Carpinaw, of course, a stupid alias to try to hide behind. But who was Andrew Octavian Kelp?

Cousin Claude and his family were early to bed, early to rise, and usually so was Querk; jail does not encourage the habit of rising late. This evening, as usual, the entire household was tucked in and dark before eleven o'clock, but this evening Querk couldn't sleep, not even if he wanted to, which he didn't. He lay in the dark in "his" room, the packed bag a dark bulk on the floor beside the bed, and he gazed at the ceiling, thinking about the plan he and Janet had worked out, seeing how good it was, how really good. They'd gone over it together he didn't know how many times, looking for flaws, finding some, correcting them. By now, the plan was honed as smooth as a river rock.

Janet almost always went to bed before Roger, and by the time he got there she would be asleep or at least pretending. Tonight, without a word, she went off to the bedroom and their separate beds just as he started watching the eleven o'clock news. He listened, and when he heard the bedroom door close he quietly got up, went to the kitchen, then through the connecting door to the garage. There was an automatic electric garage door opener, but it was very loud, and it caused a bright light to switch on for three minutes, so tonight Roger opened his car door to cause the interior light to go on, and by that light he found the red-and-white cord he could pull to separate the door from the opener, designed for emergencies like the power being off. Then he lifted the door by hand, leaned into the car to put it in neutral, and pushed it backward out of the garage. There was a slight downhill slope from garage to street, so the car did get away from him just a little bit, but there was no traffic on this residential side street this late at night, so he just followed it, and it stopped of its own accord when the rear wheels reached the street. He turned the wheel through the open window, and wrestled the car backward in a long arc until it was parked on the opposite side of the street one door down. A dark street, trees in leaf, a car like any other. Janet would have no reason to notice it. He went back to the house, into the garage, and pulled the door down. He could reattach the cord in the morning.

11:45 said Querk's bedside clock, red numbers glowing in the dark. He got up, dressed quickly and silently, picked up his bag, and tiptoed from the house. Tonight, he had parked the Honda down the block a ways. He walked to it, put the bag on the passenger seat, and drove away from there.

In their separate beds in the dark room, Janet and Roger were each convinced the other was asleep. Both were fully clothed except for their shoes under the light summer covers, and both worked very hard to breathe like a sleeping person. They had each other fooled completely.

Every time Janet, lying on her left side, cautiously opened her right eye to see the table between the beds, plus the dark mound of Roger over there, the illuminated alarm clock on the table failed to say midnight. She had no fear of accidentally falling asleep, not tonight of all nights, but why did time have to *creep* so? But then at last she opened that eye one more time and now the clock read *11:58*, and darn it, that was good enough. Being very careful, making absolutely no noise—well, a faint rustle or two—she rolled over and rose from the bed. She stooped to pick up her shoes, then carried them tiptoe from the room.

The instant he heard Janet move, Roger tensed like a bowstring. He forced himself to keep his eyes shut, believing eyes reflect whatever light might be around and she might see them and know he was awake. It wasn't until the rustle of her movements receded toward the bedroom door that he dared to look. Yes, there she goes, through the doorway, open now because it was only shut if she was in bed while he was watching television.

Janet turned left, toward the kitchen, to go out the back door and around to the car. It was too bad she'd have to start its engine so close to the house, but the bedroom was way on the other side, with the bulk of the house and the garage in between, so it should be all right. In any case, she was going.

The instant Janet disappeared from the doorway, Roger was up, stepping into his loafers, streaking silently through the house to the front door, out, and running full tilt across the street to crouch down on the far side of his car. Hunkered down there, he heard her car motor start, saw the headlights switch on, and then saw the car come out and swing away toward town, which is what he'd been hoping. It meant his car was faced the right way. He let her travel a block, then jumped into the car, started it, didn't turn the lights on, and drove off in pursuit.

12:20 by the dashboard clock, and Querk parked in the lot next to Sycamore House. There was no all-night street parking permitted in Central Sycamore, but there were always a few cars left at Sycamore House, by people whose friends had decided maybe they shouldn't drive home after all, so the Honda wouldn't attract attention. He got out and walked down the absolutely deserted silent street to the traffic light doggedly giving its signals to nothing, then crossed and walked to the entrance to Sycamore Creek and on in.

There was no problem unlocking the main gate, nor temporarily locking it again behind him. He crossed to the building, unlocked the one loading bay door with a faulty alarm he happened to know about, and made his way through the silent, dark, stuffy plant to the managers' offices, where it was a simple matter to disarm the alarm systems, running now on the backup batteries. Then he retraced his steps, out to the street.

Janet had expected to be the only person driving around this area this late at night, but partway to town another car's headlights appeared in her rearview mirror. Another night owl, she thought, and hoped he wasn't a drunken speed demon who would try to pass her. These roads were narrow and twisty. But, no; thankfully, he kept well back. She drove on into town, turned into the Sycamore House parking lot, recognized the Honda right away, and parked next to it.

Roger had kept well back, sorry he had to use his headlights at all but not wanting to run into a deer out here, the deer population having exploded in this part of the world once all of the predator animals had been removed, unless you count hunters, and don't. He followed the car ahead all the way into town, and when he saw the brake lights go on he thought at first she was braking for the traffic light up ahead, but then she suddenly made the left turn into the Sycamore House parking lot. Damn! He hadn't expected that. Should he go past? Should he stop? If he tried to park along here, you just knew some damn cop would pop out of nowhere to give him both a hard time and a ticket, while Janet got away to who knows where. Guerrera, that's where. San Cristobal, Guerrera.

He drove on by, peering in at the Sycamore House parking lot, but she'd switched her lights off and there was nothing to see. He got to the corner, and the light was against him, so he stopped, while no traffic went by in all directions. Diagonally across the street was Luigi's, the Italian restaurant, and at the far end of it, he knew, was a small parking lot, hemmed in by the fake forest. He could leave the car there and hoof it back to Sycamore House, just as soon as this damn light changed. When would it—? Ah! At last.

He drove across the empty intersection, turned left at the small and empty parking lot, and stopped, car's nose against pine branches. He switched off lights and engine, so now it was only by the vague streetlight glow well behind him that he saw, in his rearview mirror, the apparition rise from the floor behind the front seat, *exactly* like all those horror stories! He stared, convulsed with terror, and the apparition showed him a wide horrible smile, a big horrible pistol and a pair of shiny horrible handcuffs. "Didn't that tarot deck," it asked him, "tell you not to go out tonight?"

16

When Querk walked back into the Sycamore House parking lot, Janet's Chrysler Cirrus was parked next to his little Honda; a bigger, more comfortable car, though not very new. She must have seen him in the rearview mirror because she popped out of her car, the brief illumination of the interior light showing the hugeness of her smile but still the dark around her left eye. Then the door closed, the light went out, and she was in his arms.

They embraced a long time, he feeling her body tremble with the release of weeks of tension. Months. But now it was over. He was off parole, a free man. She was out of that house, a free woman. Start here.

At last he released her and whispered, "Everything's going fine. Three, four hours, it'll be all over."

"I know you'll do it," she whispered, then shook a finger at him. "Don't let them get any ideas."

"I won't."

He took his bag from the Honda and put it in the Chrysler, then kissed her one last time, got into the Honda, and drove out to the street. He turned left, ignored the red light, drove through the intersection, and stopped next to the Hess station across the street from Luigi's. Promptly, Dortmunder stepped out of the dimness inside the phone booth there, crossed the sidewalk, and slid in next to him.

Querk looked around. "Where's Kelp?"

"A couple things came up," Dortmunder told him, "nothing to do with us. He'll take care of them, then catch up with us later."

Querk didn't like this, didn't like the idea that one of his partners was going to be out of sight while the job was going down. "We're gonna need Kelp in the plant there," he said.

"He'll be there," Dortmunder promised. "He'll be right there when we get back with the truck."

There was nothing Querk could do about this development short of to call the whole thing off, which he didn't want to do, so he nodded reluctantly and said, "I hope nothing's gonna get screwed up."

"How could it? Come on, let's go."

The Combined Darby County Fire Department and Rescue Squad existed in an extremely fireproof brick building in the middle of nowhere. Seven local volunteer fire departments and two local volunteer ambulance services, each with its own firehouse or garage, had been combined into this organization, made necessary by the worsening shortage of volunteers, and political infighting had made it impossible to use any of the existing facilities. A local nob had donated land here in the middle of the responsibility area, and the building was erected, empty and alone unless a fund-raiser dinner were being held or the volunteers' beepers sounded off.

Querk parked the Honda behind the building, out of sight, and used a copy of Cousin Claude's key to unlock the right garage door. He lifted it, stepped inside, and drove out the truck, which was red like a fire engine, with high metal sides full of cubicles containing emergency equipment, a metal roof, but open at the back to show the big generator bolted to the truck body in there.

Querk waited while Dortmunder lowered the garage door and climbed up onto the seat next to him. "Pretty good machine," he said.

"It does the job," Querk said.

It was with relief that Querk saw Kelp actually standing there next to the NO TRESPASSING sign. Kelp waved, and Dortmunder waved back, while Querk drove down to the closed entrance gates. "They're unlocked," he assured Dortmunder, who climbed out to open the gates, then close them again after the truck and Kelp had both entered.

Driving slowly alongside the building toward the window he wanted, Querk saw in all his rearview mirrors, illuminated by a smallish moon, Dortmunder and Kelp walking along in his wake, talking together. Kelp must be telling Dortmunder what he'd done about whatever problem he'd gone off to fix.

Querk wondered; should he ask Kelp what the problem was? No, he shouldn't. Dortmunder had said it was nothing to do with tonight's job, so that meant it was none of his business. The fact that Kelp was here was all that mattered. A tight-lipped man knows when other people expect him to be tight-lipped.

17

Dortmunder was bored. There was nothing to do about it but admit it; he was bored.

Usually, in a heist, what you do is, you case the joint, then you plan and plan, and then there's a certain amount of tension when you break into whatever the place is, and then you *grab* what you came for and you get *out* of there.

Not this time. This time, the doors are open, the alarms are off, and nobody's around. So you just waltz in. But then you don't *grab* anything, and you certainly don't get *out* of there.

What you do instead, you shlep heavy cable off a wheel out of the generator truck, shove it through a window Querk has opened, and then shlep it across a concrete floor in the dark, around and sometimes into a lot of huge machines that are not the machine Querk wants, until at last you can hook the cables to both a machine and a control panel. This control panel also controls some lights, so finally you can see what you're doing.

Meanwhile, Querk has been collecting his supplies. He needs three different inks, and two big rolls of special paper, that he brings over with his forklift. He needs one particular size of paper cutter, a wickedly sharp big rectangle criss-crossed with extremely dangerous lines of metal, that has to be slid into an opening in the side of the machine without sacrificing any fingers to it, and which will, at the appropriate moments, descend inside the machine to slice sheets of paper into many individual siapas.

The boxes for the siapas already exist, but laid out flat, and have to be inserted into a wide slot in the back of the machine. The nasty wire bands to close the boxes—hard, springy, with extremely sharp edges—have to be inserted onto rolls and fed into the machine like feeding movie film into a projector. Having three guys for this part is a help, because it would take one guy working alone a whole lot longer just to set things up, even if he could wrestle the big paper roll into position by himself, which he probably couldn't.

But after everything was in position, then you *really* needed three guys. It was a three-guy machine. Guy number one (Querk) was at the control panel, keeping an eye on the gauges that told him how the ink flow was coming along, how the paper feed was doing, how the boxes were filling up. Guy number two (Kelp) was physically all around the machine, which was a little delicate and touchy, following Querk's orders on how to adjust the various feeds and watch the paper, which would have liked to jam up if anybody looked away for a minute.

And guy number three, Dortmunder, was the utility man. It was his job to replenish the ink supply when needed, which was rarely. It was also his job to wrestle the full boxes off the end of the chute at the back of the machine, but since in three hours there were only going to be five boxes, that didn't take up a lot of his time. It was also his job occasionally to go out to see how the generator truck was coming along, which was fine. In addition, it was his job to keep checking on the laid-out boxes inside the machine with the money stacking up on them, and the alignment of the big paper-cutter, to make sure nothing was getting off kilter and to warn Querk to shut down temporarily if something did, which only happened twice. And generally it was his job to stand chicky; but if anybody were to come into the plant that they wouldn't like to come in, it would already be too late to do anything about it.

So here he was, the gofer in a slow-motion heist, and he was bored. It was like having an actual job.

They'd started at ten after one, and it was just a few ticks after four when the last of the paper rolled into the machine and Querk started shutting its parts down, one section at a time until the fifth and final box came gliding out of the chute and Dortmunder wrestled it over onto the concrete floor with the others. Five boxes, very heavy, each containing a thousand bills compressed into the space, a thousand twenty million siapa notes per box, for a value of a hundred thousand dollars per box. In Guerrera.

Dortmunder stepped back from the final box. "Done," he said. "At last."

"Not exactly done," Querk said. "Remember, this run never happened. We gotta clean up everything in here, put it all back the way it was."

Yes; exactly like having a job.

18

Querk's nervousness, once they'd driven the generator truck actually onto the plant property, had turned into a kind of paralysis, a cauterizing in which he couldn't feel his feelings. He was just doing it, everything he'd been going over and over in his mind all this time, acting out the fantasy, reassuring Janet and himself that everything would work out just fine, playing it out in his head again and again so that, when the time came to finally *do* it, actually in the real world do it, it was as though he'd already done it and this was just remembering.

And the job went, if anything, even better than the fantasy, smooth and quick and easy. Not a single problem with the two guys he'd found to help, and that had always been one of the scarier parts of the whole thing. He couldn't do it alone, but he couldn't use locals, none of these birds around here had the faintest idea how to keep their mouths shut. Amateurs. He had to use pros, but he didn't know anybody any more.

Nevertheless, if he was going to do it, he would have to reach out, find *somebody* with the right résumé that he could talk into the job, and boy, did he come up lucky. Dortmunder and Kelp were definitely pros, but at the same time they were surprisingly gullible. He could count on them to do the job and to keep their mouths shut, and he could also count on them to never even notice what he was really up to.

The cleaning up after the print job took another half hour. The next to the last thing they did, before switching off the lights, was forklift the five boxes of siapas out to the generator truck, where they fit nicely at the back. Then it was disconnect the cables, reel them back into the truck, and drive out of there, pausing to lock the big gates on the way by.

Still dark on the streets of Sycamore. Still no vehicles for the dutiful traffic light to oversee. Dortmunder and Kelp rode on the wide bench seat of the truck beside Querk, who drove down the street to stop in front of Seven Leagues. "I'll just unlock the door," he said, as he climbed down to the street.

The story he'd told them was that the travel group going down there to Guerrera contained a bunch of evangelicals, looking for converts, so Janet would ship the boxes out of the United States as missals and hymnals. Tonight, they'd leave the boxes at Seven Leagues, and in the morning she'd cover them with all the necessary tags and stickers, and the van carrying all the tour group's luggage would come by to pick them up and take them down to JFK.

Once the boxes had been lugged into Seven Leagues and the door relocked, Querk said, "You fellas need a lift to your car?"

"No, that's okay," Kelp said, pointing vaguely north, out of town. "We're parked just up there."

Dortmunder said, "You want to get the truck back."

"I sure do."

Should he shake hands with them? He felt he should; it would be the more comradely thing to do. Sticking his hand out in Kelp's direction, he said, "It's been good working with you."

Kelp had a sunny smile, even in the middle of the night. Pumping Querk's hand, he said, "I wouldn't miss it for the world."

Shaking Dortmunder's hand, bonier than Kelp's but less powerful, Querk said, "We'll be in touch."

"You know it," Dortmunder said.

"You know where to find me."

"Sure do," Dortmunder said.

Well. That was comradely enough. "I better get this truck back before sunup," he said.

"Sure," they said, and waved at him, and he got into the truck.

He had to make a K turn to go back the other way, cumbersome with this big vehicle. He headed toward the traffic light as Dortmunder and Kelp walked off northward, disappearing almost immediately into the darkness, there being streetlights only here in the center of town.

As he drove toward the traffic light, he passed Sycamore House on his left, and resisted the impulse to tap the horn. But Janet would see him, and a horn sounding here in the middle of the night might attract attention. Attention from Dortmunder and Kelp, in any case.

So he drove on, the traffic light graciously turning green as he reached the intersection. Behind him, Janet in the Cirrus would now have seen the truck go by twice, and would know the job had gone well. He could hardly wait to get back to her.

Querk grinned all the way to the garage, where he put the truck away, backing it in the way it had been before. Then he got into the Honda for the last time in his life and drove it back to Sycamore, not only grinning now but also humming a little and at times even whistling between his teeth. To his right, the sky was just beginning to pale; dawn was on the way.

Sycamore. Once again the traffic light gave him a green. He drove through the intersection, turned into the Sycamore House parking lot, and put the Honda next to the Cirrus. He switched off the lights and the engine and stepped out to the blacktop, leaving the keys in the car. Turning to the Cirrus, he expected Janet to either start the engine or step out to speak to him. When she did neither, he bent to look into the car, and it was empty.

What? Why? They'd agreed to meet here when the job was done, so what happened? Where was she?

Maybe she'd needed to go to the bathroom. Or maybe she started to get uncomfortable in the car, after almost four hours, and decided to go wait in the office instead. The whole purpose of her being here the whole time was so he'd have his own backup means of escape in case anything were to go wrong with the job. Once she'd seen the truck, she had to know the job had gone well.

So she must be up at Seven Leagues. Querk left the parking lot and walked up the street, taking the Seven Leagues key out of his pocket. When he reached the place, there were no lights on inside. That was strange.

He unlocked the door, entered, closed the door, felt around on the wall for the light switch, found it, and stared, unbelieving.

"Surprise," Dortmunder said.

19

Between dinner and the job, in fact, Dortmunder and Kelp had found a number of things to keep them interested, if not completely surprised. Primarily, they'd wanted to know what part Janet Twilley planned to take in tonight's exercises, if any, and so had driven out to the Twilley house a little before eleven, seeing lights still on in there. They'd visited that house last week, learning more about Roger Twilley than anybody else on Earth, and had found none of it pleasant. If Janet Twilley wanted to begin life anew with Kirby Querk, they couldn't argue the case, not with what they knew of Roger, just so she didn't plan to do it with their siapas.

They were parked down the block from the Twilley residence, discussing how to play this—should Kelp drive Dortmunder back to town, to keep an eye on the plant, while Kelp kept the car and maintained an observation post chez Twilley—when Roger decided their moves for them. The first thing they saw was the garage door open over there.

"The light didn't come on," Dortmunder said.

"I knew there was something," Kelp said.

Next, a car backed out of the garage, also with no lights on, and moving very slowly. Not only that, Roger himself came trotting out of the garage right after the car, so who was driving?

Turned out, nobody. Fascinated, they watched Roger push his car around in a great loop to park it on their side of the street, about two houses away.

"He, too, knows something's up," Kelp said.

Dortmunder said, "But he doesn't know what."

"He's gonna follow her."

"So we," Dortmunder said, "follow him."

"I got a better idea," Kelp said. "Have we got that bag in the back?"

"In the trunk? Yeah."

On an outing like this, they always traveled with that bag. Small, it was packed with extra materials that, who knew, might come in handy. Tools of various kinds, ID of various kinds, weapons of various kinds, and handcuffs of just one kind.

"What do you need from it?" Dortmunder asked.

"The cuffs. I'll ride in the back of the peeping tom's car, take him out if there's a problem, borrow it myself if she doesn't come out to be followed. You stash this car in town, tell Kirby I'll meet up with you guys at the plant."

So that's what they did, Dortmunder learning some more along the way, beginning with the fact that the driver's seat had even less legroom than the passenger seat. He stashed the compact in the Sycamore House parking lot, but stayed with it, and was there when Querk arrived, parked his Honda, and went off to set things up over at the printery.

A little later, he was also about to leave when Janet Twilley drove in, shut down, but didn't get out of her car. That was interesting. Not wanting to call attention to himself, he removed the bulb from the compact's interior light so that everything remained dark when he eased out of the car and out of the parking lot to go over to the Hess station and wait for Querk.

One thing about the phone booth outside the Hess station; it had legroom. Dortmunder leaned his back against the phone, folded his arms, and watched the traffic light change. After a while he saw Querk cross the street and walk north, and then here he came in the Honda south.

After the job at the plant and the departure of Querk to return the generator truck, there'd been nothing left to do but gather up Janet Twilley, still at her post in her Chrysler Cirrus, and use her keys to gain entrance to Seven Leagues. As for her husband, he could stay where he was, trussed up on the floor of his own car down by Luigi's. Good place for him.

And now it was simply a matter of waiting for Querk. And here he is.

20

Querk stared, pole-axed with shock. Janet was gagged and tied to her office chair, wide-eyed and trembling. Even her bruise was pale. Kelp, still with that sunny smile, sat near her in the client's chair. And Dortmunder stood near Querk; not too near, but close enough so that, if Querk decided to spin around and pull the door open and run, it wouldn't happen.

Stammering, the tremble in his hands back and worse than ever, Querk said, "What? What happened?"

"We came to settle up," Dortmunder said, while Kelp got to his feet, walked back to the unused desk, took the client's chair from it, and brought it back to stand facing himself and Janet. "Take a load off," he offered.

Dortmunder said, "Andy, turn the desk light on, will you? It's too bright in here."

Kelp did, and Dortmunder switched off the overheads that Querk had switched on. It became much dimmer in the long room, the light softer, though not what Querk thought of as cozy. Watching all this, he tried desperately to think, without much success. What was going on? What were they going to do? He said, "What's wrong? Fellas? I thought everything was okay."

"Not exactly okay," Dortmunder said, as he perched on the corner of Janet's desk.

Kelp said, "Come on, Kirby, take a chair. We'll tell you all about it."

So Querk sat in the chair Kelp had brought for him, and folded his shaking hands in his lap. He could feel Janet's eyes on him, but he couldn't bring himself to look directly at her. He was supposed to make things *better* for her. Tied up in a chair by two heisters from New York wasn't *better*.

Kelp said, "You know, Kirby, the thing was, at first we believed there really was a Rodrigo." He still seemed cheerful, not angry or upset, but Querk didn't believe any of it.

"You got us there, for a while," Dortmunder agreed. He sounded sullen, and that Querk could believe.

"What we figured," Kelp said, "why would you go through this whole scheme unless you had a payout coming? So that's why we believed in Rodrigo. Until, of course, we heard about Janet. Just as a by the by."

"Just dropped in the conversation," Dortmunder said.

"And Harry Matlock said you were a better follower than a leader," Kelp said, "so we began to wonder, who exactly were you following? So when we came up here last week, I stopped in to see Janet."

What? Querk now did stare directly at Janet, and she was frantically nodding, eyebrows raised almost to her hairline. "She—" Querk had to clear his throat. "She didn't tell me."

"She didn't know," Kelp said. "See, I was a customer, I was interested in going somewhere in South America, I wasn't sure where, and we talked about, oh . . ." He looked at Janet, amiable, inquiring. "About fifteen minutes, right?" Looking at Querk again, he said, "And the funny thing, never once did she mention that tour going to Guerrera. In fact, she never even mentioned Guerrera, the whole country."

"Probably," Querk said, even though he knew it was hopeless, "the tour was full by then."

"Which gets to how easy the extra two tickets were," Kelp said. "First she can wangle one ticket, but then two tickets is easy, no sweat, you don't even have to check back with her. But I'm getting ahead of my story."

"I thought you were buying it," Querk said.

Kelp's grin got even wider. "Yeah, I know. Anyway, when I was here that time, I noticed the shiner on Janet, and you didn't seem the type—"

"We both thought that," Dortmunder said.

"Thank you," Querk said.

"So we checked out her house," Kelp said, "and that's some winner she decided to marry."

"I guess he didn't seem that bad at first," Querk said.

"Maybe," Kelp said. "Anyway, here's this bossy woman—"

Janet gave him a glare, which Kelp ignored.

"—with a shiner and a bad husband. And here's you, likes to be bossed around. So we decided, what it was, you didn't have any Rodrigo, because how is this Janet here in upstate New York gonna make that kinda connection. Also, this is not a really successful travel agency here, which you can see by the fact that the other desk isn't used, so if she ever had an assistant or a partner the business couldn't support that person. So *maybe*, just maybe, the idea is, you'll run these half million dollars' worth of siapas, and you and Janet will *drive* to Guerrera, down through Mexico and all that, maxing out your credit cards along the way. And when you get there, you find a nice place to stay, you start living on the siapas. You put 'em in a few banks down there, you can even come back up to the States sometimes and spend them like money. Of course, there wouldn't be any for *us*."

"I'm sorry," Querk said.

Dortmunder nodded. "You certainly are."

"You needed two guys," Kelp said. "You couldn't go with local amateurs, so you had to reach out for pros, and what you got was us."

"I underestimated you," Querk said.

"Don't feel bad," Kelp advised him. "That's what *we* specialize in. So here you are, you've kissed us off, and Anne Marie and me are gonna feel really stupid tomorrow night at JFK with those imitation tickets—"

"I'm sorry," Querk said again.

"We know," Dortmunder said. He didn't sound sympathetic.

"But, you know," Kelp said, "this is better for you, because *Roger* knew something was up. You know, the paranoid is sometimes right, and Roger was right. So he was following Janet tonight, and if it hadn't been for us, Roger would be making a whole lot of trouble for you people right now."

Querk was rather afraid of Roger Twilley. "Roger?" he said. "Where is he?"

"Tied up in his car, down at Luigi's."

Dortmunder said, "You owe us for that one."

"Well," Kelp said, "he owes us for the whole score."

"That's true," Dortmunder said.

Rising, Kelp said, "I'll go get our wheels, you explain it."

Kelp was the pleasant one. Why couldn't Dortmunder go get their car? But, no; Kelp nodded at Querk and left the shop, and it was Dortmunder who said, "This is what we're gonna do. We're gonna leave you one box of the siapas, that's a hundred grand you can take down to Guerrera, get you started. In six months, you come up to New York, you buy at least one more box from us, half price. Fifty grand for a hundred grand of siapas. You can buy them all then, or you can buy a box every six months."

Querk said, "Where am I gonna get that money?"

"You're gonna steal it," Dortmunder told him. "That's what you do, remember? You gave up on reform."

Querk hung his head. The thought of a Guerreran jail moved irresistably through his mind.

Meanwhile, Dortmunder said, "If you *don't* show up in six months, the four boxes go to the cops with an anonymous letter with your names and a description of the scheme and where you're hiding out, and the probable numbers on your siapas. And then you've got nothing."

"Jeez," Querk said.

"Look at it this way," Dortmunder suggested. "You lied to us, you abused our trust, but we aren't getting even, we aren't hurting you. Because all we want is what's ours. So, one way or another, you keep your side of the bargain, and we keep ours." Looking past Querk at the window, he said, "Here's the goddam compact. I hope we can fit these boxes in there. Come on, Querk, help me carry the loot."

"All right." Rising, Querk said, "What do we do about Roger?"

"Nothing," Dortmunder said. "Luigi's cook'll find him in the morning, let *him* decide what to do. Come on, grab a box."

So Querk did, the two of them shlepping the boxes one at a time, Kelp busily moving crap around inside the car. They managed to cram three of the boxes into the trunk and one on its side on the alleged back seat, with their luggage on top.

At the end, feeling humble, Querk said to them both, on the sidewalk, "I wanna thank you guys. You could of made things a lot tougher for me."

"Well," Dortmunder said, "I wouldn't say you were getting off scot free." He nodded at Seven Leagues. "Sooner or later, you're gonna have to take off that gag."

ANNE PERRY

Anne Perry is the bestselling author of two Victorian detective series that are practically mandatory reading for any aficionado of the historical mystery. Her Thomas Pitt series and the William and Hester Monk series, although both set in the same nineteenth-century London, take very different looks at English society. She is also writing another acclaimed historical series set during the French Revolution, and consisting of the books *A Dish Taken Cold* and *The One Thing More*. She has also started another series set during World War I, which launched with the acclaimed novel *No Graves As Yet*. Besides this, she has also written a fantasy duology, *Tathea* and *Come Armageddon*. But no matter what genre she writes in, her deft, detailed research, multifaceted characters, and twisting plots have garnered her fans around the world. In her spare time she lectures on writing in such places as the cruise ship the *Queen Elizabeth II*. Recent books include *A Christmas Journey*, featuring a secondary character from the Thomas Pitt novels taking center stage, and the second volume in her World War I series, *Shoulder the Sky*. She makes her home in the highlands of Scotland.

HOSTAGES

Anne Perry

Bridget folded the last pair of trousers and put them into the case. She was looking forward to the holiday so much there was a little flutter of excitement in her stomach. It would not be the west coast she loved with its clean wind off the Atlantic and the great waves pounding in, because that would mean crossing the border into Eire, and they could not do that. But the north coast held its own beauty, and it would be away from Belfast, from Connor's responsibilities to the church, and most of all to the political party. There was always something he had to do, a quarrel to arbitrate, someone's bereavement to ease, a weakness to strengthen, a decision to make, and then argue and persuade.

It had been like that as long as she had known him, as it had been for his father. But then the Irish Troubles were over three hundred years old, in one form or another. The courage with which you fought for your beliefs defined who you were.

There was room for more in the suitcase. She looked around to see what else to put in just as Liam came to the door. He was sixteen, tall and lean like Connor, not yet filled out with muscle, and very conscious of it.

"Are you packed yet?" she asked.

"You don't need that much, Mum," he said dismissively. "We're only going for a week, and you can wash things, you know! Why are we going anyway? There's nothing to do!"

"That's exactly what I want to go for," she answered with a smile. "Your father needs to do nothing."

"He'll hate it!" Liam responded. "He'll be fretting all the time in case he's missing something, and when he comes home he'll only have to work twice as hard to put right whatever they've fouled up."

"Has it ever occurred to you," she said patiently, "that nothing will go wrong, and we'll have a good time? Don't you think perhaps it would be nice to be together, with no one else to think about, no one demanding anything, just for a few days?"

Liam rolled his eyes. "No," he said candidly. "It'll bore me out of my mind, and Dad too. He'll end up half the time on the phone anyway."

"There's no phone there," she told him. "It's a beach house."

"The mobile!" he said impatiently, his voice touched with contempt. "I'm going to see Michael."

"We're leaving in a couple of hours!" she called after him as he disappeared, and she heard his footsteps light and rapid along the passage, and then the back door slammed.

Connor came into the room. "What are you taking?" he asked, looking at the case. "What have you got all those trousers for? Haven't you packed any skirts? You can't wear those all the time."

She could, and she intended to. No one would see them. For once appearance would not matter. There would be no one there to criticize or consider it was not the right example for the wife of a minister and leader of the Protestant cause. Anyway, what she wore had nothing to do with the freedom of faith he had fought for since he was Liam's age, costing him the lightheartedness and the all too brief irresponsibility of his youth.

But was it worth arguing now, on the brink of this rare time together? It would sour it from the outset, make him feel thwarted, as if she were deliberately challenging him. It always did. And she wanted this week for them to have time away from anxiety and the constant pressure and threat that he faced every day at home, or in London.

Wordlessly she took the trousers out, all but one pair, and replaced them with skirts.

He did not say anything, but she saw the satisfaction in his face. He looked tired. There was a denser network of fine lines around his eyes and he was greyer at the temples than she had realized. A tiny muscle ticked intermittently in his jaw. Although he had complained about it, denied it, he needed this holiday even more than she did. He needed days without duty, without decisions, nights of sleep without interruption from the telephone, a chance to talk without weighing every word in case it were misjudged, or misquoted. She felt the little flutter of pleasure again, and smiled at him.

He did not notice. He left, closing the door behind him.

She was crushed, even as she knew it was stupid. He had far too much else on his mind to bother with emotional trivialities. He had every right to expect that she should take such things for granted. In the twenty-four years of their marriage he had never let her down. He never let anyone down! No matter what it cost, he always kept his word. The whole of Northern Ireland knew that, Catholic and Protestant. The promise of Connor O'Malley could be trusted, it was rock solid, as immutable as the promise of God—and as hard.

She heard the words in her mind with horror. How could she even think such a thing, let alone allow it to come into her head. He was engaged in a war of the spirit, there was no room for half measures, for yielding to the seduction of compromise. And he used the right words, she could feel her own temptation to water down the chastenings, in order to achieve a little peace, to yield on truth just for respite from the constant battle. She was heart and soul weary of it. She hungered for laughter, friendship, the ordinary things of daily life, without the pressure of outward righteousness and inner anger all the time.

And he would see that as weakness, even betrayal. Right cannot ever compromise with wrong. It is the price of leadership that there can be no self-indulgence. How often had he said that, and lived up to it?

She looked at the trousers she had taken out of the case. They were comfortable, and she could wear flat, easy shoes with them. This was supposed to be a holiday. She put two pairs of them back in again, at the bottom. She would do the unpacking anyway, and he would never know.

It was not difficult to pack for him: pyjamas, underwear, socks, plenty of shirts so he would always have a clean one, sweaters, lighter coloured casual trousers, toiletries. He would bring his own books and papers; that was an area she was not expected to touch.

Three middle-sized cases and Connor's briefcase would fit into the trunk of the car easily. The bodyguards, Billy and Ian, would come separately, following in another car, and they were not her responsibility. In fact she would try to imagine they were not there. They were necessary, of course, as they always were. Connor was a target for the I.R.A., although as far as she knew they had never physically attacked him. It would be a politically stupid thing to do; it would be the one thing that would unite all the disparate Protestant factions in one solid outrage.

And for the verbal attacks, he gave as good as he received, or better. He had the gift of words, the knowledge, and above all the passion so that his sermons, and his political speeches, almost interchangeable, erupted like lava to scorch those who were against his vision of Protestant survival and freedom. Sometimes it was directed just as fiercely at those on his own side who wavered, or in his view committed the greatest sin of all, betrayal. He despised a coward even more than he hated an open enemy.

The doorbell rang, and then, before anyone had had time to answer it, she heard the door open, and then Roisin's voice call out. "Hello, Mum! Where are you?"

"Bedroom!" Bridget answered. "Just finishing the packing. Like a cup of tea?"

"I'll make it," Roisin answered, arriving in the doorway. She was twenty-three, slim, with soft, brown hair like Bridget's, only darker, no honey fair streaks. She had been married just over a year and still had that glow of surprise and happiness about her. "You all ready?" she asked.

Bridget heard a slight edge to her voice, a tension she was trying to conceal. Please heaven it was not a difference with Eamonn. They were sufficiently in love it would all iron out, but Bridget did not want to go away for a week leaving Roisin emotionally raw. She was too vulnerable, and Eamonn was like Connor, passionate about his beliefs, committed to them, and expecting the same kind of commitment from those he loved, unaware of how little of himself he gave to his family, forgetting to put into word or touch what he expected them to know. "What is it?" she said aloud.

"I've got to speak to Dad," Roisin answered. "That's what I came for, really."

Bridget opened her eyes wide.

Roisin took a quick breath. "Sorry, Mum," she apologized. "I came to wish you a good holiday too. Heaven knows, you need it. But I could have done that over the phone."

Bridget looked at her more closely. She was a little flushed and her hands were stiff at her sides. "Are you alright?" she said with a pinch of anxiety. She almost asked her if she were pregnant, there was something about her which suggested it, but it would be intrusive. If it were so, Roisin would tell her when she was ready.

"Yes, of course I am!" Roisin said quickly. "Where's Dad?"

"Is it political?" It was a conclusion more than a question. She saw the shadow deepen in Roisin's eyes, and her right hand clench. "Couldn't it wait until we get back? Please!"

Roisin's face was indefinably tighter, more closed. "Eamonn asked me to come over," she answered. "Some things don't wait, Mum. I'll put the kettle on. He's not out, is he?"

"No . . ." Before she could add anything else, Roisin twisted around and was gone. Bridget looked around, checking the room for the last time. She always forgot something, but it was usually a trivial thing she could do without. And it was not as if they were going abroad. The house on the shore was lonely, that was its greatest charm, but the nearest village was a couple of miles away, and they would have the car. Even though they took bread and potatoes and a few tins, they would still need to go for food every so often.

She went through to the kitchen and found Roisin making the tea, and Connor standing staring out of the window into the back garden. Bridget would like to have escaped the conflict, but she knew there was no point. She would hear what had been said sooner or later. If they agreed it would be a cause for celebration, and she would join in. If they didn't, it would be between them like a coldness in the house, a block of ice sitting in the kitchen to be walked around.

Roisin turned with the teapot in her hand. "Dad?"

He remained where he was, his back to the room.

She poured three cups. "Dad, Eamonn's been talking with some of the moderates about a new initiative in education . . ." She stopped as she saw his shoulders stiffen. "At least listen to them!" Her voice was tight and urgent, a kind of desperation lifting it a pitch higher. "Don't refuse without hearing what it is!"

He swung around at last. His face was bleak, almost grey in the hard light. He sounded weary and bitter. "I've heard all I need to about Catholic schools and their methods, Rosie. Wasn't it the Jesuits who said 'Give me a child until he's seven, and I'll give you the man'? It's Popish superstition founded on fear. You'll never get rid of it out of the mind. It's a poison for life."

She swallowed. "They think the same about us!" she argued. "They aren't going to give in on teaching their children as they want, they can't afford to, or they won't carry their own people!"

"Neither am I," he replied, nothing in his face yielding, his jaw set, his blue eyes cold.

Bridget ached to interrupt, but she knew better. He found her ideas woolly and unrealistic, a recipe for evasion, and inch by inch surrender without the open honesty of battle. He had said so often enough. She had never stood her ground, never found the words or the courage to argue back. Somebody had to compromise or there would never be peace. She was tired of the cost of anger, not only the destruction of lives, the injury and the bereavement, but the loss of daily sanity, laughter and the chance to build with the hope of something lasting, the freedom from having to judge and condemn.

Roisin was still trying. "But Dad, if we gave a little on the things that don't matter, then we could stick on the things that do, and at least we would have started! We would look reasonable, maybe win over some of the middle parties."

"To what?" he asked.

"To join us, of course!" She spoke as if the answer were obvious.

"For how long?" There was challenge in his voice, and something close to anger.

She looked puzzled.

"Rosie, we're different parties because we have different principles," he said wearily. "The door has always been open for them to join us, if they will. I am not adulterating my beliefs to please the crowd or to win favours of anyone. I won't do it because it's wrong, but it's also foolish. As soon as they've got one concession, they'll want another, and another, until there's nothing left of what we've fought for, and died for all these years. Each time we give in, it'll be harder to stand the next time, until we've lost all credibility, and our own can't trust us any more. You're one or another. There's no half way. If Eamonn doesn't know that now, he'll learn it bitterly."

She would not retreat. She was beaten on logic, but not on will. "But Dad, if no one ever moves on anything, we'll go on fighting each other for ever. My children will live and die for exactly the same things your parents did, and we're doing now! We've got to live together some day. Why not now?"

Connor's face softened. He had more patience with her than he did with Bridget. He picked up his cup in both hands, as if he were cold and warming himself on it. "Rosie, I can't afford to," he said quietly. "I've made promises I have to keep. If I don't, I have no right to ask for their trust. It's my job to bind them together, give them courage and hope, but I can only lead where they are willing to follow. Too far in front, and I'll lose them. Then I'll have accomplished nothing. They'll feel betrayed and choose a new leader, more extreme, and less likely to yield to anything than I am."

"But Dad, we've got to yield over something!" she persisted, her voice strained, her body awkward as she leaned across the table. "If you can't in education, then what about industry, or taxes, or censorship? There's got to be somewhere we can meet, or everything's just pointless, and we're all playing a charade that's going to go on and on forever, all our lives! All of us caught in a madman's parade, as if we hadn't the brains or the guts to see it and get out. It isn't even honest! We pretend we want peace, but we don't! We just want our own way!"

Bridget heard the hysteria in her voice, and at that moment she was sure Roisin was pregnant. She had a desperation to protect the future that was primal, higher and deeper than reason. Perhaps it was the one real hope? She stepped forward, intervening in her own instinct to shield.

"They're just people with a different faith and political aim," she said to Connor. "There must be a point where we can meet. They've moderated a lot in the last twenty years. They don't insist on Papal censorship of books any more . . ."

Connor looked at her in amazement, his eyebrows rising sharply. "Oh! And you call that moderation, do you? We should be grateful to be allowed to choose for ourselves what we can read, which works of philosophy and literature we can buy and which we can't, instead of being dictated to by the Pope of Rome?"

"Oh, come on, Dad!" Roisin waved her hand sharply. "It's not like it used to be . . ."

"We are not living under Roman Catholic laws, Roisin, not on marriage and divorce, not on birth control or abortion, not on what we can and cannot think!" His voice was grating hard, and he too leaned forward as if some physical force impelled him. "We are part of the United Kingdom of Great Britain and Northern Ireland, and that is the guarantee of our freedom to have laws that are the will of the people, not of the Roman Catholic Church. And I will die before I will give away one single right to that." His fist was clenched on the table top. "I don't move from here!"

Roisin looked pale and tired, her eyes stunned with defeat. When she spoke it was quietly. "Dad, not everyone in the party is behind you, you know. There are many who want at least to listen to the other side and make a show of being reasonable, even if at the end we don't change anything that matters." She half reached towards him, hesitated, then her hand fell away. "It's dangerous to appear as if we won't move at all." She was not looking at him, as if she dared not, in case she did not complete what she felt compelled to say. "People get impatient. We're tired of killing and dying, of seeing it going on and on without getting any better. If we're ever to heal it, we've got to begin somewhere."

There was sadness in Connor's face, Bridget could see it and pity wrenched inside her, because she knew what he was going to say. Maybe once there had been a choice, but it had gone long ago.

"We don't begin by surrendering our sovereignty, Roisin," he said. "I've tried all my life to deal with them. If we give an inch they'll take the next, and the next, until we have nothing left. They don't want accommodation, they want victory." He let his breath out in a sigh. "Sometimes I'm not even sure they want peace. Who do they hate, if not us? And who can they blame every time something goes wrong? No." He shook his head. "This is where we stand. Don't try to push me again, and tell Eamonn to do his own errands, not send you." He reached across as if to touch her hair, but she backed away, and Bridget saw the tears in her eyes.

"I'm frightened for you," Roisin said softly.

He straightened up, away from her. Her movement had hurt, and that surprised him.

"If you stand for your beliefs, there'll always be people who fight you," he answered, his lips tight, his eyes bitter. "Some of them violently."

Bridget knew he was thinking of the bombing nearly ten years ago in which his mentor had lost both his legs, and his four grandchildren with him had been killed. Something in Connor had changed then, the pain of it had withered compassion in him.

"Would you rather I were a coward?" he demanded, looking at Roisin. "There are different kinds of deaths," he went on. "I'll face mine forwards, trusting in God that He will protect me as long as I am in His service." Emotion twisted his face, startlingly naked for an instant. "Do you admire a man who bends with the wind because it might cost him to stand straight, Rosie? Is that what I've taught you?"

She shook her head, the tears spilling over. She leaned forward very quickly and brushed his cheek with her lips, but was gone past him before he could reach out his arm to hold her, and respond. She looked at Bridget for an instant, trying to smile. Her voice trembled too much to say more than a word of good-bye, and she hurried out. They heard her feet down the hall, and the front door slammed.

"It's Eamonn," Connor said grimly, avoiding meeting her eyes.

"I know," she agreed. She wanted to excuse Roisin and make him understand the fear she felt, the fierce driving need to protect the child Bridget was more than ever sure she was carrying. And she wanted to ease the hurt in Connor because he was being questioned and doubted by the daughter he loved, even if she had no idea how much, and he did not know how to tell her, or why she needed to know.

"He wants to impress her," she tried to explain. "You're the leader of Protestantism in Ireland, and he's in love with your daughter. He needs her to see him as another strong man, like you, a leader not a follower. He admires you intensely, but he can't afford to stand in your shadow—not with her."

Connor blinked and rubbed his hand wearily across his face, but at last he looked at her, surprise and a fleeting gratitude in his eyes.

Bridget smiled. "It's happened as long as young men have courted great men's daughters, and I expect it always will. It's hard to fall in love with a man who's in your own father's mould, just younger and weaker. He has to succeed for himself. Can't you see that?" She had felt that about Connor twenty-five years ago. She had seen the strength inside him, the fire to succeed. His unbreakable will had been the most exciting thing she could imagine. She had dreamed of working beside him, of sharing defeat and victory, proud just to be part of what he did. She could understand Roisin so well it was as if it were herself all over again.

Bridget had been lovely then, as Roisin was now. She had had the passion and the grace, and perhaps a little more laughter? But the cause had grown grimmer and more violent since then, and hope a little greyer. Or perhaps she had only seen more of the price of it, been to more funerals, and sat silently with more widows.

Connor stiffened. The moment was past. He looked at his watch. "It's nearly time we were going. Be ready in twenty minutes. Where's Liam?" He expected her to know, even though she had been here in the kitchen with him. The requirement for an answer was in his voice.

"He's gone to see Michael. He knows when to be back," she answered. She did not want an argument just as they were leaving, and they would have to sit together in the car all the way to the coast, verbally tiptoeing around each other. Liam would side with his father, hungry for his approval whatever the cost. She had seen his unconscious imitating of Connor, then catching himself, and deliberately doing differently, not even realizing it when he began to copy again. He was always watching, weighing, caught between admiration and judgment. He wanted to be unique and independent, and he needed to be accepted.

Connor walked past her to the door. "He'd better be here in ten minutes," he warned.

The journey to the coast was better than she had feared. The bodyguards followed behind so discreetly that most of the time she was not even aware of them. Usually she did not even know their names, only if she looked at them carefully did she notice the tension, the careful eyes, and perhaps the slight bulge of a weapon beneath their clothes if they turned a particular way, or the wind whipped a jacket hard against the outline of a body. She wondered sometimes what kind of men they were, idealists or mercenaries? Did they have wives at home, and children, mortgages, a dog? Or was this who they were all the time? They drove in the car behind, a faintly comforting presence in the rearview mirror.

She still wished they were all going west to the wildness of the Atlantic coast with its dark hills, heather-purpled in places, bog-deep, wind-scoured. It was a vast, clean land, always man's master, never his servant. But even this gentler coast would be good. They would have time together to be at ease, to talk of things that mattered only to them, and rediscover the small sanities of ordinary life.

Perhaps they would even recapture some of the laughter and the tenderness they had had before. Surely neither of them had changed too much for that?

She spoke little, content to listen to Liam and Connor talk about football, what they thought would happen in the new season, or the possibilities of getting any really good fishing in the week, where the best streams were, the best walks, the views that were worth the climb, and the secret places only the skilled and familiar could find.

She smiled at the thought of the two of them together doing things at which they were equally skilled, no leader, no follower. She was prepared to stand back and let that happen, without thinking of herself, or allowing herself to miss Connor because he gave his time, and his pleasure in it, to someone else. She was glad he had the chance to let go of the responsibility, not have to speak to anyone from the Party, and above all not to have to listen to their bickering and anger. She would be happy to walk alone along the beach and listen to the sound of the water, and let its timelessness wrap itself around her and heal the little scratches of misunderstanding that bled and ached at home.

They reached the village a little after five. The sun was still above the hills and only beginning to soften the air with gold. They stopped to buy fresh milk, eggs, an apple pie and a barbecued chicken to add to what they had brought, then drove on around the curve of the bay to the farther headland. Even Connor seemed to be excited when they pulled up at the cottage standing alone in a sheltered curve, almost on the edge of the sand. He looked around at the hills where they could climb, then across at the windows of the village where the first lights were beginning to flicker on, the dark line of the jetty cutting the golden water and the tender arch of the fading sky above. He said nothing, but Bridget saw his body relax and some of the tension iron out of his face, and she found herself smiling.

They unpacked the car, the guards, Billy and Ian, helping, Billy slender and energetic, his dark hair growing in a cowslick over his forehead, Ian fair-haired with freckles and strong, clever hands. It was he who got the gas boiler going, and unjammed the second bedroom window.

When everything was put away they excused themselves. "We'll go up the rise a little," Billy said, gesturing roughly behind him. "Set up our tent. It's camouflaged pretty well, and in the heather up there it'll be all but invisible."

"But don't worry, sir," Ian added. "One of us will be awake and with our eyes on you all the time." He gave a slight laugh. "Not that I don't feel a fraud, taking money to sit here in the sun for a week. Have a nice holiday, Mr. O'Malley. If ever a man deserved it, you do." He glanced at Bridget, smiling a little shyly. "And you, ma'am."

She thanked them and watched the two of them get back into their car and drive away up the hill until they disappeared into what seemed to be a hollow where the track ended, and she turned back and went inside. The air was growing cool and she realized how happy she was.

They ate cold chicken and salad, and apple pie. Liam went to his room with a book.

Bridget looked across at Connor. It was twilight now and the lamp on the table cast his face into shadows, emphasising the hollows under his cheeks and the lines around his mouth.

"Would you like to go for a walk along the beach?" she invited.

He looked up as if the question had intruded on his thoughts.

"Please?" she added.

"I'm tired, Bridget," he said, his voice flat. "I don't feel like talking, especially if you're going to try explaining Roisin to me. You don't need to. I understand perfectly well that she's young, thinking of having children, and she wants peace. Just leave it alone."

"I wasn't going to talk!" she said angrily. "About Roisin, or anything else. I just wanted to be outside." She added in her own mind that there used to be a time when they could have talked about anything, just for the pleasure of sharing ideas, feelings, or being together, but it sounded sentimental, and it exposed her hurt too clearly. And companionship was of no value once you had had to ask for it.

She went out of the door onto the hard earth, and then a dozen yards across it, past the washing line and through the sea grass to where the sand was softer, cool and slithering away under her feet. The evening was calm, the wave edge barely turning over, pale under the starlight. She walked without thinking, and trying to do it without even dreaming. By the time she came back her face and hands were cold, but there was a warmth inside her.

In the morning Connor seemed to be more relaxed. He was even enthusiastic about going fishing with Liam, and hummed to himself as he sorted out and chose his tackle, instructing Liam what he should take. Liam looked over his shoulder at Bridget and raised his eyebrows, but he accepted the advice goodnaturedly, secretly pleased. They took sandwiches, cold pie and bottles of water, and she watched them climb up the slope side by side, talking companionably, until they disappeared over the crest.

It was a long day without them, but she was happy knowing how much it would please Liam. Connor had sacrificed much for the cause, and perhaps one of the most costly was time with his son. He had never spoken of it, but she had seen the regret in his face, the tightening of his muscles when he had to explain why he could not be at a school prize-giving, or a football match, or why he could not simply talk, instead of working. At times it had seemed that everyone else mattered more to him than his own family, even though she knew it was not true.

At midday Ian came down to make sure everything was still working in the house, and she did not need anything. Billy had followed Connor and Liam, at a discreet distance, of course.

"It's fine, thank you," she told Ian.

He leaned against the door in the sun, and she realized with surprise that he was probably no more than thirty-two or three.

"Would you like lunch?" she offered impulsively. "There's still some apple pie—enough for one, and I don't want it."

He smiled. "I'd love it, Mrs. O'Malley, but I can't come inside for more than a moment or two. Can't see the road."

"Then I'll put the pie on a plate, and you take it," she said, going inside to fetch it before he could refuse.

He accepted it with evident pleasure, thanking her and striding away up the hill again, waving for a moment before he disappeared.

Connor and Liam came back, faces flushed, delighted with their success. For the first time in months Bridget heard him laugh.

"We've caught more than enough for us," he said triumphantly. "Do you want to go and ask Ian and Billy if they'd like a couple?" He turned to Bridget. "You'll cook them, won't you?"

"Of course," she agreed, liking the thought, and beginning immediately as Liam went out of the back door. She had them ready for the pan when he came back again, walking straight past her to the sitting room. "Dad, I can't find them!"

"Go back and look properly!" Connor said with impatience. "And hurry up! Ours'll be ready to eat in a few minutes."

"I have looked," Liam insisted. "And I called out."

"Then look again," Connor ordered. "They can't be far. At least one of them is on duty. The other one could have taken the car for something. Maybe gone to the pub to fetch a crate of Guinness."

"The car's there," Liam told him.

Connor put his newspaper down. Bridget heard the rustle of it. "Do I have to go and look myself?" he demanded.

"I'll go!" Liam was defensive, the friendship and the equality of the afternoon were gone. He marched past Bridget without looking at her, angry that she should have seen it shatter, and went outside into the darkness.

She took the frying pan off the heat.

It was another ten minutes before Liam came back alone. "They're not there," he said again, this time his voice was sharp, edged with fear.

Connor slammed the newspaper down and came out of the sitting room, his face tight and hard, the muscle jumping in his jaw. He walked past both of them and went outside. They heard him shouting, the wind carrying his voice, fading as he went up the hill.

Liam said nothing. He stood awkwardly in the kitchen, looking suddenly vulnerable, and acutely aware of it. He was waiting for Connor to return, successful where he had failed. He dreaded looking stupid in his father's eyes, far more than anything Bridget might think of him.

But when Connor came in quarter on an hour later his face was white and his body rigid, shoulders stiff. "They're not there," he said angrily. "Damn it, they must have walked over to the pub in the village." His mouth closed in a thin line and there was an icy rage in his eyes.

For the first time Bridget was touched with real fear, not of his temper but of something new, and far uglier. "They won't be far," she said aloud, and the moment the words were out of her mouth she realized how pointless they were.

He spun round on her. "They're out of earshot!" he said between his teeth. "If you screamed now, who'd hear you? For God's sake, Bridget, use your brains! They're supposed to be bodyguards! We may not be in Belfast, but we're still in Ireland! I'll have them dismissed for this."

Bridget felt the heat burn up her face, for Ian and Billy who had taken trouble to help, and even more for herself. She knew her words had been foolish, but he had had no need to belittle her in front of Liam. His lack of regard for her hurt more than she wanted to face. It was probably part of growing up, separating the man from the boy. But she was losing him, and each new widening of the gap twisted inside her.

"Don't worry, Dad," Liam said awkwardly. "No one else knows we're here. We'll be okay. We can always fry them up tomorrow."

Connor hesitated, his anger easing out of him. "Of course we will," he agreed. "It's a matter of discipline, and loyalty." He turned to Bridget, no warmth in his eyes. "You'd better put the extra fish in the fridge, and do ours. It's late."

She did as she was told, and they ate in silence. It was a long evening. Connor and Liam talked a little, but not to her. She did not intrude, she knew she would gain nothing by it, and only invite them to make her exclusion more obvious. She saw Liam glance at her once or twice, anxious and a little embarrassed, but he did not know what to say.

She went to bed early. She was still awake an hour later, and heard Connor come in, but she made no movement, and he did not attempt to waken her, as if it had not even occurred to him.

She woke to hear a steady banging, and it was several minutes before she understood what it was. There was someone at the door. It must be Billy and Ian back, probably full of remorse. They were wrong to have gone, but she wanted to protect them from Connor's anger. In theory it could have cost him his life, but actually no harm had come of it. They wouldn't have been gone no more than that brief half hour of suppertime. And no one had ever attempted to harm him physically. It was all just threat.

She swung her feet out of bed, slipped her coat over her night-gown, and went to answer before Connor heard them. She closed the bedroom door softly and tiptoed across the hall to the front door. She opened it.

It was not Billy and Ian there, but three men she had never seen before. The first was tall and lean with fair brown hair and a slightly crooked face that looked as if he laughed easily. The one to the left of him was darker, his features more regular, but there was a seriousness in him that was heavy, almost brooding. The third man was thin with bright blue eyes and hair with a strong tinge of auburn in it.

"Good morning, Mrs. O'Malley," the first one said with a smile. "It's a beautiful day, is it not?" But he did not look at the sweep of the bay, glittering in the sun, or the dark headland behind them.

It was a moment before the chill struck her that he knew her name. Then it came with a cold, tight knot.

He must have seen it in her eyes, but his expression altered only fractionally. "My name's Paddy." He gestured to the dark man. "This is Dermot." He motioned the other way. "And this is Sean. We've brought some fresh eggs with us from the farm over the way, and perhaps you'd be good enough to cook them for us, and we'll all have breakfast together—you and Mr. O'Malley, and us—and the boy, of course." He was polite, still smiling, but there was no question in his voice, no room for refusal.

She backed away from him. It occurred to her for an instant to close the door on him, but she knew he could force his way in if he wanted. "Come back in half an hour, when we're up," she said quite sure even as she spoke that he would refuse.

"We'll wait in the sitting room." He took a step towards her, holding out the open box of eggs, smooth and brown, faintly speckled. There were at least a dozen of them. "We'll have them fried, if that's alright with you? Sean here has a fresh loaf of bread, and a pound of butter as well. Here, Sean, give it to Mrs. O'Malley."

Sean held them out and Bridget took them from him. She needed time to think. She was angry at the intrusion, but she dared not show it. As she led the way to the sitting room and watched them go in easily, as if they had a right to be there, she thought how often she was angry, and suppressed it because she was afraid of making it worse, and losing what she already had. She had done it for so long it was habit.

Connor was sitting up when she returned to the bedroom.

"Where have you been?" he said irritably. "Did you go out to warn Billy and Ian? I know you!" He swung his feet out of bed and stood up. "You've no idea of the gravity of it. I don't tell you of the threats I get, there's no need for you to know, but going off as they've done is a betrayal of me—and the cause."

"No, I didn't!" she said curtly. She was frightened and angry, and the accusation was true in spirit. She would have, had they been there. "There are three men in the sitting room to speak to you . . ."

For an instant he was motionless, frozen in time and place. Then slowly he turned to stare at her. "What men?" His mouth was so dry his voice was husky. "What men, Bridget?"

She swallowed. "I don't know. But they won't go until you speak to them. They're waiting in the sitting room. They told me to get them breakfast."

He was incredulous. "They what?"

"I don't mind!" she protested, wanting to stop him from quarrelling with them needlessly. She was used to men with that hard, underlying anger in them, and the threat of violence close under the surface. Religious politics always seemed to be like that. She wanted it over as soon as possible. Let the wind and the sea wash them clean from the taste of it. She started to dress.

"Where the hell are Billy and Ian?" She heard the first cutting edge of fear in his voice, higher and sharper than the anger. It startled her. She swung around to look at him, but it was gone from his face, only fury remaining.

"Don't you dare make their breakfast!" he ordered. "Tell them to come back when I'm shaved and dressed . . . and I've eaten."

"I already did, and they won't do it," she replied, fastening her skirt. "Connor . . ." she gulped. She felt separate from him and she needed intensely to have the safety, the courage of being together. "Connor . . . they aren't going to go until they want to. Just listen to them . . . please?"

"What are they going to say? Who are they?" He demanded it as if he believed she already knew.

It was ridiculous, but her throat tightened as if she was going to cry. "I don't know." This time she went out, leaving him alone to shave and dress. In the kitchen she started making breakfast for five. Liam was still asleep, and perhaps he would stay that way until after the men had gone.

By the time Connor appeared she had laid the table and made tea and toast and was ready to serve the eggs and bacon.

"Very civil of you, Mrs. O'Malley," Paddy said appreciatively, taking the seat at the head of the table. The other two sat at the sides, leaving spaces for Connor and Bridget between them.

A flicker of annoyance crossed Connor's face, but he accepted and sat also, and started to eat. It was a race against time until either Billy or Ian should appear, or better still, both of them. They were armed and would get rid of Paddy and his friends in moments. Then Connor would crucify them for not having prevented it in the first place. She dreaded that. They were lax, but years of physical safety had left them unprepared for the reality of such intrusion. They would be horribly ashamed, and she would have given them a second chance.

"Now, Mr. O'Malley," Paddy said, putting his knife and fork together on his empty plate. "To business."

"I have no business with you," Connor replied, his eyes level, his voice flat.

"Well that's a shame now." Paddy did not lose his slight smile. "But I'm not easy put off. You see, I'm after peace, not all of a hurry, because it's not a simple thing, but just a beginning."

"So am I," Connor answered. "But only on my terms, and I doubt they're yours, but put them, if you want."

"I doubt that we can agree, Mr. O'Malley. I know right enough what your terms are. It's not as if you were backward about it, or had ever shifted your ground."

"Then where have you shifted?" Connor asked. "And who do you represent, anyway?"

Paddy leaned back in his chair, but the other two remained exactly as they were, vigilant. "Well I haven't shifted a great deal either," Paddy said. "And that's the trouble. We need to have a change, don't you think?" He did not stop long enough for Connor to answer. "This is getting nowhere, and sure enough, I don't see how it can. I'm a moderate man, Mr. O'Malley, reasonable, open to argument. And you're not."

A shred of a smile touched Connor's lips, but Bridget could see half under the table where his fists were clenched and his feet were flat on the floor to balance if he moved suddenly.

"That's the change I propose," Paddy went on.

"You've already said that you know I won't change," Connor pointed out, a very slight sneer on his face.

"Perhaps I haven't made myself plain." Paddy said it as a very slight apology. "I'm suggesting that you step down as leader, and allow a more amenable man into your place." He stopped as Connor stiffened. "Someone who's not tied by past promises," Paddy went on again. "A fresh start."

"You mean I should abandon my people?" Connor's eyebrows rose. "Walk away from them and leave the leadership open to someone of your choosing, that you can manipulate! You're a fool, Paddy—whoever you are, and you're wasting my time, and yours. You've had your breakfast, now take your friends and get out. Leave my family alone. You're . . ." He stopped.

Bridget was certain that he had been going to say that they were lucky the bodyguards had not come in and thrown them out, then he had realized that they had been here half an hour already, in fact thirty-five minutes by the kitchen clock, and neither Billy nor Ian had come. Why not? Where were they? The flicker of fear was stronger inside her and more like a bird's wing than a moth's. Was that why he had stopped, because he had felt that as well?

Paddy made no move at all, he did not even straighten in his chair. "Give it a bit of thought now, Mr. O'Malley," he persisted. "I'm sure you don't want all this trouble to go on. If there's ever going to be peace, there's got to be compromise. Just a little here and there."

"Get out," Connor repeated.

There was a slight movement in the hall doorway and as one man they all looked at Liam, in his pyjama trousers, blinking at them, his face half asleep, confused.

"And you'll be Liam," Paddy remarked. "Wanting your breakfast, no doubt. Come on in, then. Your mother'll lay a place for you. There's plenty of food left—eggs and bacon, fresh from the farm, they are."

Liam blushed. "Who are you? Where are Billy and Ian?"

"My name's Paddy, and these are my friends, Dermot and Sean. We just dropped by to have a word with your father. Have a cup of tea." He gestured to Sean. "Get up now, and let the boy have your place."

Wordlessly Sean obeyed, taking his used dishes to the sink.

Bridget stood up. "Sit," she told Liam. "I'll fry you some eggs."

Connor's face was white. "You'll do no such thing!" he said furiously. "Liam, go and get dressed! You don't come to the table like that, and you know it."

Liam turned to go.

Sean moved to the door to block his way.

Liam stopped.

Connor swivelled around in his chair.

"Come back to the table, Liam," Paddy said levelly. "It's a fine morning. You'll not be cold. Get him his breakfast, Mrs. O'Malley. Feed the boy."

Connor drew in his breath sharply, his face now twisted with anger. Bridget dreaded what punishment Ian and Billy would get when they finally showed up. It would finish their careers, perhaps even finish them ever getting work in Belfast. Connor would never forgive them for allowing him to be humiliated like this in his own house.

Then like having swallowed ice water she realized that Billy and Ian were prisoners somewhere else, just as they were here. They had not come because they could not. She turned to face Paddy and he looked across at her. She tried to mask the knowledge in her eyes, but it was too late. He had already seen it. He said nothing, but the understanding was like a rod of iron between them.

Liam sat down, looking at his father, then away again, embarrassed.

Bridget relit the gas and moved the frying pan over onto the heat.

"Are you sure you won't think again, Mr. O'Malley?" Paddy asked gently. "There are men just a little more to the centre than you are, who could afford to yield a point or two, and still hold to the rest. You've had your day at the top. It's not as if you'd not made it . . ."

"You arrogant fool!" Connor exploded. "Do you think that's what it's about—being leader?" His voice burned with contempt. He half rose in his seat, leaning across the table towards Paddy who still lounged in his chair. "It's about principle, it's about fighting for the freedom to make our own laws according to the will of the people, not the Church of Rome! I don't care that much," he snapped his fingers, "who's leader, as long as they do it with honour and the courage to yield nothing of our rights, whoever threatens them or promises money or power in exchange for the surrender of our birthright."

Liam straightened up in his chair, squaring his bare shoulders.

Bridget put bacon into the frying pan, and two eggs. She had known that was what Connor would say, and there was a kind of pride in her for his courage, but larger than that, overtaking it, was pity and anger, and sick fear.

"That's right, Mr. O'Malley," Paddy said calmly. "You're hostage to all the fine speeches you've made one time or another. I understand that you can't go back on them. You've left yourself no room. That's why I'm thinking it'd be a fine idea for you to step down now, and allow someone new to take over—someone who has a little space to move."

"Never!" Connor forced the word between his teeth. "I've never yielded to threats in my life, and I'm not beginning now. Get out of my house." He straightened up, standing tall, almost to attention. "Now!"

Paddy smiled very slightly. "Don't be hasty, Mr. O'Malley. Give it some thought before you answer."

Bridget had the frying pan in her hand, full of hot fat, the eggs and bacon sizzling.

"I wouldn't do that, Mrs. O'Malley," Paddy said warningly.

Connor swivelled around, his jaw slack for an instant, then he realized what Paddy meant. He leaned across the table and picked up the teapot and flung it not at Paddy, but at Sean standing in the doorway. It hit him in the chest, knocking him off balance and he staggered backwards.

Suddenly Dermot was on his feet, a gun in his hand. He pointed it at Liam.

"Sit down, Mr. O'Malley," Paddy said quietly, but there was no gentleness in his voice any more. "I'm sorry you won't be reasonable about this. It puts us all in an unpleasant situation. Perhaps you should consider it a little longer, don't you think? When you've finished the boy's breakfast, how about another cup of tea, Mrs. O'Malley." It was an order.

Connor sank to his chair. It seemed he had only just grasped the reality that they were prisoners. He was shaking with anger, his hands trembled and the muscle in his jaw flicked furiously.

Bridget picked up the spatula and served the eggs and bacon, using two hands because she was shaking as well, and she thought of the mess she would make on the floor if she dropped the plate.

Liam seemed about to refuse it, then met Paddy's eyes, and changed his mind.

Bridget returned the teapot to the stove, and cleaned up the spilled leaves and water on the floor. She boiled the kettle again and made more. Paddy thanked her. The minutes ticked by. No one spoke.

Liam finished his meal. "Can I go and get dressed?" he asked Paddy.

Connor's temper flared, but he did not speak.

"Sure you can," Paddy answered. "Sean'll go with you, just to make sure you don't forget to come back."

When they were gone he turned to Connor. "We've got all week, Mr. O'Malley, but it'll be nicer for everyone if you make the right decision sooner rather than later. Then you can have a nice holiday here with your family, and enjoy it just as you intended to."

"I'll see you in hell first," Connor replied.

"Now that's a shame," Paddy answered. "Hell's surely a terrible place, so I hear the preachers say. But then you're a preacher aren't you, so you'll know that already."

"You'll know it yourself, soon enough!" Connor returned.

Dermot rose to his feet. "That's your last answer, is it?"

"It is."

He shrugged. "Sean!" he called out.

Sean reappeared, Liam behind him, fully dressed now.

"Mr. O'Malley's not for changing his mind," Dermot said. "Leave the boy here. You and I have a job to do."

Sean pushed Liam, nudging him forward into the kitchen.

"What?" Connor demanded.

"You're staying here," Dermot told him. He signalled to Sean and the two of them went outside. Paddy stood up, revealing the gun in his hand also. He lounged against the door post, but it would have taken less than a second for him to straighten up and raise the barrel if one of them threatened him.

There were several moments' silence, then a shout from outside. Paddy looked up sharply, but it was Connor's name that was called. He lowered the gun and Connor walked to the outside door and opened it.

Bridget followed a step behind him.

On the tussock grass just beyond the gate Ian and Billy stood facing Dermot; their hands were tied behind their backs. Dermot jerked the gun up, gesturing with his other arm.

Billy knelt down.

Dermot put the gun to Billy's head and a shot rang out, sharp and thin in the morning air, sounding surprisingly far away. Billy fell forward. Ian swayed.

Dermot pointed again. Ian knelt. A second shot cracked. Ian fell forward.

Connor gave a strangled cry in his throat and staggered over to the sink as if he could be sick. He dry-retched and gulped air.

Bridget felt the room reel around her, her legs turn to jelly. She clasped onto the door jamb until the nausea passed, then turned to look at Liam, ashen-faced by the table, and Paddy by the stove, the gun still in his hand.

A terrible sadness overwhelmed her. It was a moment that divided forever the past from the present. Billy and Ian were dead. They had helped her, casually, smiling, not knowing what was ahead of them. They had never deserted their posts, and they were lying out there with bullets through their heads, butchered almost without thought.

Liam was ashen. Connor looked as if he might be sick.

Bridget ached to be able to help someone, help herself, undo the moment and see Billy and Ian alive again. And it was all impossible, and far too late.

She made a move towards Liam, and he jerked away from her, too hurt to be touched, blaming her in some way, as if she could have prevented it. School friends had been caught in bomb blasts. He had seen plenty of injury and bereavement, but this was the first murder he had seen. Connor went to him, holding out his hand, wordlessly. Liam took it.

Time stretched on. Bridget washed the dishes and put them away. Sean and Dermot returned. She noticed that their boots had earth on them, and there were marks of sweat on their shirts, as if they had been involved in some heavy physical exertion.

Connor stood up.

"Sit down," Dermot said pleasantly, but he stood still, waiting to be obeyed.

"I'm going to the bathroom!" Connor snapped.

"Not yet," Dermot answered. "My hands are dirty. Sean's too. We'll go and wash, then you can. And don't lock yourself in. We'll only have to break the door down, then Mrs. O'Malley'll have no privacy, and you don't want that, do you?"

"For God's sake, you can't . . ." Connor began, then he knew that they could—they would.

The morning passed slowly, all of them in the kitchen except when someone needed to use the bathroom. Bridget made them tea, and then started to peel potatoes for lunch.

"We haven't enough food for five," she pointed out. "Not beyond this evening, anyway."

"They'll be gone before then!" Connor snapped at her.

"If you've made the right decision," Paddy agreed. He turned to Bridget. "Don't worry, we've got plenty, and it's no trouble to get more. Just make what you've got, Mrs. O'Malley."

"You don't tell her what to do!" Connor turned on him.

Dermot smiled. "Sure he does, Mr. O'Malley. She knows that, don't you, Bridget?"

Connor was helpless, it was naked in his face, as if something were stripped from him.

Bridget longed to protect him, but he had made it impossible. Everything that came to her mind to say would only have made it worse, shown up the fact that she was used to being ordered around, and he was not. She realized it with a shock. Usually it was Connor, for different reasons, and now it was two strangers, but the feeling of being unable to retaliate was just the same.

"We've got to eat," she said reasonably. "I'd rather cook it myself than have one of them do it, even if I had the choice."

Connor said nothing.

Liam groaned and turned away, then slowly looked up at his father, anxiety in his face, and fear, not for himself.

Bridget dug her nails into the palms of her hands. Was Liam more afraid that Connor would be hurt, or that he would make a fool of himself, fail at what he needed to do, to be?

"You'll pay for this," Connor said at last. "No matter what you do to me, or my family, you won't change the core of the people. Is this your best argument—the gun? To hold women and children hostage?" His voice descended into sarcasm, and he did not notice Liam's sudden flush of anger and shame. "Very poor persuasion! That's really the high moral ground!"

Dermot took a step toward him, his hand clenched.

"Not yet!" Paddy said warningly. "Let him be."

Dermot glared at him, but he dropped his hand.

Bridget found herself shaking so badly she was afraid to pick up anything in case it slipped through her fingers. "I'm going to the bathroom," she said abruptly, and pushed past Sean and out of the door. No one followed her.

She closed the bathroom door and locked it, then stood by the basin, her stomach churning, nausea coming over her in waves. They were prisoners. Billy and Ian were dead. Connor was frightened and angry, but he was not going to yield, he couldn't. He had spent all his life preaching the cause, absolutism, loyalty to principles whatever the cost. Too many other men had died, and women and children, he had left himself no room to give anything away now. He might have, even yesterday, when it was only Roisin who asked him, but today it would be seen as yielding to force, and he could never do that.

They were prisoners until someone rescued them, or Dermot and Sean killed them all. Would Connor let that happen? If he gave in to save them, he would hate them for it. She knew without hesitation that he would resent them for ever for being the cause of his weakness, the abandoning of his honour, even his betrayal of all his life stood for.

How blindingly, ineffably stupid! For a sickening moment rage overtook her for the whole idiotic religious divide, which was outwardly in the name of Christianity!

But of course it wasn't. It was human arrogance, misunderstanding, rivalry, one wrong building on another, and the inability to forgive the terrible, aching losses on both sides. Religion was the excuse they clothed it in, to justify it. They created God in their own image: vengeful, partisan, too small of mind to love everyone, incapable of accepting differences. You might fear a god like that, you could not love him.

She dashed cold water over her face and dried it on the rough towel. She hung it up and saw that they were going to run out of toilet paper with six of them in the house. And laundry powder. She would have to tell Paddy that, as well as getting food.

"I'll remember," he said with a smile when she told him early in the afternoon. The others were still in the sitting room and she was in the kitchen going through the store cupboard to see what there was.

"And washing-up liquid," she added.

"Of course. Anything else?"

She straightened up and looked at him. He was still smiling, his slightly lopsided face softened by humour.

"How long are you going to stay here?" she asked.

There was a shadow around his eyes. It was the first uncertainty she had seen in him. She did not find it comforting. Suddenly she was aware, with a sharp pain of fear, how volatile the situation was. He did not know the answer. Perhaps he really had expected Connor to step down, and now that he knew he would not, he did not know how to proceed. She felt cold inside.

"That's all," she said without waiting for him to answer. "Except some bread, I suppose. And tea, if you want it." She moved past him, brushing his arm as she went back to the sitting room.

Connor was standing looking out of the window, his shoulders stiff. She could imagine the expression on his face by seeing his back. Liam was huddled in the armchair, watching his father. His unhappiness was written in every line of his body. Sean was lounging against the door. Dermot was nowhere to be seen.

The afternoon wore on in miserable silence, sporadic anger, and then silence again. Dermot returned at last. He looked at his watch. "Half past five," he observed. "I think we'll eat at seven, Mrs. O'Malley." His eyes flickered to Connor and saw the dull flash of anger in his face. A tiny smile touched his mouth. "And you can go to bed at nine, after you've done the dishes."

The muscle in Connor's jaw twitched. He was breathing slowly, trying to control himself. Liam stared at him, fear and embarrassment struggling in his eyes. He was mortified to see his father humiliated, and yet he was also deeply afraid that if he showed any courage at all he would be hurt, and then humiliated even more. Bridget found his confusion painful to watch, but she had no idea how to help. Exactly the same fear twisted inside her stomach, making her swallow to keep from being sick.

"How about a cup of tea?" Dermot went on.

She moved to obey, and saw his satisfaction.

"Get your own tea!" Connor said curtly. "Bridget! Don't wait on them!"

"I don't mind," she told him. "I've nothing else to do."

"Then do nothing!" He swung around to face her. "I told you not to wait on them. For God's sake, they're not so stupid they can't boil water!"

She saw Paddy's expression, and realized with surprise that Connor had spoken to her in exactly the same tone of voice that

Dermot had used. Was that deliberate—Dermot mimicking Connor? And she was so accustomed to obeying that she was going to do it automatically.

Now she was totally undecided. If she obeyed Dermot she would further reduce Connor, and if she did not she might provoke the violence she feared, or at best make him exert his control in some other way.

They were all watching her, waiting, particularly Liam.

"Actually I'm going to do the laundry," she said. "Just because we're prisoners here doesn't mean we shouldn't have clean underwear. If any of you can be bothered to follow me you can, but it's pretty stupid. You know I'm not going to leave. You've got my family here." And without looking at Paddy or Dermot, she walked out and went to the bedrooms to collect whatever she could find to wash. No one came after her.

The evening passed slowly, with tension in the air so brittle every time anyone moved suddenly, or made a sound with knife on china, or Liam dropped his fork, they all stiffened, and Sean in the doorway lifted the barrel of his gun.

Bridget washed the dishes and Liam dried them. They went to bed at nine o'clock, as ordered.

As soon as the bedroom door was closed Connor turned on Bridget.

"Why are you obeying them?" he said furiously, his face mottled dark with rage. "How can I make a stand against them if you defy me all the time?"

"You can't make a stand against them," she replied wearily. "They've got guns." She started to undress, hanging her skirt and blouse up in the wardrobe.

"Don't turn your back on me when I'm talking to you!" His voice shook.

She turned around. It was only one full day, not even a night, and already he was losing his mastery of himself, because nothing was in his control. She looked at him steadily, unblinking.

"We have no choice, Connor. I'm not defying you, I'm just not making them angry when there's no point. Besides, I'm used to doing what someone else tells me to."

"What do you mean by that?"

She turned back to the wardrobe. "Go to bed."

"You don't care, do you!" he accused. "You think I should give in to them, let them have whatever they want, buy our freedom now by surrendering everything we've fought for all our lives!"

"I know you can't do that." She went on undressing, looking out a clean nightgown because she had washed the other one, for something to do. "You haven't left yourself room. I don't suppose they have either. That's the trouble with all of us, we're hostage to the past we've created. Go to bed. Staying up all night isn't going to help."

"You're a coward, Bridget. I didn't think I'd ever be ashamed of my own wife."

"I don't suppose you thought about it at all," she replied. "Not really, not about me, I mean." She walked past him, putting the nightgown on and climbed into her side of the bed.

He was silent for several minutes. She heard him taking off his clothes, hanging them up as well, then she felt the bed move a little as he got in.

"I'll excuse that, because you're afraid," he said at last.

She did not answer. She was not helping him, and she felt guilty, but it was his intransigence that had made dealing with him impossible. It was a matter of principle, and she knew he could not help it, not now, anyway. He had ordered her around for years, just the way Dermot was ordering him. And it was her fault too, for obeying. She had wanted peace, wanted him happy, not always for his sake but for hers, because he was kinder then, closer to the man she wanted him to be, the man who made her laugh sometimes, who enjoyed the small things, as well as the great, and who loved her. She should have been honest years ago.

Now she could not even protect Liam from the disillusion that was already beginning to frighten him more deeply than the threat of violence from Dermot or Sean. There was nothing she could do. She slid down a little further, and pretended to be asleep.

The next day was worse. Tempers were tighter, edges more raw. There was nothing to do, and they were all cramped inside the cottage. Sean, Paddy, and Dermot took turns watching and sleeping. They had nailed the windows closed, so the air was stuffy, and there was no escape except through one of the two doors.

"What the hell are they waiting for?" Connor demanded when he and Bridget were alone in the bedroom, Sean just beyond the door.

"I don't know," she replied. "I don't know what can happen. You aren't going to change, and neither are they." What was really in her mind was Billy and Ian murdered in front of them and buried somewhere up the hillside, only she did not want to acknowledge it in words. Then she would have to face the consequences of what it meant, and the possibilities it closed off.

"Then what are they waiting for?" he repeated. "Have they asked somebody for money? Or are they going to keep me here until someone else has taken power?"

She had not thought of that. It was a relief, because it made sense. "Yes," she said aloud. "That could be it." Then doubt came to her again. She had become aware that Dermot was waiting, just small signs, a turning when there was a sound, a half listening attitude, a certain tension in him that was not in Paddy. Sean she saw far less of—in fact she had not watched him at all.

"You sound pleased," Connor said.

She looked at him. His face was deeply lined, his eyes pink-rimmed as if he had not slept at all. The muscle in his jaw jumped erratically. "I'm not pleased," she said gently. "I'm just glad you thought of something that makes sense. It's easier to deal with."

"Deal with?"

"Live with," she corrected. "I'm going back out, before they come for us." She left him alone because she did not know what more to say.

It was the third day when she was standing in the back garden, picking a handful of mint for the potatoes, and staring across the stretch of tussock grass towards the sea, when she was aware of someone behind her.

"I'm coming," she said a little tartly. Dermot was irritating her. She had watched him deliberately baiting Connor, ordering him in small, unnecessary things. She swung around, to find Paddy a yard away.

"No hurry," he answered, looking beyond her to the water, barely restless in the slight wind, the waves no more than rustling as they turned over on the sand.

She followed his glance. It had beauty, but she ached for the wilder Atlantic shore with its vast width, the skies that stretched for ever, the wind so hard and clean it blew mares tails of spume off the incoming rollers so that when they crashed on the sand the streamers of foam trailed behind them.

"I miss the west," she said impulsively.

"And of course you can't go there any more." His voice was quiet, almost gentle. "It's a high price we pay, isn't it?"

She drew in her breath to challenge him for including himself, then she realized that perhaps he too was bound by choices he had made long ago, things other people expected of him, as Connor had always expected of her.

"Yes," she agreed. "Penny by penny, over the years."

He said nothing for a little while, just watching the water, as she did.

"Do you come from the west?" she asked.

"Yes." There was regret in his voice.

She wanted to ask him how he had come to be here, holding Connor at gunpoint, what had happened in his life to change a crusade for his beliefs into this kind of violence, but she did not want to anger him with what was undoubtedly intrusive. Perhaps like her, he had started by wanting to please someone he loved, to live up to their ideas of courage and loyalty, and ended clinging onto the shreds of love, because that was all there was left, hoping for something that honesty would have told him did not exist. She had not wanted to face that. It invalidated too much she had paid for with years of trying, swinging from hope to defeat, and then creating hope again.

He started to speak, and stopped.

"What were you going to say?" she asked.

"I was going to ask you something it's none of my business to know," he replied. "And maybe I'd rather not, anyway. I know what you'd say, because you'd be loyal, and perhaps I'd believe you, perhaps not. So maybe it's better we just stand and look at the water. The tides will come and go, the seabirds will call exactly the same, whatever we do."

"He won't change," she said.

"I know. He's a hard man. His time is past, Bridget. We've got to have change. Everyone's got to yield something."

"I know. But we can't take the hard liners with us. They'll call him a traitor, and he couldn't bear that."

"Captain going down with the ship?" He had a slight, wry humour in his voice, but a knowledge of tragedy as well.

"I suppose so," she agreed.

A gull wheeled above them, and soared up in the wind. They both watched it.

She thought of asking him what they were waiting for, but she was not certain that Paddy was waiting, not as Dermot was. Should she warn him, say that Dermot was different, darker? Perhaps he already knew, and it would be disloyal to Connor if she were to say anything to Paddy that could be of help to him. Perhaps she shouldn't be speaking to him at all, more than was necessary.

"I must go in," she said aloud, turning towards the kitchen door.

He smiled at her, not moving from her path, so she passed almost close enough to brush him. She smelled a faint odour of aftershave, clean cotton from the shirt she had laundered. She forced the thoughts out of her mind and went inside.

The evening was tedious and miserable. Connor paced back and forth until Dermot lost his temper and told him to stop. Connor glared at him, and kept pacing. Dermot walked over to Liam and lifted the gun, held by the barrel.

"You don't need to do that!" Paddy said angrily. "Mr. O'Malley's going to do as he's told. He doesn't have the control of his nerves that Bridget has. He doesn't take easily to not being master of his fate."

The dull red colour rose up Connor's face, but he did not take his eyes off Dermot, the gun still within striking distance of Liam's head.

Liam sat motionless, white with misery, not fear for himself, but embarrassment for his father, and helpless anger that Bridget had been singled out for strange and double-edged praise. His loyalties were torn apart. The world which had been difficult enough had become impossible.

"I'm going to bed!" Connor said in a voice so hard it rasped on the ear.

"Good," Paddy agreed.

Dermot relaxed.

Liam stumbled to his feet. "So am I! Dad! Wait for me!"

Bridget was left alone with Paddy and Dermot. She did not want to stay, but she knew better than to follow Connor yet. He needed time on his own, to compose himself, and to pretend to be asleep when she came. There was nothing she could say to comfort him. He did not want her understanding, he would only take it for pity. He wanted respect, not companionship, honour, loyalty and obedience, not the vulnerability of love.

She would stay here for at least another hour, saying nothing, making tea for them if they wanted it, fetching and carrying, doing as she was told.

The morning began the same, but at quarter to ten suddenly Dermot stiffened, and the moment after, Bridget also heard the whine of an engine. Then it cut out. Sean went to the door. Everyone else waited.

The silence was so heavy the wind in the eaves was audible, and the far cry of seabirds. Then the footsteps came, light and quick on the path. The door opened and Roisin came in. She looked at Bridget, at her father, then at Paddy.

Paddy beckoned her to follow him, and they went into Liam's bedroom.

Dermot started to fidget, playing with the gun in his hand, his eyes moving from Connor to the door, and back again.

Connor stared at Bridget.

"I don't know," she whispered. "Some kind of a message?"

"Maybe it's money . . ." he mouthed the words.

"Where would she get money?"

"The party," Liam was close beside them. "They'd pay for you, Dad. Everybody'd give."

Bridget looked at him, he was thin, very young. In the sunlight from the window she could see the down on his cheek. He shaved, but he didn't really need to. He was desperate to believe that his father was loved, that the party respected him and valued him enough to find whatever money was demanded. She was afraid they would be politically astute enough to see the value of a martyr—three martyrs—four if Roisin were included. Please God she wasn't! Why had Eamonn sent her, instead of coming himself?

The door opened and Roisin came out, Paddy on her heels.

Dermot stared at him, the question in his eyes.

Connor was so stiff he seemed in danger of losing his balance.

Paddy faced him. "There's been a slight change, Mr. O'Malley," he said softly, his voice a trifle husky. "One of your lieutenants, Michael Adair, has gone over to the moderate camp."

"Liar," Connor said immediately. "Adair would never desert. I know him."

Bridget felt her stomach clench inside her. Connor spoke as if to change one's mind were a personal affront to him. She had felt Adair's doubt for several months, but Connor never listened to him, he always assumed he knew what he was going to say, and behaved as if he had said it. Almost as he did with her!

"It's not desertion, Dad," Roisin said awkwardly. "It's what he believes."

Connor's eyebrows rose. "Are you saying it's true? He's betrayed us?" His contempt was like a live thing in the air.

"He has either to betray you or himself," Roisin told him.

"Rubbish! You don't know what you're talking about, Rosie. I've known Adair for twenty years. He believes as I do. If he's turned his coat it's for money, or power, or because he's afraid."

Roisin seemed about to say something, then she turned away.

"Traitor!" Liam said, his pent-up fury breaking out at last. "You're best without him, Dad. Someone like that's worth nothing to them, or to us."

Connor touched his hand to Liam's shoulder in the briefest gesture, then he turned to Paddy. "It makes no difference. If you thought it would, then you're a fool!"

"Adair carries weight," Paddy answered. "He represents many. He could still carry most of your party, if you gave him your backing."

"My backing?" Connor was incredulous. "A traitor to the cause? A man who would use my imprisonment by you to seize the leadership? He's a greedy, disloyal coward, and you'd deal with him? You're an idiot! Give him a chance and he'll turn on you too."

"He's doing what he believes," Roisin repeated, but without looking at her father.

"Of course he is!" Connor spat. "He believes in opportunism, power at any price, even betrayal. That's so plain only a fool couldn't see it."

Paddy glanced at Bridget, but she knew the denial was in his eyes, and she looked away. Roisin was right. Connor had expected, bullied, ignored argument and difference, until Adair had been silenced. Now in Connor's absence, and perhaps hearing that he was hostage, he had found the courage to follow his own convictions. But she did not want Paddy even to guess that she knew that. It seemed like one more betrayal.

Paddy smiled, a funny, lopsided gesture with self-mocking in it as well as humour, and a touch of defiance. "Well, Mr. O'Malley, aren't there enough fools? But for the sake of argument, what if you were to give Adair your support, written in your own hand, for Roisin here to take back, would that not be the best choice open to you now? All things considered, as it were?"

"Ally myself with traitors?" Connor said witheringly. "Endorse what has happened, as if I'd lost my own morality? Never."

"Then maybe you could just retire, on grounds of health?" Paddy suggested. He was leaning against the kitchen bench, his long legs crossed at the ankle, the light from the window shining on his hair. The lines on his face marked his tiredness. He had seemed younger at the beginning, now it was clear he was over forty. "Give it some thought."

"There's nothing wrong with my health!" Connor said between his teeth.

Dermot twisted his gun around. "We could always do something about that," he said with a curl to the corners of his mouth that lacked even the suggestion of humour.

"And explain it as what?" Paddy rounded on him. "A hunting accident? Don't be stupid." He turned back to Connor before he saw the moment of bleak, unadulterated hatred pass over Dermot's face, making it dead, like a mask. Then he controlled it again, and was merely flat, watchful. It touched Bridget with a quite different, new fear, not just for herself but for Paddy.

"You're wasting your time," Connor answered, exactly as Bridget had known he would. He was not even considering it, not acknowledging change, he never had. Now he did not even know how to. He had made his own prison long before Paddy and his men came here with guns.

"Are you sure about that?" Paddy said softly.

"Of course he is!" Dermot cut across him. "He was never going to agree to anything. I could have told you that the day you set out." He jerked his head towards Sean, standing at the far door and the way out to the beach. Sean straightened up, holding his gun steady in front of him.

Paddy was still staring at Connor, as if he believed that he might yet change his mind. He did not see Dermot move behind him, raise his arm and bring it across sharply on the side of his jaw. Paddy crumpled to his knees, and then forward onto the floor.

"Don't!" Sean warned as Connor gasped, and Roisin made a sharp move towards Paddy. "He'll be alright."

Dermot was taking the gun out of Paddy's waistband. He stood up again, watching Bridget rather than Connor or Liam. "Just don't do anything heroic, and you'll be alright."

"Alright?" Connor was stupefied. "What the hell's the matter with you? He's your own man!"

Roisin ignored him and bent to Paddy who was already stirring. She held out her arms and helped him to climb up, slowly, his head obviously paining him. He looked confused and dizzy. He was gentle with Roisin, but did not speak to her. Awkwardly he turned to Dermot, who was careful to keep far enough away from him he was beyond Paddy's arm's length. He held the gun high and steady.

Sean was watching the rest of them. "The first one to move gets shot," he said in a high-pitched voice, rasping with tension. "None of you'd want that, now would you?"

"Dermot?" Paddy said icily.

"Don't be losing your temper, now," Dermot answered. "We did it your way, and it didn't work. Not that I thought it would, mind. O'Malley wasn't even going to change. He can't. Hasn't left himself room. But you wouldn't be told that, you and your kind. Now we'll do it our way, and you'll take the orders."

"You fool!" Paddy's voice was bitter and dangerous. "You'll make a hero out of him! Twice as many will follow him now!"

"Not the way we'll do it," Dermot answered him. "And stop giving me orders, Paddy. You're the one that'll do as you're told now."

"I'm not with you. This is the wrong way. We already decided . . ."

"You did! Now I'm in charge . . ."

"Not of me. I told you, I'm not with you," Paddy repeated.

Dermot's smile was thin as arctic sunshine. "Yes, you are, Paddy, my boy. You can't leave us. For that matter, you never could—at least not since we shot those two lads up the hill, and buried them. Markers are left, just so we could direct anyone to find them, if it were ever in our interest." He raised his black eyebrows in question.

The blood drained out of Paddy's skin, leaving him oddly grey.

He was not old, yet Bridget, looking at him, could see the image of when he would be.

"That's why you killed them . . ." he said with understanding at last.

"We killed them, Paddy," Dermot corrected. "You were part of it, just like us. Law makes no difference who pulls the trigger. Isn't that right, Mr. O'Malley?" He glanced at Connor, who was still standing motionless. Then the ease in Dermot's face vanished and his voice was savage. "Yes of course that's why we did it! You're one of us, whether you like it or not. No way out, boy, none at all. Now are you going to take your gun and behave properly? Help us to keep all these people good and obedient, until we decide exactly what's to be done with them. Now we've got the pretty Roisin as well, perhaps Mr. O'Malley will be a bit more amenable, not to mention her husband. Though to tell the truth, maybe we'd be better not to mention him for yet a while, don't you think?"

Paddy hesitated. Again there was silence in the kitchen, except for the wind and the sound of the gulls along the shore.

Liam stared at his father, waiting.

At last Paddy held out his hand.

"For the gun?" Dermot enquired. "In a little while, when I'm satisfied you've really grasped your situation. Now, Mrs. O'Malley." He turned to Bridget. "We've one extra to feed. You'd best take a good look at your rations, because there'll be no more for a while. I'm not entirely for trusting Paddy here, you see. Not enough to send him off into the village, that is. So be sparing, eh? No seconds for anyone, in fact you'd best be cutting down a bit on firsts as well. D'you understand me?"

"Of course I understand you," she replied. "We've got a whole sack of potatoes. We'll live on those if we have to. We haven't much to season them with, but I suppose that doesn't matter a lot. Connor, you'd better move in with Liam, and Roisin can come in with me. I'll wash the sheets. It's a good day for drying."

"That's a good girl, now," Dermot approved. "Always do what you're told, don't you! I'd like a woman like you for myself, one day. Or maybe with a bit more fire. You can't be much fun. But then I don't suppose Mr. O'Malley is much of a man for fun, is he? Got a face like he bit on a lemon, that one. What do you see in him, eh?"

She stopped at the doorway into the hall and looked directly at him. "Courage to fight for what he believes, without violence," she answered. "Honour to keep his word, whatever it cost him. He never betrayed anyone in his life." And without waiting to see his reaction, or Connor's, she went out across the hall and into first Liam's bedroom, taking the sheets off the bed, then her own. They could watch her launder them if they wanted to. She wouldn't have gone anywhere before, but with Roisin here as well, she was even more of a prisoner.

There was a separate laundry room with a big tub, a washboard, plenty of soap, a mangle to squeeze out the surplus water, and a laundry basket to carry them out to the line where the sea wind would blow them dry long before tonight.

She began to work, because it was so much easier than simply standing or sitting, as Connor and Liam were obliged to do.

She had filled the tub with water and was scrubbing the sheets rhythmically against the board, feeling the ridges through the cotton, when she heard the footsteps behind her. She knew it was Roisin.

"Can I help, Mum?" she asked.

"It doesn't take two of us," Bridget replied. "But stay if you want to."

"I can put them through the mangle," Roisin offered.

They worked without speaking for several minutes. Bridget didn't want to think about why Roisin was here, who had sent her with the message, but the thoughts crowded into her mind like a bad dream returning, even when her eyes were open. She was the only one they had told where they were going, not even Adair knew. Roisin had tried so hard to persuade Connor to moderate his position on education before they left. Bridget had never seen her argue with such emotion before. When he had refused, she had looked defeated, not just on a point of principle, but as if it hurt her profoundly, emotionally. The loss was somehow permanent.

"You're pregnant, aren't you?" she said aloud.

Roisin stopped, her hands holding the rinsed sheets above the mangle. The silence was heavy in the room. "Yes," she said at last. "I was going to tell you, but it's only a few weeks. It's too soon."

"No, it isn't," Bridget said quietly. "You know, that's all that matters." She wanted to be happy for her, congratulate her on the joy to come, but the words stuck in her throat. It was why Roisin had betrayed her father to the moderates, and for Eamonn. She not only wanted peace, she needed it, for her child. Everything in her now was bent on protecting it. It was part of her, tiny and vulnerable, needing her strength, her passion to feed it, keep it warm, safe, loved, defended from the violence of men who cared for ideas, not people. Perhaps Bridget would have done the same. She remembered Roisin when she was newborn. Yes, she would have done whatever was necessary to protect her, or Liam, or any child.

Roisin started the mangle again, keeping her face turned away; she did not yet realize that Bridget knew. She would have done it for Eamonn as well. He was another idealist, like Connor. Roisin was vulnerable herself. It was her first child. She might be ill with it. She would certainly be heavy, awkward, needing his love and his protection, his emotional support. She might even be afraid. Childbirth was lonely and painful, full of doubts that the baby would be well, that she would be able to look after it properly, do all the things she should to see nothing went wrong, that the tiny, demanding, infinitely precious life was cherished. She would be desperately tired at times. She would need Eamonn. Perhaps she had no choice either.

"Your father doesn't know," she said aloud.

Roisin pulled the wrung sheet out from between the rollers and put it into the basket, ready for the line. "I'll tell him in a couple of months."

"Not about the child." Bridget passed her the next sheet. "He doesn't know that you told the I.R.A., or whoever Paddy is, where we are."

Roisin froze, hands in the air. There was no sound but the dripping water.

"I know why you did it," Bridget went on. "I might have done the same, to protect you, before you were born. But don't expect him to understand. I don't think he will. Or Liam."

Roisin's face pinched, looking bruised as if some deep internal injury were finally showing. Roisin realized she had always expected her father to reject her, but she had not thought about Liam before. It was a new pain, and the reality of it might be far worse than the idea, even now.

"I thought when he realized how many of us want peace, he might change, even a little," she said. "Someone has to! We can't go on like this, year after year, hating and mourning, then starting all over again. I won't!" She bit her lips. "I want something better."

"We all do," Bridget said quietly. "The difference is in how much we are prepared to pay for it."

Roisin turned away, blinking, and bent her attention to the sheets.

When they were finished Bridget took them out and hung them on the line, propping up the middle of it with the long pole, notched at the end to hold the rope taut so the sheets did not touch the ground.

How could she protect Connor from the disillusion he would feel when he knew that it was Roisin who had betrayed him? All the reasoning in the world would not make any difference to the pain. Even if his mind understood, his emotions would not. First Adair, now his own daughter.

And what would Liam make of it? He was confused, all his previous certainties were slipping away. His father, whom he had believed to be so strong he wavered in nothing, was losing control of his temper, being ordered around by men he despised, and he did nothing about it. Now his sister was the cause of it all, and for an emotion and a loyalty he could only guess at.

She yanked up the heavy pole, awkward, tipping in her hands from the weight of the wet sheets with the wind behind them. Suddenly it eased and she lurched forward, straight into Paddy.

"Sorry," he apologized, propping the pole up for her.

"Thank you," she said abruptly, realizing he had done it to help. The wind filled the sheets, bellying them high and wide, temporarily shielding them from view of the house.

"Your husband'll work it out that it was her," he said quietly. "You can't stop it."

"I know." She was not sure if she resented his understanding, or in an obscure way it was a comfort not to face it alone. No, that was absurd. Of course she was alone. Paddy was the enemy. Except that he too had been betrayed by someone he had trusted, and it had been very neatly done, using his own plan against him, enmeshing him in a double murder so he had no retreat. He must feel like a complete fool.

"It doesn't seem as if either of us can stop much, does it?" she said drily.

He looked at her with a black laughter in his eyes, self-mocking.

He was trying to hide the hurt, and she knew in that instant that it was deep, and there were probably years of long and tangled debt behind it, and perhaps love of one sort or another. She was not sure if she wanted to know the story or not. She might understand it more than she could afford to.

She glanced at him again. He was staring out towards the horizon, his eyes narrowed against the light off the water, even though the sun was behind them.

"It didn't go where you expected, did it?" she said aloud.

"No," he admitted. "I never thought Connor would yield easily, but I thought he would, when he realized Adair had crossed over. I misjudged him. I guess the ransom for freeing him from old promises was too high. Too high for him, I mean."

"I know what you mean," she answered. "I'm not sure he knows how to escape now. He's more hostage to the past than he is to you. You're just more physically apparent, that's all. It's . . ." She thought how she was going to phrase what she wanted to say. She was thinking aloud, but if she spoke to anyone at all, it would be to Paddy.

"It's a matter of admitting it," he said for her, watching to see if she understood. "We've invested so much of ourselves, our reason for living, whatever it is that makes us think we matter, into a set of ideals. It takes a hell of a lot of courage to say that we didn't get it right—even in the silence of the small hours, staring up at the bedroom ceiling, let alone to all the angry men who've invested the same, and can't face it either. Some of us will die of pride, I think. If you don't believe in yourself, what have you got left?"

"Not much," she replied. "At least—not here. Ireland doesn't forgive—not politically. We're too good at remembering all the wrong things. We don't learn to forget and start again."

He smiled, turning to look at the water again. "Could we, do you think, then? There'd be a lot of things I'd do differently and dear God, but wouldn't I!" He swivelled suddenly to stare very directly at her. "What would you do differently, Bridget?"

She felt the colour rise up her face. His eyes were too frank, far too gentle, intruding into her thoughts, the hopes and sorrows she needed to keep locked inside herself. And yet she allowed him to go on looking at her, the wind streaming past them, the sun bright, the gulls wheeling and crying above.

"You won't tell me, will you?" he said at last, his voice urgent.

She lowered her gaze. "No, of course I won't. None of it matters anyway, because we can't."

"But I would like to have known," he said, as she started to walk back in again, forgetting the laundry basket half hidden by the blowing sheets.

She did not answer. He did know. He had seen it in her face.

Inside the house the tension was almost unbearable. Everyone was in the kitchen, so Dermot and Sean could watch them. Liam was sitting at the table swinging his legs and alternately kicking and missing the opposite chair. Dermot was glaring at him, obviously irritated. Now and then Liam looked up at him, sullen and miserable, almost daring to defy him, then backing off again.

Sean was standing in his usual place against the door frame to the hall and the bedrooms and bathroom. Connor stood by the sink and the window to the side, and the long view of the path winding up over the hill, where he and Liam had gone fishing on the first day.

Roisin was looking through the store cupboards putting things in and out, as if it made any difference.

"Stop doing that," Connor told her. "Your mother knows what we've got. We'll have to live on potatoes, until Dermot here gets tired of them."

Roisin kept her back to him, and replaced the tins and packets, such as they were, exactly where she had found them. She was stiff, her fingers fumbling. Twice she lost her grip on a tin and knocked one over. Bridget realized she was waiting for Connor to piece the facts together and realize it was she who had betrayed them.

It was still early, but she wanted to break the prickling, near silence, the tiny, meaningless remarks.

"I'll make lunch," she said to no one in particular.

"Too soon," Dermot told her. "It's only half past eleven. Wait an hour."

"I'll make a fish pie," she answered. "It takes a while. And I could bake something at the same time. There's flour."

"Don't bake for them!" Connor ordered.

"Good idea," Dermot responded instantly. "You do that, Mrs. O'Malley. Bake us something. Can you do a cake?"

"Don't be ridiculous!" Connor moved forward as if he would

stop her physically. "For God's sake, Bridget! Adair's betrayed us, told these terrorists where we are, so he can take my place and sell out the party! We're prisoners until God knows when, and you're going to bake a cake! Haven't you the faintest understanding of what's happening?"

She walked past him to the cupboard and bent down in front of it. She was aware of Paddy by the back door, and knew he was watching her. She needed to defend herself.

"Not eating isn't going to help," she replied. "And you may be perfectly happy to have potatoes for every meal, but I'd rather have something else as well. A cake is one of the few things we have the ingredients for. I'd rather bake than just stand here."

"You're playing into their hands! Don't you give a damn that Adair betrayed us? Billy and Ian are lying dead up there. Doesn't that mean something to you? You knew them for months! Ian helped you mend the gas. He stood in this kitchen only a couple of days ago." His voice was shaking. "How can you bake a cake, when this man tells you to?" He jerked his arm towards Dermot. "Are you so afraid you'll do anything at all?"

She stood up slowly and turned around to face him. "No, Connor, I'm not. I'm baking a cake because I want to. I haven't forgotten what happened to Billy and Ian, but nothing's going to change that now. Maybe we could have when we had the chance, but now it's too late. And fighting over what we eat isn't brave, it's just stupid. Please move away from the bench, so I can use it."

Connor remained where he was.

Liam was watching them, his eyes wide, the muscles in his face drawn tight with fear.

"Please, Dad?" Roisin said urgently.

He raised his head and looked at her.

Bridget watched them. It was as if time stood still. She could hear the ticking of the clock on the wall as the second hand jumped. She knew what was going to happen before it did, in the endless moment from one word to the next.

"You want me to do what he says?" Connor asked. "Why is that, Rosie? I told Adair we were going away for a week. I didn't tell him where to. Who did?"

Whether she could have lied or not, Bridget did not know, but

Roisin must have felt her face give her away. The tide of colour must have burned.

"Eamonn!" Connor said bitterly. "You told him, and he told Adair!"

"No," Roisin looked straight back at him. "Adair never knew. He still doesn't, so far as I know. I told Paddy, because you won't listen and you won't change. I'm going to have a child, and I'm tired of endless fighting and killing from one generation to the next, with no hope of ever being different. I want peace for my children to grow up in. I don't want them afraid all the time, as I am, and everyone I know. No sooner do we build something than it's broken again. Everybody I know has lost someone, either dead, or maimed. Everybody's got to move. If you won't, then we need somebody else to lead us who will!"

"You did?" He said the words as if he could hardly believe them. He swayed a little, and gripped hard on the edge of the bench, his knuckles white. "You betrayed me, the cause? My own daughter? You got Billy and Ian murdered, and the rest of us, your mother and your brother held here at gunpoint—because you're going to have a baby? Great heaven, girl, do you think you're the only woman in Ireland to have a child?"

Bridget stepped forward. "Leave her alone, Connor. She did what she thought was right. She thought you'd change. She was wrong. But I think I'd have done the same thing in her place. We protect our children. We always have."

He stared at her. "You sound as if you agree with her?" It was an accusation.

Bridget heard Paddy move a little to her left, towards Connor, but closer to her also. She was afraid he was going to say something to protect her, then she realized how stupid that was, but the feeling was still there. She rushed into speech to prevent it. "I understand. It's not the same thing. Please, Connor, this isn't the time for us to quarrel, and not here."

His face twisted in scorn. "You mean in front of this lot?" he jabbed his elbow to indicate Dermot and Sean. "Do you think I give a damn what they think about me, or anything else?"

"Perhaps you don't," she replied. "Have you considered that I might? Or Roisin, or Liam?"

"Liam's with me," he stared at her icily. "As far as Roisin is concerned, she is no longer part of my family. She is Eamonn's wife, not my daughter. That's what she has chosen." He moved fractionally so he turned his shoulder away from Roisin, as if physically cutting her out of his sight, and his knowledge.

Bridget saw her face pale, and the tears fill her eyes, but she did not defend herself. Bridget understood why Connor had said it, she could feel his hurt as if it were a tangible thing in the room, but she still was angry with him for his reaction. He should have been larger, braver of heart than to cut Roisin off. She was not betraying for money or power, but because she believed differently, even though she had deceived him.

"What she did was wrong, at least the way she did it," she said aloud. "But you contributed to that also."

"I what?" he shouted.

"You contributed to that also! You don't listen. You never really listen to anybody else, unless they agree with you." She stopped abruptly as she saw Connor's face.

Behind her Dermot was applauding. She turned and saw his smile, a wide, curling leer. His hands were held up, clapping where the others could see them.

"It's a crusade of hate, with you, isn't it!" she said to him with disgust. "It's nothing to do with religion, or freedom, or any of the other things you talk about with such affected passion. It's about power and hate. The only way you can make anybody notice you is with a gun in your hand." Her contempt was so fierce, carrying her shame for Connor, her pain for all of them, that her voice was laden with it.

Dermot swung his arm back to strike her, and Paddy lunged forward and took the blow on his forearm, sending him off balance a little, landing against the table.

Dermot swivelled to face him, his lips drawn back in a snarl. Then suddenly he stopped, and a hard, artificial smile replaced his anger. "Oh, very good!" he said sarcastically. "But I'm not that stupid, Paddy. A grandstand rescue isn't going to make any difference now. You're with us, like it or not. Remember Billy and whatever his name is, up on the hillside? You put them there just as much as we did, so you can forget trying to win Mrs. O'Malley over. She can't help you, and she won't."

"She's right," Paddy said bitterly. "You only know how to destroy."

"I know how to clear the ground, before I build," Dermot said between his teeth. "More than you do, Paddy. You're soft. You haven't the guts to go through with it, or the judgement to know who's strong and who's weak."

"Or who's honest and who isn't," Paddy added, but he did not move.

By the far door Sean relaxed a little. "I'm going to cook," Bridget said abruptly. "If you want to eat, you'll let me get on with it. If you don't, there's not much but raw potatoes. Take your choice." And without waiting for permission she went to the sink, filled the bowl with water, and took a dozen large potatoes out of the sack and began to scrub them.

Silence descended again until every movement she made sounded like a deliberate noise. The wind was rising. She heard Connor say he was going to the bathroom. There was a brief altercation with Dermot, and then he went.

She looked at Liam, still sitting at the kitchen table, and saw the misery in him. He glared back at her, as if she were the enemy. He was furious with her because she was not defending Connor. She had seen his defeat, and Liam could not forgive her for that. It confirmed it in his own mind, and made his confusion deeper. He so desperately wanted certainty, a cause to believe in and someone to admire, and in the space of a few days it had all been torn away and the flaws exposed, the fear and the weaknesses, the self-absorption.

She turned back at the potatoes. They were half done. She had to persuade Connor and Paddy both to run, in opposite directions. Paddy must know Dermot wasn't going to let them live? Was that regret deep enough in him for him to risk his life? Or would he sacrifice them all for his own chance?

And what about Connor? Would he risk himself, to save his family? Or did he really believe it was his duty to live, that only he was fit to lead the cause? She remembered him in her mind's eye as he had been when they first met, his face smooth and eager, his eyes full of dreams. There had been something beautiful in him then.

She was nearly finished with the potatoes. How long had she got left before Dermot made his decision? Once he moved it would be too late. Little time, very little. She must think of a way to persuade each person to do what she needed them to. With Paddy and Connor it would have to be without their knowing.

She cut the potatoes into manageable pieces, awkward with the one blunt slice they had left her, and put them into the largest saucepan, then covered them with cold water. They were going to be very bland. There was a little bacon left, and some eggs, but she did not want to use them now. It would betray the fact that she knew that there was no tomorrow. She must behave as if she believed rescue, or at least release, was only a matter of time. There was no ideological difference between Connor and Eamonn, or Adair, only the means to attain the goal of Protestant safety. Just as there was none between Dermot and Paddy, only the means to unite Ireland under Catholic rule. No one expected anyone to cross the gulf between them. Their quarrels with each other were nothing compared with the enmity that stretched down the generations dividing Catholic from Protestant, Southern Ireland from the North. Paddy might not be on Dermot's side, but he would never be against him. There was all the difference in the world between those two things. She must not trust him.

But she did not have to tell the truth—to anyone!

She looked at the potatoes. They needed salt, and flavour. An idea began in her mind. It was small, not very good, but there was not time to spend waiting for something better. Dermot was nervous, shifting uneasily already. How much longer would it be before he decided to act? He could shoot them, her whole family, everyone she loved most in the world. Paddy would be upset, for a while, caught in an act of barbarity he had not intended, but violence was part of Irish life. Almost every week someone was killed. It would not make any difference to him, in the long run.

"Liam!" she said suddenly. "I want to move something in my room. Will you come and help me please?"

Sean looked up suspiciously.

"In my bedroom I'd rather have my son, thank you," she said sharply. "Liam!"

He stood up slowly, unwilling. He looked for a moment at his father, and received no response. He followed Bridget along the short corridor to the bedroom.

"What is it?" he said as soon as they were inside.

"Close the door," she told him

He frowned.

"Be quick!"

"What is it?" He looked puzzled now, and a little alarmed, but he obeyed.

"Listen to me, Liam." She swallowed down the tension inside her, and deliberately banged the chair on the floor as if moving it. There was no time to think of the risk she was taking, or whether this might be the most costly mistake in her life. "Dermot can't afford to let us go. He killed Billy and Ian, and there isn't going to be any resolution to this. He'll realize it soon, and then he'll kill us."

His eyes were dark, wide with horror at what she had said, and the leap to denial.

"It's true," she said with as much firmness as she could put into her trembling voice. "One of us has to escape and get to the village."

"But, Mum . . ." he began.

"It has to be you," she cut across him. "There's no time to argue. Roisin can't do it, your father won't. I can't outrun them, but you might. I'm going to try and make Dermot think both Paddy and your father are escaping, in opposite directions, which should occupy Sean as well. When you see the chance, run for it. Don't go straight to the village, it's what they would expect. Go round the shore, and bring help back, as soon as you can. Do you understand?"

He stood silently, absorbing what she had said.

"Do you understand?" she repeated, her ears straining to catch the sound of Sean or Dermot in the passage outside. "There's no time to think of anything better."

"Are you sure?" he asked, his voice was tight, high pitched with fear.

"Yes. He can't let us go. Your father will hunt him down for ever. You know that!"

"Yes. Okay. When?"

"In a few minutes." She gulped. "If I can make Paddy and your father go in opposite directions—or I can make Dermot and Sean think they have."

"Does Dad know?"

"No. If I tell anyone else it'll raise their suspicions. Now go back and behave just the same. Go on."

He hesitated only a second, started to say something, then swallowed it back and went out. She followed a moment later.

In the kitchen everything was exactly as they had left it, Sean standing by the door, Dermot by the window behind the table,

Roisin at the stove and Connor sitting on the hard-backed chair nearest to the back door. Bridget went back to the sink and ran the tap until it was hot, replaced the water over the potatoes, put in salt, and set them on the stove.

She must do it now, before thinking about it sapped away her courage. She had nothing to lose. She must keep that in mind all the time. If Dermot realized, and acted before she did, they would all be dead.

She started to speak, but her mouth was too dry. She licked her lips and started again. "This is going to be very bland. I need something with a bit of flavour to add to it." She turned to Connor. "There are some wild onions growing up the hillside, about a hundred yards or so. Can you go and dig them up?"

He looked surprised.

"Please?" She must not make it too urgent, or Dermot would suspect. Surely worrying about food would sound so normal, so sure of tomorrow and the next day?

"Send Liam," Connor replied, without moving from his seat.

Dermot straightened up. "You're neither of you going! Do you think I'm stupid? A hundred yards up the hill, and I'd never see you again. How do I know there even are onions up there?"

Liam raised his head. "There are," he replied, without looking at Bridget.

"Then Paddy can get them," Dermot said. He looked at Paddy. "Do you know an onion when you see it?"

"Probably not," Paddy said with a half smile. "But I can smell one, or taste it." He turned to Bridget. "Do you want them dug up, or pulled, or what?"

"Dig up two or three," she told him. "There's a small garden fork just outside the back door. Thank you." She could not meet his eyes for more than a moment, but by then he was gone anyway, closing the door after him.

Now she had to get Connor to go in the other direction, or at the worst to make Dermot think he had. She glanced at Dermot. The slight sneer was still on his face. Could she trick him into doing what she wanted? Had she understood him?

She turned back to Connor. "Will you help me get the sheets in, please? It's a lot easier to fold them with two. Roisin, watch the potatoes."

"Liam can do it," Connor replied, remaining where he was.

Bridget let her annoyance show in her face. "Why can't you do something for once?" she answered back.

Liam's head turned from Bridget to Connor and back again. He was very pale.

"Liam, do as you're told," Connor said abruptly. "Help your mother with the laundry."

Uncertainly Liam started to climb to his feet.

"Sit down!" Dermot snapped. "O'Malley, she's right. You go and do something for a change. Help her fold the sheets! Move!"

Sean was smiling, leaning against the door to the passage, his gun also raised.

Slowly Connor rose to his feet, his face red, his lips in a tight, thin line. He opened the back door and Bridget followed him out. He walked ahead, without looking at her, and went straight to the line.

She hesitated. Now that the moment had come she found it desperately hard to do, almost too hard.

"Don't," she said as he unpegged the first end.

"What the hell's the matter now?" he snapped.

She moved closer to him, making him back behind the billowing sheet and he grabbed at it with his left hand.

"Connor, they won't let us go," she said levelly. "Dermot can't. And as soon as he realizes you aren't going to give in, which will be any moment, he'll shoot us. He has no choice. He'll go back over the border into Southern Ireland, and at least he'll have a head start before anybody even knows what's happened to us."

"They'll hunt him down like a rat," Connor said contemptuously.

"How? Who'll be alive to say it was him?"

The full horror of it dawned on him. She saw it in the void of his eyes.

There was a shout from the house. She could not tell from where, because the sheets were in the way, but it was Sean's voice. There was no time to hesitate.

"We've got to go! Now, while there's time," she urged. Was Sean coming after them already? What about Paddy up the hill? If he'd kept on looking for the onions, which didn't exist, he should be over the slight rise and out of sight. Why wasn't one of them looking for him? Surely after their betrayal of him they couldn't trust him, could they? Not enough to let him out of their sight, this side of the border?

Then she heard Sean's voice again, calling Paddy's name, sharp and angry.

"Is this what you intend to do?" Connor demanded. "Turn and run, and leave Liam and Rosie to take Dermot's rage when he finds we've escaped? And you were the one who said you understood Rosie putting her baby before the cause, sacrificing her morality to save her child! You disgust me, Bridget. I thought I knew you, and you were better than that. You've betrayed not only me, but everything you said you believed in, everything you are."

"Don't stand there preaching!" She heard her voice rising out of control. "Run! While there's time! For the cause, if not for yourself!"

There was a shout of rage from up the hill, and then another. They both turned towards the sound, but they could see nothing. Then there was a scream, a shot, and then silence again.

The back door slammed open and for an instant she saw Dermot's head and shoulders outlined against the house, his arm raised.

"Run!" she yelled at Connor. Then in case Dermot had not heard her, she did it again.

This time Connor obeyed. At least they were drawing one of them away from the house, and there had been no shots inside. She caught up and grasped his hand, leaping over the sea grass and running down onto the beach, towards the low rise of the sandhills twenty yards away, where at least there was a little shelter.

They were racing over the beach near the tide line where it was hard and firm when the shot rang out. Connor stumbled and pitched forward, his hand going to the scarlet stain spreading across his chest and shoulder. He rolled over and over, carried by the impetus of his speed, then lay still.

Bridget stopped abruptly, and turned back. Dermot was standing on the soft sand just in front of the sea grass, the gun still held out stiffly in front of him. He could pull the trigger again any moment, all he had to do was tighten his grip.

She waited. Oddly, she did not feel a terrible loss. As long as Liam had got away, something was saved. Perhaps Rosie had even gone with him, at least far enough to be out of sight of the house. If they were alive, that was enough. This was a clean way to go, here on the wind-scoured sand, one shot, and then oblivion. It was a bad time, but a good place to die.

Dermot lowered the gun, not right down, he still held it in his hand. He started walking towards her, slowly, evenly.

She did not know if Connor was dead or not. A chest wound might be fatal, but it looked to be closer to the shoulder. Just in case he was still alive, she moved away from him, and began to walk up towards Dermot. If he came down for her, he might shoot Connor again, to make sure. She increased her speed. Strange how she could walk so easily even where the wet sand changed to dry, slithering under her feet. She stopped a couple of yards from Dermot. He was smiling. "You don't care that I shot him, do you!" he said, his eyes wide, his face pale, with two spots of colour high on his cheeks.

"You have no idea what I care about," she answered coldly.

"You'd rather have Paddy, wouldn't you!" he said, his lip curling in disgust. "He'd use you, and throw you away."

"It really doesn't matter what you think," she said wearily, surprised that now it was almost over, that was the exact truth. All she needed was time for Liam to get away, and Rosie if possible.

He jerked the gun towards the house. "Well, let's see, shall we? Is the Reverend O'Malley's wife as cold as she looks? Or his daughter, the pretty turncoat, Roisin?"

If she refused to move, she had no doubt he'd shoot her where she stood. Walking would gain a little more time, only minutes, but minutes might count. She obeyed slowly, passing him and walking ahead. She stepped carefully through the clumps of sea grass and onto the level stretch at the beginning of the lawn, or what passed for it. The sheets were still billowing. She had no idea where Paddy or Sean were. There was no sign of life from the house, and no sound.

She reached the sheets blowing towards her. The plastic laundry basket was just in front of her, empty. Why should she go into the house with him without a fight? It was ridiculous. Rosie might be in there. Even if she wasn't, why should Bridget herself let it be easy?

She picked up the laundry basket and threw it at his feet just as he emerged between the sheets.

He had not had time to see it and dodge. It caught him below the knee, hard enough to cost him his balance. He stumbled forward, still clutching the gun. He was on his hands and knees, his face twisted with rage, already beginning to scramble up again.

She reached for the clothes prop, grasping it with both hands, yanking it out from the line and swinging it wide in a half circle, low and with all her weight behind it. The end of it caught him on the side of the head with a crack she felt all the way through her own body. He fell over sideways and lay motionless, the gun on the ground six inches away from his limp hand.

She scrambled over to him, her body shaking. She picked up the gun, then looked at him. The upper side of his head was bleeding, but not heavily. She knew from the angle of it that he had to be dead. His neck was broken.

She felt sick. But she still needed to face Sean and Paddy.

She walked shakily over to the back door and opened it. The kitchen was empty. "Roisin!" she called.

"Mum!"

The bedroom door crashed wide and Roisin came out, her eyes hollow with fear.

There was no time for hugging, for any kind of emotion. "Where's Liam?" Bridget asked. "And Sean?"

"Liam's gone, as you told him," Roisin answered. "Sean went up the hill after Paddy. I heard him shout. I don't think he came back. Where's Dad?" The look in her face betrayed that she knew.

"On the beach," Bridget replied. "Dermot's dead. I don't know how your father is, I hadn't time to look. Take the tea towels and see what you can do."

"What about you?"

"I've got the gun. I have to find Paddy and Sean."

"But . . ."

"I'll shoot them if I have to." She meant it. She could, to save herself and Roisin. "Go."

Roisin obeyed, and Bridget set off carefully up the slope, watching all the time, keeping both hands on the gun, ready to use it the moment she saw any kind of movement in the tussock and heather.

She had followed the track all the way to the ridge and beyond when she saw Paddy's body lying in a clear patch of grass, his shirt a pale blur against the green, except for the wide, bright red stain of blood across his chest, right in the middle.

Where was Sean? There was no time to allow herself grief now, or any understanding of the waste. She had heard only one shot.

Sean was alive somewhere, maybe waiting, watching her right now. Then why had he not shot her too?

She turned around slowly, searching for him, expecting the noise and the shattering weight of the bullet any moment. But all she could hear was the distant sound of the waves, and bees in the heather. She could see where it had been broken, trampled down around Paddy as if there had been a fight there. Stems were snapped off, the damp earth gouged. The trail led to the edge of a little gully.

Very carefully she walked over towards it, holding the gun in front of her, ready to squeeze the trigger. She looked from right to left, and back again. If Sean was still here, why did he do nothing?

She came to the edge and looked over. She saw him immediately, lying on his back, his body twisted, hips and legs crooked, right thigh bent half under him. His eyes were still open and the gun in his hand.

He shot at her, but it went wide. The angle was wrong, and he could not move to correct it.

She thought of shooting him, but it was cold-blooded, unnecessary. She also thought of saying something, but that was unnecessary too. His pelvis was broken, and at least one leg. He was not going to get out of the gully until someone came and carried him.

She turned away and walked back down the path to the house, and into the kitchen. It was empty. The pan of potatoes, half cooked, stood in the sink. Roisin had thought to take them off before she went into the bedroom.

She should go down to the sand and see if Connor was alive, and if she could do anything for him. At least she could help Roisin. She picked up a couple of bath towels and went out of the back door and past Dermot's body, over the edge of the sea grass and down the sand. Roisin was walking towards her, Connor lay beyond, where he had fallen, but she could not see clearly enough to know whether he was in exactly the same position or not.

Roisin stopped as Bridget reached her. Her face was wet with tears.

"He won't let me do anything," her voice choked. "He won't even listen to me."

So he was alive! And conscious. For an instant Bridget did not even know if she was glad or not. It was as if walls had closed around her again.

"Mum?"

Yes, of course she must be pleased. He didn't deserve to die. And she didn't have to stay inside the walls. It was her choice. If she paid her ransom she could escape. She must never forget that again.

"He may change his mind," she said gently, looking at Roisin. "But if he doesn't, you'll have to accept that. You made your choice, it's your husband and your child. It doesn't matter what I think, it's what you think. But if you care, I believe it's the right choice. And whether I like what you do or not, I shall always love you . . . as you will love your child." She touched Roisin for a moment, just the tips of her fingers to her cheek, then she walked on down the sand to Connor.

He looked at her as she knelt beside him. He was very white and there was a lot of blood on his shirt, but he seemed quite conscious. The tea towels were on the sand. She picked them up, rolled them into pads, and placed them firmly on the wound.

He winced and cried out.

"You should have let Rosie do it," she told him. "It would have cost you less blood."

"Never!" he said between clenched teeth, gasping as the pain washed through him in waves. "I don't have a daughter."

"That's your choice, Connor." She took one of the long towels to put it round him as well as she could to keep the pads in place. "I expect she'll forgive you for your part in this. Whether you forgive her or not is up to you, but I can tell you now, if you don't, you'll lose more than she will. By the way, you might like to know that Sean killed Paddy, but his own pelvis is broken, and he's lying up the hill in a gully. He'll be there until someone carries him out."

He stared at her as if he had never seen her before.

"And I killed Dermot." She could hardly believe her own words, though they were terribly, irrevocably true.

He blinked.

"Liam's gone for the police," she added. "I expect they'll be here soon. And a doctor."

"I can't feel my left arm," he said.

She rolled up the other towel and eased it under his head. "I'll go up to the house and get a blanket. You should be kept warm."

"No!" He breathed in and out slowly. "Stay with me!"

"Oh, I probably will," she replied. "But on my terms, Connor, not on yours. And I'm going to get the blanket. Shock can kill, if you get cold." She rose to her feet, smiling very slightly to herself, and walked back up the sand.

Joyce Carol Oates

From the publication of her first book of short stories, *By the North Gate*, in 1963, **Joyce Carol Oates** has been the most prolific of major American writers, turning out novels, short stories, reviews, essays, and plays in an unceasing flow as remarkable for its quality as its volume. Writers who are extremely prolific often risk not being taken as seriously as they should—if one can write it that fast, how good can it be? Oates, however, has largely escaped that trap, and even her increasing identification with crime fiction, at a time when the field has attracted a number of other mainstream literary figures, has not lessened her reputation as a formidable author in the least. Many of Oates's works contain at least some elements of crime and mystery, from the National Book Award winner *them*, through the Chappaquiddick fictionalization *Black Water* and the Jeffrey Dahmer-inspired serial-killer novel *Zombie*, to her controversial 738-page fictionalized biography of Marilyn Monroe, *Blonde*. The element of detection becomes explicit with the investigations of amateur sleuth Xavier Kilgarvan in the novel *The Mysteries of Winterthurn*, which, the author explains in an afterword to the 1985 paperback edition, "is the third in a quintet of experimental novels that deal, in genre form, with nineteenth- and early twentieth-century America." Why would a literary writer like Oates choose to work in such "deliberately confining structures"? Because "the formal discipline of 'genre' . . . forces us inevitably to a radical re-visioning of the world and the craft of fiction." Oates, who numbers among her honors in a related genre the Bram Stoker Award of the Horror Writers of America, did not establish an explicit crime-fiction identity until *Lives of the Twins* appeared under the pseudonym Rosamund Smith. Initially intended to be a secret, the identity of Smith was revealed almost immediately, and later novels were bylined Joyce Carol Oates (large print) writing as Rosamund Smith (smaller print). Her recent novels include *The Falls*, *I'll Take You There*, and *Rape: A Love Story*.

THE CORN MAIDEN: A LOVE STORY

Joyce Carol Oates

APRIL

YOU ASSHOLES!

Whywhy you're asking here's why her hair.

I mean *her hair*! I mean like I saw it in the sun it's pale silky gold like corn tassels and in the sun sparks might catch. And her eyes that smiled at me sort of nervous and hopeful like she could not know (but who could know?) what is Jude's wish. For I am Jude the Obscure, I am the Master of Eyes. I am not to be judged by crude eyes like yours, assholes.

There was her mother. I saw them together. I saw the mother stoop to kiss *her*. That arrow entered my heart. I thought *I will make you see me*. I would not forgive.

Okay then. More specific. Some kind of report you assholes will type up. Maybe there's a space for the medical examiner's verdict *cause of death*.

* Note: The Sacrifice of the Corn Maiden is a composite drawn from traditional sacrificial rituals of the Iroquois, Pawnee, and Blackfoot Indian tribes.

Assholes don't have a clue do you. If you did you'd know it is futile to type up reports as if such will grant you truth or even "facts."

Whywhy in the night at my computer clickclickclicking through galaxies and there was revealed on my birthday (March 11) the Master of Eyes granting me my wish that is why. *All that you wish will be made manifest in Time. If you are Master.*

Jude the Obscure he named me. In cyberspace we were twinned.

Here's why in sixth grade a field trip to the museum of natural history and Jude wandered off from the silly giggling children to stare at the Onigara exhibit of the Sacrifice of the Corn Maiden. *This exhibit is graphic in nature and not recommended for children younger than sixteen unless with parental guidance* you stepped through an archway into a fluorescent-lit interior of dusty display cases to stare at the Corn Maiden with braided black bristles for hair and flat face and blind eyes and mouth widened in an expression of permanent wonder beyond even terror and it was that vision that entered Jude's heart powerful as any arrow shot into the Corn Maiden's heart that is why.

Because it was an experiment to see if God would allow it that is why.

Because there was no one to stop me that is why.

DISCIPLES

We never thought Jude was serious!

We never thought it would turn out like it did.

We never thought . . .

. . . just *didn't*!

Never meant . . .

. . . *never*!

Nobody had anything against . . .

. . . . .

(Jude said it's Taboo to utter that name.)

Jude was the Master of Eyes. She was our leader all through school. Jude was just so cool.

Fifth grade, Jude instructed us how to get HIGH sniffing S. Where Jude got S., we didn't know.

Seventh grade, Jude gave us E. Like the older kids take. From her secret contact at the high school Jude got E.

When you're HIGH you love everybody but the secret is basically you don't give a damn.

That is what's so nice! HIGH floating above Skatskill like you could drop a bomb on Skatskill Day or your own house and there's your own family rushing out their clothes and hair on fire and screaming for help and you would smile because it would not touch you. That is HIGH.

Secrets no one else knew.

XXX videos at Jude's house.

Jude's grandmother Mrs. Trahern the widow of somebody famous.

Feral cats we fed. Cool!

Ritalin and Xanax Jude's doctors prescribed, Jude only just pretended to take that shit. In her bathroom, a supply of years.

Haagen Dazs French Vanilla ice cream we fed the Corn Maiden.

The Corn Maiden was sleepy almost at once, yawning. Ice cream tastes so good! Just one pill ground up, a half teaspoon. It was magic. We could not believe it.

Jude said you can't believe the magic you possess until somebody instructs how to unleash it.

The Corn Maiden had never been to Jude's house before. But Jude was friendly to her beginning back in March. Told us the Master of Eyes had granted her a wish on her birthday. And we were counted in that wish.

The plan was to *establish trust.*

The plan was to prepare for the Corn Maiden in the knowledge that one day there would be the magic hour when (Jude predicted) like a lightning flash lighting up the dark all would become clear.

This was so. We were in readiness, and the magic hour was so.

There is a rear entrance to the Trahern house. We came that way.

The Corn Maiden walked! On her own two feet the Corn Maiden walked, she was not forced, or carried.

Of her own volition Jude said.

It was not so in the Onigara Indian ceremony. There, the Corn Maiden did not come of her own volition but was kidnapped.

An enemy tribe would kidnap her. She would never return to her people.

The Corn Maiden would be buried, she would be laid among the corn seed in the sun and the earth covered over her. Jude told us of this like an old fairy tale to make you smile, but not to ask *Why*.

Jude did not like us to ask *Why*.

The Corn Maiden was never threatened. The Corn Maiden was treated with reverence, respect, and kindness.

(Except we had to scare her, a little. There was no other way Jude said.)

On Tuesdays and Thursdays she would come by the 7-Eleven store on the way home from school. Why this was, Jude knew. Mostly high school kids hang out there. Older kids, smoking. Crummy mini-mall on the state highway. Rug remnant store, hair and nails salon, Chinese takeout & the 7-Eleven. Behind are Dumpsters and a stink like something rotten.

Feral cats hide in the scrub brush behind the Dumpsters. Where it's like a jungle, nobody ever goes.

(Except Jude. To feed the feral cats she says are her Totem.)

At the 7-Eleven Jude had us walk separate so we would not be seen walking together.

Four girls together, somebody might notice.

A girl by herself, or two girls, nobody would notice.

Not that anybody was watching. We came by the back way.

Some old long-ago time when servants lived down the hill. When they climbed the hill to the big houses on Highgate Avenue.

Historic old Skatskill estate. That was where Jude lived with just her grandmother. On TV it would be shown. In the newspapers. In *The New York Times* it would be shown on the front page. The house would be called *an eighteenth-century Dutch-American manor house.* We never knew about that. We never saw the house from the front. We only just went into Jude's room and a few other rooms. And there was the cellar.

From Highgate Avenue you can't see the Trahern house very well, there is a ten-foot stone wall surrounding it. This wall is old and crumbling but still you can't see over it. But through the gate that's wrought iron you can see if you look fast, while you're driving by.

Lots of people drive by now I guess.

NO PARKING NO PARKING NO PARKING on Highgate. Skatskill does not welcome strangers except to shop.

The Trahern estate it would be called. The property is eleven acres. But there is a shortcut from the rear. When we brought the Corn Maiden to the house, we came from the rear. Mostly the property is woods. Mostly it is wild, like a jungle. But there are old stone steps you can climb if you are careful. An old service road that's grown over with brambles and blocked off at the bottom of the hill by a concrete slab but you can walk around the slab.

This back way, nobody would guess. Three minutes' walk from the mini-mall.

Nobody would guess! The big old houses on Highgate, way up the hill, how the rear of their property slopes down to the state highway.

Jude warned *The Corn Maiden must be treated with reverence, respect, kindness, and firmness. The Corn Maiden must never guess the fate that will be hers.*

SUBURBAN SINGLE MOM, LATCHKEY DAUGHTER

"Marissa"

The first signal something was wrong, no lights in the apartment.

The second, too quiet.

"Marissa, honey . . . ?"

Already there was an edge to her voice. Already her chest felt as if an iron band was tightening around it.

Stepped inside the darkened apartment. She would swear, no later than 8 P.M.

In a dreamlike suspension of emotion shutting the door behind her, switching on a light. Aware of herself as one might see oneself on a video monitor behaving with conspicuous normality though the circumstances have shifted, and are not normal.

A mother learns not to panic, not to betray weakness. Should a child be observing.

"Marissa? Aren't you . . . are you *home*?"

If she'd been home, Marissa would have the lights on. Marissa would be doing her homework in the living room with the TV on, loud. Or the CD player on, loud. When she was home alone Marissa was made uneasy by quiet.

Made her nervous she said. Made her think scary thoughts like about dying she said. Hear her own heartbeat she said.

But the apartment was quiet. In the kitchen, quiet.

Leah switched on more lights. She was still observing herself, she was still behaving calmly. Seeing, from the living room, down the hall to Marissa's room that the door to that room was open, darkness inside.

It was possible—it was! if only for a blurred desperate moment—to think that Marissa had fallen asleep on her bed, that was why . . . But Leah checked, there was no slender figure lying on the bed.

No one in the bathroom. Door ajar, darkness inside.

The apartment did not seem familiar somehow. As if furniture had been moved. (It had not, she would determine later.) It was chilly, drafty as if a window had been left open. (No window had been left open.)

"Marissa? Ma*riss*a?"

There was a tone of surprise and almost-exasperation in the mother's voice. As if, if Marissa heard, she would know herself just mildly scolded.

In the kitchen that was empty, Leah set the groceries down. On a counter. Wasn't watching, the bag slumped slowly over. Scarcely saw, a container of yogurt fell out.

Marissa's favorite, strawberry.

So quiet! The mother, beginning to shiver, understood why the daughter hated quiet.

She was walking through the rooms, and would walk through the few rooms of the small first-floor apartment calling *Marissa? Honey?* in a thin rising voice like a wire pulled tight. She would lose track of time. She was the mother, she was responsible. For eleven years she had not lost her child, every mother's terror of losing her child, an abrupt physical loss, a theft, a stealing-away, a *forcible abduction*.

"No. She's here. Somewhere . . ."

Retracing her steps through the apartment. There were so few rooms for Marissa to be in! Again opening the bathroom door, wider. Opening a closet door. Closet doors. Stumbling against . . . Struck her shoulder on . . . Collided with Marissa's desk chair, stinging her thigh. "Marissa? Are you *hiding*?"

As if Marissa would be hiding. At such a time.

Marissa was eleven years old. Marissa had not hidden from her mother to make Mommy seek her out giggling and squealing with excitement in a very long time.

She would protest she was not a negligent mother.

She was a working mother. A single mother. Her daughter's father had disappeared from their lives, he paid neither alimony nor child support. How was it her fault, she had to work to support her daughter and herself, and her daughter required special education instruction and so she'd taken her out of public school and enrolled her at Skatskill Day . . .

They would accuse her. In the tabloids they would crucify her.

Dial 911 and your life is public fodder. Dial 911 and your life is not yours. Dial 911 and your life is forever changed.

Suburban Single Mom. Latchkey Daughter.

Eleven-Year-Old Missing, South Skatskill.

She would protest it was not that way at all! It was not.

Five days out of seven *it was not.*

Only Tuesdays and Thursdays she worked late at the clinic. Only since Christmas had Marissa been coming home to an empty apartment.

No. It was not ideal. And maybe she should have hired a sitter except . . .

She would protest she had no choice but to work late, her shift had been changed. On Tuesdays/Thursdays she began at 10:30 A.M. and ended at 6:30 P.M. Those nights, she was home by 7:15 P.M., by 7:30 P.M. at the latest she was home. She would swear, she was! Most nights.

How was it her fault, slow-moving traffic on the Tappan Zee Bridge from Nyack then north on route 9 through Tarrytown, Sleepy Hollow, to the Skatskill town limits, and route 9 under repair. Traffic in pelting rain! Out of nowhere a cloudburst, rain! She had wanted to sob in frustration, in fury at what her life had become, blinding headlights in her eyes like laser rays piercing her brain.

But usually she was home by 8 P.M. At the latest.

Before dialing 911 she was trying to think: to calculate.

Marissa would ordinarily be home by about 4 P.M. Her last class ended at 3:15 P.M. Marissa would walk home, five and a half suburban blocks, approximately a half mile, through (mostly) a residential neighborhood. (True, 15th Street was a busy street. But Marissa didn't need to cross it.) And she would walk with school friends. (Would she?) Marissa didn't take a school bus, there was no bus for private school children, and in any case Marissa lived near the school because Leah Bantry had moved to the Briarcliff Apts. in order to be near Skatskill Day.

She would explain! In the interstices of emotion over her *missing child* she would explain.

Possibly there had been something special after school that day, a sports event, choir practice, Marissa had forgotten to mention to Leah . . . Possibly Marissa had been invited home by a friend.

In the apartment, standing beside the phone, as if waiting for the phone to ring, trying to think what it was she'd just been thinking. Like trying to grasp water with her fingers, trying to think . . .

A friend! That was it.

What were the names of girls in Marissa's class . . . ?

Of course, Leah would telephone! She was shaky, and she was upset, but she would make these crucial calls before involving the police, she wasn't a hysterical mother. She might call Leah's teacher whose name she knew, and from her she would learn the names of other girls, she would call these numbers, she would soon locate Marissa, it would be all right. And the mother of Marissa's friend would say apologetically, *But I'd thought Marissa had asked you, could she stay for supper. I'm so very sorry!* And Leah would say quickly laughing in relief, *You know how children are, sometimes. Even the nice ones.*

Except: Marissa didn't have many friends at the school.

That had been a problem in the new, private school. In public school she'd had friends, but it wasn't so easy at Skatskill Day where most students were privileged, well-to-do. Very privileged, and very well-to-do. And poor Marissa was so sweet, trusting and hopeful and easy to hurt if other girls chose to hurt her.

Already in fifth grade it had begun, a perplexing girl-meanness.

In sixth grade, it had become worse.

"Why don't they like me, Mommy?"

"Why do they make fun of me, Mommy?"

For in Skatskill if you lived down the hill from Highgate Avenue and/or east of Summit Street you were known to be *working class*. Marissa had asked what it meant? Didn't everybody work? And what was a *class* was it like . . . a class in school? A class*room?*)

But Leah had to concede: even if Marissa had been invited home by an unknown school friend, she wouldn't have stayed away so long.

Not past 5 P.M. Not past dark.

Not without calling Leah.

"She isn't the type of child to . . ."

Leah checked the kitchen again. The sink was empty. No package of chicken cutlets defrosting.

Tuesdays/Thursdays were Marissa's evenings to start supper. Marissa loved to cook, Mommy and Marissa loved to cook together. Tonight they were having chicken jambalaya which was their favorite fun meal to prepare together. "Tomatoes, onions, peppers, cajun powder. Rice . . ."

Leah spoke aloud. The silence was unnerving.

If I'd come home directly. Tonight.

The 7-Eleven out on the highway. That's where she had stopped on the way home.

Behind the counter, the middle-aged Indian gentleman with the wise sorrowful eyes would vouch for her. Leah was a frequent customer, he didn't know her name but he seemed to like her.

Dairy products, a box of tissues. Canned tomatoes. Two six-packs of beer, cold. For all he knew, Leah had a husband. *He* was the beer drinker, the husband.

Leah saw that her hands were trembling. She needed a drink, to steady her hands.

"Ma*ris*sa!"

She was thirty-four years old. Her daughter was eleven. So far as anyone in Leah's family knew, including her parents, she had been "amicably divorced" for seven years. Her former husband, a medical school drop-out, had disappeared somewhere in Northern California; they had lived together in Berkeley, having met at the university in the early 1990s.

Impossible to locate the former husband/father whose name was not Bantry.

She would be asked about him, she knew. She would be asked about numerous things.

She would explain: eleven is too old for day care. Eleven is fully capable of coming home alone . . . Eleven can be responsible for . . .

At the refrigerator she fumbled for a can of beer. She opened it and drank thirstily. The liquid was freezing cold, her head began to ache immediately: an icy spot like a coin between her eyes. *How can you! At a time like this!* She didn't want to panic and call 911 before she'd thought this through. Something was staring her in the face, some explanation, maybe?

Distraught Single Mom. Modest Apartment.

Missing Eleven-Year-Old. "Learning Disabilities."

Clumsily Leah retraced her steps through the apartment another time. She was looking for . . . Throwing more widely open those doors she'd already opened. Kneeling beside Marissa's bed to peer beneath in a burst of desperate energy.

And finding—what? A lone sock.

As if Marissa would be hiding beneath a bed!

Marissa who loved her mother, would never never wish to worry or upset or hurt her mother. Marissa who was young for her age, never rebellious, sulky. Marissa whose idea of badness was forgetting to make her bed in the morning. Leaving the bathroom mirror above the sink splattered with water.

Marissa who'd asked Mommy, "Do I have a daddy somewhere like other girls, and he knows about me?"

Marissa who'd asked, blinking back tears, "Why do they make fun of me, Mommy? Am I *slow*?"

In public school classes had been too large, her teacher hadn't had time or patience for Marissa. So Leah had enrolled her at Skatskill Day where classes were limited to fifteen students and Marissa would have special attention from her teacher and yet: still she was having trouble with arithmetic, she was teased, called "slow" . . . Laughed at even by girls she'd thought were her friends.

"Maybe she's run away."

Out of nowhere this thought struck Leah.

Marissa had run away from Skatskill. From the life Mommy had worked so hard to provide for her.

"That can't be! Never."

Leah swallowed another mouthful of beer. Self-medicating, it was. Still her heart was beating in rapid thumps, then missing a beat. Hoped to God she would not faint . . .

"Where? Where would Marissa go? *Never.*"

Ridiculous to think that Marissa would run away!

She was far too shy, passive. Far too uncertain of herself. Other children, particularly older children, intimidated her. Because Marissa was unusually attractive, a beautiful child with silky blond hair to her shoulders, brushed by her proud mother until it shone, sometimes braided by her mother into elaborate plaits, Marissa often drew unwanted attention; but Marissa had very little sense of herself and of how others regarded her.

She had never ridden a bus alone. Never gone to a movie alone. Rarely entered any store alone, without Leah close by.

Yet it was the first thing police would suspect, probably: Marissa had run away.

"Maybe she's next door. Visiting the neighbors."

Leah knew this was not likely. She and Marissa were on friendly terms with their neighbors but they never visited one another. It wasn't that kind of apartment complex, there were few other children.

Still, Leah would have to see. It was expected of a mother looking for her daughter, to check with neighbors.

She spent some time then, ten or fifteen minutes, knocking on doors in the Briarcliff Apts. Smiling anxiously into strangers' startled faces. Trying not to sound desperate, hysterical.

"Excuse me . . ."

A nightmare memory came to her, of a distraught young mother knocking on their door, years ago in Berkeley when she'd first moved in with her lover who would become Marissa's father. They'd been interrupted at a meal, and Leah's lover had answered the door, an edge of annoyance in his voice; and Leah had come up behind him, very young at the time, very blond and privileged, and she'd stared at a young Filipino woman blinking back tears as she'd asked them *Have you seen my daughter . . .* Leah could not remember anything more.

Now it was Leah Bantry who was knocking on doors. Interrupting strangers at mealtime. Apologizing for disturbing them, asking in a tremulous voice *Have you seen my daughter . . .*

In the barracks-like apartment complex into which Leah had moved for economy's sake two years before, each apartment opened directly out onto the rear of the building, into the parking area. This was a brightly lit paved area, purely functional, ugly. In the apartment complex there were no hallways. There were no interior stairs, no foyers. There were no meeting places for even casual exchanges. This was not an attractive condominium village overlooking the Hudson River but Briarcliff Apts, South Skatskill.

Leah's immediate neighbors were sympathetic and concerned, but could offer no help. They had not seen Marissa, and of course she hadn't come to visit them. They promised Leah they would "keep an eye out" and suggested she call 911.

Leah continued to knock on doors. A mechanism had been triggered in her brain, she could not stop until she had knocked on every door in the apartment complex. As she moved farther from her own first-floor apartment, she was met with less sympathy. One tenant shouted through the door to ask what she wanted. Another, a middle-aged man with a drinker's flushed indignant face, interrupted her faltering query to say he hadn't seen any children, he didn't know any children, and he didn't have time for any children.

Leah returned to her apartment staggering, dazed. Saw with a thrill of alarm she'd left the door ajar. Every light in the apartment appeared to be on. Almost, she thought Marissa must be home now, in the kitchen.

She hurried inside. "Marissa . . . ?"

Her voice was eager, piteous.

The kitchen was empty of course. The apartment was empty.

A new, wild idea: Leah returned outside, to the parking lot, to check her car which was parked a short distance away. She peered inside, though knowing it was locked and empty. Peered into the back seat.

Am I going mad? What is happening to me . . .

Still, she'd had to look. She had a powerful urge, too, to get into the car and drive along 15th Street to Skatskill Day School, and check out the building. Of course, it would be locked. The parking lot to the rear . . .

She would drive on Van Buren. She would drive on Summit. She would drive along Skatskill's small downtown of boutiques, novelty restaurants, high-priced antique and clothing stores. Out to the highway past gas stations, fast-food restaurants, mini-malls.

Expecting to see—what? Her daughter walking in the rain?

Leah returned to the apartment, thinking she'd heard the phone ring but the phone was not ringing. Another time, unable to stop herself she checked the rooms. This time looking more carefully through Marissa's small closet, pushing aside Marissa's neatly hung clothes. (Marissa had always been obsessively neat. Leah had not wished to wonder why.) Stared at Marissa's shoes. Such small shoes! Trying to remember what Marissa had worn that morning . . . So many hours ago.

Had she plaited Marissa's hair that morning? She didn't think she'd had time. Instead she had brushed it, lovingly. Maybe she was a little too vain of her beautiful daughter and now she was being punished . . . No, that was absurd. You are not punished for loving your child. She had brushed Marissa's hair until it shone and she had fastened it with barrettes, mother-of-pearl butterflies.

"Aren't you pretty! Mommy's little angel."

"Oh, Mommy. I am not."

Leah's heart caught. She could not understand how the child's father had abandoned them both. She was sick with guilt, it had to be her fault as a woman and a mother.

She'd resisted an impulse to hug Marissa, though. At eleven, the girl was getting too old for spontaneous unexplained hugs from Mommy.

Displays of emotion upset children, Leah had been warned. Of course, Leah hadn't needed to be warned.

Leah returned to the kitchen for another beer. Before dialing 911. Just a few swallows, she wouldn't finish the entire can.

She kept nothing stronger than beer in the apartment. That was a rule of her mature life.

No hard liquor. No men overnight. No exposure to her daughter, the emotions Mommy sometimes felt.

She knew: she would be blamed. For she was blameable.

Latchkey child. Working mom.

She'd have had to pay a sitter nearly as much as she made at the clinic as a medical assistant, after taxes. It was unfair, and it was impossible. She could not.

Marissa was not so quick-witted as other children her age but she was not *slow*! She was in sixth grade, she had not fallen behind. Her tutor said she was "improving." And her attitude was so hopeful. *Your daughter tries so hard, Mrs. Bantry! Such a sweet, patient child.*

Unlike her mother, Leah thought. Who wasn't sweet, and who had given up patience long ago.

"I want to report a child missing . . ."

She rehearsed the words, struck by their finality. She hoped her voice would not sound slurred.

Where was Marissa? It was impossible to think she wasn't somehow in the apartment. If Leah looked again . . .

Marissa knew: to lock the front door behind her, and to bolt the safety latch when she was home alone. (Mommy and Marissa had practiced this maneuver many times.) Marissa knew: not to answer the door if anyone knocked, if Mommy was not home. Not to answer the telephone immediately but to let the answering machine click on, to hear if it was Mommy calling.

Marissa knew: never let strangers approach her. No conversations with strangers. Never climb into vehicles with strangers or even with people she knew unless they were women, people Mommy knew or the mothers of classmates for instance.

Above all Marissa knew: come home directly from school.

Never enter any building, any house, except possibly the house of a classmate, a school friend . . . Even so, Mommy must be told about this beforehand.

(Would Marissa remember? Could an eleven-year-old be trusted to remember so much?)

Leah had totally forgotten; she'd intended to call Marissa's teacher. From Miss Fletcher, Leah would learn the names of Marissa's friends. This, the police would expect her to know. Yet she stood by the phone indecisively, wondering if she dared call the woman; for if she did, Miss Fletcher would know that something was wrong.

The ache between Leah's eyes had spread, her head was wracked with pain.

Four-year-old Marissa would climb up onto the sofa beside Leah, and stroke her forehead to smooth out the "worry lines." Wet kisses on Mommy's forehead. "Kiss to make go away!"

Mommy's vanity had been somewhat wounded, that her child saw worry lines in her face. But she'd laughed, and invited more kisses. "All right, sweetie. Kiss-to-make-go-away."

It had become their ritual. A frown, a grimace, a mournful look—either Mommy or Marissa might demand, "Kiss-to-make-go-away."

Leah was paging through the telephone directory. *Fletcher.* There were more than a dozen *Fletchers*. None of the initials seemed quite right. Marissa's teacher's first name was—Eve? Eva?

Leah dialed one of the numbers. A recording clicked on, a man's voice.

Another number, a man answered. Politely telling Leah no: there was no one named "Eve" or "Eva" at that number.

This is hopeless, Leah thought.

She should be calling ERs, medical centers, where a child might have been brought, struck by a vehicle for instance crossing a busy street . . .

She fumbled for the can of beer. She would drink hurriedly now. Before the police arrived.

Self-medicating a therapist had called it. Back in high school she'd begun. It was her secret from her family, they'd never known. Though her sister Avril had guessed. At first Leah had drunk with her friends, then she hadn't needed her friends. It wasn't for the elevated sensation, the buzz, it was to calm her nerves. To make her less anxious. Less disgusted with herself.

I need to be beautiful. More beautiful.

He'd said she was beautiful, many times. The man who was to be Marissa's father. Leah was beautiful, he adored her.

They were going to live in a seaside town somewhere in northern California, Oregon. It had been their fantasy. In the meantime he'd been a medical student, resentful of the pressure. She had taken the easier route, nursing school. But she'd dropped out when she became pregnant.

Later he would say sure she was beautiful, but he did not love her.

Love wears out. People move on.

Still, there was Marissa. Out of their coupling, Marissa.

Gladly would Leah give up the man, any man, so long as she had her daughter back.

If she had not stopped on the way home from the clinic! If she had come directly home.

She knew this: she would have to tell police where she had been, before returning home. Why she'd been unusually late. She would have to confess that, that she had been late. Her life would be turned inside-out like the pockets of an old pair of pants. All that was private, precious, rudely exposed.

The single evening in weeks, months . . . She'd behaved out of character.

But she'd stopped at the 7-Eleven, too. It was a busy place in the early evening. This wasn't out of character, Leah frequently stopped at the convenience store which was two blocks from Briarcliff Apts. The Indian gentleman at the cash register would speak kindly of her to police officers. He would learn that her name was Leah Barnty and that her daughter was missing. He would learn that she lived close by, on 15th Street. He would learn that she was a single mother, she was not married. The numerous six-packs of Coors she bought had not been for a husband but for her.

He'd seen her with Marissa, certainly. And so he would remember Marissa. Shy blond child whose hair was sometimes in plaits. He would pity Leah as he'd never had reason to pity her in the past, only just to admire her in his guarded way, the blond shining hair, the American-healthy good looks.

Leah finished the beer, and disposed of the can in the waste basket beneath the sink. She thought of going outside and dumping all the cans into a trash can, for police would possibly search the house, but there was no time, she had delayed long enough waiting for Marissa to return and everything to be again as it had been. Thinking *Why didn't I get a cell phone for Marissa, why did I think the expense wasn't worth it?* She picked up the receiver, and dialed 911.

Her voice was breathless as if she'd been running.

"I want—I want—to report a child missing."

Lone Wolves

I am meant for a special destiny. I am!

He lived vividly inside his head. She lived vividly inside her head.

He was a former idealist. She was an unblinking realist.

He was thirty-one years old. She was thirteen.

He was tall/lanky/ropey-muscled five feet ten inches (on his New York State driver's license he'd indicated 5'11"), weighing one hundred fifty-five pounds. She was four feet eleven, eighty-three pounds.

He thought well of himself, secretly. She thought very well of herself, not so secretly.

He was a substitute math teacher/ "computer consultant" at Skatskill Day School. She was an eighth grader at Skatskill Day School.

His official status at the school was *part-time employee.*

Her official status at the school was *full-tuition pupil, no exceptions.*

Part-time employee meant no medical/dental insurance coverage, less pay per hour than full-time employees, and no possibility of tenure. *Full-tuition, no exceptions* meant no scholarship aid or tuition deferral.

He was a relatively new resident of Skatskill-on-Hudson, eight miles north of New York City. She was a longtime resident who'd come to live with her widowed grandmother when she was two years old, in 1992.

To her, to his face, he was *Mr. Zallman*; otherwise, *Mr. Z.*

To him, she had no clear identity. One of those Skatskill Day girls of varying ages (elementary grades through high school) to whom he gave computer instructions and provided personal assistance as requested.

Even sixth grader Marissa Bantry with the long straight corn-tassel hair he would not recall, immediately.

The kids he called them. In a voice that dragged with reluctant affection; or in a voice heavy with sarcasm. *Those kids!*

Depending on the day, the week. Depending on his mood.

Those others she called them in a voice quavering with scorn.

They were an alien race. Even her small band of disciples she had to concede were losers.

In his confidential file in the office of the principal of Skatskill Day it was noted *Impressive credentials/recommendations, interacts well with brighter students. Inclined to impatience. Not a team player. Unusual sense of humor. (Abrasive?)*

In her confidential file (1998–present) in the principal's office it was noted in reports by numerous parties *Impressive background (maternal grandmother/legal guardian Mrs. A. Trahern, alumna/donor/trustee/ emeritus), impressive I.Q. (measured 149, 161, 113, 159 ages 6, 9, 10, 12), flashes of brilliance, erratic academic performance, lonely child, gregarious child, interacts poorly with classmates, natural leader, antisocial tendencies, lively presence in class, disruptive presence in class, hyperactive, apathetic, talent for "fantasy," poor communication skills, immature tendencies, ver-*

bal fluency, imagination stimulated by new projects, easily bored, sullen, mature for age, poor motor coordination skills, diagnosed Attention Deficit Syndrome age 5/prescribed Ritalin with good results/mixed results, diagnosed borderline dyslexic age 7, prescribed special tutoring with good results/mixed results, honor roll fifth grade, low grades/failed English seventh grade, suspended for one week Oct. 2002 "threatening" girl classmate, reinstated after three days/legal action brought against school by guardian/mandated psychological counseling with good/mixed results. (On the outside of the folder, in the principal's handwriting *A challenge*!)

He was swarthy skinned, with an olive complexion. She had pale translucent skin.

He was at the school Monday/Tuesday/Thursday unless he was subbing for another teacher which he did, on the average, perhaps once every five weeks. She was at the school five days a week, Skatskill Day was her turf!

Hate/love she felt for Skatskill Day. *Love/hate.*

(Often, as her teachers noted, she "disappeared" from classes and later "reappeared." Sulky/arrogant with no explanation.)

He was a lone wolf and yet: the great-grandson of immigrant German Jews who had come to the United States in the early 1900s. The grandson and son of partners at Cleary, McCorkle, Mace & Zallman, Wall Street brokers. She was the lone grandchild of New York State Supreme Court Justice Elias Trahern who had died before she was born and was of no more interest to her than the jut-jawed and bewigged General George Washington whose idealized image hung in the school rotunda.

His skin was dotted with moles. Not disfiguring exactly but he'd see people staring at these moles as if waiting for them to move.

Her skin was susceptible to angry-looking rashes. Nerve-rashes they'd been diagnosed, also caused by picking with her nails.

He was beginning to lose his thick-rippled dark hair he had not realized he'd been vain about. Receding at the temples so he wore it straggling over his collar. Her hair exploded in faded-rust fuzz like dandelion seed around her pointy pinched face.

He was Mikal. She was Jude.

He'd been born Michael but there were so many damn Michaels!

She'd been born Judith but—*Judith! Enough to make you want to puke.*

Lone wolves who scorned the crowd. Natural aristocrats who had no use for money, or for family connections.

He was estranged from the Zallmans. Mostly.

She was estranged from the Traherns. Mostly.

He had a quick engaging ironic laugh. She had a high-pitched nasal-sniggering laugh that surprised her suddenly, like a sneeze.

His favored muttered epithet was *What next?* Her favored muttered epithet was *Bor-ing!*

He knew: prepubescent/adolescent girls often have crushes on their male teachers. Yet somehow it never seemed very real to him, or very crucial. Mikal Zallman living in his own head.

She detested boys her own age. And most men, any age.

Making her disciples giggle and blush, at lunchtime flashing a paring knife in a swooping circular motion to indicate *cas-tra-tion: know what that is?* as certain eighth grade boys passed noisily by carrying cafeteria trays.

Boys rarely saw her. She'd learned to go invisible like a playing card turned sideways.

He lived—smugly, it seemed to some observers—inside an armor of irony. (Except when alone. Staring at images of famine, war, devastation he felt himself blinking hot tears from his eyes. He'd shocked himself and others crying uncontrollably at his father's funeral in an Upper East Side synagogue the previous year.)

She had not cried in approximately four years. Since she'd fallen from a bicycle and cut a gash in her right knee requiring nine stitches.

He lived alone, in three sparely furnished rooms, in Riverview Heights, a condominium village on the Hudson River in North Tarrytown. She lived alone, except for the peripheral presence of her aging grandmother, in a few comfortably furnished rooms in the main wing of the Trahern estate at 83 Highgate Avenue; the rest of the thirty-room mansion had long been closed off for economy's sake.

He had no idea where she lived, as he had but the vaguest idea of who she was. She knew where he lived, it was three miles from 83 Highgate Avenue. She'd bicycled past Riverview Heights more than once.

He drove a not-new metallic blue Honda CR-V, New York license TZ 6063. She knew he drove a not-new metallic blue Honda CR-V, New York license TZ 6063.

Actually he didn't always think so well of himself. Actually she didn't always think so well of herself.

He wished to think well of himself. He wished to think well of all of humanity. He did not want to think *Homo sapiens is hopeless, let's pull the plug.* He wanted to think *I can make a difference in others' lives.*

He'd been an idealist who had *burnt out, crashed* in his late twenties. These were worthy clichés. These were clichés he had earned. He had taught in Manhattan, Bronx, and Yonkers public schools through his mid-and late twenties and after an interim of recovery he had returned to Columbia University to upgrade his credentials with a master's degree in computer science and he had returned to teaching for his old idealism yet clung to him like lint on one of his worn-at-the-elbow sweaters, one thing he knew he would never emulate his father in the pursuit of money, here in Skatskill-on-Hudson where he knew no one he could work part-time mostly helping kids with computers and he would be respected here or in any case his privacy would be respected, he wasn't an ambitious private school teacher, wasn't angling for a permanent job, in a few years he'd move on but for the present time he was contentedly employed, he had freedom to *feed my rat* as he called it.

Much of the time she did not think so well of herself. Secretly.

Suicide fantasies are common to adolescents. Not a sign of mental illness so long as they remain fantasies.

He'd had such fantasies, too. Well into his twenties, in fact. He'd outgrown them now. That was what *feeding my rat* had done for Mikal Zallman.

Her suicide fantasies were cartoons, you could say. A plunge from the Tappan Zee Bridge/George Washington Bridge, footage on the 6 P.M. news. A blazing fireball on a rooftop. (Skatskill Day? It was the only roof she had access to.) If you swallowed like five, six Ecstasy pills your heart would explode (maybe). If you swallowed a dozen barbiturates you would fall asleep and then into a coma and never wake up (maybe). With drugs there was always the possibility of vomiting, waking up in an ER your stomach being pumped or waking up brain damaged. There were knives, razor blades. Bleeding into a bathtub, the warm water gushing.

Eve of her thirteenth birthday and she'd been feeling shitty and her new friend/mentor the Master of Eyes (in Alaska, unless it was Antarctica) advised her why hate yourself Jude it's bor-ing. Better to hate *those others* who surround.

She never cried, though. Really really never cried.

Like Jude O's tear ducts are dried out. Cool!

Ducts reminded her of *pubes* she had first encountered as a word in a chat room, she'd looked up in the dictionary seeing *pubes* was a nasty word for those nasty crinkly/kinky hairs that had started to sprout in a certain place, between her legs. And in her armpits where she refused to apply *deodorant* until Grandmother nagnagged.

Grandmother Trahern was half blind but her sense of smell was acute. Grandmother Trahern was skilled at nagnagnagging, you might say it was the old woman's predominant skill in the eighth decade of her life.

Mr. Z! Maybe he'd smelled her underarms. She hoped he had not smelled her crotch.

Mr. Z. in computer lab making his way along the aisle answering kids' questions most of them pretty elementary/dumb ass she'd have liked to catch his eye and exchange a knowing smirk but Mr. Z. never seemed to be looking toward her and then she was stricken with shyness, blood rushing into her face as he paused above her to examine the confusion on her screen and she heard herself mutter with childish bravado *Guess I fucked up, Mr. Zallman, huh?* wiping her nose on the edge of her hand beginning to giggle and there was sexy/cool Mr. Z. six inches from her not breaking into a smile even of playful reproach giving not the slightest hint he'd heard the forbidden F-word from an eighth grade girl's innocent mouth.

In fact Mr. Z. had heard. Sure.

Never laugh, never encourage them. If they swear or use obscene or suggestive language.

And never touch them.

Or allow them to touch you.

The (subterranean) connection between them.

He had leaned over her, typed on her keyboard. Repaired the damage. Told her she was doing very well. Not to be discouraged! He didn't seem to know her name but maybe that was just pretense, his sense of humor. Moving on to the next raised hand.

Still, she'd known there was the (subterranean) connection.

As she'd known, first glimpsing the Corn Maiden in the seventh grade corridor. Silky blond corn-tassel hair. Shy, frightened.

A new girl. Perfect.

One morning she came early to observe the Corn Maiden's mother dropping her off at the curb. Good-looking woman with the same pale blond hair, smiling at the girl and hastily leaning over to kiskiss.

Some connections go through you like a laser ray.

Some connections, you just know.

Mr. Z. she'd sent an e-message *you are a master mister z*. Which was not like Jude O. to do because any message in cyberspace can never be erased. But Mr. Z. had not replied.

So easy to reply to a fucking e-message! But Mr. Z. had not.

Mr. Z. did not exchange a knowing smile/wink with her as you'd expect.

Ignored her!

Like he didn't know which one of them she was.

Like he could confuse her with *those others* her inferiors.

And so something turned in her heart like a rusty key and she thought calmly, *You will pay for this mister asshole Z and all your progeny*.

Thought of calling the FBI reporting a suspected terrorist, Mr. Z. was dark like an Arab, and shifty-eyed. Though probably he was a Jew.

Afterward vaguely he would recall *you are a master mister z* but of course he'd deleted it. So easy to delete an e-message.

Afterward vaguely he would recall the squirmy girl at the computer with the frizz hair and glassy staring eyes, a startling smell as of unwashed flesh wafting from her (unusual at Skatskill Day as it was unusual in the affluent suburban village of Skatskill) he had not known at the time, this was January/February, was Jude Trahern. He had no homeroom students, he met with more than one hundred students sometimes within days, couldn't keep track of them and had no interest in keeping track. Though a few days later he would come upon the girl in the company of a fattish friend, the two of them rummaging in a waste basket in the computer lab but he'd taken no special note of them as they'd hurried away embarrassed and giggling together as if he'd opened a door and seen them naked.

But he would remember: the same frizz-haired girl boldly seated at his computer after school one day frowning at the screen and click-clicking keys with as much authority as if the computer were her own and this time he'd spoken sharply to her, "Excuse me?" and she'd looked up at him cringing and blind-seeming as if she thought he might hit her. And so he joked, "Here's the famous hacker, eh?"—he knew it was the kindest as it was the wisest strategy to make a joke of the audacious/inexplicable behavior of adolescents, it wasn't a good idea to confront or embarrass. Especially not a girl. And this stunted-seeming girl hunched over like she was trying make herself smaller. Papery-thin skin, short upper lip exposing her front teeth, a guarded rodent look, furtive, anxious, somehow appealing. Her eyes were of the no-color of grit, moist and widened. Eyebrows and lashes scanty, near-invisible. She was so fiercely plain and her unbeautiful eyes stared at him so *rawly* . . . He felt sorry for her, poor kid. Bold, nervy, but in another year or so she'd be left behind entirely by her classmates, no boy would glance at her twice. He could not have guessed that the tremulous girl was the lone descendent of a family of reputation and privilege though possibly he might have guessed that her parents were long divorced from one another and perhaps from her as well. She was stammering some feeble explanation *Just needed to look something up, Mr. Zallman.* He laughed and dismissed her with a wave of his hand. Had an impulse, out of character for him, to reach out and tousle that frizzed floating hair as you'd rub a dog's head partly in affection and partly to chastise.

Didn't touch her, though. Mikal Zallman wasn't crazy.

"101 DALMATIANS"

Is she breathing, d'you think?

She is! Sure she is.

Oh God what if . . .

. . . she *is*. See?

The Corn Maiden slept by candlelight. The heavy open-mouthed sleep of the sedated.

We observed her in wonder. The Corn Maiden, in our power!

Jude removed the barrettes from her hair so we could brush it. Long straight pale blond hair. We were not jealous of the Corn Maiden's hair because *It is our hair now.*

The Corn Maiden's hair was spread out around her head like she was falling.

She was breathing, yes you could see. If you held a candle close to her face and throat you could see.

We had made a bed for the Corn Maiden, that Jude called a *bier.* Out of beautiful silk shawls and a brocaded bedspread, cashmere blanket from Scotland, goose-feather pillows. From the closed-off guest wing of the house Jude brought these, her face shining.

We fumbled to remove the Corn Maiden's clothes.

You pull off your own clothes without hardly thinking but another person, even a small girl who is lying flat on her back, arms and legs limp but heavy, that's different.

When the Corn Maiden was bare it was hard not to giggle. Hard not to snort with laughter . . .

More like a little girl than she was like us.

We were shy of her suddenly. Her breasts were flat against her rib cage, her nipples were tiny as seeds. There were no hairs growing between her legs that we could see.

She was very cold, shivering in her sleep. Her lips were putty-colored. Her teeth were chattering. Her eyes were closed but you could see a thin crescent of white. So (almost!) you worried the Corn Maiden was watching us paralyzed in sleep.

It was Xanax Jude had prepared for the Corn Maiden. Also she had codeine and Oxycodone already ground to powder, in reserve.

We were meant to "bathe" the Corn Maiden, Jude said. But maybe not tonight.

We rubbed the Corn Maiden's icy fingers, her icy toes, and her icy cheeks. We were not shy of touching her suddenly, we wanted to touch her and touch and *touch.*

Inside here, Jude said, touching the Corn Maiden's narrow chest, there is a heart beating. An actual *heart.*

Jude spoke in a whisper. In the quiet you could hear the heart beat.

We covered the Corn Maiden then with silks, brocades, cashmere wool. We placed a goose-feather pillow beneath the Corn Maiden's head. Jude sprinkled perfume on the Corn Maiden with her fingertips. It was a blessing Jude said. The Corn Maiden would sleep and sleep for a long time and when she woke, she would know only our faces. The faces of her friends.

It was a storage room in the cellar beneath the guest wing we brought the Corn Maiden. This was a remote corner of the big old house. This was a closed-off corner of the house and the cellar was yet more remote, nobody would ever ever come here Jude said.

And you could scream your head off, nobody would ever hear.

Jude laughed, cupping her hands to her mouth like she was going to scream. But all that came out was a strangled choked noise.

There was no heat in the closed-off rooms of the Trahern house. In the cellar it was a damp cold like winter. Except this was meant to be a time of nuclear holocaust and no electricity we would have brought a space heater to plug in. Instead we had candles.

These were fragrant hand-dipped candles old Mrs. Trahern had been saving in a drawer since 1994, according to the gift shop receipt.

Jude said, Grandma won't miss 'em.

Jude was funny about her grandmother. Sometimes she liked her okay, other times she called her the old bat, said fuck her she didn't give a damn about Jude she was only worried Jude would embarrass her somehow.

Mrs. Trahern had called up the stairs, when we were in Jude's room watching a video. The stairs were too much for her, rarely she came upstairs to check on Jude. There was an actual elevator in the house (we had seen it) but Jude said she'd fucked it up, fooling with it so much when she was a little kid. Just some friends from school, Denise and Anita, Jude called back. You've met them.

Those times Mrs. Trahern saw us downstairs with Jude she would ask politely how we were and her snail-mouth would stretch in a grudging little smile but already she wasn't listening to anything we said, and she would never remember our names.

101 Dalmatians Jude played, one of her old videos she'd long outgrown. (Jude had a thousand videos she'd outgrown!) It was a young-kids' movie we had all seen but the Corn Maiden had never seen. Sitting cross-legged on the floor in front of the TV eating ice cream from a bowl in her lap and we finished ours and waited for her and Jude asked would she like a little more and the Corn Maidden hesitated just a moment then said *Yes thank you*.

We all had more Haagen Dazs French Vanilla ice cream. But it was not the same ice cream the Corn Maiden had not exactly!

Her eyes shining, so happy. Because we were her friends.

A sixth grader, friends with eighth graders. A guest in Jude Trahern's house.

Jude had been nice to her at school for a long time. Smiling, saying hello. Jude had a way of fixing you with her eyes like a cobra or something you could not look away. You were scared but sort of thrilled, too.

In the 7-Eleven she'd come inside to get a Coke and a package of nachos. She was on her way home from school and had no idea that two of us had followed her and one had run ahead, to wait. She was smiling to see Jude who was so friendly. Jude asked where was her mom and she said her mom was a nurse's aide across the river in Nyack and would not be home till after dark.

She laughed saying her mom didn't like her eating junk food but her mom didn't know.

Jude said what our moms don't know don't hurt them.

The Sacrifice of the Corn Maiden was a ritual of the Onigara Indians, Jude told us. In school we had studied Native Americans as they are called but we had not studied the Onigara Indians, Jude said had been extinct for two hundred years. The Iroquois had wiped out the Onigaras, it was survival of the fittest.

The Corn Maiden would be our secret. Beforehand we seemed to know it would be the most precious of our secrets.

Jude and the Corn Maiden walked ahead alone. Denise and Anita behind. Back of the stores, past the Dumpsters, we ran to catch up.

Jude asked would the Corn Maiden like to visit her house and the Corn Maiden said yes but she could not stay long. Jude said it was just a short walk. Jude pretended not to know where the Corn Maiden lived (but she knew: crummy apartments at 15th Street and Van Buren) and this was a ten-minute walk, approximately.

We climbed the back way. Nobody saw. Old Mrs. Trahern would be watching TV in her room, and would not see.

If she saw she would not seriously *see*. For at a distance her eyes were too weak.

The guest wing was a newer part of the house. It overlooked a swimming pool. But the pool was covered with a tarpaulin, Jude said nobody had swum in it for years. She could remember wading in the shallow end but it was long ago like the memory belonged to someone else.

The guest wing was never used either, Jude said. Most of the house was never used. She and her grandmother lived in just a few rooms and that was fine with them. Sometimes Mrs. Trahern would not leave the house for weeks. She was angry about something that had happened at church. Or maybe the minister had said something she found offensive. She had had to dismiss the black man who'd driven her "limo-zene." She had dismissed the black woman who'd been her cook and house cleaner for twenty years. Groceries were delivered to the house. Meals were mostly heat up in the microwave. Mrs. Trahern saw a few of her old friends in town, at the Village Woman's Club, the Hudson Valley Friends of History, and the Skatskill Garden Club. Her friends were not invited to the house to see her.

Do you love your mom? Jude asked the Corn Maiden.

The Corn Maiden nodded yes. Sort of embarrassed.

Your mom is real pretty. She's a nurse, I guess?

The Corn Maiden nodded yes. You could see she was proud of her mom but shy to speak of her.

Where is your dad? Jude asked.

The Corn Maiden frowned. She did not know.

Is your dad living?

Did not know.

When did you see your dad last?

Was not sure. She'd been so little . . .

Did he live around here, or where?

California, the Corn Maiden said. Berkeley.

My mom is in California, Jude said. Los Angeles.

The Corn Maiden smiled, uncertainly.

Maybe your dad is with my dad now, Jude said.

The Corn Maiden looked at Jude in wonderment.

In Hell, Jude said.

Jude laughed. That way she had, her teeth glistening.

Denise and Anita laughed. The Corn Maiden smiled not knowing whether to laugh. Slower and slower the spoon was being lifted to her mouth, her eyelids were drooping.

We would carry the Corn Maiden from Jude's room. Along a corridor and through a door into what Jude called the guest wing, where the air was colder, and stale. And down a stairway in the guest wing and into a cellar to the storage room.

The Corn Maiden did not weigh much. Three of us, we weighed so much more.

On the outside of the storage room door, a padlock.

Anita and Denise had to leave by 6 P.M., to return to their houses for supper. So boring!

Jude would remain with the Corn Maiden for much of the night. To *watch over*. A *vigil*. She was excited by the candle flames, the incense-smell. The pupils of her eyes were dilated, she was highhigh on Ecstasy. She would not bind the Corn Maiden's wrists and ankles, she said, until it was necessary.

Jude had a Polaroid camera, she would take pictures of the Corn Maiden sleeping on her bier.

As the Corn Maiden was being missed the next morning we would all be at school as usual. For nobody had seen us, and nobody would think of *us*.

Some pre-vert they'll think of, Jude said. We can help them with that.

Remember, the Corn Maiden has come as our guest, Jude said. It is not *kidnapping*.

The Corn Maiden came to Jude on the Thursday before Palm Sunday, in April of the year.

Breaking News

Dial 911 your life is no longer your own.

Dial 911 you become a beggar.

Dial 911 you are stripped naked.

She met them at the curb. Distraught mother awaiting police officers in the rain outside Briarcliff Apts., 15th St., South Skatskill, 8:20 P.M. Approaching officers as they emerged from the patrol car pleading, anxious, trying to remain calm but her voice rising, Help me please help my daughter is missing! I came home from work, my daughter isn't here, Marissa is eleven years old, I have no idea where she is, nothing like this has ever happened, please help me find her, I'm afraid that someone has taken my daughter!—Caucasian female, early thirties, blond, bare-headed, strong smell of beer on her breath.

They would question her. They would repeat their questions, and she would repeat her answers. She was calm. She tried to be calm. She began to cry. She began to be angry. She knew her words were being recorded, each word she uttered was a matter of public record. She would face TV cameras, interviewers with microphones outthrust like sceptors. She would see herself performing clumsily and stumbling over her lines in the genre *missing child/pleading mother*. She would see how skillfully the TV screen leapt from her anxious drawn face and bloodshot eyes to the smiling innocent wide-eyed Marissa, sweet-faced Marissa with gleaming blond hair, eleven years old, sixth grader, the camera lingered upon each of three photos of Marissa provided by her mother; then, as the distraught mother continued to speak, you saw the bland sandstone facade of the "private"—"exclusive"—Skatskill Day School and next you were looking at the sinister nighttime traffic of 15th Street, South Skatskill along which, as a neutral-sounding woman's voice explained, eleven-year-old Marissa Branty normally walked home to let herself into an empty apartment and begin to prepare supper for her mother (who worked at a Nyack medical clinic, would not be home until 8 P.M.) and herself; then you were looking at the exterior, rear of Briarcliff Apts. squat and ugly as an army barracks in the rain, where a few hardy residents stood curious staring at police officers and camera crews; then you saw again the mother of the missing girl Leah Bantry, thirty-four, obviously a negligent mother, a sick-with-guilt mother publicly pleading If anyone has seen my daughter, if anyone has any idea what might have happened to Marissa . . .

Next news item, tractor-trailer overturned on the New Jersey Turnpike, pile-up involving eleven vehicles, two drivers killed, eight taken by ambulance to Newark hospital.

So ashamed! But I only want Marissa back.

It was BREAKING NEWS! which means exciting news and by 10 P.M. of that Thursday in April each of four local TV stations was carrying the *missing Marissa* story, and would carry it at regular intervals for as long as there were developments and as long as local interest remained high. But really it was not "new" news, everyone had seen it before. All that could be "new" were the specific players and certain details to be revealed in time, with the teasing punctuality of a suspense film.

It was a good thing, the distraught mother gathered, that cases of missing/abducted children were relatively rare in the affluent Hudson Valley suburbs north of New York City, as crimes of violence in these communities were rare. This meant dramatically focused police attention, cooperation with neighboring police departments in Tarrytown, Sleepy Hollow, Irvington. This meant dramatically focused media coverage, replication of Marissa Banty's likeness, public concern and participation in the search. *Outpouring of sympathy*, it would be called. *Community involvement.* You would not find such a response in a high-crime area, Leah was told.

"Something to be grateful for. Thank you!"

She wasn't speaking ironically. Tears shone in her bloodshot eyes, she wanted only to be believed.

It was in the distraught mother's favor, too, that, if her daughter had been abducted and hadn't simply run away of her own volition, hers would be the first such case in Skatskill's history.

That was remarkable. That was truly a novelty.

"But she didn't run away. Marissa did not run away. I've tried to explain . . ."

Another novelty in the affluent Hudson Valley suburbs was the mysterious/suspicious circumstance of the "considerable" time lapse between the child's probable disappearance after school and the recorded time the mother reported her missing at 8:14 P.M. The most vigilant of the local TV stations was alert to the dramatic possibilities here. *Skatskill police will neither confirm nor deny that the department is said to be considering charging Branty, who has no previous police record, with child endangerment.*

And how it would be leaked to this same TV station, the distraught mother had evidenced signs of "inebriation" when police arrived at her home, no one at the station was in a position to say.

So ashamed! I want to die.

If I could exchange my life for Marissa's

Hours, days. Though each hour was singular, raw as a stone forced down the throat. And what were days but unchartable and unfathomable durations of time too painful to be borne except as singular hours or even minutes. She was aware of a great wheel turning, and of herself caught in this wheel, helpless, in a state of suspended panic and yet eager to cooperate with the very turning of the wheel, if it might bring Marissa back to her. For she was coming to feel, possibly yes there was a God, a God of mercy and not just justice, and she might barter her life for Marissa's.

Through most of it she remained calm. On the surface, calm. She believed she was calm, she had not become hysterical. She had called her parents in Spokane, Washington, for it could not be avoided. She had called her older sister in Washington, D.C. She had not seemed to hear in their shocked and incredulous voices any evidence of reproach, accusation, disgust; but she understood that that was to come, in time.

I am to blame. I know.

It doesn't matter about me.

She believed she was being damned calm! Answering their impudent questions and reanswering them and again repeating as in a deranged tape loop the answers that were all she had in the face of their suspicion, their doubt. She answered the officers' questions with the desperation of a drowning woman clutching a rope already fraying to haul herself into a lifeboat already leaking water. She had no idea, she had told them immediately she had no idea where Marissa's father was, for the past seven years there had been no contact between them, she had last seen him in Berkeley, California, thousands of miles away and he had had no interest in Marissa, he had sought no interest in his own daughter, and so truly she did not believe she could not believe that there was any likelihood of that man having abducted Marissa, truly she did not want to involve him, did not wish to seem in the most elliptical way to be accusing him . . . Yet they continued to question her. It was an interrogation, they sensed that she had something to hide, had she? And what was that, and why? Until finally she heard herself say in a broken defeated voice all right, yes I will give you his name and his last-known address and telephone number that was surely inoperative after so long, all right I will tell you: we were never married, his name is not my child's name, he'd pretended even to doubt that Marissa was his child, we had only lived together, he had no interest in marriage, are you satisfied now?

Her shame, she'd never told her parents. Never told her sister.

Now they would know Leah's pathetic secret. It would be another shock, a small one set beside the other. It would cause them to think less of her, and to know that she was a liar. And now she must telephone to tell them before they discovered it in the media. *I lied to you, I was never married to Andrew. There was no marriage, and there was no divorce.*

Next, they needed to know exactly where she'd been after she had left the Nyack clinic at 6:30 P.M. of the day her daughter had disappeared. Now they knew she was a liar, and a desperate woman, now they had scented blood. They would track the wounded creature to its lair.

At first Leah had been vague about time. In the shock of her daughter missing, it had been natural for the mother to be vague, confused, uncertain about time.

She'd told them that she had been stuck in traffic returning home from Nyack. The Tappan Zee Bridge, route 9 and road repair and rain but yes, she had stopped at the 7-Eleven store near her apartment to buy a few things as she often did . . .

And was that all, had that been her only stop?

Yes. Her only stop. The 7-Eleven. The clerk at the cash register would recognize her.

This was a question, a probing, that had to do with Leah Bantry's male friends. If she had any, who would have known Marissa. Who would have met Marissa. Who might simply have glimpsed Marissa.

Any male friend of the missing girl's mother who might have been attracted to the girl. Might have "abducted" her.

For Marissa might have willingly climbed into a vehicle, if it was driven by someone she knew. Yes?

Calmly Leah insisted no, no one.

She had no male friends at the present time. No serious involvements.

No one she was "seeing"?

Leah flared up, angry. In the sense of—what? What did "seeing" mean?

She was being adamant, and she was speaking forcibly. Yet her interrogators seemed to know. Especially the female detective seemed to know. An evasiveness in Leah's bloodshot eyes that were the eyes of a sick, guilty mother. A quavering in Leah's voice even as she spoke impatiently, defiantly. I told you! God damn I have told you.

There was a pause. The air in the room was highly charged.

There was a pause. Her interrogators waited.

It was explained to Leah then that she must answer the officers' questions fully and truthfully. This was a police investigation, she would be vulnerable to charges of obstruction of justice if she lied.

If she lied.

A known liar.

An exposed, humiliated liar.

And so, another time, Leah heard her voice break. She heard herself say all right, yes. She had not gone directly to the 7-Eleven store from Nyack, she had stopped first to see a friend and, yes he was a close male friend, separated from his wife and uncertain of his future and he was an intensely private man whose identity she could not reveal for he and Leah were not exactly lovers though, yes they had made love . . .

Just once, they had made love. One time.

On Sunday evening, the previous Sunday evening they had made love.

For the first time they had made love. And it wasn't certain that . . . Leah had no way of knowing whether . . .

She was almost pleading now. Blood seemed to be hemorrhaging into her swollen face.

The police officers waited. She was wiping at her eyes with a wadded tissue. There was no way out of this was there! Somehow she had known, with the sickening sensation of a doomed cow entering a slaughter chute, she had known that a part of her life would be over, when she'd dialed 911.

Your punishment, for losing your daughter.

Of course, Leah had to provide the police officers with the man's name. She had no choice.

She was sobbing, crushed. Davitt would be furious with her.

Davitt Stoop, M.D. Director of the medical clinic. He was Dr. Stoop, her superior. Her employer. He was a kindly man, yet a short-tempered man. He was not in love with Leah Banty, she knew; nor was Leah in love with him, exactly; and yet, they were relaxed together, they got along so very well together, both were parents of single children of about the same age, both had been hurt and deceived in love, and were wary of new involvements.

Davitt was forty-two, he had been married for eighteen years. He was a responsible husband and father as he had a reputation at the clinic for being an exacting physician and it had been his concern that he and Leah might be seen together prematurely. He did not want his wife to know about Leah, not yet. Still less did he want Leah's coworkers at the clinic to know. He dreaded gossip, innuendo. He dreaded any exposure of his private life.

It was the end, Leah knew.

Before it had begun between them, it would end.

They would humiliate him, these police officers. They would ask him about Leah Bantry and Leah's missing daughter, did he know the child, how well did he know the child, had he ever seen the child without the mother present, had he ever been alone with the child, had he ever given the child a ride in his car for instance this past Thursday?

Possibly they would want to examine the car. Would he allow a search, or would he insist upon a warrant?

Davitt had moved out of his family home in February and lived in an apartment in Nyack, the very apartment Leah Bantry had visited on Thursday evening after her shift. Impulsively she had dropped by. Davitt might have expected her, it hadn't been certain.

They were in the early stages of a romance, excited in each other's presence but uncertain.

This apartment. Had Marissa ever been there?

No! Certainly not.

In a faltering voice telling the officers that Davitt scarcely knew Marissa. Possibly he'd met her, once. But they had spent no time together, certainly not.

Leah had stayed in Davitt's apartment approximately a half hour.

Possibly, forty minutes.

No. They had not had sex.

Not exactly.

They had each had a drink. They had been affectionate, they had talked.

Earnestly, seriously they had talked! About the clinic, and about their children. About Davitt's marriage, and Leah's own.

(It would be revealed, Leah had led Davitt Stoop to believe she had been married, and divorced. It had seemed such a trivial and inconsequential lie at the time.)

Leah was saying, stammering, Davitt would never do such a thing! Not to Marissa, not to any child. He was the father of a ten-year-old boy, himself. He was not the type . . .

The female detective asked bluntly what did Leah mean, "type"? Was this a "type" she believed she could recognize?

Davitt forgive me! I had no choice.

I could not lie to police. I had to tell them about you. I am so very sorry, Davitt, you can understand can't you I must help them find Marissa I had no choice.

Still, Marissa remained missing.

"People who do things like this, take children, they're not rational. What they do, they do for their own purposes. We can only track them. We can try to stop them. We can't understand them."

And, "When something like this happens, it's natural for people to want to cast blame. You'd be better off not watching TV or reading the papers right now, Miss Bantry."

One of the Skatskill detectives spoke so frankly to her, she could not believe he too might be judging her harshly.

There were myriad calls, e-mail messages. Blond-haired Marissa Bantry had been sighted in a car exiting the New York Thruway at Albany. She had been sighted in the company of "hippie-type males" on West Houston Street, New York City. A Skatskill resident would recall, days after the fact, having seen "that pretty little pig-tailed blond girl" getting into a battered-looking van driven by a Hispanic male in the parking lot of the 7-Eleven store a few blocks from her home.

Still, Marissa remained missing.

. . . hours in rapid succession jarring and discontinuous as a broken film projected upon a flimsy screen she would not sleep for more than two or three hours even with sedatives and she slept without dreaming like one who has been struck on the head with a mallet and she woke hollow-headed and parch-mouthed and her heart beating in her chest like something with a broken wing.

Always as she woke in that split-second before awareness rushed upon her like a mouthful of filthy water *My daughter is gone, Marissa is lost* there was a sense of grace, a confusion in time like a prayer *It has not happened yet has it? Whatever it will be.*

Have You Seen Me?

Like a sudden bloom of daffodils there appeared overnight, everywhere in Skatskill, the smiling likeness of MARISSA BANTRY, 11.

In store windows. On public bulletin boards, telephone poles. Prominent in the foyers of the Skatskill Post Office, the Skatskill Food Mart, the Skatskill Public Library. Prominent though already dampening in April rain, on the fences of construction sites.

MISSING SINCE APRIL 10. SKATSKILL DAY SCHOOL/15TH ST. AREA.

Hurriedly established by the Skatskill police department was a

MARISSA Web site posting more photos of the missing blond girl, a detailed description of her, background information. ANYONE KNOWING ANYTHING ABOUT MARISSA BANTRY PLEASE CONTACT SKATSKILL POLICE AT THIS NUMBER.

Initially, no reward was posted. By Friday evening, an anonymous donor (prominent Skatskill philantropist, retired) had come forward to offer fifteen thousand dollars.

It was reported by the media that Skatskill police were working *round the clock*. They were *under intense pressure*, they were investigating *all possible leads*. It was reported that *known pedophiles, sex offenders, child molesters* in the area were being questioned. (Information about such individuals was confidential of course. Still, the most vigilant of area tabloids learned from an anonymous source that a sixty-year-old Skatskill resident, a retired music teacher with a sexual misdemeanor record dating back to 1987, had been visited by detectives. Since this individual refused to speak with a reporter, or consent to be photographed, the tabloid published a photograph of his front door at 12 Amwell Circle on its cover, beneath the strident headline LOCAL SEX OFFENDER QUERIED BY COPS: WHERE IS MARISSA?)

Each resident of Briarcliff Apts. was questioned, some more than once. Though no search warrants had been issued, several residents cooperated with police allowing both their apartments and their motor vehicles to be searched.

Storekeepers in the area of the Skatskill Day School and along Marissa Bantry's route home were questioned. At the 7-Eleven store in the mini-mall on the highway, so often frequented by young people, several clerks examined photographs of the missing girl, solemnly shook their heads and told police officers no, they did not believe that Marissa Bantry had been in the store recently, or ever. "There are so many children . . ." Questioned about Leah Bantry, whose photograph they were also shown, the eldest clerk said, carefully, that yes, he recognized this woman, she was a friendly woman; friendlier than most of his customers; but he could not say with certainty if she had been in his store on Thursday, with or without her daughter. "There are so many customers. And so many of them, they look like one another especially if they are blond."

Detectives queried teenagers, most of them from Skatskill High, and some no longer in school, who hung out at the mini-mall. Most of them stiffened at the approach of police officers and hurriedly shook their heads no, they had not seen the little blond girl who was missing, or anyway could not remember seeing her. A striking girl with electric blue hair and a glittering pin in her left eyebrow frowned at the photo and said finally yeah she'd maybe seen Marissa "like with her mother? But when, like maybe it wasn't yesterday because I don't think I was here yesterday, might've been last week? I don't know."

Skatskill Day School was in a stage of siege. TV crews on the front walk, reporters and press photographers at all the entrances. Crisis counsellors met with children in small groups through the day following Marissa's disappearance and there was an air in all the classrooms of shock, as if in the wake of a single violent tremor of the earth. A number of parents had kept their children home from school, but this was not advised by school authorities: "There is no risk at Skatskill Day. Whatever happened to Marissa did not happen on school grounds, and would never have happened on school grounds." It was announced that school security had been immediately strengthened, and new security measures would be begun on Monday. In Marissa Bantry's sixth grade class children were subdued, uneasy. After the counsellor spoke, and asked if anyone had a question, the class sat silent until a boy raised his hand to ask if there would be a search party "like on TV, people going through woods and fields until they find the body?"

Not after a counsellor spoke with eighth graders, but later in the day, an eighth-grade girl named Anita Helder came forward hesitantly to speak with her teacher. Anita was a heavyset girl with a low C average who rarely spoke in class, and often asked to be excused for mysterious health reasons. She was a suspected drug-taker, but had never been caught. In class, she exuded a sulky, defiant manner if called upon by her teacher. Yet now she was saying, in an anxious, faltering voice, that maybe she had seen Marissa Bantry the previous day, on 15h Street and Trinity, climbing into a minivan after school.

". . . I didn't know it was her then for sure, I don't know Marissa Bantry at all but I guess now it must've been her. Oh God I feel so bad I didn't try to stop her! I was like close enough to call out to her, 'Don't get in!' What I could see, the driver was leaning over and sort of pulling Marissa inside. It was a man, he had real dark hair kind of long on the sides but I couldn't see his face. The minivan was like silver-blue, the license plate was something like TZ 6 . . . Beyond that, I can't remember."

Anita's eyes welled with tears. She was visibly trembling, the memory so upset her.

By this time Skatskill detectives had questioned everyone on the school staff except for Mikal Zallman, thirty-one years old, computer consultant and part-time employee, who wasn't at the Skatskill Day School on Fridays.

Feeding My Rat

It was an ugly expression. It was macho-ugly, the worst kind of ugly. It made him smile.

Feeding my rat. Alone.

In Custody

Alone he'd driven out of Skatskill on Thursday afternoon immediately following his final class of the week. Alone driving north in his trim Honda minivan along the Hudson River where the river landscape so mesmerizes the eye, you wonder why you'd ever given a damn for all that's petty, inconsequential. Wondering why you'd ever given a damn for the power of others to hurt you. Or to accuse you with tearful eyes of hurting them.

He'd tossed a valise, his backpack, a few books, hiking boots and a supply of trail food into the back of the van. Always he traveled light. As soon as he left Skatskill he ceased to think of his life there. It was of little consequence really, a professional life arranged to provide him with this freedom. *Feeding my rat.*

There was a woman in Skatskill, a married woman. He knew the signs. She was lonely in her marriage and yearning to be saved from her loneliness. Often she invited him as if impulsively, without premeditation. *Come to dinner, Mikal? Tonight?* He had been vague about accepting, this time. He had not wanted to see the disappointment in her eyes. He felt a tug of affection for her, he recognized her hurt, her resentment, her confusion, she was a colleague of his at the Skatskill School whom he saw often in the company of others, there was a rapport between them, Zallman acknowledged, but he did not want to be involved with her or with any woman, not now. He was thirty-one, and no longer naive. More and more he lived for *feeding my rat.*

It was arrogant, was it, this attitude? Selfish. He'd been told so, more than once. Living so much in his own head, and for himself.

He hadn't married, he doubted he would ever marry. The prospect of children made his heart sink: bringing new lives into the uncertainty and misery of this world, in the early twenty-first century!

He much preferred his secret life. It was an innocent life. Running each morning, along the river. Hiking, mountain climbing. He did not hunt or fish, he had no need to destroy life to enhance his own. Mostly it was exulting in his body. He was only a moderately capable hiker. He hadn't the endurance or the will to run a marathon. He wasn't so fanatic, he wanted merely to be alone where he could exert his body pleasurably. Or maybe to the edge of pain.

One summer in his mid-twenties he'd gone backpacking alone in Portugal, Spain, northern Morocco. In Tangier he'd experimented with the hallucinatory *kif* which was the most extreme form of aloneness and the experience had shaken and exhilarated him and brought him back home to reinvent himself. Michael, now Mikal.

Feeding my rat meant this freedom. Meant he'd failed to drop by her house as she had halfway expected he would. And he had not telephoned, either. It was a way of allowing the woman to know he didn't want to be involved, he would not be involved. In turn, she and her her husband would not provide Mikal Zallman with an alibi for those crucial hours.

When, at 5:18 P.M. of Friday, April 11, returning to his car along a steep hiking trail, he happening to see what appeared to be a New York State troopers' vehicle in the parking lot ahead, he had no reason to think *They've come for me.* Even when he saw that two uniformed officers were looking into the rear windows of his minivan, the lone vehicle in the lot parked near the foot of the trail, because it had been the first vehicle of the day parked in the lot, the sight did not alarm or alert him. So confident in himself he felt, and so guiltless.

"Hey. What d'you want?"

Naively, almost conversationally he called to the troopers, who were now staring at him, and moving toward him.

Afterward he would recall how swiftly and unerringly the men moved. One called out, "Are you Mikal Zallman" and the other called, sharply, before Zallman could reply, "Keep your hands where we can see them, sir."

Hands? What about his hands? What were they saying about his hands?

He'd been sweating inside his T-shirt and khaki shorts and his hair was sticking against the nape of his neck. He'd slipped and fallen on the trail once, his left knee was scraped, throbbing. He was not so exuberant as he'd been in the fresh clear air of morning. He held his hands before him, palms uplifted in a gesture of annoyed supplication.

What did these men want with *him*? It had to be a mistake.

. . . staring into the back of the minivan. He'd consented to a quick search. Trunk, interior. Glove compartment. What the hell, he had nothing to hide. Were they looking for drugs? A concealed weapon? He saw the way in which they were staring at two paperback books he'd tossed onto the rear window ledge weeks ago, Roth's The Dying Animal *and Ovid's* The Art of Love. *On the cover of the first was a sensuously reclining Modligliani nude in rich flesh tones, with prominent pink-nippled breasts. On the cover of the other was a classical nude, marmoreal white female with a full, shapely body and blank, blind eyes.*

Taboo

It was Taboo to utter aloud the Corn Maiden's name.

It was Taboo to touch the Corn Maiden except as Jude guided.

For Jude was the Priest of the Sacrifice. No one else.

What does Taboo mean, it means death. If you disobey.

Jude took Polaroid pictures of the Corn Maiden sleeping on her bier. Arms crossed on her flat narrow chest, cornsilk hair spread like pale flames around her head. Some pictures, Jude was beside the Corn Maiden. We took pictures of her smiling, and her eyes shiny and dilated.

For posterity, Jude said. For the record.

It was Taboo to utter the Corn Maiden's actual name aloud and yet: everywhere in Skatskill that name was being spoken! And everywhere in Skatskill her face was posted!

Missing Girl. Abduction Feared. State of Emergency.

It is so easy, Jude said. To make the truth your own.

But Jude was surprised too, we thought. That it was so real, what had only been for so long Jude O's *idea*.

Ju*dith*!

Mrs. Trahern called in her whiny old-woman voice, we had to troop into her smelly bedroom where she was propped up in some big old antique brass bed like a nutty queen watching TV where footage of the *missing Skatskill Day girl* was being shown. Chiding, You girls! Look what has happened to one of your little classmates! Did you know this poor child?

Jude mumbled no Grandma.

Well. You would not be in a class with a retarded child, I suppose.

Jude mumbled no Grandma.

Well. See that you never speak with strangers, Judith! Report anyone who behaves strangely with you, or is seen lurking around the neighborhood. Promise me!

Jude mumbled okay. Grandma, I promise.

Denise and Anita mumbled Me, too, Mrs. Trahern. For it seemed to be expected.

Next, Mrs. Trahern made Jude come to her bed, to take Jude's hands in her clawy old-woman hands. I have not always been a good grandma, I know. As the judge's widow there are so many demands on my time. But I am your grandma, Judith. I am your only blood kin who cares for you, dear. You know that, I hope?

Jude mumbled Yes Grandma, I know.

The World as We Have Known It

Has vanished.

We are among the few known survivors.

. . . terrorist attack. Nuclear war. Fires.

New York City is a gaping hole. The George Washington Bridge is crashed into the river. Washington, D.C., is gone.

So the Corn Maiden was told. So the Corn Maiden believed in her Rapture.

Many times we said these words. Jude had made us memorize. The world as we have known it has vanished. There is no TV now. No newspapers. No electricity. We are among the few known survivors. We must be brave, everyone else is gone. All the adults are gone. All our mothers.

The Corn Maiden opened her mouth to shriek but she had not the strength. Her eyes welled with tears, lapsing out of focus.

All our mothers. So exciting!

Only candles to be lighted, solemnly. To keep away the night.

The Corn Maiden was informed that we had to ration our food supplies. For there were no stores now, all of Skatskill was gone. The Food Mart was gone. Main Street was gone. The Mall.

Jude knew, to maintain the Rapture the Corn Maiden must be fed very little. For Jude did not wish to bind her wrists and ankles, that were so fragile-seeming. Jude did not wish to gag her, to terrify her. For then the Corn Maiden would fear us and not trust and adore us as her protectors.

The Corn Maiden must be treated with reverence, respect, kindness, and firmness. She must never guess the fate that will be hers.

The Corn Maiden's diet was mostly liquids. Water, transparent fruit juices like apple, grapefruit. And milk.

It was Taboo Jude said for the Corn Maiden to ingest any foods except white foods. And any foods containing bones or skins.

These foods were soft, crumbly or melted foods. Cottage cheese, plain yogurt, ice cream. The Corn Maiden was not a retarded child as some of the TV stations were saying but she was not shrewd-witted, Jude said. For these foods we fed her were refrigerated, and she did not seem to know.

Of course, finely ground in these foods were powdery-white tranquilizers, to maintain the Rapture.

The Corn Maiden of the Onigara Sacrifice was to pass into the next world in a Rapture. Not in fear.

We took turns spooning small portions of food into the Corn Maiden's mouth that sucked like an infant's to be fed. So hungry, the Corn Maiden whimpered for more. No, no! There is no more she was told.

(How hungry we were, after these feedings! Denise and Anita went home to stuffstuff their faces.)

Jude did not want the Corn Maiden to excrete solid waste she said. Her bowels must be clean and pure for the Sacrifice. Also we had to take her outside the storage room for this, half-carrying her to a bathroom in a corner of the cobwebby cellar that was a "recreation room" of some bygone time Jude said the 1970s that is ancient history now.

Only two times did we have to take the Corn Maiden to this bathroom, half-carried out, groggy and stumbling and her head lolling on her shoulders. All other times the Corn Maiden used the pot Jude had brought in from one of the abandoned greenhouses. A fancy Mexican ceramic pot, for the Corn Maiden to squat over, as we held her like a clumsy infant.

The Corn Maiden's pee! It was hot, bubbly. It had a sharp smell different from our own.

Like a big infant the Corn Maiden was becoming, weak and trusting all her bones. Even her crying when she cried saying she wanted to go home, she wanted her mommy, where was her mommy she wanted her mommy was an infant's crying, with no strength or anger behind it.

Jude said all our mommies are gone, we must be brave without them. She would be safe with us Jude said stroking her hair. See, we would protect her better than her mommy had protected her.

Jude took Polaroid pictures of the Corn Maiden sitting up on her bier her face streaked with tears. The Corn Maiden was chalky white and the colors of the bier were so rich and silky. The Corn Maiden was so thin, you could see her collarbone jutting inside the white muslin nightgown Jude had clothed her in.

We did not doubt Jude. What Jude meant to do with the Corn Maiden we would not resist.

In the Onigara ceremony Jude said the Corn Maiden was slowly starved and her bowels cleaned out and purified and she was tied on an altar still living and a priest shot an arrow that had been blessed into her heart. And the heart was scooped out with a knife that had been blessed and touched to the lips of the priest and others of the tribe to bless them. And the heart and the Corn Maiden's body were then carried out into a field and buried in the earth to honor the Morning Star which is the sun and the Evening Star which is the moon and beg of them their blessing for the corn harvest.

Will the Corn Maiden be killed we wished to know but we could not ask Jude for Jude would be angered.

To ourselves we said Jude will kill the Corn Maiden, maybe! We shivered to think so. Denise smiled, and bit at her thumbnail, for she was jealous of the Corn Maiden. Not because the Corn Maiden had such beautiful silky hair but because Jude fussed over the Corn Maiden so, as Jude would not have fussed over Denise.

The Corn Maiden wept when we left her. When we blew out the candles and left her in darkness. We had to patrol the house we said. We had to look for fires and "gas leakage" we said. For the world as we have known it has come to an end, there were no adults now. We were the adults now.

We were our own mommies.

Jude shut the door, and padlocked it. The Corn Maiden's muffled sobs from inside. *Mommy! Mommy!* the Corn Maiden wept but there was no one to hear and even on the steps to the first floor you could no longer hear.

Out There

HATEHATEHATE you assholes Out There. The Corn Maiden was Jude O's perfect revenge.

At Skatskill Day we saw our hatred like scalding-hot lava rushing through the corridors and into the classrooms and cafeteria to burn our enemies alive. Even girls who were okay to us mostly would perish for they would rank us below the rest, wayway below the Hot Shit Cliques that ran the school and also the boys—all the boys. And the teachers, some of them had pissed us off and deserved death. Jude said Mr. Z. had "dissed" her and was the "target enemy" now.

Sometimes the vision was so fierce it was a rush better than E!

Out There it was believed that the *missing Skatskill girl* might have been kidnapped. A ransom note was awaited.

Or, it was believed the *missing girl* was the victim of a "sexual predator."

On TV came Leah Bantry, the mother, to appeal to whoever had taken her daughter saying, Please don't hurt Marissa, please release my daughter I love her so, begging please in a hoarse voice that sounded like she'd been crying a lot and her eyes haggard with begging so Jude stared at the woman with scorn.

Not so hot-shit now, are you Mrs. Brat-tee! Not so pretty-pretty.

It was surprising to Denise and Anita, that Jude hated Leah Bantry so. We felt sorry for the woman, kind of. Made us think how our mothers would be, if we were gone, though we hated our mothers we were thinking they'd probably miss us, and be crying, too. It was a new way of seeing our moms. But Jude did not have a mom even to hate. Never spoke of her except to say she was Out West in L.A. We wanted to think that Jude's mom was a movie star under some different name, that was why she'd left Jude with Mrs. Trahern to pursue a film career. But we would never say this to Jude, for sure.

Sometimes Jude scared us. Like she'd maybe hurt *us*.

Wild! On Friday 7 P.M. news came BULLETIN—BREAKING NEWS—SKATSKILL SUSPECT IN CUSTODY. It was Mr. Zallman!

We shrieked with laughter. Had to press our hands over our mouths so old Mrs. Trahern would not hear.

Jude is flicking through the channels and there suddenly is Mr.

Z. on TV! And some broadcaster saying in an excited voice that this man had been apprehended in Bear Mountain State Park and brought back to Skatskill to be questioned in the disappearance of Marissa Bantry and the shocker is: Mikal Zallman, thirty-one, is on the faculty of the Skatskill Day School.

Mr. Zallman's jaws were scruffy like he had not shaved in a while. His eyes were scared and guilty-seeming. He was wearing a T-shirt and khaki shorts like we would never see him at school and this was funny, too. Between two plainclothes detectives being led up the steps into police headquarters and at the top they must've jerked him under the arms, he almost turned his ankle.

We were laughing like hyenas. Jude crouched in front of the TV rocking back and forth, staring.

"Zallman claims to know nothing of Marissa Bantry. Police and rescue workers are searching the Bear Mountain area and will search through the night if necessary."

There was a cut to our school again, and 15th Street traffic at night. ". . . unidentified witness, believed to be a classmate of Marissa Bantry, has told authorities that she witnessed Marissa being pulled into a Honda CR-V at this corner, Thursday after school. This vehicle has been tentatively identified as . . ."

Unidentified witness. That's me! Anita cried.

And a second "student witness" had come forward to tell the school principal that she had seen "the suspect Zallman" fondling Marissa Bantry, stroking her hair and whispering to her in the computer lab when he thought no one was around, only last week.

That's *me*! Denise cried.

And police had found a mother-of-pearl butterfly barrette on the ground near Zallman's parking space, behind his condominium residence. This barrette had been "absolutely identified" by Marissa Bantry's mother as a barrette Marissa had been wearing on Thursday.

We turned to Jude who was grinning.

We had not known that Jude had planned *this*. On her bicycle she must've gone, to drop the barrette where it would be found.

We laughed so, we almost wet ourselves. Jude was just so *cool*.

But even Jude seemed surprised, kind of. That you could make the wildest truth your own and every asshole would rush to believe.

Desperate

Now she knew his name: *Mikal Zallman.*

The man who'd taken Marissa. One of Marissa's teachers at the Skatskill Day School.

It was a nightmare. All that Leah Bantry had done, what exertion of heart and soul, to enroll her daughter in a private school in which a pedophile was allowed to instruct elementary school children.

She had met Zallman, she believed. At one of the parents' evenings. Something seemed wrong, though: Zallman was young. You don't expect a young man to be a pedophile. An attractive man though with a hawkish profile, and not very warm. Not with Leah. Not that she could remember.

The detectives had shown her Zallman's photograph. They had not allowed her to speak with Zallman. Vaguely yes she did remember. But not what he'd said to her, if he had said anything. Very likely Leah has asked him about Marissa but what he'd said she could not recall.

And then, hadn't Zallman slipped away from the reception, early? By chance she'd seen him, the only male faculty member not to be wearing a necktie, hair straggling over his collar, disappearing from the noisy brightly lighted room.

He'd taken a polygraph, at his own request. The results were "inconclusive."

If I could speak with him. Please.

They were telling her no, Mrs. Bantry. Not a good idea.

This man who took Marissa if I could speak with him *please.*

In her waking state she pleaded. She would beg the detectives, she would throw herself on their mercy. Her entire conscious life was now begging, pleading, and bartering. And waiting.

Zallman is the one, isn't he? You have him, don't you? An eyewitness said she saw him. Saw him pull Marissa into a van with him. In broad daylight! And you found Marissa's barrette by his parking space *isn't that proof*!

To her, the desperate mother, it was certainly proof. The man had taken Marissa, he knew where Marissa was. The truth had to be wrung from him before it was too late.

On her knees she would beg to see Zallman promising not to become emotional and they told her no, for she would only become emotional in the man's presence. And Zallman, who had a lawyer now, would only become more adamant in his denial.

Denial! How could he . . . deny! He had taken Marissa, he knew where Marissa was.

She would beg *him*. She would show Zallman pictures of Marissa as a baby. She would plead with this man for her daughter's life if only if only if only for God's sake they would allow her.

Of course, it was impossible. The suspect was being questioned following a procedure, a strategy, to which Leah Bantry had no access. The detectives were professionals, Leah Bantry was an amateur. She was only the mother, an amateur.

The wheel, turning.

It was a very long Friday. The longest Friday of Leah's life.

Then abruptly it was Friday night, and then it was Saturday morning. And Marissa was still gone.

Zallman had been captured, yet Marissa was still gone.

He might have been tortured, in another time. To make him confess. The vicious pedophile, whose "legal rights" had to be honored.

Leah's heart beat in fury. Yet she was powerless, she could not intervene.

Saturday afternoon: approaching the time when Marissa would be missing for forty-eight hours.

Forty-eight hours! It did not seem possible.

She has drowned by now, Leah thought. She has suffocated for lack of oxygen.

She is starving. She has bled to death. Wild creatures on Bear Mountain have mutilated her small body.

She calculated: it would soon be fifty hours since Leah had last seen Marissa. Kissed her hurriedly good-bye in the car, in front of the school Thursday morning at eight. And (she forced herself to remember, she would not escape remembering) Leah hadn't troubled to watch her daughter run up the walk, and into the school. Pale gold hair shimmering behind her and just possibly (possibly!) at the door, Marissa had turned to wave goodbye to Mommy but Leah was already driving away.

And so, she'd had her opportunity. She would confess to her sister Avril *I let Marissa slip away*.

The great wheel, turning. And the wheel was Time itself, without pity.

She saw that now. In her state of heightened awareness bred of terror she saw. She had ceased to give a damn about "Leah Bantry" in the public eye. The distraught/negligent mother. Working mom, single mom, mom-with-a-drinking-problem. She'd been exposed as a liar. She'd been exposed as a female avid to sleep with another woman's husband and that husband her boss. She knew, the very police who were searching for Marissa's abductor were investigating her, too. Crude tabloids, TV journalism. Under a guise of sympathy, pity for her "plight."

None of this mattered, now. What the jackals said of her, and would say. She was bartering her life for Marissa's. Appealing to God in whom she was trying in desperation to believe. *If You would. Let Marissa be alive. Return Marissa to me. If You would hear my plea.* So there was no room to give a damn about herself, she had no scruples now, no shame. Yes she would consent to be interviewed on the cruelest and crudest of the New York City TV stations if that might help Marissa, somehow. Blinking into the blinding TV lights, baring her teeth in a ghastly nervous smile.

Never would she care again for the pieties of ordinary life. When on the phone her own mother began crying, asking why, why on earth had Leah left Marissa alone for so many hours, Leah had interrupted the older woman coldly, "That doesn't matter now, Mother. Good-bye."

Neither of the elder Bantrys was in good health, they would not fly east to share their daughter's vigil. But Leah's older sister Avril flew up immediately from Washington to stay with her.

For years the sisters had not been close. There was a subtle rivalry between them, in which Leah had always felt belittled.

Avril, an investment attorney, was brisk and efficient answering the telephone, screening all e-mail. Avril checked the *Marissa* Web site constantly. Avril was on frank terms with the senior Skatskill detective working the case, who spoke circumspectly and with great awkwardness to Leah.

Avril called Leah to come listen to a voice-mail message that had come in while they'd been at police headquarters. Leah had told Avril about Davitt Stoop, to a degree.

It was Davitt, finally calling Leah. In a slow stilted voice that was not the warm intimate voice Leah knew he was saying *A terrible thing . . . This is a . . . terrible thing, Leah. We can only pray this madman is caught and that . . .* A long pause. You would have thought that Dr. Stoop had hung up but then he continued, more forcibly, *I'm sorry for this terrible thing but Leah please don't try to contact me again. Giving my name to the police! The past twenty-four hours have been devastating for me. Our relationship was a mistake and it can't be continued, I am sure you understand. As for your position at the clinic I am sure you understand the awkwardness among all the staff if . . .*

Leah's heart beat in fury, she punched *erase* to extinguish the man's voice. Grateful that Avril, who'd tactfully left the room, could be relied upon not to ask about Davitt Stoop, nor even to offer sisterly solicitude.

Take everything from me. If You will leave me Marissa, the way we were.

Emissaries

"Mommy!"

It was Marissa's voice, but muffled, at a distance.

Marissa was trapped on the far side of a barrier of thick glass, Leah heard her desperate cries only faintly. Marissa was pounding the glass with her fists, smearing her damp face against it. But the glass was too thick to be broken. "Mommy! Help me, Mommy . . ." And Leah could not move to help the child, Leah was paralyzed. Something gripped her legs, quicksand, tangled ropes. If she could break free . . .

Avril woke her, abruptly. There was someone to see her, friends of Marissa's they said they were.

"H-Hello, Mrs. Branty . . . Bant*ry*. My name is . . ."

Three girls. Three girls from Skatskill Day. One of them, with faded-rust-red hair and glistening stone-colored eyes, was holding out to Leah an astonishing large bouquet of dazzling white flowers: long-stemmed roses, carnations, paperwhites, mums. The sharp astringent fragrance of the paperwhites prevailed.

The bouquet must have been expensive, Leah thought. She took it from the girl and tried to smile. "Why, thank you."

It was Sunday, midday. She'd sunk into a stupor after twenty hours of wakefulness. Seeing it was a warm, incongruously brightly sunny April day beyond the partly-drawn blinds on the apartment windows.

She would have to focus on these girls. She'd been expecting, from what Avril had said, younger children, Marissa's age. But these were adolescents. Thirteen, fourteen. In eighth grade, they'd said. Friends of Marissa's?

The visit would not last long. Avril, disapproving, hovered near.

Possibly Leah had invited them, the girls were seated in her living room. They were clearly excited, edgy. They glanced about like nervous birds. Leah supposed she should offer them Cokes but something in her resisted. Hurriedly she'd washed her face, dragged a comb through her snarled hair that no longer looked blond, but dust-colored. How were these girls Marissa's friends? Leah had never seen them before in her life.

Nor did their names mean anything to her. "Jude Trahern," "Denise . . ." The third name she'd failed to catch.

The girls were moist-eyed with emotion. So many neighbors had dropped by to express their concern, Leah supposed she had to endure it. The girl who'd given Leah the bouquet, Jude, was saying in a faltering nasal voice how sorry they were for what had happened to Marissa and how much they liked Marissa who was just about the nicest girl at Skatskill Day. If something like this had to happen too bad it couldn't happen to—well, somebody else.

The other girls giggled, startled at their friend's vehemence.

"But Marissa is so nice, and so sweet. Ma'am, we are praying for her safe return, every minute."

Leah stared at the girl. She had no idea how to reply.

Confused, she lifted the bouquet to her face. Inhaled the almost too rich paperwhite smell. As if the purpose of this visit was to bring Leah . . . What?

The girls were staring at her almost rudely. Of course, they were young, they knew no better. Their leader, Jude, seemed to be a girl with some confidence, though she wasn't the eldest or the tallest or the most attractive of the three.

Not attractive at all. Her face was fiercely plain as if she'd scrubbed it with steel wool. Her skin was chalky, mottled. You could sense the energy thrumming through her like an electric current, she was wound up so tightly.

The other girls were more ordinary. One was softly plump with a fattish pug face, almost pretty except for something smirky, insolent in her manner. The other girl had a sallow blemished skin, limp grease-colored hair and oddly quivering, parted lips. All three girls wore grubby blue jeans, boys' shirts, and ugly square-toed boots.

". . . so we were wondering, Mrs. Bran-, Bantry, if you would like us to, like, pray with you? Like, now? It's Palm Sunday. Next Sunday is Easter."

"What? Pray? Thank you but . . ."

"Because Denise and Anita and me, we have a feeling, we have a really strong feeling, Mrs. Bantry, that Marissa is alive. And Marissa is depending on us. So, if—"

Avril came forward quickly, saying the visit was ended.

"My sister has been under a strain, girls. I'll see you to the door."

The flowers slipped through Leah's fingers. She caught at some of them, clumsily. The others fell to the floor at her feet.

Two of the girls hurried to the door, held open by Avril, with frightened expressions. Jude, pausing, continued to smile in her earnest, pinched way. She'd taken a small black object out of her pocket. "May I take a picture, Mrs. Bantry?"

Before Leah could protest, she raised the camera and clicked the shutter. Leah's hand had flown up to shield her face, instinctively.

Avril said sharply, "Please. The visit is over, girls."

Jude murmured, on her way out, "We will pray for you anyway, Mrs. Bantry. 'Bye!"

The other girls chimed in *Bye! bye!* Avril shut the door behind them.

Leah threw the flowers away in the trash. White flowers!

At least, they hadn't brought her calla lilies.

DUTCHWOMAN

. . . in motion. Tracing and retracing The Route. Sometimes on foot, sometimes in her car. Sometimes with Avril but more often alone. "I need to get out! I can't breathe in here! I need to see what Marissa saw."

These days were very long days. And yet, in all of the hours of these days, nothing happened.

Marissa was still gone, still gone.

Like a clock's ticking: still, still gone. Each time you checked, still gone.

She had her cell phone of course. If there was news.

She walked to the Skatskill Day School and positioned herself at the front door of the elementary grades wing, which was the door Marissa would have used, would have left by on Thursday afternoon. From this position she began The Route.

To the front sidewalk and east along Pinewood. Across Pinewood to Mahopac Avenue and continue east past 12th Street, 13th Street, 14th Street, 15th Street. At 15th and Trinity, the witness had claimed to see Mikal Zallman pull Marissa Bantry into his Honda CR-V van, and drive away.

Either it had happened that way, or it had not.

There was only the single witness, a Skatskill Day student whom police would not identify.

Leah believed that Zallman was the man and yet: there was something missing. Like a jigsaw puzzle piece. A very small piece, yet crucial.

Since the girls' visit. Since the bouquet of dazzling white flowers. That small twitchy smile Leah did not wish to interpret as taunting, of the girl named Jude.

We will pray for you anyway, Mrs. Bantry. Bye!

Important for Leah to walk briskly. To keep in motion.

There is a deep-sea creature, perhaps a shark, that must keep in motion constantly, otherwise it will die. Leah was becoming this creature, on land. She believed that news of Marissa's death would come to her only if she, the mother, were still; there was a kind of deadness in being still; but if she was in motion, tracing and retracting Marissa's route . . . "It's like Marissa is with me. Is *me*."

She knew that people along The Route were watching her. Everyone in Skatskill knew her face, her name. Everyone knew why she was out on the street, tracing and retracing The Route. A slender woman in shirt, slacks, dark glasses. A woman who had made a merely perfunctory attempt to disguise herself, dusty-blond hair partly hidden beneath a cap.

She knew the observers were pitying her. And blaming her.

Still, when individuals spoke to her, as a few did each time she traced The Route, they were invariably warm, sympathetic. Some of them, both men and women, appeared to be deeply sympathetic. Tears welled in their eyes. *That bastard* they spoke of Zallman. *Has he confessed yet?*

In Skatskill the name *Zallman* was known now, notorious. That the man was—had been—a member of the faculty at the Skatskill Day School had become a local scandal.

The rumor was, Zallman had a record of prior arrests and convictions as a sexual predator. He'd been fired from previous teaching positions but had somehow managed to be hired at the prestigious Skatskill School. The school's beleaguered principal had given newspaper and TV interviews vigorously denying this rumor, yet it prevailed.

Bantry, Zallman. The names now luridly linked. In the tabloids photos of the missing girl and "suspect" were printed side by side. Several times, Leah's photograph was included as well.

In her distraught state yet Leah was able to perceive the irony of such a grouping: a mock family.

Leah had given up hoping to speak with Zallman. She supposed it was a ridiculous request. If he'd taken Marissa he was a psychopath and you don't expect a psychopath to tell the truth. If he had not taken Marissa . . .

"If it's someone else. They will never find him."

The Skatskill police had not yet arrested Zallman. Temporarily, Zallman had been released. His lawyer had made a terse public statement that he was "fully cooperating" with the police investigation. But what he had told them, what could possibly be of worth that he had told them, Leah didn't know.

Along The Route, Leah saw with Marissa's eyes. The facades of houses. On 15th Street, storefronts. No one had corroborated the eyewitness's testimony about seeing Marissa pulled into a van in full daylight on busy 15th Street. Wouldn't anyone else have seen? And who had the eyewitness been? Since the three girls had dropped by to see her, Leah was left with a new sensation of unease.

Not Marissa's friends. Not those girls.

She crossed Trinity and continued. This was a slight extension of Marissa's route home from school. It was possible, Marissa dropped by the 7-Eleven to buy a snack on Tuesdays/Thursdays when Leah returned home late.

Taped to the front plate-glass door of the 7-Eleven was

HAVE YOU SEEN ME?
MARISSA BANTRY, 11
MISSING SINCE APRIL 10

Marissa's smiling eyes met hers as Leah pushed the door open.

Inside, trembling, Leah removed her dark glasses. She was feeling dazed. Wasn't certain if this was full wakefulness or a fugue state. She was trying to orient herself. Staring at a stack of thick Sunday *New York Times*. The front page headlines were of U.S.-Iraq issues and for a confused moment Leah thought *Maybe none of it has happened yet.*

Maybe Marissa was outside, waiting in the car.

The gentlemanly Indian clerk stood behind the counter in his usual reserved, yet attentive posture. He was staring at her strangely, Leah saw, as he would never have done in the past.

Of course, he recognized her now. Knew her name. All about her. She would never be an anonymous customer again. Leah saw, with difficulty, for her eyes were watering, a second HAVE YOU SEEN ME? taped conspicuously to the front of the cash register.

Wanting to embrace the man, wordless. Wanted to press herself into his arms and burst into tears.

Instead she wandered in one of the aisles. How like an overexposed photograph the store was. So much to see, yet you saw nothing.

Thank God, there were no other customers at the moment.

Saw her hand reach out for—what? A box of Kleenex.

Pink, the color Marissa preferred.

She went to the counter to pay. Smiled at the clerk who was smiling very nervously at her, clearly agitated by the sight of her. His always-so-friendly blond customer! Leah was going to thank him for having posted the notices, and she was going to ask him if he'd ever seen Marissa in his store alone, without her, when suddenly the man said, to her astonishment, "Mrs. Bantry, I know of your daughter and what has happened, that is so terrible. I watch all the time, to see what will come of it." Behind the counter was a small portable TV, volume turned down. "Mrs. Bantry, I want to say, when the police came here, I was nervous and not able to remember so well, but now I do remember, I am more certain, yes I did see your daughter that day, I believe. She did come into the store. She was alone, and then there was another girl. They went out together."

The Indian clerk spoke in a flood of words. His eyes were repentant, pleading.

"When? When was—"

"That day, Mrs. Bantry. That the police have asked about. Last week."

"Thursday? You saw Marissa on Thursday?"

But now he was hesitating. Leah spoke too excitedly.

"I think so, yes. I can not be certain. That is why I did not want to tell the police, I did not want to get into trouble with them. They are impatient with me, I don't know English so well. The questions they ask are not so easy to answer while they wait staring at you."

Leah didn't doubt that the Indian clerk was uneasy with the Caucasian Skatskill police, she was uneasy with them herself.

She said, "Marissa was with a girl, you say? What did this girl look like?"

The Indian clerk frowned. Leah saw that he was trying to be as accurate as possible. He had probably not looked at the girls very closely, very likely he could not distinguish among most of them. He said, "She was older than your daughter, I am sure. She was not too tall, but older. Not so blond-haired."

"You don't know her, do you? Her name?"

"No. I do not know their names any of them." He paused, frowning. His jaws tightened. "Some of them, the older ones, I think this girl is one of them, with their friends they come in here after school and take things. They steal, they break. They rip open bags, to eat. Like pigs they are. They think I can't see them but I know what they do. Five days a week they come in here, many of them. They are daring me to shout at them, and if I would touch them—"

His voice trailed off, tremulous.

"This girl. What did she look like?"

". . . a white skin. More than yours, Mrs. Bantry. A strange color of hair like . . . a color of something red, faded."

He spoke with some repugnance. Clearly, the mysterious girl was not attractive in his eyes.

Red-haired. Pale-red-haired. Who?

Jude Trahern. The girl who'd brought the flowers. The girl who spoke of praying for Marissa's safe return.

Were they friends, then? Marissa had had a friend?

Leah was feeling light-headed. The fluorescent lighting began to tilt and spin. There was something here she could not grasp. *Pray with you. Next Sunday is Easter.* She had more to ask of this kindly man but her mind had gone blank.

"Thank you. I . . . have to leave now."

"Don't tell them, Mrs. Bantry? The police? Please?"

Blindly Leah pushed through the door.

"Mrs. Bantry?" The clerk hurried after her, a bag in his hand. "You are forgetting."

The box of pink Kleenex.

Flying Dutchman. Dutchwoman. She was becoming. Always in motion, terrified of stopping. Returning home to her sister.

Any news?

None.

Behind the drab little mini-mall she was drifting, dazed. She would tell the Skatskill detectives what the Indian clerk had told her—she must tell them. If Marissa had been in the store on Thursday afternoon, then Marissa could not have been pulled into a minivan on 15th Street and Trinity, two blocks back toward school. Not by Mikal Zallman, or by anyone. Marissa must have continued past Trinity. After the 7-Eleven she would have circled back to 15th Street again, and walked another half block to home.

Unless she'd been pulled into the minivan on 15th Street and Van Buren. The eyewitness had gotten the streets wrong. She'd been closer to home.

Unless the Indian clerk was confused about days, times. Or, for what purpose Leah could not bear to consider, lying to her.

"Not him! Not him, too."

She refused to think that was a possibility. Her mind simply shut blank, in refusal.

She was walking now slowly, hardly conscious of her surroundings. A smell of rancid food assailed her nostrils. Only a few employees' cars were parked behind the mini-mall. The pavement was stained and littered, a single Dumpster overflowing trash. At the back of the Chinese takeout several scrawny cats were rummaging in food scraps and froze at Leah's approach before running away in panic.

"Kitties! I'm not going to hurt you."

The feral cats' terror mocked her own. Their panic was hers, misplaced, to no purpose.

Leah wondered: what were the things Marissa did, when Leah wasn't with her? For years they had been inseparable: mother, daughter. When Marissa had been a very small child, even before she could walk, she'd tried to follow her mother everywhere, from room to room. *Mom-my! Where Mom-my going!* Now, Marissa did many things by herself. Marissa was growing up. Dropping by the 7-Eleven, with other children after school. Buying a soft drink, a bag of something crunchy, salty. It was innocent enough. No child should be punished for it. Leah gave Marissa pocket change, as she called it, for just such impromptu purchases, though she disapproved of junk food.

Leah felt a tightening in her chest, envisioning her daughter in the 7-Eleven store the previous Thursday, buying something from the Indian clerk. Then, he had not known her name. A day or two later, everyone in Skatskill knew Marissa Bantry's name.

Of course it probably meant nothing. That Marissa had walked out of the store with a classmate from school. Nothing unusual about that. She could imagine with what polite stiff expressions the police would respond to such a "tip."

In any case, Marissa would still have returned to 15th Street on her way home. So busy, dangerous at that hour of day.

It was there on 15th Street that the "unidentified" classmate had seen Marissa being pulled into the Honda. Leah wondered if the witness was the red-haired Jude.

Exactly what the girl had told police officers, Leah didn't know. The detectives exuded an air, both assuring and frustrating, of knowing more than they were releasing at the present time.

Leah found herself at the edge of the paved area. Staring at a steep hill of uncultivated and seemingly worthless land. Strange how in the midst of an affluent suburb there yet remain these stretches of vacant land, uninhabitable. The hill rose to Highgate Avenue a half mile away, invisible from this perspective. You would not guess that "historical" old homes and mansions were located on the crest of this hill, property worth millions of dollars. The hill was profuse with crawling vines, briars, and stunted trees. The accumulation of years of windblown litter and debris made it look like an informal dump. There was a scurrying sound somewhere just inside the tangle of briars, a furry shape that appeared and disappeared so swiftly Leah scarcely saw it.

Behind the Dumpster, hidden from her view, the colony of wild cats lived, foraged for food, fiercely interbred, and died the premature deaths of feral creatures. They would not wish to be "pets"—they had no capacity to receive the affection of humans. They were, in clinical terms, undomesticable.

Leah was returning to her car when she heard a nasal voice in her wake:

"Mrs. Ban-try! H'lo."

Leah turned uneasily to see the frizz-haired girl who'd given her the flowers.

Jude. Jude Trahern.

Now it came to Leah: there was a Trahern Square in downtown Skatskill, named for a Chief Justice Trahern decades ago. One of the old Skatskill names. On Highgate, there was a Trahern estate, one of the larger houses, nearly hidden from the road.

This strange glistening-eyed girl. There was something of the sleek white rat about her. Yet she smiled uncertainly at Leah, clumsily straddling her bicycle.

"Are you following me?"

"Ma'am, no. I . . . just saw you."

Wide-eyed the girl appeared sincere, uneasy. Yet Leah's nerves were on edge, she spoke sharply: "What do you want?"

The girl stared at Leah as if something very bright glared from Leah's face that was both blinding and irresistible. She wiped nervously at her nose. "I . . . I want to say I'm sorry, for saying dumb things before. I guess I made things worse."

Made things worse! Leah smiled angrily, this was so absurd.

"I mean, Denise and Anita and me, we wanted to help. We did the wrong thing, I guess. Coming to see you."

"Were you the 'unidentified witness' who saw my daughter being pulled into a minivan?"

The girl blinked at Leah, blank-faced. For a long moment Leah would have sworn that she was about to speak, to say something urgent. Then she ducked her head, wiped again at her nose, shrugged self-consciously and muttered what sounded like, "I guess not."

"All right. Good-bye. I'm leaving now."

Leah frowned and turned away, her heart beating hard. How badly she wanted to be alone! But the rat-girl was too obtuse to comprehend. With the dogged persistence of an overgrown child she followed Leah at an uncomfortably close distance of about three feet, pedaling her bicycle awkwardly. The bicycle was an expensive Italian make of the kind a serious adult cyclist might own.

At last Leah paused, to turn back. "*Do* you have something to tell me, Jude?"

The girl looked astonished.

" 'Jude'! You remember my name?"

Leah would recall afterward this strange moment. The exultant look in Jude Trahern's face. Her chalky skin mottled with pleasure.

Leah said, "Your name is unusual, I remember unusual names. If you have something to tell me about Marissa, I wish you would."

"Me? What would I know?"

"You aren't the witness from school?"

"What witness?"

"A classmate of Marissa's says she saw a male driver pull Marissa into his minivan on 15th Street. But you aren't that girl?"

Jude shook her head vehemently. "You can't always believe 'eyewitnesses,'" Mrs. Bantry."

"What do you mean?"

"It's well known. It's on TV all the time, police shows. An eyewitness swears she sees somebody, and she's wrong. Like, with Mr. Zallman, people are all saying it's him but, like, it might be somebody else."

The girl spoke rapidly, fixing Leah with her widened shining eyes.

"Jude, what do you mean, somebody else? Who?"

Excited by Leah's attention, Jude lost her balance on the bicycle, and nearly stumbled. Clumsily she began walking it again. Gripping the handlebars so tightly her bony knuckles gleamed white.

She was breathing quickly, lips parted. She spoke in a lowered conspiratorial voice.

"See, Mrs. Bantry, Mr. Zallman is like notorious. He comes on to girls if they're pretty-pretty like Marissa. Like some of the kids were saying on TV, he's got these laser-eyes." Jude shivered, thrilled.

Leah was shocked. "If everybody knows about Zallman, why didn't anybody tell? Before this happened? How could a man like that be allowed to teach?" She paused, anxious. Thinking *Did Marissa know? Why didn't she tell me?*

Jude giggled. "You got to wonder why any of them *teach*. I mean, why'd anybody want to hang out with *kids*! Not just some weird guy, but females, too." She smiled, seeming not to see how Leah stared at her. "Mr. Z. is kind of fun. He's this 'master'—he calls himself. Online, you can click onto him he's 'Master of Eyes.' Little kids, girls, he'd come onto after school, and tell them be sure not to tell anybody, see. Or they're be 'real sorry.'" Jude made a twisting motion with her hands as if wringing an invisible neck. "He likes girls with nice long hair he can brush."

"Brush?"

"Sure. Mr. Zallman has this wire brush, like. Calls it a little-doggy-brush. He runs it through your hair for fun. I mean, it used to be fun. I hope the cops took the brush when they arrested him, like for evidence. Hell, he never came on to me, I'm not pretty-pretty."

Jude spoke haughtily, with satisfaction. Fixing Leah with her curious stone-colored eyes.

Leah knew that she was expected to say, with maternal solicitude, *Oh, but you are pretty, Jude! One day, you will be.*

In different circumstances she was meant to frame the rat-girl's hot little face in her cool hands, comfort her. *One day you will be loved, Jude. Don't feel bad.*

"You were saying there might be—somebody else? Not Zallman but another person?"

Jude said, sniffing, "I wanted to tell you before, at your house, but you seemed, like, not to want to hear. And that other lady was kind of glaring at us. She didn't want us to stay."

"Jude, please. Who is this person you're talking about?"

"Mrs. Branly, Bant-ry, like I said Marissa is a good friend of mine. She is! Some kids make fun of her, she's a little slow they say but I don't think Marissa is slow, not really. She tells me all kinds of secrets, see?" Jude paused, drawing a deep breath. "She said, she missed her dad."

It was as if Jude had reached out to pinch her. Leah was speechless.

"Marissa was always saying she hates it here in Skatskill. She wanted to be with her dad, she said. Some place called 'Berkeley'—in California. She wanted to go there to live."

Jude spoke with the ingratiating air of one child informing on another to a parent. Her lips quivered, she was so excited.

Still Leah was unable to respond. Trying to think what to say except her brain seemed to be partly shutting down as if she'd had a small stroke.

Jude said innocently, "I guess you didn't know this, Mrs. Bantry?" She bit at her thumbnail, squinting.

"Marissa told you that? She told you—those things?"

"Are you mad at me, Mrs. Bantry? You wanted me to tell."

"Marissa told you—she wanted to live with her 'dad'? Not with her mother but with her 'dad'?"

Leah's peripheral vision had narrowed. There was a shadowy funnel-shape at the center of which the girl with the chalky skin and frizzed hair squinted and grinned, in a show of repentance.

"I just thought you would want to know, see, Mrs. Bantry? Like, maybe Marissa ran away? Nobody is saying that, everybody thinks it's Mr. Zallman, like the cops are thinking it's got to be him. Sure, maybe it is. But—maybe!—Marissa called her dad, and asked him to come get her? Something weird like that? And it was a secret from you? See, a lot of times Marissa would talk that way, like a little kid. Like, not thinking about her mother's feelings. And I told her, 'Your mom, she's real nice, she'd be hurt real bad, Marissa, if you—' "

Leah couldn't hold back the tears any longer. It was as if she'd lost her daughter for the second time.

Mistakes

His first was to assume that, since he knew nothing of the disappearance of Marissa Bantry, he could not be "involved" in it.

His second was not to contact a lawyer immediately. As soon as he realized exactly why he'd been brought into police headquarters for questioning.

His third seemed to be to have lived the wrong life.

Pervert. Sex offender. Pedophile.

Kidnapper/rapist/murderer.

Mikal Zallman, thirty-one. Suspect.

"Mother, it's Mikal. I hope you haven't seen the news already, I have something very disturbing to tell you . . ."

Nothing! He knew nothing.

The name MARISSA BANTRY meant nothing to him.

Well, not initially. He couldn't be sure.

In his agitated state, not knowing what the hell they were getting at with their questions, he couldn't be sure.

"Why are you asking me? Has something happened to 'Marissa Bantry'?"

Next, they showed him photographs of the girl.

Yes: now he recognized her. The long blond hair, that was sometimes plaited. One of the quieter pupils. Nice girl. He recognized the picture but could not have said the girl's name because, look: "I'm not these kids' teacher, exactly. I'm a 'consultant.' I don't have a homeroom. I don't have regular classes with them. In the high school, one of the math instructors teaches computer science. I don't get to know the kids by name, like their other instructors do."

He was speaking quickly, an edge to his voice. It was uncomfortably cold in the room, yet he was perspiring.

As in a cartoon of police interrogation. *They sweated it out of the suspect.*

Strictly speaking, it wasn't true that Zallman didn't know students' names. He knew the names of many students. Certainly, he knew their faces. Especially the older students, some of whom were extremely bright, and engaging. But he had not known Marissa Bantry's name, the shy little blond child had made so little an impression on him.

Nor had he spoken with her personally. He was certain.

"Why are you asking me about this girl? If she's missing from home what is the connection with *me*?"

That edge to Zallman's voice. Not yet angry, only just impatient.

He was willing to concede, yes: if a child has been missing for more than twenty-four hours that was serious. If eleven-year-old Marissa Bantry was missing, it was a terrible thing.

"But it has nothing to do with *me*."

They allowed him to speak. They were tape recording his precious words. They did not appear to be passing judgment on him, he was not receiving the impression that they believed him involved with the disappearance, only just a few questions to put to him, to aid in their investigation. They explained to him that it was in his best interests to cooperate fully with them, to straighten out the misunderstanding, or whatever it was, a misidentification perhaps, before he left police headquarters.

"Misidentification"? What was that?

He was becoming angry, defiant. Knowing he was God-damned innocent of any wrongdoing, no matter how trivial: traffic violations, parking tickets. *He was innocent!* So he insisted upon taking a lie-detector test.

Another mistake.

Seventeen hours later an aggressive stranger now retained as Mikal Zallman's criminal lawyer was urging him, "Go home, Mikal. If you can, sleep. You will need your sleep. Don't speak with anyone except people you know and trust and assume yourself under surveillance and whatever you do, man—don't try to contact the missing girl's mother."

Please understand I am not the one. Not the madman who has taken your beautiful child. There has been some terrible misunderstanding but I swear I am innocent, Mrs. Bantry, we've never met but please allow me to commiserate with you, this nightmare we seem to be sharing.

Driving home to North Tarrytown. Oncoming headlights blinding his eyes. Tears streaming from his eyes. Now the adrenaline rush was subsiding, leaking out like water in a clogged drain, he was beginning to feel a hammering in his head that was the worst headache pain he'd ever felt in his life.

Jesus! What if it was a cerebral hemorrhage . . .

He would die. His life would be over. It would be judged that his guilt had provoked the hemorrhage. His name would never be cleared.

He'd been so cocky and arrogant coming into police headquarters, confident he'd be released within the hour, and now. A wounded animal limping for shelter. He could not keep up with traffic on route 9, he was so sick. Impatient drivers sounded their horns. A massive SUV pulled up to within inches of Zallman's rear bumper.

He knew! Ordinarily he was an impatient driver himself. Disgusted with overly cautious drivers on route 9 and now he'd become one of these, barely mobile at twenty miles an hour.

Whoever they were who hated him, who had entangled him in this nightmare, they had struck a first, powerful blow.

Zallman's bad luck, one of his fellow tenants was in the rear lobby of his building, waiting for the elevator, when Zallman staggered inside. He was unshaven, disheveled, smelling frankly of his body. He saw the other man staring at him, at first startled, recognizing him; then with undisguised repugnance.

But I didn't! I am not the one.

The police would not have released me if.

Zallman let his fellow tenant take the elevator up, alone.

Zallman lived on the fifth floor of the so-called condominium village. He had never thought of his three sparely furnished rooms as "home" nor did he think of his mother's Upper East Side brownstone as "home" any longer: it was fair to say that Zallman had no home.

It was near midnight of an unnamed day. He'd lost days of his life. He could not have stated with confidence the month, the year. His head throbbed with pain. Fumbling with the key to his darkened apartment he heard the telephone inside ringing with the manic air of a telephone that has been ringing repeatedly.

Released for the time being. Keep your cell phone with you at all times for you may be contacted by police. Do not REPEAT DO NOT leave the area. A bench warrant will be issued for your arrest in the event that you attempt to leave the area.

"It isn't that I am innocent, Mother. I know that I am innocent! The shock of it is, people seem to believe that I might not be. A lot of people."

It was a fact. A lot of people.

He would have to live with that fact, and what it meant of Mikal Zallman's place in the world, for a long time.

Keep your hands in sight, sir.

That had been the beginning. His wounded brain fixed obsessively upon that moment, at Bear Mountain.

The state troopers. Staring at him. As if.

(Would they have pulled their revolvers and shot him down, if he'd made a sudden ambiguous gesture? It made him sick to think so. It should have made him grateful that it had not happened but in fact it made him sick.)

Yet the troopers had asked him politely enough if they could search his vehicle. He'd hesitated only a moment before consenting. Sure it annoyed him as a private citizen who'd broken no laws and as a (lapsed) member of the ACLU but why not, he knew there was nothing in the minivan to catch the troopers' eyes. He didn't even smoke marijuana any longer. He'd never carried a concealed weapon, never even owned a gun. So the troopers looked through the van, and found nothing. No idea what the hell they were looking for but he'd felt a gloating sort of relief that they hadn't found it. Seeing the way they were staring at the covers of the paperback books in the back seat he'd tossed there weeks ago and had more or less forgotten.

Female nudes, and so what?

"Good thing it isn't kiddie porn, officers, eh? That stuff is illegal."

Even as a kid Zallman hadn't been able to resist wisecracking at inopportune moments.

Now, he had a lawyer. "His" lawyer.

A criminal lawyer whose retainer was fifteen thousand dollars.

They are the enemy.

Neuberger meant the Skatskill detectives, and beyond them the prosecutorial staff of the district, whose surface civility Zallman had been misinterpreting as a tacit sympathy with him, his predicament. It was a fact they'd sweated him, and he'd gone along with it naively, frankly. Telling him he was not *under arrest* only just *assisting in their investigation*.

His body had known, though. Increasingly anxious, restless, needing to urinate every twenty minutes. He'd been flooded with adrenaline like a cornered animal.

His blood pressure had risen, he could feel pulses pounding in his ears. Damned stupid to request a polygraph at such a time but—he was an innocent man, wasn't he?

Should have called a lawyer as soon as they'd begun asking him about the missing child. Once it became clear that this was a serious situation, not a mere misunderstanding or misidentification by an unnamed "eyewitness." (One of Zallman's own students? Deliberately lying to hurt him? For Christ's sake *why*?) So at last he'd called an older cousin, a corporation attorney, to whom he had not spoken since his father's funeral, and explained the situation to him, this ridiculous situation, this nightmare situation, but he had to take it seriously since obviously he was a suspect and so: would Joshua recommend a good criminal attorney who could get to Skatskill immediately, and intercede for him with the police?

His cousin had been so stunned by Zallman's news he'd barely been able to speak. "Y-You? Mikal? You're arrested—?"

"No. I am not arrested, Andrew."

He believes I might be guilty. My own cousin believes I might be a sexual predator.

Still, within ninety minutes, after a flurry of increasingly desperate phone calls, Zallman had retained a Manhattan criminal lawyer named Neuberger who didn't blithely assure him, as Zallman halfway expected he would, that there was nothing to worry about.

TARRYTOWN RESIDENT QUESTIONED
IN ABDUCTION OF 11-YEAR-OLD

SEARCH FOR MARISSA CONTINUES
SKATSKILL DAY INSTRUCTOR IN POLICE CUSTODY

6TH GRADER STILL MISSING
SKATSKILL DAY INSTRUCTOR QUESTIONED BY POLICE
TENTATIVE IDENTIFICATION OF MINIVAN
BELIEVED USED IN ABDUCTION

MIKAL ZALLMAN, 31, COMPUTER CONSULTANT
QUESTIONED BY POLICE IN CHILD ABDUCTION

ZALLMAN: "I AM INNOCENT"
TARRYTOWN RESIDENT QUESTIONED BY POLICE
IN CHILD ABDUCTION CASE

Luridly spread across the front pages of the newspapers were photographs of the missing girl, the missing girl's mother, and "alleged suspect Mikal Zallman."

It was a local TV news magazine. Neuberger had warned him not to watch TV, just as he should not REPEAT SHOULD NOT answer the telephone if he didn't have caller I.D., and for sure he should not answer his door unless he knew exactly who was there. Still, Zallman was watching TV fortified by a half dozen double-strength Tylenols that left him just conscious enough to stare at the screen disbelieving what he saw and heard.

Skatskill Day students, their faces blurred to disguise their identities, voices eerily slurred, telling a sympathetic female broadcaster their opinions of Mikal Zallman.

Mr. Zallman, he's cool. I liked him okay.

Mr. Zallman is kind of sarcastic I guess. He's okay with the smart kids but the rest of us it's like he's trying real hard and wants us to know.

I was so surprised! Mr. Zallman never acted like that, you know—weird. Not in computer lab.

Mr. Zallman has, like, these laser eyes? I always knew he was scary.

Mr. Zallman looks at us sometimes! It makes you shiver.

Some kids are saying he had, like, a hairbrush? To brush the girls' hair? I never saw it.

This hairbrush Mr. Zallman had, it was so weird! He never used it on me, guess I'm not pretty-pretty enough for him.

He'd help you in the lab after school if you asked. He was real nice to me. All this stuff about Marissa, I don't know. It makes me want to cry.

And there was Dr. Adrienne Cory, principal of Skatskill Day, grimly explaining to a skeptical interviewer that Mikal Zallman whom she had hired two and a half years previously had excellent credentials, had come highly recommended, was a conscientious and reliable staff member of whom there had been no complaints.

No complaints! What of the students who'd just been on the program?

Dr. Cory said, twisting her mouth in a semblance of a placating smile, "Well. We never knew."

And would Zallman continue to teach at Skatskill Day?

"Mr. Zallman has been suspended with pay for the time being."

His first, furious thought was *I will sue.*

His second, more reasonable thought was *I must plead my case.*

He had friends at Skatskill Day, he believed. The young woman who thought herself less-than-happily married, and who'd several times invited Zallman to dinner; a male math teacher, whom he often met at the gym; the school psychologist, whose sense of humor dovetailed with his own; and Dr. Cory herself, who was quite an intelligent woman, and a kindly woman, who had always seemed to like Zallman.

He would appeal to them. They must believe him!

Zallman insisted upon a meeting with Dr. Cory, face to face. He insisted upon being allowed to present his side of the case. He was informed that his presence at the school was "out of the question" at the present time; a mere glimpse of Zallman, and faculty members as well as students would be "distracted."

If he tried to enter the school building on Monday morning, Zallman was warned, security guards would turn him away.

"But why? What have I done? What have I done that is anything more than rumor?"

Not what Zallman had done but what the public perceived he might have done, that was the issue. Surely Zallman understood?

He compromised, he would meet Dr. Cory on neutral territory, 8 A.M. Monday in the Trahern Square office of the school's legal counsel. He was told to bring his own legal counsel but Zallman declined.

Another mistake, probably. But he couldn't wait for Neuberger, this was an emergency.

"I need to work! I need to return to school as if nothing is wrong, in fact *nothing is wrong*. I insist upon returning."

Dr. Cory murmured something vaguely supportive, sympathetic. She was a kind person, Zallman wanted to believe. She was decent, well-intentioned, she liked him. She'd always laughed at his jokes!

Though sometimes wincing, as if Zallman's humor was a little too abrasive for her. At least publicly.

Zallman was protesting the decision to suspend him from teaching without "due process." He demanded to be allowed to meet with the school board. How could he be suspended from teaching for no reason—wasn't that unethical, and illegal? Wouldn't Skatskill Day be liable, if he chose to sue?

"I swear I did not—*do it. I am not involved.* I scarcely know Marissa Bantry, I've had virtually no contact with the girl. Dr. Cory—Adrienne—these 'eyewitnesses' are lying. This 'barrette' that was allegedly found by police behind my building—someone must have placed it there. Someone who hates me, who wants to destroy me! This has been a nightmare for me but I'm confident it will turn out well. I mean, it can't be proven that I'm involved with—with—whatever has happened to the girl—because I am not involved! I need to come back to work, Adrienne, I need you to demonstrate that you have faith in me. I'm sure that my colleagues have faith in me. Please reconsider! I'm prepared to return to work this morning. I can explain to the students—something! Give me a chance, will you? Even if I'd been arrested—which I am not, Adrienne—under the law I am innocent until proven guilty and I can't be possibly be proven guilty because I—I did not—*I did not do anything wrong.*"

He was struck by a sudden stab of pain, as if someone had driven an ice pick into his skull. He whimpered and slumped forward gripping his hand in his hands.

A woman was asking him, in a frightened voice, "Mr. Zallman? Do you want us to call a doctor?—an ambulance?"

Under Surveillance

He needed to speak with her. He needed to console her.

On the fifth day of the vigil it became an overwhelming need.

For in his misery he'd begun to realize how much worse it was for the mother of Marissa Bantry, than for him who was merely the suspect.

It was Tuesday. Of course, he had not been allowed to return to teach. He had not slept for days except fitfully, in his clothes. He ate standing before the opened refrigerator, grabbing at whatever was inside. He lived on Tylenols. Obsessively he watched TV, switching from channel to channel in pursuit of the latest news of the missing girl and steeling himself for a glimpse of his own face, haggard and hollow-eyed and disfigured by guilt as by acne. *There he is! Zallman!* The only suspect in the case whom police had actually brought into custody, paraded before a phalanx of photographers and TV cameramen to arouse the excited loathing of hundreds of thousands of spectators who would not have the opportunity to see Zallman, and to revile him, in the flesh.

In fact, the Skatskill police had other suspects. They were following other "leads." Neuberger had told him he'd heard that they had sent men to California, to track down the elusive father of Marissa Bantry who had emerged as a "serious suspect" in the abduction.

Yet, in the Skatskill area, the search continued. In the Bear Mountain State Park, and in the Blue Mountain Reserve south of Peekskill. Along the edge of the Hudson River between Peekskill and Skatskill. In parkland and wooded areas east of Skatskill in the Rockefeller State Park. These were search and rescue teams comprised of both professionals and volunteers. Zallman had wanted to volunteer to help with the search for he was desperate to do something but Neuberger had fixed him with a look of incredulity. "Mikal, that is not a good idea. Trust me."

There had been reports of men seen "dumping" mysterious objects from bridges into rivers and streams and there had been further "sightings" of the living girl in the company of her captor or captors at various points along the New York State Thruway and the New England Expressway. Very blond fair-skinned girls between the ages of eight and thirteen resembling Marissa Bantry were being seen everywhere.

Police had received more than one thousand calls and Web site messages and in the media it was announced that *all leads will be followed* but Zallman wondered at this. *All* leads?

He himself called the Skatskill detectives, often. He'd memorized their numbers. Often, they failed to return his calls. He was made to understand that Zallman was no longer their prime suspect—maybe. Neuberger had told him that the girl's barrette, so conspicuously dropped by Zallman's parking space, had been wiped clean of fingerprints: "An obvious plant."

Zallman had had his telephone number changed to an unlisted number yet still the unwanted calls—vicious, obscene, threatening, or merely inquisitive—continued and so he'd had the phone disconnected and relied now upon his cell phone exclusively, carrying it with him as he paced through the shrinking rooms of his condominium apartment. From the fifth floor, at a slant, Zallman could see the Hudson River on overcast days like molten lead but on clear days possessed of an astonishing slate-blue beauty. For long minutes he lost himself in contemplation of the view: beauty that was pure, unattached to any individual, destined to outlive the misery that had become his life.

Nothing to do with me. Nothing to do with human evil.

Desperately he wanted to share this insight with the mother of Marissa Bantry. It was such a simple fact, it might be overlooked.

He went to 15th Street where the woman lived, he'd seen the exterior of the apartment building on TV numerous times. He had not been able to telephone her. He wanted only to speak with her for a few minutes.

It was near dusk of Tuesday. A light chill mist-rain was falling. For a while he stood indecisively on the front walk of the barracks-like building, in khaki trousers, canvas jacket, jogging shoes. His damp hair straggled past his collar. He had not shaved for several days. A sickly radiance shone in his face, he knew he was doing the right thing now crossing the lawn at an angle, to circle to the rear of the building where he might have better luck discovering which of the apartments belonged to Leah Bantry.

Please I must see you.

We must share this nightmare.

Police came swiftly to intercept him, grabbing his arms and cuffing his wrists behind his back.

Sacrifice

Is she breathing?

. . . Christ!

She isn't . . . is she? *Is* she?

She is. She's okay.

. . . like maybe she's being . . . poisoned?

We were getting so scared! Anita was crying a lot, then Anita was laughing like she couldn't stop. Denise had this eating-thing, she was hungry all the time, stuffing her mouth at meals and in the cafeteria at school then poking a finger down her throat to make herself vomit into a toilet flush-flush-flushing the toilet so if she was at home nobody in her family would hear or if she was at school other girls wouldn't hear and tell on her.

More and more we could see how they were watching us at school, like *somehow they knew*.

Since giving the white flowers to the Corn Maiden's mother nothing felt right. Denise knew, and Anita. Jude maybe knew but would not acknowledge it.

Mothers don't give a shit about their kids. See, it's all pretend.

Jude believed this. She hated the Corn Maiden's mother worse than she hated anybody, just about.

Anita was worried the Corn Maiden was being poisoned, all the strong drugs Jude was making her swallow. The Corn Maiden was hardly eating anything now, you had to mush it up like cottage cheese with vanilla ice cream, open her jaws and spoon it into her mouth then close her jaws and try to make her to swallow, but half the time the Corn Maiden began choking and gagging and the white mush just leaked out of her mouth like vomit.

We were begging, Jude maybe we better . . .

. . . we don't want her to die, like do we?

Jude? *Jude?*

The fun was gone now. Seeing TV news, and all the newspapers even *The New York Times*, and the posters HAVE YOU SEEN ME? and the fifteen-thousand-dollar reward, and all that, that made us laugh like hyenas just a few days ago but wasn't anything to laugh at now, or anyway not much. Jude still scorned the assholes, she called them, and laughed at how they ran around looking for the Corn Maiden practically under their noses out Highgate Avenue.

Jude was doing these weird things. On Monday she came to school with one of the Corn Maiden's butterfly barrettes she was going to wear in her hair but we told her Oh no better not! and she laughed at us but didn't wear it.

Jude talked a lot about fire, "immolation." On the Internet she looked up some things like Buddhists had done a long time ago.

The Sacrifice of the Corn Maiden called for the heart of the captive cut out, and her blood collected in sacred vessels, but you could burn the Corn Maiden, too, and mix her ashes with the soil Jude said.

Fire is a cleaner way, Jude said. It would only hurt at the beginning.

Jude was taking Polaroids all the time now. By the end, Jude would have like fifty of these. We believed that Jude intended to post them on the Internet but that did not happen.

What was done with them, if the police took them away we would not know. They were not ever printed. Maybe they were destroyed.

These were pictures to stare at! In some of them the Corn Maiden was lying on her back in the bier in the beautiful silky fabrics and brocades and she was *so little*. Jude posed her naked and with her hair fanned out and her legs spread wide so you could see the little pink slip between her legs Jude called her cut.

The Corn Maiden's cut was not like ours, it was a little-girl cut and nicer, Jude said. It would never grow *pubic hairs* Jude said, the Corn Maiden would be spared that.

Jude laughed saying she would send the TV stations these pictures they could not use.

Other poses, the Corn Maiden was sitting up or kneeling or on her feet if Jude could revive her, and slap-slap her face so her eyes were open, you would think she was awake, and smiling this wan little smile leaning against Jude, their heads leaning together and Jude grinning like Jude O and the Corn Maiden were floating somewhere above the earth in some Heaven where nobody could reach them, only just look up at them wondering how they'd got there!

Jude had us take these pictures. One of them was her favorite, she said she wished the Corn Maiden's mother could see it and maybe someday she would.

That night, we thought the Corn Maiden would die.

She was shivering and twitching in her sleep like she'd been mostly doing then suddenly she was having like an epileptic fit, her mouth sprang open *Uh-uh-uh* and her tongue protruded wet with spittle and really ugly like a freak and Anita was backing off and whimpering She's going to die! oh God she's going to die! Jude do something she's going to die! and Jude slapped Anita's face to shut her up, Jude was so disgusted. Fat ass, get away. What the fuck do you know. Jude held the Corn Maiden down, the Corn Maiden's skinny arms and legs were shaking so, it was like she was trying to dance laying down and her eyes came open unseeing like a doll's dead glass eyes and Jude was kind of scared now and excited and climbed up onto the bier to lay on her, for maybe the Corn Maiden was cold, so skinny the cold had gotten into her bones, Jude's arms were stretched out like the Corn Maiden's arms and her hands were gripping the Corn Maiden's hands, her legs quivering stretched out the Corn Maiden's legs, and the side of her face against the Corn Maiden's face like they were twin girls hatched from the same egg. I am here, I am Jude I will protect you, in the Valley of the Shadow of Death I will protect you forever AMEN. Till finally the Corn Maiden ceased convulsing and was only just breathing in this long shuddering way, but she was breathing, she would be okay.

Still, Anita was freaked. Anita was trying not to laugh this wild hyena laugh you'd hear from her at school sometimes, like she was being tickled in a way she could not bear so Jude became disgusted and slapped Anita SMACK-SMACK on both cheeks calling her fat ass and stupid cunt and Anita ran out of the storage room like a kicked dog crying, we heard her on the stairs and Jude said, She's next.

On darkspeaklink.com where Jude O bonded with the Master of Eyes Jude showed us IF THERE IS A PERSON THERE IS A PROBLEM. IF THERE IS NO PERSON THERE IS NO PROBLEM. (STALIN)

Jude had never told the Master of Eyes that she was female or male and so the Master of Eyes believed her to be male. She had told him she had taken her captive, did he give her permission to Sacrifice? and the Master of Eyes shot back you are precocious/precious if 13 yrs old & where do you live Jude O? but the thought came to Jude suddenly the Master of Eyes was not her friend who dwelled in several places of the earth simultaneously but an FBI agent pretending to be her soul mate in order to capture her so Jude O disappeared from darkspeaklink.com forever.

YOU ASSHOLES! A SUICIDE NOTE

Jude O knew, it was ending. Four days preceding the Sacrifice and this was the sixth day. No turning back.

Denise was breaking down. Dull/dazed like she'd been hit over the head and in morning homeroom the teacher asked, Denise are you ill and at first Denise did not hear then shaking her head almost you could not hear her *no*.

Anita had not come to school. Anita was hiding away at home, and would betray Jude. And there was no way to get to Anita now, Jude was unable to silence the traitor.

Jude's disciples, she had trusted. Yet she had not truly trusted them knowing they were inferiors.

Denise was begging, Jude I think we better . . .

. . . let the Corn Maiden go?

Because because if she, if . . .

The Corn Maiden becomes Taboo. The Corn Maiden can never be released. Except if somebody takes the Corn Maiden's place the Corn Maiden can never be released.

You want to take the Corn Maiden's place?

Jude, she isn't the Corn Maiden she's M-Marissa Ban—

A flame of righteous fury came over Jude O, SMACK-SMACK with the palm and back of her hand she slapped the offensive face.

When spotted hyenas are born they are usually twins. One twin is stronger than the other and at once attacks the other hoping to tear out its throat and why, because the other would try to kill it otherwise. There is no choice.

At the table at the very rear of the cafeteria where Jude O and her disciples perceived as pathetic misfit losers by their Skatskill Day classmates usually ate their lunches together except today only Jude O and Denise Ludwig, and it was observed how Denise was whimpering and pleading with Jude wiping at her nose in a way repellent to the more fastidious girl who said through clenched jaws I forbid you to cry, I forbid you to make a spectacle of yourself, but Denise continued, and Denise whimpered and begged, and at last a flame of indignation swept over Jude who slapped Denise and Denise stumbled from the table overturning her chair, ran blubbering from the cafeteria in full view of staring others, and in that same instant it seemed that wily Jude O fled through a rear exit running crouched over to the middle school bicycle rack, and fueled by that same passion of indignation Jude bicycled 2.7 miles home to the old Trahern house on Highgate Avenue several times nearly struck by vehicles that swerved to avoid the blind-seeming cyclist and she laughed for she was feeling absolutely no fear now like a hawk riding the crest of an updraft scarcely needing to move its wings to remain aloft, and lethal. A hawk! Jude O was a hawk! If her bicycle had been struck and crushed, if she'd died on Highgate Avenue the Corn Maiden would molder in her bier of silks and brocades, unseen. No one would find the Corn Maiden for a long time.

It is better this way, we will die together.

She would not have requested a jury trial, you had to utter such bullshit to sway a jury. She would have requested a judge merely.

A judge is an aristocrat. Jude O was an aristocrat.

She would have been tried as an adult! Would have insisted.

In the gardener's shed there was a rusted old lawnmower. A can of gasoline half full. You poured the gasoline through the funnel if you could get it open. Jude had experimented, she could get it open.

Her grandmother's old silver lighter engraved with the initials *G.L.T.* Click-click-click and a transparent little bluish-orange flame appeared pretty as a flicking tongue.

She would immolate the Corn Maiden first.

No! Better to die together.

Telling herself calmly *It will only hurt at first. Just for a few seconds and by then it will be too late.*

She laughed to think of it. Like already it was done.

Stealthily entering the house by the rear door. So the old woman watching afternoon TV would not hear.

She was very excited! She was determined to make no error. Already forgetting that perhaps she had erred, allowing both her disciples to escape when she'd known that they were weakening. And confiding in the Master of Eyes believing she could trust him as her twin not recalling the spotted hyena twin, of course you could not trust.

Well, she had learned!

Forced herself to compose the Suicide Note. In her thoughts for a long time (it seemed so, now!) Jude had been composing this with care knowing its importance. It was addressed to *you assholes* for there was no one else.

Smiling to think how *you assholes* would be amazed.

On TV and on-line and in all the papers including *The New York Times* front page.

Whywhy you're asking here's why her hair.

I mean *her hair*! I mean like I saw it in the sun . . .

So excited! Heart beating fast like she'd swallowed a dozen E's. Unlocking the padlock with trembling hands. If Denise had told, already! *Should have killed them both last night. When I had the chance.* Inside the storage room, the Corn Maiden had shifted from the lying-on-her-side position in which Jude had left her that morning after making her eat. This was proof, the Corn Maiden was shrewdly pretending to be weaker than she was. Even in her sickness there was deceit.

Jude left the storage room door open, to let in light. She would not trouble to light the scented candles, so many candles there was not time. And flame now would be for a different purpose.

Squatting breathless over the Corn Maiden, with both thumbs lifting the bruised eyelids.

Milky eyes. Pupils shrunken.

Wake up! It's time it's time.

Feebly the Corn Maiden pushed at Jude. She was frightened, whimpering. Her breath smelled of something rotted. She had not been allowed to brush her teeth since coming to Jude's house, she had not been allowed to bathe herself. Only as Jude and her disciples had bathed her with wetted soapy washclothes.

Know what time it is it's time it's time it's timetimetime!

Don't hurt me please let me go . . .

Jude was the Taboo Priest. Seizing the Corn Maiden's long silky hair in her fist and forcing her down onto the bier scolding No no no no *no* like you would scold a baby.

A baby that is flesh of your flesh but you must discipline.

The immolation would have to be done swiftly, Jude knew. For that traitor-cunt Denise had babbled by now. Fat ass Anita had babbled. Her disciples had betrayed her, they were unworthy of her. They would be so sorry! She would not forgive them, though. Like she would not forgive the Corn Maiden's mother for staring at her like she was a bug or something, loathsome. What she regretted was she would not have time to cut out the Corn Maiden's heart as the Sacrifice demanded.

Lay still, I said it's *time.*

A new thought was coming to her now. She had not hold of it yet, the way you have not yet hold of a dream until it is fully formed like a magnificent bubble inside your head.

Jude had dragged the gasoline can into the storage room, and was spilling gasoline in surges. This could be the priest blessing the Corn Maiden and her bier. The stink of gasoline was strong, that was why the Corn Maiden was revived, her senses sharpening.

No! no! Don't hurt me let me go! I want my mother.

Jude laughed to see the Corn Maiden so rebellious. Actually pushing free of Jude, so weak she could not stand but on hands and knees naked crawling desperately toward the door. Never had Jude left the door open until now and yet the Corn Maiden saw, and comprehended this was escape. Jude smiled seeing how desperate the Corn Maiden, stark naked and her hair trailing the floor like an animal's mane. Oh so skin-and-bones! Her ribs, bony hips, even the ankle bones protruding. Skinny haunches no bigger than Jude's two hands fitted together. And her hinder. *Hinder* was a funny word, a word meant to make you smile. A long time ago a pretty curly-haired woman had been humming and singing daubing sweet-smelling white powder onto Jude's little *hinder* before drawing up her rubber underpants, pulling down Jude's smock embroidered with dancing kittens or maybe it had been a nightgown, and the underpants had been a diaper.

Jude watched, fascinated. She had never seen the Corn Maiden disobey her so openly! It was like a baby just learning to crawl. She had not known the Corn Maiden so desired to live. Thinking suddenly *Better for her to remain alive, to revere me. And I have made my mark on her she will never forget.*

The Priest was infused with the power. The power of life-and-death. She would confer life, it was her decision. Climbing onto the bier spilling gasoline in a sacred circle around her. The stink of gasoline made her sensitive nostrils constrict, her eyes were watering so she could barely see. But she had no need to see. All was within, that she wished to see. *It will only hurt at first. Then it will be too late.* Click-click-clicking the silver lighter with gasoline-slippery fingers until the bright little flame-tongue leapt out.

See what I can do assholes, you never could.

SEPTEMBER

The Little Family

It was their first outing together, at the Croton Falls Nature Preserve. The three of them, as a family.

Of course, Zallman was quick to concede, not an actual *family.*

For the man and woman were not married. Their status as friends/lovers was yet undefined. And the girl was the woman's child, alone.

Yet if you saw them, you would think *family.*

It was a bright warm day in mid-September. Zallman who now measured time in terms of before/after was thinking the date was exactly five months *after.* But this was a coincidence merely.

From Yonkers, where he now lived, Zallman drove north to Mahopac to pick up Leah Bantry and her daughter Marissa at their new home. Leah and Marissa had prepared a picnic lunch. The Croton Falls Nature Preserve, which Leah had only recently discovered, was just a few miles away.

A beautiful place, Leah had told Zallman. So quiet.

Zallman guessed this was a way of saying *Marissa feels safe here.*

Leah Bantry was working now as a medical technician at Woman/Space, a clinic in Mahopac, New York. Mikal Zallman was temporarily teaching middle school math at a large public school in Yonkers where he also assisted the soccer/basketball/baseball coach.

Marissa was enrolled in a small private school in Mahopac without grades or a formal curriculum in which students received special tutoring and counseling as needed.

Tuition at the Mahopac Day School was high. Mikal Zallman was helping with it.

No one can know what you and your daughter went through. I feel so drawn to you both, please let me be your friend!

Before Zallman had known Leah Bantry, he had loved her. Knowing her now he was confirmed in his love. He vowed to bear this secret lightly until Leah was prepared to receive it.

She wanted no more emotion in her life, Leah said. Not for a long time.

Zallman wondered: what did that mean? And did it mean what it meant, or was it simply a way of saying *Don't hurt me! Don't come near.*

He liked it that Leah encouraged Marissa to call him Uncle Mikal. This suggested he might be around for a while. So far, in Zallman's presence at least, Marissa did not call him anything at all.

Zallman saw the girl glance at him, sometimes. Quick covert shy glances he hesitated to acknowledge.

There was a tentative air about them. The three of them.

As if (after the media nightmare, this was quite natural) they were being observed, on camera.

Zallman felt like a tightrope walker. He was crossing a tightrope high above a gawking audience, and there was no safety net beneath. His arms were extended for balance. He was terrified of falling but he must go forward. If at this height your balance is not perfect, it will be lethal.

In the nature preserve in the bright warm autumnal sunshine the adults walked together at the edge of a pond. To circle the pond required approximately thirty minutes. There were other visitors to the preserve on this Sunday afternoon, families and couples.

The girl wandered ahead of the adults, though never far ahead. Her behavior was more that of a younger child than a child of eleven. Her movements were tentative, sometimes she paused as if she were out of breath. Her skin was pale and appeared translucent. Her eyes were deep-socketed, wary. Her pale blond hair shimmered in the sun. It had been cut short, feathery, falling to just below her delicate eggshell ears.

After her ordeal in April, Marissa had lost much of her beautiful long hair. She'd been hospitalized for several weeks. Slowly she had regained most of the weight she'd lost so abruptly. Still she was anemic, Leah was concerned that there had been lasting damage to Marissa's kidneys and liver. She suffered from occasional bouts of tachycardia, of varying degrees of severity. At such times, her mother held her tight, tight. At such times the child's runaway heartbeat and uncontrollable shivering seemed to the mother a demonic third presence, a being maddened by terror.

Both mother and daughter had difficulty sleeping. But Leah refused prescription drugs for either of them.

Each was seeing a therapist in Mahopac. And Marissa also saw Leah's therapist for a joint session with her mother, once a week.

Leah confided in Zallman, "It's a matter of time. Of healing. I have faith, Marissa will be all right."

Leah never used such terms as *normal, recovered.*

Mikal Zallman had been the one to write to Leah Bantry of course. He had felt the desperate need to communicate with her, even if she had not the slightest wish to communicate with him.

I feel that we have shared a nightmare. We will never understand it. I don't know what I can offer you other than sympathy, commiseration. During the worst of the nightmare I had almost come to think that I was responsible . . .

After Marissa was discharged from the hospital, Leah took her away from Skatskill. She could not bear living in that apartment another day, she could not bear all that reminded her of the nightmare. She was surrounded by well-intentioned neighbors, and through the ordeal she had made several friends; she had been offered work in the area. If she'd wished to return to work at the Nyack Clinic, very likely Davitt Stoop would have allowed her to return. He had reconciled with his wife, he was in a forgiving mood. But Leah had no wish to see the man again, ever. She had no wish to drive across the Tappan Zee Bridge again, ever.

Out of the ordeal had come an unexpected alliance with her sister Avril. While Marissa was in the hospital, Avril had continued to stay in Skatskill; one or the other of the two sisters was always in Marissa's hospital room. Avril had taken an unpaid leave from her job in Washington, she helped Leah find another job and to relocate in Mahopac, fifty miles north in hilly Putnam County.

Enough of Westchester County! Leah would never return.

She was so grateful for Avril's devotion, she found herself at a loss for words.

"Leah, come on! It's what any sister would do."

"No. It is not what any sister would do. It's what my sister would do. God damn I love you, Avril."

Leah burst into tears. Avril laughed at her. The sisters laughed together, they'd become ridiculous in their emotions. Volatile and unpredictable as ten-year-olds.

Leah vowed to Avril, she would never take anyone for granted again. Never anything. Not a single breath! Never again.

When they'd called her with the news: *Marissa is alive.*

That moment. Never would she forget that moment.

In their family only Avril knew: police had tracked Marissa's elusive father to Coos Bay, Oregon. There, he had apparently died in 1999 in a boating mishap. The medical examiner had ruled the cause of death "inconclusive." There had been speculation that he'd been murdered . . .

Leah hadn't been prepared for the shock she'd felt, and the loss.

Now, he would never love her again. He would never love his beautiful daughter again. He would never make things right between them.

She had never spoken his name aloud to Marissa. She would never speak it aloud. As a younger child Marissa used to ask Where is Daddy? When will Daddy come back? But now, never.

The death of Marissa's father in Coos Bay, Oregon, was a mystery, but it was a mystery Leah Bantry would not pursue. She was sick of mystery. She wanted only clarity, truth. She would surround herself with good decent truthful individuals for the remainder of her life.

Mikal Zallman agreed. No more mysteries!

You become exhausted, you simply don't care. You care about surviving. You care about the banalities of life: *closure, moving on.* Before the nightmare he'd have laughed at such TV talk-show jargon but now, no.

Of Leah Bantry and Mikal Zallman, an unlikely couple, Zallman was the more verbal, the more edgy. He was from a tribe of talkers, he told Leah. Lawyers, financiers, high-powered salesmen. A rabbi or two. For Zallman, just to wake up in the morning in Yonkers, and not in Skatskill, was a relief. And not in April, during that siege of nightmare. To lift his head from the pillow and not wince with pain as if broken glass were shifting inside his skull. To be able to open a newspaper, switch on TV news, without seeing his own craven likeness. To breathe freely, not-in-police-custody. Not the object of a mad girl's vengeance.

Mad girl was the term Zallman and Leah used, jointly. Never would they utter the name *Jude Trahern.*

Why had the mad girl abducted Marissa? Why, of all younger children she might have preyed upon, had she chosen Marissa? And why had she killed herself, why in such a gruesome way, self-immolation like a martyr? These questions would never be answered. The cowed girls who'd conspired with her in the abduction had not the slightest clue. Something about an Onigara Indian sacrifice! They could only repeat brainlessly that they hadn't thought the mad girl was serious. They had only just followed her direction, they had wanted to be her friend.

To say that the girl had been *mad* was only a word. But the word would suffice.

Zallman said in disgust, "To know all isn't to forgive all. To know all is to be sickened by what you know." He was thinking of the Holocaust, too: a cataclysm in history that defied all explanation.

Leah said, wiping at her eyes, "I would not forgive her, under any circumstances. She wasn't 'mad,' she was evil. She took pleasure in hurting others. She almost killed my daughter. I'm glad that she's dead, she's removed herself from us. But I don't want to talk about her, Mikal. Promise me."

Zallman was deeply moved. He kissed Leah Bantry then, for the first time. As if to seal an understanding.

Like Leah, Zallman could not bear to live in the Skatskill area any longer. Couldn't breathe!

Without exactly reinstating Zallman, the principal and board of trustees of Skatskill Day had invited him back to teach. Not immediately, but in the fall.

A substitute was taking his place at the school. It was believed to be most practical for the substitute to finish the spring term.

Zallman's presence, so soon after the ugly publicity, would be "distracting to students." Such young, impressionable students. And their anxious parents.

Zallman was offered a two-year renewable contract at his old salary. It was not a very tempting contract. His lawyer told him that the school feared a lawsuit, with justification. But Zallman said the hell with it. He'd lost interest in combat.

And he'd lost interest in computers, overnight.

Where he'd been fascinated by the technology, now he was bored. He craved something more substantial, of the earth and time. Computers were merely technique, like bodiless brains. He would take a temporary job teaching math in a public school, and he would apply to graduate schools to study history. A Ph.D. program in American studies. At Columbia, Yale, Princeton.

Zallman didn't tell Leah what revulsion he sometimes felt, waking before dawn and unable to return to sleep. Not for computers but for the Zallman who'd so adored them.

How arrogant he'd been, how self-absorbed! The lone wolf who had so prided himself on aloneness.

He'd had enough of that now. He yearned for companionship, someone to talk with, make love with. Someone to share certain memories that would otherwise fester in him like poison.

In late May, after Leah Bantry and her daughter Marissa had moved away from Skatskill—a departure excitedly noted in the local media—Zallman began to write to her. He'd learned that Leah had taken a position at a medical clinic in Mahopoc. He knew the area, to a degree: an hour's drive away. He wrote single-page, thoughtfully composed letter to her not expecting her to reply, though hoping that she might. *I feel so close to you! This ordeal that has so changed our lives.* He'd studied her photographs in the papers, the grieving mother's drawn, exhausted face. He knew that Leah Bantry was a few years older than he, that she was no longer in contact with Marissa's father. He sent her postcards of works of art: Van Gogh's sunflowers, Monet's water lilies, haunted landscapes of Caspar David Friedrich and gorgeous autumnal forests of Wolf Kahn. In this way Zallman courted Leah Bantry. He allowed this woman whom he had never met to know that he revered her. He would put no pressure on her to see him, not even to respond to him.

In time, Leah Bantry did respond.

They spoke on the phone. They made arrangements to meet. Zallman was nervously talkative, endearingly awkward. He seemed overwhelmed by Leah's physical presence. Leah was more wary, reticent. She was a beautiful woman who looked her age, she wore no makeup, no jewelry except a watch; her fair blond hair was threaded with silver. She smiled, but she did not speak much. She liked it that this man would do the talking, as men usually did not. Mikal Zallman was a personality of a type Leah knew, but at a distance. Very New York, very intense. Brainy, but naive. She guessed that his family had money, naturally Zallman scorned money. (But he'd been reconciled with his family, Zallman said, at the time of the ordeal. They had been outraged on his behalf and had insisted upon paying his lawyer's exorbitant fees.) During their conversation, Leah recalled how they'd first met at the Skatskill school, and how Zallman the computer expert had walked away from her. So arrogant! Leah would tease him about that, one day. When they became lovers perhaps.

Zallman's hair was thinning at the temples, there was a dented look to his cheeks. His eyes were those of a man older than thirty-one or -two. He'd begun to grow a beard, a goatee, to disguise his appearance, but you could see that it was a temporary experiment, it would not last. Yet Leah thought Mikal Zallman handsome, in his way rather romantic. A narrow hawkish face, brooding eyes. Quick to laugh at himself. She would allow him to adore her, possibly one day she would adore him. She was not prepared to be hurt by him.

Eventually she would tell him the not-quite-true *I never believed you were the one to take Marissa, Mikal. Never!*

The little family, as Zallman wished to think them, ate their picnic lunch, and what a delicious lunch it was, on a wooden table on the bank of a pond, beneath a willow tree so exquisitely proportioned it looked like a work of art in a children's storybook. He noted that Marissa still had trouble with food, ate slowly and with an air of caution, as if, with each mouthful, she was expecting to encounter broken glass. But she ate most of a sandwich, and half an apple Leah peeled for her, since "skins" made her queasy. And afterward tramping about the pond admiring snowy egrets and great blue herons and wild swans. Everywhere were lushly growing cattails, rushes, flaming sumac. There was a smell of moist damp earth and sunlight on water and in the underbrush red-winged blackbirds were flocking in a festive cacophony. Leah lamented, "But it's too soon! We're not ready for winter." She sounded genuinely hurt, aggrieved.

Zallman said, "But Leah, snow can be nice, too."

Marissa, who was walking ahead of her mother and Mr. Zallman, wanted to think this was so: *snow, nice.* She could not clearly remember snow. Last winter. Before April, and after April. She knew that she had lived for eleven years and yet her memory was a windowpane covered in cobwebs. Her therapists were kindly soft-spoken women who asked repeatedly about what had happened to her in the cellar of the old house, what the bad girls had done to her, for it was healthy to remember, and to speak of what she remembered, like draining an absess they said, and she should cry, too, and be angry; but it was difficult to have such emotions when she couldn't remember clearly. What are you feeling, Marissa, she was always being asked, and the answer was *I don't know* or *Nothing!* But that was not the right answer.

Sometimes in dreams she saw, but never with opened eyes.

With opened eyes, she felt blind. Sometimes.

The bad girl had fed her, she remembered. Spoon-fed. She'd been so hungry! So grateful.

All adults are gone. All our mothers.

Marissa knew: that was a lie. The bad girl had lied to her.

Still, the bad girl had fed her. Brushed her hair. Held her when she'd been so cold.

The sudden explosion, flames! The burning girl, terrible shrieks and screams—Marissa had thought at first it was herself, on fire and screaming. She was crawling upstairs but was too weak and she fainted and someone came noisy and shouting to lift her in his arms and it was three days later Mommy told her when she woke in the hospital, her head so heavy she could not lift it.

Mommy and Mr. Zallman. She was meant to call him "Uncle Mikal" but she could not.

Mr. Zallman had been her teacher in Skatskill. But he behaved as if he didn't remember any of that. Maybe Mr. Zallman had not remembered her, Marissa had not been one of the good students. He had only seemed to care for the good students, the others were invisible to him. He was not "Uncle Mikal" and it would be wrong to call him that.

At this new school everybody was very nice to her. The teachers knew who she was, and the therapists and doctors. Mommy said they had to know or they could not help her. One day, when she was older, she would move to a place where nobody knew Marissa Bantry. Away out in California.

Mommy would not wish her to leave. But Mommy would know why she had to leave.

At this new school, that was so much smaller than Skatskill Day, Marissa had a few friends. They were shy wary thin-faced girls like herself. They were girls who, if you only just glanced at them, you would think they were missing a limb; but then you would see, no they were not. They were *whole girls*.

Marissa liked her hair cut short. Her long silky hair the bad girls had brushed and fanned out about her head, it had fallen out in clumps in the hospital. Long hair made her nervous now. Through her fingers at school sometimes lost in a dream she watched girls with hair rippling down their backs like hers used to, she marveled they were oblivious to the danger.

They had never heard of the Corn Maiden! The words would mean nothing to them.

Marissa was a reader now. Marissa brought books everywhere with her, to hide inside. These were storybooks with illustrations. She read slowly, sometimes pushing her finger beneath the words. She was fearful of encountering words she didn't know, words she was supposed to know but did not know. Like a sudden fit of coughing. Like a spoon shoved into your mouth before you were ready. Mommy had said Marissa was safe now from the bad girls and from any bad people, Mommy would take care of her but Marissa knew from reading stories that this could not be so. You had only to turn the page, something would happen.

Today she had brought along two books from the school library: *Watching Birds!* and *The Family of Butterflies*. They were books for readers younger than eleven, Marissa knew. But they would not surprise her.

Marissa is carrying these books with her, wandering along the edge of the pond a short distance ahead of Mommy and Mr. Zallman. There are dragonflies in the cattails like floating glinting needles. There are tiny white moth-butterflies, and beautiful large orange monarchs with slow-pulsing wings. Behind Marissa, Mommy and Mr. Zallman are talking earnestly. Always they are talking, it seems.

Maybe they will be married and talk all the time and Marissa will not need to listen to them, she will be invisible.

A red-winged blackbird swaying on a cattail calls sharply to her.

In the Valley of the Shadow of Death I will protect you AMEN.

Walter Mosley

Walter Mosley has forged a successful mystery career in the tradition of authors like Chester Himes and Carroll John Daly, but he added the complex issue of race relations and an in-depth look at the lethal heart of a major city that few authors can even come close to. He is the author of twenty books and has been translated into twenty-one languages. His popular mysteries featuring Easy Rawlins and his friend Raymond "Mouse" Alexander began with *Devil in a Blue Dress*, which was made into the film of the same name starring Denzel Washington and Jennifer Beals. Others in the series were *A Red Death*, *White Butterfly*, *Black Betty*, *A Little Yellow Dog*, and *Bad Boy Brawley Brown*; a prequel to the Rawlins mysteries, *Gone Fishin'*, and a series of short stories collected in *Six Easy Pieces*. His other character, ex-con Socrates Fortlow, lives in Los Angeles, infusing his episodic tales with ethical and political considerations. Excerpts from his collection *Always Outnumbered, Always Outgunned: The Socrates Fortlow Stories* have been published in *Esquire*, *GQ*, *USA Weekend*, *Buzz*, and *Mary Higgins Clark Mystery Magazine*. One of these new stories was an O. Henry Award winner for 1996 and is featured in *Prize Stories 1996: The O. Henry Awards*, edited by William Abraham. In 1996 he was named the first Artist-in-Residence at the Africana Studies Institute, New York University. Since that residency, he has continued to work with the department, creating an innovative lecture series entitled "Black Genius" which brings diverse speakers from art, politics, and academe to discuss practical solutions to contemporary issues. Designed as a "public classroom" these lectures have included speakers ranging from Spike Lee to Angela Davis. In February 1999, a collection of these lectures was published with the title *Black Genius*, with a Mosley introduction and essay. This past year, Mosley returned to the mystery world with the debut of a new series. *Fearless Jones* is now available. Set in 1950s Los Angeles and introducing secondhand bookstore owner Paris Minton and his best friend, war veteran Fearless Jones, the novel is already garnering early praise. His most recent novels include a look at men in shades of black and white in *The Man in My Basement* and the novel *47*.

ARCHIBALD LAWLESS, ANARCHIST AT LARGE: WALKING THE LINE

Walter Mosley

1

I saw the first ad on a Tuesday in the *Wall Street Journal.*

> REQUIRED: SCRIBE
> A. LAWLESS IN THE TESSLA BUILDING

The next notice appeared on Thursday in the classified section of the daily *New York Times.*

> AAL LTD. SEEKS SCRIBE
> APPLY AT OFFICES IN TESSLA BUILDING

Then, the next week, on the back page of the *Village Voice* and in the classified section of the *Amsterdam News.*

> SCRIBE SOUGHT KL-5-8713

The last ads gave no address but I knew that it had to be put there by A. Lawless at AAL Ltd. in the Tessla Building. I called and got an answering machine.

"If you are applying for the position leave your name and number," a throaty woman's voice said. "And please let us know where you heard about the position."

Then came the tone.

"Felix Orlean," I said. I gave my phone number and added, "I saw your ad in the *Times*, the *Journal*, the *Amsterdan News*, and the *Village Voice*."

Much later that night, hours after I'd gone to sleep, the phone rang giving me a sudden fright. I was sure that my mother or father had gotten sick down home. I grabbed the phone and whined, "What? What's wrong?"

"Mr. Orlean?" He said *or-leen* not *or-le-ahn* as I pronounce my name.

"Yes? What's wrong?"

"Nothing's wrong, son," he sad in a deep gravelly voice that reminded me of Wallace Beery from the old films. "Why would you think something's wrong?"

"What time is it?"

"I just went through the tape," he said. "You were the only one who saw all four ads. Do you read all those New York papers?"

"Yeah," I said. "The *Washington Post* too. And the *International Herald Tribune* when I can get it."

I turned on the light next to my bed to see the clock but was blinded by the glare.

"Are you a student?" he asked.

"Yeah," I said. "At Columbia." If I had been more awake I wouldn't have been so open.

"Come to the office this morning," he said. "I'll be in by five but you don't have to get there till ten to six."

"Huh?"

He hung up and my eyesight cleared enough to see that it was three forty-five.

I wondered what kind of man did his work at that time. And what would possess him to call a potential employee hours before the sun came up? Was he crazy? Must be, I thought. Of course I had no intention of going to his office at six A.M. or at any other time. I turned out the light and pulled the covers up to my chin but sleep did not return.

I had been intrigued for days about the job description of *scribe*. I had thought it was just a fancy way to say secretary who takes dictation. But after the call I wasn't so sure. Who was A. Lawless? Was it that cool woman's voice on the answering machine? No. It had to be the raspy late-night caller.

What kind of job could it be?

"It's too bad yo' daddy and them named you Felix," Aunt Alberta, the Ninth Ward fence, said to me once. And when I asked her why she said, " 'Cause that's a cartoon cat and we all know what curiosity do for a cat."

I loved my Aunt Alberta. She's the one who encouraged me when I wanted to come up to New York to study journalism. My parents had always planned on me becoming a lawyer like my father, and his father. Even my great grandfather had studied law, although he wasn't able to get a license to practice in Louisiana. In those days colored lawyers, even extremely light ones, were rare down south.

My father had harangued me for a week to stop my foolishness and make a decision about which law school to attend. I finally told him that Alberta thought it was a good idea for me to try journalism.

"And how would you know what Alberta thinks?" he asked. My father is a big man but I'm just small, taking after the men on my mother's side.

"I asked her," I said shaking a little under the shadow of JP Orlean.

"You what?"

"I went down to the county jail and saw her, poppa." I closed my eyes involuntarily, expecting to be knocked on my can.

I had been hit by my father before. He was a violent man. *Stern but fair*, my mother used to say. But I never saw what was fair about whipping a child with a strap until red welts rose up all over his body.

"I thought I told you that Alberta Hadity is no longer to be considered family," my father said in a voice as quiet as the breeze.

And that was my chance. After twenty-one years of obeying my father, or lying to him, the gate was open. All I had to do was stay quiet. All I had to do was keep my mouth shut and he would see it as insubordination.

I looked down at his brown shoes. Blutcher's we called them down south. They're known as wing tips in New York. Chub Wilkie, I knew, had shined those shoes that morning. He shined my father's shoes every week day morning. JP used to say that Chub Wilkie was the finest man in the law building where he practiced. But he never invited Mr. Wilkie to dinner as he did the law partners at Hermann, Bledsoe, and Orlean.

Mr. Wilkie was too dark-skinned and too poor to be seen on our social level.

My father and mother were no more than café au lait in their coloring. My sister and I were lighter even than that.

"Well?" my father said. I could feel the weight of his stare on my neck.

It was a great concession for him to ask anything of me. I was supposed to say that I was sorry, that I would never speak to my felon auntie again. The words formed in my mouth but I kept my teeth clamped down on them.

"I expect you out of the house before your mother returns home," he said.

But still he hesitated.

I knew that he expected me to fold, to gasp out an apology and beg for his indulgence. I had always lived at home, never worked a day in my life. But as dependent as I was on my father I was just as stubborn too.

After another minute the shoes carried him from the family den. I looked up and out of the glass doors that led to the garden at the back of the house. I knew then that it would be the last time I ever saw my mother's orchid and lily garden.

I almost yelled for joy.

After reliving my exile from the Orlean family sleep was impossible. At five I got out of bed and went to the tiny kitchen that separated my room from my soccer-star roommate, Lonnie McKay. I heated water in a saucepan instead of the kettle so as not to wake him.

Lonnie had a full scholarship in the engineering school for captaining the fledgling Columbia Ciceros (pronounced by those in the know as Kickeros). I had to borrow the thirty thousand dollars a year and then get part-time jobs to pay the outrageous rent and for anything else I might need—like instant coffee.

I poured the hot water and mixed in the freeze-dried flakes. The coffee was bitter and yet tasteless but that was all right by me. The bitter taste was my life, that's what I was thinking.

And then I looked up.

The long red velvet curtain that covered Lonnie's doorway fluttered and a young woman walked through. There was only the small forty-watt bulb lighting the kitchen but I could see that she was naked except for the tan bikini panties. An inch shorter than I with smallish but shapely breasts. Her hair was long curly brown and her eyes were large. She was slender and pale skinned but somehow I knew that she was a colored woman, girl really—not more than nineteen. When she saw me she smiled, crossed her hands over her breasts, and sat down on the chair across from where I was standing.

"Hi," she said, smiling with false modesty.

"Hi." I looked away to hide my embarrassment.

"You must be Felix."

Forcing my head back I looked her in the eye. Eyes. They were light brown and laughing, full of life and encouraging me to stay where I was, not to run back to my room which is what I wanted to do more than anything.

"Yes," I said. I stepped forward and held out my hand like I always did when someone called me by name.

She looked at my hand, hesitated, then shifted, managing to keep her modesty and take my hand at the same time.

"Arrett," she said. "I'm a friend of Lonnie's."

"Pleased to meet you," I said.

We stared at each other for a moment, and then a moment more. Arrett seemed to be suppressing a laugh. I would have loved to see that laugh.

"Why are you up so early?" she asked.

"Going to apply for a job," I said. And there it was. My future was sealed. A near naked woman stumbling across my path in the early hours of the morning and I was thrown out of my orbit. My whole life had changed because of a girl I'd probably never see again.

Mr. Lawless would have said that it was my fate, that the moment he heard my light New Orleans drawl he knew that we were meant to come together.

"What kind of job?" she asked.

"I don't know."

She grinned and I felt my heart swell up in my chest.

A sound issued from Lonnie's room. It might have been her name.

"He wants me," she said. It was almost a question.

I almost said, *don't go*.

"Ari," Lonnie called from behind the red curtain.

She got up, forgetting her modesty, and said, "We'll see each other at school," and then ran through the red fabric into my roommate's den.

I sat down and considered going back to bed. But then Lonnie's first sigh of pleasure pierced the air. I hurried to my room, dressed and left the apartment before they could fill the house with their love.

2

The Tessla building is on West 38th Street. It's not the biggest building in midtown Manhattan but it's up there. Sixty-nine stories. The glass doors are modern but the lobby is thirties art deco to the max. Black, white, and red tiles of marble cover the floor in vaguely Egyptian designs. The marble on the walls is gray and light blue. A huge painting behind the guard's stone counter is of a bare-breasted, golden skinned Joan of Arc leading her French army out of a sun that you just know represents God.

"Yes?" the guard asked me. "Can I help you?"

"AAL Limited," I said.

The man behind the counter was African, I believed. His features were purely Negroid. The round head and almost almond shaped eyes, the dark skin had no blemishes and his lips seemed chiseled they were so perfect. My sister went out with a man like this for two weeks once and our parents decided to send her to Paris for two years. She was still there for all that I knew.

The man's eyes rose as a smile curved his sensual mouth.

"Mr. Lawless wants to see you?"

"I guess," I said. "He said to get here by ten to six."

"That's Mr. Lawless. No visitors after five fifty-five. He told me that himself," the guard said, sounding a little like he'd learned to speak English from an Englishman. "What do you do?"

"I'm a student," I said. "I study journalism."

This answer seemed to disappoint the young guard. He shrugged his shoulders as if to say, too bad.

"Fifty-two eleven," he said. "Take the last elevator on the right. It's the only one we have working this early."

It was a utility elevator. Thick matting like gray bedspreads were hung over the walls to protect them from harm when heavy objects were moved. I pushed the button and the door closed but there was no sense of motion. A couple of times I looked up at the small screen that should have shown the floors as they passed by but the number was stuck at twelve.

Finally, after a long interval the doors opened and I got out wondering if I was on the right floor. The walls were painted the palest possible green and the floor was tiled with white stone veined in violet and dark jade. Two arrows on the wall opposite the elevator door pointed in either direction. Right was 5220 to 5244 and left was 5200 to 5219.

I turned left. After I passed the first few offices I realized that the door at the dead end of the hall was my destination.

That door was different than the rest. From the distance it seemed to be boarded up as if it were under construction or condemned. Five or six weathered boards were nailed into place, lengthwise but not neatly at all. Two shorter boards were nailed across these, more or less vertically. There was something that I couldn't discern hanging midway down the left side of the door.

I passed Tweed's Beads and then Thunderstruck, Personal Dating Service. I was wondering what other kind of date there was, other than personal that is, when I realized that the object hanging from the door at the end of the hall was a handmade doll with a black face and a striped yellow and red dress. The dress was painted on the cylindrical body made from a toilet paper roll or something like that.

The voodoo doll stopped me for moment. I'd seen many such fetishes in Louisiana. They're all over the French Quarter, for tourists mainly. But hanging there, from that boarded-up door, the manißkin took on a sinister air.

What the hell was a voodoo doll doing there on the fifty-second floor of a skyscraper in New York City?

I gritted my teeth and took a deep breath through my nostrils. Then I walked forward.

There wasn't any doorknob or door that I could see. Just the grayed planking nailed to either side of the doorway covering something black and wooden behind. The doll had a slack grin painted on her round head. She seemed to be leering at me.

"Go on," I said to the doll.

I rapped on the boards.

No answer.

After a reasonable pause I knocked again.

No answer.

My fear of the doll was quickly being replaced by fury. What kind of trick was being played on me? Was the guard downstairs in on it? Did Lonnie put Arrett out there to run me out of the house?

My fingernails were pressing hard against my palms when a voice said, "Who's out there?"

There was no mistaking that raspy tone.

"Mr. Lawless?"

"Orleen?"

"Yes. I mean yes sir." The latter was added because I was raised on good manners down home.

The door opened into the room, which surprised me. The planks were arranged to give the illusion of a boarded-up portal but really they were cut to allow the door, boards and all, to open inward.

The man standing there before me had no double in the present day world or in history. He stood a solid six three or four with skin that was deep amber. His hair, which was mostly dark brown and gray, had some reddish highlights twined into a forest of thick dreadlocks that went straight out nine inches from his head, sagging only slightly. The hair resembled a royal headdress, maybe even a crown of thorns but Mr. A. Lawless was no victim. His chest and shoulders were unusually broad even for a man his size. His eyes were small and deep set. The forehead was round and his high cheekbones cut strong slanting lines down to his chin which gave his face a definite heart shape. There was no facial hair and no wrinkles except at the corners of his eyes.

His stomach protruded from his open fatigue jacket but it didn't sag or seem soft against the buttoned-up rose colored shirt. His pants were tan and shapeless. His big feet were bare.

A. Lawless was forty-five or maybe sixty. But even a rowdy with a baseball bat would have thought twice before taking a swing at him.

"Orleen?" he asked me again.

"Yes sir."

"Come in, come." He gestured with hands that were small compared to the rest of the him. But that only reminded me of stories I'd read about the Brown Bomber, Joe Louis. He had small hands too.

Mr. Lawless went around me to close the boarded door. He threw three bolts down the side and then flipped down a bronze piece of metal at the base that served a buttress against anyone forcing their way in.

"Just so we don't have any unwanted guests," he said. Then he led the way back to the interior.

I followed my host through a moderate sized room that had a dark wood floor and wooden furniture that wasn't of this century or the last. Just a couple of tables with a chair and a cushionless couch. The thick pieces had seen a lot of use in the past hundred years or so but they were well varnished and sturdy.

There were two doors at the back of the room. Straight ahead was a frosted glass door that had no writing on it. Immediately to the left was an oak door upon which the word STORAGE was stenciled in highlighted gold lettering.

We went through the untitled glass door into a smallish room that I figured to be his office. At the back of the room was a window that had an unobstructed view of the Hudson River and New Jersey beyond. It was about six and the sun was just falling upon our misty neighbor state. There was a dark wood swivel chair next to the window, behind a small desk which was only large enough for the laptop computer that sat on it.

The room was filled with a musky odor that, while neither sweet nor sour, carried a pleasant notion. This odor I later came to associate with Archibald Lawless's life. He pervaded any situation with his presence and half-civilized genius.

The wall to my left had a series of shelves that held various oddities. There was a crusty old toy chest and a child's baby doll with a red sash around its throat. There was a rattlesnake suspended in fluid in a large jar, a parchment scroll tied with string, a replica of a human skull, a small stuffed animal (I didn't know what species at the time), and a necklace: a piece of costume jewelry in a plastic case held up by a W-shaped metal frame. This necklace was made up of gaudy pieces of glass representing emeralds and rubies mainly, with a ribbon of fake diamonds snaking through. There were other pieces on the shelves but that's all I was able to make out on first sight.

The wall opposite the shelves was dominated by a giant blown-up photograph rendered in sepia tones. It was the face of some German or Russian from a bygone age. The man, whoever he was, had a big mustache and a wild look in his eye. I would have said it was a picture of Nietzsche but I knew it wasn't him because I had just finished reading *Thus Spoke Zarathustra* for a class called the History of the West and there was a photograph of the German philosopher on the cover of the book.

"Bakunin," A. Lawless said. "It's Bakunin."

"The anarchist?"

"He's why I'm here today talking to you. And he's why you're here today talking to me."

"Oh," I said trying to think of a way into the conversation.

"Sit down," the big man said.

I noticed that there were two tree trunks diagonally across from the swivel chair. Real tree trunks, plucked right out of the ground. Each one was about two and a half feet high with curves carved into them for a comfortable seat.

I sat.

"Archibald Lawless Anarchist at Large," my host said formally. He sat in the swivel chair and leaned back.

"What does that mean exactly?"

"What do you think it means?"

"That you plan to overthrow the government in hopes of causing a perpetual state of chaos throughout the world?"

"They aren't much on reality at Xavier or Columbia, are they?"

I didn't remember telling him that I did my undergrad work at Xavier but I didn't remember much before Arrett.

"What do you do?" I asked.

"I walk the line."

"What line?"

"Not," he said raising an instructive finger, "what line but the line between what forces?"

"Okay," I said. "The line between what forces?"

"I walk the line between chaos and the man."

3

Archibald Lawless brought two fingers to his lower lip speculating, it seemed, about me and how I would fill the job opening.

But by then I had decided against taking the position. I found his presence disturbing. If he offered me a cup of tea I'd take it out of civility, but I wouldn't swallow a drop.

Still, I was intrigued. The line between chaos and the man seemed a perfect personal realization of the philosophy he followed. It brought to mind a wild creature out at the edges of some great, decaying civilization. Interesting for a college paper but not as a profession.

I had just begun considering how to refuse if he offered me the job when a knock came on the front door of the office. Three fast raps and then two slower ones.

"Get that will you, Felix?" Lawless said.

I didn't want to sound off so I went back through the Americana room and said, "Yes," through the door.

"Carlos for A L," a slightly Spanish, slightly street accented voice answered.

I didn't know what to do so I threw the locks, kicked up the buttress, and opened the door.

The man was my height, slight and obviously with a preoccupation for the color green. He wore a forest green three-button suit over a pale green shirt with a skinny dark green tie.

His shoes were reptile definitely and also green. His skin was olive. He was past forty, maybe past fifty.

"Hey, bro," Carlos said and I really didn't know what to make of him.

"Wait here please," I said.

He nodded and I went back to Archibald Lawless's office. The anarchist was sitting back in his chair, waiting for my report.

"It's a guy named Carlos. He's all in green. I didn't ask what he wanted."

"Come on in, Carlos!" Archibald shouted.

The green man came in pushing open the office door.

"Hey, Mr. Big," Carlos greeted.

"What you got for me?"

"Not too much. They say he was drinking, she wasn't but she was just some girl he'd picked up at the bar."

"Couldn't you get any more?" Lawless wasn't upset but there was a certain insistence to his query.

"Maria tried, man, but they don't have it on the computer and the written files were sent to Arizona three hours after they were done. The only reason she got that much was that she knows a guy who works in filing. He sneaked a look for her."

Lawless turned away from Carlos and me and looked out over New Jersey.

"How's your mother?" Lawless asked Hoboken.

"She's fine," Carlos responded. "And Petey's doin' real good in that school you got him into."

"Tell him hello for me when you see him," Lawless said. He swiveled around and leveled his murky eyes at the green man. "See you later, Carlos."

"You got it, Mr. Big. Any time."

Carlos turned to go. I noticed that he seemed nervous. Not necessarily scared but definitely happy to be going. I followed him to the front door and threw all the locks into place after him.

When I returned Lawless was pulling on heavy work boots. He nodded toward a tree stump and I sat.

"Do you know what a scribe does?" he asked.

"I don't know if I'm really interested—"

"Do you know what a scribe does?" he asked again, cutting me off.

"They were monks or something," I said. "They wrote out copies of the bible before there was printing or moveable type."

"That's correct," he said sounding like one of my professors. "They also wrote for illiterate lords. Contracts, peace treaties, even love letters." Lawless smiled. "How much do you know about Bakunin?"

"Just his name."

"He was a great man. He knew about all the gross injustices of Stalin before Stalin was born. He was probably the greatest political thinker of the twentieth century and he didn't even live in that century. But do you know what was wrong with him?"

"No sir."

"He was a man of action and so he didn't spend enough time writing cohesive documents of his ideas. Don't get me wrong, he wrote a lot. But he never created a comprehensive document detailing a clear idea of anarchist political organization. After he died the writing he left behind made many small-minded men see him as a crackpot and a fool. I don't intend for my legacy to be treated like that."

"And that's why you need a scribe?"

"Mainly." He turned to watch Jersey again. "But also I need a simple transcriber. Someone to take my notes and scribbles and to make sense out of them. To document what I'm trying to do."

"That's all?"

"Mostly. There'll be some errands. Maybe even a little research, you know—investigative work. But any good journalism student should love doing some field work."

"I didn't tell you I was a journalism student."

"No, you didn't. But I know a lot about you, Felix Orlean," he said, pronouncing my name correctly this time. "That's why I put that old doll of mine on the door, I wanted to see if you were superstitious. I know about your father too, Justin Proudfoot Orlean, a big time lawyer down in Louisiana. And your mother, Katherine Hadity, was a medical student before she married your father and decided to commit her life to you and your sister Rachel who now goes by the name Angela in the part of London called Brixton."

He might as well have hit me over the head with a twelve-pound ham. I didn't know that my mother had been a medical student but it made sense since she had always wanted Rachel to be a doctor. I didn't know that Rachel had moved to England.

"Where'd you get all that?"

"And that's another thing." Lawless cut his eyes at the laptop on the tiny desk. Then he held up that educational finger. "No work that you do for me goes on the computer. I want to wait until we get it right to let the world in on our work."

"I'm not w-working for you, Mr. Lawless," I said, hating myself for the stutter skip.

"Why not?"

"I don't know what you do for one thing," I said. "And I don't like people calling me at any hour of the night. You have your doors boarded up and you call yourself an anarchist. Some guy who looks like a street thug comes in to make some kind of report."

"I told you what I do. I'm an anarchist who wants to keep everything straight. From the crazed politico who decides that he can interfere with the rights of others because he's got some inside track on the truth to the fascist mayor trying to shut down the little guy so he can fill his coffers with gold while reinventing the police state.

"I'm the last honest man, an eastern cowboy. And you, Mr. Orlean, you are a young man trying to make something of himself. Your father's a rich man but you pay your own way. He wanted you to become a lawyer, I bet, and you turned your back on him in order to be your own man. That's half the way to me, Felix. Why not see what more there is?"

"I can take care of my own life, Mr. Lawless," I said. "The only thing I need from a job is money."

"How much money?"

"Well, my rent which is five-fifty a month and then my other expenses. . . ."

"So you need forty-two thousand, before taxes, that is if you pay taxes." I had come up with the same number after an afternoon of budgeting.

"Of course I pay my taxes," I said.

"Of course you do," Lawless said, smiling broadly. "I'll pay you what you need for this position. All you have to do is agree to try it out for a few weeks."

I glanced at the blow-up of Bakunin and thought about the chance this might be. I needed the money. My parents wouldn't even answer one of my letters much less finance my education.

"I'm not sure," I said.

"About what?"

"The line you're talking about," I said. "It sounds like some kind of legal boundary. One side is law abiding and the other isn't."

"You're just an employee, Felix. Like anyone working for Enron or Hasbro. No one there is held responsible for what their employers may or may not have done."

"I won't do anything illegal."

"Of course you won't," Lawless said.

"I have to put my school work first."

"We can make your hours flexible."

"If I don't like what's happening I'll quit immediately," I said. "No prior notice."

"You sound more like a law student than a news hound," Lawless said. "But believe me I need you, Felix. I don't have the time to read every paper. If I know you're going through five or six of the big ones that'll take a lot of pressure off of me. And you'll learn a lot here. I've been around. From the guest of royalty in Asia to the prisons of Turkey and Mexico."

"No law breaking for me," I said again.

"I heard you." Lawless took a piece of paper from the ledge on the window behind him and handed it to me. "Over the next couple of days I'd like you to check up on these people."

"What do you mean?"

"Nothing questionable, simply check to see that they're around. Try to talk to them yourself but if you can't just make sure that they're there, and that they're okay."

"You think these people might be in trouble?"

"I don't worry about dolls hanging from doorknobs," he said. "They don't mean a thing to me. I'm just looking into a little problem that I picked up on the other day."

"Maybe you should call the police."

"The police and I have a deal. I don't talk to them and they don't listen to me. It works out just fine."

4

I wanted to talk more but Lawless said that he had his day cut out for him.

"I've got to go out but you can stay," he said. "The room next door will be your workplace. Here let me show you."

My new employer stood up. As I said, he's a big man. There seemed to be something important in even this simple movement. It was as if some stone monolith were suddenly sentient and moving with singular purpose in the world.

The room labeled STORAGE was narrow, crowded with boxes and untidy. There was a long table covered with papers, both printed and handwritten, and various publications. The boxes were cardboard, some white and some brown. The white ones had handwritten single letters on their fitted lids, scrawled in red. The brown ones on the whole were open at the top with all sorts of files and papers stacked inside.

"The white ones are my filing cabinet," Lawless said. "The

brown ones are waiting for you to put them in order. There's a flat stack of unconstructed file boxes in the corner under the window. When you need a new one just put it together." He waved at a pile of rags set upon something in the corner.

"What's that?" I asked, pointing at a pink metal box that sat directly under the window.

"It's the only real file cabinet but we don't keep files in there." He didn't say anything else about it and I was too busy trying to keep up to care.

Through the window an ocean liner was making its way up river. It was larger than three city blocks.

"The papers are all different," Lawless said. "The legal sheets are my journal entries, reports, and notes. These you are to transcribe. The mimeod sheets are various documents that have come to me. I need you to file them according to the way the rest of the files work. If you have any questions just ask me."

The liner let out a blast from its horn that I heard faintly through the closed window.

"And these newsletters," he said and then paused.

"What about them?"

"These newsletters I get from different places. They're very, very specialized." He was holding up a thick stack of printed materials. "Some of them come from friends around the world. Anarchist and syndicalist communes in America and elsewhere, in the country and the cities too. One of them's an Internet commune. That one will be interesting to keep tabs on; see if they got something there."

The big man stopped speaking for a moment and considered something. Maybe it was the Internet anarchist commune or maybe it was a thought that passed through his mind while talking. In the weeks to come I was to learn how deeply intuitive this man was. He was like some pre-Columbian shaman looking for signs in everything; talking to gods that even his own people had no knowledge of.

"Then there are the more political newsletters. The friendlies include various liberation movements and ecological groups. And of course there's Red Tuesday. She gathers up reports of problems brewing around the world. Dictators rising, infrastructures failing, and the movements of various players in the international killkill games."

"The what?"

"How do you kill a snake?" he asked grabbing me by the arm with a frighteningly quick motion.

I froze and wondered if it was too late to tell him that I didn't want the job.

"Cut off his head," Lawless informed me. "Cut off his head." He let me go and held out his hands in wonder. "To the corporations and former NATO allies this whole world is a nest of vipers. They have units, killkill boys Red Tuesday calls them. These units remove the heads of particularly dangerous vipers. Some of them are well known. You see them on TV and in courtroom cases. Others move like shadows. Red tries to keep tabs on them. She has a special box for the killkill boys and girls just so they know that somebody out there has a machete for their fangs too."

He said this last word like a breathy blast on a toy whistle. It made me laugh.

"Not funny," he told me. "Deadly serious. If you read Red's letters you will know more than any daily papers would ever dare tell you."

I wondered, not for the last time, about my employer's sanity.

"She's crazy of course," Lawless said as though he had read my mind.

"Excuse me?"

"Red. She's crazy. She also has a soap box about the pope. She's had him involved in every conspiracy from that eyeball on the dollar bill to frozen aliens in some Vatican subbasement."

"So how can you trust anything she says?"

"That's just it, son," Lawless said boring those pinpoint eyes into mine. "You can't trust anyone, not completely. But you can't afford not to listen. You have to listen, examine, and then make up your own mind."

The weight of his words settled in on me. It was a way of thinking that produced a paranoia beyond paranoia.

"That sounds like going into the crazy house and asking for commentary on the nightly news," I said, trying to make light of his assertions.

"If the world is insane then you'd be a fool to try and look for sanity to answer the call." Archibald Lawless looked at me with that great heart-shaped face. His bright skin and crown of thorns caused a quickening in my heart.

"The rest of these newsletters and whatnot are from the bad guys. White supremacist groups, pedophile target lists, special memos from certain key international banks. Mostly it's nothing but sometimes it allows you to make a phone call, or something." Again he drifted off into space.

I heard the threat in his voice with that *or something* but by then I knew I had to spend at least a couple of hours with those notes. My aunt Alberta was right about my curiosity. I was always sticking my nose where it didn't belong.

"So you can spend as much time as you want making yourself at home around here. The phone line can be used calling anywhere on the planet but don't use the computer until I show you what's what there." He seemed happy, friendly. He imparted that élan to me. "When you leave just shut the door. It will engage all the locks by itself, electrically."

As he opened the door to leave my storage office, I asked, "Mr. Lawless?"

"Yeah, son?"

"I don't get it."

"Get what?"

"With all this Red Tuesday, pedophiliac, white supremacist stuff how can you know that you should trust me? I mean all you've done is read some computer files. All that could be forged, couldn't it?"

He smiled and instead of answering my question he said, "You're just like a blank sheet of paper, Orleen. Maybe a name and a date up top but that's all and it's in pencil. You could be my worst nightmare, Felix. But first we've got to get some words down on paper." He smiled again and went out of his office. I followed.

He threw the bolts open and kicked up the buttress. Then he pulled open the door. He made to go out and then thought of something, turned and pointed that teacher's finger at me again.

"Don't open this door for anybody. Not for anyone but me. Don't answer it. Don't say anything through it. You can use this," he tapped a small video monitor that was mounted on the wall to the right of the door, "to see, but that's it."

"W-why?" I stammered.

"The landlord and I have a little dispute going."

"What kind of dispute?"

"I haven't paid rent in seven years and he thinks that it's about time that I did."

"And you don't?"

"The only truth in the bible is where it says that stuff about money and evil," he said and then he hurried out. The door closed behind him, five seconds later the locks all flipped down and the buttress lowered. I noticed then that there was a network of wires that led from the door to a small black box sitting underneath the cushionless couch.

The box was connected to an automobile battery. Even in a blackout Archibald Lawless would have secure doors.

5

I spent that morning inside the mind of a madman or a genius or maybe outside of what Lawless refers to as *the hive mind, the spirit that guides millions of heedless citizens through the aimless acts of everyday life.*

The mess on my office table was a treasure trove of oddities and information. Xeroxed copies of *wanted* posters, guest lists to conservative political fund raisers, blueprints of corporate offices and police stations. Red Tuesday's newsletter had detailed information about the movements of certain *killkills* using their animal code names (like Bear, Ringed Hornet, and Mink). She was less forthcoming about certain saboteurs fighting for anything from ecology to the liberation of so-called political prisoners. For these groups she merely lauded their actions and gave veiled warnings about how close they were to discovery in various cities.

Lawless was right about her and the Catholic Church. She also had a box in each issue surrounded by a border of red and blue crosses in which she made tirades against Catholic crack houses paying for political campaigns and other such absurdities. Even the language was different. This article was the only one that had misspellings and bad grammar.

At the back of every Red Tuesday newsletter, on page four, was an article signed only in the initials AAL. Everything else was written by Red Tuesday. This regular column had a title, REVOLUTIONARY NOTES. After flipping through about fifteen issues I found one column on Archie and the rent.

Never give an inch to the letter of the law if it means submitting to a lie. Your word is your freedom not your bond. If you make a promise, or a promise is made to you, it is imperative that you make sure the word, regardless of what the law says, is upheld. Lies are the basis for all the many crimes that we commit every day. From petty theft to genocide it is a lie that makes it and the truth that settles the account.

Think of it! If only we made every candidate for office responsible for every campaign promise she made. Then you'd see a democracy that hasn't been around for a while. My own landlord promised me whitewashed walls and a red carpet when I agreed to pay his lousy rent. He thought the lie would go down easy, that he could evict me because I never signed a contract. But he had lied. When I took his rooms for month to month he needed the rent and told me that a contract wasn't necessary. He told me that he'd paint and lay carpet, but all that was lies.

It's been years and I'm still here. He hasn't painted or made a cent. I brought him to court and I won. And then, because a man who lies cannot recognize the truth, he sent men to run me out . . .

Never lie and never lie down for a lie. Live according to your word and the world will find its own balance.

I was amazed by the almost innocent and idealistic prattle of such an obviously intelligent man.

The thought of a landlord sending up toughs to run me out of the rooms stopped my lazy reading and sent me out on the job I had been given.

The first person on my list was Valerie Lox. She was a commercial real estate broker on Madison Avenue, just above an exclusive jewelry store. I got there at about eleven forty-five. The offices were small but well appointed. The building was only two floors and the roof had a skylight making it possible for all of the lush green plants to flourish between the three real estate agents' desks.

"Can I help you?" a young Asian man at the desk closest to the door asked.

I suppressed the urge to correct him. *May I*, my mother inside me wanted to say. But I turned my head instead looking out of the window onto posh Madison. Across the street was a furrier, a fancy toy store, and a German pen shop.

"Yes," I said. "I want to see Ms. Lox."

The young man looked me up and down. He didn't like my blue jeans and ratty, secondhand Tibetan sweater—this college wear wasn't designed for Madison Avenue consumption.

"My father is thinking of opening a second office in Manhattan and he wanted me to see what was available," I further explained.

"And your father is?" Another bad sentence.

"JP Orlean of Herman, Bledsoe, and Orlean in New Orleans."

"Wait here." The young man uttered these words, rose from his chair, and walked away.

The two young women agents, one white and the other honey brown, looked from me to the young man as he made his way past them and through a door at the back of the garden room.

I was missing my seminar on the History of the West but that didn't bother me much. I could always get the notes from my friend Claude. And working for Lawless promised to hone my investigative potentials.

"Making sense out of a seemingly incomprehensible jumble of facts." That's what Professor Ortega said at the first lecture I attended at Columbia. His class was called the Art in Article.

I wasn't sure what Lawless was looking for but that didn't worry me. I knew enough from my father's practice to feel safe from involvement in any crime. The test was that even if I went to the police there was nothing concrete I could tell them that they didn't already know.

I was beginning to wonder where the agent had gone when he and a small woman in a dark blue dress came out of the door in back. He veered off and the woman walked straight toward me.

"Mr. Orlean?" she asked with no smile.

"Ms. Lox?" I did smile.

"May I see some form of identification?"

This shocked. When did a real estate agent ask for anything but a deposit? But I took out my wallet and showed her my student ID and Louisiana driver's license. She looked them over carefully and then invited me to follow her into the back.

The head woman's office was no larger than an alcove, there was no skylight or window. Her workstation was a one-piece, salmon pink high school desk next to which sat a short black filing cabinet. She sat and put on a telephone headset, just an earphone and a tiny microphone in front of her mouth.

I stayed standing even though there was a visitor's chair, because I had my manners to maintain.

"Sit," she said, not unkindly.

I did so.

Valerie Lox was a mild blend of contradictions. Her pale skin seemed hard, almost ceramic. Her tightly wound blond hair was in the final phase of turning to white. The hint of yellow was illusive. The face was small and sharp, and her features could have been lightly sculpted and then painted on. Her birdlike body was slender and probably as hard as the rest of her but the blue dress was rich in color and fabric. It was like a royal cloak wrapped around the shoulders of a white twig.

"Why did you need to see my ID?"

"This is an exclusive service, Mr. Orlean," she said with no chink of humanity in her face. "And we like to know exactly who it is we're dealing with."

"Oh," I said. "So it wasn't because of my clothes or my race?"

"The lower races come in all colors, Mr. Orlean. And none of them get back here."

Her certainty sent a shiver down my spine. I smiled to hide the discomfort.

She asked of what assistance she could be to my father. I told her some lies but I forget exactly what. Lying comes easily to me. My aunt Alberta had once told me that lying was a character trait of men on my father's side of the family. That was why they all became lawyers.

"Lawyer even sounds like liar," she used to say. "That's a good thing and it's a bad thing. You got to go with the good, honey chile, no matter what you do."

I spent forty-five minutes looking over photographs and blueprints of offices all over the Madison Avenue area. Nothing cost less than three hundred and fifty thousand a year and Ms. Lox got a whole year's rent as commission. I was thinking maybe I could marry a real estate agent while I worked the paper trade.

Ms. Lox didn't press me. She showed me one office after another asking strategic questions now and then.

"What sort of law would he be practicing?" she asked at one point. "I mean would he need a large waiting room?"

"If he did," I answered, "I wouldn't be here talking to you. Any lawyer with a waiting room is just two steps away from ambulance chasing."

That was the only time I saw her smile.

"Is your father licensed to practice in New York?" she asked at another time.

"You should know," I said.

"Come again?"

"I gave your assistant my father's name and he came back here for five minutes or more. If I were you I would have looked up JP Orlean in the ABA Internet service. There I would have seen that he is not licensed in this state. But you must be aware that he has many clients who have investments and business in the city. A lawyer is mostly mind and a license is easy to rent." These last words were my father's. He used them all the time to out-of-state clients who didn't understand the game.

It struck me as odd that Ms. Lox was so suspicious of me. I was just looking at pictures of commercial spaces. There was nothing top secret that I could steal.

The young Asian man, Brian, brought me an espresso with a coconut cookie while I considered. And when I was through he led me to the front door and said good-bye using my name. I told him, as I had told Valerie Lox, that I would be in touch in a few days after my father and I had a chance to talk.

As I was leaving I saw Valerie Lox standing at the door in back looking after me with something like concern on her porcelain face.

The next stop was a construction site on 23rd Street. Kenneth Cornell, the man I came to see, was some kind of supervisor there. The crew was excavating a deep hole getting ready for the roots of a skyscraper. There were three large cranes moving dirt and stone from the lower depths to awaiting trucks on a higher plane. There was a lot of clanging and whining motors, men, and a few women, shouting, and the impact of hammers, manual and automatic, beating upon the poor New York soil, trying once again to make her submit to their architectural dreams.

I walked in, stated my business, was fitted with a hard hat, and shown into the pit.

They led me to a tin shack half the way down the dirt slope. The man inside the shack was yelling something out of the paneless window at workers looking up from down below. I knew that he was yelling to be heard over the noise but it still gave me the impression that he was a man in a rage. And, being so small, I always stood back when there was rage going on.

Cornell was tall but a bit lanky for construction I thought. His pink chin was partly gray from afternoon shadow and his gray eyes were unsettling because they seemed to look a bit too deeply into my intentions.

"Yeah?"

"Mr. Cornell?"

"Yeah?"

"I'm Orlean," I said pronouncing it *or-leen* as Lawless had done.

"That supposed to mean something to me?"

"I called your office last week—about getting a job," I said.

His eyes tightened, it felt as though they were squeezing my lungs.

"Who are you?" he asked me.

It suddenly occurred to me that I was way out of my depth.

Cornell's hands folded up into fists as if to underscore the epiphany.

"Get the hell out of here," he said.

I didn't exactly run out of that hole but if I had been competing in a walking race I wouldn't have come in last.

6

Lana Drexel, fashion model, was the last name on my list. She was the one I most wanted to see but I didn't make it that day.

Henry Lansman was my second to last stop. He was an easy one, a barber at Crenshaw's, a popular place down in Greenwich Village. There was almost always a line at Crenshaw's. They were an old time barbershop that catered to the conservative thirty-something crowd. They gave classic haircuts in twelve minutes and so could afford to undercut, so to speak, the competition.

The shop, I knew from friends, had nine barber chairs that were all busy all of the time. But because this was a Tuesday at two-thirty there were only about ten or twelve customers waiting in line at the top of the stairwell of the shop. You had to go down a half flight of stairs to get into the establishment. I can't say what the inside of the place looked like because I never made it there.

"Hey," someone said in tone that was opening to fear. "Hey, mister."

"Excuse me," a man in a red parka said before he shouldered me aside hard enough to have thrown me down the stairwell if there hadn't been a portly gentleman there to block my fall.

"Hey, man! What the fuck!" the big man I fell against hollered. He was wearing some kind of blue uniform.

I wanted to see who it was that pushed me. I did catch a glimpse of the top of the back of his head. It had partly gray close-cut hair. He was crouching down and the parka disguised his size, and, anyway, the big guy I slammed into needed an apology.

"I'm sorry . . ." I said and then the shouting started.

"Hey, mister. Mister! Hey I think this guy's havin' a heart attack!"

The big man had put his hand on my shoulder but the terror in the crackling tone distracted him long enough for me to rush to the side of the young man who was screaming. I wish I could say that it was out of concern for life that moved me so quickly but I really just wanted to save myself from being hit.

The screamer was a white man, tall and well built. He was tan and wore an unbuttoned black leather jacket and a coal colored loose-knit shirt that was open at the neck revealing a thick gold chain that hung around his throat. He had a frightened child's eyes. His fear was enough to convince me to clear out before the danger he saw could spread. I would have run away if it wasn't for the dying man at my feet.

I crouched down on one knee to get a closer look at the heart attack victim. There was a fleck of foam at the corner of his mouth. The lips were dark, the panic in his wide eyes was fading into death. He wore a short-sleeved nylon shirt which was odd because this was late October and on the chilly side. His gray slacks rode a little high. He was almost completely bald.

The struggle in his eyes was gone by the time I had noticed these things. I cradled the back of his head with my hand. A spasm went through his neck. His back arched and I thought he was trying to rise. But then he slumped back down. Blood seeped out of his left nostril.

"He's dead," the someone whispered.

Men and women all around were voicing their concern but I only made out one sentence, "Mr. Bartoli, it's Henry, Henry Lansman!" a man's voice shouted.

I was watching the color drain from the dead man's face thinking that I should clear out or tell somebody what I knew. But all I could do was kneel there holding the heavy head, watching the drop of blood making its way down his jowl.

"Out of the way! Let him go!" a man ordered.

A round man, hard from muscle, pushed me aside. He was wearing a white smock. At first I thought it was a doctor. But then I realized it must be someone from the barbershop.

I moved aside and kept on going. The screamer with the gold chain was leaning against the window of the shoe store next door. His tan had faded. I remember thinking that some poor woman would have to have sex with him all night long before the color came back.

Henry Lansman was dead. People were shouting for someone to call an ambulance. I stayed watching until I heard the first far-off whine of the siren then I walked away from the scene feeling guilty though not knowing why.

I went over to Saint Mark's Place, a street filled with head shops, twelve-step programs, and wild youths with punk hair and multiple piercings. There was a comic book store that I frequented and a quasi-Asian restaurant that was priced for the college student pocketbook.

I ordered soba noodles with sesame sauce and a triple espresso. I finished the coffee but only managed about half of the entrée. I sat there thinking about the ceramic woman, the angry man, and the dead barber. That morning I was just a college student looking for a job. By afternoon I had witnessed a man dying.

I considered my options. The first one was calling my father. He knew lawyers in New York. Good ones. If I told him what was wrong he'd be on the next plane. JP would be there. He'd body block anyone trying to hurt me. He'd do anything to save me from danger. But then he'd take me back down to Louisiana and tell me how stupid I was and which law school I was to attend. He might even tell me that I had to live at home for a while.

And how could I say no if I begged him to save me?

And anyway it looked like a heart attack that killed Lansman. I decided that I was just being oversensitive to the paranoia of Lawless and Red Tuesday.

The man was just sick.

"Didn't you like it?" the slightly overweight, blue-haired, black waitress asked. Actually her hair was brown with three bright blue streaks running back from her forehead.

"I like you," I said, completely out of character.

She gave me a leery look and then walked away to the kitchen. She returned with my bill a few moments later. At the bottom was her telephone number and her name, Sharee.

I called Lawless's answering machine from a pay phone on the street.

"Lox and Cornell are fine," I said after the tone. "But Lansman died of a heart attack. He fell dead just when I got there. I didn't get to Drexel and I quit too. You don't have to pay me."

From there I went up to the special lab room that was set up for us at Columbia. There were three computers that were connected to AP, UPI, and Reuters news databases. There were also lines connected to police and hospital reports in Manhattan. Lansman's death wasn't even listed. That set my mind at ease some. If there was no note of his death it had to be some kind of medical problem and not foul play.

I followed breaking news in the Middle East and Africa until late that night. There had been a car bomb near the presidential residence in Caracas, Venezuela. I wondered, briefly, what Red Tuesday would have made of that.

It was midnight by the time I got to 121st Street. I made it to our apartment house, the Madison, and climbed six floors. I was walking down the hall when a tall man in a dark suit appeared before me.

"Mr. Orlean?"

"Yes?"

"We need to speak to you."

"It's late," I complained and then made to walk around him.

He moved to block my way.

Backing up I bumped into something large and soft so I turned. Another obstacle in the form of a man in a suit stood before me.

The first man was white, the second light brown.

"We need to talk to you at the station," the brown man informed me.

"You're the police?"

Instead of speaking he produced a badge.

"What do you want with me?" I asked, honestly confused. I had put my dealings with Archibald Lawless that far behind me.

"You're a witness to a possible crime," the man behind me said.

I turned and looked at him. He had a big nose with blue and red veins at the surface. His breath carried the kind of halitosis that you had to take pills for.

The brown man pulled my arms behind my back and clapped handcuffs on my wrists.

"You don't arrest witnesses," I said.

"You've been moving around a lot, son," the white cop said, exhaling a zephyr of noxious fumes. "And we need to know some answers before we decide if we're going to charge you with something or not."

"Where's your warrant?" I said in a loud voice intended to waken my roommate. But I was cut short by the quick slap from the man I came to know as August Morganthau.

7

They took me to the 126th Street station. There were police cars parked up and down the block. I was taken past a waiting room full of pensive looking citizens. They weren't manacled or guarded so I figured they were there to make complaints or to answer warrants. I *was* a felon in their eyes, cuffed and manhandled, shoved past them like a thief.

They took me to a Plexiglas booth where a uniformed officer filled out what I came to know later as an entry slip.

"Name?" the sentry asked.

I was looking at the floor to avoid the nausea caused by Morganthau's breath.

"Name?"

I realized that I was expected to answer the question. It seemed unfair. Why should I tell him my name? I didn't ask to be there.

"Felix Orlean," I said taking great pleasure in withholding my middle names.

"Middle name?"

I shook my head.

"Case number?"

"I don't know," I said, trying now to be helpful. I regretted the childish withholding of my name.

"Of course you don't, stupid," Morganthau said. He shoved me too.

"Case six-three-two-two-oh, homicide," the chubby brown man, Tito Perez, said.

"Charges?"

"Pending," Officer Morganthau grunted.

There was a Plexiglas wall next to the booth with a rude door cut into it. The edges were all uneven and it had only a makeshift wire hanger handle. I got the impression that one day the police realized that if someone got loose with a gun there would be a lot of casualties unless they put up a bulletproof barrier between them and the phantom shooter. So they bought some used Plexiglas and cut it into walls and doors and whatnot. After that they never thought about it again.

Perez pulled open the door. It wasn't locked, couldn't be as far as I could see. They pushed me along an aisle of cubicles. Men and women wearing headsets were sitting behind the low-cut walls talking to the air or each other. Some of them were in uniform, some not. Mostly it was women. Almost all of them white. The room was shabby. The carpet under my feet was worn all the way to the floor in places. The cubicles were piled high with folders, scraps of pink and white papers, coffee cups, and small heaps of sweaters, shirts, and caps. The tan cubicle walls weren't all straight. A few were missing, some were half rotted away or stained from what must have been water damage of some sort.

If this was the nerve center of police intelligence for that neighborhood, crime was a good business opportunity to consider.

I see how slipshod the police seemed now. But that night, while I merely recorded what I saw with my eyes, my mind was in a state of full-blown horror. As soon as I got to a phone I was going to call my father's twenty-four-hour service. Betty was the woman on the late night shift. She'd get to him no matter where he was.

We reached a large cubicle that was not only disheveled but it also smelled. The smell was sharp and unhealthy. Morganthau sat down on one of a pair of gray steel desks that faced each other. He indicated the chair that sat at the desk for me.

"Can you take these things off my hands?" I asked.

"Sorry," he said with an insincere gray smile. "Policy."

I lifted my arms to go behind the back of the chair and sat slightly hunched over.

"I'm Morganthau and this is Officer Perez," he said. "Tell us what you know about Hank Lansman."

The "Hank" threw me off for a second. I frowned trying to connect it.

"Come on, kid," Perez said. "You were seen at the barbershop. We know you were there."

My mind flooded with thoughts. How did they know I was there? Was Lansman murdered? Even if someone saw me how would they know my name? I didn't tell anyone. I don't have a record or even any friends in that part of town.

All of this was going on just barely in the range of consciousness. Most of what I felt was fear and discomfort. Morganthau's breath was beginning to reach my nostrils again. That coupled with the sharp odor of the cubicle started to seriously mess with my stomach.

"I want to make a phone call."

"Later," Perez said. His voice was soft.

"I have a right . . ." I began but I stopped when Morganthau put his shod foot, sole down, on my lap.

"I asked you a question," he said.

"A man named Archibald Lawless hired me to see about four people. He didn't tell me why." I gave them the names of Lox, Lansman, Drexler, and Cornell. "He said that I should go see these people, make sure I saw them in the flesh."

"And then what?"

"That's all he said. He said see them. I suppose he wanted me to make a report but we didn't get that far."

"What were you supposed to say to these people when you saw them?" Perez asked.

"What was said didn't matter. Just make sure I saw them, that's all. Listen. I don't know anything about this. I answered an ad in the paper. It was for Lawless. He said that he wanted a scribe . . ."

"We know all about Lawless," Morganthau said. "We know about his *scribes* and we know about you too."

"There's nothing about me that has to do with him."

"One dead man," Perez suggested.

"I thought he had a heart attack?"

The officers looked at each other.

"We don't need any shit, kid," Morganthau said. "Who else is in the cell?"

It was at that moment I began to fear that even my father could not save me.

I had to swallow twice before saying, "What do you mean?"

Morganthau's foot was still in my lap. He increased the weight a little and said, "This is about to get ugly."

I felt cold all of a sudden. My head was light and my tongue started watering.

"Shit!" Morganthau shouted. He pulled his foot back from my thighs but not before I vomited soba noodles all over his pant leg. "Damn!"

He skipped away. Perez flung open a drawer in his desk and threw a towel to his partner who began wiping his pants as he went back down the corridor we came from.

"You're in trouble now, kid," Perez said.

If I had seen it on a TV show I would have sneered at the weak dialogue. But in that chair I was scared to death. I retched twice more and steeled my neck to keep from crying.

After he was sure that I was through being sick, Perez jerked me up by the arm and dragged me down another corridor until we came to a big room where there were other chained prisoners. All of them male.

The center of the room was empty of furniture except for a small table in the middle of the floor where a lone sentry sat. Along three walls ran metal benches that were bolted to the floor. Every four feet or so along each bench there was a thick eyebolt also planted in the concrete floor. There were three eyebolts along each bench. Six men were attached to these stations by manacles that also held their feet. All of these men were negroes.

"Finney," Perez said. "Grab me some bracelets for this one."

Finney was my age with pale strawberry hair. He was tall and long limbed. He had to stand up in order to kneel down and reach under the table for the restraints. Perez undid my handcuffs, made me sit at a station next to a big brown man who was rocking backward and forth and talking to himself. He was smiling through his words, which were mostly indistinct, and tapping his right foot on the concrete. Two places away, on the other side was a man so big that it didn't seem as if the chains he wore could possibly hold him. Across the way was a young, very mean looking man. All he wore was a pair of tattered jeans. His eyes bored into mine. It was as if I were his worst enemy and finally my throat was within his reach.

Perez didn't say anything to me or even look me in the face. He simply attached the new manacles to my ankles and wrists and secured the chains to the eyebolt in the floor. Then he went to fill out a form on Finney's table. After they exchanged words, which I couldn't make out, Perez left through the door we had entered.

8

I was relieved to be away from Morganthau's putrid breath. At least I had a few moments to think about what happened so far. If Lansman was murdered the man in the red parka had something to do with it. I wanted to tell the police about him but they seemed so sure of my guilt that I thought they might construe any information I gave them as confirmation of my culpability. I wasn't very experienced with police procedure but I knew a lot about the law from my father and grandfather, LJ Orlean.

I knew that I needed to speak to a lawyer before I could have any kind of meaningful dialogue with the law. But they didn't seem ready to allow me my Constitutional phone call. I was screwing up my courage to ask the midwestern looking Finney for my one call when the big guy two spaces to my left began speaking to me.

"You look like a cherry," he said. It was almost a question.

"Cherry, cherry, cherry . . ." the grinning rocker on the other side chanted.

"You might need a friend," the big man suggested.

"I'm all right," I said with nary a break in my voice.

". . . cherry, cherry, cherry . . ."

"You dissin' me, bitch?" the big man asked, this time it was hardly a question.

I didn't know what to say. An apology seemed inappropriate and getting down on my knees to beg was not what a man should do in such a situation.

The man across from me mouthed a sentence that was either announcing his intention of killing or kissing me, I didn't know which.

"Officer," I said. "Officer."

". . . cherry, cherry, cherry, cherry . . ."

"Officer."

"Shut up," Finney said.

"Officer, I haven't been given the right to a phone call yet. I want to make that call now."

The strawberry blond didn't respond. He was reading something. I honestly believe that he no longer heard me.

"I'ma bust you up, punk," the big man to my left proclaimed.

I started thinking about the possibility of weapons at my disposal.

A man is only as strong as his th'oat or his groin. My aunt Alberta's words came back to me with a flash of heat and then cold passing over my scalp. *Just remember, baby—don't hesitate, not for a minute.*

". . . cherry, cherry . . ."

I glanced at the big man. He had fists the width of a small tree's trunk. I decided that when I got the chance I'd go in low on him: hit him hard and ruin him for life. Jail had turned me into a felon and I hadn't been there an hour.

A phone rang, which in itself was not unusual but I couldn't see a phone anywhere in the room. It rang again.

". . . cherry, cherry, I want some," the rocking man sang.

The shirtless man across the way was still mouthing his violent flirtation.

The phone rang for the third time.

The guard turned the page of his magazine.

The big man on the left suddenly yanked on his chains with all his might. My heart leapt. I was sure that he'd break those flimsy shackles.

"Settle down, Trainer," the blond guard said. Then he got up and walked to the wall where there was a space between the benches.

The phone rang.

"You gonna suck my toes, niggah," the man called Trainer promised.

The kid across the way made me another promise.

The phone rang. The room started spinning. The guard located a hidden door in the wall and pulled it open. He reached in and came out with a yellow phone receiver connected to a black cord.

"Finney here," he said.

". . . cherry, cherry the best dessert," the rocking man said. "Cherry, cherry in the dirt."

Maybe he didn't say those words but that's what I remember. The room was spinning and my sweater smelled of vomit. Finney looked at me.

". . . cherry . . ."

". . . suck on my big black dick . . ."

". . . Orlean?" Finney said.

"What?"

"Are you Felix Orlean?" he asked.

"Yes sir."

"*Yes sir,*" Trainer said. He was trying to make fun of me but I think he realized that I might soon be beyond his reach.

"He's here," Finney said into the receiver.

He hung up the phone and went back to his chair and magazine.

"Hm," Trainer said. "Looks like they just wanted to make sure you was up here wit' me."

"Fuck you," I said. I didn't mean to, I really didn't. But I was sick and he was stupid . . .

"What did you say?"

"I said, fuck you, asshole."

Trainer's eyes widened. The veins on his neck were suddenly engorged with blood. His lips actually quivered. And then I did the worst thing I could have done to such a man—I laughed.

What did I have to lose? He was going to brutalize me if he could anyway. Maybe I could catch him by the nuts like my aunt Alberta had advised.

"You a dead man," Trainer promised.

"Mash his cherry, Jerry," the rocking man tapped his toe for each syllable.

I lowered my head and tried to remember the Lord's prayer.

I could not.

Then I heard the door to the strange room open. I looked up to see a white man walking through. He was tall and dressed in an expensive gray suit.

"Which one is Orlean?" the white man asked Blondie.

"Over there." Finney gestured with his chin.

"Unlock him."

"Rules are you need two guards to remove a recal," the guard replied.

"Get up off your ass, kid, or I will have you mopping up vomit in the drunk tank for a month of Sundays." The gray suit had a deadly certain voice.

The guard got up and unlocked my fetters. I stood up and smiled at Trainer and the shirtless man across the way.

"This way, Felix," the man in the gray suit said.

"I'm gonna remember you, Felix Orlean," the prisoner Trainer said.

"Whatever you say, loser," I said smiling. "Maybe you'll learn something."

Again the prisoner named Trainer strained at his bonds. He jumped at me but there was no give to his chains. I was scared to death. The only way I kept from going crazy was taunting my helpless tormentor.

The man in the gray suit took me by the shoulder and guided me out of the room. The shirtless detainee spat on the floor as I left. Trainer screeched like a mad elephant.

We walked down a long corridor coming to a small elevator at last. The car went up seven floors and opened into a room that was almost livable. There were carpets and stuffed chairs and the smell of decent coffee.

"You can go in there and clean up," the suit said, pointing toward a closed door.

"What's your name?" I asked him.

"Captain Delgado."

The door led to a large restroom and shower area. I took off my college clothes and got under a spigot for at least fifteen minutes. After the shower I washed the vomit from my sweater. Between the lateness of the hour, the heat, dehydration, and fear I was so tired that it was hard to keep moving.

I staggered back to the room where Delgado waited. He was sitting in a big red chair, reading a newspaper.

"Feel better?"

"Uh-huh."

"Let's go then."

We retraced every step I'd taken through the station. Me sticking close to the slick policeman and him leading the way. Nobody stopped us, nobody questioned our passing.

We went to a '98 Le Sabre parked out in front of the station and Delgado drove us up further into Harlem.

"Where we going?" I asked.

"Up on One Fifty-sixth," he said.

"I'd like to go home."

"No you wouldn't. Take my word on that."

"What's going on, Captain?"

"I haven't the slightest idea, son."

We stopped in front of a large stone apartment building on 156th Street. Even though it was late there were young men and women hanging out around the front stoop.

"Eight twenty-one," Delgado said.

"What?"

"Apartment eight twenty-one. That's where you're going."

"I want to go home."

"Get out."

"Are you coming?"

"No."

I had never felt more vulnerable in my life.

I opened the door and all the faces from the stoop turned toward me.

"Who's up there?" I asked Delgado.

He pulled my door shut and drove off.

"You a cop, man?" a young man asked me.

He had climbed down from his seat on the top step of the stoop.

"No. No. He just gave me a ride."

My inquisitor was probably a year or two younger than I. His skin was very dark. Even though the air was chilly he wore only a T-shirt. His arms were slender but knotty with muscle.

"You fuckin' wit' me, man?"

"No. I'm supposed to go to an apartment upstairs."

Two other angry looking youths climbed down from the stoop. They flanked my interlocutor, searching me with their eyes.

"What for?" the youth asked.

"They told me that the man who had me released is up there."

I started walking. I had to go around my three new friends. Up the stoop I went and into the dark corridor of the first floor.

There was no light and I could almost feel the young men they followed me so closely. As we climbed the stairs they spoke to me.

"You with the cops you ain't gonna get outta here, mothahfuckah," one of them said.

"We should take him now, Durkey," another suggested.

"Let's see where he go," Durkey, the first one who had approached me, said. "Let's check it out."

I was breathing hard by the time I got to the eighth floor landing. Most of the journey was made through semi-darkness. Along the way there was some light from open apartment doors. Silent sentinels came to mark our passing: children, old people, women, and some men. But no one asked Durkey and his henchmen why they were following me.

I had been in places like this before, in the Ninth Ward, New Orleans. But I was always under the protection of my aunt Alberta and her boyfriends. Being from a light-skinned family of the upper crust of colored society I was always seen as an outsider.

I knocked on the door to apartment eight twenty-one and waited—and prayed.

"Nobody there," Durkey said.

He put a hand on my shoulder.

The door opened flooding the hallway with powerful light. I winced. Durkey's hand fled my shoulder.

Archibald Lawless appeared in the doorway.

"Mr. Madison," he said loudly. "I see that you've accompanied my guest upstairs."

"Hey, Lawless," Durkey said with deference. "I didn't know he was your boy."

"Uh-huh," the anarchist said. "You can go now."

My retinue of toughs backed away. My recent, and ex, boss smiled.

"Come on in, Felix. You've had a busy day."

9

It was an opulent room. The floors were covered in thick, rose-colored carpets. On the walls hung a dozen eighteenth century paintings of countrysides and beautiful young men and women of all races. There was a fireplace with a gas blaze raging and a large dark-wood table set with cheeses, meats, fruits, and bottles of wine.

"Have a seat," Lawless said.

There was a big backless couch upholstered with the rough fur of bear or maybe beaver.

"What's going on?" I asked.

"Are you hungry?"

"I don't know. I threw up at the police station."

"Wine then," Archibald said. He took a dark green bottle and a slender water glass from the table. He filled the glass halfway with the dark red liquid and handed it to me.

It was the finest burgundy I'd ever tasted. Rich, fruity, almost smoky.

"Cheese?" Lawless asked.

"In a minute," I said. "Is this your apartment?"

"I own the building," he said blandly. "Bought it when the prices were still depressed."

"You're a landlord?"

"Building manager is the title I prefer. I collect a certain amount of rent from my tenants until they've paid for the cost of their unit. After that they pay whatever maintenance is necessary for taxes and upkeep."

I must have been gaping at him.

"It's the way Fidel does it in Cuba," he said.

"Castro's a dictator."

"And Bush is a democratically elected official," he replied.

"But . . ." I said.

Lawless held up his hand.

"We'll have enough time to discuss politics on slow days at the office," he said. "Right now we have some more pressing business."

I'd drunk the half glass and he replenished it.

"I left you a message," I said. "Did you get it?"

"Tell me about the murder," he replied.

"But I quit."

"No."

The wine felt good in my belly and in my blood. It warmed me and slowed the fear I'd felt since being taken by the police. I was safe, even hidden, with a man who seemed to be a force of nature all on his own. His refusal to accept my resignation made me tired. I took another swig, sat the glass down on an antique wooden crate used as a table, and let my head loll backward.

"I'm not working for you," I said. And then my eyes closed. I forced them open but couldn't keep focus. I closed my eyes again and I must have fallen asleep for a while.

The next thing I knew there was somebody whimpering somewhere . . .

"Ohhhhh the wolverines. The maggots and the ticks. Blood suckers and whores . . ."

The voice was high which somehow fit with the headache threaded behind my eyes. I sat up and regretted it. My stomach was still unsteady, my tongue dry as wood.

". . . whores and pimps and teachers sticking sticks in your ass . . ."

Lawless was rolling on the floor, whining out these complaints. At first I thought he must have had too much wine. I went to him, touched his shoulder.

He rose under me like the ground in a terrible upheaval. Grabbing me by my hair and right shoulder he lifted me high above the floor.

"Don't you fuck with me, mother fucker!" he shouted.

His small eyes were almost large with the fear.

"It's me, Mr. Lawless," I said. "Felix. Your scribe."

He lowered me slowly, painfully because of his hold on my hair.

"I'm sick," he cried when he'd released me. "Sick."

He swayed left then right and then fell in a heap like a young child in despair. I looked around the room for something that might help him. I didn't see anything so I took a doorway that led me into a master bedroom painted dark blue with a giant bed in the center. There was a skylight in this room. Light came in from an outside source somewhere. There was a white bag on the bed made from the skin of what seemed to be an albino crocodile. You had to open the mouth and reach in past the sharp teeth to see what was inside. Therein I found a knife and pistol, an English bible and an old copy of the Koran in both English and Arabic. There was a clear plastic wallet filled with one-dollar bills and a small amber vial which contained a dozen or so tiny tablets.

There was no label on the glass tube.

Archibald Lawless had stripped off his clothes by the time I returned to the living room. He was squatting down and rocking not unlike the man in the police station.

I knelt down next him, held up the small bottle, and asked, "How many do you take, Mr. Lawless?"

His eyes opened wide again.

"Who are you?"

"Felix Orlean, your scribe. You hired me yesterday."

"Are you killkill?"

"I'm not on any of Red Tuesday's lists."

For some reason this made him laugh. He took the bottle from me and dumped all the pills in his mouth. He chewed them up and said, "I better get into the bed before I go unconscious—or dead."

I helped him into the bedroom. I think he was asleep before his head hit the mattress.

For the next few hours I hung around the big bed. Lawless was unconscious but fitful. He talked out loud in his sleep speaking in at least four different languages. I understood the Spanish and German but the other dialects escaped me. Most of his utterances were indistinct. But his tone was plaintive enough that I could feel the pain.

Now and then I went back into the living room. I had some

cheddar and a sip of burgundy. After a while I started putting the food away in the kitchen, which was through a door opposite the bedroom entrance.

I stayed because I was afraid to leave. The police might still be after me for all I knew. Delgado seemed to owe a debt to Lawless but that didn't mean that Perez and Morganthau wouldn't grab me again. And somehow I'd been implicated in a murder. I had to know what was going on.

But there was more to it than that. The self-styled anarchist seemed so helpless when I'd come to. His mental state was definitely unstable and he did get me out of jail. I felt that I should wait, at least until he was aware and able to take care of himself.

There was a bookshelf in the bathroom. The books were composed of two dominant genres: politics and science fiction. I took out a book entitled *Soul of the Robot* by the author Barrington J. Bayley. It was written in the quick style of pulp fiction, which I liked because there was no pretension to philosophy. It was just a good story with incredible ideas.

I'd been reading on the bear or beaver couch for some while when there came a knock on the front door. Five quick raps and then silence. I didn't even take a breath.

I counted to three and the knock came again.

Still I didn't make a sound.

I might have stayed there silently, breathing only slightly. But then the doorknob jiggled.

I moved as quietly as I could toward the door.

"Who is it?" I called.

The doorknob stopped moving.

"Who is that?" a woman's voice asked.

"I'm Felix. I work for Mr. Lawless."

"Open the door, Felix." Her voice was even and in charge.

"Who are you?"

"My name is Maddie. I need to see Archie." A sweetness came into her voice.

I tried to open the door but there were three locks down the side that required specialized attention. One had a knob in a slot shaped like a simple maze. The next one had a series of three buttons that needed to be pressed.

"Are you going to let me in, Felix?" Maddie asked.

"Trying to get the locks."

The last lock was a bolt. The knob was on a spring that allowed it be pushed in. I squashed the knob inward but the bolt refused to slide. I tried pulling it out but that didn't work either.

"Felix?"

"I'm trying."

The hand on my shoulder made me jump into the door.

"What's wrong?" Maddie asked from her side.

"Nothing, M," Archibald Lawless said from behind me.

"Archie," the woman called.

"Meet me at Sunshine's at noon," Lawless said to the door, his hand still on my shoulder.

"Will you be there?" she asked.

"Absolutely. I can't let you in right now because I'm in the middle of something, something I have to finish."

"You promise to meet me," the disembodied woman said.

"You have my word."

He had on camouflage pants and a black T-shirt, black motorcycle boots and a giant green inlaid ring on the point finger of his left hand.

"Okay," Maddie said.

I inhaled deeply.

"You've got the job," he said.

10

Lawless drank a glass of wine, said, "Sleep on the couch," and stumbled back toward his bedroom.

I lay down not expecting to sleep a wink but the next thing I knew there was sunlight coming through a window and the smell of food in the air. There was a small table at the far end of the narrow kitchen. The chairs set there looked out of a window, down on the playground of an elementary school. He made griddle cakes with a sweet pecan sauce, spicy Andouille sausage, and broiled grapefruit halves with sugar glazed over the top, set off by a few drops of bourbon.

I tried to ask him questions while he was cooking but he put them all off asking me instead about parts of New Orleans that I knew well.

I loved talking about my city. The music and the food, the racial diversity and the fact that it was the only really French city in the United States.

"I used to go down there a lot," Lawless told me while flipping our cakes. "Not to the city so much as the swamplands. There's some people out around there who live like human beings."

When the breakfast was finally served he sat down across from me. There was a girl in the asphalt yard calling up to her mother in some apartment window. I couldn't discern what they were saying because I was studying the madman's eyes.

"I have a few disorders," he said after passing a hand over his food.

"You mean about last night?"

"Bipolar, mildly schizophrenic," he continued. "One doctor called it a recurring paranoid delusional state but I told him that if he had seen half the things that I have that he'd live in Catatonia and eat opium to wake up."

His laugh was only a flash of teeth and a nod. Everything Lawless did seemed pious and sacred—though I was sure he did not believe in God.

"Are you under a doctor's care?" I asked him.

"You might say that," he said. "I have a physician in New Delhi. A practitioner of ancient lore. He keeps me stocked with things like those pills you fed me. He keeps the old top spinning."

Lawless pointed at his head.

"Maybe you're addicted," I suggested.

"Tell me about the murder," he replied.

"I'm not working for you."

"Are you going to work for yourself?" he asked.

"What does that mean?"

"It means that it would be in your best interest to give me the information you have. That way I can make sure that the police and anybody else will leave you alone."

He was right of course. But I didn't want to admit it. I felt as if I had been tricked into my problems and I blamed A. Lawless for that.

"First I want *you* to answer some questions," I said.

Lawless smiled and held his palms up—as in prayer.

"Who was that guy in the green suit talking about in your office yesterday?" I asked.

"A diamond dealer named Benny Lamarr. He was from South Africa originally but he relocated to New York about five years ago."

"Why did you want to know about him?"

Lawless smiled. Then he nodded.

"I have a friend in the so-called intelligence center here in New York. She informs me when the government takes an interest in the arrests, detainments, deaths, or in the liberation of citizens, aliens, and government officials."

"This is someone in your employ?" I asked.

"In a manner of speaking. I maintain Nelly, but she only gives me information that is, or should be, public record. You know, Felix, the government and big business hide behind a mountain of data. They hide, in plain sight, the truth from us. I tease out that truth so that at least one man knows what's going on."

"What did this Nelly tell you?" I asked.

"The diamond dealer died in an automobile accident. There was no question of foul play on the local level but still the death was covered up. His files were sealed and sent to Arizona."

"Arizona?"

"There's a government facility outside of Phoenix where certain delicate information is handled."

"Did you know this Lamarr?" I asked.

"No."

"Then why are you so concerned with him?"

"When I looked into Lamarr's past I found that he had recently been seen in the company of a man named Tellman Drake. Drake had also moved to New York and changed his name to Kenneth Cornell. When I looked into both men together I found the other names on our list."

"So what?"

Archibald Lawless smiled.

"What are you grinning about?" I asked him.

"You're good at asking questions," he said. "That's a fine trait and something to know about you."

"You're only going to know me long enough to get me out of this trouble you started."

Lawless held up his palms again. "Lamarr was in diamonds. Valerie Lox leases expensive real estate around the world. Tellman Drake—"

"Kenneth Cornell," I said to make sure that I was following the story.

"Yes," the anarchist said. "Kenny Cornell is a world class demolitions expert. Henry Lansman was an assassin when he lived in

Lebanon, and Lana Drexel . . . Well, Lana Drexel learned when she was quite young that men, and women too, would give up their most guarded secrets in the light of love."

"And the government was looking into all of these people?"

"I'm looking into them."

"Why?"

"Because Lamarr's murder was covered up."

"You said it was an accident."

"The facts were smothered, sent to Arizona," Lawless said. "That's enough for me."

"Enough for you to what?"

"Walk the line."

The words chilled me in spite of my conviction to treat Lawless as an equal.

"Are you working for someone?" I managed to ask.

"For everyone. For the greater good," Lawless said. "But now I've answered your questions. You tell me what happened when you saw Henry Lansman die."

"One more question." I said.

"Okay."

"Who is Captain Delgado to you?"

"An ambitious man. Not a man to trust but someone to be used. He wants to advance in the department and he knows that I have a reach far beyond his own. We get together every month or so. I point him where I might need some assistance and, in return, he answers when I call."

"It all sounds very shady."

"I need you, Felix," Archibald Lawless said then. "I need someone who can ask questions and think on his feet. Stick with me a day or two. I'll pay you and I'll make sure that all the problems that have come up for you will be gone."

"What is it that you're asking me to do?" I asked.

I thought I was responding to his offer of exoneration. But now, when I look back, I wonder if maybe it wasn't his unashamed admission of need that swayed me.

"Tell me about the death of Henry Lansman," he said for the third time.

I gave him every detail I remembered down to the waitress and the half-eaten meal.

"We need to talk to at least one of these players," Lawless said. "I want to know what's going on."

"Which one?"

"Lana Drexel I should think," he said. "Yes definitely Lana . . ."

He stood up from the table and strode back toward the living room. I followed. From under the fur divan he pulled a slender briefcase. When he opened it, I could see that it contained twenty amber colored bottles in cozy velvet insets.

"These are the medicines that Dr. Meta has prescribed for me. Here . . ." From the upper flap of the briefcase he pulled three sheets of paper that were stapled together. "These are the instructions about what chemical I need in various manifest states. This last bottle is an aerosol spray. You might need it to subdue me in case my mind goes past reason."

"You want me to tote this around behind you?"

"No," he said. "I just want you to see it. I have a variety of these bags. If I start slipping all I need is for you to help me out a little."

Hearing his plea I felt a twinge of emotion and then the suspicion that Archibald Lawless was messing with my mind.

11

"Lana Drexel," the anarchist was saying to me a while later. We were having a glass of fresh lemonade that he'd prepared in the kitchen. "She's the most dangerous of the whole bunch."

"What do you mean?"

"Valerie Lox or Kenny Cornell are like nine-year-old hall guards compared to her."

"She's the smallest," I said, "and the youngest."

"She swallows down whole men three times her age and weight," Lawless added. "But she's fair to look at and you're only young once no matter how long you live."

"Are you going to your meeting?" I asked him.

"What meeting?"

"The one with the woman you talked to through the door."

"Oh no," he said, shaking his head. "No. Never. Not me."

I was thinking about our conversation when I entered the Rudin apartment building on East 72nd.

Lawless had given me one of his authentic Afghan sweaters to make up for the sweater I vomited on. I looked a little better than I had before but not good enough to saunter past the doorman at Lana Drexel's building.

"Yes?" the sentry asked. He wore a dark blue coat festooned with dull brass buttons, a pair of pale blue pants with dark stripes down the side, and light blue gloves.

"Drexel," I said.

The doorman—who was also a white man and a middle-aged man—sneered.

"And your name is?" he asked as if he expected me to say, *Mud.*

"Lansman," I replied smugly. "Henry Lansman."

The doorman reached into his glass alcove-office and pulled out a phone receiver. He pressed a few digits on the stem, waited and then said, "A Mr. Lansman."

It was a pleasure to see his visage turn even more sour. I think, when he looked to me that he was still half inclined to turn me away.

"Back elevator," he said. "Twenty-fifth floor."

"What's the apartment number?" I asked.

"It's the only door," he said getting at least some pleasure out of my naiveté.

The elevator was small but well-appointed, lined with rosewood, floored in plush maroon carpeting, and lit by a tasteful crystal chandelier. The doors slid opened revealing a small red room, opposite a pink door. This door was held ajar by a small olive-skinned woman who had eyes twice the size they should have been. Her hair was thick, bronze and golden of color. Her cheekbones were high and her chin just a shade lower than where you might have expected it to be. She was beautiful the way the ocean is beautiful. Not a human charm that you could put your arms around but all the exquisiteness of a wild orchid or a distant explosion. It was a cold beauty that you knew was burning underneath. But there was no warmth or comfort in the pull of Lana Drexel's magnetism. There was only a jungle and, somewhere in the thickness of that hair, a tiger's claws.

She looked me up and down with and said, "You're not Lansman."

"Sorry," I said. "But he's dead."

I had practiced that line for two hours. Lawless had given me the job of getting in to see the fashion model and of convincing her to come to his office and share what she knew about the other names on his list. It was my idea to pretend that I was the dead man. I also decided that shock might loosen her tongue.

But if she was in any way alarmed I couldn't see it.

"He is?" she said.

"Yeah. The people around thought that it was a heart attack but then the police arrested me and said something about murder."

"So he was murdered?" she asked.

"I thought I'd come here and ask you."

"Why?"

"Because the police for some reason suspect me of being involved with you guys and your business. You see, I'm just a journalism student and I'd like them to leave me alone."

"Excuse me," she said, still holding the door against my entrée, still unperturbed by the seriousness of our talk, "but what is your real name?"

It was her turn to frighten me. I thought that if she was to know my name then she could send someone after me. I lamented, not for the last time, agreeing to work for the anarchist.

"I'm a representative of Archibald Lawless," I said, "Anarchist at large."

Lana Drexel's confident expression dissolved then. She fell back allowing the door to come open. She wandered into the large room behind her.

I followed.

I began to think that you could understand the strange nature of denizens that peopled Archibald Lawless's world by their sense of architecture and design. The room I entered was as beautiful and intense as young Lana Drexel. The ceilings were no less than eighteen feet high and the room was at least that in width—and more in length. The outer wall was one large pane of glass. There was no furniture in the room except for the wide, cushioned bench that ran from the front door to the picture window. Nine feet up on either side were large platforms that made for rooms without walls. Underneath the platform on the right everything was painted dark gray. The room formed underneath the platform on the left was white.

Miss Drexel threw herself down in the middle of the banquette. She was wearing a maroon kimono that barely came down to the tops of her thighs. This garment exposed shapely legs and powerful hamstrings. Her toenails were painted bright orange.

I sat down a few feet from her, near the window that looked south upon midtown.

"What does he want?" Lana said covering her eyes with an upturned hand.

"I don't really know," I said. "But he seems to think that you and Lansman and a few others are in trouble."

"Who?" She sat up and leaned toward me. The intensity of her stare was captivating and cold.

"Valerie Lox, Henry Lansman, Kenneth Cornell, Benny Lamarr, and you," I said. "Lamarr is also dead."

"How did he die?"

"A car accident I think. He was with a woman."

"What was her name?"

"I don't know."

The beauty lowered her face to her hands, causing her hair to fall forward. I could see her breasts under the mane of hair but somehow that didn't matter much.

"What does he want from me?" she asked.

"He wants to see you," I said.

She looked up at me again. "Will you protect me from him?"

"Yes," I said without hesitation. My heart went out to her and I think I might have even challenged A. Lawless for her smile.

12

We reached the Tessla building at about two in the afternoon. There were various business types coming in and out. The guard sitting in front of the Joan of Arc mural was an elderly white man with a big mustache and a head full of salt and pepper hair.

"Hello, Mr. Orlean," he hailed. "Mr. Lawless is expecting you and the lady."

"He is?"

"Yes sir."

The guard's eyes strayed over to Lana. She wore a Japanese ensemble of work pants and jacket made from rough cotton. The color was a drab green but still it accented her beauty.

"What's your name?" I asked the guard.

"Andy."

"I thought Lawless was in trouble with the building, Andy."

"No sir, Mr. Orlean. Why would you say that?"

"It was something about the rent."

"Oh," he said. Andy's smile was larger even than his mustache. "You mean the owners don't like him. Well, that might be true but you know the *men* in this building, the union men, they love Mr. Lawless. He's a legend in unions all over the city and the world. The reason they can't trick him outta here is that no real union man would ever turn a key on him."

In the elevator Lana stood close to me. When the doors slid open she squeezed my left forearm. I touched her hand. She kissed me lightly on the lips and smiled.

In the six seconds between the door opening and our departure she raised my blood pressure to a lethal level.

Archibald was waiting for us. He opened the door before I could knock and ushered us into chairs in the outer room.

I was later to learn that Lawless never had anyone but his closest confidants in his office.

"Miss Drexel," he said, smiling broadly.

Timidly, and leaning toward me on the hardback sofa, she said, "I hope that you'll be kind."

"I'll do you one better, lady," he said. "I'll be honest and I'll be fair."

She shivered.

I put a hand on her shoulder.

Archibald Lawless laughed.

"Let's get something straight from the start, Lana," he said. "Felix is working for me. He won't jump, lady, so straighten up and talk to me."

Lana did sit up. The woman who met me at the pink door returned. She was self-possessed and distant, a European princess being held for ransom in a Bedouin camp.

"What do you want?" she asked.

"Why did you come?" he replied.

"Because your employee told me that Hank Lansman and Benny Lamarr had been murdered."

Lawless smiled. I think he liked Lana.

"Why would that bother you?"

"Don't you know?"

He shook his head then shrugged his shoulders. "Someone in the government has gone to great lengths to hide the accidental deaths of your two friends. You got precious gems, hide away real estate, explosives, security, and a siren all mixed up together and then the hammer drops . . ."

Lana's eyes cut toward me for a moment then she turned them on the madman.

"What are you in this for?" she asked.

Walking the line, I said in my mind.

"I've been hired by the insurance company to locate some property that has been—temporarily misplaced," he said.

I was lost. Every step along the way he had presented himself as a dedicated anarchist, a man of the people. Now all of a sudden he was working for the Man.

Lana sat back. She seemed to relax.

"How much will they pay?" she asked.

"Five percent with a conviction," he said. "Eight if I can keep things quiet."

"Four million is a lot of revolution," she said. "But the full fifty could topple a nation."

"Are you worried about surviving or retiring?" Archibald asked the beauty.

It was her turn to smile enigmatically.

"Because you know," Lawless continued, "whoever it was killed Lansman and Lamarr will certainly come to your door one day soon."

"I'll die one day anyway," she admitted with a half pouting lower lip. "But to stay alive you have to keep on moving."

How old was she? I wondered. Four years and a century older than I.

"I ask you again," Lawless said. "Why did you come here?"

"No one says no to Mr. Archibald Lawless," she opined. "Just ask Andy downstairs."

"What do you want?" Lawless asked Lana.

"Hardly anything. Two hundred and fifty thousand will pay for my ticket out of town. And, of course, I expect exemption from arrest."

"Of course."

Lana stretched, looked at his murky eyes, and then nodded.

"Who were you working for?" he asked after an appreciative pause.

"Lamarr."

"To do what?"

"To go with him to a party in the Hamptons," she said sounding bored. "To meet a man named Strangman. To make friends with his bedroom."

"And did you?"

Her stare was her response.

"And then what?" Archibald asked.

"I met with Lansman, told him where the hidey hole was and collected my fee."

"That's all?"

"I met with the other people on your list," she admitted.

"When?"

"The morning after I spent with Strangman," she said. "He was really a jerk."

"Where did you meet?" Lawless asked.

"A vacant house that Val was selling. They wanted to go over the layout with me."

"And this Strangman," Lawless asked. "He was in the same business that Lamarr was in, I suppose?"

"I suppose," she replied.

"And was the operation a success?"

"I was paid."

"By who?" Lawless asked.

I wanted to correct his grammar but held my tongue.

"Lamarr." Lana hesitated. Her vast eyes were seeing something that had been forgotten.

"There was a guy with Lamarr," she said. "Normal looking. White. Forties."

"Was his hair short?" I asked.

"I think so."

"With a little gray?"

She turned to me, bit her lower lip, and then shook her head.

"I don't remember," she said. "He didn't make much of an impression. I thought that maybe he worked for Lamarr. Actually I'm pretty sure of it."

"So we have Stangman and a fortyish white man that might have worked for Lamarr," Lawless said.

"And Valerie Lox and Kenneth Cornell," I added.

The existentialist detective shook his head.

"No," he said. "Cornell made a mistake with a blasting cap yesterday afternoon and took off the top of his skull. Valerie Lox has disappeared. Maybe she's just smart but I wouldn't put a dollar on seeing her breathing again."

"What about me?" Lana Drexel asked.

"You're still breathing," he said.

"What should I do?"

"Nothing you've ever done before. Don't go home. Don't use your credit cards. Don't call anyone who has been on your phone bill in the last three years."

The young woman had a slight smile on her face as she listened to the anarchist's commandments.

"Do you have a suggestion of where I should go?" she asked.

"Sure. I'm full of advice. You just wait out here for a few minutes while I give my operative here his walking orders. Come on, Felix," he said to me. "Let's go in my office for a minute or two."

13

"She needs to be put somewhere very safe," Lawless told me, his profile set against the New Jersey landscape.

"Where?"

"There's a small chapel in Queens," he said. "Run by a defrocked priest I know."

"A friend of Red Tuesday's?"

He turned toward me and smiled. "That's why we're going to get along, kid," he said. "Because you know how to be funny."

"Do you want me to take her there?" I asked.

"No. If I let her spend more than an hour with you the next thing I know there you'd be face down with a knife in your back in some back alley in Cartegena."

His swampy eyes were laughing but I knew he believed what he said. *I* believed it. Inwardly I was relieved that I didn't have to accompany Lana Drexel to Queens.

"No," Lawless continued, "Lana can take care of herself and besides—I might have a little job for her."

"What kind of job?"

"The kind I wouldn't give you," he said.

"What should I do?"

"Follow the same plan I laid out for Miss Drexel. Don't do anything that you've done before."

"How can I not do anything I've done?" I asked. "I only have seven dollars on me. I don't know anything but my routine."

The anarchist smiled.

"Your first baby step outside the lies they have you living, young man."

"That doesn't help me."

"There's a hotel on East Thirty-fifth," he said. "Over by Park. It's called the Barony. Go there when you get tired. Tell Frederick that I told you to stay there tonight. Other than that you can do anything. Anything that you've never done before."

"Can I get an advance to eat with?"

"Frederick will feed you."

"What if want to go to a movie?"

Lawless shook his head. I could see his thoughts: *Here the child could do anything and all he can come up with is a movie.*

"Or maybe opera tickets," I added.

"I never carry more than ten dollars in cash myself," he said.

"But I don't have a credit card."

"Neither do I." He held his pious palms upward.

"How do you make it with only ten bucks in your pocket?"

"It's a challenge," he said. "And challenge is what makes life sing."

I must have looked miserable because he gave me his quick laugh and said, "In your office. The bottom half of the pink file. Eighteen, eighteen, nine."

With that he rose and went to the door.

"When do I see you again?" I asked.

"I'll call you," he said. "Be prepared."

With that he left the office. I heard him say a few words to Lana Drexel. She laughed and said something. And then they were gone.

I felt uncomfortable staying in his private office. It seemed so personal in there. There were private letters on his closed laptop and all those curiosities along the walls. I went to the storage room, what he called my office, and sat at the long table in a chair that seemed to be made from stoneware pottery clay. It was glazed a shiny dark red and slender in every aspect. I wouldn't have been surprised if it broke under the weight of a man Lawless's size.

I perused a couple of Red Tuesday's newsletters. The paranoia struck a note with me though and so I put them down.

I wondered about what Lawless had said; that we lived in a skein of lies. So many things he said seemed to be anchored in some greater truth. In many ways he was like my father, certain and powerful—with all of the answers, it seemed.

But Lawless was wild. He took chances and had received some hard knocks. He lived with severe mental illness and shrugged off threats that would turn brave men into jellyfish.

Don't do anything you've done before, he told me. I experienced the memory of his words like a gift.

I picked up the phone and entered a number from a slip of paper in my pocket.

"Hello?" she answered. "Who is this?"

There was a lot of noise in the background, people talking and the clatter of activity.

"Felix."

"Who?"

"The guy you gave your number yesterday at lunch . . . I had the soba noodles."

"Oh. Hi."

"I was wondering if you wanted to get together tonight. After work I mean."

"Oh. I don't know. I was going to go with some of the guys here to . . . But I don't have to. What did you want to do?"

"I'm pretty open," I said. "Anything you been really wanting to do?"

"Well," she hesitated.

"What?"

"There's a chamber music concert up at the Cloisters tonight. It's supposed to be wonderful up there."

"That sounds great," I said, really meaning it.

"But the tickets are seventy-five dollars . . . each."

"Hold on," I said.

I stretched the phone cord over to the tiny pink file cabinet. The drawers were facing the wall so I turned it around—it was much heavier than I expected.

I could see that the bottom drawer was actually a safe with a combination lock.

"Are you still there?" Sharee said.

"Oh yeah. Listen, Sharee . . ."

"What?"

"Can I call you right back?"

"Okay."

It took me a moment to recall the numbers eighteen eighteen nine. The combination worked the first time.

There was more cash in that small compartment than I had ever seen. Stacks of hundred-dollar bills and fifties and twenties. English pounds and piles of euros. There were pesos and other bills in white envelopes that were from other, more exotic parts of the world.

"Wow."

I took two hundred and fifty dollars leaving an IOU in its place. Then I hit the redial button.

"Felix?" she answered.

"What time do you get off work?"

Sharee was a music student at Julliard. She studied oboe and flute. There was an oboe in the quartet and a violin that made my heart thrill. After the concert we walked along the dark roads of the Cloisters' park. I kissed her against a moss covered stone wall and she ran her hands up under my sweater scratching her long fingernails across my shoulder blades.

We took a taxi down to the Barony. At first the desk clerk didn't want to get Frederick but when I mentioned Mr. Lawless he jumped to the task.

Frederick was a tall man, white from his hair to his shoes. He guided us to a small elevator and brought us to a room that was small and lovely. It was red and purple and mostly bed.

I must have kissed Sharee's neck for over an hour before trying to remove her muslin blouse. She pulled the waistband of her skirt up over her belly and said, "Don't look at me. I'm fat."

That's when I started kissing around her belly button. It was an inny and very deep. Every time I pressed my tongue down there she gasped and dug her nails into my shoulders.

"What are you doing to me?" she said.

"Didn't anybody ever kiss you here before?" I asked her. "It's just so sexy." And then I jammed my tongue down deep.

We spent the night finding new places on each other. It was almost a game and we were almost children. We didn't even go to the bathroom alone.

At five I ordered room service. Salami sandwiches and coffee.

"Who are you, Felix Orlean?" she asked me as we stared at each other over the low coffee table that held our early morning meal.

"Just a journalism student," I said. "In over my head every way that I look."

She was wearing my sweater and nothing else. I wanted to kiss her belly but she looked too comfortable to unfold out of that chair.

"I have a kinda boyfriend," she said.

"Huh?"

"Are you mad?"

"How could I be mad?" I said. "What you gave me last night was exactly what I needed. And you're so beautiful."

"But I'm not very nice," she said, experimenting with the thought of being beautiful while at the same time feeling guilty about her deceit.

"I think you are."

"But here I am smelling like you in your sweater and he's in the East Village sleeping in his bed."

"And here you are and here I am," I said. "Everybody's got to be someplace."

She came over and began kissing my navel then.

The phone rang. It was the last thing in the world that I wanted but I knew that I had to answer.

Sharee moaned in distress.

"Just a minute, honey," I said. "It might be business. Hello?"

"Between Sixth and Seventh on the north side of Forty-seventh Street," Archibald Lawless said. "Deluxe Jewelers. Nine thirty. I'll meet you out front."

The moment I hung up the phone Sharee whispered in my ear, "Give me three days and I'm yours."

I grunted and pulled her blue-streaked hair so that her lips met mine. And for a long time I didn't think about big-eyed models or anarchy or where the day might end.

14

I was standing across the street from the jewelry store at nine fifteen, sipping coffee from a paper cup and rubbing the sand from my eyes. When I say jewelry store I should be more specific. That block is all jewelers. Almost every doorway and almost every floor. There were Arabs and India Indians and Orthodox Jews, white men and Asian men and every other race counted on that block. Big black security guards joked with small wizened dealers. I heard French and Spanish, Hebrew and Yiddish, Chinese and even a Scandinavian tongue casually spoken by passersby.

I had put Sharee in a taxi an hour before. She said that she was going to get some sleep and that I should call her later that day. I told her that I'd call that day if I could and she asked if I was in trouble.

"Why you say that?"

"My daddy was always in trouble and you remind me of him."

"I like it when you call me daddy," I said before kissing her and closing the yellow cab door.

Deluxe Jewelers was just a glass door with unobtrusive gold letters telling of its name. There was an older brown man, with an almond shaped head accented by a receding hairline, sitting on a fold-up metal chair inside the door. There were many more impressive stores on that block. Stores with display cases lined with precious stones set in platinum and gold.

I figured that the people who worked at Deluxe were Lawless's low-rent toehold in this world of unending wealth.

"Hey, kid," Archibald Lawless said.

He was standing there next to me as if he had appeared out of thin air.

"Mr. Lawless."

"Being on time is a virtue in this world," he said. I wasn't sure if that was a compliment or an indictment. "Shall we?"

We crossed the street and went through the modest entrance.

"Mr. Lawless," the seated guard hailed. "You here for Sammy?"

"I think I need Applebaum today, Larry."

The sentry nodded and said, "Go on then."

The room he sat in was no more than a vestibule. There was a black tiled floor, his chair, and an elevator door. Lawless pressed the one button on the panel and the door opened immediately. On the panel inside there were twelve buttons, in no particular order, marked only by colors. The anarchist chose orange and the car began to descend.

When the door opened we entered into another small and nondescript room. It was larger than Larry's vestibule but with no furniture and a concrete floor.

There was a closed door before us.

This opened and a small Asian woman came out. Her face was as hard as a Brazil nut until she saw Lawless. She smiled and released a stream of some Asian dialect. Archibald answered in the same language, somewhat slower but fluent still and all.

We followed the woman down a hall of open doorways, each one leading to rooms with men and women working on some aspect of gemstones. In one room there was an elderly Jewish man looking down on a black velvet-lined board. On the dark material lay at least a dozen diamonds, every one large enough to choke a small bird.

At the end of the hall was a doorless doorway through which I could see a dowdy office and an unlikely man.

He stood up to meet us but wasn't much taller than am I. He was brown with blond hair and striking emerald green eyes. He was both hideous and beautiful, qualities that don't come together well in men.

"Archie," he said in an accent I couldn't place. "It's been so long."

They shook hands.

"Vin, this is Felix. He's working for me," Lawless said.

"So happy to meet you." The jeweler took my hand and gazed into my eyes.

I suppressed a shudder and said, "Me too."

There were chairs and so we sat. Vin Applebaum went behind his battered oak desk. We were underground and so there were no windows. The office, which wasn't small, had been painted so long ago that it was a toss-up what color it had been originally. The lighting was fluorescent and the Persian carpet was threadbare where it had been regularly traversed.

Applebaum, who was somewhat over forty, wore an iridescent silver and green suit. It was well tailored with three buttons. His shirt was black and open at the throat.

The most surprising thing to me about his dress was that he wore no jewelry. No ring or chain or even a watch. He was like a gay male pimp who specialized in women or a vegan butcher.

"Strangman," Lawless said.

"Lionel," Vin replied.

"If you say so. What about him?"

"He was the luckiest man in the world there for a while. Through an investment syndicate he made a purchase that kings salivate over. Now he's in bad trouble. As bad as it can be."

"He was robbed?"

"That word doesn't begin to explain the loss of twenty-three nearly red diamonds."

"Red?" Lawless said. "I thought the most you could get in a diamond was pink or purple."

Applebaum nodded. "Yes. You might say that these stones, not one of which is less than six karats, are a deep or dark pink. But to the eye beholding they are red."

"Fifty million dollars red?"

"If you could sell the whole collection," Applebaum said, nodding. "Yes. Think of the necklace you could make with just nine of those gems."

"My scales run to starving, dying millions," Lawless said.

"You could feed a small country with Strangman's find."

"What about Lamarr?" Archibald Lawless asked then.

I wondered if he were really working for an insurance company. I realized that even if he had a client that their needs might dovetail like the interests of a gem dealer and a mad anarchist in a basement room in Manhattan.

"Benny?" Applebaum asked. "What about him?"

"Did he know Strangman?"

"Everyone knows Lionel. He's been on the periphery of our business for many years. Do you think that Benny had anything to do with the theft?"

"The diamonds were definitely stolen then?" Lawless asked.

"Definitely."

"Who has them?"

Applebaum shook his head.

"Who insured them then?" Lawless asked.

"Auchschlous, Anterbe, and Grenell. An Australian company." Again the odd jeweler shook his head.

"What's wrong with them?"

"Strangman is old-fashioned. He likes to carry stones around in his pocket," the ugly diamond dealer said. "A lot of the old-timers are like that. Somebody says that all they would need is fifty thousand dollars and life would even out and Strangman would pull two hundred thousand in diamonds out of his vest pocket just to show them how small they really are. Stupid."

"The insurance didn't cover personal delivery?" I asked just to feel that I wouldn't blend in with the colorless walls.

"That's right," Applebaum said with a generous smile. "Somebody made a deal with Strangman. A deal so sweet and so secure that he brought the stones home and made an appointment with the buyer."

Archibald Lawless's eyes were closed. His hands were held upward. He began nodding his head as if he were listening to a subtle tune coming from a bit too far off.

"Who is the investigating agent?" he asked behind still closed eyes.

"Jules Vialet," Applebaum said without hesitation.

The anarchist opened his eyes and asked, "How did you know that so quickly?"

"Because he's AAG's best man and even though they have a clause saying that he couldn't carry the jewels without proper protection he still might be able to make a case against them."

"And what about Strangman," Lawless asked. "Is he still around?"

"Up at Obermann's Sanitarium on sixty-eighth."

"He's fakin' it?"

"I doubt it," Vin said. "He never had much money or much power. Those stones represented a whole new life for him on these streets. All he needed was that collection in his vault and he would have had the respect of the whole community. Now, of course, all of that is gone."

There was great deal of pleasure Applebaum felt about the professional demise of Lionel Strangman. I got the feeling that life in the jewelry district wasn't friendly or safe.

15

There was a silver-gray Cadillac waiting for us when we came out. A dark man with broad shoulders, and a neck an inch too short, climbed out of the driver's seat to greet us.

"Mr. Lawless," he said in a Caribbean-English accent. "Where do you wish to go, sir?"

"This is Felix Orlean," Lawless said. "Felix, meet Derek Chambers."

The chauffeur's hands were rough and strong. He was shorter than Lawless, only about six feet.

"Pleased to meet you, Derek," I said.

"We're going to an address somewhere in Manhattan," Lawless said. "I'll need the phone books."

Derek opened the back door and Lawless slipped in, moving all the way to the other side in order to make room for me. I got in and the door shut behind me. The chauffeur went to the rear of the car, opened the trunk and closed it. After he'd climbed into the driver's seat he handed my temporary employer the white book and Yellow Pages for New York City.

Derek drove off and Lawless began thumbing through the Yellow Pages, the business to business volume.

"Corruption on this level is always pretty easy to crack," he was saying. "Big companies, rich men, and the government are all too arrogant to waste time hiding their crimes. They have official avenues to follow and reports to make, agents with health benefits and paramours who nurse aspirations of their own.

"Derek, take us to Second Avenue between Fifty-fourth and Fifty-fifth."

"Yes sir, Mister Lawless."

"Is that your real name?" I asked. "Lawless?"

The nihilist smiled at me and patted my knee.

"You would even question a man's name?" he asked, amazed.

"I mean what are the odds?" I said. "An anarchist named Lawless? That's just too perfect."

"What if my parents were revolutionists? What if I looked up my name and decided that that's what I'd become?"

"Your parents were revolutionaries that changed their names?" I asked.

"I am Archibald Lawless," he said. "I'm sitting here before you. You are looking into my eyes and questioning what you see and what you hear. On the streets you meet Asian men named Brian, Africans named Joe Cramm. But you don't questions their obviously being named for foreign devils. You accept their humiliation. You accept their loss of history. You accept them being severed from long lines of heritage by their names. Why wouldn't you accept just as simply my liberating appellation?"

"I . . ." I said.

"Here we are," Derek announced.

The building must have been considered futuristic and quirky when it was newly built. It still had a personality, if somewhat cold. Gray steel and stone relieved by thick glass windows that were accented by just a touch of green tinting. Two guards sat at a violet kidney-shaped desk with computer screens embedded in the top.

"Yes?" the smaller one asked me.

"Lawless," I said. "Archibald and associate for Mr. Vialet."

There were lights on in the entranceway but darkness hovered at the corners of the room. That gloom ascended to the roof.

The guard flipped through a screen, found a number and then dialed it on an old-fashioned rotary phone.

"A man named Lawless and somebody else for Mr. Vialet," the guard said.

He listened for a beat or two and then said to us, "Please have a seat. Someone'll be down to get you."

There was a whole tree that had been split down the middle and then cut to the length of a twelve-foot bench for us to sit on. The tree-half had been heavily lacquered and fitted with dowels to keep it from rolling around when someone sat on it.

"They rule the world," Archibald Lawless hissed.

He was sitting next to me with his hands on his knees. He still wore black slacks and an army jacket buttoned half the way up his chest. Now that his jacket was open I noticed that he wore a necklace too. It was strung with chicken bones that were white from age and being exposed to the sun. The bones had a crazy clattery way about them. There wasn't much doubt why the security guard decided to ask me about our business.

"Who?" I asked.

"People in buildings like this one. They own farms in Turkey and solar generation plants in the Gobi desert. They decide on foreign legislation and cry over the deaths of their children. Even their love is hypocritical. Even with their deaths they cannot pay for their crimes . . ."

He would have said more but a young man in a lavender suit approached us.

"Mr. Lawless?" he asked me.

"No," I said.

The kid was pale and definitely an ectomorph. But he'd been doing his exercises. There was muscle under his lapels and on his toothpick shoulders. In his eyes however he was still a ninety-pound weakling. He stared at Lawless as if the big man were a plains lion hungry for a pale-boy snack.

"You're Lawless?"

"Mr. Archibald Lawless."

"Yes," the young man said. "I'm Grant Harley, Mr. Vialet's assistant. Please follow me."

He led us through a hallway that had as a path a raised ramp that went over a hall-long pond filled with oversized, multicolored carp. Bamboo sprouted from planters along the sides of the walls. We entered into a large room inhabited by five secretaries, each at her own pastel colored desk. The were windows in this room and classical flute playing instead of Muzak.

One of the secretaries, a forty-year-old black woman with a broad chest and small eyes, got up and approached us.

"You Lawless?" she asked me.

"I'm Mr. Lawless," Archibald said.

The woman didn't seem to like his sense of self-worth but I think she was more intimidated by his size and growl.

"This way," she said.

We went through a smallish doorway into a long dark hall. At the end of this hall was a white door. The secretary opened the door and brought us into a large room with a sunken office at its center. We had to walk down five stairs to get on an even plane with the desk behind which sat a man who was almost indescribable he was so plain.

He stood to his five foot nine height and looked at us with bland brown eyes. His hair was brown and his skin was off-white. His hands were as normal as you could be. The suit he wore was medium gray and the shirt might have had a few blue threads in the depths of all that white.

"Archibald," he said to the right man.

"Do I know you?" my would-be employer asked.

"No. But I sure know a lot about you. There was an emerald necklace that we lost in Sri Lanka six years ago that no one ever thought we'd recover. One day you just walked in and dropped it off. Gave the fee to some charity as I remember."

"Can we sit down, Mr. Vialet?"

"Certainly. Forgive me. What is your friend's name?"

"Felix," I said. "Orlean."

"Have a seat, Felix, Archibald. Right here on the sofa."

It was a fuzzy white sofa that sat across from his desk. There was a dark stained walnut coffee table before us. Vialet sat in a plain walnut chair.

"Anything to drink?" he offered.

"Lets talk about red diamonds," Lawless replied.

"I like a man who gets down to business," Jules Vialet said. "Business is what makes the world turn."

". . . like a stone over the bones of the innocent," Lawless added. "Who do you suspect in the theft?"

"I'm really not at liberty to discuss the disposition of any active case that we are pursuing, Mr. Lawless. But if—"

Archibald stood up.

"Come on, Felix," he said.

Before I could rise the insurance investigator was on his feet, holding up both hands.

"Don't be like that," he said. "You know there are rules that I have to follow."

"I don't have time for your rules, Mr. Insurance Man. People have been dying out there and your government is covering it up. There's something rotten in this business and I'm the one's going to sanitize and bleach it clean."

"What do you mean about the government?" Vialet asked.

"You answer me, Mr. Insurance Man, and then I'll share."

"That's hardly fair, you know," Vialet said. "What if I give you all my information and then you turn around and leave or tell me that you really don't know anything?"

"I'm not the liar here," Lawless said. "You are. This whole building is a lie. Your pale-faced boy and your snotty secretaries are lies. Maybe if you ate raw flesh at your desk and kept a pot of shit at each doorway then maybe you'd be halfway to the truth about something. No. I'm not a liar, Mr. Insurance Man. I'm the only true thing you've seen all year."

His voice sounded a little high, strained. I worried that maybe one of his psychological maladies was manifesting itself.

"Mr. Lawless," I said.

When he turned toward me I could see the madness in his eyes.

"What?"

"We don't have the briefcase with us so I won't be able to make complete notes."

For a moment he was bewildered but then his mind grabbed hold. He laughed and said, "It's okay, Felix. We'll just wing it until we have the case." He looked back at Vialet and said, "Tell me, who do you suspect in the theft?"

Vialet looked at us and sighed. He sat down and so did Lawless.

"A man named Lamarr," the insurance man said.

"Benny," Lawless agreed. "Him and Lana Drexel. And Valerie Lox, Kenneth Cornell, and Henry Lansman. We know the soldiers. What we want is the bankroll."

I could see that Vialet was concentrating on the names Lawless threw out.

"You seem to know more than I do," he said.

"Who is the man who has been traveling with Lamarr lately?" Archibald asked. "A white man in his forties. He has short hair, maybe graying, maybe not."

"Wayne Sacorliss," Vialet said without hesitation. "He's been around Lamarr for a few years. Just as toady as far as we can tell. He has an office on Lexington, just south of Forty-first."

"Who's the buyer?" Lawless asked.

"We think it's a Canadian name Rudolph Bickell. He's a very rich man and a collector of rare gems. He lives in Las Vegas half the year."

"How does he make his money?"

"Buying and selling," Vialet said. "Your grain to bakeries, cotton to sweatshops in Asia, metal to gun makers and guns to the highest bidder."

"Weapons?"

"Anything," Vialet said. "He'd been making noise to Strangman about buying the gemstones until about three months ago. We figure that when he came up with the plan he stopped calling."

"How much?" Lawless asked.

"We'll go as high as three million. That's all the stones in perfect condition. No trouble to cover either."

"Will corroboration by the police about my central role in reclaiming the jewels be enough?" Lawless asked in flawless business contract style.

"Certainly," Vialet allowed.

"Come on, Felix," Archibald said.

We were out of the gray insurance building in less than five minutes.

16

"I thought that you were an anarchist," I was saying, "a political purist, a man of the people."

Lawless was sitting next to me in the back seat of Derek Chambers's limo, scanning the white pages.

"That sounds right to me," he said. "But mostly, Felix, like I told you before, I walk that line."

"So the three million means nothing to you?"

"That money will pay for a lot of walking, son. Slaves walking across borders, bound men dancing again—that's what it'll pay for, and more."

He gave Derek an address on Lexington.

Sacorliss ran an optical glass frame distribution business on the fourteenth floor. Many of the offices around him were empty. The reception room had been uninhabited for some while. There was dust on the blotter and no evidence that the phone was even plugged in. I wondered if Wayne Sacorliss had moved on to LensCrafters or some other larger optical business.

"Hello," I called.

There was a doorway beyond the reception desk leading to a passageway formed from opaque glass panels. This hallway was in the form of an L that one would suspect led to the main office.

"Who's there?" a mild mannered male voice inquired.

"Archibald Lawless," I said, "and his assistant." I couldn't get my tongue around the word scribe.

A man appeared in the glass angle. From the front he could have been the man I saw running from the death of Henry Lansman. Only this man wore a light brown suit instead of a red parka.

"Who?" he asked.

"We've come to ask you about Benny Lamarr," Lawless said.

Sacorliss had light blue eyes and a broad face. His eyes were elliptical in both shape and manner. His lips were so sensual they belonged on a younger man, or a slightly perverse demigod. His features were all that he showed. There wasn't even a glimmer of recognition for the man he assisted.

He didn't respond at all.

"Can we go into your office, Mr. Sacorliss?" I asked.

"Are you here to buy frames?"

"No."

"Then I don't see what we have to talk about."

"Henry Lansman for one thing," I said.

From the corner of my eye I saw Lawless swivel his head to regard me.

"I don't know who that is," Sacorliss was saying, "but if you must come in then follow me."

At the end of the L-shaped glass hall was a round room lined on one side by waist-high, old fashioned windows that were furbished with brown tinted glass. I could see people in offices not twenty feet away. Some were working and others talking. It was a pleasant proletariat view of the inner workings of a big city's commerce.

This room was also quite desolate. One maple desk with a square-cut oak chair, a telephone with a bare cord that ran across the room to find the jack in the opposite wall. There was a laptop computer on the floor and not one scrap of paper anywhere.

Sacorliss was a few inches taller than I and maybe twenty pounds more than he should have been. But he moved with grace and self-confidence. Once we were in the room he closed the door.

Lawless's eyes never left the smaller man. His wariness made me nervous but I didn't know what to do. So I perched myself on the edge of the maple desk while Wayne Sacorliss and Archibald faced each other.

"What is it you want from me?" Sacorliss asked the amber king before him.

"There's no need for trouble here, Wayne. I'm just interested in why the government wants to cover up Lansman's death, his and a few others whom you might or might not know."

Lawless's mouth turned up in a smile but his eyes were dull.

The baby finger of his left hand twitched.

Sacorliss moved a few inches to his right so that his back was turned fully toward me. Seeing his head from this position I was sure that he was the same man I saw fleeing the scene of Henry Lansman's death. I wanted to signal Lawless that we had what we needed but all of his attention was on the killer.

"I furnish frames for optical lenses, Mr. um, Lawless, wasn't it?"

"There's no need for conflict between us, Wayne," Lawless said in a uncharacteristically placating tone. "Felix here and I just want to know about who would want to hide the murders of international criminals. Especially when those murders were so well executed that no doctor would suspect foul play."

What happened next took me a few days to work out. Sacorliss lifted his right shoulder in a way that made me think he was about to deny any knowledge of Lawless's insinuations. Then Archibald took half a step backwards. Sacorliss moved the same distance forward by taking a step with his left foot. Then the assassin shouted and I felt a powerful impact against my chest. I flew backward over the desk, hit the floor and slid into the wall.

While I was still en route to the wall Sacorliss produced a very slender ten-inch blade from somewhere in his suit. He lunged at his anarchist inquisitor and stabbed him in the chest.

Lawless wasn't slow, however. He grabbed Sacorliss's arm at the elbow so that the tip of the blade went less than half an inch into his body.

I struggled to my feet coughing hard. The vision I saw was surreal: Before me the two men were struggling like the titans in Goya's black painting. Sacorliss's knife was still piercing Lawless's chest but the larger man was managing to impede the progress of the blade. Through the window two women were talking, a whole office full of workers were walking back and forth, there was even a man looking up from his keyboard staring dreamily toward the battle.

Sacorliss kicked Lawless in the thigh with a quick movement. He did this twice more and I knew that sooner or later the man I came in with would be dead. I tried the door but it was locked. I was still coughing and stunned from the roundhouse kick the killer had hit me with. I looked for something to hit him with. I tried to lift his oak chair but it was too heavy to get up over my head.

I was about to go for the laptop when Sacorliss tried another kick. Lawless moved his thigh and the assassin lost his balance. Lawless then lifted him up over his head. That's when the most amazing thing happened. Somehow Archibald managed to disarm Sacorliss so that when he slammed him down on the floor he also stabbed him through the chest.

Sacorliss kicked Lawless away and jumped to his feet. He looked at me and then at the computer. He took a step toward the laptop but his foot betrayed him and he went down on one knee. He looked at his killer then.

"Who are you?" I heard him ask. And then he fell face forward and I think he was dead.

Blood seeped toward the laptop.

Lawless turned Sacorliss over with a toe.

"Get the computer," he said to me.

While I did that, he wiped the haft of the knife clean of fingerprints.

People were still gabbing and working in the office building across the way.

On the way out, Lawless made sure that the doorknob was clean of prints. By the time we were back in Derek's limo, I was so cold that my teeth were chattering. Soon after that I lost consciousness.

17

When I woke up it was dark. I was still dressed and on my back on a bed that was fully made. There was a scented candle burning and mild recorder music wafting in from somewhere. I felt odd, both peaceful and numb. My hands were lying at my sides and I felt no need to move them. I remembered the death of Wayne Sacorliss and the bizarre witnesses from the windows across the way. I thought about the blood across the barren wood floor but none of that bothered me. I supposed that Lawless had given me some kind of sedative from his medical case; something to relax my nerves. I was grateful for whatever he'd done because I knew that unaided I would have been in the depths of anxious despair.

A feathery touch skimmed my brow. I turned to see a woman, somewhere near fifty but still very attractive, sitting at my side.

"You had quite a scare," she said.

"Where am I?"

"Have you ever been to Queens?" she asked with a smile.

"Kennedy Airport."

She was slight and pale with crystalline blue eyes and long fingers. She wore a cream colored dress. The bodice was raw silk and the rest was made from the more refined version of that material. It seemed as if her hair were platinum blonde instead of white.

"Who are you?" I asked.

"A friend of Archibald," she said. "He's downstairs now. Would you like to see him?"

"I don't know if I can get up."

"Once you start moving it wears off," she said.

She took my hand and stood up, pulling me. She had no strength but I followed her lead. I worried that when I got to my feet I'd be dizzy but I wasn't. As a matter of fact I felt very good.

Outside the bedroom was a short hallway that shared space with a staircase leading down. Everything was covered in thick green carpeting and so our footsteps were silent.

On the first floor was a sitting room with two sofas and three stuffed chairs. Archibald Lawless, wearing a gold colored two-piece suit and a ochre shirt was sitting in one of the chairs with his feet up on a small stool.

"Felix. How are you, son?"

"You killed that man."

"I certainly did. Maybe if you hadn't told him about Lansman I could have kept him alive but—"

"You mean you blame you killing him on me?"

"As soon as you mentioned Lansman he was sure that we had identified him as the assassin. It was either us or him. I tried to tell him that I didn't care but he was a professional and he had to at least try and kill us."

I sat down on the corner of a sofa nearest to him.

"How can you be so cavalier about a murder?" I asked.

"I did not murder him," he replied. "I saved our lives. That man was a stone cold killer. If I hadn't been keeping up with my tai chi he would have gutted me and then cut your throat."

I remembered the impact of his kick against my chest and the speed with which he attacked the seemingly unassailable Lawless.

"What about all those witnesses?"

"There were no witnesses."

"The people in the windows across the way. We were in plain sight of them."

"Oh no," Lawless said, shaking his spiky head. "Those windows were one-way panes. I've used the same brand myself."

"So no one saw?"

"No. And even if they did. He was trying to kill us. That was self-defense, Felix."

"Would either of you boys like to have some tea?" our hostess asked.

"I'd like some English Breakfast if you have it, ma'am," I said.

She smiled at me and said, "I like this one, Arch. You should hold onto him."

"He doesn't want to work for me, Red. Thinks that it's too dangerous."

She smiled again. "Green tea for you?"

Lawless nodded and she made her way out of the room.

"What did you call her?" I asked.

"Red."

"Red Tuesday?"

"Has she asked you if you were Catholic yet?"

For some reason I hadn't thought that Red Tuesday was a real person. At least not a beautiful middle-aged woman living in a standard working class home.

"If she does," Lawless continued, "Tell her that your parents are but that you have lapsed in your faith."

"Okay."

"Now," he said. "Lets talk about what we have to do tonight."

"Tonight? I'm not doing anything with you tonight or any other time. You killed that man."

"Did I have a choice?"

"*I* have a choice," I said. "The choice not to be in the same room with you."

"Yes," he said, nodding at me. "But this is a deep problem, Felix. You can see that even I'm in danger here. Sacorliss was an assassin. We certainly ran the danger of a violent confrontation with such a man. But now we're going to a sanitarium, to see a sick man. There's no danger involved."

"Why the hell do you need me in the first place?" I said. "You never even knew me before three days ago. How can I possibly help someone like you?"

"My kind of work is lonely, Felix. And maybe it's a little bit crazy. I've spent a whole lifetime trying to fix broken systems, making sure that justice is served. Lately I've been lagging a little. Slowing down, breaking down, making mistakes that could be fatal. Having you by me has given me a little bit of an edge, some confidence that I hadn't even known was eroded.

"All I ask is that you stick with me until we find the answer to why Sacorliss was activated. Just stick with me until the police believe they have the killer of Henry Lansman."

"I thought he had a heart attack?"

"No. He was accosted by an aerosol toxin. The autopsy showed that last night. And there's a warrant out for your arrest in connection with that killing."

"Me?"

"English Breakfast," Red Tuesday said as she came into the room. "And green tea for man who watches his health and the health of the enslaved world."

She carried the delicate teacups on a silver tray, proffering us our drinks.

"Felix?" she said.

"Yes, Ms. Tuesday?"

"Are you a Catholic by any chance?"

"My parents are, ma'am, but I never went after I was twelve."

Oberman's Sanitarium had only a small brass sign on the wall to identify itself. Otherwise you would have thought it was a residential prewar building like all its neighbors on the block.

It was twelve-fifteen by the time Derek dropped us off.

Lawless rang the bell and stood there in his gold suit, carrying his medical briefcase. He looked like a rattlesnake in a Sunday bonnet, a stick of dynamite with chocolate coating up to the fuse.

I was sickened by events of the day but still I knew I had to stay with the anarchist because that was the only way for me to keep on top of what was happening. If I left then, even if I ran and went back to New Orleans, I would be vulnerable to dangerous people who could get at me without me ever knowing they were near. And there would still be a warrant out for my arrest.

The door was opened by a woman wearing all white. She was young, tall, and manlike in her demeanor and visage.

"Lawless?" she asked me.

"It's him," I said.

"Come quickly."

We hustled into the building.

She led us to an elevator made for two and took us to the sixth floor.

When we got out she said, "Do you have it?"

Lawless took out a large wallet from his front pocket and counted out five one-hundred-dollar bills. He handed these to the manly nurse.

"No funny stuff," she said as she folded the bills into her white apron.

"What room is he in?" Lawless responded.

"Seven."

18

I was surprised by the hominess of the room. Darkish yellow walls with a real wood-framed bed and knickknacks on the shelves and bureaus. On the wall with the largest expanse hung a framed picture that was at least six feet wide and almost that in height. The colors were buff and pale blue. It was a beach at first light. Almost devoid of details it seemed to me a commentary on the beginning of the world.

In a small padded chair next to the one window a thin white man sat looking out on the street. He wore a gray robe over striped blue and white pajamas. His elbows were on his knees, his small mustache was crooked.

"I, I, I thought you were here for me," he said softly.

The only clue that we were in some kind of medical facility was metal tray-table at the foot of the bed. There was a medical form on a clipboard hanging from the side. Lawless unhooked the clipboard and began to read.

"Yes," he said to the patient. "I was told that you're suffering from a mild breakdown. I was called by Dr. Samson to administer Cronomicin."

"Wh-what's that?"

Lawless put his briefcase on the metal table and opened it. He took out a hypodermic needle that had already been filled with a pinkish fluid.

Gesturing at the needle, he said, "This will alleviate your anxiety and impose a feeling of calm that will allow you to sleep and wake up without a care in the world."

I wondered if he had given me some of the same juice.

"Why haven't they, why haven't they given it to me before?" Lionel Strangman asked.

"Cronomicin is very expensive. There was a hang-up with the insurance." Lawless's smile was almost benign.

"You don't look like a doctor." Strangman seemed to be speaking to someone behind the big amber liar.

"Catch me at office hours and I'll have on my smock just like everybody else."

"Maybe I should—" Strangman started.

"Give me your arm," Lawless commanded.

The thin white man did as he was told.

Lawless took a cotton swab and alcohol from his briefcase, cleaned a spot on Strangman's arm, and then began to search for a vein. I turned my back on them. I don't know why exactly. Maybe I thought if I didn't see the injection I couldn't bear witness in court.

I went to the picture on the wall. It wasn't a print, as I had at first thought, but an original oil painting. It was old too. From a few feet distant the beige sky and faint water looked to be seamless. But up close I could make out thousands of small brushstrokes composed of dozens of colors. I imagined some asylum patient of another century making this painting for the inmates of today.

"How are you feeling, Mr. Strangman?" Archibald Lawless was asking the man in the chair.

"Good," he said without hesitation. "Peaceful. Maybe I should lie down."

"In a minute. First I'd like to ask you a few questions."

"Okay."

"Dr. Samson told me that you had the collapse after a theft."

"Yes," he said. He looked down at his hands. "Funny, it doesn't seem so important now. They were beautiful, you know. Almost like rubies."

"They were stolen from a safe in your home?" Dr. Lawless asked.

"Yes." Strangman looked up. His eyes were beatific as if they were meant to be paired with that painting of the primordial first day. "I woke up and they were gone. They must have drugged me because the police said that they used an explosive on the safe."

He brought hands to lips as a reflex of grief but the sorrow was forgotten now with Lawless's elixir in his veins.

"Do you know Benny Lamarr?" Lawless asked.

"Why yes. How did you know that?"

"He called to ask how you were doing. Him and his friend Wayne Sacorliss."

"Wayne. To look at him you'd never think that he was from Lebanon, would you?"

"No," Lawless said carelessly. "It surprised me that he was a Moslem."

"Oh no," Strangman said in high feminine voice. "Christian. Christian. His mother was from Armenia. But he's an American now."

"Did you work with him?"

"No. He works for Benny. Poor Benny."

"Why do you say that?" Lawless asked.

"He brought his fiancée to a party at my house. The next night she was in my bed." Even under the spell of the narcotic Strangman was a dog.

"Who are you?" I asked Archibald Lawless.

We were sitting in the window seat of a twenty-four-hour diner on the West Side Highway at 2:57 A.M.

"You're not questioning my name again, are you?"

"No. Not that. How did you get into that clinic? How did you know what drug to give Strangman? How did you know what that killer was thinking? No one man can do all these things."

"You're right."

"I thought so. Who do you work for? Really."

"You're a very intelligent young man, Felix. But intelligence alone doesn't help you rise above. You see clearly, more clearly, than most, but you don't apprehend.

"I am, everyone is, a potential sovereignty, a nation upon my own. I am responsible for every action taken in my name and for every step that I take—or that I don't take. When you get to the place that you can see yourself as a completely autonomous, self-governing entity then everything will come to you; everything that you will need."

A waiter brought us coffee then. I sat there drinking, thinking about the past few days. I had missed two seminars and a meeting with my advisor. I hadn't been home, though I doubted if my roommate would notice. I had been arrested for suspicion of my involvement in a murder, made love to by a woman I didn't really know, I had been an accessory to a killing, and party to the illegal impersonation of a doctor—in addition to the unlawful administration of contraband drugs. I was temporarily in the employ of a madman and involved in the investigation of the theft of millions of dollars in diamonds. And, even though I was aware of all those aspects of the past few days, I was still almost totally in the dark.

"What are we doing, Mr. Lawless? What are we involved in?"

He smiled at me. The swamp of his eyes grew to an endless, hopeless vista.

"Can't you put it together yet, Felix?"

"No sir."

He smiled and reached over to pat my forearm. There was something very calming about this gesture.

"To answer one of your questions," he said. "I once saved the life of the daughter of a man who is very influential at the St. Botolph Hospital."

"So?"

"Botolph funds Oberman's Sanitarium. I called this man and asked him to intervene. A price was set and there you are."

"I thought all you wanted me to do was take notes," I said, exhausted by the stretch of Lawless's reach.

"Tonight we'll go to a place I know across the river and tomorrow we'll come back to clear it all up." He reached in his pocket and came out with two dollar bills. "Oh. I seem to be a little short. Do you have any cash, son?"

"What about that big fat wallet you paid the nurse from?"

"I only had what I needed for the bribe. Don't you have some money left from that IOU you left me?"

I paid the bill and we left.

There was a motorboat waiting for us off a dilapidated pier across the West Side Highway. Because there were no stairs we had to jump down onto the launch, which then took us up river and deposited us at strange river inn on the Jersey side of the Hudson.

The inn had its own small dock. The boat captain, who was dark-skinned and utterly silent, let us off there. The key to the door was in a coffee can nailed to a wall. Lawless brought us in an area that was at least partially submerged in the River.

There was no one else in residence, at least no one there that I could see. The door Lawless opened led to a circular room that had four closed doors and led to an open hallway.

"Room two is yours," the anarchist told me. "Breakfast will be at the end of the hall when you wake up."

The bed was bunklike but very comfortable. Maybe the drug I'd been given before was still in effect but whatever the circumstance I was asleep as soon as I lay down.

19

The sunrise over Manhattan was magnificent. It sparkled on the water and shone brightly in my little cockleshell room. For almost the first full minute of consciousness I forgot my problems.

The respite was soon over, however. By the time I sat up anxiety was already clouding my mind. I dressed quickly. The hall outside my door led to a wide room under a low roof that was dominated by an irregularly shaped table—set for two.

"Good morning, Felix."

Archibald Lawless was eating scrambled eggs. A small Asian woman sat on a small stool against the wall. When I entered the room she stood up and pulled out the seat next to the anarchist. She nodded for me to sit and when I did so she scuttled out of the room.

"Mr. Lawless."

"Don't look so sad, son. Today all of our problems will be solved."

"Where are we?" I asked.

"Oh," he said, half smiling, looking like the main deity of some lost Buddhist tribe that found itself marooned in Africa an eon ago. "This is a halfway house. One of many such places where certain unpopular foreign dignitaries and agents come when they have to do business in America."

"Like who?" I asked.

"Militants, dethroned dictators, communist sympathizers, even anarchists have stayed here. Presidents and kings unpopular with current American regimes have slept in the same bed that you have, waiting to meet with clandestine mediators or diplomats from the UN."

"But there's no security."

"None that you've seen," Lawless said, bearing that saintly mien. "But there's enough protection close at hand to fend off an NYPD swat team."

"You're joking," I said.

"All right," he replied. "Have it your way."

The small woman returned with a plate of eggs and herring, a small bowl of rice and a mug full of smoky flavored tea. After serving me she returned to her perch against the wall.

I ate for a while. Lawless looked out of the window at Manhattan.

"So at the office you look at New Jersey and here you look at New York."

He cackled and then laughed. He grabbed my neck with his powerful hand and said, "I like you, boy. You know how to make me laugh."

"Who do you plan to kill today?"

He laughed again.

"I talked to your girlfriend last night," he said.

"Who?" I wondered if he had somehow gotten in touch with Sharee.

"Lana," he said articulating her name as an opera singer might in preparation for singing it later on. "She and Mr. Lamarr practised being engaged before she seduced Strangman."

"Okay."

"He told her things."

"What things?"

"People he trusted . . . places where certain transactions were to transpire."

"And where might that be?" I asked, sucked into the rhythm of his improvisational operetta.

"Today we go to Peninsula Hotel," he said. "There all of our problems will come to an end."

We exited the Refugee Inn (Lawless's term for it) by climbing a steep trail which led to a dirt path that became a paved lane after a quarter mile or so. There Derek was waiting for us. He drove off without asking for a destination.

On the way Lawless talked to me about my duties as his scribe. I was tired of arguing with him, and just a little frightened after seeing how easily he killed the assassin Wayne Sacorliss, and so I let him go on without contradiction.

A block away from the hotel I began to get nervous.

"What are we going to do here?" I asked.

"Have breakfast."

"We just had breakfast."

"The sacrifices we must make for the movement," he said. "Sometimes you have to wallow with the fat cats and follow their lead. Here, put these on."

He handed me a pair of glasses that had thick black rims and a blond wig.

"What are these for?"

"You're going to be incognito."

I donned the glasses and wig because I had already learned that there was logic to every move that my would-be employer made. I also half believed that the outlandish getup would get us thrown out of the hotel.

We entered the restaurant at about ten-thirty. No one gave me a second look.

When Lawless introduced himself the maître d' guided us to a table in an isolated corner of the main dining room. Lawless put himself in a seat with his back to rest of the room. I was seated in an alcove, hidden from view by the bauguette.

He ordered salmon hash with shirred eggs and I had the Marscapone pancakes with a side of apple smoked bacon.

After the breakfast was served I said, "I'm not going to work for you, you know."

"I know that you don't expect to take the job but the day is young."

"No. I'm not working for you under any condition. I don't even know what we're doing now. How can I take a job where I don't even know where I'll wake up in the morning?"

"You'd rather have a job where you'll know where you'll be every day for the rest of your life?" he asked.

"No. Of course not, but, I mean I don't want to be involved with criminals and dirty politics."

"You're the one who said that he always pays his taxes, Felix," he said. "That makes you a part of an elite criminal and political class. If you buy gasoline or knitted sweaters or even bananas then you belong to the greatest crime family on Earth."

I don't know why I argued with him. I had been around people like him ever since college. *Politico dingbats* is what my father calls them. People who see conspiracies in our economic system, people who believe America is actually set against the notion of liberty.

I talked about the Constitution. He talked about the millions dead in Africa, Cambodia, Vietnam, and Nagasaki. I talked about the freedom of speech. He came back with the millions of dark-skinned men and women who spend most of their lives in prison. I talked about international terrorism. He brushed that off and concentrated on the embargos imposed on Iraq, Iran, Cuba, and North Korea.

I was about to bring out the big guns: the American peoples and the part they played in World War Two. But just then a familiar man came up and sat down at our table.

"Right on time, Ray," Archibald Lawless said.

Our guest was dressed in a dark blue suit with a white shirt held together at the cuffs by sapphire studs. *Raymond*, I supposed his first name was. The only title I knew him by was Captain Delgado.

"Archie," he said. "Felix. What's up?"

The way he said my name was respectful, as if I deserved a place at the table. As much as I wanted to deny it, I liked that feeling.

"Two tables over to your right," Lawless told the police captain. "A man and a woman talking over caviar and scrambled eggs."

I leaned over and slanted my eyes to see them. Through the clear glass frames of my disguise I recognized Valerie Lox, the Madison Avenue real estate agent. The whole time we had been talking she was there meeting with a man who was unknown to me.

She was wearing a red Chanel suit and an orange scarf. I'd never seen the man she was with. He was porcine and yet handsome. His movements were self-assured to the degree where he almost seemed careless.

"You were recently made aware of a diamond theft, were you not, Captain Delgado?" Lawless asked.

"Are you telling me or digging?" the cop asked back.

"Red diamonds," Lawless replied. "Millions of dollars' worth. A syndicate represented by Lionel Strangman reported it to their insurance company."

"You have my attention."

"Is Felix still being sought in connection with the murder of Henry Lansman?"

"Until we find another candidate."

"Wait," I said. "Why would you even think of me?"

Delgado shrugged but said nothing.

"The boy has a right to know why he's being sought," Archibald said.

"The gems," the police captain said as if it were patently obvious. "A special unit started investigating Lamarr as soon as the theft was reported. They had Lansman, Brexel, Cornell, and Ms. Lox over there under surveillance. There was a tap on her phone. When she called Cornell we picked up your name. Then when you were photographed at the scene of Lansman's murder you became a suspect."

"Why not Sacorliss?" I asked.

"He's out of bounds," Delgado said. "Works as an informant for the FBI."

"Regardless," Lawless said. "Sacorliss is your killer."

"Who does he work for?" Delgado asked.

"As you indicated," Lawless said with a sense of the dramatic in his tone, "the same people that you work for. He also killed Benny Lamarr and Kenneth Cornell. If you look into the records of those deaths you will find that they have disappeared. Gone to Arizona, I hear."

"Fuckin' meatheads," Delgado muttered.

"I agree," Lawless said. "You have another problem however."

"What's that?"

"The man sitting with Ms. Lox is Rudolph Bickell, one of the richest men in Canada. She is passing the diamonds to him. She may have already done so."

"You want me to arrest the richest man in Canada on your say-so?"

"It's a toss-up, my friend. Take the plunge and maybe you'll lose everything. Don't take it and pass up the chance of a lifetime."

Lawless gestured for the bill and then said to Delgado, "You can pay for our meal, officer. Because even just the arrest of Wayne Sacorliss will keep you in good standing with your superiors.

"Come on, Felix," he said then.

And he left without paying another bill.

20

Even the *Wall Street Journal* covered the arrest of the billionaire Rudolph Bickell. They also asked how the mysterious entrepreneur was able to make bail and flee the country within three hours of his arrest at the posh Peninsula Hotel in New York City. Bickell's spokesperson in Toronto told reporters that the industrialist had no knowledge that the diamonds he was purchasing were stolen; that there was no law against acquiring the gemstones from the legal representative of a diamond dealer. Valerie Lox, who *was* in jail, was working for a man named Benny Lamarr who had died in an unrelated auto accident.

The *Journal* didn't cover the murder of optical materials dealer Wayne Sacorliss. I had to read about that in the Metro Section of *The New York Times*. The police had no motive for the crime but they had not ruled out theft. It seemed that Sacorliss was known to carry large sums of cash.

No one connected Sacorliss with Lamarr.

There were no policemen waiting at my door either.

The next morning at five-fifty I was at the front desk of the Tessla building marveling bleary eyed at the saintliness of Joan of Arc.

"Mr. Orlean," a young red-headed guard said.

"How do you know my name?"

"Mr. Lawless gave us a picture of you so that we'd know to let you in even if you came in after five fifty-five."

He answered the door before I knocked. That morning he wore white overalls and a bloodred shirt. At his gesture I went into his office and sat on the tree trunk I'd used a few days before.

"What was it all about?" I asked him.

"That why you're here, Felix?"

"Yes sir."

"You want to know why," he said with a smile. "It bothers you to sit alone in your room thinking that the papers might have gotten it wrong, that the police might be covering up a crime. It's troubling that you can be exonerated from suspicion in a murder case with a few words over an expensive breakfast in midtown Manhattan. That's not the world you thought you were living in."

If I were superstitious I might have believed that he was a mind reader. As it was, I thought that he had incredible logical and intuitive faculties.

"Yes," I said, "but there's something else."

"First," he said, "let me tell you what I know."

He sat back in his chair and brought his hands together in front of his face as if in Christian prayer.

"There was, in the works of Agineau Armaments, a shipment being readied for delivery in Ecuador at the end of next month. The company slated to receive the shipment is a dummy corporation owned by a conservative plantation owner in Venezuela. It's not hard to see where the shipment is bound for and who will use the guns."

"So Bickell is funding conservative guerrillas in Venezuela?" I asked.

"Bickell wanted the diamonds. Sacorliss wanted to fund the revolution."

"Why?"

"That, my friend, is an argument that we will have over and over again. For my money Sacorliss is a well-trained operative of the United States government. His job was to plan a robbery set to fund our clandestine interests in South America. You probably believe that it isn't such a far-reaching conspiratorial act. Only time, and blood, will tell."

"What about Valerie Lox and Lana Drexel?"

"Lox was released from jail. She claimed that she knew nothing about stolen gems, that Lamarr had always been a reputable dealer. The prosecutors decided to believe her which makes me believe that she is also a government operative. I sent Drexel her money. She's moving to Hollywood. I've been trying to decipher the code of Sacorliss's computer. One day I'll succeed and prove to you that I'm right. All we have to discuss now are the final terms of your employment."

"What do you mean?" I asked. "You don't expect that I'm going to come work for you after what I've been through."

"Sure I do."

"Why?"

"Because of your aunt, of course. You'll agree to work for me for a specified amount of time and I will agree to do what your father refused to do, free your aunt from jail."

The hairs on the back of my neck rose up then. I hadn't even considered this option until the middle of the night before. My face must have exposed my surprise.

"I need you, Felix," Lawless said. "You complete a faulty circuit in my head. You give me the three years that your aunt has left on her sentence and I will make sure that she's out of the joint by Sunday next."

"I still won't be involved in any crimes," I said.

"Agreed. I won't knowingly put you in the position of breaking the law. You will write down everything of import that I say, regardless of your own opinions. I in turn will open your eyes to a whole new world. As a journalist you will learn more from me than from a thousand seminars."

There was no reason for me to argue.

"Okay," I said. "But I have two needs and one question."

"And what might those be?"

"First is salary."

"Forty-two thousand dollars a year payable from a fund set up by Auchschlous, Anterbe, and Grenell, the world's largest insurers of rare gems. They prepared the account at my behest."

"Two," I said, "is that you agree not to lie to me. If I ask you a question you answer to the best of your ability."

"Agreed," Lawless replied, "depending upon circumstances. It might be that the truth would be giving away someone else's secret and that I have no right to do."

"Okay. Fine. Then I agree. Three years terminable if you decide I can't do the job or if you break your word to me. All of course contingent upon the release of my aunt Alberta."

"You had a question," Lawless reminded me.

"Oh. Yeah. It didn't have to do with our contract."

"Ask anyway."

"Who was the woman who came to your apartment door, the one in Harlem? I think she said her name was Maddie."

"Oh. No one. She had nothing to do with our business."

"But who was she?" I asked.

"My fiancée," he said. "She's been looking for me for a couple of years now."

I'm still in school, still out of contact with my parents. My aunt Alberta was freed from jail on a technicality that a colleague of my father turned up. She's coming to live in New York.

I work for the anarchist at least four days a week. We argue almost every day I'm there. I still think he's crazy but I've learned that doesn't always mean he's wrong.

Sharyn McCrumb

Sharyn McCrumb holds degrees from the University of North Carolina and Virginia Tech. She lives in Virginia's Blue Ridge Mountains but travels the United States and the world lecturing on her work, most recently leading a writer's workshop in Paris in summer 2001. Her Ballad series, beginning with *If Ever I Return, Pretty Peggy-O* (1990), has won her numerous honors, including the Appalachian Writers Association's Award for Outstanding Contribution to Appalachian Literature and several listings as *New York Times* and *Los Angeles Times* notable books. In the introduction to her short-story collection *Foggy Mountain Breakdown and Other Stories*, she details the family history in North Carolina and Tennessee that contributed to her Appalachian fiction. One of the continuing characters, Sheriff Spencer Arrowood, takes his surname from ancestors on her father's side, while Frankie Silver ("the first woman hanged for murder in the state of North Carolina"), whose story McCrumb would incorporate in *The Ballad of Frankie Silver*, was a distant cousin. "My books are like Appalachian quilts," she writes. "I take brightly colored scraps of legends, ballads, fragments of rural life, and local tragedy, and I place them together into a complex whole that tells not only a story, but also a deeper truth about the nature of the mountain south." The seventh and most recent title in the Ballad series, *Ghost Riders*, appeared in 2003. Her most recent novel is *St. Dale.*

THE RESURRECTION MAN

Sharyn McCrumb

Haloed in lamplight the young man stands swaying on the threshold for an instant, perhaps three heartbeats, before the scalpel falls from his fingers, and he pitches forward into the dark hallway, stumbling toward the balcony railing where the stairwell curves around the rotunda. From where he stands outside the second floor classroom, it is thirty feet or more to the marble floor below.

The old man in the hall is not surprised. He has seen too many pale young men make just such a dash from that room, from its stench of sweet decay, hardly leavened by the tobacco spit that coats the wooden floor. They chew to mask the odor—this boy is new, and does not yet know that trick. The tobacco will make him as sick as the other at first. It is all one.

He makes no move to take hold of the sufferer. They are alone in the building, but even so, these days such a thing would not be proper. The young man might take offense, and there is his own white linen suit to be thought of. He is not working tonight. He only came to see why there was a light in the upstairs window. More to the point, he has long ago lost the desire to touch human flesh. He stays in the shadows and watches the young man lunge for cold air in the cavernous space beneath the dome.

But the smell of the dissecting room is not escaped so easily, and the old man knows what will happen if the student does not get fresh air soon. Somebody will have to clean up the hall floor. It won't be the old man. He is too grand for that, but it will be one of the other employees, some acquaintance of his, and it is easy enough to spare a cleaner more work and the young man more embarrassment. Easy enough to offer the fire bucket as an alternative.

A gallon bucket of sand has been set outside the dissection room in case a careless student overturns an oil lamp, and in one fluid motion he hoists it, setting it in front of the iron railing, directly in the path of the young man, who has only to bend over and exhale to make use of it, which he does, for a long time. He coughs and retches until he can manage only gasps and dry heaves. By the time he is finished he is on his knees, hunched over the bucket, clutching it with both hands. The retching turns to sobbing and then to soft cursing.

A few feet away the old man waits, courteously and without much interest in the purging process. If the student should feel too ill to return to his work, he will call someone to tend to him. He will not offer his shoulder unless the tottering young man insists. He does not care to touch people: The living are not his concern. Most of the students know him, and would shrink from him, but this one is new. He may not know whom he has encountered in the dark hallway. For all the boy's momentary terror and revulsion, he will be all right. He will return to his task, if not tonight then tomorrow. It is the night before his first dissection class, after all, and many a queasy novice has conquered his nerves and gone on to make a fine doctor.

The young man wipes his face with a linen handkerchief, still gulping air as if the motion *in* will prevent the motion *out.* "I'm all right," he says, aware of the silent presence a few feet away.

"Shouldn't come alone," the old man says. "They make you work together for a reason. 'Cause you joke. You prop up one another's nerve. Distractions beguile the mind, makes it easier, if you don't think too much."

The young man looks up then, recognizing the florid speech and the lilt of a Gullah accent beneath the surface. Pressing the handkerchief to his mouth, he takes an involuntary step backward. He does know who this is. He had been expecting to see a sweeper, perhaps, or one of the professors working here after hours, but this apparition, suddenly recognized, legendary and ancient even in his father's student days, fills him with more terror than the shrouded forms in the room he has just quit.

He is standing in the hall, beside a bucket filled with his own vomit, and his only companion is this ancient black man, still straight and strong-looking in a white linen suit, his grizzled hair shines about his head in the lamplight like a halo, and the student knows that he looks a fool in front of this old man who has touched more dead people than live ones. He peers at the wrinkled face to see if there is some trace of scorn in the impassive countenance.

"I was here because I was afraid," he says, glancing back at the lamp-lit room of shrouded tables. He does not owe this man an explanation, and if asked, he might have replied with a curt dismissal, but there is only silence, and he needs to feel life in the dark hall. "I thought I might make a fool of myself in class tomorrow—" He glances toward the bucket, and the old man nods. "—And so I came along tonight to try to prepare myself. To see my—well, to see it. Get it over with. Put a cloth over its eyes." He dabbed at his mouth with the soiled handkerchief. "You understand that feeling, I guess."

"I can't remember," said the old man. He has always worked alone. He pulls a bottle out of the pocket of his black coat, pulls out the cork, and passes it to the young man. It is half full of grain alcohol, clear as water.

The young man takes a long pull on the bottle and wipes his mouth with the back of his hand. The two of them look at each other and smile. Not all of the students would drink from the same bottle as a black man. Not in this new century. Maybe once, but not now. The prim New Englanders would not, for his race is alien to them, and while they preach equality, they shrink from proximity. The crackers would not, because they must always be careful to enforce their precarious rank on the social ladder, even more so since Reconstruction. But this boy is planter class, and he has no need for such gestures. He has traded sweat and spit with Negroes since infancy, and he has no self-consciousness, no need for social barriers. It is the way of his world. They understand each other.

"You don't remember?" The young man smiles in disbelief as he hands back the bottle. "But how could you not recall the first time you touched the dead?"

Because it has been nigh on sixty years, the old man thinks. He points to the bucket. "Do you remember the first time you ever did that?"

His life is divided into *before the train* and *after the train*. Not after the war. Things for him did not so much change after the war as this new century's white folks might suppose. The landmark of his life was that train ride down from Charleston. He remembers some of his earliest life, or perhaps he has imagined parts of it for so long that they have taken on a reality in his mind. He remembers a rag quilt that used to lay atop his corn shuck mattress. It had been pieced together from scraps of cloth—some of the pieces were red and shiny, probably scavenged from silk dresses worn by the ladies up at the house. His memories are a patchwork as well: a glimpse of dark eyes mirroring firelight; the hollowed shell of a box turtle . . . someone, an old man, is making music with it, and people are dancing . . . he is very young, sitting on a dirt floor, watching legs and calico skirts flash past him, brushing him sometimes, as the dancers stamped and spun, the music growing louder and faster . . .

There was a creek, too . . . He is older by then . . . Squatting on a wet rock a little way out into the water, waiting for the frog . . . waiting . . . So still that the white birds come down into the field for the seeds as if he were not there . . . Then crashing through the cattails comes Dog, reeking of creek water and cow dung, licking his face, thrashing the water with his muddy tail . . . frogs scared into kingdom come. What was that dog's name? It is just sounds now, that name, and he isn't sure he remembers them right, but once they meant something inside his head, those sounds . . . He has never heard them since.

Older still . . . Now he has seen the fields for what they are: not a place to play. Sun up to sun down . . . Water in a bucket, dispensed from a gourd hollowed out to make a dipper . . . the drinking gourd. He sits in the circle of folks in the dark field, where a young man with angry eyes is pointing up at the sky. The *drinking gourd* is a pattern of stars. They are important. They lead you somewhere, as the Wise Men followed stars . . . But he never set off to follow those stars, and he does not know what became of the angry young man who did. It is long ago, and he resolved to have nothing to do with drinking gourds—neither stars nor rice fields.

He listened to the old people's stories, of how the trickster rabbit smiled and smiled his way out of danger, and how the fox never saw the trap for the smile, and he reckoned he could do that. He could smile like honey on a johnny cake. Serenity was his shield. You never looked sullen, or angry, or afraid. Sometimes bad things happened to you anyway, but at least, if they did, you did not give your tormentor the gift of your pain as well. So he smiled in the South Carolina sunshine and waited for a door to open somewhere in the world, and presently it did.

The sprawling white house sat on a cobblestone street near the harbor in Charleston. It had a shady porch that ran the length of the house, and a green front door with a polished brass door knocker in the shape of a lion's head, but that door did not open to the likes of him. He used the back door, the one that led to the kitchen part of the house.

The old woman there was kind. To hear anyone say otherwise would have astonished her. She kept slaves as another woman might have kept cats—with indulgent interest in their habits, and great patience with their shortcomings. Their lives were her theatre. She was a spinster woman, living alone in the family house, and she made little enough work for the cook, the maid, and the yard man, but she must have them, for the standards of Charleston's quality folk must be maintained.

The old woman had a cook called Rachel. A young girl with skin the color of honey, and still so young that the corn pone and gravy had not yet thickened her body. She was not as pretty as some, but he could tell by her clothes and the way she carried herself that she was a cherished personage in some fine house. He had met her at church, where he always took care to be the cleanest man there with the shiniest shoes. If his clothes were shabby, they were as clean and presentable as he could make them, and he was handsome, which went a long ways toward making up for any deficiency in station. By then he was a young man, grown tall, with a bronze cast to his skin, not as dark as most, and that was as good as a smile, he reckoned, for he did not look so alien to the white faces who did the picking and choosing. He was a townsman, put to work on the docks for one of the ship's chandlers at the harbor. He liked being close to the sea, and his labors had made him strong and lean, but the work was hard, and it led nowhere. The house folk in the fine homes fared the best. You could tell them just by looking, with their cast-off finery and their noses in the air, knowing their station—higher than most folks.

The fetching little cook noticed him—he took care that this should be so, but he was patient in his courting of her, for he had more on his mind than a tumble on a corn shuck mattress. For many weeks he was as gentlemanly as a prince in a fairy story, taking no more liberties than pressing her hand in farewell as they left the church service. Finally when the look in her eyes told him that she thought he'd hung the moon, he talked marriage. He could not live without her, he said. He wanted no more of freedom than the right to grow old at her side.

Presently the determined Rachel ushered him into the presence of her mistress, the old woman who kept her servants as pets, and he set out to charm her with all the assurance of golden youth, condescending to old age. The gambit would not work forever, but this time it did, and he received the mistress's blessing to wed the pretty young cook. The mistress would buy him, she said, and he could join the household, as butler and coachman—or whatever could be done by an assiduous young man with strength and wit.

The joining took place in a proper white frame church, presided over by a stately clergyman as dignified and elegant as any white minister in Charleston. No broom jumping for the likes of them. And the mistress herself even came to the wedding, sat there in the pew with two of her lady friends and wept happy tears into a lace handkerchief.

Then the newlyweds went back to their room behind the kitchen that would be their home for the next dozen years. Being a town servant was easy, not like dock work. The spinster lady didn't really need a coachman and butler, not more than a few hours a week, so she let him hire out to the inn to work as a porter there, and she even let him keep half of what he earned there. He could have saved up the coins, should have perhaps. One of the cooks there at the inn had been salting away his pay to purchase his freedom, but he didn't see much point in that. As it was, he and Rachel lived in a fine house, ate the same good food as the old lady, and never had to worry about food or clothes or medicine. The free folks might give themselves airs, but they lived in shacks and worked harder than anybody, and he couldn't see the sense of that. Maybe someday they'd think about a change, but no use to deprive himself of fine clothes and a drink or two against that day, for after all, the old missus might free them in her will, and then all those years of scrimping would have been for naught.

All this was *before the train ride . . .*

Dr. George Newton—1852

Just as Lewis Ford and I were setting out from the college on Telfair Street, one of the local students, young Mr. Thomas, happened along in his buggy and insisted upon driving us over the river to the depot at Hamburg so that we could catch the train to Charleston. When Thomas heard our destination, he began to wax poetic about the beauties of that elegant city, but I cut short his rhapsody. "We are only going on business, Dr. Ford and I," I told him. "We shall acquire a servant for the college and come straight back tomorrow."

The young man left us off the depot, wishing us godspeed, but I could see by his expression that he was puzzled, and that only his good manners prevented his questioning us further. *Going to Charleston for a slave?* he was thinking. *Whatever for? Why not just walk down to sale at the Lower Market on Broad Street here in Augusta?*

Well, we could hardly do that, but I was not at liberty to explain the nature of our journey to a disinterested party. We told people that we had gone to secure a porter to perform custodial services for the medical college, and so we were, but we wanted no one with any ties to the local community. Charleston was just about far enough away, we decided.

For all that the railroad has been here twenty years, Lewis claims he will never become accustomed to jolting along at more than thirty miles per hour, but he allows that it does make light of a journey that would have taken more than a day by carriage. I brought a book along, though Lewis professes astonishment that I am able to read at such a speed. He contented himself with watching the pine trees give way to cow pastures and cotton fields and back again.

After an hour he spoke up. "I suppose this expense is necessary, Newton."

"Yes, I think so," I said, still gazing out the window. "We have all discussed it, and agreed that it must be done."

"Yes, I suppose it must. Clegg charges too much for his services, and he really is a most unsatisfactory person. He has taken to drink, you know."

"Can you wonder at it?"

"No. I only hope he manages to chase away the horrors with it. Still, we cannot do business with him any longer, and we have to teach the fellows somehow."

"Exactly. We have no choice."

He cleared his throat. "Charleston. I quite understand the need for acquiring a man with no ties to Augusta, but Charleston is a singular place. They have had their troubles there, you know."

I nodded. Thirty years ago the French Caribbean slave Denmark Vesey led an uprising in Charleston, for which they hanged him. All had been quiet there since, but Dr. Ford is one of nature's worriers. "You may interview the men before the auction if it will ease your mind. You will be one-seventh owner," I reminded him. We had all agreed on that point: All faculty members to own a share in the servant, to be bought out should said faculty member leave the employ of the college.

He nodded. "I shall leave the choosing to you, though, Newton, since you are the dean."

"Very well," I said. Dr. Ford had been my predecessor—the first dean of the medical college—but after all it was he who had engaged the services of the unsatisfactory Clegg, so I thought it best to rely upon my judgment this time.

"Seven hundred dollars, then," said Ford. "One hundred from each man. That sum should be sufficient, don't you think?"

"For a porter, certainly," I said. "But since this fellow will also be replacing Clegg, thus saving us the money we were paying out to him, the price will be a bargain."

"It will be if the new man has diligence and ingenuity. And if he can master the task, of which we are by no means certain," said Ford.

"He will have to. Only a slave can perform the task with impunity."

We said little else for the duration of the journey, but I was hoping for a good dinner in Charleston. After my undergraduate days at the University of Pennsylvania, I went abroad to study medicine in Paris.

There I acquired a taste for the fine food and wines that Charleston offers in abundance. It is the French influence—all those refugees from the French Caribbean improved the cuisine immeasurably.

When we had disembarked and made our way to the inn to wash off the dust of the journey, there were yet a few hours of daylight before dinner, and after I noted down the costs of our train fares and lodging for the college expense record, I decided that it would be prudent to visit the market in preparation for the next day's sale. Slaves who are to be auctioned are housed overnight in quarters near the market, and one may go and view them, so as to be better prepared to bid when the time came.

It was a warm afternoon, and I was mindful of the mix of city smells and sea air as I made my way toward the old market. I presented myself at the building quartering those who were to be sold the next day, and a scowling young man ushered me inside. No doubt the keeping of this establishment made for unpleasant work, for some of its inhabitants were loudly lamenting their fate, while others called out for water or a clean slop bucket, and above it all were the wails of various infants and snatches of song from those who had ceased to struggle against their lot.

It was a human zoo with but one species exhibited, but there was variation enough among them, save for their present unhappiness. I wanted to tell them that this was the worst of it—at least I hoped it was.

I made my way into the dimly lit barracks, determined to do my duty despite the discomfort I felt. *Slave* . . . We never use that word. *My servant*, we say, or *my cook*, or *the folks down on my farm* . . . *my people* . . . *Why, he's part of the family*, we say . . . We call the elderly family retainers by the courtesy title of Uncle or Aunt . . . Later, when we have come to know and trust them and to presume that they are happy in our care, it is all too easy to forget by what means they are obtained. From such a place as this.

In truth, though, it hardly matters that I am venturing into slave quarters, for I am not much at ease anywhere in the company of my fellow creatures. Even at the orphan asylum supported by my uncle, my palms sweat and I shrink into my clothes whenever I must visit there, feeling the children's eyes upon me with every step I take. I find myself supposing that every whisper is a mockery of me, and that all eyes upon me are judging me and finding me wanting. It is a childish fear, I suppose, and I would view it as such in anyone other than myself, but logic will not lay the specter of ridicule that dogs my steps, and so I tread carefully, hearing sniggers and seeing scorn whether there be any or not.

Perhaps that is why I never married, and why, after obtaining my medical degree, I chose the role of college administrator to that of practicing physician—I hope to slip through life unnoticed. But I hope I do my duty, despite my personal predilections, and that evening my duty was to enter this fetid human stable and to find a suitable man for the college. I steeled myself to the sullen stares of the captives and to the cries of their frightened children. The foul smell did not oppress me, for the laboratories of the college are much the same, and the odor permeates the halls and even my very office. No, it was the eyes I minded. The cold gaze of those who fear had turned to rage. I forced myself to walk slowly, and to look into the face of each one, nodding coolly, so that they would not know how I shrank from them.

"Good evening, sir." The voice was deep and calm, as if its owner were an acquaintance, encountering me upon some boulevard and offering a greeting in passing.

I turned, expecting to see a watchman, but instead I met with a coffee-colored face, gently smiling: an aquiline nose, pointed beard, and sharp brown eyes that took in everything and gave out nothing. The man looked only a few years younger than myself—perhaps thirty-five—and he wore the elegant clothes of a dandy, so that he stood out from the rest like a peacock among crows.

The smile was so guileless and open that I abandoned my resolve of solemnity and smiled back. "How do you do?" I said. "Dreadful place, this. Are you here upon the same errand as I?" Charleston has a goodly number of half castes, a tropical mixture of Martinique slaves and their French masters. They even have schools here to educate them, which I think a good thing, although it is illegal to do so in Georgia. There are a good many freedmen in every city who have prospered and have taken it in turn to own slaves themselves, and I supposed that this light-colored gentleman must be such a free man in need of a workman.

There was a moment's hesitation and then the smile shone forth again. "Almost the same," he said. "Are you here in search of a servant? I am in need of a new situation."

In momentary confusion I stared at his polished shoes, and the white shirt that shone in the dimness. "Are you—"

He nodded, and spoke more softly as he explained his position. For most of his adult life he had been the principal manservant of a spinster lady in Charleston, and he had also been permitted in his free time to hire out to a hotel in the city, hence his mannered speech and the clothes of a dandy.

"But—you are to be sold?"

He nodded. "The mistress is ailing, don't you know. Doesn't need as much help as before, and needs cash money more. The bank was after her. So I had to go. Made me no never mind. I'll fetch a lot. I just hope for a good place, that's all. I'm no field hand."

I nodded, noting how carefully he pronounced his words, and how severely clean and well-groomed his person. Here was a man whose life's course would be decided in seconds tomorrow, and he had done all he could to see that it went well.

"And the mistress, you know, she cried and carried on to see me go. And she swore that she would never part with my wife."

I nodded. It is regrettable that such things happen. Money is the tyrant that rules us all. I said, "I am the dean of a medical college in Augusta. In Georgia. Do you know where that is?"

"A good ways off, sir."

"Half a day's journey south by train. Over the Savannah River and into the state of Georgia."

"A college. That sounds like a fine situation indeed, sir. What kind of place is it?"

"We teach young men to be doctors and surgeons."

"No, sir," He smiled again. "The *place*. The position you've come here wanting to fill."

"Oh, that." I hesitated. "Well—Porter, I suppose you'd say. General factotum about the college. And *something else*, for which, if the man were able to do it, we should *pay*." I did not elaborate, but I thought he could read expressions much better than I, for he looked thoughtful for a few moments, and then he nodded.

"You'd pay . . . Enough for train fare?"

"If the work is satisfactory. Perhaps enough, if carefully saved, to make a larger purchase than that. But the extra duty . . . it is not pleasant work."

He smiled. "If it was pleasant, you wouldn't pay."

And so it was done. It was not the sordid business of buying a life, I told myself, but more of a bargain struck between two men of the world. True, he would have to leave his wife behind in Charleston, but at least we were saving him from worse possible fates. From cane fields farther south, or from someone who might mistreat him. He could do worse, I told myself. And at least I saved him from one ordeal—that of standing upon the block not knowing what would become of him. I thought the man bright enough and sufficiently ambitious for the requirements of our institution. It may seem odd that I consulted him beforehand as if he had a choice in his fate, but for our purposes we needed a willing worker, not a captive. We needed someone dependable, and I felt that if this man believed it worth his while to join us, we would be able to trust him.

They must have thought him wonderfully brave the next day. On the block, before upturned white faces like frog spawn, peering up at him, he stood there smiling like a missionary with four aces. It was over in the space of a minute, only a stepping stone from one life to the next, crossed in the blink of an eye.

Seven hundred dollars bid and accepted in the span of ten heart-beats, and then the auctioneer moved on to the next lot, and we went out. As we counted out the gold pieces for the cashier, and signed the account book, Lewis Ford was looking a little askance at the whole procedure.

"So you're certain of this fellow, Newton?"

"Well, as much as one can be, I suppose," I said. "I talked at length with him last evening. Of course I did not explain the particulars of the work to him. That would have been most imprudent."

Lewis Ford grunted. "Well, he has the back for it, I grant you that. And, as you say, perhaps the temperament as well. But has he the stomach for it? After our experience with Clegg, that's what I wonder."

"Well, *I* would, Dr. Ford. If my choice in life was the work we have in store for this fellow or a short, hard life in the cane fields further south, by God, I would have the stomach for it."

"Indeed. Well, I defer to your judgment. I don't suppose what we're asking of him is much worse than what we do for a living, after all."

"We'll be serving the same master, anyhow," I said. "The college, you know, and the greater good of medicine."

"What is the fellow's name, do you know?"

I nodded. "He told me. It is Grandison. Grandison Harris."

"Odd name. I mean they *have* odd names, of course. Xerxes and Thessalonians, and all that sort of thing. People will give slaves and horses the most absurd appellations, but I wouldn't have taken Grandison for a slave name, would you?"

I shrugged. "Called after the family name of his original owner, I should think. And judging by the lightness of his skin, there's some might say he's entitled to it."

Grandison Harris had never been on a train before, and his interest in this new experience seemed to diminish what regrets he might have about leaving his home in Charleston. When the train pulled out of the depot, he leaned out the window of the car and half stood until he could see between the houses and over the people all the way to the bay—a stand of water as big as all creation, it looked from here. Water that flowed into the sky itself where the other shore ought to be. The glare of the afternoon sun on the water was fierce, but he kept on twisting his head and looking at the diminishing city and the expanse of blue.

"You'll hurt your eyes staring out at the sun like that," I said.

He half turned and smiled. "Well, sir, Doctor," he said, "I mean to set this place in my memory like dye in new-wove cloth. My eyes may water a little, but I reckon that's all right, for dyes are sot in salt. Tears will fix the memories to my mind to where they'll never come out."

After that we were each left alone with our thoughts for many miles, to watch the unfamiliar landscapes slide past the railway carriage, or to doze in relief that, although the future might be terrible, at least this day was over.

Instead of the sea, the town of Augusta had the big Savannah River running along beside it, garlanded in willows, dividing South Carolina from the state of Georgia. From the depot in Hamburg they took a carriage over the river into town, but it was dark by then, and he couldn't see much of the new place except for the twinkling lights in the buildings. Wasn't as big as Charleston, though. They boarded him for the night with a freed woman who took in lodgers, saying that they would come to fetch him in the morning for work.

For a moment in the lamplight of the parlor, he had taken her for a white woman, this haughty lady with hair the brown of new leather and green eyes that met everybody's gaze without a speck of deference. Dr. Newton took off his hat to her when they went in, and he shook her hand and made a little bow when he took his leave.

When he was alone with this strange landlady, he stared at her in the lamplight and said, "Madame, you are a red bone, not?"

She shrugged. "I am a free person of color. Mostly white, but not all. They've told you my name is Alethea Taylor. I'll thank you to call me Miz Taylor."

"You sure look white," he said. *Act it, too*, he thought.

She nodded. "My mama was half-caste and my daddy was white. So was my husband, whose name I ought to have. But it was Butts, so maybe I don't mind so much."

She smiled at that and he smiled back.

"We married up in Carolina where I was born. It's legal up there. I was given schooling as well. So don't think this house is any low class place, because it isn't. We have standards."

The new lodger looked around at the tidy little parlor with its worn but elegant mahogany settee and a faded turkey carpet. A book shelf stood beside the fireplace, with a big leather Bible on top in pride of place. "Your white husband lives here, too?" he asked.

"Of course not." Her face told him that the question was foolish. "He was rich enough to buy up this whole town, Mr. Butts was. But he's dead now. Set me and our children free, though, when he passed. Seven young'uns we had. So now I do fine sewing for the town ladies, and my boys work to keep us fed. Taking in a lodger helps us along, too. Though I'm particular about who I'll accept. Took you as a favor to Dr. George Newton. Would you tell me your name again?"

"Grandison Harris," he said. "I guess the doctors told you: I'm the porter at the college."

She gave him a scornful look. "'Course you are. Dr. Newton's uncle Tuttle is my guardian, so I know all about the college."

"Guardian?"

"Here in Georgia, freed folk have to have white guardians."

"What for?"

She shrugged. "To protect us from other white men, I suppose. But Mr. Isaac Tuttle is a good man. I can trust him."

He watched her face for some sign that this Tuttle was more to her than a disinterested legal guardian, but she seemed to mean no more than what she said. It made no difference to him, though. Who she shared her bed with was none of his business, and never would be. She had made her opinion of him plain. He was a slave, and she was a free woman, his landlady, and a friend of his owners. You couldn't cross that gulf on a steamboat.

"It's late," she said, "But I expect you are hungry as well as tired. I can get you a plate of beans if you'd care to eat."

"No, ma'am, I'm good 'til morning. Long day."

She nodded, and her expression softened. "Well, it's over now. You've landed on your feet."

"The college—It's a good place, then?" he asked.

"Hard work," she said. She paused as if she wanted to say more, but then she shook her head. "Better than the big farms, anyhow. Dr. George is a good man. Lives more in his books than in the world, but he means well. Those doctors are all right. They treat sick black folks, same as white. You will be all right with them if you do your job. They won't beat you to show they're better than you." She smiled. "Doctors think they are better than most everybody else, anyhow, so they don't feel the need to go proving it with a bull whip."

"That's good to hear."

"Well, just you mind how *you* treat *them*," she said. "You look like you wouldn't be above a little sharp practice, and those doctors can be downright simple. Oh, they know a lot about doctoring and a lot about books, but they're not very smart about people. They don't expect to be lied to. So you take care to be straight with them so that you can keep this good place."

He followed her meekly to a clean but spartan room. A red rag quilt covered the bed, and a chipped white pitcher and basin stood on a small pine table next to a cane-seat chair. Compared to the faded splendor of Miz Taylor's parlor, the room was almost a prison cell, but he was glad enough to have it. Better here with a family than in some makeshift room at the medical college. He wasn't sure whether the doctors kept sick people around the place, but he didn't like the thought of sleeping there all the same. In a place of death. The best thing about this small bare room was what it did *not* contain: no shackles, no lock on the door or barred window. He was a boarder in a freedman's house.

He turned to the woman, who stood on the threshold holding the lamp.

"Aren't they afraid I'll run off?" he asked.

She sighed. "I told you. They don't have good sense about people. I reckon they figure you'd be worse off running than staying here. You know what happens to runaways."

He nodded. He had seen things in Charleston, heard stories about brandings and toes lopped off. And of course the story of Denmark Vesey, whose rebellion had consisted mostly of talk, was never far from the surface of any talk about running or disobedience.

She set the lamp beside the basin. "I'll tell you what's the truth, Mr. Harris. If you give satisfaction at the college—do your work and don't steal, or leastways don't get caught at it—those doctors won't care about what you do the rest of the time. They won't remember to. They don't want to have to take care of a servant as if he were a pet dog. All they want is a job done with as few ructions as possible, and the less trouble you give them, the happier they'll be. You do your job well, you'll become invisible. Come and go as you please. You'll be a freedman in all but name. That's what I think. And I know the doctors, you see?"

"I won't give them no trouble," he said.

"See you don't. Can you read, Mr. Harris?"

He shook his head. There had been no call for it, and the old miss in Charleston wasn't averse to her folks getting book learning, but she had needed him to work.

"Well," she said, "I school my young'uns every evening. If you would like to join us, one of my girls can start by teaching you your letters."

"I thank you."

She nodded and turned to leave. "Reading is a good skill," she said as she closed the door. "You can write out your own passes."

He had seen fine buildings in Charleston, but even so, the Medical College on Telfair Street was a sight to behold. A white temple, it was, with four stone columns holding up the portico and a round dome atop the roof, grand as a cathedral, it was. You stepped inside to an open space that stretched all the way up to the dome, with staircases curving up the sides that led to the upper floor rooms. The wonder of it wore off before long, but it was grand while it lasted. Soon enough the architectural splendor failed to register, and all he saw were floors that needed mopping and refuse bins that stank.

For the first couple of days he chopped firewood, and fetched pails of water when they needed them.

"Just until you are settled in," Dr. Newton had said. "Then we will have a talk about why you are here."

He didn't see much of the doctors during the couple of days they gave him to get acquainted with his new surroundings. Perhaps they were busy with more pressing matters, and, remembering Alethea Taylor's advice about giving no trouble, he got on with his work and bothered no one. At last, though, clad in one of the doctors' clean cast-off suits, he was summoned into the presence, a little shy before the all-powerful strangers, but not much afraid, for they had paid too much good money for him to waste it by harming him.

For a night or two he had woken up in the dark, having dreamed that the doctors were going to cut him open alive, but this notion was so patently foolish that he did not even mention it to his landlady, whose scorn would have been withering.

George Newton was sitting behind his big desk, tapping his fingers together, looking as if his collar were too tight. "Now Grandison," he began, "you have settled in well? Good. You seem to be a good worker, which is gratifying. So now I think we can discuss that other task that your duties entail."

He paused, perhaps to wait for a question, but he saw only respectful interest in the man's face. "Well, then . . . This is a place where men are taught to be doctors. And also to be surgeons. A grim task, that: the cutting open of living beings. Regrettably necessary. A generation ago there was an English surgeon who would vomit before every operation he performed. Do you know why?"

The listener shook his head.

"Because the patient is awake for the operation, and because the pain is so terrible that many die of it. We lose half the people on whom we operate, even if we do everything right. They die of shock, of heart failure, perhaps, from the pain. But despite these losses, we are learning. We *must* learn. We must help more people, and lessen the torture of doing so. This brings me to your function here at the college." He paused and tapped his pen, waiting in case the new servant ventured a question, but the silence stretched on. At last he said, "It was another English surgeon who said, *we must mutilate the dead in order not to mutilate the living.*" Another pause. "What he meant was that we physicians must learn our way around the human body, and we must practice our surgical skills. It is better to practice those skills upon a dead body rather than a living one. Do you see the sense of that?"

He swallowed hard, but finally managed to nod. "Yes, sir."

George Newton smiled. "Well, if you *do* understand that, Grandison, then I wish you were the governor of Georgia, because *he* doesn't. The practice is against the law in this state—indeed, in all states—to use cadavers for medical study. People don't want us defiling the dead, they say—so, instead, out of ignorance, we defile the living. And that cannot be permitted. We must make use of the dead to help the living."

"Yes, sir," he said. The doctor still seemed lost in thought, so he added encouragingly, "It's all right with me, sir."

Again the smile. "Well, thank you, Grandison. I'm glad to have your permission, anyhow. But I'm afraid we will need more than that. Tell me, do you believe that the spirits of the dead linger in the graveyard? Object to being disturbed? That they'd try to harm anyone working on their remains?"

He tried to picture dead people loitering around the halls of the college, waiting for their bodies to be returned. This was a place of death. He didn't know whether to smile or weep. Best not to think of it at all, he decided. "They are gone, ain't they?" he said at last. "Dead. Gone to glory. They're not sitting around waiting for Judgment Day in the grave, are they?"

Another doctor sighed. "Well, Grandison, to tell you the truth, I don't know where the souls of the dead are. That is something we don't teach in medical college. However, I don't believe they're sitting out there in the graveyard, tied to their decaying remains. I think we can be sure of that."

"And you need the dead folks to learn doctoring on?"

Dr. Ford nodded. "Each medical student should have a cadaver to work on, so that he can learn his trade without killing anyone in the learning process. That seems a sufficiently noble reason to rob graves, doesn't it?"

He considered it, more to forestall the rest of the conversation than anything else. "You could ask folks before they dies," he said. "Tell them how it is, and get them to sign a paper for the judge."

"But since the use of cadavers is against the law, no judge would honor such a paper, even if people could be persuaded to sign it, which most would not. I wish there were easy answers, but there aren't. You know what we must ask of you."

"You want me to bring you dead folks? Out the graveyard?"

"Yes. There is a cemetery on Watkins Street, not half a mile from here, so the journey would not be long. You must go at night, of course."

He stood quite still for some time before he spoke. It was always best to let white folks think you took everything calmly and agreed with them on every particular. To object that such a deed would frighten or disgust him would make no difference. The doctor would dismiss his qualms as fear or superstition. The doctors had explained the matter to him, when they could have simply given him an order. That was something, anyhow. At last he nodded. The matter was settled, and the only considerations now were practical ones. "If I get caught, what then?"

"I don't suppose you will *get caught*, as you put it, if you are the least bit clever about it, but even if you should, remember that slaves are not prosecuted for any crime. They are considered property and therefore not subject to prosecution. The authorities simply hand them back over to their masters." Newton smiled. "And you don't suppose that *we* would punish you for it, do you?"

The others nodded in agreement, and the matter was settled.

He was given a lantern and a shovel, and a horse-drawn cart. Dr. Newton had written out a pass, saying that the bearer, Grandison Harris, servant of the medical college, was allowed to be abroad that night to pick up supplies for the doctors. "I doubt very much that the city's watchmen can read," Newton had told him. "Just keep this pass until it wears out, and then one of us will write you a new one."

He kept the pass in his jacket pocket, ready to produce if anyone challenged him, but he had met no one on his journey from Telfair Street to the burying ground. It was well after midnight, and the sliver of moon had been swallowed by clouds, so he made his way in darkness. Augusta was a smaller place than Charleston. He had walked around its few streets until he knew it by day and by night, and he had been especially careful of the route to Cedar Grove, where the town buried its slaves and freedmen. Now he could navigate the streets without the help of the lantern. Only the horse's footfalls broke the silence. Nearer to the town center, perhaps, people might still be out drinking and wagering at cards, but no sounds of merriment reached him here on the outskirts of town. He would have been glad of the sound of laughter and music, but the silence blanketed everything, and he did not dare to whistle to take his mind off his errand.

Do you want me to dig up just any old grave? he had asked the doctor.

No. There were rules. A body rots quick. Well, he knew that. Look at a dead cat in the road, rippling with maggots. After two, three days, you'd hardly know what it was. *Three days buried and no more*, the doctor told him. *After that, there's no point in bringing the corpse back up; it's too far gone to teach us anything. Look for a newly-dug grave*, Newton told him. Flowers still fresh on a mound of newly-spaded earth. *Soon*, he said, *you will get to know people about the town, and you will hear about deaths as they happen. Then you can be ready. This time, though, just do the best you can.*

He knew where he was going. He had walked in the graveyard that afternoon, and found just such a burial plot a few paces west of the gate: a mound of brown dirt, encircled by clam shells, and strewn across it a scattering of black-eyed susans and magnolia flowers, wilting in the Georgia sun, but newly placed there.

He wondered whose grave it was. No mourners were there when he found it. Had there been, he would have hesitated to inquire, for fear of being remembered if the theft were ever discovered. There was no marker to tell him, either, even if he had been able to read. The final resting place of a slave—no carved stone. Here and there, crude wooden crosses tilted in the grass, but they told him nothing.

He reached the cemetery gate. Before he began to retrace his steps to the new grave, he lit the lantern. No one would venture near a burying ground so late at night, he thought, and although he had paced off the steps to the grave, he would need the light for the task ahead.

Thirty paces with his back to the gates, then ten paces right. He saw the white shape of shells outlining the mound of earth, and smelled the musk of decaying magnolia. He stood there a long time staring down at the flower-strewn grave, a colorless shape in the dimness. All through the long afternoon he had thought it out, while he mopped the classroom floors and emptied the waste bins, and waited for nightfall. His safety lay in concealment: No one must suspect that a grave had been disturbed. No one would look for a grave robber if they found no trace of the theft. The doctor had told him over and over that slaves were not jailed for committing a crime, but he did not trust laws. Public outrage over this act might send him to the end of a rope before anyone from the college could intervene. Best not to get caught.

He would memorize the look of the burial plot: the position of the shells encircling the mound, and how the flowers were placed, so that when he had finished his work he could replace it all exactly as it had been before.

Only when he was sure that he remembered the pattern of the grave did he thrust his shovel into the soft earth. He flinched when he heard the rasp of metal against soil, and felt the blade connect with the freshly-spaded dirt. The silence came flowing back. What had he expected? A scream of outrage from beneath the mound? When he had first contemplated the task before him, he had thought he could endure it by thinking only of the physical nature of the work: It is like digging a trench, he would tell himself. Like spading a garden. It is just another senseless task thought up by the white people to keep you occupied. But here in the faint lantern light of a burying ground, he saw that such pretenses would not work. The removing of dirt from a newly-filled hole was the least of it. He must violate consecrated ground, touch a corpse, and carry it away in darkness to be mutilated. He could not pretend otherwise.

All right, then. If the spirits of the dead hovered outside the lantern light, watching him work, so be it. Let them see. Let them hear his side of it, and judge him by that.

"Don't you be looking all squinty-eyed at me," he said to the darkness as he worked. "Wasn't my doing. You all know the white folks sent me out here. Say they need to study some more on your innards."

The shovel swished in the soft earth, and for a moment a curve of moon shimmered from behind a cloud, and then it was gone. He was glad of that. He fancied that he could make out human shapes in the shadows beneath the trees. Darkness was better. "You all long dead ones don't have no quarrel with me," he said, more loudly now. "Doctors don't want you if you gone ripe. You all like fish—after three days, you ain't good for nothing except fertilizer."

He worked on in the stillness, making a rhythm of entrenchment. The silence seemed to take a step back, giving him breathing room as he worked. Perhaps two hours now before cock crow.

He struck wood sooner than he had expected to. Six feet under, people always said. But it wasn't. Three feet, more like. Just enough to cover the box and then some for top soil. Deep enough, he supposed, since the pine boards would rot and the worms would take care of the rest.

He didn't need to bring up the coffin itself. That would disturb too much earth, and the doctors had no use for the coffin, anyhow. Dr. Newton told him that. It might be stealing to take a coffin, he had said. Wooden boxes have a monetary value. Dead bodies, none.

He stepped into the hole, and pushed the dirt away from the top of the box. The smell of wet soil made him dizzy, and he willed himself not to feel for worms in the clods of earth. He did not know whose grave this was. They had not told him, or perhaps they didn't know.

"You didn't want to be down there anyhow," he said to the box. "Salted away in the wet ground. You didn't want to end up shut away in the dark. I came to bring you back. If the angels have got you first, then you won't care, and if they didn't, then at least you won't be alone in the dark any more."

He took the point of the shovel and stove in the box lid, pulling back when he heard the wood splinter, so that he would not smash what lay beneath it. On the ground beside the grave, he had placed a white sack, big enough to carry away the contents of the box. He pulled it down into the hole, and cleared away splinters of wood from the broken box, revealing a face, inches from his own.

Its eyes were closed. Perhaps—this first time—if they had been open and staring up at him, he would have dropped the shovel and run from the graveyard. Let them sell him south rather than to return to such terrors. But the eyes were shut. And the face in repose was an old woman, scrawny and grizzled, lying with her hands crossed over her breast, and an expression of weary resignation toward whatever came next.

He pulled the body out through the hole in the coffin lid, trying to touch the shroud rather than the flesh of the dead woman. She was heavier than he had expected from the look of her frail body, and the dead weight proved awkward to move, but his nerves made him hurry, and to finish the thing without stopping for breath: only get her into the sack and be done with it.

He wondered if the spirit of the old woman knew what was happening to her remains, and if she cared. He was careful not to look too long at the shadows and pools of darkness around trees and gravestones, for fear that they would coalesce into human shapes with burning eyes.

"Bet you ain't even surprised," he said to the shrouded form, as he drew the string tight across the mouth of the sack. "Bet you didn't believe in that business about eternal rest, no more'n the pigs would. Gonna get the last drop of use out you, same as pigs. But never mind. At least it ain't alone in the dark."

She lay there silent in the white sack while he spent precious long minutes refilling the hole, smoothing the mound, and placing the shells and flowers back exactly as he had found them.

He never found out who the old woman was, never asked. He had trundled the body back to the porter's entrance of the medical college, and steeped her in the alcohol they'd given him the money to buy as a preservative. Presently, when the body was cured and the class was ready, the old woman was carried upstairs to perform her last act of servitude. He never saw her again—at least not to recognize. He supposed that he had seen remnants of her, discarded in bits and pieces as the cutting and the probing progressed. That which remained, he put in jars of whiskey for further study or scattered in the cellar of the building, dusting it over with quicklime to contain the smell. What came out of the classes was scarcely recognizable as human, and he never tried to work out whose remains he was disposing of in a resting place less consecrated than the place from which he had taken them.

"Well, I suppose the first one is always the worst," said Dr. Newton the next day when he had reported his success in securing a body for the anatomy class. He had nodded in agreement, and pocketed the coins that the doctor gave him, mustering up a feeble smile in response to the pat on the back and the hearty congratulations on a job well done.

The doctor had been wrong, though. The first one was not the worst. There were terrors in the unfamiliar graveyard, that was true, and the strange feel of dead flesh in his hands had sent him reeling into the bushes to be sick, so that even he had believed that the first time was as bad as it could get, but later he came to realize that there were other horrors to take the place of the first ones. That first body was just a lump of flesh, nothing to him but an unpleasant chore to be got over with as quick as he could. And he would have liked for them all to be that way, but he had a quota to fill, and to do that he had to mingle with the folks in Augusta, so that he could hear talk about who was ailing and who wasn't likely to get well.

He joined the Springfield Baptist Church, went to services, learned folks' names, and passed the time of day with them if he happened to be out and about. Augusta wasn't such a big town that a few months wouldn't make you acquainted with almost the whole of it. He told people that he was the porter up to the medical college, which was true enough as far as it went, and no one seemed to think anything more about him. Field hands would have been surprised by how much freedom you could have if you were a town servant in a good place. There were dances and picnics, camp meetings and weddings. He began to enjoy this new society so much that he nearly forgot that they would see him as the fox in the henhouse if they had known why he was set among them.

Fanny, Miz Taylor's eldest girl, made sport of him because of his interest in the community. "I declare, Mister Harris," she would say, laughing, "You are worse than two old ladies for wanting to know all the goings-on, aren't you?"

"I take an interest," he said.

She shook her head. "Who's sick? Who's in the family way? Who's about to pass?—Gossip! I'd rather talk about books!" Miss Fanny, with her peach-gold cheeks and clusters of chestnut curls, was a pretty twelve-year-old. She and her young sister Nannie were soon to be sent back to South Carolina for schooling, so she had no time for the troubles of the old folks in dull old Augusta.

When she thought he was out of earshot, Fanny's mother reproved her for her teasing. "Mary Frances," she said. "You should not poke fun at our lodger for taking an interest in the doings of the town. Do you not think he might be lonely, with no family here, and his wife back in Charleston? It is our Christian duty to be kind to him."

"Oh, *duty*, mama!"

"And, Fanny, remember that a lady is always kind."

But he had not minded Miss Fanny's teasing. To be thought a nosey "old lady" was better than to be suspected of what he really was. But in the few months before she left for school, Miss Fanny had made an effort to treat him with courtesy. She was well on her way to being a lady, with her mother's beauty and her father's white skin. He wondered what would become of her.

He was in the graveyard again, this time in the cold drizzle of a February night. He barely needed a lantern anymore to find his way to a grave, so accustomed had he become to the terrain of that hallowed field. And this time he would try to proceed without the light, not from fear of discovery but because he would rather not see the face of the corpse. Cheney Youngblood, a soft-spoken young woman whose sweet serenity made her beautiful, had gone to death with quiet resignation on Saturday night. It had been her first child, and when the birthing went wrong, the midwife took to drink and wouldn't do more than cry and say it weren't her fault. At last Miz Taylor was sent for, and she had dispatched young Jimmie to fetch Dr. Newton. He had come readily enough, but by then the girl had been so weak that nothing could have saved her. "I'd have to cut her open, Alethea," Dr. Newton had said. "And she'd never live through that, and I think the baby is dead already. Why give her more pain when there's nothing to be gained from it?"

At dawn the next morning he had just been going out the door to light the fires at the college when Alethea Taylor came home, red-eyed and disheveled from her long night's vigil. "It's over," she told him, and went inside without another word.

The funeral had been held the next afternoon. Cheney Youngblood in her best dress had been laid to rest in a plain pine box, her baby still unborn. He had stood there before the flower-strewn grave with the rest of the mourners, and he'd joined in the singing and in the prayers for her salvation. And when the minister said, *Rest in peace*, he had said "Amen" with the rest of them. But he knew better.

Three-quarters of an hour in silence, while the spadefuls of earth fell rhythmically beside the path. He would not sing. He could not pray. And he tried not to look at the shadows that seemed to grow from the branches of the nearby azaleas. At last he felt the unyielding wood against his spade, and with hardly a pause for thought, he smashed the lid, and knelt to remove the contents of the box. There had been no shroud for Cheney Youngblood, but the night was too dark for him to see her upturned face, and he was glad.

"Now, Cheney, I'm sorry about this," he whispered, as he readied the sack. "You must be in everlasting sorry now that you ever let a man touch you, and here I am seeing that you will get more of the same. I just hope you can teach these fool doctors something about babies, Cheney. So's maybe if they see what went wrong, they can help the next one down the road."

He stood at the head of the coffin, gripping her by the shoulders, and pulled until the flaccid body emerged from the box. Fix his grip beneath her dangling arms, and it would be the act of a moment to hoist the body onto the earth beside the grave, and then into the sack. He did so, and she was free of the coffin, but not free.

Attached by a cord.

He stood there unmoving in the stillness, listening. Nothing.

He lit the lamp, and held it up so that he could see inside the box.

The child lay there, its eyes closed, fists curled, still attached to its mother's body by the cord.

His hand was shaking as he set down the lantern on the edge of the grave, and reached down for the child. After so much death, could he possibly restore to life . . . He took out his knife, but when he lifted the cord, it was withered and cold—like a pumpkin vine in winter.

Dr. Newton sat before the fire in his study, clad in a dressing gown and slippers. First light was a good hour away, but he had made no complaint about being awakened by the trembling man who had pounded on his door in the dead of night, and, when the doctor answered, had held out a sad little bundle.

He was sitting now in a chair near the fire, still shaking, still silent.

Dr. Newton sighed, poured out another glass of whiskey, and

held it out to his visitor. "You could not have saved it, Grandison," he said again. "It did not live."

The resurrection man shook his head. "I went to the burying, Doctor. I was there. I saw. Cheney died trying to birth that baby, but she never did. She was big with child when they put her in the ground."

"And you think the baby birthed itself there in the coffin and died in the night?"

He took a gulp of whiskey, and shuddered. "Yes."

"No." Newton was silent for a moment, choosing his words carefully. "I saw a man hanged once. I was in medical school in those days, and we were given the body for study. When we undressed the poor fellow in the dissecting room, we found that he had soiled himself in his death agonies. The professor explained to us that when the body dies, all its muscles relax. The bowels are voided . . . And, I think, the muscles that govern the birth process must also relax, and the gases build up as the body decays, so that an infant in the birth canal is released in death."

"And it died."

"No. It never lived. It never drew breath. It died when its mother did, not later in the coffin when it was expelled. But it does you credit that you tried to save it."

"I thought the baby had got buried alive." The doctor shook his head, and Grandison said, "But people do get buried alive sometimes, don't they?"

Newton hesitated, choosing his words carefully. "It has happened," he said at last. "I have never seen it, mind you. But one of my medical professors in Paris told the tale of a learned man in medieval times who was being considered for sainthood. When the church fathers dug him up, to see if his body was in that uncorrupted state that denotes sanctity, they found the poor soul lying in the coffin on his back, splinters under his fingernails and a grimace of agony frozen on his withered features." He sighed. "To add insult to injury, they denied the fellow sainthood on the grounds that he seemed to be in no hurry to meet his Maker."

They looked at each other and smiled. It was a grim story, but not so terrible as the sight of a dead child wrapped in its mother's winding sheet. Besides, first light had just begun to gray the trees and the lawn outside. That night was over.

Cheney Youngblood had been early on, though. And he was sorry for her, because she was young and kindly, and he had thought her child had lived, however briefly. A year or so after that—it was hard to remember after so long a time, with no records kept—a steaming summer brought yellow fever into Augusta, and many died, burning in their delirium and crying for water. Day after day wagons stacked with coffins trundled down Telfair Street, bound for the two cemeteries, black and white. The old people and the babies died first, and here and there someone already sick or weakened by other ailments succumbed as well. New graves sprouted like skunk cabbage across the green expanse of the burying field.

Now he could dig and hoist with barely a thought to spare for the humans remains that passed through his hands. By now there had been too many dark nights, and too many still forms to move him to fear or pity. His shovel bit into the earth, and his shoulders heaved as he tossed aside the covering soil, but his mind these days ranged elsewhere.

"I want to go home," he told George Newton one night, after he had asked for the supplies he needed.

The doctor looked up, surprised and then thoughtful. "Home, Grandison?"

His answer was roundabout. "I do good work, do I not, doctor? Bring you good subjects for the classes, without causing you any trouble. Don't get drunk. Don't get caught."

"Yes. I grant you all that, but where is home, Grandison?"

"I have a wife back in Charleston."

Dr. Newton considered it. "You are lonely? I know that sometimes when people are separated by circumstance, they find other mates. I wonder if you have given any thought to that—or perhaps she—"

"We were married legal," he said. "I do good work here. Y'all trust me."

"Yes. Yes, we do. And you want to go back to Charleston to see your wife?"

He nodded. No use in arguing about it until the doctor thought it out.

At last Newton said, "Well, I suppose it might be managed. We could buy you a train ticket. Twelve dollars is not such a great sum, divided by the seven of us who are faculty members." He tapped his fingers together as he worked it out. "Yes, considered that way, the cost seems little enough, to ensure the diligence of a skilled and steady worker. I think I can get the other doctors to go along. You would have to carry a pass, stating that you have permission to make the journey alone, but that is easily managed."

"Yes. I'd like to go soon, please." He was good at his job for just this reason, so that it would be easier to keep him happy than to replace him.

Not everyone could do his job. The free man who was his predecessor had subsided into a rum-soaked heap; even now he could be seen shambling along Bay Street, trying to beg or gamble up enough money to drown the nightmares.

Grandison Harris had no dreams.

"Excuse me, Dr. Newton, but it's time for my train trip again, and Dr. Eve said it was your turn to pay."

"Hmm . . . what? Already?"

"Been four weeks." He paused for a moment, taking in the rumpled figure elbow-deep in papers at his desk. "I know you've had other things on your mind, sir. I'm sorry to hear about your uncle's passing."

"Oh, yes, thank you, Grandison." George Newton ran a hand through his hair, and sighed. "Well, it wasn't a shock, you know. He was a dear old fellow, but getting up in years, you know. No, it isn't so much that. It's the chaos he's left me."

"Chaos?"

"The mess. In his will my uncle left instructions that his house be converted to use as an orphanage, which is very commendable, I'm sure, but he had a houseful of family retainers, you know. And with the dismantling of his household on Walker Street, they have all moved in with me on Greene Street. I can't walk for people. Eleven of them! Women. Children. Noise. Someone tugging at my sleeve every time I turn around. And the Tuttle family heirlooms, besides. It's bedlam. And Henry, my valet, is at his wit's end. He's getting on in years, you know, and accustomed to having only me to look after. I would not dream of turning them out, of course, but . . ."

Grandison nodded. Poor white folks often thought that servants solved all the problems rich people could ever have, but he could see how they could be problems as well. They had to be fed, clothed, looked after when they got sick. It would be one thing if Dr. George had a wife and a busy household already going—then maybe a few extra folks wouldn't make much difference, but for a bachelor of forty-five used to nobody's company but his own, this sudden crowd of dependents might prove a maddening distraction. It would never occur to George Newton to sell his uncle's slaves, either. That was to his credit. Grandison thought that things ought to be made easier for them so he wouldn't be tempted to sell those folks to get some peace. He considered the situation, trying to think of a way to lighten the load. He said, "Have you thought about asking Miz Alethea if she can help you sort it out, Doctor?"

"Alethea Taylor? Well, I am her guardian now, I know." Newton smiled. "Is she also to be mine?"

"You know she does have seven young'uns. She's used to a house full. Maybe she could set things in order for you."

George Newton turned the idea over in his mind. Women were better at managing a household and seeing to people's needs. He had more pressing matters to contend with here at the medical school. He reached into his pocket and pulled out a roll of greenbacks. "Well, we must get you to Charleston," he said. "Twelve dollars for train fare, isn't it? And, thanks. I believe I will take your advice and ask Alethea to help me."

George Newton's problems went out of his head as soon as the door shut behind him. He went off to the depot to wait for the train, and he wanted no thought of Augusta to dampen his visit to Rachel.

Three days later he walked into Alethea Taylor's parlor near suppertime, and found that one of the family was missing. "Where's Miss Mary Frances?" he asked as they settled around the big table.

Young Joseph waved a drumstick and said, "Oh, Mama sent her over to Dr. George's house. You know how he's been since Mr. Tuttle passed. People just running all over him, asking for things right and left. And Mr. George he can't say no to anybody, and he has about as much common sense as a day-old chick. He asked Mama to come help him, but she's too busy with her sewing work. So we sent Fanny instead."

Jane, who was ten, said, "Mama figured Fanny would put a stop to that nonsense. She'll sort them all out, that's certain. Ever since she got back from that school in South Carolina she's been bossing all of us something fierce, so I'm glad she's gone over there. It'll give us a rest."

"But she's what—seventeen?"

Joseph laughed. "Sixteen going-on-thirty," he said. "Those folks at Newton's will think a hurricane hit 'em. Fanny's got enough sand to take on the lot of them, and what's more she won't need a pass to go there, either."

Harris nodded. No, she wouldn't need a pass. Fanny Taylor was a gray-eyed beauty, whiter than some of the French Creole belles he'd seen in Charleston. With her light skin, her education and her poise, she could go anywhere unchallenged, and she had the same fire and steel as Miss Alethea, so he didn't think she'd be getting any back talk from the Newton household.

"She's living over there now?"

Jim laughed. "No-oo, sir! Mama wouldn't sit still for that." He glanced at his mother to see if it was safe to say more, but her expression was not encouraging.

"She'll be home directly," said Anna. "She goes first thing in the morning and she comes home after dinner time."

Miss Alethea spoke up then. "Children, where are your manners? Pass Mr. Harris those fresh biscuits and some gravy, and let him talk for once. Hand round the chicken, Jim. Mr. Harris, how was your journey?"

"The day was fine for a train ride," he said, careful to swallow the last bit of chicken before he spoke. The Taylors were sticklers for table manners. "Though we did have to stop once for some cows had got out and would not leave the track."

Miss Alethea was not interested in cows. "And your wife, Mr. Harris? I hope you found her well?"

"She's well enough." He hesitated. "She is with child."

Miss Alethea glanced at her own brood, and managed to smile. "Why, don't say that news with such a heavy heart, Mr. Harris. This will be your first born, won't it! You should be joyful!"

He knew it was his child. The old miss would never permit any goings-on in her house. Not that he thought Rachel would have countenanced it anyhow. But a child was one more millstone of Charleston to burden him. He couldn't be with his child, couldn't protect it. And the old missus professed to be delighted at this new addition to the household, but he was afraid that a baby on the premises would be more annoying to her than she anticipated. He thought of Dr. George's fractious household. Might the old missus part with Rachel and the infant to restore her house to its former peacefulness? Was it any wonder that he was worried?

Miss Alethea gave her children a look, and one by one they left the table, as if a command had been spoken aloud. When the two of them were alone, she said, "It's not right to separate a husband from his wife. I don't know what Dr. George was thinking when he brought you here to begin with."

"No, I asked him to. It seemed for the best. And my Rachel wasn't to be sold, so there wasn't any question of bringing her, too."

"Be that as it may, you have been here now, what? Three years? It is high time that Medical College did something about your situation. And a baby on the way as well. Yes, they must see about that."

"I suppose the doctors thought—"

"I know what they thought. They thought what all you men think—that you'd replace your wife and be glad of the chance. Folks said that about Mr. Butts, too, but they were wrong. Seven children we had, and he stayed with me until the day he died. Those doctors must see by now that you have not deserted your wife. You going so faithful on the train to see her every chance you get. Well, it's early days still. The baby not born yet, and many a slip, as they say. Let us wait and see if all goes well, and if it does, one day we will speak to Dr. George about it."

The anatomy classes did not often want babies. He was glad of that. He thought he might take to drink as old Clegg had done if he'd had to lift shrouded infants out of the ground during the months that he waited for his own child to be born in Charleston.

Women died in childbirth. No one knew better than he. The men he pulled from their shrouds in Cedar Grove were either old husks of humanity, worn out by work and weariness at a great age, or else young fools who lost a fight, or died of carelessness, their own or someone else's. But the women . . . It was indeed the curse of Eve. Sometimes the women died old, too, of course. Miss Alethea herself had borne seven babies, and would live to make old bones. She came of sturdy stock. But he saw many a young woman put into the clay before her time, with her killer wrapped in swaddling cloths and placed in her arms.

And the doctors did want those young mothers. Their musculature was better for study than the stringy sinews of old folks, Dr. Newton had told him. "A pregnant woman will make a good subject," he said, examining the body Grandison had brought in just before dawn. "Midwives see to all the normal births, of course, but when something goes wrong, they'll call in a doctor. When we attend a birth, it's always a bad sign. We need to know all we can."

"But why does birthing kill them?" Grandison had asked. It was when he'd first learned about Rachel, and he wondered if the doctors here had some new sliver of knowledge that might save her, if it came to that. Surely this long procession of corpses had amounted to something.

George Newton thought the matter over carefully while he examined the swollen form of the young woman on the table before them. In the emptiness of death she looked too young to have borne a child. Well, she did not bear it. It remained inside her, a last secret to take away with her. Grandison stared at her, trying to remember her as a living being. He must have seen her among the crowds at the city market, perhaps, or laughing among the women on the lawn outside the church. But he could not place her. Whoever she had been was gone, and he was glad that he could summon no memory to call her back. It was easier to think of the bodies as so much cordwood to be gathered for the medical school. Had it not been for her swollen belly, he would not have given her a thought.

At last Dr. Newton said, "Why do they die? Now that's a question for the good Reverend Wilson over at the Presbyterian church across the street. He would tell you that their dying was the will of God, and the fulfillment of the curse on Eve for eating the apple, or some such nonsense as that. But I think . . ." He paused for a moment, staring at the flame of his match as if he'd forgotten the question.

"Yes, doctor? Why do you think they die?"

"Well, Grandison, I spent my boyhood watching the barn cats give birth and the hounds drop litters of ten at a time, and the hogs farrow a slew of piglets. And you know, those mothers never seemed to feel any pain in those birthings. But women are different. It kills some and half kills the rest. And I asked myself why, same as you have, and I wondered if we could find something other than God to blame for it."

"Did you? Find something to blame besides God?"

Dr. Newton smiled. "Ourselves, I guess. The problem in childbirth is the baby's head. The rest of that little body slides through pretty well, but it's the head that gets caught and causes the problems. I suppose we need those big heads because our brains are bigger than a dog's or a pig's, but perhaps over the eons our heads have outgrown our bodies."

He thought it over. "But there's nothing I can do about that," he said, "I can't help Rachel."

The doctor nodded. "I know," he said. "Perhaps in this case Reverend Wilson would be more help to you than we doctors are. He would prescribe prayer, and I have nothing better to offer."

Newton turned to go, but another thought occurred to him. "Grandison, why don't you come in to class today?" He nodded toward the girl's swollen body. "She will be our subject today. Perhaps you'll feel better if you understood the process."

Grandison almost smiled. It would never occur to the studious bachelor that a man with a pregnant wife might be appalled by such a sight. Dr. George considered learning a cure in itself. Grandison did not think that was the case, but since learning was often useful for its own sake, he would not refuse the offer. And he would take care not to show disgust or fear, because that might prevent other offers to learn from coming his way. Doctoring would be a good skill to know. He had seen enough of death to want to fight back.

He had watched while the doctors cut open the blank-faced woman, and now he knew that the womb looked like a jellyfish from the Charleston docks, and that the birth canal made him think of a snake swallowing a baby rabbit, but the knowledge did nothing to allay his fears about Rachel's confinement. It was all right, though, in the end. Whether the prayers accomplished their object or whether his wife's sturdy body and rude good health had been her salvation, the child was safely delivered, and mother and baby thrived. He called that first son "George," in honor of Dr. Newton, hoping the gesture would make the old bachelor feel benevolent toward Rachel and the boy.

After that he got into the habit of sitting in on the medical classes when he could spare the time from his other duties. Apart from the big words the doctors used, the learning didn't seem too difficult. Once you learned what the organs looked like and how to find them in the body, the rest followed logically. They were surprised to learn that he could read—his lessons with the Taylor children had served him well. After a while, no one took any notice of him at all in the anatomy classes, and presently the doctors grew accustomed to calling on him to assist them in the demonstrations. He was quiet and competent, and they noticed his helpfulness, rather than the fact that he, too, was learning medicine.

He had been in Augusta four years. By now he was as accustomed to the rhythm of the academic year as he had once been attuned to the seasonal cadence of the farm. He had taken Alethea Taylor's advice and made himself quietly indispensable, so that at work the doctors scarcely had to give him a thought, except to hand over money for whatever supplies he needed for the task at hand or for his personal use. No one ever questioned his demands for money these days. They simply handed over whatever he asked for, and went back to what they had been doing before he had interrupted.

Sixteen bodies per term for the anatomy class. He could read well now, thanks to the Taylor daughters, although they would be shocked if they knew that he found this skill most useful in reading the death notices in the *Chronicle.* When there were not enough bodies available in the county to meet this need, Grandison was authorized to purchase what he needed. A ten-dollar gold piece for each subject. Two hundred gallons of whiskey purchases each year for the preservation of whole corpses or of whatever organs of interest the doctors wished to keep for further study, and if he bought a bit more spirits than that amount, no one seemed to notice. It never went to waste.

He tapped on the door of George Newton's office. "Morning, Dr. George. It's train time again."

The doctor looked up as if he had forgotten where he was. "Train time?—Oh, yes, of course. Your family. Sit down, Grandison. Perhaps we should talk."

He forced himself to keep smiling, because it didn't do any good to argue with a man who could break your life in two. He wasn't often asked to sit down when he talked to the doctors, and he made no move toward the chair. He assumed an expression of anxious concern. "Is there anything I can help you with, Dr. George?" he said.

The doctor tapped his pen against the ledger. "It's just that I've been thinking, you know. Twelve dollars a month for train fare, for you to go and see your wife."

"And child," said Grandison, keeping his voice steady.

"Yes, of course. Well, I was thinking about it, and I'll have to talk it over with the rest of the faculty—"

I could take a second job, he was thinking. *Maybe earn the money for train fare myself . . .*

But Dr. George said, "I shall persuade them to purchase your family."

It took him a moment to sort out the words, so contrary were they to the ones he had anticipated. He had to bite back the protests that had risen in his throat. "Buy Rachel and George?"

The doctor smiled. "Oh, yes. I shall explain that we could save enough money in train fare to justify the purchase price within a few years. It does make fiscal sense. Besides, I have lately come to realize how much you must miss them."

Grandison turned these words over in his mind. If one of the cadavers had got up from the dissecting table and walked away, he could not have been more surprised. He never mentioned his wife and son except to respond with a vague pleasantry on the rare occasion that someone asked after them. Why had the doctor suddenly taken this charitable notion? Why not when the baby was first born? Dr. George was a kind man, in an absent-minded sort of way, but he hardly noticed his own feelings, let alone anybody else's. Grandison stood with his back to the door, the smile still frozen to his lips, wondering what had come over the man.

George Newton rubbed his forehead and sighed. He started to speak, and then shook his head. He began again, "It may be a few months before we can find the money, mind you. It should take about thirteen hundred dollars to buy both your wife and son. That should do it, surely. I'll write to your wife's mistress in Charleston to negotiate the purchase."

Grandison nodded. "Thank you," he whispered. The joy would come later, when the news had sunk in. Just now he was still wondering what had come over Dr. George.

"I'm going to be moving out one of these days," he told Alethea Taylor that night after supper.

She sat in her straight-backed chair closest to the lamp, embroidering a baby dress. "You'll be needing to find a place for your family to live," she said, still intent upon her work.

He laughed. "The world can't keep nothing from you, Miz Taylor. Dr. George told you?"

"Fanny told me." She set the baby dress down on the lamp table, and wiped her eyes. "She's been after George to bring them here, and he promised he would see to it."

"I wondered what put it into his head. Saying he was going to buy them, right out of the blue, without me saying a word about it. I can't make out what's come over him."

She made no reply, but her frown deepened as she went on with her sewing.

"I don't suppose you know what this is all about?"

She wiped her eyes on the hem of the cloth. "Yes. I know. I may as well tell you. Dr. George and Fanny are—well, man and wife, I would say, though the state of Georgia won't countenance it. Fanny has a baby coming soon."

He was silent for a bit, thinking out what to say. Dr. George was in his forties, and looked every minute of it. Fanny was a slender and beautiful sixteen. He knew how it would sound to a stranger, but he had known Dr. George five years now, and for all the physician's wealth and prominence, he couldn't help seeing him as a gray-haired mole, peering out at the world from his book-lined burrow, while the graceful Fanny seemed equal to anything. He knew—he *knew*—of light-skinned women forced to become their owners' mistresses, but Fanny was free, and besides he couldn't see her mother allowing such a thing to happen. Miss Alethea did not have all the rights of a white woman, though you'd take her for one to look at her, but still, there were some laws to protect free people of color. Through her dress-making business, Miss Alethea had enough friends among her lady clientele that if she'd asked, some lady's lawyer husband would have intervened. The white ladies hated the idea of their menfolk taking colored mistresses, and they'd jump at the chance to put a stop to it. Someone would have been outraged by such a tale, and they would have been eager to save Miss Alethea's young daughter from a wicked seducer. But . . . *Dr. George?* He couldn't see it. Why, for all his coolness in cutting up the dead, when it came to dealing with live folks, Dr. George wouldn't say boo to a goose.

"He didn't . . . force her?" he asked, looking away as he said it. But when he looked back and saw Miss Alethea's expression, his lips twitched, and then they both began to laugh in spite of it all.

Miss Alethea shook her head. "*Force? Dr. George?* Oh, my. I can't even think it was his idea, Mr. Harris. You know how he is."

"Well, is Miss Fanny happy?" he said at last.

"Humph. Sixteen years old and a rich white doctor thinks she hung the moon. What do you think?" She sighed. "When a man falls in love for the first time when he's past forty, it hits him hard. Seems like he's taken leave of his senses."

"Oh. Well," he cast about for some word of comfort, and settled on, "I won't tell anybody."

She stabbed her needle at the cloth. "Shout it from the rooftops if you feel like it, Mr. Harris. It's not as if *they're* keeping it a secret. He wants to marry her."

He smiled. "Anybody would, Miss Alethea. Mary Frances is a beautiful girl."

"You misunderstand, Mr. Harris. I'm saying that he *means* to marry her."

"And stay here? And let folks know about it?"

She nodded. "I'm saying. Live as man and wife, right there on Greene Street."

Now he realized why George Newton had suddenly understood the pain of his separation from Rachel, but he felt that the doctor's newfound wisdom had come at the price of folly. St. Paul's seeing the light on the road to Damascus might have been a blessed miracle, but Dr. George's light was more likely to be a thunderbolt. "He can't do that," he said. "Set her up as his wife."

"Not without losing his position he can't." The needle stabbed again. "Don't you think I've told them that?"

"And what did he say?"

"He's going to resign from the medical school, that's what. Says he has money enough. Going to continue his work in a laboratory at home. Huh!" She shook her head at the folly of it.

He thought about it. Perhaps in Charleston such a thing might work. Down in the islands, certainly. Martinique. Everybody knew that the French . . . But *here*?

"I even asked him, Mr. Harris, I said straight out, *Do you remember Richard Mentor Johnson?*" His expression told her that he did not remember, either. But she did. "Richard Mentor Johnson of Kentucky. He was the vice president of the United States, back when I was a girl. Under President Van Buren. Folks said that he had killed the Indian chief Tecumseh, which they thought made him a hero. But then he had also married a woman of color, and when word of that got out, they tried to run him out of office on account of it. When his first term was over, he gave up and went home to Kentucky. And, do you know, Mr. Johnson's wife wasn't even alive by that time. She had died before he ever went to Washington to be vice president. Just the memory of her was enough to ruin him. Now, how well does Dr. George think he will fare in Georgia with a *live* colored wife in his house?"

"But Miss Fanny—to look at her—"

"I know. She's whiter to look at than some of the doctors' wives, but that makes no difference. This is a small town, Mr. Harris. Everybody knows everybody. Fanny can't pass in Augusta, and they both say they've no mind to go elsewhere."

He thought he had made all the proper expressions of sympathy and commiseration, but he was thinking just as much about the effect that Dr. George's folly would have on him. Would this change of heart mean no more robbing Cedar Grove? Or in his madness would the doctor insist on obtaining an equal number of bodies from the white burying ground? Equality was a fine thing, but not if it got him hanged by a white lynch mob.

He swept the upstairs hall four times that morning, waiting for Dr. George to be alone in his office. Finally the last visitor left, and he tapped on the door quickly before anyone else could turn up. "Excuse me, Dr. George. We're getting low on supplies for the anatomy classes," he said.

He always said "supplies" instead of "bodies" even when they were alone, just in case anyone happened to overhear.

Dr. George gave him a puzzled frown. "Supplies? Oh—oh, I see. Not filled our quota yet? Well, are there any fresh ones to be had?"

"A burying today," he said. "Little boy fell off a barn roof. I just wondered if you wanted me to take him."

"Yes, I suppose so. He's needed. Though we could use a yellow fever victim if you hear of one. Must teach the Southern diseases, you know. Medical schools up north don't know a thing about them." Dr. George looked up. "Why did you ask about this boy in particular? Do you know him?"

That didn't matter. He had known them all for years now. Some he minded about more than others, but all of them had long ceased to be merely lumps of clay in his hands. "It's all right," he said. "I don't mind bringing him in. I just wondered what you wanted me to do, and if there's to be a new dean—"

The doctor leaned back in his chair and sighed. "Yes, I see, Grandison. You have heard."

"Yes."

"It's true that I am resigning the post of dean. I felt that it was better for the college if I did so." He picked up a sheaf of papers from his desk and held it out with a bemused smile. "But it seems that I shall be staying on as Emeritus Professor of Anatomy, after all. This is a petition, signed by all of the students and faculty, asking that I stay. And the Board of Trustees has acceded to their request."

"Do they know?"

"About Fanny? They do. They profess not to care. I suppose when one is a doctor, one sees how little difference there really is between the races. Just a thin layer of skin, that's all, and then it's all the same underneath. Whatever the reason, they insist that I stay on in some capacity, and I shall."

"So nothing will change? For me, I mean?"

George Newton shook his head. "We still must have bodies, and the only safe place to obtain them is from Cedar Grove. That has not changed. And I fancy that I shall still have enough influence to bring your family to Augusta. I do not intend to shirk my duty, so you may go and see to yours."

Madison Newton was born on the last day of February, red-faced, fair-haired, and hazel-eyed, looking like a squashed cabbage leaf, but a white one, after all.

"It's a fine baby," he had said to Fanny, when she brought the baby to her mother's house on a mild day in March.

Fanny switched the blanket back into place, so that only the infant's nose peeped out. "People only want to look at him to see what color he is," she said. "What do they expect? He had sixteen great-great grandparents, same as everybody, and only one of them was colored. All the rest of him from then on down is white. Of course, that doesn't change what he is to most folks' way of thinking."

He had kept smiling and said the plain truth: that the infant was a fortunate child, but he had been angry, and his annoyance had not left him. That night in Cedar Grove in a fine mist of rain, he dug as if he could inflict an injury upon the earth itself. "I reckon Miss Fanny is whiter in her head than she is on her face," he said to the darkness, thrusting the shovel deep into the ground. "Feeling sorry for a light-eyed baby born free, his daddy a rich white doctor. I guess pretty Miss Fanny wants the moon, even when it's raining."

He spared hardly a thought for the man in the box below. Some drunken laborer from the docks, hit too hard over the head in a brawl. He had even forgotten the name. An easy task tonight. No shells or flowers decorated this grave site. The dead man had been shunted into the ground without grief or ceremony. Just as well take him to the doctors, where he could do some good for once. His thoughts returned to his grievance. Spoiled Miss Fanny had never given a thought to his baby when she was complaining about her own son's lot in life. How would she have liked to be Rachel—separated from her husband, and left to raise a child without him, knowing that at any time old missus might take a notion to sell that child, and nothing could be done to stop it.

He brushed the dirt from the pine box, and stove in the lid with his shovel point. Miss Fanny Taylor didn't know what trouble was, complaining about—

A sound.

Something like a moan, coming from inside the smashed coffin. He forgot about Fanny and her baby, as he knelt in the loose dirt of the open grave, pressing his ear close to the lid of the box. He held his breath, straining to hear a repetition of the sound. In the stillness, with all his thoughts focused on the dark opening before him, he realized that something else was wrong with the grave site. The smell was wrong. The sickly sweet smell of newly decaying flesh should have been coming from the box, but it wasn't. Neither was the stench of voided bowels, the last letting-go of the dead. All he smelled was rotgut whiskey.

He gripped the corpse under the armpits and pulled it out of the grave, but instead of sacking it up, he laid the body out on the damp grass. It groaned.

He had heard such sounds from a corpse before. The first time it happened, he had been unloading a sack from the wagon into the store room at the medical college. He had dropped the sack and gone running to Dr. George, shouting that the deader from the burying ground had come back to life.

George Newton had smiled for an instant, but without a word of argument, he'd followed the porter back to the store room and examined the sacked-up body. He had felt the wrist and neck for a pulse, and even leaned into the dead face to check for breath, but Grandison could tell from his calm and deliberate movements that he knew what he would find. "The subject is dead," he said, standing up, and brushing traces of dirt from his trousers.

"It just died then. I heard it moan."

Dr. George smiled gently. "Yes, I believe you did, Grandison, but it was dead all the same."

"A ghost then?"

"No. Merely a natural process. When the body dies, there is still air trapped within the lungs. Sometimes when that air leaves the lungs it makes a moaning sound. Terrifying, I know. I heard it once myself in my student days, but it is only a remnant of life, not life itself. This poor soul has been dead at least a day."

He never forgot that sound, though in all the bodies that had passed through his hands on the way to the dissecting table, he had never heard it since.

The sound coming now from the man stretched out on the grass was different. And it changed—low and rumbling at first, and then louder. He knelt beside the groaning man and shook his shoulder.

"Hey!" he said. "Hey, now—" His voice was hoarse and unnaturally loud in the still darkness of Cedar Grove. *What can you say to a dead man?*

The groan changed to a cough, and then the man rolled over and vomited into the mound of spaded earth.

He sighed, and edged away a few feet. He had seen worse. Smelled worse. But finding a live body in the graveyard complicated matters. He sat quietly, turning the possibilities over in his mind, until the retching turned to sobbing.

"You're all right," he said, without turning around.

"This is the graveyard. Badger Benson done killed me?"

"I guess he tried. But you woke up. Who are you, anyhow?"

"I was fixing to ask you that. How did you come to find me down in the ground? You don't look like no angel."

He smiled. "Might be yours, though. You slave or free, boy?"

"Belong to Mr. Johnson. Work on his boat."

"Thought so. Well, you want to go back to Mr. Johnson, do you?"

The man stretched and kicked his legs, stiff from his interment. "I dunno," he said. "Why you ask me that?"

" 'Cause you were dead, boy, as far as anybody knows. They buried you this morning. Now if you was to go back to your master, there'd be people asking me questions about how I come to find you, and they'd take you back to Johnson's, and you'd still be a slave, and like as not I'd be in trouble for digging you up. But if you just lit out of here and never came back, why nobody would ever even know you were gone and that this grave was empty. You're dead. You don't let 'em find out any different, and they'll never even know to hunt for you."

The man rubbed the bruise on the back of his head. "Now how did you come to find me?"

Grandison stood up and retrieved the shovel. "This is where the medical school gets the bodies to cut up for the surgery classes. The doctors at the college were fixing to rip you open. And they still can, I reckon, unless you light out of here. Now, you tell me, boy, do you want to be dead again?"

The young man raised a hand as if to ward off a blow. "No. No!—I understand you right enough. I got to get gone."

"And you don't go back for nothing. You don't tell nobody goodbye. You are dead, and you leave it at that."

The young man stood up and took a few tentative steps on still unsteady legs. "Where do I go then?"

Grandison shrugged. "If it was me, I would go west. Over the mountains into Indian country. You go far enough, there's places that don't hold with slavery. I'd go there."

The man turned to look at him. "Well, why don't you then?" he said. "Why don't *you* go?"

"Don't worry about me. I'm not the one who's dead. Now are you leaving or not?"

"Yeah. Leaving."

"You've got three hours before sunup." He handed the shovel to the resurrected man. "Help me fill in your grave, then."

Dr. George Newton—December 1859

It is just as well that I stepped down as dean of the medical college. I haven't much time to wind up my affairs, and the fact that Ignatius Garvin is ably discharging my former duties leaves me with one less thing to worry about. If I can leave my dear Fanny and the babies safely provided for, I may leave this world without much regret. I wish I could have seen my boy grow up . . . wish I could have grown old with my dearest wife . . . And I wish that God had seen fit to send me an easier death.

No one knows yet that I am dying, and it may yet be weeks before the disease carries me off, but I do not relish the thought of the time before me, for I know enough of this illness to tremble at the thought of what will come. I must not do away with myself, though. I must be brave, so as not to cause Fanny any more pain than she will feel at losing me so soon.

So many papers to sift through. Investments, deeds, instructions for the trustees—my life never felt so complicated. Soon the pain will begin, and it may render me incapable of making wise decisions to safeguard my little family. At least I have safeguarded the family of our faithful college servant, Grandison Harris. Thank God I was able to do that in time, for I had long promised him that I would bring his Rachel and her boy to Augusta, so I did a few months back. I am not yet fifty, sound in body and mind, and newly married. I thought I had many years to do good works and to continue my medical research. I suppose that even a physician must think that he will never face death. Perhaps we would go mad if we tried to live thinking otherwise.

I wonder how it happened. People will say it was the buggy accident just before Christmas, and perhaps it was. That gelding is a nervous horse, not at all to be depended upon in busy streets of barking dogs and milling crowds. I must remember to tell Henry to sell the animal, for I would not like to think of Fanny coming to harm if the beast became spooked again. I was shaken and bruised when he dumped me out of the carriage and into the mud, but did I sustain any cuts during the fall? I do not remember any blood.

Dr. Eve came to look me over, and he pronounced me fit enough, with no bones broken, and no internal injuries. He was right as far as it went. My fellow physicians all stopped by to wish us good cheer at Christmas, and to pay their respects to their injured friend. They did not bring their wives, of course. No respectable white woman accepts the hospitality of this house, for it is supposed that Fanny's presence taints the household. We are not, after all, legally married in the eyes of the law here. Fanny professes not to care. *Dull old biddies*, anyhow, she declares. But she has certainly charmed the gentlemen, who consider me a lucky man. And so I was, until this tragedy struck—though none of those learned doctors suspected it.

I wish that I had not. I wish that I could go innocently into the throes of this final illness, as would a child who had stepped on a rusty nail, not knowing what horrors lay before me. But I am a trained physician. I do know. And the very word clutches at my throat with cold fingers.

Tetanus.

Oh, I know too much, indeed. Too much—and not enough. I have seen people die of this. The muscles stretch and spasm, in the control of the ailment rather than the patient, an agonizing distension such as prisoners must have felt upon the rack in olden days. The body is tortured by pain beyond imagining, but beyond these physical torments, the patient's mind remains clear and unaffected. I doubt that the clarity is a blessing. Delirium or madness might prove a release from the agony, yet even that is denied to the sufferer. And there is no cure. Nothing can stop the progression of this disease, and nothing can reverse its effects. I have, perhaps, a week before the end, and I am sure that by then I will not dread death, but rather welcome it as a blessed deliverance.

Best not to dwell on it. It will engulf me soon enough. I must send for James Hope. I can trust him. As the owner of the cotton mill, he will be an eminently respectable guardian for my wife's business interests, and since James is a Scotsman by birth, and not bound by the old Southern traditions of race and caste, he will see Fanny as the gentlewoman that she is. He treats her with all the courtly gentility he would show to a duchess, and that endears him to both of us. Yes, I must tell James what has happened, and how soon he must pick up where I am forced to leave off.

My poor Fanny! To be left a widow with two babies, and she is not yet twenty. I worry more over her fate than I do my own. At least mine will be quick, but Fanny has another forty years to suffer if the world is unkind to her. I wish that the magnitude of my suffering could be charged against any sorrow God had intended for her. I must speak to James Hope. How aptly named he is! I must entrust my little family to him.

It was nearly Christmas, and Rachel had made a pound cake for the Newtons. He was to take it around to Greene Street that afternoon, when he could manage to get away from his duties. Grandison looked at the cake, and thought that Dr. George might prefer a specimen from the medical school supply for his home laboratory, but he supposed that such a gesture would not be proper for the season. Rachel would know best what people expected on social occasions. She talked to people, and visited with her new friends at church, while he hung back, dreading the prospect of talking to people that he might be seeing again some day.

He took the cake to the Newton house, and tapped on the back door, half expecting it to open before his hand touched the wood. He waited a minute, and then another, but no one came. He knocked again, harder this time, wondering at the delay. As many servants as the Newtons had, that door ought to open as soon as his foot hit the porch. What was keeping them so busy?

Finally, after the third and loudest spate of knocking, Fanny herself opened the door. He smiled and held out his paper-wrapped Christmas offering, but the sight of her made him take a step backward. His words of greeting stuck in his throat. She was big-bellied with child again, he knew that. She looked as if it could come at any moment, but what shocked him was how ill she looked, as if she had not eaten or slept for a week. She stared out at him, hollow-eyed and trembling, her face blank with weariness. For a moment he wondered if she recognized him.

"My Rachel made y'all a pound cake. For Christmas," he said.

She nodded, and stepped back from the door to admit him to the kitchen. "Put it on the table," she said.

He set down the cake. The house was unnaturally quiet. He listened for sounds of baby Madison playing, or the bustle of the servants, who should have been making the house ready for the holiday, but all was still. He looked back at Fanny, who was staring down at the parcel as if she had never seen one before, as if she had forgotten how it got there, perhaps.

"Are you all right?" he asked. "Shall I fetch Miss Alethea for you?"

Fanny shook her head. "She's been already. She took Madison so that I can stay with George," she whispered. "And I've sent most of the others around there, too. Henry stayed here, of course. He won't leave George."

Something was the matter with Dr. George, then. It must be bad. Fanny looked half dead herself. "Shall I go for Dr. Eve?" he asked.

"He was here this morning. So was Dr. Garvin. Wasn't a bit of use. George told me that from the beginning, but I wouldn't have it. I thought with all those highfalutin doctors somebody would be able to help him, but they can't. They can't."

"Is he took bad?"

"He's dying. It's the lockjaw. You know what that is?"

He nodded. Tetanus. Oh, yes. They had covered it in one of the medical classes, but not to consider a course of treatment. Only to review the terrible symptoms and to hope they never saw them. He shivered. "Are they sure?"

"George is sure. Diagnosed himself. And the others concur. I was the only one who wouldn't believe it. I do now, though. I sit with him as long as I can. Hour after hour. Watch him fighting the pain. Fighting the urge to scream. And then I go and throw up, and I sit with him some more."

"I could spell you a while."

"*No!*" She said it so harshly that he took a step back in surprise. She took a deep breath, and seemed to swallow her anger. "No, thank you very kindly, Mr. Harris, but I will not let you see him."

"But if Dr. George is dying—"

"That's exactly why. Don't you think I know what you do over there at the medical college? Porter, they call you. *Porter.* I know what your real duties are, Mr. Harris. Known for a long time. And that's fine. I know doctors have to learn somehow, and that nothing about doctoring is pretty or easy. But you are not going to practice your trade in this house. You are not going to take my husband's body, do you hear?"

He said softly, "I only wanted to help you out, and maybe to tell him good-bye."

"So you say. But he is weak now. Half out of his mind with the pain, and he'd promise anything. He might even suggest it himself, out of some crazy sense of duty to the medical college, but I won't have it. My husband is going to have a proper burial, Mr. Harris. He has suffered enough!"

It doesn't hurt, he wanted to tell her. *You don't feel it if you're dead.* He did not bother to speak the words. He knew whose pain Fanny was thinking of, and that whatever Dr. George's wishes might be, it was the living who mattered, not the dead. Best to soothe her quickly and with as little argument as possible. He did not think that the other doctors would accept George Newton's body anyhow. That would be bringing death too close into the fold, and he was glad that he would not be required to carry out that task. Let the doctor lie in consecrated ground: There were bodies enough to be had in Augusta.

"I'll go now, Miss Fanny," he said, putting on his best white folks manners, if it would give her any comfort. "But I think one of the doctors should come back and take a look at you." He nodded toward her distended belly. "And we will pray for the both of you, my Rachel and I. Pray that he gets through this." It was a lie. He never prayed, but if he did, it would be for Dr. George's death to come swiftly—the only kindness that could be hoped for in a case of tetanus.

Dr. George died after the new year in 1860. The illness had lasted only two weeks, but the progress of the disease was so terrible that it had begun to seem like months to those who could do nothing but wait for his release from the pain. Grandison joined the crowd at the doctor's funeral, though he took care to keep clear of Fanny, for fear of upsetting her again. In her grief she might shout out things that should not be said aloud in Augusta's polite society. The doctors knew his business, of course, but not the rest of the town. He reckoned that most of Augusta would have been at the funeral if it weren't for the fact of the doctor's awkward marriage arrangements. As it was, though, his fellow physicians, the students, and most of the town's businessmen came to pay their respects, while their wives and daughters stayed home, professing themselves too delicate to endure the sight of the doctor's redbone widow. Not that you could see an inch of her skin, whatever its color, for she was swathed from head to foot in black widow's weeds and veils, leaning on the arm of Mr. James Hope, as if he were the spar of her sinking ship.

"Left a widow at eighteen," said Miss Alethea, regal in her black dress, her eyes red from tears of her own. "I had hoped for better for my girl."

He nodded. "She will be all right," he said. "Dr. George would have seen to that."

Miss Alethea gave him the look usually reserved for one of her children talking foolishness. "She's back home again, you know. Dr. George was too clouded at the last to do justice to a will, and Mr. James Hope had to sell the house on Greene Street. He vows to see her settled in a new place, though, over on Ellis, just a block from Broad Street. Having it built. There's all Dr. George's people to be thought of, you know, and the Tuttle folks, as well. Fanny has to have a house of her own, but I'm glad to have her by me for now, for the new baby is due any day—if it lives through her grief. We must pray for her, Mr. Harris."

Grandison looked past her at the tall, fair-haired Scotsman, who was still hovering protectively beside the pregnant young widow, and wondered if the prayer had already been answered.

The cellar was paved with bones now. Each term when the anatomy class had finished with its solemn duties of dissection, the residue was brought to him to be disposed of. He could hardly rebury the remains in any public place or discard them where they might be recognized for what they were. The only alternative was to layer them in quicklime in the basement on Telfair Street. How many hundred had it been now? He had lost count. Mercifully the faces and the memories of the subjects' resurrection were fading with the familiarity of the task, but sometimes he wondered if the basement resounded with cries he could not hear, and if that was why the building's cat refused to set foot down there. The quicklime finished taking away the flesh and masked the smell, but he wondered what part of the owners remained, and if that *great getting up in the morning* that the preacher spoke of was really going to come to pass on Judgment Day. And who would have to answer for the monstrous confusion and scramble of bones that must follow? Himself? Dr. George? The students who carved up the cadavers? Sometimes as he scattered the quicklime over a new batch of discarded bones, he mused on Dr. George peering over the wrought iron fence of white folks' heaven at an angry crowd of colored angels shaking their fists at him.

"Better the dead than the living, though," he would tell himself.

Sometimes on an afternoon walk to Cedar Grove, he would go across to the white burying ground to pay his respects to Dr. George, lying there undisturbed in his grave, and sometimes he would pass the time of day with the grassy mound, as if the doctor could still hear him. "Miss Mary Frances finally birthed that baby," he said one winter day, picking the brown stems of dead flowers off the grave. "Had a little girl the other day. Named her Georgia Frances, but everybody calls her Cissie, and I think that's the name that's going to stick. She's a likely little thing, pale as a Georgia peach. And Mr. James Hope is building her that house on Ellis like he promised, and she's talking about having her sister Nannie and young Jimmie move in along with her. I thought maybe Mr. James Hope would be moving in, too, the way he dotes on her, but he's talking about selling the factory here and going back to New York where his family is, so I don't think you need to linger on here if you are, sir. I think everything is going to be all right."

Dr. George hadn't been gone hardly more than two years when the war came, and that changed everything. Didn't look like it would at first, though. For the rest of the country, the war began in April in Charleston, when Fort Sumpter fell, but Georgia had seceded in

January, leaving Augusta worried about the arsenal on the hill, occupied by federal troops. Governor Joe Brown himself came to town to demand the surrender of the arsenal, and the town was treated to a fine show of military parades in the drizzling rain. Governor Brown himself stood on the porch of the Planters Hotel to watch the festivities, but Captain Elzey, who was in command of the eighty-two men at the arsenal, declined to surrender it. He changed his mind a day or so later when eight hundred soldiers and two brigadier generals turned up in the rain to show the arsenal they meant business. Then Captain Elzey sent for the governor to talk things over, and by noon the arsenal and its contents had been handed over to the sovereign State of Georgia, without a shot fired. That, and a lot of worrying, was pretty much all that happened to Augusta for the duration of the war.

When the shooting actually started in Charleston, he was glad that Rachel and the boy were safe in Augusta, instead of being caught in the middle of a war, though personally he would have liked to see the battle for the novelty of it. Everybody said the war was only going to last a few weeks, and he hated to have missed getting a glimpse of it.

Folks were optimistic, but they were making preparations anyhow. Two weeks after Fort Sumpter, Augusta organized a local company of home guards, the Silver Grays, composed mostly of men too old to fight in the regular army. Mr. James Hope came back from New York City to stand with the Confederacy and got himself chosen second member of the company, after Rev. Joseph Wilson, who was the first. Rev. Wilson's boy Tommy and little Madison Newton were the same age, and they sometimes played together on the lawn of the Presbyterian church, across the road from the college. Sometimes the two of them would come over and pepper him with questions about bodies and sick folks, and he often thought that you'd have to know which boy was which to tell which one wasn't the white child. Fanny kept young Madison as clean and well-dressed as any quality child in Augusta.

The months went by, and the war showed no signs of letting up. One by one the medical students drifted away to enlist in regiments back home.

"I don't suppose you'll have to worry about procuring any more cadavers for classes, Grandison," Dr. Garvin told him.

"No, sir," he said. "I've heard a lot of the students are fixing to quit and join up."

Dr. Garvin scowled. "I expect they will, but even if the school stays open, this war will produce enough cadavers to supply a thousand medical schools before it's over."

There wasn't any fighting in Augusta, but they saw their share of casualties anyhow. A year into the war, the wounded began arriving by train from distant battlefields, and the medical school suspended operation in favor of setting up hospitals to treat the wounded. The City Hotel and the Academy of Richmond County were turned into hospitals in '62 to accommodate the tide of injured soldiers flowing into the city from far off places with unfamiliar names, like Manassas and Shiloh. Many of the faculty members had gone off to serve in the war as well. Dr. Campbell was in Virginia with the Georgia Hospital Association, seeing to the state's wounded up there; Dr. Miller and Dr. Ford were serving with the Confederate forces at different places up in Virginia, and Dr. Jones was somewhere on the Georgia coast contributing his medical skills to the war effort.

Grandison worked in one of the hospitals, assisting the doctors at first, but as the number of casualties strained their ability to treat them, he took on more and more duties to fill the gap.

"I don't see why you are working so hard to patch those Rebels up," one of the porters said to him one day, when he went looking for a roll of clean bandages. "The Federals say they are going to end slavery, and here you are helping the enemy."

He shrugged. "I don't see any Federals in Augusta, do you? I don't see any army coming here to hand me my freedom. So meanwhile I do what I'm supposed to do, and we'll see what transpires when the war is over." Besides, he thought, it was one thing to wish the Confederacy to perdition, and quite another to ignore the suffering of a single boy soldier who couldn't even grow a proper beard yet.

Sometimes he wondered what had happened to the man he "resurrected" who wasn't dead—whether the fellow had made it to some free state beyond the mountains, and whether that had made any difference.

He didn't know if freedom was coming, or what it would feel like, but for the here and now there was enough work for ten of him.

So he stitched, and bandaged, and dressed wounds. *I've handled dead people*, he told himself. *This isn't any worse than that.*

But of course it was.

The boy was a South Carolina soldier, eighteen or so, with copper-colored hair and a sunny nature that not even a gaping leg wound could dampen. The pet of the ward, he was, and he seemed to be healing up nicely what with all the rest and the mothering from Augusta's lady hospital visitors. The nurses were already talking about the preparations to send him home.

Grandison was walking down the hall that morning, when one of the other patients came hobbling out into the hall and clutched at his coat sleeve. "You got to come now!" the man said. "Little Will just started bleeding a gusher."

He hurried into the ward past the crippled soldier and pushed his way through the patients clustered around the young man's cot. A blood-soaked sheet was pulled back revealing a skinny white leg with a spike of bone protruding through the skin. Jets of dark blood erupted from the bone splinter's puncture. Without a word Grandison sat down beside the boy and closed his fingers over the ruptured skin.

"I just tried to walk to the piss pot," the boy said. He sounded close to passing out. "I got so tired of having to be helped all the time. I felt fine. I just wanted to walk as far as the wall."

He nodded. The mending thigh bone had snapped under the boy's weight, severing a leg artery as the splintered bone slid out of place. The men crowded around the bed murmured among themselves, but no one spoke to the boy.

"Shall I fetch the surgeon?" one of the patients asked Grandison.

He shook his head. "Surgeon's amputating this morning. Wouldn't do no good to call him anyhow."

The boy looked up at him. "Can you stop it, sir?"

He looked away, knowing that the *sir* was for his medical skills and not for himself, but touched by it all the same. The red-haired boy had a good heart. He was a great favorite with his older and sadder comrades.

"Get a needle?" somebody said. "Sew it back in?"

He kept his fingers clamped tight over the wound, but he couldn't stay there forever. He wanted to say: *Y'all ever see a calf killed? Butcher takes a sharp knife and slits that cord in his throat, and he bleeds out in—what? A minute? Two?* It was the same here. The severed artery was not in the neck, no, but the outcome would be the same—and it was just as inevitable.

"But I feel all right," said the boy. "No pain."

He ignored the crowd around the bed and looked straight into the brown eyes of the red-haired boy. "Your artery's cut in two," he said. "Can't nothing remedy that."

"Can you stop the bleeding?"

He nodded toward his fingers pressed against the pale white skin. The warmth of the flesh made him want to pull away. He took a deep breath. "I have stopped it," he said, nodding toward his hand stanching the wound. "But all the time you've got is until I let go."

The boy stared at him for a moment while the words sunk in. Then he nodded. "I see," he said. "Can you hold on a couple minutes? Let me say a prayer."

Somebody said, "I got paper here, Will. You ought to tell your folks good-bye. I'll write it down."

The boy looked the question at Grandison, who glanced down at his hand. "Go ahead," he said. "I can hold it."

In a faltering voice the boy spoke the words of farewell to his parents. He sounded calm, but puzzled, as if it were happening to someone else. That was just as well. Fear wouldn't change anything, and it was contagious. They didn't need a panic in the ward. The room was silent as the boy's voice rose and fell. Grandison turned away from the tear-stained faces to stare at a fly speck on the wall, wishing that he could be elsewhere while this lull before dying dragged on. These last minutes of life should not be witnessed by strangers.

The letter ended, and a few minutes after that the prayers, ending with a whispered amen as the last words of the Lord's Prayer trailed off into sobs.

He looked at the boy's sallow face, and saw in it a serenity shared by no one else in the room. "All right?" he said.

The boy nodded, and Grandison took his hand away.

A minute later the boy was dead. Around the bedstead the soldiers wept, and Grandison covered the still form with the sheet and went back to his duties. He had intended to go to the death room later to talk to the boy, to tell him that death was a release from worse horrors and to wish him peace, but there were so many wounded, and so much to be done that he never went.

The war came to Augusta on stretchers and in the form of food shortages and lack of mercantile goods—but never on horseback with flags flying and the sound of bugles. Augusta thought it would, of course. When Sherman marched to the sea by way of Savannah, troops crowded into the city to defend it, and the city fathers piled up bales of cotton, ready to torch them and the rest of the town with it to keep the powder works and the arsenal out of Union hands, but Sherman ignored them and pushed on north into South Carolina.

Three months later the war ended, and federal troops did come to occupy the city.

"I am a throne, Grandison!" Tommy Wilson announced one May morning. "And Madison here, he's only a dominion."

"That's fine," he said without a glance at the two boys. He was cleaning out the little work room at the college on Telfair Street. It had been his headquarters and his storage room for thirteen years now, but the war was over and he was free. It was time to be his own master now somewhere else. He thought he might cross the river to Hamburg. Folks said that the Yankees over there were putting freedmen into jobs to replace the white men. He would have to see.

Tommy Wilson's words suddenly took shape in his mind. "A throne?" he said. "I thought a throne was a king's chair."

"Well, a throne can be that," said Tommy, with the air of one who is determined to be scrupulously fair. "But it's also a rank of angels. We're playing angels, me and Madison. We're going to go out and convert the heathens."

"Well, that's a fine thing, boys. You go and—*what* heathens?"

"The soldiers," said Madison.

Tommy nodded. "They misbehave something awful, you know. They drink and fight and take the Lord's name in vain."

"And by God we're gonna fix 'em," said Madison.

"Does your father know where you are?"

Tommy nodded. "He said I could play outside."

Madison Newton shrugged. "Mr. Hope don't care where I go.

He's living up at my house now, but he's not my daddy. He says he's gonna take Momma and their new babies up north with him, but me and Cissie can't go."

Grandison nodded. Fanny Newton was now called Fanny Hope, and she had two more babies with magnolia skin and light eyes. He wondered what would become of Dr. George's two children.

"Don't you go bothering the soldiers now," he told the boys. "They might shoot the both of you."

Tommy Wilson grinned happily. "Then we shall be angels for real."

"Do we call you *judge* now, Mr. Harris?" Either the war or the worry of family had turned Miss Alethea into an old woman. Her hair was nearly white now, and she peered up at him now through the thick lenses of rimless spectacles.

He had taken his family to live across the river in South Carolina, but he still came back to Augusta on the occasional errand. That morning he had met Miss Alethea as she hobbled along Broad Street, shopping basket on her arm, bound for the market. He smiled and gave her a courtly bow. "Why, you may call me judge if it pleases you, ma'am," he said. "But I don't expect I'll be seeing you in court, Miss Alethea. I'll be happy to carry your shopping basket in exchange for news of your fine family. How have you been?"

"Oh, tolerable," she said with a sigh. "My eyes aren't what they used to be—fine sewing in a bad light, you know. The boys are doing all right these days, grown and gone you know. But I do have young Madison and Cissie staying with me now. Mr. James Hope has taken their mother off to New York with him. Their little girls, too. You know they named the youngest after me? Little Alethea." She sighed. "I do miss them. But tell me about you, Mr. Harris. A judge now, under the new Reconstruction government! What's that like?"

He shrugged. "I don't do big law. Just little matters. Fighting drunks. Disturbing the peace. Stealing trifling things—chickens, not horses." They both smiled. "But when I come into the court, they all have to stand up and show me respect. I do like that. I expect Fanny—er, Mrs. Hope—knows what I mean, being up there in New York and all."

The old woman sighed. "She hates it up there—would you credit it? Poor James Hope is beside himself with worry. Thought he was handing her heaven on a plate, I reckon. Come north where there's been no slaves for fifty years, and maybe where nobody knows that Fanny is a woman of color anyhow. Be really free." She shook her head. "Don't you suppose he expected her to thank God for her deliverance and never want to come back."

"I did suppose it," he said.

"So did the Hopes. But she's homesick and will not be swayed. Why, what do you suppose Mr. James Hope did? He took Fanny to meet with Frederick Douglass. The great man himself! As if Mr. Douglass didn't have better things to do than to try to talk sense into a little Georgia girl. He did his best, though, to convince her to stay. She'll have none of it."

"Do you hear from her, Miz Alethea?"

She nodded. "Regular as clockwork. In every letter she sounds heartbroken. She misses me and her brothers and sisters. Misses Madison and Cissie something fierce. She says she hates northern food. Hates the cold weather and that ugly city full of more poor folks and wickedness than there is in all of Georgia. Fanny has her heart set on coming home."

"But if she stays up there, she could live white, and her children could be white folks."

Alethea Taylor stared. "Why would she want to do that, Mr. Harris?"

She already knew the answer to that, of course, but stating the truth out loud would only incur her wrath, so he held his peace, and wished them all well.

A year later, James and Fanny Hope did return to take up residence in Augusta, and perhaps it was best that they had, for Miz Alethea died before another year was out. At least she got to be reunited with her family again, and he was glad of that.

He did not go to the burying. They laid her to rest in Cedar Grove, and he forced himself to go for the sake of their long acquaintance. At least she would rest in peace. He alone was sure of that.

He wished that she had lived to see her new grandson, who was born exactly a year after his parents returned from the North. The Hopes named the boy John, and he was as blond and blue-eyed as any little Scotsman.

Privately Grandison had thought Fanny had been crazy to come back south when she could have passed in New York and dissolved her children's heritage in the tide of immigrants. But before the end of the decade, he knew he had come round to her way of thinking, for he quit his post of judge in South Carolina, and went back over the river to work at the medical school. Perhaps there were people talking behind his back then, calling him a graven fool, as he had once thought Fanny Hope, but now he had learned the hard way. For all the promises of the Reconstruction men, he got no respect as a judge. The job was a sham whose purpose was not to honor him or his people, but to shame the defeated Rebels. He grew tired of being stared at by strangers whose hatred burned through their feigned respect, and as the days went by, he found himself remembering the medical school with fondness.

He had been good at his job, and the doctors had respected his skills. Sometimes he even thought they forgot about his color. Dr. George had said something once about the difference being a thin layer of skin, and then underneath it was all the same. Many of the faculty had left during the war, but one by one they were coming back now to take up their old jobs at the medical college, and he knew that he was wishing he could join them as well.

He was wearing his white linen suit, a string tie, and his good black shoes. He stood in front of the desk of Dr. Louis Dugas, hat in hand, waiting for an answer.

Dugas, a sleek; clean-shaven man who looked every inch a French aristocrat, had taken over as dean of the college during the war years. In his youth he had studied in Paris, as Dr. George had, and it was Dugas who had traveled to Europe to purchase books for Augusta's medical library. It was said that he had dined with Lafayette himself. Now he looked puzzled. Fixing his glittering black eyes on Harris's face in a long-nosed stare, he said, "Just let me see if I understand you, my good man. You wish to leave a judiciary position across the river and come back here to work as a porter."

Grandison inclined his head. "I do, sir."

"Well, I don't wish to disparage the virtues of manual labor, as I am sure that the occupation of porter is an honorable and certainly a necessary one, but could you just tell me why it is that you wish to abandon your exalted legal position for such a job?"

He had been ready for this logical question, and he knew better than to tell the whole truth. The law had taught him that, at least. Best not to speak of the growing anger of defeated white men suddenly demoted to second-class citizens by contemptuous strangers. He'd heard tales of a secret society that was planning to fight back at the conquerors and whoever was allied with them. But as much as the rage of the locals made him uneasy, the patronizing scorn of his federal overseers kindled his own anger. They treated him like a simpleton, and he came to realize that he was merely a pawn in a game between the white men, valued by neither side. It would be one thing to have received a university education and then to have won the job because one was qualified to do it. Surely they could have found such a qualified man of color in the North, and if not, why not? But to be handed the job only as a calculated insult to others—that made a mockery of his intelligence and skills. At least the doctors had respected him for his work and valued what he did. Fifteen years he'd spent with them.

Best not to speak of personal advantage—of the times in the past when he had prevailed upon one or another of the doctors to treat some ailing neighbor or an injured child who might otherwise have died. The community needed a conduit to the people in power—he could do more good there than sentencing his folks to chain gangs across the river.

Best not to say that he had come to understand the practice of medicine and that, even as he approached his fiftieth year, he wanted to know more.

At last he said simply, "I reckon I miss y'all, Dr. Dugas."

Louis Dugas gave him a cold smile that said that he himself would never put sentiment before other considerations, but loyalty to oneself is a hard fault to criticize in a supplicant. "Even with the procuring of the bodies for the dissection table? You are willing to perform that task again as before?"

We must mutilate the dead so that we do not mutilate the living. He must believe that above all.

He nodded. "Yes, sir."

"Very well then. Of course we must pay you now. The rate is eight dollars per month, I believe. Give your notice to the South Carolina court and you may resume your post here."

And it was done. What he had entered into by compulsion as a slave so many years before, he now came to of his own volition as a free man. He would return to the cart and the lantern and the shovel and begin again.

Well, all that was a long time ago. It is a new century now, and much has changed, not all of it for the better.

He steps out into the night air. The queasy medical student has tottered away to his rooms, and now the building can be locked again for the night. He still has his key, and he will do it himself, although his son George is the official porter now at the medical college—not as good as he himself once was, but what of that? Wasn't the faculty now packed with pale shadows—the nephews and grandsons of the original doctors? A new century, not a patch on the old one for all its motorcars and newfangled gadgets.

He will walk home down Ellis Street, past the house where James and Fanny Hope had raised their brood of youngsters. One of the Hope daughters lived there now, but that was a rarity these days. There was a colored quarter in Augusta now, not like the old days when people lived all mixed together and had thought nothing about it.

James and Fanny Hope had enjoyed eight years in that house on Ellis Street, before a stroke carried him off in 1876. They had let his white kinfolk take him back to New York for burying. Better to have him far away, Fanny Hope had said, than separated from us by a cemetery wall here in Augusta.

Fanny raised her brood of eight alone, and they did her credit. She had lived three years into the twentieth century, long enough to see her offspring graduate from colleges and go on to fine careers. Little blue-eyed John Hope was the best of them, folks said. He had attended Brown University up north, and now he was president of a college in Atlanta. So was little Tommy Wilson, the white preacher's son, who now went by his middle name of Woodrow, and was a "throne" at Princeton College up north. You never could tell about a child, how it would turn out.

Though he never told anyone, Grandison had hoped that Dr. George's son Madison might be the outstanding one of Fanny's children, but he had been content to work at low wage jobs in Augusta and to care for his aging mother. He and Dr. George had that in common—neither of the sons had surpassed them.

Funny to think that he had outlived the beautiful Fanny Hope. In his mind she is still a poised and gentle young girl, and sometimes he regrets that he did not go to her burying in Cedar Grove. The dead rested in peace there now, for the state had legalized the procuring of cadavers by the medical schools some twenty years back, but around that time, rumors had surfaced in the community about grave robbing. Where had the doctors got the bodies all those years for their dissecting classes? Cedar Grove, of course. There was talk of a riot. Augusta had an undertaker now for people of color. The elegant Mr. Dent, with his fancy black oak hearse with the glass panels, and the plumed horses to draw it along in style. Had John or Julia Dent started those rumors to persuade people to be embalmed so the doctors wouldn't get you? There had been sharp looks and angry mutterings at the time, for everyone knew who had been porter at the medical college for all these years, but he was an old man by then, a wiry pillar of dignity in his white suit, and so they let him alone, but he did not go to buryings any more.

The night air is cool, and he takes a deep breath, savoring the smell of flowers borne on the wind. He hears no voices in the wind, and dreams no dreams of dead folks reproaching him for what he has done. In a little while, a few months or years at most, for he is nearly ninety, he too will be laid to rest in Cedar Grove among the empty grave sites, secret monuments to his work. He is done with this world, with its new machines and the new gulf between the races. Sometimes he wonders if there are two heavens, so that Fanny Hope will be forever separated from her husbands by some celestial fence, but he rather hopes that there is no hereafter at all. It would be simpler so. And in all his dissecting he has never found a soul.

He smiles on the dark street, remembering a young minister who had once tried to persuade him to attend a funeral. "Come now, Mr. Harris," the earnest preacher had said. "There is nothing to fear in a cemetery. Surely those bodies are simply the discarded husks of our departed spirits. Surely the dead are no longer there."

Bibliography

Allen, Lane. "Grandison Harris, Sr.: Slave, Resurrectionist and Judge." Athens, GA: *Bulletin of the Georgia Academy of Science*, 34:192–199.

Ball, James M. *The Body Snatchers*. New York: Dorset Press, 1989.

Blakely, Robert L., and Judith M. Harrington. *Bones in the Basement: Post Mortem Racism in Nineteenth Century Medical Training*. Washington, DC: Smithsonian Institution, 1997.

Burr, Virginia Ingraham, ed. *The Secret Eye: The Journal of Ella Gertrude Clanton Thomas, 1848–1889*. Chapel Hill, NC: UNC Press, 1990.

Cashin, Edward J. *Old Springfield: Race and Religion in Augusta, Georgia*. Augusta, GA: The Springfield Village Park Assoc. 1995.

Corley, Florence Fleming. *Confederate City: Augusta, Georgia 1860–1865*. Columbia, SC: The USC Press; Rpt. Spartanburg, SC: The Reprint Company, 1995.

Davis, Robert S. *Georgia Black Book: Morbid Macabre and Disgusting Records of Genealogical Value*. Greenville, SC: Southern Historical Press, 1982.

Fido, Martin. *Body Snatchers: A History of the Resurrectionists*. London: Weidenfeld & Nicolson, 1988.

Fisher, John Michael. Fisher & Watkins Funeral Home, Danville, VA. Personal Interview, March 2003.

Kirby, Bill. *The Place We Call Home: A Collection of Articles About Local History from the Augusta Chronicle*. Augusta, GA: *The Augusta Chronicle*, 1995.

Lee, Joseph M. III. *Images of America: Augusta and Summerville*. Charleston, SC: Arcadia Publishing, 2000.

Spalding, Phinizy. *The History of the Medical College of Georgia*. Athens, GA: The University of Georgia Press, 1997.

Torrence, Ridgely. *The Story of John Hope*. New York: Macmillan, 1948.

United States Census Records: Richmond County, GA: 1850; 1860; 1870; 1880; 1990.

Ed McBain

Ed McBain was born in 1956, when Evan Hunter was thirty years old. I am both of these people. What happened was that Pocket Books, Inc., had published the paperback edition of *The Blackboard Jungle* (by Evan Hunter) and wanted to know if I had any ideas for a mystery series. I came up with the notion of the 87th Precinct, and they gave me a contract for three paperback books, "to see how it goes." I was advised to put a pseudonym on the new series because "If it becomes known that Evan Hunter is writing mystery novels, it could be damaging to your career as a serious novelist," quote, unquote. When I finished the first book, *Cop Hater*, I still didn't have a new name. I went out into the kitchen, where my wife was feeding my twin sons, and I said, "How's Ed McBain?" She thought for a moment, and then said, "Good."

Fiddlers, which will be published this year, is the fifty-sixth title in the 87th Precinct series; frankly, I can't see that the Evan Hunter career has suffered at all. Between them, Hunter and McBain have written more than a hundred novels. McBain has never written a screenplay, but Hunter has written several, including *The Birds* for Alfred Hitchcock. The most recent Hunter novel was *The Moment She Was Gone*. The most recent McBain was *Alice in Jeopardy*, the first in a new mystery series.

But only once have they ever *actually* written anything together: Hunter wrote the first half of *Candyland* and McBain wrote the second half.

They still speak to each other.

MERELY HATE

Ed McBain

A blue Star of David had been spray-painted on the windshield of the dead driver's taxi.

"This is pretty unusual," Monoghan said.

"The blue star?" Monroe asked.

"Well, that, too," Monoghan agreed.

The two homicide detectives flanked Carella like a pair of bookends. They were each wearing black suits, white shirts, and black ties, and they looked somewhat like morticians, which was not a far cry from their actual calling. In this city, detectives from Homicide Division were overseers of death, expected to serve in an advisory and supervisory capacity. The actual murder investigation was handled by the precinct that caught the squeal—in this case, the Eight-Seven.

"But I was referring to a cabbie getting killed," Monoghan explained. "Since they started using them plastic partitions . . . what, four, five years ago? . . . yellow-cab homicides have gone down to practically zip."

Except for tonight, Carella thought.

Tall and slender, standing in an easy slouch, Steve Carella looked like an athlete, which he wasn't. The blue star bothered him. It bothered his partner, too. Meyer was hoping the blue star wasn't the start of something. In this city—in this world—things started too fast and took too long to end.

"Trip sheet looks routine," Monroe said, looking at the clipboard he'd recovered from the cab, glancing over the times and locations handwritten on the sheet. "Came on at midnight, last fare was dropped off at one-forty. When did you guys catch the squeal?"

Car four, in the Eight-Seven's Adam Sector, had discovered the cab parked at the curb on Ainsley Avenue at two-thirty in the morning. The driver was slumped over the wheel, a bullet hole at the base of his skull. Blood was running down the back of his neck, into his collar. Blue paint was running down his windshield. The uniforms had phoned the detective squadroom some five minutes later.

"We got to the scene at a quarter to three," Carella said.

"Here's the ME, looks like," Monoghan said.

Carl Blaney was getting out of a black sedan marked with the seal of the Medical Examiner's Office. Blaney was the only person Carella knew who had violet eyes. Then again, he didn't know Liz Taylor.

"What's this I see?" he asked, indicating the clipboard in Monroe's hand. "You been compromising the crime scene?"

"Told you," Monoghan said knowingly.

"It was in plain sight," Monroe explained.

"This the vic?" Blaney asked, striding over to the cab and looking in through the open window on the driver's side. It was a mild night at the beginning of May. Spectators who'd gathered on the sidewalk beyond the yellow CRIME SCENE tapes were in their shirt sleeves. The detectives in sport jackets and ties, Blaney and the homicide dicks in suits and ties, all looked particularly formal, as if they'd come to the wrong street party.

"MCU been here yet?" Blaney asked.

"We're waiting," Carella said.

Blaney was referring to the Mobile Crime Unit, which was called the CSI in some cities. Before they sanctified the scene, not even the ME was supposed to touch anything. Monroe felt this was another personal jab, just because he'd lifted the goddamn clipboard from the front seat. But he'd never liked Blaney, so fuck him.

"Why don't we tarry over a cup of coffee?" Blaney suggested, and without waiting for company, started walking toward an all-night diner across the street. This was a black neighborhood, and this stretch of turf was largely retail, with all of the shops closed at three-fifteen in the morning. The diner was the only place ablaze with illumination, although lights had come on in many of the tenements above the shuttered shops.

The sidewalk crowd parted to let Blaney through, as if he were a visiting dignitary come to restore order in Baghdad. Carella and Meyer ambled along after him. Monoghan and Monroe lingered near the taxi, where three or four blues stood around scratching their asses. Casually, Monroe tossed the clipboard through the open window and onto the front seat on the passenger side.

There were maybe half a dozen patrons in the diner when Blaney and the two detectives walked in. A man and a woman sitting in one of the booths were both black. The girl was wearing a purple silk dress and strappy high-heeled sandals. The man was wearing a beige linen suit with wide lapels. Carella and Meyer each figured them for a hooker and her pimp, which was profiling because for all they knew, the pair could have been a gainfully employed, happily married couple coming home from a late party. Everyone sitting on stools at the counter was black, too. So was the man behind it. They all knew this was the Law here, and the Law frequently spelled trouble in the hood, so they all fell silent when the three men took stools at the counter and ordered coffee.

"So how's the world treating you these days?" Blaney asked the detectives.

"Fine," Carella said briefly. He had come on at midnight, and it had already been a long night.

The counterman brought their coffees.

Bald and burly and blue-eyed, Meyer picked up his coffee cup, smiled across the counter, and asked, "How you doing?"

"Okay," the counterman said warily.

"When did you come to work tonight?"

"Midnight."

"Me, too," Meyer said. "Were you here an hour or so ago?"

"I was here, yessir."

"Did you see anything going down across the street?"

"Nossir."

"Hear a shot?"

"Nossir."

"See anyone approaching the cab there?"

"Nossir."

"Or getting out of the cab?"

"I was busy in here," the man said.

"What's your name?" Meyer asked.

"Whut's my name got to do with who got aced outside?"

"Nothing," Meyer said. "I have to ask."

"Deaven Brown," the counterman said.

"We've got a detective named Arthur Brown up the Eight-Seven," Meyer said, still smiling pleasantly.

"That right?" Brown said indifferently.

"Here's Mobile," Carella said, and all three men hastily downed their coffees and went outside again.

The chief tech was a Detective/First named Carlie . . .

"For Charles," he explained.

. . . Epworth. He didn't ask if anyone had touched anything, and Monroe didn't volunteer the information either. The MCU team went over the vehicle and the pavement surrounding it, dusting for prints, vacuuming for fibers and hair. On the cab's dashboard, there was a little black holder with three miniature American flags stuck in it like an open fan. In a plastic holder on the partition facing the back seat, there was the driver's pink hack license. The name to the right of the photograph was Khalid Aslam. It was almost four A.M. when Epworth said it would be okay to examine the corpse.

Blaney was thorough and swift.

Pending a more thorough examination at the morgue, he proclaimed cause of death to be a gunshot wound to the head—

Big surprise, Monroe thought, but did not say.

—and told the assembled detectives that they would have his written report by the end of the day. Epworth promised likewise, and one of the MCU team drove the taxi off to the police garage where it would be sealed as evidence. An ambulance carried off the stiff. The blues took down the CRIME SCENE tapes, and told everybody to go home, nothing to see here anymore, folks.

Meyer and Carella still had four hours to go before their shift ended.

"Khalid Aslam, Khalid Aslam," the man behind the computer said. "Must be a Muslim, don't you think?"

The offices of the License Bureau at the Taxi and Limousine Commission occupied two large rooms on the eighth floor of the old brick building on Emory Street all the way downtown. At five in the morning, there were only two people on duty, one of them a woman at another computer across the room. Lacking population, the place seemed cavernous.

"Most of the drivers nowadays are Muslims," the man said. His name was Lou Foderman, and he seemed to be close to retirement age, somewhere in his mid-sixties, Meyer guessed.

"Khalid Aslam, Khalid Aslam," he said again, still searching. "The names these people have. You know how many licensed yellow-cab drivers we have in this city?" he asked, not turning from the computer screen. "Forty-two thousand," he said, nodding. "Khalid Aslam, where are you hiding, Khalid Aslam? Ninety percent of them are immigrants, seventy percent from India, Pakistan, and Bangladesh. You want to bet Mr. Aslam here is from one of those countries? How much you wanna bet?"

Carella looked up at the wall clock.

It was five minutes past five.

"Back when *I* was driving a cab," Foderman said, "this was during the time of the Roman Empire, most of your cabbies were Jewish or Irish or Italian. We still got a couple of Jewish drivers around, but they're mostly from Israel or Russia. Irish and Italian, forget about it. You get in a cab nowadays, the driver's talking Farsi to some other guy on his cell phone, you think they're planning a terrorist attack. I wouldn't be surprised Mr. Aslam was talking on the phone to one of his pals, and the passenger shot him because he couldn't take it anymore, you said he was shot, correct?"

"He was shot, yes," Meyer said.

He looked up at the clock, too.

"Because he was babbling on the phone, I'll bet," Foderman said. "These camel jockeys think a taxi is a private phone booth, never mind the passenger. You ask them to please stop talking on the phone, they get insulted. We get more complaints here about drivers talking on the phone than anything else. Well, maybe playing the radio. They play their radios with all this string music from the Middle East, sitars, whatever they call them. Passengers are trying to have a decent conversation, the driver's either playing the radio or talking on the phone. You tell him please lower the radio, he gives you a look could kill you on the spot. Some of them even wear turbans and carry little daggers in their boots, Sikhs, they call themselves. 'All Singhs are Sikhs,'" Forderman quoted, "'but not all Sikhs are Singhs,' that's an expression they have. Singhs is a family name. Or the other way around, I forget which. Maybe it's 'All Sikhs are Singhs,' who knows? Khalid Aslam, here he is. What do you want to know about him?"

Like more than thousands of other Muslim cab drivers in this city, Khalid Aslam was born in Bangladesh. Twelve years ago, he came to America with his wife and one child. According to his updated computer file, he now had three children and lived with his family at 3712 Locust Avenue in Majesta, a neighborhood that once—like the city's cab drivers—was almost exclusively Jewish, but which now was predominately Muslim.

Eastern Daylight Savings Time had gone into effect three weeks ago. This morning, the sun came up at six minutes to six. There was already heavy early-morning rush-hour traffic on the Majesta Bridge. Meyer was driving. Carella was riding shotgun.

"You detect a little bit of anti-Arab sentiment there?" Meyer asked.

"From Foderman, you mean?"

"Yeah. It bothers me to hear another Jew talk that way."

"Well, it bothers me, too," Carella said.

"Yeah, but you're not Jewish."

Someone behind them honked a horn.

"What's with him?" Meyer asked.

Carella turned to look.

"Truck in a hurry," he said.

"I have to tell you," Meyer said, "that blue star on the windshield bothers me. Aslam being Muslim. A bullet in the back of his head, and a Star of David on the windshield, that bothers me."

The truck driver honked again.

Meyer rolled down the window and threw him a finger. The truck driver honked again, a prolonged angry blast this time.

"Shall we give him a ticket?" Meyer asked jokingly.

"I think we should," Carella said.

"Why not? Violation of Section Two Twenty-One, Chapter Two, Subchapter Four, Noise Control."

"Maximum fine, eight hundred and seventy-five smackers," Carella said, nodding, enjoying this.

"Teach him to honk at cops," Meyer said.

The driver behind them kept honking his horn.

"So much hate in this city," Meyer said softly. "So much hate."

Shalah Aslam opened the door for them only after they had both held up their shields and ID cards to the three inches of space allowed by the night chain. She was wearing a blue woolen robe over a long white cotton nightgown. There was a puzzled look on her pale face. This was six-thirty in the morning, she had to know that two detectives on her doorstep at this hour meant something terrible had happened.

There was no diplomatic way to tell a woman that her husband had been murdered.

Standing in a hallway redolent of cooking smells, Carella told Shalah that someone had shot and killed her husband, and they would appreciate it if she could answer a few questions that might help them find whoever had done it. She asked them to come in. The apartment was very still. In contrast to the night before, the day had dawned far too cold for May. There was a bleak chill to the Aslam dwelling.

They followed her through the kitchen and into a small living room where the detectives sat on an upholstered sofa that probably had been made in the mountains of North Carolina. The blue robe Shalah Aslam was wearing most likely had been purchased at the Gap. But here on the mantel was a clock shaped in the form of a mosque, and there were beaded curtains leading to another part of the apartment, and there were the aromas of strange foods from other parts of the building, and the sounds of strange languages wafting up from the street through the open windows. They could have been somewhere in downtown Dhakar.

"The children are still asleep," Shalah explained. "Benazir is only six months old. The two other girls don't catch their school bus until eight-fifteen. I usually wake them at seven."

She had not yet cried. Her pale narrow face seemed entirely placid, her dark brown eyes vacant. The shock had registered, but the emotions hadn't yet caught up.

"Khalid was worried that something like this might happen," she said. "Ever since 9/11. That's why he had those American flags in his taxi. To let passengers know he's American. He got his citizenship five years ago. He's American, same as you. We're all Americans."

They had not yet told her about the Star of David painted on her husband's windshield.

"Seven Bangladesh people died in the towers, you know," she said. "It is not as if we were not victims, too. Because we are Muslim, that does not make us terrorists. The terrorists on those planes were Saudi, you know. Not people from Bangladesh."

"Mrs. Aslam, when you say he was worried, did he ever say specifically . . . ?"

"Yes, because of what happened to some other drivers at Regal."

"Regal?"

"That's the company he works for. A Regal taxi was set on fire in Riverhead the very day the Americans went into Afghanistan. And another one parked in Calm's Point was vandalized the week after we invaded Iraq. So he was afraid something might happen to him as well."

"But he'd never received a specific death threat, had he? Or . . ."

"No."

". . . a threat of violence?"

"No, but the fear was always there. He has had rocks thrown at his taxi. He told me he was thinking of draping a small American flag over his hack license, to hide his picture and name. When passengers ask if he's Arab, he tells them he's from Bangladesh."

She was still talking about him in the present tense. It still hadn't sunk in.

"Most people don't even know where Bangladesh is. Do you know where Bangladesh is?" she asked Meyer.

"No, ma'am, I don't," Meyer said.

"Do you?" she asked Carella.

"No," Carella admitted.

"But they know to shoot my husband because he is from Bangladesh," she said, and burst into tears.

The two detectives sat opposite her clumsily, saying nothing.

"I'm sorry," she said.

She took a tiny, crochet-trimmed handkerchief from the pocket of the robe, dabbed at her eyes with it.

"Khalid was always so careful," she said. "He never picked up anyone wearing a ski cap," drying her cheeks now. "If he got sleepy, he parked in front of a twenty-four-hour gas station or a police precinct. He never picked up anyone who didn't look right. He didn't care what color a person was. If that person looked threatening, he wouldn't pick him up. He hid his money in his shoes, or in an ashtray, or in the pouch on the driver-side door. He kept only a few dollars in his wallet. He was a very careful man."

Meyer bit the bullet.

"Did your husband know any Jewish people?" he asked.

"No," she said. "Why?"

"Mama?" a child's voice asked.

A little girl in a white nightgown, six, seven years old, was standing in the doorway to one of the other rooms. Her dark eyes were big and round in a puzzled face Meyer had seen a thousand times on television these past several years. Straight black hair. A slight frown on the face now. Wondering who these strange men were in their living room at close to seven in the morning.

"Where's Daddy?" she asked.

"Daddy's working," Shalah said, and lifted her daughter onto her lap. "Say hello to these nice men."

"Hello," the little girl said.

"This is Sabeen," Shalah said. "Sabeen is in the first grade, aren't you, Sabeen?"

"Uh-huh," Sabeen said.

"Hello, Sabeen," Meyer said.

"Hello," she said again.

"Sweetie, go read one of your books for a while, okay?" Shalah said. "I have to finish here."

"I have to go to school," Sabeen said.

"I know, darling. I'll just be a few minutes."

Sabeen gave the detectives a long look, and then went out of the room, closing the door behind her.

"Did a Jew kill my husband?" Shalah asked.

"We don't know that," Carella said.

"Then why did you ask if he knew any Jews?"

"Because the possibility exists that this might have been a hate crime," Meyer said.

"My husband was not a Palestinian," Shalah said. "Why would a Jew wish to kill him?"

"We don't know for a fact . . ."

"But you must at least *suspect* it was a Jew, isn't that so? Otherwise, why would you ask such a question? Bangladesh is on the Bay of Bengal, next door to India. It is nowhere near Israel. So why would a Jew . . . ?"

"Ma'am, a Star of David was painted on his windshield," Meyer said.

The room went silent.

"Then it *was* a Jew," she said, and clasped her hands in her lap.

She was silent for perhaps twenty seconds.

Then she said, "The rotten bastards."

"I shouldn't have told her," Meyer said.

"Be all over the papers, anyway," Carella said. "Probably make the front page of the afternoon tabloid."

It was ten minutes past seven, and they were on their way across the bridge again, to where Regal Taxi had its garage on Abingdon and Hale. The traffic was even heavier than it had been on the way out. The day was warming up a little, but not much. This had been the worst damn winter Carella could ever remember. He'd been cold since October. And every time it seemed to be warming up a little, it either started snowing or raining or sleeting or some damn thing to dampen the spirits and crush all hope. Worst damn shitty winter ever.

"What?" Meyer said.

"Nothing."

"You were frowning."

Carella merely nodded.

"When do you think she'll tell the kids?" Meyer asked.

"I think she made a mistake saying he was working. She's got to tell them sooner or later."

"Hard call to make."

"Well, she's not gonna send them to school today, is she?"

"I don't know."

"Be all over the papers," Carella said again.

"I don't know what I'd do in a similar situation."

"When my father got killed, I told my kids that same day," Carella said.

"They're older," Meyer said.

"Even so."

He was silent for a moment.

"They really loved him," he said.

Meyer figured he was talking about himself.

There are times in this city when it is impossible to catch a taxi. Stand on any street corner between three-fifteen and four o'clock and you can wave your hand at any passing blur of yellow, and—forget about it. That's the forty-five minutes when every cabbie is racing back to the garage to turn in his trip sheet and make arrangements for tomorrow's tour of duty. It was the same with cops. The so-called night shift started at four P.M. and ended at midnight. For the criminally inclined, the shift change was a good time for them to do their evil thing because that's when all was confusion.

Confusion was the order of the day at the Regal garage when Meyer and Carella got there at seven-thirty that morning. Cabs were rolling in, cabs were rolling out. Assistant managers were making arrangements for tomorrow's short-terms, and dispatchers were sending newly gassed taxis on their way through the big open rolling doors. This was the busiest time of the day. Even busier than the pre-theater hours. Nobody had time for two flatfoots investigating a homicide.

Carella and Meyer waited.

Their own shift would end in—what was it now?—ten minutes, and they were bone-weary and drained of all energy, but they waited patiently because a man had been killed and Carella had been First Man Up when he answered the phone. It was twelve minutes after eight before the manager, a man named Dennis Ryan, could talk to them. Tall, and red-headed, and fortyish, harried-looking even though all of his cabs were on their way now, he kept nodding impatiently as they told him what had happened to Khalid Aslam.

"So where's my cab?" he asked.

"Police garage on Courtney," Meyer told him.

"When do I get it back? That cab is money on the hoof."

"Yes, but a man was killed in it," Carella said.

"When I saw Kal didn't show up this morning . . ."

Kal, Carella thought. Yankee Doodle Dandy.

". . . I figured he stopped to say one of his bullshit prayers."

Both detectives looked at him.

"They're supposed to pray five times a day, you know, can you beat it? Five times! Sunrise, early afternoon, late afternoon, sunset, and then before they go to bed. Five friggin times! And two *optional* ones if they're *really* holy. Most of them recognize they have a job to do here, they don't go flopping all over the sidewalk five times a day. Some of them pull over to a mosque on their way back in, for the late afternoon prayer. Some of them just do the one before they come to work, and the sunset one if they're home in time, and then the one before they go to bed. I can tell you anything you need to know about these people, we got enough of them working here, believe me."

"What kind of a worker was Aslam?" Carella asked.

"I guess he made a living."

"Meaning?"

"Meaning, it costs eighty-two bucks a shift to lease the cab. Say the driver averages a hundred above that in fares and tips. Gasoline costs him, say, fifteen, sixteen bucks? So he ends up taking home seventy-five, eighty bucks for an eight-hour shift. That ain't bad, is it?"

"Comes to around twenty grand a year," Meyer said.

"Twenty, twenty-five. That ain't bad," Ryan said again.

"Did he get along with the other drivers?" Carella asked.

"Oh, sure. These friggin Arabs are thick as thieves."

"How about your non-Arab drivers? Did he get along with them?"

"What non-Arab drivers? Why? You think one of my drivers done him?"

"Did he ever have any trouble with one of the other drivers?"

"I don't think so."

"Ever hear him arguing with one of them?"

"Who the hell knows? They babble in Bangla, Urdu, Sindi, Farsi, who the hell knows what else? They all sound the same to me. And they *always* sound like they're arguing. Even when they got smiles on their faces."

"Have you got any Jewish drivers?" Meyer asked.

"Ancient history," Ryan said. "I ain't *ever* seen a Jewish driver at Regal."

"How about anyone who might be sympathetic to the Jewish cause?"

"Which cause is that?" Ryan asked.

"Anyone who might have expressed pro-Israel sympathies?"

"Around here? You've got to be kidding."

"Did you ever hear Aslam say anything *against* Israel? Or the Jewish people?"

"No. Why? Did a Jew kill him?"

"What time did he go to work last night?"

"The boneyard shift goes out around eleven-thirty, quarter to twelve, comes in around seven, seven-thirty—well, you saw. I guess he must've gone out as usual. Why? What time was he killed?"

"Around two, two-thirty."

"Where?"

"Up on Ainsley and Twelfth."

"Way up there, huh?" Ryan said. "You think a nigger did it?"

"We don't know if who did it was white, purple, or black, was the word you meant, right?" Carella said, and looked Ryan dead in the eye.

And fuck you, too, Ryan thought, but said only, "Good luck catching him," making it sound like a curse.

Meyer and Carella went back to the squadroom to type up their interim report on the case.

It was almost a quarter to nine when they finally went home.

The day shift had already been there for half an hour.

Detectives Arthur Brown and Bert Kling made a good salt-and-pepper pair.

Big and heavyset and the color of his surname, Brown looked somewhat angry even when he wasn't. A scowl from him was usually enough to cause a perp to turn to Kling for sympathy and redemption. A few inches shorter than his partner—*everybody* was a few inches shorter than Brown—blond and hazel-eyed, Kling looked like a broad-shouldered farm boy who'd just come in off the fields after working since sunup. God Cop-Bad Cop had been invented for Kling and Brown.

It was Brown who took the call from Ballistics at 10:27 that Friday morning.

"You handling this cabbie kill?" the voice said.

Brown immediately recognized the caller as a brother.

"I've been briefed on it," he said.

"This is Carlyle, Ballistics. We worked that evidence bullet the ME's office sent over, you want to take this down for whoever's running the case?"

"Shoot," Brown said, and moved a pad into place.

"Nice clean bullet, no deformities, must've lodged in the brain matter, ME's report didn't say exactly where they'd recovered it. Not that it matters. First thing we did here, bro . . ."

He had recognized Brown's voice as well.

". . . was compare a rolled impression of the evidence bullet against our specimen cards. Once we got a first-sight match, we did a microscopic examination of the actual bullet against the best sample bullet in our file. Way we determine the make of an unknown firearm is by examining the grooves on the bullet and the right or left direction of twist—but you don't want to hear all that shit, do you?"

Brown had heard it only ten thousand times before.

"Make a long story short," Carlyle said, "what we got here is a bullet fired from a .38-caliber Colt revolver, which is why you didn't find an ejected shell in the taxi, the gun being a revolver and all. Incidentally, there are probably a hundred thousand unregistered, illegal .38-caliber Colts in this city, so the odds against you finding it are probably eighty to one. End of story."

"Thanks," Brown said. "I'll pass it on."

"You see today's paper?" Carlyle asked.

"No, not yet."

"Case made the front page. Makes it sound like the Israeli army invaded Majesta with tanks, one lousy Arab. Is this true about a Jewish star on the windshield?"

"That's what our guys found."

"Gonna be trouble, bro," Carlyle said.

He didn't know the half of it.

While Carella and Meyer slept like hibernating grizzlies, Kling and Brown read their typed report, noted that the dead driver's widow had told them the Aslams' place of worship was called Majid Hazrat-i-Shabazz, and went out at eleven that morning to visit the mosque.

If either of them had expected glistening white minarets, arches, and domes, they were sorely disappointed. There were more than a hundred mosques in this city, but only a handful of them had been originally designed as such. The remainder had been converted to places of worship from private homes, warehouses, storefront buildings, and lofts. There were, in fact, only three requirements for any building that now called itself a mosque: that males and females be separated during prayer; that there be no images of animate objects inside the building; and that the *quibla*—the orientation of prayer in the direction of the Kabba in Mecca—be established.

A light rain began falling as they got out of the unmarked police sedan and began walking toward a yellow brick building that had once been a small supermarket on the corner of Lowell and Franks. Metal shutters were now in place where earlier there'd been plate glass display windows. Grafitti decorated the yellow brick and the green shutters. An ornately hand-lettered sign hung above the entrance doors, white on a black field, announcing the name of the mosque: Majid Hazrat-i-Shabazz. Men in flowing white garments and embroidered prayer caps, other men in dark business suits and pillbox hats milled about on the sidewalk with young men in team jackets, their baseball caps turned backward. Friday was the start of the Muslim sabbath, and now the faithful were being called to prayer.

On one side of the building, the detectives could see women entering through a separate door.

"My mother knows this Muslim lady up in Diamondback," Brown said, "she goes to this mosque up there—lots of blacks are Muslims, you know . . ."

"I know," Kling said.

"And where she goes to pray, they got no space for this separation stuff. So the men and women all pray together in the same open hall. But the women sit *behind* the men. So this fat ole sister gets there late one Friday, and the hall is already filled with men, and they tell her there's no room for her. Man, she takes a fit! Starts yelling, 'This is America, I'm as good a Muslim as any man here, so how come they's only room for *brothers* to pray?' Well, the imam—that's the man in charge, he's like the preacher—he quotes scripture and verse that says only men are *required* to come to Friday prayer, whereas women are not. So they have to let the men in first. It's as simple as that. So she quotes right back at him that in Islam, women are *spose* to be highly respected and revered, so how come he's dissing her this way? And she walked away from that mosque and never went back. From that time on, she prayed at home. That's a true story," Brown said.

"I believe it," Kling said.

The imam's address that Friday was about the dead cab driver. He spoke first in Arabic—which, of course, neither Kling nor Brown understood—and then he translated his words into English, perhaps for their benefit, perhaps in deference to the younger worshippers in the large drafty hall. The male worshippers knelt at the front of the hall. Behind a translucent, moveable screen, Brown and Kling could perceive a small number of veiled female worshippers.

The imam said he prayed that the strife in the Middle East was not now coming to this city that had known so much tragedy already. He said he prayed that an innocent and hard-working servant of Allah had not paid with his life for the acts of a faraway people bent only on destruction—

The detectives guessed he meant the Israelis.

—prayed that the signature star on the windshield of the murdered man's taxi was not a promise of further violence to come.

"It is foolish to grieve for our losses," he said, "since all is ordained by Allah. Only by working for the larger nation of Islam can we understand the true meaning of life."

Men's foreheads touched the cement floor.

Behind the screen, the women bowed their heads as well.

The imam's name was Muhammad Adham Akbar.

"What we're trying to find out," Brown said, "is whether or not Mr. Aslam had any enemies that you know of."

"Why do you even ask such a question?" Akbar said.

"He was a worshipper at your mosque," Kling said. "We thought you might know."

"Why would he have enemies here?"

"Men have enemies everywhere," Brown said.

"Not in a house of prayer. If you want to know who Khalid's enemy was, you need only look at his windshield."

"Well, we have to investigate every possibility," Kling said.

"The star on his windshield says it all," Akbar said, and shrugged. "A Jew killed him. That would seem obvious to anyone."

"Well, a Jew may have committed those murders," Kling agreed. "But . . ."

"May," the imam said, and nodded cynically.

"But until we catch him, we won't know for sure, will we?" Kling said.

Akbar looked at him.

Then he said, "The slain man had no enemies that I know of."

Just about when Carella and Meyer were each and separately waking up from eight hours of sleep, more or less, the city's swarm of taxis rolled onto the streets for the four-to-midnight shift. And as the detectives sat down to late afternoon meals which for each of them were really hearty breakfasts, many of the city's more privileged women were coming out into the streets to start looking for taxis to whisk them homeward. Here was a carefully coiffed woman who'd just enjoyed afternoon tea, chatting with another equally stylish woman as they strolled together out of a midtown hotel. And here was a woman who came out of a department store carrying a shopping bag in each hand, shifting one of the bags to the other hand, freeing it so she could hail a taxi. And here was a woman coming out of a Korean nail shop, wearing paper sandals to protect her freshly painted toenails. And another coming out of a deli, clutching a bag with baguettes showing, raising one hand to signal a cab. At a little before five, the streets were suddenly alive with the leisured women of this city, the most beautiful women in all the world, all of them ready to kill if another woman grabbed a taxi that had just been hailed.

This was a busy time for the city's cabbies. Not ten minutes later, the office buildings would begin spilling out men and women who'd been working since nine this morning, coming out onto the pavements now and sucking in great breaths of welcome spring air. The rain had stopped, and the sidewalk and pavements glistened, and there was the strange aroma of freshness on the air. This had been one hell of a winter.

The hands went up again, typists' hands, and file clerks' hands, and the hands of lawyers and editors and agents and producers and exporters and thieves, yes, even thieves took taxis—though obvious criminal types were avoided by these cabbies steering their vehicles recklessly toward the curb in a relentless pursuit of passengers. These men had paid eighty-two dollars to lease their taxis. These men had paid fifteen, twenty bucks to gas their buggies and get them on the road. They were already a hundred bucks in the hole before they put foot to pedal. Time was money. And there were hungry mouths to feed. For the most part, these men were Muslims, these men were gentle strangers in a strange land.

But someone had killed one of them last night.

And he was not yet finished.

Salim Nazir and his widowed mother left Afghanistan in 1994, when it became apparent that the Taliban were about to take over the entire country. His father had been one of the mujahideen killed fighting the Russian occupation; Salim's mother did not wish the wrath of "God's Students" to fall upon their heads if and when a new regime came to power.

Salim was now twenty-seven years old, his mother fifty-five. Both had been American citizens for three years now, but neither approved of what America had done to their native land, the evil Taliban notwithstanding. For that matter they did not appreciate what America had done to Iraq in its search for imaginary weapons of mass destruction. (Salim called them "weapons of mass deception.") In fact, Salim totally disapproved of the mess America had made in what once was his part of the world, but he rarely expressed these views out loud, except when he was among other Muslims who lived—as he and his mother did now—in a ghettolike section of Calm's Point.

Salim knew what it was like to be an outsider in George W. Bush's America, no matter how many speeches the president made about Islam being a peaceful religion. With all his heart, Salim knew this to be true, but he doubted very much that Mr. Bush believed what he was saying.

Just before sundown that Friday, Salim pulled his yellow taxi into the curb in front of a little shop on a busy street in Majesta. Here in Ikram Hassan's store, devout Muslims could purchase whatever food and drink was considered *halal*—lawful or permitted for consumption as described in the Holy Koran.

The Koran decreed, "Eat of that over which the name of Allah hath been mentioned, if ye are believers in His revelations." Among the acceptable foods were milk (from cows, sheep, camels, or goats), honey, fish, plants that were not intoxicant, fresh or naturally frozen vegetables, fresh or dried fruits, legumes (like peanuts, cashews, hazelnuts, and walnuts), and grains such as wheat, rice, barley, and oats.

Many animals, large and small, were considered *halal* as well, but they had to be slaughtered according to Islamic ritual. Ikram Hassan was about to slay a chicken just as his friend Salim came into the shop. He looked up when a small bell over his door sounded.

"Hey there, Salim," he said in English.

There were two major languages in Afghanistan, both of them imported from Iran, but Pushto was the official language the two men had learned as boys growing up in Kandahar, and this was the language they spoke now.

Salim fidgeted and fussed as his friend hunched over the chicken; he did not want to be late for the sunset prayer. Using a very sharp knife, and making certain that he cut the main blood vessels without completely severing the throat, Ikram intoned "*Bismillah Allah-u-Albar*" and completed the ritual slaughter.

Each of the men then washed his hands to the wrists, and cleansed the mouth and the nostrils with water, and washed the face and the right arm and left arm to the elbow, and washed to the ankle first the right foot and then the left, and at last wiped the top of the head with wet hands, the three middle fingers of each hand joined together.

Salim consulted his watch yet another time.

Both men donned little pillbox hats.

Ikram locked the front door to his store, and together they walked to the mosque four blocks away.

The sun had already set.

It was ten minutes to seven.

Among other worshippers, Salim and Ikram stood facing Mecca, their hands raised to their ears, and they uttered the words, "*Allahu Akbar*," which meant "Allah is the greatest of all." Then they placed the right hand just below the breast and recited in unison the prayer called *istiftah*.

"Surely I have turned myself, being upright holy to Him Who originated the heavens and the earth and I am not of the polytheists. Surely my prayer and my sacrifice and my life and my death are for Allah, the Lord of the worlds, no associate has He; and this I am commanded and I am one of those who submit. Glory to Thee, O Allah, and Thine is the praise, and blessed is Thy name, and exalted is Thy majesty, and there is none to be served besides Thee."

A'udhu bi-llahi minash-shaitani-r-rajim.

"I seek the refuge of Allah from the accursed devil."

Six hours later, Salim Nazir would be dead.

In this city, all the plays, concerts, and musicals let out around eleven, eleven-thirty, the cabarets around one, one-thirty. The night clubs wouldn't break till all hours of the night. It was Salim's habit during the brief early-morning lull to visit a Muslim friend who was a short-order cook at a deli on Culver Avenue, a mile and a half distant from all the midtown glitter. He went into the deli at one-thirty, enjoyed a cup of coffee and a chat with his friend, and left twenty minutes later. Crossing the street to where he'd parked his taxi, he got in behind the wheel, and was just about to start the engine when he realized someone was sitting in the dark in the back seat.

Startled, he was about to ask what the hell, when the man fired a bullet through the plastic divider and into his skull.

The two Midtown South detectives who responded to the call immediately knew this killing was related to the one that had taken place uptown the night before; a blue Star of David had been spray-painted on the windshield. Nonetheless, they called their lieutenant from the scene, and he informed them that this was a clear case of First Man Up, and advised them to wait right there while he contacted the Eight-Seven, which had caught the original squeal. The detectives were still at the scene when Carella and Meyer got there at twenty minutes to three.

Midtown South told Carella that both MCU and the ME had already been there and gone, the corpse and the vehicle carried off respectively to the morgue and the PD garage to be respectively dissected and impounded. They told the Eight-Seven dicks that they'd talked to the short-order cook in the deli across the street, who informed them that he was a friend of the dead man, and that he'd been in there for a cup of coffee shortly before he got killed. The vic's name was Salim Nazir, and the cab company he worked for was called City Transport. They assumed the case was now the Eight-Seven's and that Carella and Meyer would do all the paper shit and send them dupes. Carella assured them that they would.

"We told you about the blue star, right?" one of the Midtown dicks said.

"You told us," Meyer said.

"Here's the evidence bullet we recovered," he said, and handed Meyer a sealed manila envelope. "Chain of Custody tag on it, you sign next. Looks like you maybe caught an epidemic."

"Or maybe a copycat," Carella said.

"Either way, good luck," the other Midtown dick said.

Carella and Meyer crossed the street to the deli.

Like his good friend, Salim, the short-order cook was from Afghanistan, having arrived here in the city seven years ago. He offered at once to show the detectives his green card, which made each of them think he was probably an illegal with a counterfeit card, but they had bigger fish to fry and Ajmal Khan was possibly a man who could help them do just that.

Ajmal meant "good-looking" in his native tongue, a singularly contradictory description for the man who now told them he had heard a shot outside some five minutes after Salim finished his coffee. Dark eyes bulging with excitement, black mustache bristling, bulbous nose twitching like a rabbit's, Ajmal reported that he had rushed out of the shop the instant he heard the shot, and had seen a man across the street getting out of Salim's taxi on the driver's side, and leaning over the windshield with a can of some sort in his hand.

Ajmal didn't know what he was doing at the time but he now understood the man was spray-painting a Jewish star on the windshield.

"Can you describe this man?" Carella asked.

"Is that what he was doing? Painting a Star of David on the windshield?"

"Apparently," Meyer said.

"That's bad," Ajmal said.

The detectives agreed with him. That was bad. They did not believe this was a copycat. This was someone specifically targeting Muslim cab drivers. But they went through the routine anyway, asking the questions they always asked whenever someone was murdered: Did he have any enemies that you know of, did he mention any specific death threats, did he say he was being followed or harassed, was he in debt to anyone, was he using drugs?

Ajmal told them that his good friend Salim was loved and respected by everyone. This was what friends and relatives always said about the vic. He was a kind and gentle person. He had a wonderful sense of humor. He was thoughtful and generous. He was devout. Ajmal could not imagine why anyone would have done this to a marvelous person like his good friend Salim Nazir.

"He was always laughing and friendly, a very warm and outgoing man. Especially with the ladies," Ajmal said.

"What do you mean?" Carella asked.

"He was quite a ladies' man, Salim. It is written that men may have as many as four wives, but they must be treated equally in every way. That is to say, emotionally, sexually, and materially. If Salim had been a wealthy man, I am certain he would have enjoyed the company of many wives."

"How many wives did he actually *have*?" Meyer asked.

"Well, none," Ajmal said. "He was single. He lived with his mother."

"Do you know where?"

"Oh yes. We were very good friends. I have been to his house many times."

"Can you give us his address?"

"His phone number, too," Ajmal said. "His mother's name is Gulalai. It means 'flower' in my country."

"You say he was quite a ladies' man, is that right?" Carella asked.

"Well, yes. The ladies liked him."

"More than one lady?" Carella said.

"Well, yes, more than one."

"Did he ever mention any jealousy among these various ladies?"

"I don't even know who they were. He was a discreet man."

"No reason any of these ladies might have wanted to shoot him?" Carella said.

"Not that I know of."

"But he *did* say he was seeing several women, is that it?"

"In conversation, yes."

"He said he was in *conversation* with several women?"

"No, he said to *me* in conversation that he was enjoying the company of several women, yes. As I said, he was quite a ladies' man."

"But he didn't mention the names of these women."

"No, he did not. Besides, it was a man I saw getting out of his taxi. A very tall man."

"Could it have been a very tall woman?"

"No, this was very definitely a man."

"Can you describe him?"

"Tall. Wide shoulders. Wearing a black raincoat and a black hat." Ajmal paused. "The kind rabbis wear," he said.

Which brought them right back to that Star of David on the windshield.

Two windshields.

This was not good at all.

This was a mixed lower-class neighborhood—white, black, Hispanic. These people had troubles of their own, they didn't much care about a couple of dead Arabs. Matter of fact, many of them had sons or husbands who'd fought in the Iraqi war. Lots of the people Carella and Meyer spoke to early that morning had an "Army of One," was what it was called nowadays, who'd gone to war right here from the hood. Some of these young men had never come back home except in a box.

You never saw nobody dying on television. All them reporters embedded with the troops, all you saw was armor racing across the desert. You never saw somebody taking a sniper bullet between the eyes, blood spattering. You never saw an artillery attack with arms and legs flying in the air. You could see more people getting killed right here in the hood than you saw getting killed in the entire Iraqi war. It was an absolute miracle, all them embedded newspeople out there reporting, and not a single person getting killed for the cameras. Maybe none of them had a camera handy when somebody from the hood got killed. So who gave a damn around here about a few dead Arabs more or less?

One of the black women they interviewed explained that people were asleep, anyway, at two in the morning, wun't that so? So why go axin a dumb question like did you hear a shot that time of night? A Hispanic man they interviewed told them there were *always* shots in the barrio; nobody ever paid attention no more. A white woman told them she'd got up to go pee around that time, and thought she heard something but figured it was a backfire.

At 4:30 A.M., Meyer and Carella spoke to a black man who'd been blinded in Iraq. He was in pajamas and a bathrobe, and he was wearing dark glasses. A white cane stood angled against his chair. He could remember President Bush making a little speech to a handful of veterans like himself at the hospital where he was recovering, his eyes still bandaged. He could remember Bush saying something folksy like, "I'll bet those Iraqi soldiers weren't happy to meet *you* fellas!" He could remember thinking, I wun't so happy to meet *them*, either. I'm goan be blind the ress of my life, Mr. Pres'dunt, how you feel about *that*?

"I heerd a shot," he told the detectives.

Travon Nelson was his name. He worked as a dishwasher in a restaurant all the way downtown. They stopped serving at eleven, he was usually out by a little before one, took the number 17 bus uptown, got home here around two. He had just got off the bus, and was walking toward his building, his white cane tapping the sidewalk ahead of him . . .

He had once thought he'd like to become a Major League ballplayer.

. . . when he heard the sharp crack of a small-arms weapon, and then heard a car door slamming, and then a hissing sound, he didn't know what it was . . .

The spray paint, Meyer thought.

. . . and then a man yelling.

"Yelling at *you*?" Carella asked.

"No, sir. Must've been some girl."

"What makes you think that?"

"Cause whut he yelled was 'You *whore*!' An' then I think he must've hit her, cause she screamed an' kepp right on screamin an' screamin."

"Then what?" Meyer asked.

"He run off. She run off, too. I heerd her heels clickin away. High heels. When you blind . . ."

His voice caught.

They could not see his eyes behind the dark glasses.

". . . you compensate with yo' other senses. They was the sound of the man's shoes runnin off and then the click of the girl's high heels."

He was silent for a moment, remembering again what high heels on a sidewalk sounded like.

"Then evy'thin went still again," he said.

Years of living in war-torn Afghanistan had left their mark on Gulalai Nazir's wrinkled face and stooped posture; she looked more like a woman in her late sixties than the fifty-five-year-old mother of Salim. The detectives had called ahead first, and several grieving relatives were already in her apartment when they got there at six that Saturday morning. Gulalai—although now an American citizen—spoke very little English. Her nephew—a man who at the age of sixteen had fought with the mujahideen against the Russians—translated for the detectives.

Gulalai told them what they had already heard from the short-order cook.

Her son was loved and respected by everyone. He was a kind and gentle person. A loving son. He had a wonderful sense of humor. He was thoughtful and generous. He was devout. Gulalai could not imagine why anyone would have done this to him.

"Unless it was that Jew," she said.

The nephew translated.

"Which Jew?" Carella asked at once.

"The one who killed that other Muslim cab driver uptown," the nephew translated.

Gulalai wrung her hands and burst into uncontrollable sobbing. The other women began wailing with her.

The nephew took the detectives aside.

His name was Osman, he told them, which was Turkish in origin, but here in America everyone called him either Ozzie or Oz.

"Oz Kiraz," he said, and extended his hand. His grip was firm and strong. He was a big man, possibly thirty-two, thirty-three years old, with curly black hair and an open face with sincere brown eyes. Carella could visualize him killing Russian soldiers with his bare hands. He would not have enjoyed being one of them.

"Do you think you're going to get this guy?" he asked.

"We're trying," Carella said.

"Or is it going to be the same song and dance?"

"Which song and dance is that, sir?" Meyer said.

"Come on, this city is run by Jews. If a Jew killed my cousin, it'll be totally ignored."

"We're trying to make sure that doesn't happen," Carella said.

"I'll bet," Oz said.

"You'd win," Meyer said.

The call from Detective Carlyle in Ballistics came at a quarter to seven that Saturday morning.

"You the man I spoke to yesterday?" he asked.

"No, this is Carella."

"You workin this Arab shit?"

"Yep."

"It's the same gun," Carlyle said. "This doesn't mean it was the same *guy*, it coulda been his cousin or his uncle or his brother pulled the trigger. But it was the same .38-caliber Colt that fired the bullet."

"That it?"

"Ain't that enough?"

"More than enough," Carella said. "Thanks, pal."

"Buy me a beer sometime," Carlyle said, and hung up.

At 8:15 that morning, just as Carella and Meyer were briefing Brown and Kling on what had happened the night before, an attractive young black woman in her mid twenties walked into the squadroom. She introduced herself as Wandalyn Holmes, and told the detectives that she'd been heading home from baby-sitting her sister's daughter last night—walking to the corner to catch the number 17 bus downtown, in fact—when she saw this taxi sitting at the curb, and a man dressed all in black spraying paint on the windshield.

"When he saw I was looking at him, he pointed a finger at me . . ."

"Pointed . . . ?"

"Like this, yes," Wandalyn said, and showed them how the man had pointed his finger. "And he yelled 'You! Whore!' and I screamed and he came running after me."

"You whore?"

"No, two words. First 'You!' and *then* 'Whore!' "

"Did you know this man?"

"Never saw him in my life."

"But he pointed his finger at you and called you a whore."

"Yes. And when I ran, he came after me and caught me by the back of the coat, you know what I'm saying? The collar of my coat? And pulled me over, right off my feet."

"What time was this, Miss Holmes?" Carella asked.

"About two in the morning, a little after."

"What happened then?"

"He kicked me. While I was laying on the ground. He seemed mad as hell. I thought at first he was gonna rape me. I kept screaming, though, and he ran off."

"What'd you do then?" Brown asked.

"I got up and ran off, too. Over to my sister's place. I was scared he might come back."

"Did you get a good look at him?"

"Oh yes."

"Tell us what he looked like," Meyer said.

"Like I said, he was all in black. Black hat, black raincoat, black everything."

"Was he himself black?" Kling asked.

"Oh no, he was a white man."

"Did you see his face?"

"I did."

"Describe him."

"Dark eyes. Angry. Very angry eyes."

"Beard? Mustache?"

"No."

"Notice any scars or tattoos?"

"No."

"Did he say anything to you?"

"Well, yes, I told you. He called me a whore."

"*After* that."

"No. Nothing. Just pulled me over backward, and started kicking me when I was down. I thought he was gonna rape me, I was scared to death." Wandalyn paused a moment. The detectives caught the hesitation.

"Yes?" Carella said. "Something else?"

"I'm sorry I didn't come here right away last night, but I was too scared," Wandalyn said. "He was very angry. *So* angry. I was scared he might come after me if I told the police anything."

"You're here now," Carella said. "And we thank you."

"He *won't* come after me, right?" Wandalyn asked.

"I'm sure he won't," Carella said. "It's not you he's angry with."

Wandalyn nodded. But still looked skeptical.

"You'll be okay, don't worry," Brown said, and led her to the gate in the slatted wooden railing that divided the squadroom from the corridor outside.

At his desk, Carella began typing up their Detective Division report. He was still typing when Brown came over and said, "You know what time it is?"

Carella nodded and kept typing.

It was 9:33 A.M. when he finally printed up the report and carried it over to Brown's desk.

"Go home," Brown advised, scowling.

They had worked important homicides before, and these had also necessitated throwing the schedule out the window. What was new this time around—

Well, no, there was also a murder that had almost started a race riot, this must've been two, three years back, they hadn't got much sleep that time, either. This was similar, but different. This was two Muslim cabbies who'd been shot to death by someone, obviously a Jew, eager to take credit for both murders.

Meyer didn't know whether he dreamt it, or whether it was a brilliant idea he'd had before he fell asleep at nine that morning.

Dream or brilliant idea, the first thing he did when the alarm clock rang at three that afternoon was find a fat felt-tipped pen and a sheet of paper and draw a big blue Star of David on it.

He kept staring at the star and wondering if the department's handwriting experts could tell them anything about the man or men who had spray-painted similar stars on the windshields of those two cabs.

He was almost eager to get to work.

Six hours of sleep wasn't bad for what both detectives considered a transitional period, similar to the decompression a deep-sea diver experienced while coming up to the surface in stages. Actually, they were moving back from the midnight shift to the night shift, a passage that normally took place over a period of days, but which given the exigency of the situation occurred in the very same day. Remarkably, both men felt refreshed and—in Meyer's case at least—raring to go.

"I had a great idea last night," he told Carella. "Or maybe it was just a dream. Take a look at this," he said, and showed Carella the Star of David he'd drawn.

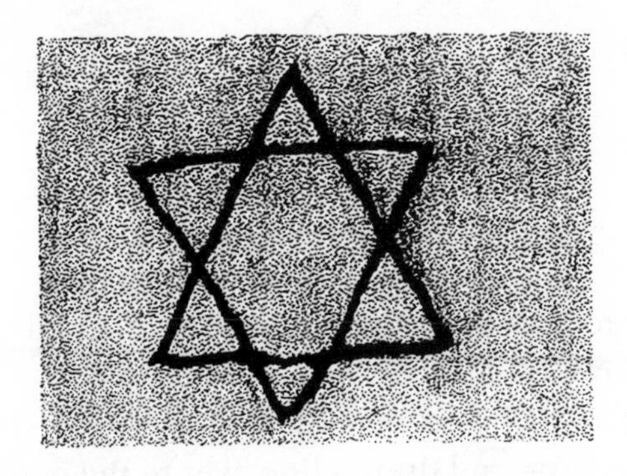

"Okay," Carella said.

"I'm right-handed," Meyer said. "So what I did . . ."

"So am I," Carella said.

"What I did," Meyer said, "was start the first triangle here at the northernmost point of the star . . . there are six points, you know, and they mean something or other, I'm not really sure what. I am not your ideal Jew."

"I never would have guessed."

"But religious Jews know what the six points stand for."

"So what's your big idea?"

"Well, I was starting to tell you. I began the first triangle at the very top, and drew one side down to this point here," he said, indicating the point on the bottom right . . .

". . . and then I drew a line across to the left . . ."

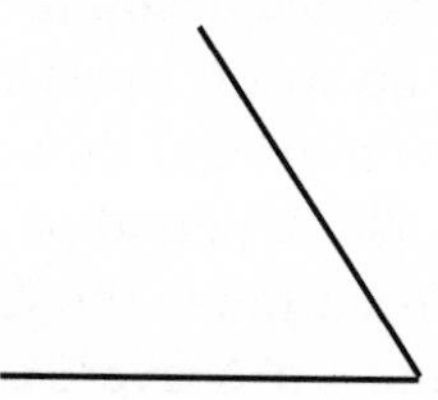

". . . and another line up to the northern point again, completing the first triangle."

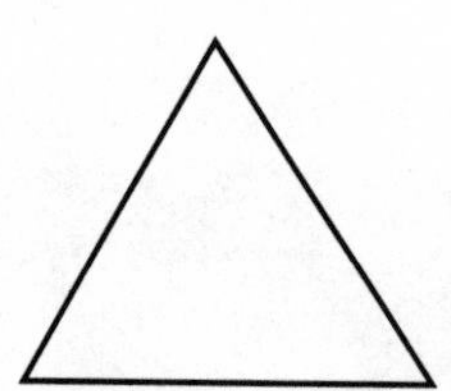

"Okay," Carella said, and picked up a pen and drew a triangle in exactly the same way.

"Then I started the second triangle at the western point—the one here on the left—and drew a line over to the east here . . ."

". . . and then down on an angle to the south . . ."

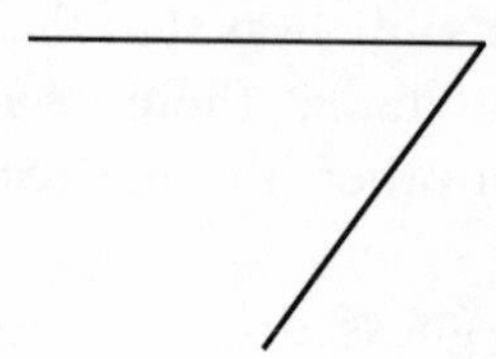

". . . and back up again to . . . northwest, I guess it is . . . where I started."

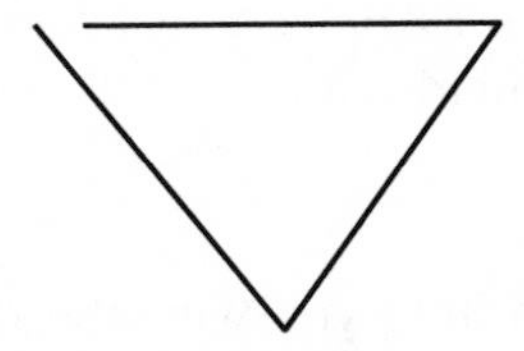

Carella did the same thing.

"That's right," he said. "That's how you do it."

"Yes, but we're both right-handed."

"So?"

"I think a left-handed person might do it differently."

"Ah," Carella said, nodding.

"So I think we should call Documents and get them to look at both those cabs. See if the same guy painted those two stars, and find out if he was right-handed or left-handed."

"I think that's brilliant," Carella said.

"You don't."

"I do."

"I can tell you don't."

"I'll make the call myself," Carella said.

He called downtown, asked for the Documents Section, and spoke to a detective named Jackson who agreed that there would be a distinct difference between left- and right-handed handwriting, even if the writing instrument—so to speak—was a spray can. Carella told him they were investigating a double homicide . . .

"Those Muslim cabbies, huh?"

. . . and asked if Documents could send someone down to the police garage to examine the spray-painting on the windshields of the two impounded taxis. Jackson said it would have to wait till tomorrow morning, they were a little short-handed today.

"While I have you," Carella said, "can you switch me over to the lab?"

The lab technician he spoke to reported that the paint scrapings from the windshields of both cabs matched laboratory samples of a product called Redi-Spray, which was manufactured in Milwaukee, Wisconsin, distributed nationwide, and sold in virtually every hardware store and supermarket in this city. Carella thanked him and hung up.

He was telling Meyer what he'd just learned, when Rabbi Avi Cohen walked into the squadroom.

"I think I may be able to help you with the recent cab driver murders," the rabbi said.

Carella offered him a chair alongside his desk.

"If I may," the rabbi said, "I would like to go back to the beginning."

Would you be a rabbi otherwise? Meyer thought.

"The beginning was last month," the rabbi said, "just before Passover. Today is the sixteenth day of the Omer, which is one week and nine days from the second day of Passover, so this would have been before Passover. Around the tenth of April, a Thursday I seem to recall it was."

As the rabbi remembers it . . .

This young man came to him seeking guidance and assistance. Was the rabbi familiar with a seventeen-year-old girl named Rebecca Schwartz, who was a member of the rabbi's own congregation? Well, yes, of course, Rabbi Cohen knew the girl well. He had, in fact, officiated at her *bat mitzvah* five years ago. Was there some problem?

The problem was that the young man was in love with young Rebecca, but he was not of the Jewish faith—which, by the way, had been evident to the rabbi at once, the boy's olive complexion, his dark brooding eyes. It seemed that Rebecca's parents had forbidden her from seeing the boy ever again, and this was why he was here in the synagogue today, to ask the rabbi if he could speak to Mr. Schwartz and convince him to change his mind.

Well.

The rabbi explained that this was an Orthodox congregation and that anyway there was a solemn prohibition in Jewish religious law against a Jew marrying anyone but another Jew. He went on to explain that this ban against intermarriage was especially pertinent to our times, when statistics indicated that an alarming incidence of intermarriage threatened the very future of American Jewry.

"In short," Rabbi Cohen said, "I told him I was terribly sorry, but I could never approach Samuel Schwartz with a view toward encouraging a relationship between his daughter and a boy of another faith. Do you know what he said to me?"

"What?" Carella asked.

" 'Thanks for nothing!' He made it sound like a threat."

Carella nodded. So did Meyer.

"And then the e-mails started," the rabbi said. "Three of them all together. Each with the same message. 'Death to all Jews.' And just at sundown last night . . ."

"When was this?" Meyer asked. "The e-mails?"

"Last week. All of them last week."

"What happened last night?" Carella asked.

"Someone threw a bottle of whiskey with a lighted wick through the open front door of the synagogue."

The two detectives nodded again.

"And you think this boy . . . the one who's in love with Rebecca . . . ?"

"Yes," the rabbi said.

"You think he might be the one responsible for the e-mails and the Molotov . . ."

"Yes. But not only that. I think he's the one who killed those cab drivers."

"I don't understand," Carella said. "Why would a Muslim want to kill *other* Mus . . . ?"

"But he's *not* Muslim. Did I say he was Muslim?"

"You said this was related to the . . ."

"Catholic. He's a Catholic."

The detectives looked at each other.

"Let me understand this," Carella said. "You think this kid . . . how old is he, anyway?"

"Eighteen, I would guess. Nineteen."

"You think he got angry because you wouldn't go to Rebecca's father on his behalf . . ."

"That's right."

"So he sent you three e-mails, and tried to fire-bomb your temple . . ."

"Exactly."

". . . and also killed two Muslim cab drivers?"

"Yes."

"Why? The Muslims, I mean."

"To get even."

"With?"

"With me. And with Samuel Schwartz. And Rebecca. With the entire Jewish population of this city."

"How would killing two . . . ?"

"The *magen David*," the rabbi said.

"The Star of David," Meyer explained.

"Painted on the windshields," the rabbi said. "To let people think a Jew was responsible. To enflame the Muslim community against Jews. To cause trouble between us. To cause more killing. That is why."

The detectives let this sink in.

"Did this kid happen to give you a name?" Meyer asked.

Anthony Inverni told the detectives he didn't wish to be called Tony.

"Makes me sound like a wop," he said. "My grandparents were born here, my parents were born here, my sister and I were both born here, we're Americans. You call me Tony, I'm automatically *Italian*. Well, the way I look at it, Italians are people who are born in Italy and live in Italy, not Americans who were born here and live here. And we're not *Italian*-Americans, either, by the way, because *Italian*-Americans are people who came here from Italy and *became* American citizens. So don't call me Tony, okay?"

He was nineteen years old, with curly black hair, and an olive complexion, and dark brown eyes. Sitting at sunset on the front steps of his building on Merchant Street, all the way downtown near Ramsey University, his arms hugging his knees, he could have been any Biblical Jew squatting outside a baked-mud dwelling in an ancient world. But Rabbi Cohen had spotted him for a *goy* first crack out of the box.

"Gee, who called you Tony?" Carella wanted to know.

"You were about to. I could feel it coming."

Calling a suspect by his first name was an old cop trick, but actually Carella hadn't been about to use it on the Inverni kid here. In fact, he agreed with him about all these proliferating hyphenated Americans in a nation that broadcast the words "United We Stand" as if they were a newly minted advertising slogan. But his father's name had been Anthony. And his father had called himself Tony.

"What would you like us to call you?" he asked.

"Anthony. Anthony could be British. In fact, soon as I graduate, I'm gonna change my last name to Winters. Anthony Winters. I could be the prime minister of England, Anthony Winters. That's what Inverni means anyway, in Italian. Winters."

"Where do you go to school, Anthony?" Carella asked.

"Right here," he said, nodding toward the towers in the near distance. "Ramsey U."

"You studying to be a prime minister?" Meyer asked.

"A writer. Anthony Winters. How does that sound for a writer?"

"Very good," Meyer said, trying the name, "Anthony Winters, excellent. We'll look for your books."

"Meanwhile," Carella said, "tell us about your little run-in with Rabbi Cohen."

"What run-in?"

"He seems to think he pissed you off."

"Well, he did. I mean, why *wouldn't* he go to Becky's father and put in a good word for me? I'm a straight-A student, I'm on the dean's list, am I some kind of pariah? You know what that means, 'pariah'?"

Meyer figured this was a rhetorical question.

"I'm not even *Catholic*, no less pariah," Anthony said, gathering steam. "I gave up the church the minute I tipped to what they were selling. I mean, am I supposed to believe a *virgin* gave birth? To the son of *God*, no less? That goes back to the ancient Greeks, doesn't it? All their Gods messing in the affairs of humans? I mean, give me a break, man."

"Just how pissed off were you?" Carella asked.

"Enough," Anthony said. "But you should've seen *Becky*! When I told her what the rabbi said, she wanted to go right over there and kill him."

"Then you're still seeing her, is that it?"

"Of course I'm still seeing her! We're gonna get married, what do you think? You think her bigoted father's gonna stop us? You think Rabbi Cohen's gonna stop us? We're in *love*!"

Good for you, Meyer thought. And *mazeltov*. But did you kill those two cabbies, as the good *rov* seems to think?

"Are you on the internet?" he asked.

"Sure."

"Do you send e-mails?"

"That's the main way Becky and I communicate. I can't phone her because her father hangs up the minute he hears my voice. Her mother's a little better, she at least lets me talk to her."

"Ever send an e-mail to Rabbi Cohen?"

"No. Why? An e-mail? Why would . . . ?"

"Three of them, in fact."

"No. What kind of e-mails?"

" 'Death to all Jews,' " Meyer quoted.

"Don't be ridiculous," Anthony said. "I love a Jewish *girl*! I'm gonna *marry* a Jewish girl!"

"Were you anywhere near Rabbi Cohen's synagogue last night?" Carella asked.

"No. Why?"

"You didn't throw a fire-bomb into that synagogue last night, did you?"

"No, I did not!"

"Sundown last night? You didn't . . . ?"

"Not at sundown and not at *any* time! I was with *Becky* at sundown. We were walking in the park outside school at sundown. We were trying to figure out our next *move*."

"You may love a Jewish girl," Meyer said, "but how do you feel about *Jews*?"

"I don't know what that means."

"It means how do you feel about all these *Jews* who are trying to keep you from marrying this Jewish *girl* you love?"

"I did not throw a fucking fire-bomb . . ."

"Did you kill two Muslim cabbies . . . ?"

"What!"

". . . and paint Jewish stars on their windshields?"

"Holy shit, is *that* what this is about?"

"Did you?"

"Who said I did?" Anthony wanted to know. "Did the rabbi say I did such a thing?"

"Did you?"

"No. Why would . . . ?"

"Because you were pissed off," Meyer said. "And you wanted to get even. So you killed two Muslims and made it look like a Jew did it. So Muslims would start throwing fire-bombs into . . ."

"I don't give a damn about Muslims or Jews *or* their fucking problems," Anthony said. "All I care about is Becky. All I care about is marrying Becky. The rest is all bullshit. I did not send any e-mails to that jackass rabbi. I did not throw a fire-bomb into his dumb temple, which by the way won't let women sit with men. I did not kill any Muslim cab drivers who go to stupid temples of their own, where *their* women aren't allowed to sit with men, either. That's a nice little plot you've cooked up there, and I'll use it one day, when I'm Anthony Winters the best-selling writer. But right now, I'm still just Tony Inverni, right? And that's the only thing that's keeping me from marrying the girl I love, and that is a shame, gentlemen, that is a fucking crying shame. So if you'll excuse me, I really don't give a damn about *your* little problem, because Becky and I have a major problem of our own."

He raised his right hand, touched it to his temple in a mock salute, and went back into his building.

At nine the next morning, Detective Wilbur Jackson of the Documents Section called to say they'd checked out the graffiti—

He called the Jewish stars graffiti.

—on the windshields of those two evidence cabs and they were now able to report that the handwriting was identical in both instances and that the writer was right-handed.

"Like ninety percent of the people in this city," he added.

That night, the third Muslim cabbie was killed.

"Let's hear it," Lieutenant Byrnes said.

He was not feeling too terribly sanguine this Monday morning. He did not like this at all. First off, he did not like murder epidemics. And next, he did not like murder epidemics that could lead to full-scale riots. White-haired and scowling, eyes an icy-cold blue, he glowered across his desk as though the eight detectives gathered in his corner office had themselves committed the murders.

Hal Willis and Eileen Burke had been riding the midnight horse when the call came in about the third dead cabbie. At five-eight, Willis had barely cleared the minimum height requirement in effect before women were generously allowed to become police officers, at which time five-foot-two-eyes-of-blue became threatening when one was carrying a nine-millimeter Glock on her hip. That's exactly what Eileen was carrying this morning. Not on her hip, but in a tote bag slung over her shoulder. At five-nine, she topped Willis by an inch. Red-headed and green-eyed, she provided Irish-setter contrast to his dark, curly-haired, brown-eyed, cocker-spaniel look. Byrnes was glaring at both of them. Willis deferred to the lady.

"His name is Ali Al-Barak," Eileen said. "He's a Saudi. Married with three . . ."

"That's the most common Arabic name," Andy Parker said. He was slumped in one of the chairs near the windows. Unshaven and unkempt, he looked as if he'd just come off a plant as a homeless wino. Actually, he'd come straight to the squadroom from home, where he'd dressed hastily, annoyed because he wasn't supposed to come in until four, and now another fuckin Muslim had been aced.

"Al-Barak?" Brown asked.

"No, Ali," Parker said. "More than five million men in the Arab world are named Ali."

"How do you know that?" Kling asked.

"I know such things," Parker said.

"And what's it got to do with the goddamn price of fish?" Byrnes asked.

"In case you run into a lot of Alis," Parker explained, "you'll know it ain't a phenomenon, it's just a fact."

"Let me hear it," Byrnes said sourly, and nodded to Eileen.

"Three children," she said, picking up where she'd left off. "Lived in a Saudi neighborhood in Riverhead. No apparent connection to either of the two other vics. All three even worshipped at different mosques. Shot at the back of the head, same as the other two. Blue star on the windshield . . ."

"The other two were the same handwriting," Meyer said.

"Right-handed writer," Carella said.

"Anything from Ballistics yet?" Byrnes asked Eileen.

"Slug went to them, too soon to expect anything."

"Two to one, it'll be the same," Richard Genero said.

He was the newest detective on the squad and rarely ventured comments at these clambakes. Taller than Willis—hell, *everybody* was taller than Willis—he nonetheless looked like a relative, what with the same dark hair and eyes. Once, in fact, a perp had asked them if they were brothers. Willis, offended, had answered, "I'll give you brothers."

"Which'll mean the same guy killed all three," Byrnes said.

Genero felt rewarded. He smiled in acknowledgment.

"Or the same gun, anyway," Carella said.

"Widow been informed?"

"We went there directly from the scene," Willis said.

"What've we got on the paint?"

"Brand name sold everywhere," Meyer said.

"What's with this Inverni kid?"

"He's worth another visit."

"Why?"

"He has a thing about religion."

"What kind of thing?"

"He thinks it's all bullshit."

"Doesn't everyone?" Parker said.

"I don't," Genero said.

"That doesn't mean he's going around killing Muslims," Byrnes said. "But talk to him again. Find out where he was last night at . . . Hal? What time did the cabbie catch it?"

"Twenty past two."

"Be nice if Inverni's our man," Brown said.

"Yes, that would be very nice."

"In your dreams," Parker said.

"You got a better idea?"

Parker thought this over.

"You're such an expert on Arabian first names . . ."

"Arabic."

". . . I thought maybe you might have a better idea," Byrnes said.

"How about we put undercovers in the cabs?"

"Brilliant," Byrnes said. "You know any Muslim cops?"

"Come to think of it," Parker said, and shrugged again.

"Where'd this last one take place?"

"Booker and Lowell. In Riverhead," Eileen said. "Six blocks from the stadium."

"He's ranging all over the place."

"Got to be random," Brown said.

"Let's scour the hood," Kling suggested. "Must be somebody heard a shot at two in the morning."

"Two-twenty," Parker corrected.

"I'm going to triple-team this," Byrnes said. "Anybody not on vacation or out sick, I want him on this case. I'm surprised the commissioner himself hasn't called yet. Something like this . . ."

The phone on his desk rang.

"Let's get this son of a bitch," Byrnes said, and waved the detectives out of his office.

His phone was still ringing.

He rolled his eyes heavenward and picked up the receiver.

THIRD HATE KILLING

MUSLIM MURDERS MOUNT

All over the city, busy citizens picked up the afternoon tabloid, and read its headline, and then turned to the story on page three. Unless the police were withholding vital information, they still did not have a single clue. This made people nervous. They did not want these stupid killings to escalate into the sort of situation that was a daily occurrence in Israel. They did not want retaliation to follow retaliation. They did not want hate begetting more hate.

But they were about to get it.

The first of what the police hoped would be the last of the bombings took place that very afternoon, the fifth day of May.

Parker—who knew such things—could have told the other detectives on the squad that the fifth of May was a date of vast importance in Mexican and Chicano communities, of which there were not a few in this sprawling city. *Cinco de Mayo*, as it was called in Spanish, celebrated the victory of the Mexican Army over the French in 1862. Hardly anyone today—except Parker maybe—knew that *La Battala de Puebla* had been fought and won by Mestizo and Zapotec Indians. Nowadays, many of the Spanish-speaking people in this city thought the date commemorated Mexican independence, which Parker could have told you was September 16, 1810, and not May 5, 1862.

Some people suspected Parker was an idiot savant, but this was only half true. He merely read a lot.

On that splendid, sunny, fifth day of May, as the city's Chicano population prepared for an evening of folklorico dancing and mariachi music and margaritas, and as the weary detectives of the Eight-Seven spread out into the three sections of the city that had so far been stricken with what even the staid morning newspaper labeled "The Muslim Murders," a man carrying a narrow Gucci dispatch case walked into a movie theater that was playing a foreign film about a Japanese prostitute who aspires to become an internationally famous violinist, took a seat in the center of the theater's twelfth row, watched the commercials for furniture stores and local restaurants and antique shops, and then watched the coming attractions, and finally, at 1:37 P.M.—just as the feature film was about to start—got up to go to the men's room.

He left the Gucci dispatch case under the seat.

There was enough explosive material in that sleek leather case to blow up at least seven rows of seats in the orchestra. There was also a ticking clock set to trigger a spark at 3:48 P.M., just about when the Japanese prostitute would be accepted at Juilliard.

Spring break had ended not too long ago, and most of the students at Ramsey U still sported tans they'd picked up in Mexico or Florida. There was an air of bustling activity on the downtown campus as Meyer and Carella made their way through crowded corridors to the Registrar's Office, where they hoped to acquire a program for Anthony Inverni. This turned out to be not as simple as they'd hoped. Each and separately they had to show first their shields and next their ID cards, and still had to invoke the sacred words "Homicide investigation," before the yellow-haired lady with a bun would reveal the whereabouts of Anthony Inverni on this so-far eventless Cinco de Mayo.

The time was 1:45 P.M.

They found Inverni already seated in the front row of a class his program listed as "Shakespearean Morality." He was chatting with a girl wearing a blue scarf around her head and covering her forehead. The detectives assumed she was Muslim, though this was probably profiling. They asked Inverni if he would mind stepping outside for a moment, and he said to the girl, "Excuse me, Halima," which more or less confirmed their surmise, but which did little to reinforce the profile of a hate criminal.

"So what's up?" he asked.

"Where were you at two this morning?" Meyer asked, going straight for the jugular.

"That, huh?"

"That," Carella said.

"It's all over the papers," Inverni said. "But you're still barking up the wrong tree."

"So where were you?"

"With someone."

"Who?"

"Someone."

"The someone wouldn't be Rebecca Schwartz, would it? Because as an alibi . . ."

"Are you kidding? You think old Sam would let her out of his sight at two in the morning?"

"Then who's this 'someone' we're talking about?"

"I'd rather not get her involved."

"Oh? Really? We've got three dead cabbies here. You'd better start worrying about *them* and not about getting *someone* involved. Who is she? Who's your alibi?"

Anthony turned to look over his shoulder, into the classroom. For a moment, the detectives thought he was going to name the girl with the blue scarf. Hanima, was it? Halifa? He turned back to them again. Lowering his voice, he said, "Judy Manzetti."

"Was with you at two this morning?"

"Yes."

His voice still a whisper. His eyes darting.

"Where?"

"My place."

"Doing what?"

"Well . . . you know."

"Spell it out."

"We were in bed together."

"Give us her address and phone number," Carella said.

"Hey, come on. I told you I didn't want to get her involved."

"She's already involved," Carella said. His notebook was in his hand.

Inverni gave him her address and phone number.

"Is that it?" he asked. "Cause class is about to start."

"I thought you planned to marry Becky," Meyer said.

"Of *course* I'm marrying Becky!" Inverni said. "But meanwhile . . ."—and here he smiled conspiratorially—". . . I'm fucking Judy."

No, Meyer thought. It's Becky who's getting fucked.

The time was two P.M.

As if to confirm Parker's fact-finding acumen, the two witnesses who'd heard the shot last night were both named Ali. They'd been coming home from a party at the time, and each of them had been a little drunk. They explained at once that this was not a habit of theirs. They fully understood that the imbibing of alcoholic beverages was strictly forbidden in the Koran.

"*Haram*," the first Ali said, shaking his head. "Most definitely *haram*."

"Oh yes, unacceptable," the second Ali agreed, shaking his head as well. "Forbidden. Prohibited. In the Koran, it is written, 'They ask thee concerning wine and gambling. In them is great sin, and some profit, for men; but the sin is greater than the profit.' "

"But our friend was celebrating his birthday," the first Ali said, and smiled apologetically.

"It was a party," the second Ali explained.

"Where?" Eileen asked.

The two Alis looked at each other.

At last, they admitted that the party had taken place at a club named Buffers, which Eileen and Willis both knew was a topless joint, but the Alis claimed that no one in their party had gone back to the club's so-called private room but had instead merely enjoyed the young ladies dancing around their poles.

Eileen wondered *whose* poles?

The young ladies' poles?

Or the poles of Ali and Company?

She guessed she maybe had a dirty mind.

At any rate, the two Alis were staggering out of Buffers at two o'clock in the morning when they spotted a yellow cab parked at the curb up the block. They were planning on taking the subway home, but one never argued with divine providence so they decided on the spot to take a taxi instead. As they tottered and swayed toward the idling cab—the first Ali raising his hand to hail it, the second Ali breaking into a trot toward it and almost tripping—they heard a single shot from inside the cab. They both stopped dead still in the middle of the pavement.

"A man jumped out," the first Ali said now, his eyes wide with the excitement of recall.

"What'd he look like?" Eileen asked.

"A tall man," the second Ali said. "Dressed all in black."

"Black suit, black coat, black hat."

"Was he bearded or clean-shaven?"

"No beard. No."

"You're sure it was a man?"

"Oh yes, positive," the second Ali said.

"What'd he do after he got out of the cab?"

"Went to the windshield."

"Sprayed the windshield."

"You saw him spraying the windshield?"

"Yes."

"Oh yes."

"Then what?"

"He ran away."

"Up the street."

"Toward the subway."

"There's an entrance there."

"For the subway."

Which could have taken him anywhere in the city, Eileen thought.

"Thanks," Willis said.

It was 2:15 P.M.

Parker and Genero were the two detectives who spoke once again to Ozzie Kiraz, the cousin of the second dead cabbie.

Kiraz was just leaving for work when they got there at a quarter past three that afternoon. He introduced them to his wife, a diminutive woman who seemed half his size, and who immediately went into the kitchen of their tiny apartment to prepare tea for the men. Fine-featured, dark-haired and dark-eyed, Badria Kiraz was a woman in her late twenties, Parker guessed. Exotic features aside, she looked very American to him, sporting lipstick and eye shadow, displaying a nice ass in beige tailored slacks, and good tits in a white cotton blouse.

Kiraz explained that he and his wife both worked night shifts at different places in different parts of the city. He worked at a pharmacy in Majesta, where he was manager of the store. Badria worked as a cashier in a supermarket in Calm's Point. They both started work at four, and got off at midnight. Kiraz told them that in Afghanistan he'd once hoped to become a schoolteacher. That was before he started fighting the Russians. Now, here in America, he was the manager of a drugstore.

"Land of the free, right?" he said, and grinned.

Genero didn't know if he was being a wise guy or not.

"So tell us a little more about your cousin," he said.

"What would you like to know?"

"One of the men interviewed by our colleagues . . ."

Genero liked using the word "colleagues." Made him sound like a university professor. He consulted his notebook, which made him feel even more professorial.

"Man named Ajmal, is that how you pronounce it?"

"Yes," Kiraz said.

"Ajmal Khan, a short-order cook at a deli named Max's in Midtown South. Do you know him?"

"No, I don't."

"Friend of your cousin's," Parker said.

He was eyeing Kiraz's wife, who was carrying a tray in from the kitchen. She set it down on the low table in front of the sofa, smiled, and said, "We drink it sweet, but I didn't add sugar. It's there if you want it. Cream and lemon, too. Oz," she said, "do you know what time it is?"

"I'm watching it, Badria, don't worry. Maybe you should leave."

"Would that be all right?" she asked the detectives.

"Yes, sure," Genero said, and both detectives rose politely. Kiraz kissed his wife on the cheek. She smiled again and left the room.

They heard the front door to the apartment closing. The men sat again. Through the open windows, they could heard the loud-speakered cry of the muezzin calling the faithful to prayer.

"The third prayer of the day," Kiraz explained. "The *Salat al-'Asr*," and added almost regretfully, "I never pray anymore. It's too difficult here in America. If you want to be American, you follow American ways, am I right? You do what Americans do."

"Oh sure," Parker agreed, even though he'd never had any problem following American ways or doing what Americans do.

"Anyway," Genero said, squeezing a little lemon into one of the tea glasses, and then picking it up, "this guy at the deli told our colleagues your cousin was dating quite a few girls . . ."

"That's news to me," Kiraz said.

"Well, that's what we wanted to talk to you about," Parker said. "We thought you might be able to help us with their names."

"The names of these girls," Genero said.

"Because this guy in the deli didn't know who they might be," Parker said.

"I don't know, either," Kiraz said, and looked at his watch.

Parker looked at his watch, too.

It was twenty minutes past three.

"Ever *talk* to you about any of these girls?" Genero asked.

"Never. We were not that close, you know. He was single, I'm married. We have our own friends, Badria and I. This is America. There are different customs, different ways. When you live here, you do what Americans do, right?"

He grinned again.

Again, Genero didn't know if he was getting smart with them.

"You wouldn't know if any of these girls were Jewish, would you?" Parker asked.

"Because of the blue star, you mean?"

"Well . . . yes."

"I would sincerely doubt that my cousin was dating any Jewish girls."

"Because sometimes . . ."

"Oh sure," Kiraz said. "Sometimes things aren't as simple as they appear. You're thinking this wasn't a simple hate crime. You're thinking this wasn't a mere matter of a Jew killing a Muslim simply because he *was* a Muslim. You're looking for complications. Was

Salim involved with a Jewish girl? Did the Jewish girl's father or brother become enraged by the very *thought* of such a relationship? Was Salim killed as a warning to any other Muslim with interfaith aspirations? Is that why the Jewish star was painted on the windshield? Stay away! Keep off!"

"Well, we weren't thinking *exactly* that," Parker said, "but, yes, that's a possibility."

"But you're forgetting the *other* two Muslims, aren't you?" Kiraz said, and smiled in what Genero felt was a superior manner, fuckin guy thought he was Chief of Detectives here.

"No, we're not forgetting them," Parker said. "We're just trying to consider all the possibilities."

"A mistake," Kiraz said. "I sometimes talk to this doctor who comes into the pharmacy. He tells me, 'Oz, if it has stripes like a zebra, don't look for a horse.' Because people come in asking me what I've got for this or that ailment, you know? Who knows why?" he said, and shrugged, but he seemed pleased by his position of importance in the workplace. "I'm only the manager of the store, I'm not a pharmacist, but they ask me," he said, and shrugged again. "What's good for a headache, or a cough, or the sniffles, or this or that? They ask me all the time. And I remember what my friend the doctor told me," he said, and smiled, seemingly pleased by this, too, the fact that his friend was a doctor. "If it has the symptoms of a common cold, don't go looking for SARS. Period." He opened his hands to them, palms up, explaining the utter simplicity of it all. "Stop looking for zebras," he said, and smiled again. "Just find the fucking Jew who shot my cousin in the head, hmm?"

The time was 3:27 P.M.

In the movies these days, it was not unusual for a working girl to become a princess overnight, like the chambermaid who not only gets the hero onscreen but in real life as well, talk about Cinderella stories! In other movies of this stripe, you saw common working class girls who aspired to become college students. Or soccer players. It was a popular theme nowadays. America was the land of opportunity. So was Japan, apparently, although Ruriko—the prostitute in the film all these people were waiting on line to see— was a "working girl" in the truest sense, and she didn't even want to become a princess, just a concert violinist. She was about to become just that in about three minutes.

The two girls standing on line outside the theater box office also happened to be true working girls, which was why they were here to catch the four o'clock screening of the Japanese film. They had each separately seen *Pretty Woman*, another Working Girl Becomes Princess film, and did not for a moment believe that Julia Roberts had ever blown anybody for fifty bucks, but maybe it would be different with this Japanese actress, whatever her name was. Maybe this time, they'd believe that these One in a Million fairy tales could really happen to girls who actually did this sort of thing for a living.

The two girls, Heidi and Roseanne, looked and dressed just like any secretary who'd got out of work early today . . .

It was now 3:46 P.M.

. . . and even sounded somewhat like girls with junior college educations. As the line inched closer to the box office, they began talking about what Heidi was going to do to celebrate her birthday tonight. Heidi was nineteen years old today. She'd been hooking for two years now. The closest she'd got to becoming a princess was when one of her old-fart regulars asked her to come to London with him on a weekend trip. He rescinded the offer when he learned she was expecting her period, worse luck.

"You doing anything special tonight?" Roseanne asked.

"Jimmy's taking me out to dinner," Heidi said.

Jimmy was a cop she dated. He knew what profession she was in.

"That's nice."

"Yeah."

In about fifteen seconds, it would be 3:48 P.M.

"I still can't get over it," Roseanne said.

"What's that, hon?"

"The *coincidence*!" Roseanne said, amazed. "Does your birthday *always* fall on Cinco de Mayo?"

A couple sitting in the seats just behind the one under which the Gucci dispatch case had been left were seriously necking when the bomb exploded.

The boy had his hand under the girl's skirt, and she had her hand inside his unzippered fly, their fitful manual activity covered by the raincoat he had thrown over both their laps. Neither of them really gave a damn about whether or not Ruriko passed muster with the judges at Juilliard, or went back instead to a life of hopeless despair in the slums of Yokohama. All that mattered to them was achieving mutual orgasm here in the flickering darkness of the theater while the soulful strains of Aram Khacaturian's *Spartacus* flowed from Ruriko's violin under the expert coaxing of her talented fingers.

When the bomb exploded, they both thought for the tiniest tick of an instant that they'd died and gone to heaven.

Fortunately for the Eight-Seven, the movie-theater bombing occurred in the Two-One downtown. Since there was no immediate connection between this new outburst of violence and the Muslim Murders, nobody from the Two-One called uptown in an attempt to unload the case there. Instead, because this was an obvious act of terrorism, they called the Joint Terrorist Task Force at One Federal Square further downtown, and dumped the entire matter into their laps. This did not, however, stop the talking heads on television from linking the movie bombing to the murders of the three cabbies.

The liberal TV commentators noisily insisted that the total mess we'd made in Iraq was directly responsible for this new wave of violence here in the United States. The conservative commentators wagged their heads in tolerant understanding of their colleagues' supreme ignorance, and then sagely suggested that if the police in this city would only learn how to handle the problems manifest in a gloriously diverse population, there wouldn't be any civic violence at all.

It took no more than an hour and a half before all of the cable channels were demanding immediate arrests in what was now perceived as a single case. On the six-thirty network news broadcasts, the movie-theater bombing was the headline story, and without fail the bombing was linked to the cab-driver killings, the blue Star of David on the windshields televised over and over again as the unifying leitmotif.

Ali Al-Barak, the third Muslim victim, had worked for a company that called itself simply Cabco. Its garage was located in the shadow of the Calm's Point Bridge, not too distant from the market under the massive stone supporting pillars on the Isola side of the bridge. The market was closed and shuttered when Meyer and Carella drove past it at a quarter to seven that evening. They had trouble finding Cabco's garage and drove around the block several times, getting entangled in bridge traffic. At one point, Carella suggested that they hit the hammer, but Meyer felt use of the siren might be excessive.

They finally located the garage tucked between two massive apartment buildings. It could have been the underground garage for either of them, but a discreet sign identified it as Cabco. They drove down the ramp, found the dispatcher's office, identified themselves, and explained why they were there.

"Yeah," the dispatcher said, and nodded. His name was Hazhir Demirkol. He explained that like Al-Barak, he too was a Muslim, though not a Saudi. "I'm a Kurd," he told them. "I came to this country ten years ago."

"What can you tell us about Al-Barak?" Meyer asked.

"I knew someone would kill him sooner or later," Demirkol said. "The way he was shooting up his mouth all the time."

Shooting *off*, Carella thought, but didn't correct him.

"In what way?" he asked.

"He kept complaining that Israel was responsible for all the trouble in the Arab world. If there was no Israel, there would have been no Iraqi war. There would be no terrorism. There would be no 9/11. Well, he's a Saudi, you know. His countrymen were the ones who *bombed* the World Trade Center! But he was being foolish. It doesn't matter how you feel about Jews. I feel the same way. But in this city, I have learned to keep my thoughts to myself."

"Why's that?" Meyer asked.

Demirkol turned to him, looked him over. One eyebrow arched. Sudden recognition crossed his face. This man was a Jew. This detective was a Jew.

"It doesn't matter why," he said. "Look what happened to Ali. *That* is why."

"You think a Jew killed him, is that it?"

"No, an angel from Paradise painted that blue star on his windshield."

"Who might've heard him when he was airing all these complaints?" Carella asked.

"Who knows? Ali talked freely, *too* freely, you ask me. This is a democracy, no? Like the one America brought to Iraq, no?" Demirkol asked sarcastically. "He talked everywhere. He talked here in the garage with his friends, he talked to his passengers, I'm sure he talked at the mosque, too, when he went to prayer. Freedom of speech, correct? Even if it gets you killed."

"You think he expressed his views to the wrong person, is that it?" Meyer asked. "The wrong *Jew*."

"The *same* Jew who killed the other drivers," Demirkol said, and nodded emphatically, looking Meyer dead in the eye, challenging him.

"This mosque you mentioned," Carella said. "Would you know . . . ?"

"Majid At-Abu," Demirkol said at once. "Close by here," he said, and gestured vaguely uptown.

Now *this* was a mosque.

This was what one conjured when the very word was uttered. This was straight out of *Arabian Nights*, minarets and domes, blue tile and gold leaf. This was the real McCoy.

Opulent and imposing, Majid At-Abu was not as "close by" as Demirkol had suggested, it was in fact a good mile and a half uptown. When the detectives got there at a little past eight that night, the faithful were already gathered inside for the sunset prayer. The sky beyond the mosque's single glittering dome was streaked with the last red-purple streaks of a dying sun. The minaret from which the muezzin called worshippers to prayer stood tall and stately to the right of the arched entrance doors. Meyer and Carella stood on the sidewalk outside, listening to the prayers intoned within, waiting for an opportune time to enter.

Across the street, some Arabic-looking boys in T-shirts and jeans were cracking themselves up. Meyer wondered what they were saying. Carella wondered why they weren't inside praying.

"Ivan Sikimiavuçlyor!" one of the kids shouted, and the others all burst out laughing.

"How about Alexandr Siksallandr?" one of the other kids suggested, and again they all laughed.

"Or Madame Döllemer," another boy said.

More laughter. Carella was surprised they didn't all fall to the sidewalk clutching their bellies. It took both of the detectives a moment to realize that these were *names* the boys were bandying about. They had no idea that in Turkish "Ivan Sikimiavuçlyor" meant "Ivan Holding My Cock," or that "Alexandr Siksallandr" meant "Alexander Who Swings a Cock," or that poor "Madame Döllemer" was just a lady "Sucking Sperm." Like the dirty names Meyer and Carella had attached to fictitious book titles when they themselves were kids . . .

The Open Robe by Seymour Hare.

The Russian Revenge by Ivana Kutchakokoff.

The Chinese Curse by Wan Hong Lo.

Hawaiian Paradise by A'wana Leia Oo'aa.

. . . these Arab teenagers growing up here in America were now making puns on their parents' native tongue.

"Fenasi Kerim!" one of the boys shouted finally and triumphantly, and whereas neither of the detectives knew that this invented name meant "I Fuck You Bad," the boys' ensuing exuberant laughter caused them to laugh as well.

The sunset prayer had ended.

They took off their shoes and placed them outside in the foyer—alongside the loafers and sandals and jogging shoes and boots and laced brogans parked there like autos in a used-car lot—and went inside to find the imam.

"I never heard Ali Al-Barak utter a single threatening word about the Jewish people, or the Jewish state, or any Jew in particular," Mohammad Talal Awad said.

They were standing in the vast open hall of the mosque proper, a white space the size of a ballroom, with arched windows and tiled floors and an overhead clerestory through which the detectives could see the beginnings of a starry night. The imam was wearing white baggy trousers and a flowing white tunic and a little while pillbox hat. He had a long black beard, a narrow nose and eyes almost black, and he directed his every word to Meyer.

"Nor is there anything in the Koran that directs Muslims to kill anyone," he said. "Not Jews, not anyone. There is nothing there. Search the Koran. You will find not a word about murdering in the name of Allah."

"We understand Al-Barak made remarks some people might have found inflammatory," Carella said.

"Political observations. They had nothing to do with Islam. He was young, he was brash, perhaps he was foolish to express his opinions so openly. But this is America, and one may speak freely, isn't that so? Isn't that what democracy is all about?"

Here we go again, Meyer thought.

"But if you think Ali's murder had anything to do with the bombing downtown . . ."

Oh? Carella thought.

". . . you are mistaken. Ali was a pious young man who lived with another man his own age, recently arrived from Saudi Arabia. In their native land, they were both students. Here, one drove a taxi and the other bags groceries in a supermarket. If you think Ali's friend, in revenge for his murder, bombed that theater downtown . . ."

Oh? Carella thought again.

". . . you are very sadly mistaken."

"We're not investigating that bombing," Meyer said. "We're investigating Ali's murder. And the murder of two other Muslim cab drivers. If you can think of anyone who might possibly . . ."

"I know no Jews," the imam said.

You know one now, Meyer thought.

"This friend he lived with," Carella said. "What's his name, and where can we find him?"

The music coming from behind the door to the third-floor apartment was very definitely rap. The singers were very definitely black, and the lyrics were in English. But the words weren't telling young kids to do dope or knock women around or even up. As they listened at the wood, the lyrics the detectives heard spoke of intentions alone not being sufficient to bring reward . . .

When help is needed, prayer to Allah is the answer . . .

Allah alone can assist in . . .

Meyer knocked on the door.

"Yes?" a voice yelled.

"Police," Carella said.

The music continued to blare.

"Hello?" Carella said. "Mind if we ask you some questions?"

No answer.

"Hello?" he said again.

He looked at Meyer.

Meyer shrugged. Over the blare of the music, he yelled, "Hello in there!"

Still no answer.

"This is the police!" he yelled. "Would you mind coming to the door, please?"

The door opened a crack, held by a night chain.

They saw part of a narrow face. Part of a mustache. Part of a mouth. A single brown eye.

"Mr. Rajab?"

"Yes?"

Wariness in the voice and in the single eye they could see.

"Mind if we come in? Few questions we'd like to ask you."

"What about?"

"You a friend of Ali Al-Barak?"

"Yes?"

"Do you know he was murdered last . . . ?"

The door slammed shut.

They heard the sudden click of a bolt turning.

Carella backed off across the hall. His gun was already in his right hand, his knee coming up for a jackknife kick. The sole of his shoe collided with the door, just below the lock. The lock held.

"The yard!" he yelled, and Meyer flew off down the stairs.

Carella kicked at the lock again. This time, it sprang. He followed the splintered door into the room. The black rap group was still singing praise to Allah. The window across the room was open, a curtain fluttering in the mild evening breeze. He ran across the room, followed his gun hand out the window and onto a fire escape. He could hear footsteps clattering down the iron rungs to the second floor.

"Stop!" he yelled. "Police!"

Nobody stopped.

He came out onto the fire escape, took a quick look below, and started down.

From below, he heard Meyer racketing into the backyard. They had Rajab sandwiched.

"Hold it right there!" Meyer yelled.

Carella came down to the first-floor fire escape, out of breath, and handcuffed Rajab's hands behind his back.

They listened in total amazement as Ishak Rajab told them all about how he had plotted instant revenge for the murder of his friend and roommate, Ali Al-Barak. They listened as he told them how he had constructed the suitcase bomb . . .

He called the Gucci dispatch case a suitcase.

. . . and then had carefully chosen a movie theater showing so-called art films because he knew Jews pretended to culture, and there would most likely be many Jews in the audience. Jews had to be taught that Arabs could not wantonly be killed without reprisal.

"Ali was killed by a Jew," Rajab said. "And so it was fitting and just that Jews be killed in return."

Meyer called the JTTF at Fed Square and told them they'd accidentally lucked into catching the guy who did their movie-theater bombing.

Ungrateful humps didn't even say thanks.

It was almost ten o'clock when he and Carella left the squadroom for home. As they passed the swing room downstairs, they looked in through the open door to where a uniformed cop was half-dozing on one of the couches, watching television. One of cable's most vociferous talking heads was demanding to know when a terrorist was *not* a terrorist.

"Here's the story," he said, and glared out of the screen. "A green-card Saudi-Arabian named Ishak Rajab was arrested and charged with the wanton slaying of sixteen movie patrons and the wounding of twelve others. Our own police and the Joint Terrorist Task Force are to be highly commended for their swift actions in this case. It is now to be hoped that a trial and conviction will be equally swift.

"However . . .

"Rajab's attorneys are already indicating they'll be entering a plea of insanity. Their reasoning seems to be that a man who *deliberately* leaves a bomb in a public place is not a terrorist—have you got that? *Not* a terrorist! Then what is he, huh, guys? Well, according to his attorneys, he was merely a man blinded by rage and seeking retaliation. The rationale for Rajab's behavior would seem to be his close friendship with Ali Al-Barak, the third victim in the wave of taxi-driver slayings that have swept the city since last Friday: Rajab was Al-Barak's roommate.

"Well, neither I nor any right-minded citizen would condone the senseless murder of Muslim cab drivers. That goes without saying. But to invoke a surely inappropriate Biblical—*Biblical*, mind you—'eye for an eye' defense by labeling premeditated mass murder 'insanity' is in itself insanity. A terrorist is a terrorist, and this was an act of terrorism, pure and simple. Anything less than the death penalty would be gross injustice in the case of Ishak Rajab. That's my opinion, now let's hear yours. You can e-mail me at . . ."

The detectives walked out of the building and into the night.

In four hours, another Muslim cabbie would be killed.

The police knew at once that this wasn't their man.

To begin with, none of the other victims had been robbed.

This one was.

All of the other victims had been shot only once, at the base of the skull.

This one was shot three times through the open driver-side window of his cab, two of the bullets entering his face at the left temple and just below the cheek, the third passing through his neck and lodging in the opposite door panel.

Shell casings were found on the street outside the cab, indicating that the murder weapon had been an automatic, and not the revolver that had been used in the previous three murders. Ballistics confirmed this. The bullets and casings were consistent with samples fired from a Colt .45 automatic.

Moreover, two witnesses had seen a man leaning into the cab window moments before they heard shots, and he was definitely not a tall white man dressed entirely in black.

There were only two similarities in all four murders. The drivers were all Muslims, and a blue star had been spray-painted onto each of their windshields.

But the Star of David had six points, and this new one had only five, and it was turned on end like the inverted pentagram used by devil-worshippers.

They hoped to hell yet *another* religion wasn't intruding its beliefs into this case.

But they knew for sure this wasn't their man.

This was a copycat.

CABBIE SHOT AND KILLED
FOURTH MUSLIM MURDER

So read the headline in the Metro Section of the city's staid morning newspaper. The story under it was largely put together from details supplied in a Police Department press release. The flak that had gone out from the Public Relations Office on the previous three murders had significantly withheld any information about the killer himself or his MO. None of the reporters—print, radio, or television—had been informed that the killer had been dressed in black from head to toe, or that he'd fired just a single shot into his separate victims' heads. They were hoping the killer himself—if ever they caught him—would reveal this information, thereby incriminating himself.

But this time around, because the police knew this was a copycat, the PR release was a bit more generous, stating that the cabbie had been shot three times, that he'd been robbed of his night's receipts, and that his assailant, as described by two eyewitnesses, was a black man in his early twenties, about five feet seven inches tall, weighing some hundred and sixty pounds and wearing blue jeans, white sneakers, a brown leather jacket, and a black ski cap pulled low on his forehead.

The man who'd murdered the previous three cabbies must have laughed himself silly.

Especially when another bombing took place that Tuesday afternoon.

The city's Joint Terrorist Task Force was an odd mix of elite city detectives, FBI Special Agents, Homeland Security people, and a handful of CIA spooks. Special Agent in Charge Brian Hooper and a team of four other Task Force officers arrived at The Merrie Coffee

Bean at three that afternoon, not half an hour after a suicide bomber had killed himself and a dozen patrons sitting at tables on the sidewalk outside. Seven wounded people had already been carried by ambulance to the closest hospital, Abingdon Memorial, on the river at Condon Street.

The coffee shop was a shambles.

Wrought iron tables and chairs had been twisted into surreal and smoldering bits of modern sculpture. Glass shards lay all over the sidewalk and inside the shop gutted and flooded by the Fire Department.

A dazed and dazzled waitress, wide-eyed and smoke-smudged but remarkably unharmed otherwise, told Hooper that she was at the cappuccino machine picking up an order when she heard someone yelling outside. She thought at first it was one of the customers, sometimes they got into arguments over choice tables. She turned from the counter to look outside, and saw this slight man running toward the door of the shop, yelling at the top of his lungs . . .

"What was he yelling, miss, do you remember?" Hooper asked.

Hooper was polite and soft-spoken, wearing a blue suit, a white shirt, a blue tie, and polished black shoes. Two detectives from the Five-Oh had also responded. Casually, dressed in sport jackets, slacks, and shirts open at the throat, they looked like bums in contrast. They stood by trying to look interested and significant while Hooper conducted the questioning.

"Something about Jews," the waitress said. "He had a foreign accent, you know, so it was hard to understand him to begin with. And this was like a rant, so that made it even more difficult. Besides, it all happened so fast. He was running from the open sidewalk down this, like, *space* we have between the tables? Like an *aisle* that leads to the front of the shop? And he was yelling Jews-this, Jews-that, and waving his arms in the air like some kind of nut? Then all at once there was this terrific explosion, it almost knocked *me* off my feet, and I was all the way inside the shop, near the cap machine. And I saw . . . there was like sunshine outside, you know? Like shining through the windows? And all of a sudden I saw all body parts flying in the air in the sunshine. Like in silhouette. All these people getting blown apart. It was, like, awesome."

Hooper and his men went picking through the rubble.

The two detectives from the Five-Oh were thinking this was very bad shit here.

If I've already realized what I hoped to accomplish, why press my luck, as they say? The thing has escalated beyond my wildest expectations. So leave it well enough alone, he told himself.

But that idiot last night has surely complicated matters. The police aren't fools, they'll recognize at once that last night's murder couldn't possibly be linked to the other three. So perhaps another one *was* in order, after all. To nail it to the wall. Four would round it off, wouldn't it?

To the Navajo Indians—well, Native Americans, as they say—the number four was sacred. Four different times of day, four sacred mountains, four sacred plants, four different directions. East was symbolic of Positive Thinking. South was for Planning. West for Life itself. North for Hope and Strength. They believed all this, the Navajo people. Religions were so peculiar. The things people believed. The things he himself had once believed, long ago, so very long ago.

Of course the number four wasn't *truly* sacred, that was just something the Navajos believed. The way Christians believed that the number 666 was the mark of the beast, who was the Antichrist and who—well, of course, what else?—had to be Jewish, right? There were even people who believed that the Internet acronym "www" for "World Wide Web" really transliterated into the Hebrew letter "*vav*" repeated three times, *vav, vav, vav*, the numerical equivalent of 666, the mark of the beast. *Let him that hath understanding count the number of the beast: for it is the number of a man; and his number is six hundred threescore and six*, Revelations 13. Oh yes, I've read the Bible, thank you, *and* the Koran, *and* the teachings of Buddha, and they're all total bullshit, as they say. But there are people who believe in a matrix, too, and not all of them are in padded rooms wearing straitjackets.

So, yes, I think there should be another one tonight, a tip of the hat, as they say, to the Navajo's sacred number four, and that will be the end of it. The last one. The same signature mark of the beast, the six-pointed star of the Antichrist. Then let them go searching the synagogues for me. Let them try to find the murdering Jew. After tonight, I will be finished!

Tonight, he thought.

Yes.

Abbas Miandad was a Muslim cab driver, and no fool.

Four Muslim cabbies had already been killed since Friday night, and he didn't want to be number five. He did not own a pistol—carrying a pistol would be exceedingly stupid in a city already so enflamed against people of the Islamic faith—nor did he own a dagger or a sword, but his wife's kitchen was well stocked with utensils and before he set out on his midnight shift he took a huge bread knife from the rack . . .

"Where are you going with that?" his wife asked.

She was watching television.

They were reporting that there'd been a suicide bombing that afternoon. They were saying the bomber had not been identified as yet.

"Never mind," he told her, and wrapped a dishtowel around the knife and packed it in a small tote bag that had BARNES & NOBLE lettered on it.

He had unwrapped the knife the moment he drove out of the garage. At three that Wednesday morning, it was still in the pouch on the driver's side of the cab. He had locked the cab when he stopped for a coffee break. Now, he walked up the street to where he'd parked the cab near the corner, and saw a man dressed all in black, bending to look into the back seat. He walked to him swiftly.

"Help you, sir?" he asked.

The man straightened up.

"I thought you might be napping in there," he said, and smiled.

"No, sir," he said. "Did you need a taxi?"

"Is this your cab?"

"It is."

"Can you take me to Majesta?" he said.

"Where are you going, sir?"

"The Boulevard and a Hundred Twelfth."

"Raleigh Boulevard?"

"Yes."

Abbas knew the neighborhood. It was residential and safe, even at this hour. He would not drive anyone to neighborhoods that he knew to be dangerous. He would not pick up black men, even if they were accompanied by women. Nowadays, he would not pick up anyone who looked Jewish. If you asked him how he knew whether a person was Jewish or not, he would tell you he just knew. This man dressed all in black did not look Jewish.

"Let me open it," he said, and took his keys from the right-hand pocket of his trousers. He turned the key in the door lock and was opening the door when, from the corner of his eye, he caught a glint of metal. Without turning, he reached for the bread knife tucked into the door's pouch.

He was too late.

The man in black fired two shots directly into his face, killing him at once.

Then he ran off into the night.

"Changed his MO," Byrnes said. "The others were shot from the back seat, single bullet to the base of the skull . . ."

"Not the one Tuesday night," Parker said.

"Tuesday was a copycat," Genero said.

"Maybe this one was, too," Willis suggested.

"Not if Ballistics comes back with a match," Meyer said.

The detectives fell silent.

They were each and separately hoping this newest murder would not trigger another suicide bombing someplace. The Task Force downtown still hadn't been able to get a positive ID from the smoldering remains of the Merrie Coffee Bean bomber.

"Anybody see anything?" Byrnes asked.

"Patrons in the diner heard shots, but didn't see the shooter."

"Didn't see him painting that blue star again?"

"I think they were afraid to go outside," Carella said. "Nobody wants to get shot, Pete."

"Gee, no kidding?" Byrnes said sourly.

"Also, the cab was parked all the way up the street, near the corner, some six cars back from the diner, on the same side of the street. The killer had to be standing on the passenger side . . ."

"Where he could see the driver's hack license . . ." Eileen said.

"Arab name on it," Kling said.

"Bingo, he had his victim."

"Point is," Carella said, "standing where he was, the people in the diner couldn't have seen him."

"Or just didn't *want* to see him."

"Well, sure."

"Cause they *could've* seen him while he was painting the star," Parker said.

"That's right," Byrnes said. "He had to've come around to the windshield."

"They could've at least seen his back."

"Tell us whether he was short, tall, what he was wearing . . ."

"But they didn't."

"Talk to them again."

"We talked them deaf, dumb, and blind," Meyer said.

"Talk to them *again*," Byrnes said. "And talk to anybody who was in those coffee shops, diners, delis, whatever, at the scenes of the other murders. These cabbies stop for coffee breaks, two, three in the morning, they go back to their cabs and get shot. That's no coincidence. Our man knows their habits. And he's a night-crawler. What's with the Inverni kid? Did his alibi stand up?"

"Yeah, he was in bed with her," Carella said.

"In bed with who?" Parker asked, interested.

"Judy Manzetti. It checked out."

"Okay, so talk to everybody *else* again," Byrnes said. "See who might've been lurking about, hanging around, casing these various sites *before* the murders were committed."

"We *did* talk to everybody again," Genero said.

"Talk to them *again* again!"

"They all say the same thing," Meyer said. "It was a Jew who killed those drivers, all we have to do is look for a goddamn Jew."

"You're too fucking sensitive," Parker said.

"I'm telling you what we're getting. Anybody we talk to thinks it's an open-and-shut case. All we have to do is round up every Jew in the city . . ."

"Take forever," Parker said.

"What does that mean?"

"It means there are millions of Jews in this city."

"And what does *that* mean?"

"It means you're too fucking sensitive."

"Knock it off," Byrnes said.

"Anyway, Meyer's right," Genero said. "That's what we got, too. You know that, Andy."

"What do I know?" Parker said, glaring at Meyer.

"They keep telling us all we have to do is find the Jew who shot those guys in the head."

"Who told you that?" Carella said at once.

Genero looked startled.

"Who told you they got shot in the head?"

"Well . . . they *all* did."

"No," Parker said. "It was just the cousin, whatever the fuck his name was."

"What cousin?"

"The second vic. His cousin."

"Salim Nazir? *His* cousin?"

"Yeah, Ozzie something."

"Osman," Carella said. "Osman Kiraz."

"That's the one."

"And he said these cabbies were shot in the *head*?"

"Said his cousin was."

"Told us to stop looking for zebras."

"What the hell is that supposed to mean?" Byrnes asked.

"Told us to just find the Jew who shot his cousin in the head."

"The *fucking* Jew," Parker said.

Meyer looked at him.

"Were his exact words," Parker said, and shrugged.

"How did he know?" Carella asked.

"Go get him," Byrnes said.

Ozzie Kariz was asleep when they knocked on his door at nine-fifteen that Wednesday morning. Bleary-eyed and unshaven, he came to the door in pajamas over which he had thrown a shaggy blue robe, and explained that he worked at the pharmacy until midnight each night and did not get home until one, one-thirty, so he normally slept late each morning.

"May we come in?" Carella asked.

"Yes, sure," Kariz said, "but we'll have to be quiet, please. My wife is still asleep."

They went into a small kitchen and sat at a wooden table painted green.

"So what's up?" Kariz asked.

"Few more questions we'd like to ask you."

"Again?" Kariz said. "I told those other two . . . what were their names?"

"Genero and Parker."

"I told them I didn't know any of my cousin's girlfriends. Or even their names."

"This doesn't have anything to do with his girlfriends," Carella said.

"Oh? Something new then? Is there some new development?"

"Yes. Another cab driver was killed last night."

"Oh?"

"You didn't know that."

"No."

"It's already on television."

"I've been asleep."

"Of course."

"Was he a Muslim?"

"Yes."

"And was there another . . . ?"

"Yes, another Jewish star on the windshield."

"This is bad," Kiraz said. "These killings, the bombings . . ."

"Mr. Kiraz," Meyer said, "can you tell us where you were at three o'clock this morning?"

"Is that when it happened?"

"Yes, that's exactly when it happened."

"Where?"

"You tell us," Carella said.

Kiraz looked at them.

"What is this?" he asked.

"How'd you know your cousin was shot in the head?" Meyer asked.

"Was he?"

"That's what you told Genero and Parker. You told them a Jew shot your cousin in the head. How did you . . . ?"

"And did a Jew also shoot this man last night?" Kiraz asked. "In the head?"

"Twice in the face," Carella said.

"I asked you a question," Meyer said. "How'd you know . . . ?"

"I saw his body."

"You saw your cousin's . . ."

"I went with my aunt to pick up Salim's corpse at the morgue. After the people there were finished with him."

"When was this?" Meyer asked.

"The day after he was killed."

"That would've been . . ."

"Whenever. I accompanied my aunt to the morgue, and an ambulance took us to the mosque where they bathed the body according to Islamic law . . . they have rules, you know. Religious Muslims. They have many rules."

"I take it you're not religious."

"I'm American now," Kiraz said. "I don't believe in the old ways anymore."

"Then what were you doing in a mosque, washing your cousin's . . . ?"

"My aunt asked me to come. You saw her. You saw how distraught she was. I went as a family duty."

"I thought you didn't believe in the old ways anymore," Carella said.

"I don't believe in any of the *religious* bullshit," Kiraz said. "I went with her to help her. She's an old woman. She's alone now that her only son was killed. I went to help her."

"So you washed the body . . ."

"No, the *imam* washed the body."

"But you were there when he washed the body."

"I was there. He washed it three times. That's because it's written that when the daughter of Muhammad died, he instructed his followers to wash her three times, or more than that if necessary. Five times, seven, whatever. But always an *odd* number of times. Never an *even* number. That's what I mean about all the religious *bullshit.* Like having to wrap the body in *three* white sheets. That's because when Muhammad died, he himself was wrapped in three white sheets. From Yemen. That's what's written. So God forbid you should wrap a Muslim corpse in *four* sheets! Oh no! It has to be three. But you have to use *four* ropes to tie the sheets, not *three*, it has to be four. And the ropes each have to be seven feet long. Not three, or four, but *seven*! Do you see what I mean? All mumbo-jumbo bullshit."

"So you're saying you saw your cousin's body . . ."

"Yes."

". . . while he was being washed."

"Yes."

"And that's how you knew he was shot in the head."

"Yes. I saw the bullet wound at the base of his skull. Anyway, where *else* would he have been shot? If his murderer was sitting behind him in the taxi . . ."

"How do you know that?"

"What?"

"How do you know his murderer was inside the taxi?"

"Well, if Salim was shot at the back of the head, his murderer *had* to be sitting . . ."

"Oz?"

She was standing in the doorway to the kitchen, a diminutive woman with large brown eyes, her long ebony hair trailing down the back of the yellow silk robe she wore over a long white nightgown.

"Badria, good morning," Kiraz said. "My wife, gentlemen. I'm sorry, I've forgotten your names."

"Detective Carella."

"Detective Meyer."

"How do you do?" Badria said. "Have you offered them coffee?" she asked her husband.

"I'm sorry, no."

"Gentlemen? Some coffee?"

"None for me, thanks," Carella said.

Meyer shook his head.

"Oz? Would you like some coffee?"

"Please," he said. There was a faint amused smile on his face now. "As an illustration," he said, "witness my wife."

The detectives didn't know what he was talking about.

"The wearing of silk is expressly forbidden in Islamic law," he said. " 'Do not wear silk, for one who wears it in the world will not wear it in the Hereafter.' That's what's written. You're not allowed to wear yellow clothing, either, because 'these are the clothes usually worn by nonbelievers,' quote unquote. But here's my beautiful wife wearing a yellow silk robe, oh shame unto her," Kiraz said, and suddenly began laughing.

Badria did not laugh with him.

Her back to the detectives, she stood before a four-burner

stove, preparing her husband's coffee in a small brass pot with a tin lining.

"'A man was wearing clothes dyed in saffron,'" Kiraz said, apparently quoting again, his laughter trailing, his face becoming serious again. "'And finding that Muhammad disapproved of them, he promised to wash them. But the Prophet said, *Burn* them!'" That's written, too. So tell me, Badria. Should we burn your pretty yellow silk robe? What do you think, Badria?"

Badria said nothing.

The aroma of strong Turkish coffee filled the small kitchen.

"You haven't answered our very first question," Meyer said.

"And what was that? I'm afraid I've forgotten it."

"Where were you at three o'clock this morning?"

"I was here," Kiraz said. "Asleep. In bed with my beautiful wife. Isn't that so, Badria?"

Standing at the stove in her yellow silk robe, Badria said nothing.

"Badria? Tell the gentlemen where I was at three o'clock this morning."

She did not turn from the stove.

Her back still to them, her voice very low, Badria Kiraz said, "I don't know where you were, Oz."

The aroma of the coffee was overpowering now.

"But you weren't here in bed with me," she said.

Nellie Brand left the District Attorney's Office at eleven that Wednesday morning and was uptown at the Eight-Seven by a little before noon. She had cancelled an important lunch date, and even before the detectives filled her in, she warned them that this better be real meat here.

Osman Kiraz had already been read his rights and had insisted on an attorney before he answered any questions. Nellie wasn't familiar with the man he chose. Gulbuddin Amin was wearing a dark-brown business suit, with a tie and vest. Nellie was wearing a suit, too. Hers was a Versace, and it was a deep shade of green that complimented her blue eyes and sand-colored hair. Amin had a tidy little mustache and he wore eyeglasses. His English was impeccable, with a faint Middle-Eastern accent. Nellie guessed he might originally have come from Afghanistan, as had his client. She guessed he was somewhere in his mid fifties. She herself was thirty-two.

The police clerk's fingers were poised over the stenotab machine. Nellie was about to begin the questioning when Amin said, "I hope this was not a frivolous arrest, Mrs. Brand."

"No, counselor . . ."

". . . because that would be a serious mistake in a city already fraught with Jewish-Arab tensions."

"I would not use the word frivolous to describe this arrest," Nellie said.

"In any case, I've already advised my client to remain silent."

"Then we have nothing more to do here," Nellie said, briskly dusting the palm of one hand against the other. "Easy come, easy go. Take him away, boys, he's all yours."

"Why are you afraid of her?" Kiraz asked his lawyer.

Amin responded in what Nellie assumed was Arabic.

"Let's stick to English, shall we?" she said. "What'd you just say, counselor?"

"My comment was privileged."

"Not while your man's under oath, it isn't."

Amin sighed heavily.

"I told him I'm afraid of no woman."

"Bravo!" Nellie said, applauding, and then looked Kiraz dead in the eye. "How about you?" she asked. "Are *you* afraid of me?"

"Of course not!"

"So would you like to answer some questions?"

"I have nothing to hide."

"Yes or no? It's your call. I haven't got all day here."

"I would like to answer her questions," Kiraz told his lawyer.

Amin said something else in Arabic.

"Let us in on it," Nellie said.

"I told him it's his own funeral," Amin said.

Q: Mr. Kiraz, would you like to tell us where you were at three this morning?
A: I was at home in bed with my wife.
Q: You wife seems to think otherwise.
A: My wife is mistaken.
Q: Well, she'll be subpoenaed before the grand jury, you know, and

she'll have to tell them under oath whether you were in bed with her or somewhere else.

A: I was home. She was in bed with me.

Q: You yourself are under oath right this minute, you realize that, don't you?

A: I realize it.

Q: You swore on the Koran, did you not? You placed your left hand on the Koran and raised your right hand . . .

A: I know what I did.

Q: Or does that mean anything to you?

Q: Mr. Kiraz?

Q: Mr. Kiraz, does that mean anything to you? Placing your hand on the Islamic holy book . . .

A: I heard you.

Q: May I have your answer, please?

A: My word is my bond. It doesn't matter whether I swore on the Koran or not.

Q: Well, good, I'm happy to hear that. So tell me, Mr. Kiraz, where were you on these *other* dates at around two in the morning? Friday, May second . . . Saturday, May third . . . and Monday, May fifth. All at around two in the morning, where were you, Mr. Kiraz?

A: Home asleep. I work late. I get home around one, one-fifteen. I go directly to bed.

Q: Do you know what those dates signify?

A: I have no idea.

Q: You don't read the papers, is that it?

A: I read the papers. But those dates . . .

Q: Or watch television? You don't watch television?

A: I work from four to midnight. I rarely watch television.

Q: Then you don't know about these Muslim cab drivers who were shot and killed, is that it?

A: I know about them. Is that what those dates are? Is that when they were killed?

Q: How about Saturday, May third? Does that date hold any particular significance for you?

A: Not any more than the other dates.

Q: Do you know who was killed on that date?

A: No.

Q: Your cousin. Salil Nazir.

A: Yes.

Q: Yes what?

A: Yes. Now I recall that was the date.

Q: Because the detectives spoke to you that morning, isn't that so?

In your aunt's apartment? Gulalai Nazir, right? Your aunt? You spoke to the detectives at six that morning, didn't you?

A: I don't remember the exact time, but yes, I spoke to them.

Q: And told them a Jew had killed your cousin, isn't that so?

A: Yes. Because of the blue star.

Q: Oh, is that why?

A: Yes.

Q: And you spoke to Detective Genero and Parker, did you not, after a third Muslim cab driver was killed? This would have been on Monday, May fifth, at around three in the afternoon, when you spoke to them. And at that time you said, correct me if I'm wrong, you said, "Just find the fucking Jew who shot my cousin in the head," is that correct?

A: Yes, I said that. And I've already explained how I knew he was shot in the head. I was there when the imam washed him. I saw the bullet wound . . .

Q: Did you know any of these other cab drivers?

A: No.

Q: Khalid Aslam . . .

A: No.

Q: Ali Al-Barak?

A: No.

Q: Or the one who was killed last night, Abbas Miandad, did you know any of these drivers?

A: I told you no.

Q: So the only one you knew was your cousin, Salim Nazir.

A: Of course I knew my cousin.

Q: And you also knew he was shot in the head.

A: Yes. I told you . . .

Q: Like all the other drivers.

A: I don't know how the other drivers were killed. I didn't see the other drivers.

Q: But you saw your cousin while he was being washed, is that correct?

A: That is correct.

Q: Would you remember the name of the imam who washed him?

A: No, I'm sorry.

Q: Would it have been Ahmed Nur Kabir?

A: It could have. I had never seen him before.

Q: If I told you his name was Ahmed Nur Kabir, and that the name of the mosque where your cousin's body was prepared for burial is Masjid Al-Barbrak, would you accept that?

A: If you say that's where . . .

Q: Yes, I say so.

A: Then, of course, I would accept it.

Q: Would it surprise you to learn that the detectives here—Detectives Carella and Meyer—spoke to the imam at Masjid Al-Barbrak?
A: I would have no way of knowing whether or not they . . .
Q: Will you accept my word that they spoke to him?
A: I would accept it.
Q: They spoke to him and he told them he was alone when he washed your cousin's body, alone when he wrapped the body in its shrouds. There was no one in the room with him. He was alone, Mr. Kiraz.
A: I don't accept that. I was with him.
Q: He says you were waiting outside with your aunt. He says he was alone with the corpse.
A: He's mistaken.
Q: If he was, in fact, alone with your cousin's body . . . ?
A: I told you he's mistaken.
Q: You think he's lying?
A: I don't know what . . .
Q: You think a holy man would lie?
A: *Holy* man! *Please*!
Q: If he was alone with the body, how do you explain seeing a bullet wound at the back of your cousin's head?
Q: Mr. Kiraz?
Q: Mr. Kiraz, how did you know your cousin was shot in the head? None of the newspaper or television reports . . .
Q: Mr. Kiraz? Would you answer my question, please?
Q: Mr. Kiraz?
A: Any man would have done the same thing.
Q: What would any man . . . ?
A: She is not one of his *whores*! She is my *wife*!

I knew, of course, that Salim was seeing a lot of women. That's okay, he was young, he was good-looking, the Koran says a man can take as many as four wives, so long as he can support them emotionally and financially. Salim wasn't even married, so there's nothing wrong with dating a lot of girls, four, five, a dozen, who cares? This is America, Salim was American, we're all Americans, right? You watch television, the bachelor has to choose from *fifteen* girls, isn't that so? This is America. So there was nothing wrong with Salim dating all these girls.

But not my wife.

Not Badria.

I don't know when it started with her. I don't know when it

started between them. I know one night I called the supermarket where she works. This was around ten o'clock one night, I was at the pharmacy. I manage a pharmacy, you know. People ask me all sorts of questions about what they should do for various ailments. I'm not a pharmacist, but they ask me questions. I know a lot of doctors. Also, I read a lot. I have time during the day, I don't start work till four in the afternoon. So I read a lot. I wanted to be a teacher, you know.

They told me she had gone home early.

I said, Gone home? Why?

I was alarmed.

Was Badria sick?

The person I spoke to said my wife had a headache. So she went home.

I didn't know what to think.

I immediately called the house. There was no answer. Now I became really worried. Was she seriously ill? Why wasn't she answering the phone? Had she fainted? So I went home, too. I'm the manager, I can go home if I like. This is America. A manager can go home if he likes. I told my assistant I thought my wife might be sick.

I was just approaching my building when I saw them. This was now close to eleven o'clock that night. It was dark, I didn't recognize them at first. I thought it was just a young couple. Another young couple. Only that. Coming up the street together. Arm in arm. Heads close. She turned to kiss him. Lifted her head to his. Offered him her lips. It was Badria. My wife. Kissing Salim. My cousin.

Well, they knew each other, of course. They had met at parties, they had met at family gatherings, this was my *cousin*! "Beware of getting into houses and meeting women," the Prophet said. "But what about the husband's brother?" someone asked, and the Prophet replied, "The husband's brother is like death." He often talked in riddles, the Prophet, it's all such bullshit. The Prophet believed that the influence of an evil eye is *fact*. Fact, mind you. The evil eye. The Prophet believed that he himself had once been put under a spell by a Jew and his daughters. The Prophet believed that the fever associated with plague was due to the intense heat of Hell. The Prophet once said, "Filling the belly of a person with pus is better than stuffing his brain with poetry." Can you believe that? I *read* poetry! I read a lot. The Prophet believed that if you had a bad dream, you should spit three times on your left side. That's what Jews do when they want to take the curse off something, you know, they spit on their fingers, ptui, ptui, ptui. I've seen elderly Jews doing that on the street. It's the same thing, am I right? It's all bullshit, all of it. Jesus turning water into wine, Jesus raising the dead! I mean, come on! Raising the *dead*? Moses parting the Red Sea? I'd love to see that one!

It all goes back to the time of the dinosaurs, when men huddled in caves in fear of thunder and lightning. It all goes back to God-fearing men arguing violently about which son of Abraham was the true descendant of the one true God, and whether or not Jesus was, in fact, the Messiah. As if a one *true* God, if there *is* a God at all, doesn't know who the hell he himself is! All of them killing each other! Well, it's no different today, is it? It's all about killing each other in the name of God, isn't it?

In the White House, we've got a born-again Christian who doesn't even realize he's fighting a holy war. An angry dry-drunk, as they say, full of hate, thirsting for white wine, and killing Arabs wherever he can find them. And in the sand out there, on their baggy-pantsed knees, we've got a zillion Muslim fanatics, full of hate, bowing to Mecca and vowing to drive the infidel from the Holy Land. Killing each other. All of them killing each other in the name of a one true God.

In my homeland, in my village, the tribal elders would have appointed a council to rape my wife as punishment for her transgression. And then the villagers would have stoned her to death.

But this is America.

I'm an American.

I knew I had to kill Salim, yes, that is what an American male would do, protect his wife, protect the sanctity of his home, kill the intruder. But I also knew I had to get away with it, as they say, I had to kill the violator and still be free to enjoy the pleasures of my wife, my position, I'm the manager of a pharmacy!

I bought the spray paint, two cans, at a hardware store near the pharmacy. I thought that was a good idea, the Star of David. Such symbolism! The six points of the star symbolizing God's rule over the universe in all six directions, north, south, east, west, up and down. Such bullshit! I didn't kill Salim until the second night, to make it seem as if he wasn't the true target, this was merely hate, these were hate crimes. I should have left it at three. Three would have been convincing enough, weren't you convinced after three?

Especially with the bombings that followed? Weren't you convinced? But I had to go for four. Insurance. The Navajos think four is a sacred number, you know. Again, it has to do with religion, with the four directions. They're all related, these religions. Jews, Christians, Muslims, they're all related. And they're all the same bullshit.

Salim shouldn't have gone after my wife.

He had enough whores already.

My wife is not a whore.

I did the right thing.

I did the American thing.

They came out through the back door of the station house—a Catholic who hadn't been to church since he was twelve, and a Jew who put up a tree each and every Christmas—and walked to where they'd parked their cars early this morning. It was a lovely bright afternoon. They both turned their faces up to the sun and lingered a moment. They seemed almost reluctant to go home. It was often that way after they cracked a tough one. They wanted to savor it a bit.

"I've got a question," Meyer said.

"Mm?"

"Do you think I'm too sensitive?"

"No. You're not sensitive at all."

"You mean that?"

"I mean it."

"You'll make me cry."

"I just changed my mind."

Meyer burst out laughing.

"I'll tell you one thing," he said. "I'm sure glad this didn't turn out to be what it looked like at first. I'm glad it wasn't hate."

"Maybe it was," Carella said.

They got into their separate cars and drove toward the open gate in the cyclone fence, one car behind the other. Carella honked "Shave-and-a-hair-cut," and Meyer honked back "Two-bits!" As Carella made his turn, he waved so long. Meyer tooted the horn again.

Both men were smiling.

Stephen King

There are certain things that are almost always mentioned when the name **Stephen King** comes up. How many books he's sold. What he's doing in and for literature today. One thing almost never mentioned—and not generally perceived—is that he single-handedly made popular fiction grow up. While there were many good bestselling writers before him, King, more than anybody since John D. MacDonald, brought reality to genre novels with his minutely detailed examinations of life and the people of mythical towns in New England that seem to exist due to his amazing talent for making them real in every detail. Of course, combined with the elements of supernatural terror, novels such as *It*, *The Stand*, *Insomnia*, and *Bag of Bones* have propelled him to the top of the bestseller lists time after time. He's often remarked that *Salem's Lot* was "Peyton Place Meets Dracula." And so it was. The rich characterization, the careful and caring social eye, the interplay of story line and character development announced that writers could take worn themes such as vampirism or ghosts and make them fresh again. Before King, many popular writers found their efforts to make their books serious blue-penciled by their editors. Stuff like that gets in the way of the story, they were told. Well, it's stuff like that that has made King so popular, and helped free the popular name from the shackles of simple genre writing. He is a master of masters. Recently he has been completing his magnum opus fantasy series The Dark Tower, with book six, *Song of Susannah*, published, and the last book, *The Dark Tower*, just out.

THE THINGS THEY LEFT BEHIND

Stephen King

The things I want to tell you about—the ones they left behind—showed up in my apartment in August of 2002. I'm sure of that, because I found most of them not long after I helped Paula Robeson with her air conditioner. Memory always needs a marker, and that's mine. She was a children's book illustrator, good-looking (hell, *fine*-looking), husband in import-export. A man has a way of remembering occasions when he's actually able to help a good-looking lady in distress (even one who keeps assuring you she's "very married"); such occasions are all too few. These days the would-be knight errant usually just makes matters worse.

She was in the lobby, looking frustrated, when I came down for an afternoon walk. I said *Hi, howya doin'*, the way you do to other folks who share your building, and she asked me in an exasperated tone that stopped just short of querulousness why the super had to be on vacation *now*. I pointed out that even cowgirls get the blues and even supers go on vacation; that August, furthermore, was an extremely logical month to take time off. August in New York (and in Paris, *mon ami*) finds psychoanalysts, trendy artists, and building superintendents mighty thin on the ground.

She didn't smile. I'm not sure she even got the Tom Robbins reference (obliqueness is the curse of the reading class). She said it might be true about August being a good month to take off and go to the Cape or Fire Island, but her damned apartment was just about burning *up* and the damned air conditioner wouldn't so much as burp. I asked her if she'd like me to take a look, and I remember the glance she gave me—those cool, assessing gray eyes. I remember thinking that eyes like that probably saw quite a lot. And I remember smiling at what she asked me: *Are you safe?* It reminded me of that movie, not *Lolita* (thinking about *Lolita*, sometimes at two in the morning, came later) but the one where Laurence Olivier does the impromptu dental work on Dustin Hoffman, asking him over and over again, *Is it safe?*

I'm safe, I said. *Haven't attacked a woman in over a year. I used to attack two or three a week, but the meetings are helping.*

A giddy thing to say, but I was in a fairly giddy mood. A *summer* mood. She gave me another look, and then *she* smiled. Put out her hand. *Paula Robeson*, she said. It was the left hand she put out—not normal, but the one with the plain gold band on it. I think that was probably on purpose, don't you? But it was later that she told me about her husband being in import-export. On the day when it was my turn to ask *her* for help.

In the elevator, I told her not to expect too much. Now, if she'd wanted a man to find out the underlying causes of the New York City Draft Riots, or to supply a few amusing anecdotes about the creation of the smallpox vaccine, or even to dig up quotes on the sociological ramifications of the TV remote control (the most important invention of the last fifty years, in my 'umble opinion), I was the guy.

Research is your game, Mr. Staley? she asked as we went up in the slow and clattery elevator.

I admitted that it was, although I didn't add that I was still quite new to it. Nor did I ask her to call me Scott—that would have spooked her all over again. And I certainly didn't tell her that I was trying to forget all I'd once known about rural insurance. That I was, in fact, trying to forget quite a lot of things, including about two dozen faces.

You see, I may be trying to forget, but I still remember quite a lot. I think we all do, when we put our minds to it (and sometimes, rather more nastily, when we don't). I even remember something one of those South American novelists said—you know, the ones they call the Magical Realists? Not the guy's name, that's not important, but this quote: *As infants, our first victory comes in grasping some bit of the world, usually our mothers' fingers. Later we discover that the world, and the things of the world, are grasping us, and have been, all along.* Borges? Yes, it might have been Borges. Or it might have been Remarquez. That I *don't* remember. I just know I got her air conditioner running, and when cool air started blowing out of the convector, it lit up her whole face. I also know it's true, that thing about how perception switches around and we come to realize that the things we thought we were holding are actually holding us. Keeping us prisoner, perhaps—Thoreau certainly thought so—but also holding us in place. That's the trade-off. And no matter what Thoreau might have thought, I believe the trade is mostly a fair one. Or I did then; now, I'm not so sure.

And I know these things happened in late August of 2002, not quite a year after a piece of the sky fell down and everything changed for all of us.

On an afternoon about a week after Sir Scott Staley donned his Good Samaritan armor and successfully battled the fearsome air conditioner, I took my afternoon walk to the Staples on Eighty-third Street to get a box of Zip discs and a ream of paper. I owed a fellow forty pages of background on the development of the Polaroid camera (which is more interesting a story as you might think). When I got back to my apartment, there was a pair of sunglasses with red frames and very distinctive lenses on the little table in the foyer where I keep bills that need to be paid, claim checks, overdue-book notices, and things of that nature. I recognized the glasses at once, and all the strength went out of me. I didn't fall, but I dropped my packages on the floor and leaned against the side of the door, trying to catch my breath and staring at those sunglasses. If there had been nothing to lean against, I believe I would have swooned like a miss in a Victorian novel—one of those where the lustful vampire appears at the stroke of midnight.

Two related but distinct emotional waves struck me. The first was that sense of horrified shame you feel when you know you're about to be caught in some act you will never be able to explain. The memory that comes to mind in this regard is of a thing that happened to me—or almost happened—when I was sixteen.

My mother and sister had gone shopping in Portland and I supposedly had the house to myself until evening. I was reclining naked on my bed with a pair of my sister's underpants wrapped around my cock. The bed was scattered with pictures I'd clipped from magazines I'd found in the back of the garage—the previous owner's stash of *Penthouse* and *Gallery* magazines, very likely. I heard a car come crunching into the driveway. No mistaking the sound of that motor; it was my mother and sister. Peg had come down with some sort of flu bug and started vomiting out the window. They'd gotten as far as Poland Springs and turned around.

I looked at the pictures scattered all over the bed, my clothes scattered all over the floor, and the foam of pink rayon in my left hand. I remember how the strength flowed out of my body, and the terrible sense of lassitude that came in its place. My mother was yelling for me—"Scott, Scott, come down and help me with your sister, she's sick"—and I remember thinking, "What's the use? I'm caught. I might as well accept it, I'm caught and this is the first thing they'll think of when they think about me for the rest of my life: Scott, the jerk-off artist."

But more often than not a kind of survival overdrive kicks in at such moments. That's what happened to me. I might go down, I decided, but I wouldn't do so without at least an effort to save my dignity. I threw the pictures and the panties under the bed. Then I jumped into my clothes, moving with numb but sure-fingered speed, all the time thinking of this crazy old game-show I used to watch, *Beat the Clock*.

I can remember how my mother touched my flushed cheek when I got downstairs, and the thoughtful concern in her eyes. "Maybe you're getting sick, too," she said.

"Maybe I am," I said, and gladly enough. It was half an hour before I discovered I'd forgotten to zip my fly. Luckily, neither Peg nor my mother noticed, although on any other occasion one or both of them would have asked me if I had a license to sell hot dogs (this was what passed for wit in the house where I grew up). That day one of them was too sick and the other was too worried to be witty. So I got a total pass.

Lucky me.

What followed the first emotional wave that August day in my apartment was much simpler: I thought I was going out of my mind. Because those glasses couldn't be there. Absolutely could. Not. No way.

Then I raised my eyes and saw something else that had most certainly not been in my apartment when I left for Staples half an hour before (locking the door behind me, as I always did). Leaning in the corner between the kitchenette and the living room was a baseball bat. Hillerich & Bradsby, according to the label. And while I couldn't see the other side, I knew what was printed there well enough: CLAIMS ADJUSTOR, the words burned into the ash with the tip of a soldering iron and then colored deep blue.

Another sensation rushed through me: a third wave. This was a species of surreal dismay. I don't believe in ghosts, but I'm sure that at that moment I looked as though I had just seen one.

I felt that way, too. Yes indeed. Because those sunglasses had to be gone—long-time gone, as the Dixie Chicks say. Ditto Cleve Farrell's Claims Adjustor. ("Besboll been bery-bery good to mee," Cleve would sometimes say, waving the bat over his head as he sat at his desk. "In-SHOO-rance been bery-bery bad.")

I did the only thing I could think of, which was to grab up Sonja D'Amico's shades and trot back down to the elevator with them, holding them out in front of me the way you might hold out something nasty you found on your apartment floor after a week away on vacation—a piece of decaying food, or the body of a poisoned mouse. I found myself remembering a conversation I'd had about Sonja with a fellow named Warren Anderson. *She must have looked like she thought she was going to pop back up and ask somebody for a Coca-Cola,* I had thought when he told me what he'd seen. Over drinks in the Blarney Stone Pub on Third Avenue, this had been, about six weeks after the sky fell down. After we'd toasted each other on not being dead.

Things like that have a way of sticking, whether you want them to or not. Like a musical phrase or the nonsense chorus to a pop song that you just can't get out of your head. You wake up at three in the morning, needing to take a leak, and as you stand there in front of the bowl, your cock in your hand and your mind about ten per cent awake, it comes back to you: *Like she thought she was going to pop back up. Pop back up and ask for a Coke.* At some point during that conversation Warren had asked me if I remembered her funny sunglasses, and I said I did. Sure I did.

Four floors down, Pedro the doorman was standing in the shade of the awning and talking with Rafe the FedEx man. Pedro was a serious hardboy when it came to letting deliverymen stand in front of the building—he had a seven-minute rule, a pocket watch with which to enforce it, and all the beat cops were his buddies—but he got on with Rafe, and sometimes the two of them would stand there for twenty minutes or more with their heads together, doing the old New York Yak. Politics? Besboll? The Gospel According to Henry David Thoreau? I didn't know and never cared less than on that day. They'd been there when I went up with my office supplies, and were still there when a far less carefree Scott Staley came back down. A Scott Staley who had discovered a small but noticeable hole in the column of reality. Just the two of them being there was enough for me. I walked up and held my right hand, the one with the sunglasses in it, out to Pedro.

"What would you call these?" I asked, not bothering to excuse myself or anything, just butting in head-first.

He gave me a considering stare that said, "I am surprised at your rudeness, Mr. Staley, truly I am," then looked down at my hand. For a long moment he said nothing, and a horrible idea took possession of me: he saw nothing because there was nothing to see. Only my hand outstretched, as if this were Turnabout Tuesday and I expected *him* to tip *me*. My hand was empty. Sure it was, had to be, because Sonja D'Amico's sunglasses no longer existed. Sonja's joke shades were a long time gone.

"I call them sunglasses, Mr. Staley," Pedro said at last. "What else would I call them? Or is this some sort of trick question?"

Rafe the FedEx man, clearly more interested, took them from me. The relief of seeing him holding the sunglasses and looking at them, almost *studying* them, was like having someone scratch that exact place between your shoulder blades that itches. He stepped out from beneath the awning and held them up to the day, making a sunstar flash off each of the heart-shaped lenses.

"They're like the ones the little girl wore in that porno movie with Jeremy Irons," he said at last.

I had to grin in spite of my distress. In New York, even the deliverymen are film critics. It's one of the things to love about the place.

"That's right, *Lolita*," I said, taking the glasses back. "Only the heart-shaped sunglasses were in the version Stanley Kubrick directed. Back when Jeremy Irons was still nothing but a putter." That one hardly made sense (even to me), but I didn't give Shit One. Once again I was feeling giddy . . . but not in a good way. Not this time.

"Who played the pervo in that one?" Rafe asked.

I shook my head. "I'll be damned if I can remember right now."

"If you don't mind me saying," Pedro said, "you look rather pale, Mr. Staley. Are you coming down with something? The flu, perhaps?"

No, that was my sister, I thought of saying. *The day I came within about twenty seconds of getting caught masturbating into her panties while I looked at a picture of Miss April.* But I hadn't been caught. Not then, not on 9/11, either. Fooled ya, beat the clock again. I couldn't speak for Warren Anderson, who told me in the Blarney Stone that he'd stopped on the third floor that morning to talk about the Yankees with a friend, but not getting caught had become quite a specialty of mine.

"I'm all right," I told Pedro, and while that wasn't true, knowing I wasn't the only one who saw Sonja's joke shades as a thing that actually existed in the world made me feel better, at least. If the sunglasses were in the world, probably Cleve Farrell's Hillerich & Bradsby was, too.

"Are those *the* glasses?" Rafe suddenly asked in a respectful, ready-to-be-awestruck voice. "The ones from the first *Lolita*?"

"Nope," I said, folding the bows behind the heart-shaped lenses, and as I did, the name of the girl in the Kubrick version of the film came to me: Sue Lyon. I still couldn't remember who played the pervo. "Just a knock-off."

"Is there something special about them?" Rafe asked. "Is that why you came rushing down here?"

"I don't know," I said. "Someone left them behind in my apartment."

I went upstairs before they could ask any more questions and looked around, hoping there was nothing else. But there was. In addition to the sunglasses and the baseball bat with CLAIMS ADJUSTOR burned into the side, there was a Howie's Laff-Riot Farting Cushion, a conch shell, a steel penny suspended in a Lucite cube, and a ceramic mushroom (red with white spots) that came with a ceramic Alice sitting on top of it. The Farting Cushion had belonged to Jimmy

Eagleton and got a certain amount of play every year at the Christmas party. The ceramic Alice had been on Maureen Hannon's desk—a gift from her granddaughter, she'd told me once. Maureen had the most beautiful white hair, which she wore long, to her waist. You rarely see that in a business situation, but she'd been with the company for almost forty years and felt she could wear her hair any way she liked. I remembered both the conch shell and the steel penny, but not in whose cubicles (or offices) they had been. It might come to me; it might not. There had been lots of cubicles (and offices) at Light and Bell, Insurers.

The shell, the mushroom, and the Lucite cube were on the coffee table in my living room, gathered in a neat pile. The Farting Cushion was—quite rightly, I thought—lying on top of my toilet tank, beside the current issue of Spenck's Rural Insurance Newsletter. Rural insurance used to be my specialty, as I think I told you. I knew all the odds.

What were the odds on this?

When something goes wrong in your life and you need to talk about it, I think that the first impulse for most people is to call a family member. This wasn't much of an option for me. My father put an egg in his shoe and beat it when I was two and my sister was four. My mother, no quitter she, hit the ground running and raised the two of us, managing a mail-order clearinghouse out of our home while she did so. I believe this was a business she actually created, and she made an adequate living at it (only the first year was really scary, she told me later). She smoked like a chimney, however, and died of lung cancer at the age of forty-eight, six or eight years before the Internet might have made her a dot-com millionaire.

My sister Peg was currently living in Cleveland, where she had embraced Mary Kay Cosmetics, the Indians, and fundamentalist Christianity, not necessarily in that order. If I called and told Peg about the things I'd found in my apartment, she would suggest I get down on my knees and ask Jesus to come into my life. Rightly or wrongly, I did not feel Jesus could help me with my current problem.

I was equipped with the standard number of aunts, uncles, and cousins, but most lived west of the Mississippi, and I hadn't seen any of them in years. The Killians (my mother's side of the family) have never been a reuning bunch. A card on one's birthday and at Christmas were considered sufficient to fulfill all familial obligations. A card on Valentine's Day or at Easter was a bonus. I called my sister on Christmas or she called me, we muttered the standard crap about getting together "sometime soon," and hung up with what I imagine was mutual relief.

The next option when in trouble would probably be to invite a good friend out for a drink, explain the situation, and then ask for advice. But I was a shy boy who grew into a shy man, and in my current research job I work alone (out of preference) and thus have no colleagues apt to mature into friends. I made a few in my last job—Sonja and Cleve Farrell, to name two—but they're dead, of course.

I reasoned that if you don't have a friend you can talk to, the next-best thing would be to rent one. I could certainly afford a little therapy, and it seemed to me that a few sessions on some psychiatrist's couch (four might do the trick) would be enough for me to explain what had happened and to articulate how it made me feel. How much could four sessions set me back? Six hundred dollars? Maybe eight? That seemed a fair price for a little relief. And I thought there might be a bonus. A disinterested outsider might be able to see some simple and reasonable explanation I was just missing. To my mind the locked door between my apartment and the outside world seemed to do away with most of those, but it was *my* mind, after all; wasn't that the point? And perhaps the problem?

I had it all mapped out. During the first session I'd explain what had happened. When I came to the second one, I'd bring the items in question—sunglasses, Lucite cube, conch shell, baseball bat, ceramic mushroom, the ever-popular Farting Cushion. A little show and tell, just like in grammar school. That left two more during which my rent-a-pal and I could figure out the cause of this disturbing tilt in the axis of my life and set things straight again.

A single afternoon spent riffling the Yellow Pages and dialing the telephone was enough to prove to me that the idea of psychiatry was unworkable in fact, no matter how good it might be in theory. The closest I came to an actual appointment was a receptionist who told me that Dr. Jauss might be able to work me in the following January. She intimated even that would take some inspired shoehorning. The others held out no hope whatsoever. I tried half a dozen therapists in Newark and four in White Plains, even a hypnotist in Queens, with the same result. Mohammed Atta and his Suicide Patrol might have been very bery-bery bad for the city of New York (not to mention for the in-SHOO-rance business), but it was clear to me from that single fruitless afternoon on the telephone that they had been a boon to the psychiatric profession, much as the psychiatrists themselves might wish otherwise. If you wanted to lie on some professional's couch in the summer of 2002, you had to take a number and wait in line.

I could sleep with those things in my apartment, but not well. They whispered to me. I lay awake in my bed, sometimes until two, thinking about Maureen Hannon, who felt she had reached an age (not to mention a level of indispensability) at which she could wear her amazingly long hair any way she damn well liked. Or I'd recall the various people who'd gone running around at the Christmas party, waving Jimmy Eagleton's famous Farting Cushion. It was, as I may have said, a great favorite once people got two or three drinks closer to New Year's. I remembered Bruce Mason asking me if it didn't look like an enema bag for elfs—"elfs," he said—and by a process of association remembered that the conch shell had been his. Of course. Bruce Mason, Lord of the Flies. And a step further down the associative food-chain I found the name and face of James Mason, who had played Humbert Humbert back when Jeremy Irons was still just a putter. The mind is a wily monkey; sometime him take-a de banana, sometime him don't. Which is why I'd brought the sunglasses downstairs, although I'd been aware of no deductive process at the time. I'd only wanted confirmation. There's a George Seferis poem that asks, *Are these the voices of our dead friends, or is it just the gramophone?* Sometimes it's a good question, one you have to ask someone else. Or . . . listen to this.

Once, in the late eighties, near the end of a bitter two-year romance with alcohol, I woke up in my study after dozing off at my desk in the middle of the night. I staggered off to my bedroom, where, as I reached for the light switch, I saw someone moving around. I flashed on the idea (the near *certainty*) of a junkie burglar with a cheap pawnshop .32 in his trembling hand, and my heart almost came out of my chest. I turned on the light with one hand and was grabbing for something heavy off the top of my bureau with the other—anything, even the silver frame holding the picture of my mother, would have done—when I saw the prowler was me. I was staring wild-eyed back at myself from the mirror on the other side of the room, my shirt half-untucked and my hair standing up in the back. I was disgusted with myself, but I was also relieved.

I wanted this to be like that. I wanted it to be the mirror, the gramophone, even someone playing a nasty practical joke (maybe someone who knew why I hadn't been at the office on that day in September). But I knew it was none of those things. The Farting Cushion was there, an actual guest in my apartment. I could run my thumb over the buckles on Alice's ceramic shoes, slide my finger down the part in her yellow ceramic hair. I could read the date on the penny inside the Lucite cube.

Bruce Mason, alias Conch Man, alias Lord of the Flies, took his big pink shell to the company shindig at Jones Beach one July and blew it, summoning people to a jolly picnic lunch of hotdogs and hamburgers. Then he tried to show Freddy Lounds how to do it. The best Freddy had been able to muster was a series of weak honking sounds like . . . well, like Jimmy Eagleton's Farting Cushion. Around and around it goes. Ultimately, every associative chain forms a necklace.

In late September I had a brainstorm, one of those ideas so simple you can't believe you didn't think of it sooner. Why was I was holding onto this unwelcome crap, anyway? Why not just get rid of it? It wasn't as if the items were in trust; the people who owned them weren't going to come back at some later date and ask for them to be returned. The last time I'd seen Cleve Farrell's face it had been on a poster, and the last of those had been torn down by November of '01. The general (if unspoken) feeling was that such homemade homages were bumming out the tourists, who'd begun to creep back to Fun City. What had happened was horrible, most New Yorkers opined, but America was still here and Matthew Broderick would only be in *The Producers* for so long.

I'd gotten Chinese that night, from a place I like two blocks over. My plan was to eat it as I usually ate my evening meal, watching Chuck Scarborough explain the world to me. I was turning on the television when the epiphany came. They *weren't* in trust, these unwelcome souvenirs of the last safe day, nor were they evidence. There had been a crime, yes—everyone agreed to that—but the perpetrators were dead and the ones who'd set them on their crazy course were on the run. There might be trials at some future date, but Scott Staley would never be called to the stand, and Jimmy Eagleton's Farting Cushion would never be marked Exhibit A.

I left my General Tso's chicken sitting on the kitchen counter with the cover still on the aluminum dish, got a laundry bag from the shelf above my seldom-used washing machine, put the things into it (sacking them up, I couldn't believe how light they were, or how long I'd waited to do such a simple thing), and rode down in the elevator with the bag sitting between my feet. I walked to the corner of 75th and Park, looked around to make sure I wasn't being watched (God knows why I felt so furtive, but I did), then put litter in its place. I took one look back over my shoulder as I walked away. The handle of the bat poked out of the basket invitingly. Someone would come along and take it, I had no doubt. Probably before Chuck Scarborough gave way to John Seigenthaler or whoever else was sitting in for Tom Brokaw that evening.

On my way back to my apartment, I stopped at Fun Choy for a fresh order of General Tso's. "Last one no good?" asked Rose Ming, at the cash register. She spoke with some concern. "You tell why."

"No, the last one was fine," I said. "Tonight I just felt like two."

She laughed as though this were the funniest thing she'd ever heard, and I laughed, too. Hard. The kind of laughter that goes well beyond giddy. I couldn't remember the last time I'd laughed like that, so loudly and so naturally. Certainly not since Light and Bell, Insurers, fell into West Street.

I rode the elevator up to my floor and walked the twelve steps to 4-B. I felt the way seriously ill people must when they awaken one day, assess themselves by the sane light of morning, and discover that the fever has broken. I tucked my takeout bag under my left arm (an awkward maneuver but workable in the short run) and then unlocked my door. I turned on the light. There, on the table where I leave bills that need to be paid, claim checks, and overdue-book notices, were Sonja D'Amico's joke sunglasses, the ones with the red frames and the heart-shaped Lolita lenses. Sonja D'Amico who had, according to Warren Anderson (who was, so far as I knew, the only other surviving employee of Light and Bell's home office), jumped from the one hundred and tenth floor of the stricken building.

He claimed to have seen a photo that caught her as she dropped, Sonja with her hands placed primly on her skirt to keep it from skating up her thighs, her hair standing up against the smoke and blue of that day's sky, the tips of her shoes pointed down. The description made me think of "Falling," the poem James Dickey wrote about the stewardess who tries to aim the plummeting stone of her body for water, as if she could come up smiling, shaking beads of water from her hair and asking for a Coca-Cola.

"I vomited," Warren told me that day in the Blarney Stone. "I never want to look at a picture like that again, Scott, but I know I'll never forget it. You could see her face, and I think she believed that somehow . . . yeah, that somehow she was going to be all right."

I've never screamed as an adult, but I almost did so when I looked from Sonja's sunglasses to Cleve Farrell's CLAIMS ADJUSTOR, the latter once more leaning nonchalantly in the corner by the entry to the living room. Some part of my mind must have remembered that the door to the hallway was open and both of my fourth-floor neighbors would hear me if I did scream; then, as the saying is, I would have some 'splainin to do.

I clapped my hand over my mouth to hold it in. The bag with the General Tso's chicken inside fell to the hardwood floor of the foyer and split open. I could barely bring myself to look at the resulting mess. Those dark chunks of cooked meat could have been anything.

I plopped into the single chair I keep in the foyer and put my face in my hands. I didn't scream and I didn't cry, and after a while I was able to clean up the mess. My mind kept trying to go toward the things that had beaten me back from the corner of 75th and Park, but I wouldn't let it. Each time it tried to lunge in that direction, I grabbed its leash and forced it away again.

That night, lying in bed, I listened to conversations. First the things talked (in low voices), and then the people who had owned the things replied (in slightly louder ones). Sometimes they talked about the picnic at Jones Beach—the coconut odor of suntan lotion and Lou Bega singing "Mambo Number Five" over and over from Misha Bryzinski's boom box. Or they talked about Frisbees sailing under the sky while dogs chased them. Sometimes they discussed children puddling along the wet sand with the seats of their shorts and their bathing suits sagging. Mothers in swimsuits ordered from the Land's End catalogue walking beside them with white gloop on their noses. How many of the kids that day had lost a guardian Mom or a Frisbee-throwing Dad? Man, that was a math problem I didn't want to do. But the voices I heard in my apartment *did* want do it. They did it over and over.

I remembered Bruce Mason blowing his conch shell and proclaiming himself the Lord of the Flies. I remembered Maureen Hannon once telling me (not at Jones Beach, not this conversation) that *Alice in Wonderland* was the first psychedelic novel. Jimmy Eagleton telling me one afternoon that his son had a learning disability to go along with his stutter, two for the price of one, and the kid was going to need a tutor in math and another one in French if he was going to get out of high school in the foreseeable future. "Before he's eligible for the AARP discount on textbooks" was how Jimmy had put it. His cheeks pale and a bit stubbly in the long afternoon light, as if that morning the razor had been dull.

I'd been drifting toward sleep, but this last one brought me fully awake again with a start, because I realized the conversation must have taken place not long before September Eleventh. Maybe only days. Perhaps even the Friday before, which would make it the last day I'd ever seen Jimmy alive. And the l'il putter with the stutter and the learning disability: had his name actually been Jeremy, as in Jeremy Irons? Surely not, surely that was just my mind (sometimes him take-a de banana) playing its little games, but it had been *close* to that, by God. Jason, maybe. Or Justin. In the wee hours everything grows, and I remember thinking that if the kid's name *did* turn out to be Jeremy, I'd probably go crazy. Straw that broke the camel's back, baby.

Around three in the morning I remembered who had owned the Lucite cube with the steel penny in it: Roland Abelson, in Liability. He called it his retirement fund. It was Roland who had a habit of saying "Lucy, you got some 'splainin to do." One night in the fall of '01, I had seen his widow on the six o'clock news. I had talked with her at one of the company picnics (very likely the one at Jones Beach) and thought then that she was pretty, but widowhood had refined that prettiness, winnowed it into severe beauty. On the news report she kept referring to her husband as "missing." She would not call him "dead." And if he *was* alive—if he ever turned up—he would have some 'splainin to do. You bet. But of course, so would she. A woman who has gone from pretty to beautiful as the result of a mass murder would certainly have some 'splainin to do.

Lying in bed and thinking of this stuff—remembering the crash of the surf at Jones Beach and the Frisbees flying under the sky—filled me with an awful sadness that finally emptied in tears. But I have to admit it was a learning experience. That was the night I came to understand that *things*—even little ones, like a penny in a Lucite cube—can get heavier as time passes. But because it's a weight of the mind, there's no mathematical formula for it, like the ones you can find in an insurance company's Blue Books, where the rate on your whole life policy goes up *x* if you smoke and coverage on your crops goes up *y* if your farm's in a tornado zone. You see what I'm saying?

It's a weight of the mind.

The following morning I gathered up all the items again, and found a seventh, this one under the couch. The guy in the cubicle next to mine, Misha Bryzinski, had kept a small pair of Punch and Judy dolls on his desk. The one I spied under my sofa with my little eye was Punch. Judy was nowhere to be found, but Punch was enough for me. Those black eyes, staring out from amid the ghost-bunnies, gave me a terrible sinking feeling of dismay. I fished the doll out, hating the streak of dust it left behind. A thing that leaves a trail is a real thing, a thing with weight. No question about it.

I put Punch and all the other stuff in the little utility closet just off the kitchenette, and there they stayed. At first I wasn't sure they would, but they did.

My mother once told me that if a man wiped his ass and saw blood on the toilet tissue, his response would be to shit in the dark for the next thirty days and hope for the best. She used this example to illustrate her belief that the cornerstone of male philosophy was "If you ignore it, maybe it'll go away."

I ignored the things I'd found in my apartment, I hoped for the best, and things actually got a little better. I rarely heard those voices whispering in the utility closet (except late at night), although I was more and more apt to take my research chores out of the house. By the middle of November, I was spending most of my days in the New York Public Library. I'm sure the lions got used to seeing me there with my PowerBook.

Then, just before Thanksgiving, I happened to be going out of my building one day and met Paula Robeson, the maiden fair whom I'd rescued by pushing the reset button on her air conditioner, coming in.

With absolutely no forethought whatsoever—if I'd had time to think about it, I'm convinced I never would have said a word—I asked her if I could buy her lunch and talk to her about something.

"The fact is," I said, "I have a problem. Maybe you could push my reset button."

We were in the lobby. Pedro the doorman was sitting in the corner, reading the *Post* (and listening to every word, I have no doubt—to Pedro, his tenants were the world's most interesting daytime drama). She gave me a smile both pleasant and nervous. "I guess I owe you one," she said, "but . . . you know I'm married, don't you?"

"Yes," I said, not adding that she'd shaken with me wrong-handed so I could hardly fail to notice the ring.

She nodded. "Sure, you must've seen us together at least a couple of times, but he was in Europe when I had all that trouble with the air conditioner, and he's in Europe now. Edward, that's his name. Over the last two years he's been in Europe more than he's here, and although I don't like it, I'm very married in spite of it." Then, as a kind of afterthought, she added: "Edward is in import-export."

I used to be in insurance, but then one day the company exploded, I thought of saying. Came *close* to saying, actually. In the end, I managed something a little more sane.

"I don't want a date, Ms. Robeson," No more than I wanted to be on a first-name basis with her, and was that a wink of disappointment I saw in her eyes? By God, I thought it was. But at least it convinced her. I was still *safe.*

She put her hands on her hips and looked at me with mock exasperation. Or maybe not so mock. "Then what *do* you want?"

"Just someone to talk to. I tried several shrinks, but they're . . . busy."

"*All* of them?"

"It would appear so."

"If you're having problems with your sex life or feeling the urge to race around town killing men in turbans, I don't want to know about it."

"It's nothing like that. I'm not going to make you blush, I promise." Which wasn't quite the same as saying *I promise not to shock you* or *You won't think I'm crazy.* "Just lunch and a little advice, that's all I'm asking. What do you say?"

I was surprised—almost flabbergasted—by my own persuasiveness. If I'd planned the conversation in advance, I almost certainly would have blown the whole deal. I suppose she was curious, and I'm sure she heard a degree of sincerity in my voice. She may also have surmised that if I was the sort of man who liked to try his hand picking up women, I would have had a go on that day in August when I'd actually been alone with her in her apartment, the elusive Edward in France or Germany. And I have to wonder how much actual desperation she saw in my face.

In any case, she agreed to have lunch with me at Donald's Grill down the street on Friday. Donald's may be the least romantic restaurant in all of Manhattan—good food, fluorescent lights, waiters who make it clear they'd like you to hurry. She did so with the air of a woman paying an overdue debt about which she's nearly forgotten. This was not exactly flattering, but it was good enough for me. Noon would be fine for her, she said. If I'd meet her in the lobby, we could walk down there together. I told her that would be fine for me, too.

That night was a good one for me. I went to sleep almost immediately, and there were no dreams of Sonja D'Amico going down beside the burning building with her hands on her thighs, like a stewardess looking for water.

As we strolled down 86th Street the following day, I asked Paula where she'd been when she heard.

"San Francisco," she said. "Fast asleep in a Wradling Hotel suite with Edward beside me, undoubtedly snoring as usual. I was coming back here on September twelfth and Edward was going on to Los Angeles for meetings. The hotel management actually rang the fire alarm."

"That must have scared the hell out of you."

"It did, although my first thought wasn't fire but earthquake. Then this disembodied voice came through the speakers, telling us that there was no fire in the hotel, but a hell of a big one in New York."

"Jesus."

"Hearing it like that, in bed in a strange room . . . hearing it come down from the ceiling like the voice of God . . ." She shook her head. Her lips were pressed so tightly together that her lipstick almost disappeared. "That was very frightening. I suppose I understand the urge to pass on news like that, and immediately, but I still haven't entirely forgiven the management of the Wradling for doing it that way. I don't think I'll be staying there again."

"Did your husband go on to his meetings?"

"They were canceled. I imagine a lot of meetings were canceled that day. We stayed in bed with the TV on until the sun came up, trying to get our heads around it. Do you know what I mean?"

"Yes."

"We talked about who might have been there that we knew. I suppose we weren't the only ones doing that, either."

"Did you come up with anyone?"

"A broker from Shearson, Lehman and the assistant manager of the Borders book store in the mall," she said. "One of them was all right. One of them . . . well, you know, one of them wasn't. What about you?"

So I didn't have to sneak up on it, after all. We weren't even at the restaurant yet and here it was.

"*I* would have been there," I said. "I *should* have been there. It's where I worked. In an insurance company on the hundred and tenth floor."

She stopped dead on the sidewalk, looking up at me, eyes wide. I suppose to the people who had to veer around us, we must have looked like lovers. "Scott, *no!*"

"Scott, yes," I said. And finally told someone about how I woke up on September eleventh expecting to do all the things I usually did on weekdays, from the cup of black coffee while I shaved all the way to the cup of cocoa in front of the midnight news summary on Channel Thirteen. A day like any other day, that was what I had in mind. I think that is what Americans had come to expect as their right. Well, guess what? That's an airplane! Flying into the side of a skyscraper! Ha-ha, asshole, the joke's on you, and half the goddam world's laughing!

I told her about looking out my apartment window and seeing the seven A.M. sky was perfectly cloudless, the sort of blue so deep you think you can almost see through it to the stars beyond. Then I told her about the voice. I think everyone has various voices in their heads and we get used to them. When I was sixteen, one of mine spoke up and suggested it might be quite a kick to masturbate into a pair of my sister's underpants. *She has about a thousand pairs and surely won't miss one, y'all,* the voice opined. (I did not tell Paula Robeson about this particular adolescent adventure.) I'd have to call that the voice of utter irresponsibility, more familiarly known as Mr. Yow, Git Down.

"Mr. Yow, Git Down?" Paula asked doubtfully.

"In honor of James Brown, the King of Soul."

"If you say so."

Mr. Yow, Git Down had had less and less to say to me, especially since I'd pretty much given up drinking, and on that day he awoke from his doze just long enough to speak a dozen words, but they were life-changers. Life-*savers.*

The first five (that's me, sitting on the edge of the bed): *Yow, call in sick, y'all!* The next seven (that's me, plodding toward the shower and scratching my left buttock as I go): *Yow, spend the day in Central Park!* There was no premonition involved. It was clearly Mr. Yow, Git Down, not the voice of God. It was just a version of my very own voice (as they all are), in other words, telling me to play hooky. *Do a little suffin fo' yo'self, Gre't God!* The last time I could recall hearing this version of my voice, the subject had been a karaoke contest at a bar on Amersterdam Avenue: *Yow, sing along wit' Neil Diamond, fool—git up on stage and git ya bad self down!*

"I guess I know what you mean," she said, smiling a little.

"Do you?"

"Well . . . I once took off my shirt in a Key West bar and won ten dollars dancing to 'Honky-Tonk Women.'" She paused. "Edward doesn't know, and if you ever tell him, I'll be forced to stab you in the eye with one of his tie tacks."

"Yow, you go, girl," I said, and her smile became a rather wistful grin. It made her look younger. I thought this had a chance of working.

We walked into Donald's. There was a cardboard turkey on the door, cardboard Pilgrims on the green tile wall above the steam table.

"I listened to Mr. Yow, Git Down and I'm here," I said. "But some other things are here, too, and he can't help with them. They're things I can't seem to get rid of. Those are what I want to talk to you about."

"Let me repeat that I'm no shrink," she said, and with more than a trace of uneasiness. The grin was gone. "I majored in German and minored in European history."

You and your husband must have a lot to talk about, I thought. What I said out loud was that it didn't have to be her, necessarily, just someone.

"All right. Just as long as you know."

A waiter took our drink orders, decaf for her, regular for me. Once he went away she asked me what things I was talking about.

"This is one of them." From my pocket I withdrew the Lucite cube with the steel penny suspended inside it and put it on the table. Then I told her about the other things, and to whom they had belonged. Cleve "Besboll been bery-bery good to me" Farrell. Maureen Hannon, who wore her hair long to her waist as a sign of her corporate indispensability. Jimmy Eagleton, who had a divine nose for phony accident claims, a son with learning disabilities, and a Farting Cushion he kept safely tucked away in his desk until the Christmas party rolled around each year. Sonja D'Amico, Light and Bell's best accountant, who had gotten the Lolita sunglasses as a bitter divorce present from her first husband. Bruce "Lord of the Flies" Mason, who would always stand shirtless in my mind's eye, blowing his conch on Jones Beach while the waves rolled up and expired around his bare feet. Last of all, Misha Bryzinski, with whom I'd gone to at least a dozen Mets games. I told her about putting everything but Misha's Punch doll in a trash basket on the corner of Park and 75th, and how they had beaten me back to my apartment, possibly because I had stopped for a second order of General Tso's chicken. During all of this, the Lucite cube stood on the table between us. We managed to eat at least some of our meal in spite of his stern profile.

When I was finished talking, I felt better than I'd dared to hope. But there was a silence from her side of the table that felt terribly heavy.

"So," I said, to break it. "What do you think?"

She took a moment to consider that, and I didn't blame her. "I think that we're not the strangers we were," she said finally, "and making a new friend is never a bad thing. I think I'm glad I know about Mr. Yow, Git Down and that I told you what I did."

"I am, too." And it was true.

"Now may I ask you two questions?"

"Of course."

"How much of what they call 'survivor guilt' are you feeling?"

"I thought you said you weren't a shrink."

"I'm not, but I read the magazines and have even been known to watch *Oprah.* That my husband *does* know, although I prefer not to rub his nose in it. So . . . how much, Scott?"

I considered the question. It was a good one—and, of course, it was one I'd asked myself on more than one of those sleepless nights. "Quite a lot," I said. "Also, quite a lot of relief, I won't lie about that. If Mr. Yow, Git Down was a real person, he'd never have to pick up another restaurant tab. Not when I was with him, at least." I paused. "Does that shock you?"

She reached across the table and briefly touched my hand. "Not even a little."

Hearing her say that made me feel better than I would have believed. I gave her hand a brief squeeze and then let it go. "What's your other question?"

"How important to you is it that I believe your story about these things coming back?"

I thought this was an excellent question, even though the Lucite cube was right there next to the sugar bowl. Such items are not exactly rare, after all. And I thought that if she *had* majored in psychology rather than German, she probably would have done fine.

"Not as important as I thought an hour ago," I said. "Just telling it has been a help."

She nodded and smiled. "Good. Now here's my best guess: someone is very likely playing a game with you. Not a nice one."

"Trickin' on me," I said. I tried not to show it, but I'd rarely been so disappointed. Maybe a layer of disbelief settles over people in certain circumstances, protecting them. Or maybe—probably—I hadn't conveyed my own sense that this thing was just . . . happening. *Still* happening. The way avalanches do.

"Trickin' on you," she agreed, and then: "But you don't believe it."

More points for perception. I nodded. "I locked the door when I went out, and it was locked when I came back from Staples. I heard the clunk the tumblers make when they turn. They're loud. You can't miss them."

"Still . . . survivor guilt is a funny thing. And powerful, at least according to the magazines."

"This . . ." *This isn't survivor guilt* was what I meant to say, but it would have been the wrong thing. I had a fighting chance to make a new friend here, and having a new friend would be good, no matter how the rest of this came out. So I amended it. "I don't think this is survivor guilt." I pointed to the Lucite cube. "It's right there, isn't it? Like Sonja's sunglasses. You see it. I do, too. I suppose I could have bought it myself, but . . ." I shrugged, trying to convey what we both surely knew: *anything* is possible.

"I don't think you did that. But neither can I accept the idea that a trapdoor opened between reality and the Twilight Zone and these things fell out."

Yes, that was the problem. For Paula the idea that the Lucite cube and the other things which had appeared in my apartment had some supernatural origin was automatically off-limits, no matter how much the facts might seem to support the idea. What I needed to do was to decide if I needed to argue the point more than I needed to make a friend.

I decided I did not.

"All right," I said. I caught the waiter's eye and made a check-writing gesture in the air. "I can accept your inability to accept."

"Can you?" she asked, looking at me closely.

"Yes." And I thought it was true. "If, that is, we could have a cup of coffee from time to time. Or just say hi in the lobby."

"Absolutely." But she sounded absent, not really in the conversation. She was looking at the Lucite cube with the steel penny inside it. Then she looked up at me. I could almost see a lightbulb appearing over her head, like in a cartoon. She reached out and grasped the cube with one hand. I could never convey the depth of the dread I felt when she did that, but what could I say? We were New Yorkers in a clean, well-lighted place. For her part, she'd already laid down the ground rules, and they pretty firmly excluded the supernatural. The supernatural was out of bounds. Anything hit there was a do-over.

And there was a light in Paula's eyes. One that suggested Ms.

Yow, Git Down was in the house, and I know from personal experience that's a hard voice to resist.

"Give it to me," she proposed, smiling into my eyes. When she did that I could see—for the first time, really—that she was sexy as well as pretty.

"Why?" As if I didn't know.

"Call it my fee for listening to your story."

"I don't know if that's such a good—"

"It is, though," she said. She was warming to her own inspiration, and when people do that, they rarely take no for an answer. "It's a *great* idea. I'll make sure this piece of memorabilia at least doesn't come back to you, wagging its tail behind it. We've got a safe in the apartment." She made a charming little pantomime gesture of shutting a safe door, twirling the combination, and then throwing the key back over her shoulder.

"All right," I said. "It's my gift to you." And I felt something that might have been mean-spirited gladness. Call it the voice of Mr. Yow, You'll Find Out. Apparently just getting it off my chest wasn't enough, after all. She hadn't believed me, and at least part of me *did* want to be believed and resented Paula for not getting what it wanted. That part knew that letting her take the Lucite cube was an absolutely terrible idea, but was glad to see her tuck it away in her purse, just the same.

"There," she said briskly. "Mama say bye-bye, make all gone. Maybe when it doesn't come back in a week—or two, I guess it all depends on how stubborn your subconscious wants to be—you can start giving the rest of the things away." And her saying that was her real gift to me that day, although I didn't know it then.

"Maybe so," I said, and smiled. Big smile for the new friend. Big smile for pretty Mama. All the time thinking, You'll find out.

Yow.

She did.

Three nights later, while I was watching Chuck Scarborough explain the city's latest transit woes on the six o'clock news, my doorbell rang. Since no one had been announced, I assumed it was a package, maybe even Rafe with something from Federal Express. I opened the door and there stood Paula Robeson.

This was not the woman with whom I'd had lunch. Call this

version of Paula Ms. Yow, Ain't That Chemotherapy *Nasty*. She was wearing a little lipstick but nothing else in the way of makeup, and her complexion was a sickly shade of yellow-white. There were dark brownish-purple arcs under her eyes. She might have given her hair a token swipe with the brush before coming down from the fifth floor, but it hadn't done much good. It looked like straw and stuck out on either side of her head in a way that would have been comic-strip funny under other circumstances. She was holding the Lucite cube up in front of her breasts, allowing me to note that the well-kept nails on that hand were gone. She'd chewed them away, right down to the quick. And my first thought, God help me, was *yep, she found out.*

She held it out to me. "Take it back," she said.

I did so without a word.

"His name was Roland Abelson," she said. "Wasn't it?"

"Yes."

"He had red hair."

"Yes."

"Not married but paying child support to a woman in Rahway."

I hadn't known that—didn't believe *anyone* at Light and Bell had known that—but I nodded again, and not just to keep her rolling. I was sure she was right. "What was her name, Paula?" Not knowing why I was asking, not yet, just knowing I had to know.

"Tonya Gregson." It was as if she was in a trance. There was something in her eyes, though, something so terrible I could hardly stand to look at it. Nevertheless, I stored the name away. *Tonya Gregson, Rahway*. And then, like some guy doing stockroom inventory: *One Lucite cube with penny inside.*

"He tried to crawl under his desk, did you know that? No, I can see you didn't. His hair was on fire and he was crying. Because in that instant he understood he was never going to own a catamaran or even mow his lawn again." She reached out and put a hand on my cheek, a gesture so intimate it would have been shocking had her hand not been so cold. "At the end, he would have given every cent he had, and every stock option he held, just to be able to mow his lawn again. Do you believe that?"

"Yes."

"The place was full of screams, he could smell jet fuel, and *he un-*

derstood it was his dying hour. Do you understand that? Do you understand the *enormity* of that?"

I nodded. I couldn't speak. You could have put a gun to my head and I still wouldn't have been able to speak.

"The politicians talk about memorials and courage and wars to end terrorism, but burning hair is apolitical." She bared her teeth in an unspeakable grin. A moment later it was gone. "He was trying to crawl under his desk with his hair on fire. There was a plastic thing under his desk, a what-do-you-call it—"

"Mat—"

"Yes, a mat, a plastic mat, and his hands were on that and he could feel the ridges in the plastic and smell his own burning hair. Do you understand that?"

I nodded. I started to cry. It was Roland Abelson we were talking about, this guy I used to work with. He was in Liability and I didn't know him very well. To say hi to is all; how was I supposed to know he had a kid in Rahway? And if I hadn't played hooky that day, my hair probably would have burned, too. I'd never really understood that before.

"I don't want to see you again," she said. She flashed her gruesome grin once more, but now she was crying, too. "I don't care about your problems. I don't care about any of the shit you found. We're quits. From now on you leave me alone." She started to turn away, then turned back. She said: "They did it in the name of God, but there is no God. If there was a God, Mr. Staley, He would have struck all eighteen of them dead in their boarding lounges with their boarding passes in their hands, but no God did. They called for passengers to get on and those fucks just got on."

I watched her walk back to the elevator. Her back was very stiff. Her hair stuck out on either side of her head, making her look like a girl in a Sunday Funnies cartoon. She didn't want to see me anymore, and I didn't blame her. I closed the door and looked at the steel Abe Lincoln in the Lucite cube. I looked at him for quite a long time. I thought about how the hair of his beard would have smelled if U.S. Grant had stuck one of his everlasting cigars in it. That unpleasant frying aroma. On TV, someone was saying that there was a mattress blowout going on at Sleepy's. After that, Len Berman came on and talked about the Jets.

That night I woke up at two in the morning, listening to the voices whisper. I hadn't had any dreams or visions of the people who owned the objects, hadn't seen anyone with their hair on fire or jumping from the windows to escape the burning jet fuel, but why would I? I knew who they were, and the things they left behind had been left for me. Letting Paula Robeson take the Lucite cube had been wrong, but only because she was the wrong person.

And speaking of Paula, one of the voices was hers. *You can start giving the rest of the things away,* it said. And it said, *I guess it all depends on how stubborn your subconscious wants to be.*

I lay back down and after a while I was able to go to sleep. I dreamed I was in Central Park, feeding the ducks, when all at once there was a loud noise like a sonic boom and smoke filled the sky. In my dream, the smoke smelled like burning hair.

I thought about Tonya Gregson in Rahway—Tonya and the child who might or might not have Roland Abelson's eyes—and thought I'd have to work up to that one. I decided to start with Bruce Mason's widow.

I took the train to Dobbs Ferry and called a taxi from the station. The cabbie took me to a Cape Cod house on a residential street. I gave him some money, told him to wait—I wouldn't be long—and rang the doorbell. I had a box under one arm. It looked like the kind that contains a bakery cake.

I only had to ring once, because I'd called ahead and Janice Mason was expecting me. I had my story carefully prepared and told it with some confidence, knowing that the taxi sitting in the driveway, its meter running, would forestall any detailed cross-examination.

On September seventh, I said—the Friday before—I had tried to blow a note from the conch Bruce kept on his desk, as I had heard Bruce himself do at the Jones Beach picnic. (Janice, Mrs. Lord of the Flies, nodding; she had been there, of course.) Well, I said, to make a long story short, I had persuaded Bruce to let me have the conch shell over the weekend so I could practice. Then, on Monday morning, I'd awakened with a raging sinus infection and a horrible headache to go with it. (This was a story I had already told several people.) I'd been drinking a cup of tea when I heard the boom and saw the rising smoke. I hadn't thought of the conch shell again until just this week. I'd been cleaning out my little utility closet and by damn, there it was. And I just thought . . . well, it's not much of a keepsake, but I just thought maybe you'd like to . . . you know . . .

Her eyes filled up with tears just as mine had when Paula brought back Roland Abelson's "retirement fund," only these weren't accompanied by the look of fright that I'm sure was on my own face as Paula stood there with her stiff hair sticking out on either side of her head. Janice told me she would be glad to have any keepsake of Bruce.

"I can't get over the way we said good-bye," she said, holding the box in her arms. "He always left very early because he took the train. He kissed me on the cheek and I opened one eye and asked him if he'd bring back a pint of Half and Half. He said he would. That's the last thing he ever said to me. When he asked me to marry him, I felt like Helen of Troy—stupid but absolutely true—and I wish I'd said something better than 'Bring home a pint of Half and Half.' But we'd been married a long time, and it seemed like business as usual that day, and . . . we don't know, do we?"

"No."

"Yes. Any parting could be forever, and we don't know. Thank you, Mr. Staley. For coming out and bringing me this. That was very kind." She smiled a little then. "Do you remember how he stood on the beach with his shirt off and blew it?"

"Yes," I said, and looked at the way she held the box. Later she would sit down and take the shell out and hold it on her lap and cry. I knew that the conch, at least, would never come back to my apartment. It was home.

I returned to the station and caught the train back to New York. The cars were almost empty at that time of day, early afternoon, and I sat by a rain- and dirt-streaked window, looking out at the river and the approaching skyline. On cloudy and rainy days, you almost seem to be creating that skyline out of your own imagination, a piece at a time.

Tomorrow I'd go to Rahway, with the penny in the Lucite cube. Perhaps the child would take it in his or her chubby hand and look at it curiously. In any case, it would be out of my life. I thought the only difficult thing to get rid of would be Jimmy Eagleton's Farting Cushion—I could hardly tell Mrs. Eagleton I'd brought it home for the weekend in order to practice using it, could I? But necessity is the mother of invention, and I was confident that I would eventually think of some halfway plausible story.

It occurred to me that other things might show up, in time. And I'd be lying if I told you I found that possibility entirely unpleasant. When it comes to returning things which people believe have been lost forever, things that have *weight*, there are compensations. Even if they're only little things, like a pair of joke sunglasses or a steel penny in a Lucite cube . . . yeah. I'd have to say there are compensations.

John Farris

John Farris began writing fiction in high school. At 22, while he was studying at the University of Missouri, his first major novel, *Harrison High*, was published; it became a bestseller. He has worked in many genres—suspense, horror, mystery—while transcending each through the power of his writing. The *New York Times* noted his talent for "masterfully devious plotting" while reviewing *The Captors. All Heads Turn When the Hunt Goes By* was cited in an essay published in *Horror: 100 Best Books*, which concluded, "The field's most powerful individual voice . . . when John Farris is on high-burn, no one can match the skill with which he puts words together." In the 1990s he turned exclusively to thrillers, publishing *Dragonfly, Soon She Will Be Gone, Solar Eclipse*, and *Sacrifice*, of which Richard Matheson wrote, "John Farris has once again elevated the terror genre into the realm of literature." Commenting on *Dragonfly*, Ed Gorman said, "*Dragonfly* has style, heart, cunning, terror, irony, suspense, and genuine surprise—and an absolutely fearless look into the souls of people very much like you and me." And *Publishers Weekly* concluded, "(he writes with) a keen knowledge of human nature and a wicked sense of humor." John Farris received the 2001 Lifetime Achievement Award from the Horror Writers Association. His latest novel is *Phantom Nights*.

THE RANSOME WOMEN

John Farris

One

Echo Halloran first became aware of the Woman in Black during a visit to the Highbridge Museum of Art in Cambridge, Massachusetts. Echo and her boss were dealing that day with the chief curator of the Highbridge, a man named Charles Carwood. The Highbridge was in the process of deacquisitioning, as they say in the trade, a number of paintings, mostly by twentieth-century artists whose stock had remained stable in the fickle art world. The Highbridge was in difficulty with the IRS and Carwood was looking for around thirty million for a group of Representationalists.

Echo's boss was Stefan Konine, director of Gilbard's, the New York auction house. Stefan was a big man, florid as a poached salmon, who lied about his age and played the hayburners for recreation. He wore J. Dege & Sons suits with the aplomb of royalty. He wasn't much interested in Representationalists and preferred to let Echo, who had done her thesis at NYU on the Boquillas School, carry the ball while the paintings were reverently brought, one by one, to their attention in the seventh floor conference room. The weather outside was blue and clear. Through a nice spread of windows the view to the south included the Charles River.

Echo had worked for Konine for a little over a year. They had established an almost familial rapport. Echo kept busy with her laptop on questions of provenance while Stefan sipped Chablis and regarded each painting with the same dyspeptic expression, as if he were trying to digest a bowling ball he'd had for lunch. His mind was mostly on the Trifecta he had working at Belmont, but he was alert to the nuances of each glance Echo sent his way. They were a team. They knew each other's signals.

Carwood said, "And we have this exquisite David Herrera from the Oppenheim estate, probably the outstanding piece of David's Big Bend Cycle."

Echo smiled as two museum assistants wheeled in the oversize canvas. She was drinking 7-Up, not Chablis.

The painting was in the style of Georgia O'Keeffe during her Santa Fe incarnation. Echo looked down at her laptop screen, hit a few keys, looked up again. It was a long stare, as if she were trying to see all the way to the Big Bend country of Texas. After a couple of minutes Stefan raised a spikey eyebrow. Carwood fidgeted on his settee. His eyes were on Echo. He had done some staring himself, from the moment Echo was introduced to him.

There are beauties who stop traffic and there are beauties who grow obsessively in the hearts of the susceptible; Echo Halloran was one of those. She had a full mane of wraparound dark hair. Her eyes were large and round and dark as polished buckeyes, deeply flecked with gold. Spright as a genie, endowed with a wealth of breeding and self-esteem, she viewed the world with an intensity of favor that piqued the wonder of strangers.

When she cleared her throat Carwood started nervously. Stefan looked lazily at his protégée, with the beginning of a wise smile. He sensed an intrigue.

Carwood said, "Perhaps you'd care to have a closer look, Miss Halloran? The light from the windows—"

"The light is fine." Echo settled back in her seat. She closed her eyes and touched the center of her forehead with two fingers. "I've seen enough. I'm very sorry, Mr. Carwood. But that canvas isn't David Herrera's work."

"Oh, my *dear*," Carwood said, drawing a pained breath as if he were trying to decide whether a tantrum or a seizure was called for, "you must be extremely careful about making potentially actionable judgments—"

"I am," Echo said, and opened her eyes wide, "always careful. It's a fake. And not the first fake Herrera I've seen. Give me a couple of hours and I'll tell you which of his students painted it, and when."

Carwood attempted to appeal to Stefan, who held up a cautionary finger.

"But that will cost you a thousand dollars for Miss Halloran's time and expertise. A thousand dollars an hour. I would advise you to pay it. She's very good. As for the lot you've shown us today—" Stefan got to his feet with a nod of good cheer. "Thank you for considering Gilbard's. I'm afraid our schedule is unusually crowded for the fall season. Why don't you try Sotheby's?"

For a man of his bulk, Stefan did a good job of imitating a capering circus bear in the elevator going down to the lobby of the Highbridge.

"Now, Stefan," Echo said serenely.

"But I *loved* seeing dear old Carwood go into the crapper."

"I didn't realize he was another of your old enemies."

"Enemy? I don't hold Charles in such high regard. He's simply a pompous ass. If he were mugged for his wits, he would only impoverish the thief. So tell me, who perpetrated the fraud?"

"Not sure. Either Fimmel or Arzate. Anyway, you can't get a fake Herrera past me."

"I'm sure it helps to have a photographic memory."

Echo grinned.

"Perhaps you should be doing my job."

"Now, Stefan." Echo reached out to press the second-floor button.

"Some day you *will* have my job. But you'll have to pry it from my cold, dead fingers."

Echo grinned again. The elevator stopped on two.

"What are you doing? Aren't we leaving?"

"In a little while." Echo stepped off the elevator and beckoned to Stefan. "This way."

"What? Where are you dragging me to? I'm desperate to have a smoke and find out how My Little Margie placed in the fourth."

Echo looked at her new watch, a twenty-second birthday present from her fiancé that she knew had cost far more than either of them should have been spending on presents.

"There's time. I want to see the Ransome they've borrowed for their show of twentieth-century portraitists."

"Oh, dear God!" But he got off the elevator with Echo. "I detest Ransome! Such transparent theatrics. I've seen better art on a sailor's ass."

"Really, Stefan?"

"Although not all that recently, I'm sorry to say."

The gallery in which the exhibition was being mounted was temporarily closed to the public, but they wore badges allowing them access to any part of the Highbridge. Echo ignored frowns from a couple of dithering functionaries and went straight to the portrait by Ransome that was already in place and lighted.

The subject was a seated nude, blond, Godiva hair. Ransome's style was impressionistic, his canvas flooded with light. The young woman was casually posed, like a Degas girl taking a backstage break, her face partly averted. Stefan had his usual attitude of near-suicidal disdain. But he found it hard to look away. Great artists were hypnotists with a brush.

"I suppose we must give him credit for his excellent eye for beauty."

"It's marvelous," Echo said softly.

"As Delacroix said, 'One never paints violently enough.' We must also give Ransome credit for doing violence to his canvases. And I must have an Armagnac, if the bar downstairs is open. Echo?"

"I'm coming," she said, hands folded like an acolyte's in front of her as she gazed up at the painting with a faintly worshipful smile.

Stefan shrugged when she failed to budge. "I don't wish to impose on your infatuation. Suppose you join me in the limo in twenty minutes?"

"Sure," Echo murmured.

Absorbed in her study of John Leland Ransome's technique, Echo didn't immediately pay attention to that little barb at the back of her neck that told her she was being closely observed by someone.

When she turned she saw a woman standing twenty feet away ignoring the Ransome on the wall, staring instead at Echo.

The woman was dressed all in black, which seemed to Echo both obsessive and oppressive in high summer. But it was elegant, tasteful couture. She wasn't wearing jewelry. She was, perhaps, excessively made up, but striking nonetheless. Mature, but Echo couldn't guess her age. Her features were immobile, masklike. The directness of her gaze, a burning in her eyes, gave Echo a couple of bad moments. She knew a pickup line was coming. She'd averaged three of these encounters a week since puberty.

But the stare went on, and the woman said nothing. It had the effect of getting Echo's Irish up.

"Excuse me," Echo said. "Have we met?" Her expression read, *Whatever you're thinking, forget it, Queenie.*

Not so much as a startled blink. After a few more seconds the woman looked rather deliberately from Echo to the Ransome painting on the wall. She studied that for a short time, then turned and walked away as if Echo no longer existed, heels clicking on the gallery floor.

Echo's shoulders twitched in a spidery spasm. She glanced at a portly museum guard who also was eyeing the woman in black.

"Who is *that*?"

The guard shrugged. "Beats me. She's been around since noon. I think she's from the gallery in New York." He looked up at the Ransome portrait. "His gallery. You know how fussy these painters get about their placement in shows."

"Uh-huh. Doesn't she talk?"

"Not to me," the guard said.

The limousine Stefan had hired for the day was parked in a taxi zone outside the Highbridge. Stefan was leaning on the limo getting track updates on his BlackBerry. There was a *Racing Form* lying on the trunk.

He put away his BlackBerry with a surly expression when Echo approached. My Little Margie must have finished out of the money.

"So the spell is finally broken. I suppose we could have arranged for a cot to be moved in for the night."

"Thanks for being so patient with me, Stefan."

They lingered on the sidewalk, enjoying balmy weather. New York had been a stewpot when they'd left that morning.

"It's all hype, you know," Stefan said, looking up at the gold and glass façade of the Cesar Pelli–designed building. "The Ransomes of the art world excel at manipulation. The scarcity of his work only makes it more desirable to the *Vulturati*."

"No, I think it's the quality that's rare, Stefan. Courbet, Bonnard, he shares their sense of . . . call it a divine melancholy."

"'Divine melancholy.' Nicely put. I must remember to filch that one for my *Art News* column. Where are we having dinner tonight? You *did* remember to make reservations? Echo?"

Echo was looking past him at the Woman in Black, who had walked out of the museum and was headed for a taxi.

Stefan turned. "Who, or what, is that?"

"I don't know. I saw her in the gallery. Caught her staring at me." Uncanny, Echo thought, how much she resembled the black queen on Echo's chessboard at home.

"Apparently, from her lack of interest now, you rebuffed her."

Echo shook her head. "No. Actually she never said a word. Dinner? Stefan, I'm sorry. You're set at Legal's with the Bronwyns for eight-thirty. But I have to get back to New York. I thought I told you. Engagement party tonight. Peter's sister."

"Which sister? There seems to be a multitude."

"Siobhan. The last one to go."

"Not that huge, clumsy girl with the awful bangs?"

"Hush. She's really very sweet."

"Now that Peter has earned his gold shield, am I correct to assume the next engagement party will be yours?"

"Yes. As soon as we all recover from this one."

Stefan looked deeply aggrieved. "Echo, have you any idea what child-bearing will do to your lovely complexion?"

Echo looked at her watch and smiled apologetically.

"I can just make the four o'clock Acela."

"Well, then. Get in."

Echo was preoccupied with answering e-mail during their short trip up Memorial Drive and across the river to Boston's North Station.

She didn't notice that the taxi the Woman in Black had claimed was behind them all the way.

> Hi Mom
> Busy day. I had to hustle but I made the four o'clock train. I'll probably go straight to Queens from the station so won't be home until after midnight. Scored points with the boss today; tell you all about it at breakfast. Called Uncle Rory at the Home, but the Sister on his floor told me he probably wouldn't know who I was . . .

The Acela was rolling quietly through a tunnel on its way out of the city. In her coach seat Echo, riding backwards, looked up from the laptop she'd spent too much time with today. Her vision was blurry, the back of her neck was stiff and she had a headache. She looked at her reflection in the window, which disappeared as the train emerged into bright sunlight. She winced and closed her laptop after sending the message to her mother, rummaged in her soft-leather shoulder bag for Advil and swallowed three with sips of designer water. Then she closed her eyes and rubbed her temples.

When she looked up again she saw the Woman in Black, looking solemnly at her before she opened the vestibule door and disappeared in the direction of the club car.

The look didn't mean anything. The fact that they were on the same train didn't mean anything either. Even so for a good part of the trip to New York, while Echo tried to nap, she couldn't get the woman out of her mind.

Two

After getting eight stitches to close the cut near his left eye at the hospital in Flatbush, Peter O'Neill's partner Ray Scalla drove him to the 7-5 station house, where Pete retrieved his car and continued home to Bayside, Queens. By then he'd put in a twelve-hour day, but he had a couple of line-of-duty off days coming.

The engagement party for his sister Siobhan was roaring along by the time he got to the three-story brick-and-shingle house on

Compton Place, and he had to hunt for a parking space a block and a half away. Walked back to the house swapping smack with neighborhood kids on their bikes and skateboards. The left eye felt swollen. He needed an ice bag, but a cold beer would be the first order of business. Make it two beers.

The O'Neill house was lit up to the roof line. Floodlights illuminated half a dozen guys playing a scuffling game of basketball in the driveway. Peter was related one way or another to all of them, and to everyone on the teeming porch.

His brother Tommy, a freshman at Hofstra on a football scholarship, fished in a tub of cracked ice and pitched Pete a twelve-ounce Rolling Rock as he walked up to the stoop. Kids with Gameboys cluttered the steps. His sister Kathleen, just turned thirty, was barefoot on the front lawn, gently rocking to sleep an infant on her shoulder. She gave Pete a kiss and frowned at the patched eye.

"So when's number four due?"

"You mean number five," Kathleen said. "October ninth, Petey."

"Guess I got behind on the count when I was workin' undercover." Pete popped the tab top on the icy Rock and drank half of it while he watched some of the half-court action on the driveway. He laughed. "Hey, Kath. Tell your old man to give up pasta or give up hoops."

Brother Tommy came down to the walk and put an arm around him. He was a linebacker, three inches taller than the five-eleven Peter but no wider in the shoulders. Big shoulders were a family hallmark, unfortunately for the women.

One of the basketball players got stuffed driving for a layup, and they both laughed.

"Hey, Vito!" Pete called. "Come on hard or keep it in your pants!" He finished off the beer and crushed the can. "Echo make it back from Boston?" he asked Tommy.

"She's inside. Nice shiner."

Pete said ruefully, "My collar give it to me."

"Too bad they don't hand out Purple Hearts downtown."

"Yeah, but they'll throw you a swell funeral," Pete said, forgetting momentarily what a remark like that meant to the women in a family of cops. Kathleen set him straight with a stinging slap to the back of his head. Then she crossed herself.

"God and Blessed Mother! Don't you ever say that again, Petey!"

Like the rest of the house, the kitchen was full of people helping themselves to beer and food. Peter gave his mom a kiss and looked at Echo, who was taking a pan of hors d'oeuvres out of the oven with insulated mittens. She was moist from the heat at her temples and under her eyes. She gave Pete, or the butterfly patches above his eye, a look and sat him down on a stool near the door to the back porch for a closer appraisal. Pete's middle sister Jessie handed him a bulging hero.

"Little bitty girl," Pete said. "One of those wiry types, you know? She was on crank and I don't know what else."

"Just missed your eye," Echo said, tight-lipped.

"Live and learn." Peter bit into his sandwich.

"You get a tetanus booster?"

"Sure. How was your day?"

"I did great," Echo said, still finding small ways to fuss over him: brushing his hair back from his forehead with the heel of one hand, dabbing at a drip of sauce on his chin with a napkin. "I deserve a raise."

"About time. How's your mom?"

"Didn't have a real good day, Julia said. Want another beer?"

"Makes you think I had one already?"

"Ha-ha," Echo said; she went out to the porch to fish the beer from the depths of the cooler. Peter's sister Siobhan, the bride-to-be, followed her unsteadily inside, back on her heels from an imaginary gale in her face. Her eyes not tracking well. She embraced Peter with a goofy smile.

"I'm so happy!"

"We're happy for you, Siobhan." At thirty-five she was the oldest of the seven O'Neill children, and the least well favored. Putting it mildly.

Her fiancé appeared in the doorway behind Siobhan. He was a head shorter, gap-toothed, had a bad haircut. A software salesman. Doing very well. He drove a Cadillac, had put a down payment on a condo in Vally Stream and was planning an expensive honeymoon cruise. The diamond on Siobhan's finger was a big one.

Peter saluted the fiancé with his can of beer. Siobhan straightened unsteadily and embraced Echo too, belching loudly.

"Oops. Get any on ya?"

"No, sweetie," Echo said, and passed her on to the fiancé, who chuckled and guided her through the kitchen to a bathroom. Peter shook his head.

"What they say about opposites."

"Yeah."

"Siobhan has a lot to learn. She still thinks 'fellatio' is an Italian opera."

"You mean it's not?" Echo said, wide-eyed. Then she patted his cheek. "Lay off. I love Siobhan. I love all your family."

Peter put the arm on his fourteen-year-old brother Casey as he came inside from the porch, and crushed him affectionately.

"Even the retards?"

"Get outta here," Casey said, fighting him off.

"Casey's no retard, he's a lover," Echo said. "Gimme kiss, Case."

"No way!" But Echo had him grinning.

"Don't waste those on that little fart," Pete said.

Casey looked him over. "Man, you're gonna have a shiner."

"I know." Pete looked casually at Echo and put his sandwich down. "It's a sweatbox in here. Why don't we go upstairs a little while?"

Casey smiled wisely at them. "Uh-uh. Aunt Pegeen put the twins to sleep on your bed." He waited for the look of frustration in Peter's eyes before he said, "But I could let you use my room if you guys want to make out. Twenty bucks for an hour sound okay?"

"Sounds like you think I'm a hooker," Echo said to Casey. Staring him down. Casey's shoulders dropped; he looked away uneasily.

"I didn't mean—"

"Now you got a good reason not to skip confession again this week," Peter said. Glancing at Echo, and noticing how tired she looked, having lost her grip on her upbeat mood.

Driving Echo back to the city, Pete said, "I just keep goin' round and round with the numbers, like a dog chasin' its tail. You know?"

"Same here."

"Jesus, I'm twenty-six, ought to have my own place already instead of living home."

"*Our* own place. Trying to save anything these days. The taxes.

Both of us still paying off college loans. Forty thousand each. My mom sick. Your mom was sick—"

"We both got good jobs. The money'll come together. But we'll need another year."

Peter exited from the Queensboro Bridge and took First uptown. They were nearing 78th when Echo said, "A year. How bad can that be?" Her tone of voice said, *miserable.*

They waited on the light at 78th, looking at each other as if they were about to be cast into separate dungeons.

"Gotta tell you, Echo. I'm just goin' nuts. You know."

"I know."

"It hasn't been easy for you either. Couple close calls, huh?" He smiled ruefully.

She crossed her arms as if he'd issued a warning. "Yeah."

"You know what I'm sayin". We are gonna be married. No doubt about that. Is there?"

"No."

"So—how big a deal is it, really? An act of contrition—"

"Pete, I'm not happy being probably the only twenty-two-year-old virgin on the face of the earth. But confession's not the same as getting a ticket fixed. You know how I was brought up. It's *God's law.* That has to mean something, or none of it does."

The light changed. Peter drove two blocks and parked by a fire hydrant a few doors down from Echo's brownstone.

"Both your parents were of the cloth," he said. "They renounced their vows and they made you. Made you for me. I can't believe God thought that was a sin."

Blue and unhappy, Echo sank lower in her seat, arms still crossed, over her breasts and her crucifix.

"I love you so much. And I swear to Him, I'll always take care of you."

After a long silence Echo said, "I know. What do you want me to do, Pete?"

"Has to be your call."

She sighed. "No motels. I feel cheap that way, I can't help myself. Just know it wouldn't work."

"There's this buddy of mine at the squad, he was in my year at the Academy, Frank Ringer. Like maybe you met him at the K of C picnic in July?"

"Oh. Yeah. Got a twitch in one eye? Really ripped, though."

"Right. Frank Ringer. Well, his uncle's got a place out on the Island. Way out, past Riverhead on Peconic Bay I think."

"Uh-huh."

"Frank's uncle travels a lot. Frank says he could make arrangements for us to go out there, maybe this weekend—"

"So you and Frank been having these discussions about our sex life?"

"Nothing like that. I just mentioned we'd both like to get off somewhere for some R and R, that's all."

"Uh-huh."

"So in exchange for the favor I'd cover Frank's security job for him sometime. Echo?"

"Guess I'd better be getting on up, see how mom is. Might be a long night; you know, I read to her when she can't—"

"So what do I tell Frank?"

Echo hesitated after she opened the door.

"This weekend sounds okay," she said. "Does his uncle have a boat?"

Three A.M. and John Leland Ransome, the painter, was up and prowling barefoot around his apartment at the Pierre Hotel on Fifth Avenue. The doors to his terrace were open; the sounds of the city's streets had dwindled to the occasional swish of cabs or a bus seven stories below. There was lightning in the west, a plume of yellow-tinged dark clouds over New Jersey or the Hudson. Some rain moving into Manhattan, stirring the air ahead of it. A light wind that felt good on his face.

Ransome had a woman on his mind. Not unusual; his life and career were dedicated to capturing the essence of a very few uniquely stunning creatures. But this was someone he'd never seen or heard of until approximately eight o'clock of the night before. And the few photos he'd seen, taken with a phonecam, hadn't revealed nearly enough of Echo Halloran to register her so strongly on his imagination.

Anyway, it was too soon, he told himself. Better just to forget this one, the potential he'd glimpsed. His new show, the first in four years, was being mounted at his gallery. Five paintings only, his usual output after as much as eighteen painful months of work. He wouldn't be ready to pick up a brush for at least that length of time. If ever again.

And half the world's population was women. More or less. A small but dependable percentage of them physically ravishing.

But this one was a painter herself, which intrigued him more than the one good shot of her he'd seen, taken on the train, Echo sitting back in her seat with her eyes closed, unaware that she was being photographed.

Ransome wondered if she had promise as a painter. But he could easily find out.

He lingered on the terrace until the first big drops of rain fell. He went inside, closing the doors, walked down a marble hall to the room in which Taja, wearing black silk lounging pajamas, was watching *Singin' in the Rain* on DVD. Another insomniac. She saw his reflection on the plasma screen and looked around. There was a hint of a contrite wince in his smile.

"I'll want more photos," he said. "Complete background check, of course. And order a car for tomorrow. I'd like to observe her myself."

Taja nodded, drew on a cigarette and returned her attention to the movie. Donald O'Connor falling over a sofa. She didn't smile. Taja never smiled at anything.

Three

It rained all day Thursday; by six-thirty the clouds over Manhattan were parting for last glimpses of washed-out blue; canyon walls of geometric glass gave back the brassy sunset. Echo was able to walk the four blocks from her Life Studies class to the 14th Street IRT station without an umbrella. She was carrying her portfolio in addition to a shoulder tote and computer, having gone directly from her office at Gilbard's to class.

The uptown express platform was jammed, the atmosphere underground thick and fetid. Obviously there hadn't been a train for a while. There were unintelligible explanations or announcements on the P.A. Someone played a violin with heroic zeal. Echo edged her way up the platform to find breathing room where the first car would stop when the train got there.

Half a dozen Hispanic boys were scuffling, cutting up; a couple of the older ones gave her the eye. One of them, whom she took in at a glance, looked like trouble. Tats and piercings. Full of himself.

A child of the urban jungle, Echo was skilled at minding her own business, building walls around herself when she was forced to linger in potentially bad company.

She pinned her bulky portfolio between her knees while she retrieved a half-full bottle of water from her tote. She was jostled from behind by a fat woman laden with shopping bags and almost lost her balance. The zipper on her portfolio had been broken for a while. A few drawings spilled out. Echo grimaced, nodded at the woman's brusque apology and tried to gather up her life studies before someone else stepped on them.

One of the younger Hispanic kids, wearing a do-rag and a Knicks jersey, came over to give her a hand. He picked up a charcoal sketch half-soaked in a puddle of water. Echo's problem had attracted the attention of all the boys.

The one she'd had misgivings about snatched the drawing from the hand of the Knicks fan and looked it over. A male nude. He showed it around, grinning. Then backed off when Echo held out a hand, silently asking for the return of her drawing. She heard the uptown express coming.

The boy looked at her. He wore his Cholo shirt unbuttoned to his navel.

"Who's this guy? Your boyfriend?"

"Give me a break, will you? I've had a long day, I'm tired, and I don't want to miss my train."

The boy pointed to the drawing and said, "Man, I seen a bigger tool on a gerbil."

They all laughed as they gathered around, reinforcing him.

"No," Echo said. "*My* boyfriend is on the cops, and I can arrange for you to meet him."

That provoked whistles, snorts, and jeers. Echo looked around at the slowing express train, and back at the boy who was hanging onto her drawing. Pretending to be an art critic.

"Hey, you're good, you know that?"

"Yes, I know."

"You want to do me, I can *arrange* the time." He grinned around at his buddies, one of whom said, "*Draw* you."

"Yeah, man. That's what I said." He feigned confusion. "That ain't what I said?" He looked at Echo and shrugged magnanimously. "So first you draw me, then you can *do* me."

Echo said, "Listen, you fucking little idiot, I want my drawing *now*, or you'll be in shit up to your bull ring."

The express screeched to a stop behind her. A local was also approaching on the inside track. The boy made a show of being astonished by her threat. As if he were trembling in fright, his hands jerked and the drawing tore nearly in half.

"Oh, sorry, man. Now I guess you need to get yourself another naked guy." He finished ripping her drawing.

Echo, losing it, dropped her computer case and hooked a left at his jaw. She was quick on her feet; it just missed. The *cholo* danced away with the halves of the drawing in each hand, and bumped into a woman walking the yellow platform line of the local track as if she were a ballet dancer. The headlight of the train behind her winked on the slim blade of a knife in her right hand.

With her left hand she took hold of the boy by his bunchy testicles and lifted him up on his toes until they were at eye level.

The Woman in Black stared at him, and the point of the knife was between two of his exposed ribs. Echo's throat dried up. She had no doubt the woman would cut him if he didn't behave. The boy's mouth was open, but he could have screamed without being heard as the train thundered in a couple of feet away from them.

The woman cast a long look at Echo, then nodded curtly toward the express.

The kid in the Knicks jersey picked up Echo's computer and shoved it at her as if he suspected that she too might have a blade. The doors of the local opened and there was a surge of humanity across the platform to the parked express. Echo let herself be carried along with it, looking back once as she boarded. Another glimpse of the Woman in Black, still holding the *cholo* helpless, getting a few looks but no interference. Echo's pulses throbbed. The woman was like a walking superstition, with a temperament as dark and lurking as paranoia.

Who was she? And why, Echo wondered as the doors closed, does she keep showing up in *my* life?

She rode standing up to 86th in the jam of commuters, her face expressionless, presenting a calm front but inside just a blur, like a traumatized bird trying to escape through a sealed window.

Echo didn't say anything to Peter about the Woman in Black until Friday evening, when they were slogging along in oppressive traffic on the 495 eastbound, on their way to Mattituck and the cozy weekend they'd planned at the summer house of Frank Ringer's uncle.

"No idea who she is?" Peter said. "You're sure you don't know her from somewhere?"

"Listen, she's the kind, see her once, you never forget her. I'm talking spooky."

"She pulled a knife in the subway? Switchblade?"

"Maybe. I don't know much about knives. It was the look in her eyes, man. That *cholo* must've went in his pants." Echo smiled slightly, then her expression turned glum. "So, the first couple times, okay. Coincidence. A third time in the same week, uh-uh, I don't buy it. She must've been following me around." Echo shrugged again, and her shoulders stayed tight. "I didn't sleep so good last night, Pete."

"You ever see her again, make it your business to call me right away."

"I wonder if maybe I should—"

"*No*. Stay away from her. Don't try to talk to her."

"You're thinking she could be some sort of psycho?"

"That's New York. Ten people go by in the street, one or two out of the ten, something's gonna be seriously wrong with them mentally."

"Great. Now I'm scared."

Peter put an arm around her.

"You just let me handle this. Whatever it is."

"Engine's overheating." Echo observed.

"Yeah. Fucking traffic. Weekend, it'll be like this until ten o'clock. Might as well get off, get something to eat."

The cottage that had been lent to them for the weekend wasn't impressive in the headlights of Peter's car; it looked as if Frank Ringer's uncle had built it on weekends using materials taken from various construction or demolition sites. Mismatched windows, missing clapboards, a stone chimney on one side that obviously was out of plumb; the place had all the eye appeal of a bad scab.

"Probably charming inside," Echo said, determined to be upbeat about a slow start to their intimate weekend.

Inside the small rooms smelled of mildew from a leaky roof. There were curbsides in Manhattan that were better furnished on trash pickup days.

"Guess it's kind of like men only out here," Pete said, not concealing his disbelief. "I'll open a couple of windows."

"Do you think we could clean it up some?" Echo said.

Peter took another look around.

"More like burn it down and start over."

"It's such a beautiful little cove."

There was so much dismay in her face it started him laughing. He put an arm around her, guided her outside, and locked the door behind them.

"Live and learn," he said.

"Your house or mine?" Echo said.

"Bayside's closest."

The O'Neill house in Bayside didn't work out, either; overrun with relatives. At a few minutes past ten Echo unlocked the door of the Yorktown apartment where she lived with her mother and Aunt Julia, from her late father's side of the family. She looked at Peter, sighed, kissed him.

Rosemay and Julia were playing Scrabble at the dining room table when Echo walked in with Peter. She had left her weekend luggage in the hall by her bedroom door.

"This is a grand surprise," Rosemay said. "Echo, I thought you were stayin' over in Queens."

Echo cleared her throat and shrugged, letting Peter handle this one.

Peter said, "My uncle Dennis, from Philly? Blew into town with his six kids. Our house looks like a day camp. They been redoin' the walls with grape jelly." He bent over Rosemay, putting his arms around her. "How're you, Rosemay?"

Rosemay was wearing lounging pajamas and a green eyeshade.

There were three support pillows in the chair she occupied, and one under her slippered feet.

"A little fatigued, I must say."

Julia was a roly-poly woman who wore thick eyeglasses. "Spent most of the day writing," she said of Rosemay. "Talk to your ma about eating, Echo."

"Eat, mom. You promised."

"I had my soft-boiled egg with some tea. It was, oh, about five o'clock, wasn't it, Julia?"

"Soft-boiled eggs. Wants nought but her bit of egg."

"They go down easy," Rosemay said, massaging her throat. Words didn't come easily, at least at this hour of the night. But for Rosemay sleep was elusive as well.

"All that cholesterol," Peter chided.

Rosemay smiled. "Nothing to worry about. I already have one fatal disease."

"None of that," Peter said sternly.

"Go on, Petey. You say what is. At least my mind will be the last of me to go. Pull up some chairs, we'll all play."

The doorbell rang. Echo went to answer it.

Peter was arranging chairs around the table when he heard Echo unlock the door, then cry out.

"Peter!"

"Who is it, Echo?" Rosemay called, as Peter backtracked through the front room to the foyer. The door to the hall stood half open. Echo had backed away from the door and from the Woman in Black who was standing outside.

Peter took Echo by an elbow and flattened her against the wall behind the door, saying to the Woman in Black, "Excuse me, can I talk to you? I'm the police."

The Woman in Black looked at him for a couple of seconds, then reached into her purse as Peter filled the doorspace.

"Don't do that!"

The woman shook her head. She pulled something from her purse but Peter had a grip on her gloved wrist before her hand fully cleared. She raised her eyes to him but didn't resist. There was a white business card between her thumb and forefinger.

Still holding onto her wrist, Peter took the card from her with his left hand. Glanced at it. He felt Echo at his back, looking at the woman over his shoulder. The woman looked at Echo, looked back at Peter.

"What's going on?" Echo said, as Rosemay called again.

Peter let go of the Woman in Black, turned and handed Echo the card.

"Echo! Peter!"

"Everything's fine, mom," Echo said, studying the writing on the card in the dim foyer light.

Peter said to the Woman in Black, "Sorry I got a little rough. I heard about that knife you carry, is all."

This time it was Echo who moved Peter aside, opening the door wider.

"Peter, she can't—"

"Talk. I know." He didn't take his eyes off the woman in black. "You've got another card, tells me who you are?"

She nodded, glanced at her purse. Peter said, "Yeah, okay." This time the woman produced her calling card, which Echo took from her.

"Your name's Taja? Am I saying that right?"

The woman nodded formally.

"Taja what?"

She shrugged slightly, impatiently; as if it didn't matter.

"So I guess you know who *I* am. What did you want to see me about? Would you like to come in?"

"Echo—" Peter objected.

But the woman shook her head and indicated her purse again. She made an open-palm gesture, hand extended to Echo, slow enough so Peter wouldn't interpret it as hostile.

"You have something for me?" Echo said, baffled.

Another nod from Taja. She looked appraisingly at Peter, then returned to her purse and withdrew a cream-colored envelope the size of a wedding announcement.

Peter said, "Echo tells me you've been following her places. What's that about?"

Taja looked at the envelope in her hand as if it would answer all of their questions. Peter continued to size the woman up. She used cosmetics in almost theatrical quantities; that overload plus Botox, maybe, was enough to obscure any hint of age. She wore a flat-crowned hat and a long skirt with large fabric-covered buttons down one side. A scarlet puff of neckerchief was Taja's only concession to color. That, and the rose flush of her cheeks. Her eyes were almond-shaped, creaturely bold, intelligent. One thing about her, she didn't blink very often, which enhanced a certain robotic effect.

Echo took the envelope. Her name, handwritten, was on it. She smiled uncertainly at Taja, who simply looked away—something dismissive in her lack of expression, Peter thought.

"Just a minute. I'd like to ask you—"

The Woman in Black paused on her way to the stairs.

Echo said, "Pete? It's okay. Taja?"

Taja turned.

"I wanted to say—thank you. You know, for the subway, the other day?"

Taja, after a few moments, did something surprisingly out of character, considering her previous demeanor, the rigid formality. She responded to Echo with an emphatic thumbs-up before soundlessly disappearing down the stairs. Peter had the impression she'd enjoyed intimidating the *cholo* kid. Might have enjoyed herself even more if she'd used the knife on him.

Echo had a hand on his arm, sensing his desire to follow the Woman in Black.

"Let's see what this is," she said, of the envelope in her other hand.

"She looks Latin to me, what d'you think?" Peter said to Echo as they returned to the front room. Rosemay and Julia began talking at the same time, wanting to know who was at the door. "Messenger," Peter said to them, and looked out the windows facing the street.

Echo, preoccupied, said, "You're the detective." She looked for a letter opener on Rosemay's writing table.

"Jesus above," Julia said. "Sounded like a ruckus. I was reachin' for me heart pills."

Peter saw the Woman in Black get into a waiting limousine.

"Travels first class, whoever she is." He caught the license plate number as the limo pulled away, jotted it down on the inside of his left wrist with a ballpoint pen.

Rosemay and Julia were watching Echo as she slit the envelope open.

"What is it, dear, an invitation?"

"Looks like one."

"Now, who's getting married this time?" Julia said. "Seems like you've been to half a dozen weddings already this year."

"No, it's—" Echo's throat seemed to close up on her. She sat down slowly on one of a pair of matched love seats.

"Good news or bad?" Peter said, adjusting the blinds over the window.

"My . . . God!"

"Echo!" Rosemay said, mildly alarmed by her expression.

"This is so . . . utterly . . . fantastic!"

Peter crossed the room and took the invitation from her.

"But why me?" Echo said.

"Part of your job, isn't it? Going to these shows? What's so special about this one?"

"Because it's John Leland Ransome. And it's the event of the year. You're invited."

"I see that. 'Guest.' Real personal. I'm overwhelmed. Let's play." He took out his cell phone. "After I run a plate."

Echo wasn't paying attention to him. She had taken the invitation back and was staring at it as if she were afraid the ink might disappear.

Stefan Konine's reaction was predictable when Echo showed him the invitation. He pouted.

"Not to disparage your good fortune but, yes, why you? If I wasn't aware of your high moral standards—"

Echo said serenely, "Don't say it, Stefan."

Stefan began to look over a contract that one of his assistants had silently slipped onto his desk. He picked up his pen.

"I confess that it took me literally *weeks* to finagle my way onto the guest list. And I'm not just anyone's old hand job in this town."

"I thought you didn't like Ransome. Something about art on a sailor's—"

Stefan slashed through an entire paragraph on the contract and looked up at Echo.

"I don't worship the man, but I adore the event. Don't you have work to do?"

"I'm not strong on the pre-Raphaelites, but I called around. There's a definite lack of viability in today's market."

"Call it what it is, an Arctic chill. Tell the appraiser for the Chandler estate that he might do better on one of those auction-junkie internet sites." Stefan performed strong-arm surgery on another page of the contract. "You will want to appear in something singularly ravishing for the Ransome do. All of us at Gilbard's can only benefit from your reflected glory."

"May I put the gown on my expense account?"

"Of course not."

Echo winced slightly.

"But perhaps," Stefan said, twiddling his gold pen, "we can do something about that raise you've been whining about for weeks."

Four

Cyrus Mellichamp's personal quarters took up the fourth floor of his gallery on East 58th Street. They were an example of what wealth and unerring taste could accomplish. So was Cy himself. He not only looked pampered by the best tailors, dieticians, physical therapists, and cosmeticians, he looked as if he truly deserved it.

John Ransome's fortune was to the tenth power of what Cy Mellichamp had managed to acquire as a kingpin of the New York art world, but on the night of the gala dedicated to himself and his new paintings, which he had no plans to attend, he was casually dressed. Tennis sweater, khakis, loafers. No socks. While the Mellichamp Gallery's guests were drinking Moët and Chandon below, Ransome sipped beer and watched the party on several TV monitors in Cy's study.

There was no sound, but thanks to the gallery owner's expensive surveillance system, it was possible, if he wanted, to tune in on nearly every conversation on the first two floors of the gallery, swarming with media—annointed superstars. Name a profession with glitter appeal, there was an icon, a living legend, or a superstar in attendance.

Cy Mellichamp had coaxed one of his very close friends, from a list that ran in the high hundreds, to prepare dinner for Ransome and his guests for the evening, both of whom were still unaware they'd been invited.

"John," Cy said, "Monsieur Rapaou wanted to know if there was a special dish you'd like added to his menu for the evening."

"Why don't we just scrap the menu and have cheeseburgers," Ransome said.

"Oh my God," Cy said, after a shocked intake of breath. "Scrap—? John, Monsieur Rapaou is one of the most honored chefs on four continents."

"Then he ought to be able to make a damn fine cheeseburger."

"Johnnn—"

"We're having dinner with a couple of kids. Basically. And I want them to be at ease, not worrying about what fork to use."

A dozen of the gallery's guests were being admitted at one time to the room in which the Ransome exhibition was mounted. To avoid damaged egos, the order in which they were being permitted to view the new Ransomes had been chosen impartially by lot. Except for Echo, Peter, and Stefan Konine, arbitrarily assigned to the second group. Ransome, for all of his indolence at his own party, was impatient to get on with his prime objective of the evening.

All of the new paintings featured the same model: a young black woman with nearly waist-length hair. She was, of course, smashing, with the beguiling quality that differentiates mere looks from classic beauty.

Two canvases, unframed, were wall-mounted. The other three, on easels, were only about three feet square. A hallmark of all Ransome's work were the wildly primeval, ominous or threatening landscapes in which his models existed aloofly.

Two minutes after they entered the room Peter began to fidget, glancing at Echo, who seemed lost in contemplation.

"I don't get it."

Echo said in a low firm tone, "Peter."

"What is it, like High Mass, I can't talk?"

"Just—keep it down, please."

"Five paintings?" Peter said, lowering his voice. "That's what all the glitz is about? The movie stars? Guy that plays James Bond is here, did you notice?"

"He only does five paintings at a time. Every three years."

"Slow, huh?"

"Painstaking." Peter could hear her breathing, a sigh of rapture. "The way he uses light."

"You've been staring at that one for—"

"Go away."

Peter shrugged and joined Stefan, who was less absorbed.

"Does Ransome get paid by the square yard?"

"The square inch, more likely. It takes seven figures just to buy into the playoff round. And I'm told there are already more than four hundred prospective buyers, the cachet-stricken."

"For five paintings? Echo, just keep painting. Forget about your day job."

Echo gave him a dire look for breaking her concentration. Peter grimaced and said to Stefan, "I think I've seen this model somewhere else. *Sports Illustrated*. Last year's swimsuit issue."

"Doubtful," Stefan said. "No one knows who Ransome's models are. None of them have appeared at the shows, or been publicized. Nor has the genius himself. He might be in our midst tonight, but I wouldn't recognize him. I've never seen a photo."

"You saying he's shy?"

"Or exceptionally shrewd."

Peter had been focusing on a nude study of the unknown black girl. Nothing left to the imagination. Raw sensual appeal. He looked around the small gallery, as if his powers of detection might reveal the artist to him. Instead who he saw was Taja, standing in a doorway, looking at him.

"Echo?"

She looked around at Peter with a frown, then saw Taja herself. When the Woman in Black had her attention she beckoned. Echo and Peter looked at each other.

"Maybe it's another special delivery," Peter said.

"I guess we ought to find out."

In the center of the gallery's atrium a small elevator in a glass shaft rose to Cy Mellichamp's penthouse suite. A good many people who considered themselves important watched Peter and Echo rise to the fourth floor with Taja. Stefan took in some bemused and outright envious speculation.

A super-socialite complained, "I've spent seventeen million with Cy, and *I've* never been invited to the penthouse. Who *are* they?"

"Does Ransome have children?"

"Who knows?"

A talk-show host with a sneaky leer and a hard-drive's capacity for gossip said, "The dark one, my dear, is John Ransome's mistress. He abuses her terribly. So I've been told."

"Or perhaps it's the other way around," Stefan said, feeling a flutter of distress in his stomach that had nothing to do with the quantity of hors d'oeuvres he'd put away. Something was up, obviously it involved Echo, and even more obviously it was none of his business. Yet his impression, as he watched Echo step off the elevator and vanish into Cy's sanctum, was of a lovely doe being deftly separated from a herd of deer.

Taja ushered Echo and Peter into Cy Mellichamp's presence and closed the door to the lush sitting room, a gallery in itself that was devoted largely to French Impressionists. A very large room with a high tray ceiling. French doors opened onto a small terrace where there was a candlelit table set for three and two full-dress butlers in attendance.

"Miss Halloran, Mr. O'Neill! I'm Cyrus Mellichamp. Wonderful that you could be here tonight. I hope you're enjoying yourselves."

He offered his hand to Echo, and a discreet kiss to one cheek, somewhere between businesslike and avuncular, Peter noted. He shook hands with the man and they were eye to eye, Cy with a pleasant smile but no curiosity.

"We're honored, Mr. Mellichamp," Echo said.

"May I call you Echo?"

"Yes, of course."

"What do you think of the new Ransomes, Echo?"

"Well, I think they're—magnificent. I've always loved his work."

"He will be very pleased to hear that."

"Why?" Peter said.

They both looked at him. Peter had, deliberately, his cop face on. Echo didn't appreciate that.

"This is a big night for Mr. Ransome. Isn't it? I'm surprised he's not here."

Cy said smoothly, "But he is here, Peter."

Pete spread his hands and smiled inquiringly as Echo's expression soured.

"It's only that John has never cared to be the center of attention. He wants the focus to be solely on his work. But let John tell you himself. He's wanted very much to meet you both."

"Why?" Peter said.

"*Peter*," Echo said grimly.

"Well, it's a fair question," Peter said, looking at Cy Mellichamp, who wore little gold tennis racket cuff links. A fair question, but not a lob. Straight down the alley, no time for footwork, spin on the return.

Cy blinked and his smile got bigger. "Of course it is. Would you mind coming with me? Just in the other room there, my study. Something we would like for you to see."

"You and Mr. Ransome," Peter said.

"Why, yes."

He offered Echo his arm. She gave Peter a swift dreadful look as she turned her back on him. Peter simmered for a couple of moments, took a breath and followed them.

The study was nearly dark. Peter was immediately interested in the array of security monitors, including three affording different angles on the small gallery where the newest Ransome paintings were on display. Where he had been with Echo a few minutes ago. The idea that they'd been watched from this room, maybe by Ransome himself, caused Peter to chew his lower lip. No reason Cy Mellichamp shouldn't have the best possible surveillance equipment to protect millions of dollars' worth of property. But so far none of this—Taja following Echo around town, the special invitations to Ransome's showing—added up, and Peter was more than ready to cut to the chase.

There was a draped, spotlighted easel to one side of Mellichamp's desk. The dealer walked Echo to it, smiling, and invited her to remove the drape.

"It's a work in progress, of course. John would be the first to say it doesn't do his subject justice."

Echo hesitated, then carefully uncovered the canvas, which revealed an incomplete study of—Echo Halloran.

Jesus, Peter thought, growing tense for no good reason. Even though what there was of her on the canvas looked great.

"Peter! Look at this!"

"I'm looking," Peter said, then turned, aware that someone had come into the room behind them.

"No, it doesn't do you justice," John Ransome said. "It's a beginning, that's all." He put out a hand to Peter. "Congratulations on your promotion to detective."

"Thanks," Peter said, testing Ransome's grip with no change of expression.

Ransome smiled slightly. "I understand your paternal grandfather was the third most-decorated officer in the history of the New York City police force."

"That's right." Cy Mellichamp had blue-ribbon charm and social graces and the inward chilliness of a shark cruising behind the glass of a seaquarium tank. John Ransome looked at Peter as if every detail of his face were important to recall at some later time. He held his grip longer than most men, but not too long. He was an inch taller than Peter, with a thick head of razor-cut hair silver over the ears, a square jawline softening with age, deep folds at the corners of a sensual mouth. He talked through his nose, yet the effect was sonorous, softly pleasing, as if his nose were lined with velvet. His dark eyes didn't veer from Peter's mildly contentious gaze. They were the eyes of a man who had fought battles, won only some of them. They wanted to tell you more than his heart could let go of. And that, Peter divined in a few moments of hand-to-hand contact with the man, was the major source of his appeal.

Having made Peter feel a little more at home Ransome turned his attention again to Echo.

"I had only some photographs," he said of the impressionistic portrait. "So much was missing. Until now. And now that I'm finally meeting you—I see how very much I've missed."

By candlelight and starlight they had cheeseburgers and fries on the terrace. And they *were* damn good cheeseburgers. So was the beer. Peter concentrated on the beer because he didn't like eating when something was eating him. Probably Echo's star-struck expression. As for John Leland Ransome—there was just something about aging yuppies (never mind the aura of the famous and reclusive artist) who didn't wear socks with their loafers that went against Peter's Irish grain.

Otherwise maybe it wasn't so hard to like the guy. Until it became obvious that Ransome or someone else had done a thorough job of prying into Echo's life and family relations. Now hold on, just a damn minute.

"Your name is given as Mary Catherine on your birth and baptismal certificates. Where did 'Echo' come from?"

"Oh—well—I was talking a blue streak at eighteen months. Repeated everything I heard. My father would look at me and say, 'Is there a little echo in here?'"

"Your father was a Jesuit, I understand."

"Yes. That was his—vocation, until he met my mother."

"Who was teaching medieval history at Fordham?"

"Yes, she was."

"Now retired because of her illness. Is she still working on her biography of Bernard of Clairvaux? I'd like to read it sometime. I'm a student of history myself."

Peter allowed his beer glass to be filled for a fourth time. Echo gave him a vexed look as if to say, *Are you here or are you not here?*

Ransome said, "I see the beer is to your liking. It's from an exceptional little brewery in Dortmund that's not widely known outside of Germany."

Peter said with an edge of hostility, "So you have it flown in by the keg, something like that?"

Ransome smiled. "Corner deli. Three bucks a pop."

Peter shifted in his seat. The lace collar of his tux was irritating his neck. "Mr. Ransome—mind if I ask you something?"

"If you'll call me John."

"Okay—John—what I'd like to know is, why all the detective work? I mean, you seem to know a h— a lot about Echo. Almost an invasion of her privacy, seems to me."

Echo looked as if she would gladly have kicked him, if her gown hadn't been so long. She smiled a tight apology to Ransome, but Peter had the feeling she was curious too, in spite of the hero-worship.

Ransome took the accusation seriously, with a hint of contrition in his downcast eyes.

"I understand how that must appear to you. It's the nature of detective work, of course, to interpret my curiosity about Echo as suspicious or possibly predatory behavior. But if Echo and I are going to spend a year together—"

"What?" Peter said, and Echo almost repeated him before pressing a napkin to her lips and clearing her throat.

Ransome nodded his point home with the confidence of those who are born and bred in the winner's circle; someone, Peter thought resentfully, who wouldn't break a sweat if his pants were on fire.

"—I find it helpful in my work as an artist," Ransome continued, "if there are other areas of compatibility with my subjects. I like good conversation. I've never had a subject who wasn't well read and articulate." He smiled graciously at Echo. "Although I'm afraid that I've tended to monopolize our table-talk tonight." He shifted his eyes to Peter. "And Echo is also a painter of promise. I find that attractive as well."

Echo said incredulously, "Excuse me, I fell off at that last turn."

"Did you?" Ransome said.

But he kept his gaze on Peter, who had the look of a man being cunningly outplayed in a game without a rule book.

With the party over, the gallery emptied and cleanup crews at work, John Ransome conducted a personal tour of his latest work while Cy Mellichamp entertained Stefan Konine and a restless Peter, who had spent the better part of the last hour obviously wishing he were somewhere else. With Echo.

"Who is she?" Echo asked of Ransome's most recent model. "Or is that privileged information?"

"I'll trust your discretion. Her name is Silkie. Oddly enough, my previous subjects have remained anonymous at their own request. To keep the curious at arm's length. I suppose that during the year of our relationships each of them absorbed some of my own passion for—letting my work speak for itself."

"The year of your relationships? You don't see them any more?"

"No."

"Is that at your request?"

"I don't want it to seem to you as if I've had affairs that all turned out badly. That's far from the truth."

With her lack of expression Echo kept a guarded but subtle emotional distance from him.

"Silkie. The name describes her perfectly. Where is she from?"

"South Africa. Taja discovered her, on a train from Durban to Capetown."

"And Taja discovered me? She does get around."

"She's found all of my recent subjects—by 'recent' I mean the last twenty years." He smiled a bit painfully, reminded of how quickly the years passed, and how slowly he worked. "I very much depend on Taja's eye and her intuition. I depend on her loyalty. She was an artist herself, but she won't paint any more. In spite of my efforts to—inspire her."

"Why can't she speak?"

"Her tongue was cut out by agents of one of those starkly repressive Cold War governments. She wouldn't reveal the whereabouts of dissident members of her family. She was just thirteen at the time."

"Oh God, that's so awful!"

"I'm afraid it's the least of what was done to Taja. But she has always been like a—for want of a better word, *talisman* for me."

"Where did you meet her?"

"She was a sidewalk artist in Budapest, living down an alley with whores and thieves. I first saw her during one of my too-frequent sabbaticals in those times when I wasn't painting well. Nor painting very much at all. It's still difficult for me, nearly all of the time."

"Is that why you want me to pose for—a year?"

"I work for a year with my subject. Take another year to fully realize what we've begun together. Then—I suppose I just agonize for several months before finally packing my pictures off to Cy. And finally—comes the inevitable night."

He made a weary, sweeping gesture around the "Ransome Room," then brightened.

"I let them go. But this is the first occasion when I've had the good fortune of knowing my next subject and collaborator before my last paintings are out of our hands."

"I'm overwhelmed, really. That you would even consider me. I'm sorry that I have to say—it's out of the question. I can't do it."

Echo glanced past at him, to the doorway where Peter was standing around with the other two men, trying not to appear anxious and irritable.

"He's a fine young man," Ransome said with a smile.

"It isn't just Peter, I mean, being away from him for so long. That would be hard. But there's my mother."

"I understand. I didn't expect to convince you at our first meeting. It's getting late, and I know you must be tired."

"Am I going to see you again?" Echo said.

"That's for you to decide. But I need you, Mary Catherine. I hope to have another chance to convince you of that."

Neither Echo nor Peter were the kind to be reticent about getting into it when there was an imagined slight or a disagreement to be settled. They were city kids who had grown up scrappy and contentious if the occasion called for it.

Before Echo had slipped out of the new shoes that had hurt her feet for most of the night she was in Peter's face. They were driving up Park. Too fast, in her opinion. She told him to slow down.

"Or put your flasher on. You just barely missed that cabbie."

"I can get suspended for that," Peter said.

"Why are you so *angry*?"

"Said I was angry?"

"It was a wonderful evening, and now you're spoiling it for me. *Slow down.*"

"When a guy comes on to you like that Ransome—"

"Oh, please. Comes *on* to me? That is so—so—I don't want to say it."

"Go ahead. We say what is, remember?"

"Im-mature."

"Thank you. I'm immature because the guy is stuffing me in the face and I'm supposed to—"

"Peter, I never said I was going to do it! I've got my job to think about. My mom."

"So why did he say he hoped he'd be hearing from you soon? And you just smiled like, *sure*. I can hardly wait."

"You don't just blow somebody off who has gone out of his way to—"

"Why not?"

"Peter. Look. I was paid an incredible compliment tonight, by a painter who I think is—I mean, I can't be flattered? Come on."

Peter decided against racing a red light and settled back behind the wheel.

"You come on. You got something arranged with him?"

"For the last time, *no*." Her face was red, and she had chewed most of the gloss off her lower lip. In a softer tone she said, "You know it's not gonna happen, have some sense. The ball is over. Just let Cinderella enjoy her last moments, okay?—They're honking because the light is green, Petey."

Six blocks farther uptown Peter said, "Okay. I guess I—"

"Overreacted, what else is new? Sweetie, I love you."

"How much?"

"Infinity."

"Love you too. Oh God. Infinity."

Rosemay and Julia were asleep when Echo got home. She hung up the gown she'd worn to John Leland Ransome's show in her small closet, pulled on a sleep shirt and went to the bathroom to pee and brush her teeth. She spent an uncharacteristic amount of time studying her face in the mirror. It wasn't vanity; more as if she were doing an emotional self-portrait. She smiled wryly and shrugged and returned to her bedroom.

There she took down from a couple of shelves of cherished art books a slim oversized volume entitled *The Ransome Women*. She curled up against a bolster on her studio bed and turned on a reading lamp, spent an absorbed half hour looking over the thirty color plates and pages with areas of detail that illustrated aspects of the artist's technique.

She nodded off about three, then awoke with a start, the book sliding off her lap to the floor. Echo left it there, glanced at a landscape on her easel that she'd been working on for several weeks, wondering what John Ransome would think of it. Then she turned off the light and lay face-up in the dark, her rosary gripped unsaid in her fist. Thinking *what if, what if.*

But such a dramatic change in her life was solely in her imagination, or in a parallel universe. And *Cinderella* was a fairy tale.

Five

Peter O'Neill was working the day watch with his partner Ray Scalla, investigating a child-abuse complaint, when he was abruptly pulled off the job and told to report to the Commissioner's Office at One Police Plaza.

It was a breezy, unusually cool day in mid September. Pete's lieutenant couldn't give him a reason for what was officially described as a "request."

"Downtown, huh?" Scalla said. "Lunch with your old man?"

"Jesus, don't ask me," Peter said, embarrassed and uncomfortable.

The offices of the Police Commissioner for the City of New York were on the fourteenth floor. Peter walked into reception to find his father also waiting there. Corin O'Neill was wearing his dress uniform, with the two stars of a borough commander. Pete would have been slightly less surprised to see Elvis Presley.

"What's going on, pop?"

Corin O'Neill's smile was just a shade uneasy. "Beats me. Any problems on the job, Petey?"

"I'd've told you first."

"That you would."

The commissioner's executive assistant came out of her office. "Good morning, Peter. Glad you could make it."

As if he had a choice. Pete made an effort to look calm and slightly unimpressed. Corin said, "Well, Lucille. Let's find out how the wind's blowin' today."

"I just buzzed him. You can go right in, Commander."

But the commissioner opened his own door, greeting them heartily. His name was Frank Mullane.

"Well, Corin! Pleasure, as always. How is Kate? You know we've had a lot of concern."

"She's nearly a hundred percent now, and she'll be pleased you were askin'."

Mullane looked past him at Peter, then gave the young detective a partial embrace: handshake, bicep squeeze. "When's the last time I saw you, Peter? Rackin' threes for Cardinal Hayes?"

"I think so, yes, sir."

Mullane kept a hand on Peter's arm. "Come in, come in. So are you likin' the action in the 7–5?"

"That's what I wanted, sir."

As soon as they were inside the office, Lucille closing the door behind them, Peter saw John Ransome, wearing a suit and a tie today. It had been more than a month since the artist's show at the Mellichamp Gallery. Echo hadn't said another two words about Ransome; Peter had forgotten about him. Now he had a feeling that a brick was sinking to the pit of his stomach.

"Peter," Mullane said, "you alreadly know John Ransome." Pete's father gave him a quick look. "John, this is Corin O'Neill, Pete's father, one of the finest men I've had on my watch."

The older men shook hands. Peter just stared at Ransome.

"John's an artist, I suppose you know," Mullane said to Corin. "My brother owns one of his paintings. And John has been a big supporter of police charities since well before I came to the office. Now, he has a little request, and we're happy to oblige him." Mullane turned and winked at Peter. "Special assignment for you. John will explain."

"I'm sure he will," Peter said.

A chartered helicopter flew Peter and John Ransome to the White Plains airport, where a limousine picked them up. They traveled north through Westchester County on route 22 to Bedford. Estate country. They hadn't talked much on the helicopter, and on the drive through some of the most expensive real estate on the planet Ransome had phone calls to make. He was apologetic. Peter just nodded and looked out the window. Feeling that his time was being wasted. He was sure that, eventually, Ransome was going to bring up Echo. He hadn't forgotten about her, and in his own quiet way he was a determined guy.

Once Ransome was off the phone for good Peter decided to go on the offensive.

"You live up this way?"

"I was raised here," Ransome said. "Bedford Village."

"So that's where we're going, your house?"

"No. The house I grew up in is no longer there. I let go of all but a few acres after my parents died."

"Must've been worth a bundle."

"I didn't need the money."

"You were rich already, is that it?"

"Yes."

"So—this special assignment the commissioner was talking about? You need for somebody to handle a, what, situation for you? Somebody causing you a problem?"

"You're my only problem at the moment, Peter."

"Okay, well, maybe I guessed that. So this is going to be about Echo?"

Ransome smiled disarmingly. "Do you think I'm a rich guy out to steal your girl, Peter?"

"I'm not worried. Echo's not gonna be your—what do you call it, your 'subject?' You know that already."

"I think there is more of a personal dilemma than you're willing to admit. It affects both you and Echo."

Peter shrugged, but the back of his neck was heating up.

"I don't have any personal dilemmas, Mr. Ransome. That's for guys who have too much time and too much money on their hands. You know? So they try to amuse themselves messin' around in other people's lives, who would just as soon be left alone."

"Believe me. I have no intention of causing either of you the slightest—" He leaned forward and pointed out the window.

"This may interest you. One of my former subjects lives here."

They were passing an estate enclosed by what seemed to be a quarter mile of low stone walls. Peter glimpsed a manor house in a grove of trees, and a name on a stone gatepost. Van Lier.

"I understand she's quite happy. But we haven't been in touch since Anne finished sitting for me. That was many years ago."

"Looks to be plenty well-off," Peter said.

"I bought this property for her."

Peter looked at him with a skeptical turn to his lips.

"All of my former subjects have been well provided for—on the condition that they remain anonymous."

"Why?"

"Call it a quirk," Ransome said, with a smile that mocked Peter's skepticism. "Us rich guys have all these quirks." He turned his attention to the road ahead. "There used to be a fruit and vegetable stand along this road that had truly wonderul pears and apples at this season. I wonder—yes, there it is."

Peter was thirsty and the cider at the stand was well chilled. He walked around while Ransome was choosing apples. Among the afternoon's shoppers was a severely disabled young woman in a wheelchair that looked as if it cost almost as much as a sports car.

When Ransome returned to the limo he asked Peter, "Do you like it up here?"

"Fresh air's giving me a headache. Something is." He finished his cider. "How many have there been, Mr. Ransome? Your 'subjects,' I mean."

"Echo will be the eighth. If I'm able to persuade—"

"No *if.* You're wasting your time." Peter looked at the helpless young woman in the wheelchair as she was being power-lifted into a van.

"ALS is a devastating disease, Peter. How long before Echo's mother can no longer care for herself?"

"She's probably got two or three years."

"And after that?"

"No telling. She could live to be eighty. If you want to call it living."

"A terrible burden for Echo to have to bear. Let's be frank."

Peter stared at him, crushing his cup.

"Financially, neither of you will be able to handle the demands of Rosemay's illness. Not and have any sort of life for yourselves. But I can remove that burden."

Peter put the crushed paper cup in a trash can from twenty feet away, turning his back on Ransome.

"Did you fuck all of them?"

"You know I have no intention of answering a question like that, Peter. I will say this: there can never be any conflict, any—hidden tension between my subjects and myself that will adversely affect my work. The work is all that really matters."

Peter looked around at him as blandly as he could manage, but the sun was in his eyes and they smarted.

"Here's what matters to us. Echo and me are going to be married. We know there're problems. We've got it covered. We don't need your help. Was there anything else?"

"I'm happy that we've had this time to become acquainted. Would you mind one more stop before we head back to the city?"

"Take your time. I'm on the clock, pop said. So far it's easy money."

At the end of a winding uphill gravel drive bordered by stacked rock walls that obviously had been there for a century or longer, the limousine came to a pretty Cotswold-style stone cottage with slate roofs that overlooked a lake and a wildfowl sanctuary.

They parked on a cobblestone turnaround and got out. A caterer's van and a blue Land Rover stood near a separate garage.

"That's Connecticut a mile or so across the lake. In another month the view turns—well, as spectacular as a New England fall can be. In winter, of course, the lake is perfect for skating. Do you skate, Peter?"

"Street hockey," Peter said, taking a deep breath as he looked around. The sun was setting west of a small orchard behind the cottage; there was a good breeze across the hilltop. "So this is where you grew up?"

"No. The caretaker lived here. This cottage and about ten acres of woods and orchard are all that's left of the five hundred acres my family owned. All of it is now deeded public land. No one can build another house within three-quarters of a mile."

"Got it all to yourself? Well, this is definitely where I'd work if I were you. Plenty of peace and quiet."

"When I was much younger than you, just beginning to paint, the woods in all their form and color were like an appetite. Paraphrasing Wordsworth, a different kind of painter—poetry being the exotic pigment of language." He looked slowly around, eyes brimming with memory. "Almost six years since I was up here. Now I spend most of my time in Maine. But I recently had the cottage redecorated, and added an infinity pool on the lake side. Do you like it, Peter?"

"I'm impressed."

"Why don't you have a look around inside?"

"Looks like you've got company. Anyway, what's the point?"

"The point is, the cottage is yours, Peter. A wedding present for you and Echo."

Peter had hit a Trifecta two years ago at Aqueduct, which rewarded him with twenty-six hundred dollars. He'd been thrilled by the windfall. Now he was stunned. When his heartbeat was more or less under control he managed to say, "Wait a minute. You . . . can't do this."

"It's done, Peter. Echo is in the garden, I believe. Why don't you join her? I'll be along in a few minutes."

"Omigod, Peter, do you *believe* it?"

She was on the walk that separated garden and swimming pool, the breeze tugging her hair across her eyes. There were a lot of roses in the garden, he noticed. He felt, in spite of the joy he saw in Echo's face, a thorn in his heart. And it was a crushing effort for him just to breathe.

"Jesus, Echo—what've you done?"

"Peter—"

He walked through the garden toward her. Echo sat on a teakwood bench, hands folded in her lap, her pleasure dimmed to a defensive smile because she knew what was coming. He could almost see her stubborn streak surfacing, like a shark's fin in bloodied waters. Peter made an effort to keep his tone reasonable.

"Wedding present? That's china and toasters and things. How do we rate something like this? Nobody in his right mind would give away—"

"I haven't done anything," Echo said. "And it isn't ours. Not yet."

"I'm usually in my right mind," John Ransome said pleasantly. Peter stopped, halfway between Echo and Ransome, who was in the doorway to the garden, the setting sun making of his face a study in sanguinity. He held a large thick envelope in one hand. "Escrow to the cottage and grounds will close in one year, when Mary Catherine has completed her obligation to me." He smiled. "I don't expect an invitation to the wedding. But I wish you both a lifetime of happiness. I'll leave this inside for you to read." Nobody said anything for a few moments. They heard a helicopter. Ransome glanced up. "My ride is here," he said. "Make yourselves at home for as long as you like, and enjoy the dinner I've had prepared for you. My driver will take you back to the city when you're ready to go."

The night turned unseasonably chilly for mid September, temperature dropping into the low fifties by nine o'clock. One of the caterers built a fire on the hearth in the garden room while Echo and Peter were served after-dinner brandies. They sipped and read the contract John Ransome had left for Echo to sign, Peter passing pages to her as he finished reading.

A caterer looked in on them to say, "We'll be leaving in a few minutes, when we've finished cleaning up the kitchen."

"Thank you," Echo said. Peter didn't look up or say a word until he'd read the last page of the contract. Wind rattled one of the stained-glass casement windows in the garden room. Peter poured more brandy for himself, half a snifter's worth, as if it were cherry Coke. He drank all of it, got up and paced while Echo read by firelight, pushing her reading glasses up the bridge of her nose with a forefinger when they slipped.

When she had put the twelve pages in order, Peter fell back into the upholstered chair opposite Echo. They looked at each other. The fire crackled and sparked.

"I can't go up there to see you? You can't come home, unless it's an emergency? He doesn't want to paint you, he wants to own you!"

They heard the caterer's van drive away. The limo chauffeur had enjoyed his meal in a small apartment above the garage.

"I understand his reasons," Echo said. "He doesn't want me to be distracted."

"Is that what I am? A distraction?"

"Peter, you don't have a creative mind, so I really don't expect you to get it." Echo frowned; she knew when she sounded condescending. "It's only for a year. I can *do* this. Then we're set." She looked around the garden room, a possessive light in her eyes. "My Lord, this place, I've never even dreamed of— I want mom to see it! Then, if she approves—"

"What about my approval?" Peter said with a glower, drinking again.

Echo got up and stretched. She shuddered. In spite of the fire it was a little chilly in the room. He watched the rise and fall of her breasts with blurred yearning.

"I want that too."

"And you want this house."

"Are you going to sulk the rest of the evening?"

"Who's sulking?"

She took the glass from his hand, sat down in his lap and cradled her head on a wide shoulder, closing her eyes.

"With real estate in the sky, best we could hope for is a small house in, you know, Yonkers or Port Chester. This is *Bedford*."

Peter cupped the back of her head with his hand.

"He's got you wanting, instead of thinking. He's damn good at it. And that's how he gets what *he* wants."

Echo slipped a hand over his heart. "So angry." She trembled. "I'm cold, Peter. Warm me up."

"Isn't what we've always planned good enough any more?"

"Oh, Peter. I love you and I'm going to marry you, and nothing will ever change that."

"Maybe we should get started home."

"But what if this *is* home, Peter? Our home." She slid off his lap, tugged nonchalantly at him with one hand. "C'mon. You haven't seen everything yet."

"What did I miss?" he said reluctantly.

"Bedroom. And there's a fireplace too."

She dealt soothingly with his resistance, his fears that he wasn't equal to the emotional cost that remained to be exacted for their prize. He wasn't steady on his feet. The brandy he had drunk was hitting him hard.

"Just think about it," Echo said, leading him. "How it could be. Imagine that a year has gone by—so fast—" Echo kissed him and opened the bedroom door. Inside there was a gas log fire on a corner hearth. "—and here we are." She framed his his face lovingly with her hands. "What do you want to do now?" she said, looking solemnly into his eyes.

Peter swallowed the words he couldn't speak, glancing at the four-poster bed that dominated the room.

"I know what I want you to do," she said.

"Echo—"

She tugged him into the room and closed the door with her foot.

"It's all right," she said as he wavered. "Such a perfect place to spend our first night together. I want you to appreciate just how much I love you."

She left him and went to a corner of the room by the hearth where she undressed quickly, a quick-change artist down to the skin, slipping then beneath covers, to his fuming eyes a comely shadow.

"Peter?"

He touched his belt buckle; dropped his hands. He felt at the point of tears; ardor and longing were compromised by too much drink. His heartbeat was fueled by inchoate anger.

"Peter? What's wrong?"

He took a step toward her, stumbled, fell against a chair with a lyre back. Heavy, but he lifted it easily and slammed it against the wall. His unexpected rage had her cowering, his insulted hubris a raw wound she was too inexperienced to deal with. She hugged herself in shock and pain.

Peter opened the bedroom door.

"I'll wait in the fuckin' limo. You—you stay here if you want! Stay all night. Do whatever the hell you think you've got to do to make yourself happy, and just never mind what it'll do to us!"

Six

The first day of fall, and a good day for riding in convertibles: unclouded blue sky, temperatures on the East Coast in the sixties. The car John Ransome drove uptown and parked opposite Echo's building was a Mercedes two-seater. Not a lot of room for luggage, but she'd packed frugally: the clothes she would need for wintering on a small island off the coast of Maine. And her paintbox.

He didn't get out of the car right away; cell phone call. Echo lingered an extra few moments at her bedroom windows hoping to see Peter's car. They'd talked briefly about one A.M., and he'd sounded okay, almost casual about her upcoming enforced absence from his life. Holidays included. He was trying a little too hard not to show a lack of faith in her. Neither of them mentioned John Ransome. As if he didn't exist, and she was leaving to study painting in Paris for year.

Echo picked up her duffels from the bed and carried them out to the front hall. She left the door ajar and went into the front room where Julia was reading to Rosemay from the *National Enquirer*. Julia was a devotee of celebrity gossip.

Commenting on an actress who had been photographed trying to slip out of a California clinic after a makeover, Julia said, "Sure and she's at an age where she needs to give up plastic surgery and place her bets with a good taxidermist."

Rosemay smiled, her eyes on her daughter. Rosemay's lips trembled perceptibly; her skin was china-white, mimicking the tone of the bones within. Echo felt a strong pulse of fear; how frail her mother had become in just three months.

"Mom, I'm leaving my cell phone with you. It doesn't work on the island, John says. But there's a dish for Internet, no problem with e-mail."

"That's a blessing."

"Peter comin' to see you off?" Julia asked.

Echo glanced at her watch. "He wasn't sure. They were working a triple homicide last night."

"Do we have time for tea?" Rosemay asked, turning slowly away from her computer and looking up at Echo through her green eyeshade.

"John's here already, mom."

Then Echo, to her surprise and chagrin, just lost it, letting loose a flood of tears, sinking to her knees beside her mother, laying her head in Rosemay's lap as she had when she was a child. Rosemay stroked her with an unsteady hand, smiling.

Behind them John Ransome appeared in the hallway. Rosemay saw his reflection on a window pane. She turned her head slowly to acknowledge him. Julia, oblivious, was turning the pages of her gossip weekly.

The expression in Rosemay's eyes was more of a challenge than a welcome to Ransome. Her hands came together protectively over Echo. Then she prayerfully bowed her head.

Peter double-parked in the street and was running up the stairs of Echo's building when he met Julia coming down with her Save the Trees shopping bag.

"They're a half hour gone, Peter. I was just on my way to do the marketing."

Peter shook his head angrily. "I only got off a half hour ago! Why couldn't she wait for me, what was the big rush?"

"Would you mind sittin' with Rosemay while I'm out? Because it's goin' down hard for her, Peter."

He found Rosemay in the kitchen, a mug of cold tea between her hands. He put the kettle on again, fetched a mug for himself and sat down wearily with Rosemay. He took one of her hands in his.

"A year. A year until she's home again. Peter, I only let her do this because I was afraid—"

"It's okay. I'll be comin' around myself, two, three times a week, see how you are."

"—not afraid for myself," Rosemay said, finishing her thought. "Afraid of what my illness could do to you and Echo."

They looked at each other wordlessly until the kettle on the stove began whistling.

"Listen, we're gonna get through this," Peter said, grim around the mouth.

Rosemay's head drooped slowly, as if she hadn't the strength to hold it up any longer.

"He came, and took her away. Like the old days of lordship, you see. A privilege of those who ruled."

Echo didn't see much of Kincairn Island that night when they arrived. The seven-mile ferry trip left her so sick and sore from heaving she couldn't fully straighten up once they docked at the fishermen's quay. There were few lights in the clutter of a town occupying a small cove. A steady wind stung her ears on the short ride cross-island by Land Rover to the house facing two thousand miles of open ocean.

A sleeping pill knocked her out for eight hours.

At first light the cry of gulls and waves booming on the rocks a hundred feet below her bedroom windows woke her up. She had a hot shower in the recently updated bathroom. Some eyedrops got the red out. By then she thought she could handle a cup of black coffee. Outside her room she found a flight of stairs to the first-floor rear of the house. Kitchen noises below. John Ransome was an early riser; she heard him talking to someone.

The kitchen also had gone through a recent renovation. But the architect hadn't disturbed quaint and mostly charming old features: a hearth for baking in one corner, hand-hewn oak beams overhead.

"Good morning;" John Ransome said. "Looks as if you got your color back."

"I think I owe you an apology," Echo mumbled.

"For getting sick on the ferry? Everybody does until they get used to it. The fumes from that old diesel banger are partly to blame. How about breakfast? Ciera just baked a batch of her cinnamon scones."

"Coffeecoffeecoffee," Echo pleaded.

Ciera was a woman in her sixties, olive-skinned, with tragic dark eyes. She brought the coffeepot to the table.

"Good morning," Echo said to her. "I'm Echo."

The woman cocked her head as if she hadn't heard correctly.

"It's just a—a nickname. I was baptized Mary Catherine."

"I like Mary Catherine," Ransome said. He was smiling. "So why don't we call you by your baptismal name while you're here."

"Okay," Echo said, with a glance at him. It wasn't a big thing; nicknames were childish anyway. But she felt a slight psychic disturbance. As if, in banishing "Echo," he had begun to invent the person whom he really wanted to paint, and to live within a relationship that he firmly controlled.

Foolish, Echo thought. *I know who I am.*

The rocky path to Kincairn light, where Ransome had his studio, took them three hundred yards through scruffy stunted hemlock and blueberry barrens, across lichen-gilded rock, thin earth and frost-heaves. At intervals the path wended close to the high-tide line. Too close for Echo's peace of mind, although she tried not to appear nervous. Kincairn Island, about eight and a half crooked miles by three miles wide with a high, forested spine, was only a granitic pebble confronting a mighty ocean, blue on this October morning beneath a lightly cobwebbed sky.

"The light is fantastic," she said to Ransome.

"That's why I'm here, in preference to Cascais or Corfu for instance. Clear winter mornings are the best. The town is on the lee side of the island facing Penobscot. There's a Catholic church, by the way, that the diocese will probably close soon, or Unitarian for those who prefer Religion Lite."

"Who else lives here?" Echo asked, blinking salt spume from her eyelashes. The tide was in, wind from the southeast.

"About a hundred forty permanent residents, average age fifty-five. The economy is lobsters. Period. At the turn of the century Kincairn was a lively summer community, but most of the old saltbox cottages are gone; the rest belong to locals."

"And you own the island?"

"The original deed was recorded in 1794. You doing okay, Mary Catherine?"

The ledge they were crossing was only about fifty feet above the breakers and a snaggle of rocks close to shore.

"I get a little nervous . . . this close."

"Don't you swim?"

"Only in pools. The ocean—I nearly drowned on a beach in New Jersey. I was five. The waves that morning were nothing, a couple of feet high. I had my back to the water, playing with my pail and shovel. All of a sudden there was a huge wave, out of nowhere, that caught everybody by surprise."

"Rogue wave. We get them too. My parents were sailing off the light, just beyond that nav buoy out there, when a big one capsized their boat. They never had a chance."

"Good Lord. When was this?"

"Twenty-eight years ago." The path took a turn uphill, and the lighthouse loomed in front of them. "I'm a strong swimmer. Very cold water doesn't seem to get to me as quickly as other people. When I was nineteen—and heavily under the influence of Lord Byron—I swam the Hellespont. So I've often wondered—" He paused and looked out to sea. "If I had been with my mother and father that day, could I have saved them?"

"You must miss them very much."

"No. I don't."

After a few moments he looked around at her, as if her gaze had made him uncomfortable.

"Is that a terrible thing to say?"

"I guess I— I don't understand it. Did you love your parents?"

"No. Is that unusual?"

"I don't think so. Were they abusive?"

"Physically? No. They just left me alone, most of the time. As if I didn't exist. I don't know if there's a name for that kind of pain."

His smile, a little dreary, suggested that they leave the topic alone. They walked on to the lighthouse, brilliantly white on the highest point of the headland. Ransome had remodeled it, to considerable outrage from purists, he'd said, installing a modern, airport-style beacon atop what was now his studio.

"I saw what it cost you," Ransome said, "to leave your mother—your life. I'd like to think that it wasn't only for the money."

"Least of all. I'm a painter. I came to learn from you."

He nodded, gratified, and touched her shoulder.

"Well. Shall we have a look at where we'll both be working, Mary Catherine?"

Peter didn't waste a lot of time taking on a load at the reception following his sister Siobhan's wedding to the software salesman from Valley Stream. Too much drinking gave him the mopes, followed by a tendency to take almost anything said to him the wrong way.

"What've you heard from Echo?" a first cousin named Fitz said to him.

Peter looked at Fitz and had another swallow of his Irish in lieu of making conversation. Fitz glanced at Peter's cousin Rob Flaherty, who said, "Six tickets to the Rangers tonight, Petey. Good seats."

Fitz said, "That's two for Rob and his girl, two for me and Colleen, and I was thinkin'—you remember Mary Mahan, don't you?"

Peter said ungraciously, "I don't feel like goin' to the Rangers, and you don't need to be fixin' me up, Fitz." His bow tie was hanging limp and there was fire on his forehead and cheekbones. A drop of sweat fell unnoticed from his chin into his glass. He raised the glass again.

Rob Flaherty said with a grin, "You remind me of a lovesick camel, Petey. What you're needin' is a mercy hump."

Peter grimaced hostilely. "What I need is another drink."

"Mary's had a thing for you, how long?"

"She's my mom's godchild, asshole."

Fitz let the belligerence slide. "Well, you know. It don't exactly count as a mortal sin."

"Leave it, Fitz."

"Sure. Okay. But that is exceptional pussy you're givin' your back to. I can testify."

Rob said impatiently, "Ah, let him sit here and get squashed. Echo must've tied a knot in his dick before she left town with her artist friend."

Peter was out of his chair with a cocked fist before Fitz could step between them. Rob had reach on Peter and jabbed him just hard enough in the mouth to send him backwards, falling against another of the tables ringing the dance floor, scarcely disturbing a mute couple like goggle-eyed blowfish, drunk on senescence. Pete's mom saw the altercation taking shape and left her partner on the dance floor. She took Peter gently by an elbow, smiled at the other boys, telling them with a motion of her elegantly coiffed head to move along. She dumped ice out of a glass onto a napkin.

"Dance with your old ma, Peter."

Somewhat shamefaced, he allowed himself to be led to the dance floor, holding ice knotted in the napkin to his lower lip.

"It's twice already this month I see you too much in drink."

"It's a wedding, ma." He put the napkin in a pocket of his tux jacket.

"I'm thinking it's time you get a grip on yourself," Kate said as they danced to a slow beat. "You don't hear from Echo?"

"Sure. Every day."

"Well, then? She's doing okay?"

"She says she is." Peter drew a couple of troubled breaths. "But it's e-mail. Not like actually—you know, hearin' her voice. People are all the time sayin' what they can't put into words, you just have to have an ear for it."

"So—maybe there's things she wants you to know, but can't talk about?"

"I don't know. We've never been apart more than a couple days since we met. Maybe Echo's found out—it wasn't such a great bargain after all." He had a tight grip on his mother's hand.

"Easy now. If you trust Echo, then you'll hold on. Any man can do that, Petey, for the woman he loves."

"I'll always love her," Peter said, his voice tight. He looked into Kate's eyes, a fine simmer of emotion in his own eyes. "But I don't trust a man nobody knows much about. He's got walls around him you wouldn't believe."

"A man who values his privacy. That kind of money, it's not surprising." Kate hesitated. "You been digging for something? Unofficially, I mean."

"Yeah."

"No beefs?"

"No beefs. The man's practically invisible where public records are concerned."

"Then let it alone."

"If I could see Echo, just for a little while. I'm half nuts all the time."

"God love you, Peter. Long as you have Sunday off, why don't the two of us go to visit Rosemay, take her for an outing? Been a while since I last saw her."

"I don't think I can, ma. I, uh—need to go up to Westchester, talk to somebody."

"Police business, is it?"

Peter shook his head.

"Her name's Van Lier. She posed for John Ransome once."

Seven

The Van Lier residence was a copy—an exact copy, according to a Web site devoted to descriptions of Westchester County's most spectacular homes—of a sixteenth-century English manor house. All Peter saw of the inside was a glimpse of slate floor and dark wainscotting through a partly opened front door.

He said to the houseman who had answered his ring, "I'd like to see Mrs. Van Lier."

The houseman was an elderly Negro with age spots on his caramel-colored face like the spots on a leopard.

"There's no *Mrs.* Van Lier at this residence."

Peter handed him his card.

"Anne Van Lier. I'm with the New York police department."

The houseman looked him over patiently, perhaps hoping if his appraisal took long enough Peter would simply vanish from their doorstep and he could go back to his nap.

"What is your business about, Detective? Miss Anne don't hardly care to see nobody."

"I'd like to ask her a few questions."

They played the waiting game until the houseman reluctantly took a Motorola TalkAbout from a pocket of the apron he wore over his Sunday suit and tried to raise her on a couple of different channels. He frowned.

"Reckon she's laid hers down and forgot about it," he said.

"Well, likely you'll find Miss Anne in the greenhouse this time of the day. But I don't expect she'll talk to you, police or no police."

"Where's the greenhouse?"

"Go 'round the back and walk toward the pond, you can't hardly miss it. When you see her, tell Miss Anne I did my best to raise her first, so she don't throw a fit my way."

Peter approached the greenhouse through a squall of copper beech leaves on a windy afternoon. The slant roofs of the long greenhouse reflected scudding clouds. Inside a woman he assumed was Anne Van Lier was visible through a mist from some overhead pipes. She wore gloves that covered half of her forearms and a gardening hat with a floppy brim that, along with the mist float above troughs of exotic plants, obscured most of her face. She was working at a potting bench in the diffused glimmer of sunlight.

"Miss Van Lier?"

She stiffened at the sound of an unfamiliar voice but didn't look around. She was slight-boned in dowdy tan coveralls.

"Yes? Who is it?" Her tone said that she didn't care to know. "You're trespassing."

"My name is Peter O'Neill. New York City police department."

Peter walked a few steps down a gravel path toward her. With a quick motion of her head she took him in and said, "Stay where you are. Police?"

"I'd like to show you some identification."

"What is this about?"

He held up his shield. "John Leland Ransome."

She dropped a three-pronged tool from her right hand onto the bench and leaned against it as if suddenly at a loss for breath. Her back was to Peter. A dry scuttle of leaves on the overhead glass cast a kaleidoscope of shadow in the greenhouse. He wiped mist from his forehead and continued toward her.

"You posed for Ransome."

"What of it? Who told you that?"

"He did."

She'd been rigidly still; now Anne Van Lier seemed pleasurably agitated.

"You *know* John? You've seen him?"

"Yes."

"When?"

"A couple of months ago." Peter had closed the distance between them. Anne darted another look his way, a gloved hand covering her profile as if she were a bashful child; but she no longer appeared to be concerned about him.

"How is John?" Her voice was suddenly rich with emotion. "Did he—mention me?"

"That he did," Peter said reassuringly, and dared to ask, "Are you still in love with Ransome?"

She shuddered, protecting herself with the glove as if he'd thrown a stone, seeming to cower.

"What did John say about me? *Please.*"

Knowing he'd touched a nerve, Peter said soothingly, "Told me the year he spent with you was one of the happiest of his life."

Still it bothered him when, after a few moments, she began softly to weep. He moved closer to Anne, put a hand on her arm.

"Don't," she pleaded. "Just go."

"How long since you seen him last, Anne?"

"Eighteen years," she said despondently.

"He also said—it was his understanding that you were very happy."

Anne Van Lier gasped. Then she began shaking with laughter, as if at the cruelest joke she'd ever heard. She turned suddenly to Peter, knocking his hand away from her, snatching off her gardening hat as she stared up at him.

The shock she gave him was like the electric jolt from a hard jab to the solar plexus.

Because her once-lovely face was a horror. She had been brutally, deeply slashed. Attempts had been made to correct the damage, but plastic surgeons could do only so much. Repairing damage to severed nerves was beyond any surgeon's skill. Her mouth drooped on one side. She had lost the sight of her left eye, filled now with a bloom of suffering.

"Who did this to you? Was it Ransome?"

Jarred by the blurted question, she backed away from Peter.

"What? *John?* How dare you think that!"

Gloved fingers prowled the deep disfiguring lines on her face.

"I never saw my attacker. It happened on a street in the East Village. He could have been a mugger. I didn't resist him, so why, *why*?"

"The police—"

"Never found him." She stared at Peter, and through him, at the past. "Or is that what you've come to tell me?"

"No. I don't know anything about the case. I'm sorry."

"Oh. Well." Her fate was dead weight on her mind. "So many years ago."

She put her gardening hat back on, adjusted the brim, gave Peter a vague look. She was in the past again.

"You can tell John—I won't always look like this. Just one more operation, they promised. I've had ten so far. Then I'll—finally be ready for John." She anticipated the question Peter wasn't about to ask. "To pose again!" A vaguely flirtatious smile came and went. "Otherwise I've kept myself up, you know. I do my exercises. Tell John—I bless him for his patience, but it won't be much longer."

In spite of the humidity and the drifting spray in the greenhouse Peter's throat was dry. His own attempt at a smile felt like hardening plaster on his face. He knew he had only glimpsed the depths of her psychosis. The decent thing to do now was to leave her with some assurance that her fantasy would be fulfilled.

"I'll tell him, Miss Van Lier. That's the news he's been waiting for."

The following Saturday night Peter was playing pool with his old man at the Knights of Columbus, and letting Corin win. The way he used to let him win at Horse when Corin was still spry enough for some basketball: *just a little off my game tonight*, Peter would always say, pretending annoyance. Corin bought the beers afterward and they relaxed in a booth at their favorite sports bar.

"Heard you was into the cold case files in the Ninth," Corin said, wiping some foam off his mustache. He looked at one of the big screens around the room. The Knicks were at the Heat, and tonight they couldn't throw one in the ocean.

"You hear everything, Pop," Pete said admiringly.

"In my borough. What's up?"

"Just something I got interested in, I had a little spare time." He explained about the Van Lier slashing.

"How many times was she cut?"

"Ten slashes, all on her face. He just kept cutting on her, even after she was down. That sound like all he wanted was a purse?"

"No. Leaves three possibilities. A psycho, hated women. Or an old boyfriend she gave the heave-ho to, his ego couldn't take it. But you said the vic didn't make him."

"No."

"Then somebody hired it done. Tell me again what your interest is in the vic?"

"Eighteen, nineteen years ago, she posed for John Ransome."

Corin rubbed a temple and managed to keep his disapproval muted. "Jeez Marie, Petey."

"My girl is up there in Maine with him, pop!"

"And you're lettin' your imagination— I see your mind workin'. But it's far-fetched, lad. Far-fetched."

"I suppose so," Peter mumbled in his beer.

"How many young women do you think have posed for him in his career?"

"Seven that anybody knows about. Not counting Echo."

Corin spread his hands.

"But nobody knows who they are, or where they are. Almost nobody, it's some kind of secret list. I'm tellin' you, pop, there is too much about him that don't add up."

"That's not cop sense, that's your emotions talkin'."

"Two damn months almost, I don't see her."

"That was his deal. His and hers, and there's good reasons why Echo did it."

"Didn't tell you this before. That woman friend of his, whore, whatever: she carries a knife and Echo saw her almost use it on a kid in the subway."

"Jeez Marie, where's this goin' to end with you?" Corin sat back in the booth and rapped the table once with the knuckles of his right fist. "Tell you where it ends. Right here, tonight. You know why? Too much money, Petey. That's what it's always about."

"Yeah, I know. I saw the commissioner's head up Ransome's ass."

"Remember that." He stared at Peter until exasperation softened into forgiveness. "Echo have any problems up there she's told you about?"

"No," Peter admitted. "Ransome's just doing a lot of sketches of her, and she has time to paint. I guess everything's okay."

"Give her credit for good sense, then. And do your part."

"Yeah, I know. Wait." His expression was pure naked longing

and remorse. "Two months. And you know what, Pop? It's like one of us died. Only I don't know which one, yet."

As she had done almost every day since arriving on Kincairn Echo took her breakfast in chilly isolation in a corner of the big kitchen, then walked to the lighthouse. Frequently she could only see a few feet along the path because of fog. But sometimes there was no fog; the air was sharp and windless as the rising sun cast upon the copper face of the sea a great peal of morning.

She'd learned early on that John Ransome was an insomniac who spent most of the deep night hours reading in his second-floor study or taking long walks by himself in the dark, with only a flashlight along island paths he'd been familiar with since he was a boy.

Sleep would come easier for him, Ransome assured her, as if apologizing, once he settled down to doing serious painting. But the unfinished portrait he'd begun in New York on a big rectangle of die board had remained untouched on his easel for nearly six weeks while he devoted himself to making postcard-size sketches of Echo, hundreds of them, or silently observing her own work take shape. Late at night he would leave Post-it notes of praise or criticism on her easel.

When they were together he was always cordial but preferred letting Echo carry the conversation. He seemed endlessly curious about her life. About her father, who had been a Jesuit until the age of fifty-one, when he met Rosemay, a Maryknoll nun. He never asked about Peter.

There were days when Echo didn't see him at all. She felt his absence from the island but had no idea of where he'd gone, or why. Not that it was any of her business. But it wasn't the working relationship she'd bargained for. His inability to resume painting made her uneasy. And it wasn't her nature to put up with being ignored, or feeling slighted, for long.

"Is it me?" she'd asked him at dinner the night before.

Her question, the mood of it, startled him.

"No. Of course not, Mary Catherine." He looked distressed, random gestures substituting for the words he couldn't find to reassure her. "Case of nerves, that's all. It always happens. I'm afraid I'll begin and—then I'll find myself drawing from a dry well." He paused to pour himself more wine. He'd been drinking more before and after dinner than was his custom; his aim was a little off and he grimaced. "Afraid that everything I do will be trite and awful."

Echo had sensed his vulnerability—all artists had it. But she wasn't quite sure how to deal with his confession.

"You're a great painter."

Ransome shook his head, shying from the burden of her suggestion.

"If I ever believe that, then I will be finished." Echo got up, pinched some salt from a silver bowl and spread it over the wine stain on the fine linen tablecloth. She looked hesitantly at him.

"How can I help?"

He was looking at the salted stain. "Does that work?"

"Usually, if you do it right away."

"If human stains were so easy to remove," he said with sudden vehemence.

"God's always listening," she said, then thought it was probably too glib, patronizing and unsatisfactory. She felt God, but she also felt there was little point in trying to explain Him to someone else.

After a silence the unexpected flood of his passion ebbed.

"I don't believe as easily as you, Mary Catherine," he said with a tired smile that became tense. "But if we do have your God watching us, then I think it likely that his revenge is to do nothing."

Ransome pushed his chair back and stood, looked at Echo, put out a hand and lifted her head slightly with thumb and forefinger on her chin. He said, studying her as if for the first time, "The light in your eyes is the light from your heart."

"That's sweet," Echo said demurely, knowing what was coming next. She'd been thinking about it, and how to handle it, for weeks.

He kissed her on the forehead, not the lips. As if bestowing a blessing. That was sweet too. But the erotic content, enough to cause her lips to part and put a charge in her heartbeat, took her by surprise.

"I have to leave the island for a few days," he said then.

Ransome's studio had replaced the closetlike space that once had held the Kincairn Light and reflecting mirror. It sat upon the spindle of the lighthouse shaft like a flying saucer made mostly of glass that was thirty feet in diameter. There was an elevator inside, another addition, but Echo always used the circular stairs coming and going. Ciera was a very good cook and the daily climb helped Echo shed the pounds that had a tendency to creep aboard like hitchhikers on her hips.

She had decided, because the day was neither blustery enough to blow her off her Vespa nor bitterly cold, to pack up her paints and easel and go cross-island for an exercise in plein air painting on the cove and dock.

Approaching Kincairn village, Echo saw John Ransome at the end of the town dock unmooring a cabin cruiser that had been tied up alongside Wilkins' Marine and the mail/ferry boat slip. She stopped her puttering scooter in front of the cottage where a lone priest, elderly and in virtual exile in this most humble of parishes, lived with an equally old housekeeper. Echo had no reason for automatically keeping her distance from Ransome until she also saw Taja at the helm of the cruiser. Which wasn't much of a reason either. She hadn't seen the Woman in Black nor given her much thought since the night of the artist's show at Cy Mellichamp's. Ransome never mentioned her. Apparently she seldom visited the island.

Friend, business associate, confidante? Mistress, of course. But if she kept some distance between them now, perhaps that was in the past. Even if they were no longer lovers Echo assumed she might still be emotionally supportive, a rare welcome visitor to his isolato existence; his stiller doom, Echo thought with a certain poignancy, remembering a phrase of Charlotte Bronte's from Echo's favorite novel, *Jane Eyre.*

Watching Ransome jump into the bow of the cruiser, Echo felt frustrated for his sake. Obviously he was not going to be painting anytime soon. She also felt a dim sense of betrayal that made no sense to her. Yet it lingered like the spectral imprint of a kiss that had made her restless during a night of confused, otherworldly dreams; dreams of Ransome, dreams of being as naked in his studio as a snail on a thorn.

Echo watched Taja back the cruiser from the dock and turn it toward the mainland. Pour on the power. She decided to take a minute to go into the empty church. Was it time to ring the bell for a confession of her own? She couldn't make up her mind about that, and her heart was no help either.

Cy Mellichamp was using a phone at a gallery associate's desk in the second-floor office when Peter was brought in by a secretary. Mellichamp glanced at him with no hint of welcome. Two more associates, Mellichamp's morale-boosting term for salespeople, were working the phones and computers. In another large room behind the office paintings were being uncrated.

Mellichamp smiled grievously at something he was hearing and fidgeted until he had a chance to break in.

"Really, Allen, I think your affections are misplaced. There is neither accomplishment nor cachet in the accident of Roukema's success. And at six million—no, I don't want to have this conversation. *No.* The man should be doing frescoes in tombs. You wanted my opinion, which I freely give to you. Okay, please think it over and come to your senses."

Cy rang off and looked again at Peter, with the fixed smile of a man who wants you to understand he could be doing better things with his time.

"Why," he asked Peter, "do otherwise bright young people treat inherited fortunes the way rednecks treat junk cars?" He shrugged. "Mr. O'Neill! Delighted to see you again. How can I help you?"

"Have you heard anything from Mr. Ransome lately?"

"We had dinner two nights ago at the Four Seasons."

"Oh, he was in town?" Cy waited for a more sensible question. "His new paintings sell okay?"

"We did very, very well. And how is Echo?"

"I don't know. I'm not allowed to see her, I might be a distraction. I thought Ransome was supposed to be slaving away at his art up there in Maine."

Cy looked at his watch, looked at Peter again uncomprehendingly.

"I was hoping you could give me some information, Mr. Mellichamp."

"In regard to?"

"The other women Ransome has painted. I know where one of them lives. Anne Van Lier." The casual admission was calculated to provoke a reaction; Peter didn't miss the slight tightening of Cy Mellichamp's baby blue eyes. "Do you know how I can get in touch with the others?"

Cy said after a few moments, "Why should you want to?" with a muted suggestion in his gaze that Peter was up to no good.

"Do you know who and where those women are?"

An associate said to Cy, "Princess Steph on three."

Distracted, Cy looked over his shoulder. "Find out if she's on St. Barts. I'll get right back to her."

While Cy wasn't watching him Peter glanced at a computer on a nearby desk where nobody was working. But the person whose desk it was had carelessly left his user ID on the screen.

Cy looked around at Peter again. "I could not help you if I did know," he said curtly. "Their whereabouts are none of my business."

"Why is Ransome so secretive about those women?"

"That, of course, is John's prerogative. Now if you wouldn't mind—it *has* been one of those days—" He summoned a moment of the old charm. "I'm sorry."

"Thanks for taking the time to see me, Mr. Mellichamp."

"If there should be a next time, unless it happens to be official, you would do well to leave that gold shield in your pocket."

EIGHT

Peter got home from his watch at twenty past midnight. He fixed himself a sardine sandwich on sourdough with a smelly slice of gouda and some salsa dip he found in the fridge. He carried the sandwich and a bottle of Sam Adams up the creaky back stairs to the third floor he shared with his brother Casey. The rest of the house was quiet except for his father's distant whistling snore. But with no school for two days Case was still up with his iMac. Graphics were Casey's passion: his ambition was to design the cars of the future.

Peter changed into sweats. The third floor was drafty; a wind laced with the first fitful snow of the season was belting them.

There was an e-mail on the screen of his laptop that said only *missyoumissyoumissyou*. He smiled bleakly, took a couple of twenties from his wallet and walked through the bathroom he shared with Casey, pausing to kick a wadded towel off the floor in the direction of the hamper.

"Hi, Case."

Casey, mildly annoyed at the intrusion, didn't look around.

"That looks like the Batmobile," Peter said of the sleek racing machine Casey was refining with the help of some Mac software.

"It is the Batmobile."

Peter laid a twenty on the desk where Casey would see it out of the corner of his eye.

"What's that for?"

"For helping me out."

"Doing what?"

"See, I've got this user ID, but there's probably gonna be a log-on code too—"

"Hack a system?"

"I'm not stealing anything. Just want to look at some names, addresses."

"It's against the law."

Peter laid the second twenty on top of the first.

"Way I see it, it's kind of a gray area. There's something going on, maybe involves Echo, I need to know about. Right away."

Casey folded the twenties with his left hand and slid them under his mouse pad.

"If I get in any trouble," he said, "I'm givin' your ass up first."

After nearly a week of Ransome's absence, Echo was angry at him, fed up with being virtually alone on an island that every storm or squawl in the Atlantic seemed to make a pass at almost on a daily basis, and once again dealing with acute bouts of homesickness. Never mind that her bank account was automatically fattening twice a month, it seemed to be payment for emotional servitude, not the pleasant collaboration she'd anticipated. Only chatty e-mails from girl friends, from Rosemay and Stefan and even Kate O'Neill, plus Peter's maddeningly noncommittal daily communications (he was hopeless at putting feelings into words), provided balance and escape from depression through the long nights. They reminded her that the center of her world was a long way from Kincairn Island.

She had almost no one to talk to other than the village priest, who seemed hard-put to remember her name at each encounter, and Ransome's housekeeper. But Ciera's idea of a lively conversation was two sentences an hour. Much of the time, perhaps affected by the dismal weather that smote their rock or merely the oppression of passing time, Ciera's face looked as if Death had scrawled an "overdue" notice on it.

Echo had books and her music and DVDs of recent movies arrived regularly. She had no difficulty in passing the time when she wasn't working. But she hated the way she'd been painting lately, and missed the stealth insights from her employer and mentor. Day after day she labored at what she came to judge as stale, uninspired landscapes, taking a palette knife to them as soon as the light began to fade. She didn't know if it was the creeping ennui or a faltering sense of confidence in her talent.

November brought fewer hours of the crystal lambency she'd discovered on her first day there. Ransome's studio was equipped with full-spectrum artificial light, but she always preferred painting outdoors when it was calm enough, no tricky winds to snatch her easel and fling it out to sea.

The house of John Ransome, built to outlast centuries, was not a house in which she would ever feel at home, in spite of his library and collection of paintings that included some of his own, youthful work that would never be shown anywhere. These she studied with the avid eye of an archaeologist in a newly unearthed pyramid. The house was stone and stout enough but at night in a hard gale had its creepy, shadowy ways. Hurricane lamps had to be lit two or three times a week at about the same time her laptop lost satellite contact and the screen's void reflected her dwindled good cheer. Reading by lamplight hurt her eyes. Even with earplugs she couldn't fall asleep when the wind was keening a single drawn-out note or slapdash, grabbing at shutters, mewling under the eaves like a ghost in a well.

Nothing to do then but lie abed after her rosary and cry a little as her mood worsened. And hope John Ransome would return soon. His continuing absence a puzzle, an irritant; yet working sorcery on her heart. When she was able to fall asleep it was Ransome whom she dreamed about obsessively. While fitful and half awake she recalled every detail of a self portrait and the faces of his women. Had any of his subjects felt as she now did? Echo wondered about the depth of each relationship he'd had with his unknown beauties. One man, seven young women—had Ransome slept with any of them? Of course he had. But perhaps not every one.

His secret. Theirs. And what might other women to come, lying awake in this same room on a night as fierce as this one, adrift in loneliness and sensation of their own, imagine about Echo's involvement with John Leland Ransome?

Echo threw aside her down comforter and sat on the edge of the bed, nervous, heart-heavy. Except for hiking shoes she slept fully dressed, with a small flame in one of the tarnished lamp chimneys for company and a hammer on the floor for security, not knowing who in that island community might take a notion, no matter what the penalty. Ciera went home at night to be with her severely arthritic husband, and Echo was alone.

She rubbed down the lurid gooseflesh on her arms, feeling guilty in the sight of God for what raged in her mind. For sexual cravings like nettles in the blood. She put her hand on the Bible beside her bed but didn't open it. *Dear Lord, I'm only human.* She felt, honestly, that it was neither the lure of his flesh nor the power of his talent but the mystery of his torment that ineluctably drew her to Ransome.

A shutter she had tried to secure earlier was loose again to the incessant prying of the wind, admitting an almost continual flare of lightning centered in this storm. She picked up the hammer and a small eyebolt she'd found in a tool chest along with a coil of picture wire.

It was necessary to crank open one of the narrow lights of the mullioned window, getting a faceful of wind and spume in the process. As she reached for the shutter that had been flung open she saw by a run of lightning beneath boiling clouds a figure standing a little apart from the house on the boulders that formed a sea wall. A drenched white shirt ballooned in the wind around his torso. He faced the sea and the brawling waves that rose ponderously to foaming heights only a few feet below where he precariously stood. Waves that crashed down with what seemed enough force to swamp islands larger than Kincairn.

John Ransome had returned. Echo's lips parted to call to him, small-voiced in the tumult, her skin crawling coldly from fear, but the shutter slammed shut on her momentary view of the artist.

When she pushed it open again and leaned out slightly to see him, her eyelashes matting with salt spray, hair whipping around her face, Ransome had vanished.

Echo cranked the window shut and backed away, tingling in her hands, at the back of her neck. She took a few deep breaths, wiping at her eyes, then turned, grabbed a flashlight and went to the head of the stairs down the hall from her room, calling his name in the darkness, shining the beam of the light down the stairs, across the foyer to the front door, which was closed. There was no trace of water on the floor, as she would have expected if he'd come in out of the storm.

"ANSWER ME, JOHN! ARE YOU HERE?"

Silence, except for the wind.

She bolted down the stairs, grabbed a hooded slicker off the wall-mounted coat tree in the foyer and let herself out.

The three-cell flashlight could throw a brilliant beam for well over a hundred yards. She looked around with the light, shuddering in the cold, lashed in a gale that had to be more than fifty knots. She heard thunder rolling above the shriek of the wind. She was scared to the marrow. Because she knew she had to leave the relative shelter afforded by the house at her back and face the sea where she'd last seen him.

With her head low and an arm protecting her face, she made her way to the sea wall, the dash of waves terrifying in the beam of the flashlight. Her teeth were clenched so tight she was afraid of chipping them. Remembering the shock of being engulfed on what had been a calm day at the Jersey shore, pulled tumbling backwards and almost drowning in the sandy undertow.

But she kept going, mounted the seawall and crouched there, looking down at the monster waves. It was near to freezing. In spite of the hood and slicker she was already soaked and trembling so badly she was afraid of losing her grip on the flashlight as she crawled over boulders. Looking down into crevices where he might have fallen, to slowly drown at each long roll of a massive wave.

Thought she saw something—something alive like an animal caught in discarded plastic wrap. Then she realized it was a face she was looking at in the down-slant of the flashlight, and it wasn't plastic, it was Ransome's white shirt. He lay sprawled on his back a few feet below her, dazed but not unconscious. His eyelids squinched in the light cast on his face.

Echo got down from the boulder she was on, found some footing, got her hands under his arms and tugged.

One of his legs was awkwardly wedged between boulders. She couldn't tell if it was broken as she turned her efforts to pulling his foot free. Hurrying. Her strength ebbing fast. Battling him and the storm and sensing something behind her, still out to sea but coming her way with such size, unequaled in its dark momentum, that it would drown them both in one enormous downfall like a building toppling.

"MOVE!"

Echo had him free at last and pushed him frantically toward the top of the sea wall. She'd managed to lose her grip on the flashlight but it didn't matter, there was lightning around their heads and all of the deep weight of the sea coming straight at them. She couldn't make herself look back.

Whatever the condition of his leg, Ransome was able to hobble with her help. They staggered toward the house, whipsawed by the wind, until the rogue wave she'd anticipated burst over the seawall and sent them rolling helplessly a good fifty feet before its force was spent.

When she saw Ransome's face again beneath the flaring sky he was blue around the mouth but his eyes had opened. He tried to speak but his chattering teeth chopped off the words.

"WHAT?"

He managed to say what was on his mind between shudders and gasps.

"I'm n-n-not w-worth it, y-you know."

Hot showers, dry clothing. Soup and coffee when they met again in the kitchen. When she had Ransome seated on a stool she looked into his eyes for sign of a concussion, then examined the cut on his forehead, which was two inches long and deep enough so that it would probably scar. She pulled the edges of the cut together with butterfly bandages. He sipped his coffee with steady hands on the mug and regarded her with enough alertness so that she wasn't worried about that possible concussion.

"How did you learn to do this?" he asked, touching one of the bandages.

"I was a rough-and-tumble kid. My parents weren't always around, so I had to patch myself up."

He put an inquisitive fingertip on a small scar under her chin.

"Street hockey," she said. "And this one—"

Echo pulled her bulky fisherman's sweater high enough to reveal a larger scar on her lower rib cage.

"Stickball. I fell over a fire hydrant."

"Fortunately . . . nothing happened to your marvelous face."

"Thanks be to God." Echo repacked the first aid kit and ladled clam chowder into large bowls, straddled a stool next to him. "Ought to see my knees," she said, as an afterthought. She was ravenous, but before dipping the spoon into her chowder she said, "You need to eat."

"Maybe in a little while." He uncorked a bottle of brandy and poured an ounce into his coffee.

Echo bowed her head and prayed silently, crossed herself. She dug in. "And thanks be to God for saving our lives out there."

"I didn't see anyone else on those rocks. Only you."

Echo reached for a box of oyster crackers. "Do I make you uncomfortable?"

"How do you mean, Mary Catherine?"

"When I talk about God."

"I find that . . . endearing."

"But you don't believe in Him. Or do you?"

Ransome massaged a sore shoulder.

"I believe in two gods. The god who creates, and the god who destroys."

He leaned forward on the stool, folded his arms on the island counter, which was topped with butcher's block, rested his head on his arms. Eyes still open, looking at her as he smiled faintly.

"The last few days I've been keeping company with the god who destroys. You have a good appetite, Mary Catherine."

"Haven't been eating much. I don't like eating alone at night."

"I apologize for—being away for so long."

Echo glanced thoughtfully at him.

"Will you be all right now?"

He sat up, slipped off his stool, stood behind her and put a hand lightly on the back of her neck.

"I think the question is—after your experience tonight, will *you* be all right—with me?"

"John, were you trying to kill yourself?"

"I don't think so. But I don't remember what I was thinking out there. I'm also not sure how I happened to find myself sitting naked on the floor of the shower in my bathroom, scrubbed pink as a boiled lobster."

Echo put her spoon down. "Look, I cut off your clothes with scissors and sort of bullied you into the shower and loofah'd you to get your blood going. Nothing personal. Something I thought I'd better do, or else. I left clothes out for you then went upstairs and took a shower myself."

"You must have been as near freezing as I was. But you helped me first. You're a tough kid, all right."

"You were outside longer than me. How much longer I didn't know. But I knew hypothermia could kill you in a matter of minutes. You had all of the symptoms."

Echo resumed eating, changing hands with the spoon because she felt as if her right hand was about to cramp; it had been doing that for an hour.

She had cut off his clothes because she wanted him naked. Not out of prurience; she'd been scared and angry and needed to distance herself from his near-death folly and the hard reality of the impulse that had driven him outside in his shirt and bare feet to freeze or drown amid the rocks. Nude, barely conscious and semicoherent, the significance of *Ransome* was reduced in her mind and imagination; sitting on the floor of the shower and shuddering as the hot water drove into him, he was to her like an anonymous subject in a life class, to be viewed objectively without unreliable emotional investment. It gave her time to think about the situation. And decide. If it was only creative impotence there was still a chance she could be of use to him. Otherwise she might as well be aboard when the ferry left at sunrise.

"Mary Catherine?"

"Yes?"

"I've never loved a woman. Not one. Not ever. But I may be in love with you."

She thought that was too pat to take seriously. A compliment he felt he owed her. Not that she minded the mild pressure of his palm on her neck. It was soothing, and she had a headache.

Echo looked around at Ramsome. "You're bipolar, aren't you?"

He wasn't surprised by her diagnosis.

"That's the medical term. Probably all artists have a form of it. Soaring in the clouds or morbid in the depths, too blue and self-pitying to take a deep breath."

Echo let him hold her with his gaze. His fingers moved slowly along her jawline to her chin. She felt that, all right. Maybe it was going to become an issue. He had the knack of not blinking very often that could be mesmerizing in a certain context. She lifted her chin away from his hand.

"My father was manic-depressive," she said. "I learned to deal with it."

"I know that he didn't kill himself."

"Nope. Chain-smoking did the job for him."

"You were twelve?"

"Just twelve. He died on the same day that I got—my—when I—"

She felt that she had blundered. *Way too personal, Echo; and shut up.*

"Became a woman. One of the most beautiful women I've been privileged to know. I feel that in a small way I may do your father honor by preserving that beauty for—who knows? Generations to come."

"Thank you," Echo said, still resonant from his touch, her brain on lull. Then she got what he was saying. She looked at Ransome again in astonishment and joy. He nodded.

"I feel it beginning to happen," he said. "I need to sleep for a few hours. Then I want to go back to that portrait of you I began in New York. I have several ideas." He smiled rather shyly. "About time, don't you think?"

NINE

After a few days of indecision, followed by an unwelcome intrusion that locked two seemingly unrelated incidents together in his mind, Cy Mellichamp made a phone call, then dropped around to the penthouse apartment John Ransome maintained at the Pierre Hotel. It was snowing in Manhattan. Thanksgiving had passed, and jingle bell season dominated Cy's social calendar. Business was brisk at the gallery.

The Woman in Black opened the door to Cy, admitting him to the large gloomy foyer. Where she left him standing, still wearing his alpaca overcoat, muffler, and cossack's hat. Cy swallowed his dislike and mistrust of Taja and pretended he wasn't being slighted by John Ransome's gypsy whore. And who knew what else she was to Ransome in what had the appearance, to Mellichamp, of a *folie à deux* relationship.

"We were hacked last night," he said. "Whoever it was now has the complete list of Ransome women. Including addresses, of course."

Taja cocked her head slightly, waiting, the low light of a nearby sconce repeated in her dark irises.

"The other, ah, visitation might not be germane, but I can't be sure. Peter O'Neill came to the gallery a few days ago. There was belligerence in his manner I didn't care for. Anyway, he claimed to know Anne Van Lier's whereabouts. Whether he'd visited her he didn't say. He wanted to know who the other women are. Pressing me for information. I said I couldn't help him. Then, last night as I've said, someone very resourceful somehow plucked that very information from our computer files." He gestured a little awkwardly, denying personal responsibility. There was no such thing as totally secure in a world managed by machines. "I thought John ought to know."

Taja's eyes were unwinking in her odd, scarily immobile face for a few moments longer. Then she abruptly quit the foyer, moving soundlessly on slippered feet, leaving the sharp scent of her perfume behind—perfume that didn't beguile, it mugged you. She disappeared down a hallway lined with a dozen hugely valuable portraits and drawings by Old Masters.

Mellichamp licked his lips and waited, hat in hand, feeling obscurely humiliated. He heard no sound other than the slight wheeze of his own breath within the apartment.

"I, I really must be going," he said to a bust of Hadrian and his own backup reflection in a framed mirror that once had flattered royalty in a Bavarian palace. But he waited another minute before opening one of the bronze doors and letting himself out into the elevator foyer.

Gypsy whore, he thought again, extracting some small satisfaction from this judgment. Fortunately he seldom had to deal with her. Just to lay eyes on the Woman in Black with her bilious temperament and air of closely held violence made him feel less secure in the world of social distinction that, beginning with John Ransome's money, he had established for himself: a magical, intoxicating, uniquely *New York* place where money was in the air always, like pixie dust further enchanting the blessed.

Money and prestige were both highly combustible, however. In circumstances such as a morbid scandal could arrange, disastrous events turned reputations to ash.

The elevator arrived.

Not that he was legally culpable, Cy assured himself while descending. It had become his mantra. On the snowy bright-eyed street he headed for his limo at the curb, taking full breaths of the heady winter air. Feeling psychologically exonerated as well, blamelessly distanced from the tragedy he now accepted must be played out for the innocent and guilty alike.

Peter O'Neill arrived in Las Vegas on an early flight and signed for his rental car in the cavernous baggage claim area of McCarran airport.

"Do you know how I can find a place called the King Rooster?"

The girl waiting on him hesitated, smiled ironically, looked up and said softly, "Now I wouldn't have thought you were the type."

"What's that mean?"

"First trip to Vegas?"

"Yeah."

She shrugged. "You didn't know that the King Rooster is, um, a brothel?"

"No kidding?"

"They're not legal in Las Vegas or Clark County." She looked thoughtfully at him. "If you don't mind my saying—you probably could do better for yourself. But it's none of my business, is it?" She had two impish dimples in her left cheek.

Next, Peter thought, she was going to tell him what time she got off from work. He smiled and showed his gold shield.

"I'm not on vacation."

"Ohhh. NYPD Blue, huh? I hated it when Jimmy Smits died." She turned around the book of maps the car company gave away and made notations on the top sheet with her pen. "When you leave the airport, take the Interstate south to exit thirty-three, that's Route 160 west? Blue Diamond Road. You want to go about forty miles past Blue Diamond to Nye County. When you get there you'll see this big mailbox on the left with a humungous, um, red cock—the crowing kind—on top of it. That's all, no sign or anything. Are you out here on a big case?"

"Too soon to tell," Peter said.

The whorehouse, when he got there, wasn't much to look at. The style right out of an old western movie: two square stories of cedar with a long deep balcony on three sides. In the yard that was dominated by a big cottonwood tree the kind of discards you might see at a flea market were scattered around. Old wagonwheels, an art-glass birdbath, a dusty carriage in the lean-to of a blacksmith's shed. There was a roofed wishing well beside the flagstone walk to the house. A chain-link fence that clashed with the rustic ambience surrounded the property. The gate was locked; he had to be buzzed in.

Inside it was cool and dim and New Orleans rococo, with paintings of reclining nudes that observed the civilities of *Fin de Siècle*. Nothing explicit to threaten a timid male; their pussies were as chaste as closed prayerbooks. A Hispanic maid showed Peter into a separate parlor. Drapes were drawn. The maid withdrew, closing pocket doors. Peter waited, turning the pages of an expensive-looking leather-bound book featuring porn etchings in a time of derbies and bustles. The maid returned with a silver tray, delicate china cups and coffee service.

She said, "You ask for Eileen. But she is indispose this morning. There is another girl she believe you will like, coming in just a—"

Peter flashed his shield and said, "Get Eileen in here. Now."

Ten more minutes passed. Peter opened the drapes and looked at sere mountains, the mid-range landscape pocked and rocky. A couple of wild burros were keeping each other company out there. He drank coffee. The doors opened again. He turned.

She was tall, a little taller than Peter in her high heels. She wore pale green silk lounging pajamas and a pale green harem mask that clung to the contours of her face but revealed only her eyes: they were dark, plummy, febrile in pockets of mascara. Tiny moons of sclera showed beneath the pupils.

"I'm Eileen."

"Peter O'Neill."

"Is there a problem?"

"What's with the mask, Eileen?"

"That's why you asked for me, isn't it? All part of the show you want."

"No. I didn't know about—. Mind taking the mask off?"

"But that's for upstairs," she protested, her tone demure. She began running her hands over her breasts, molding the almost sheer material of the draped pajamas around dark nipples. She cupped her breasts, making of them an offering.

"Listen, I didn't come here to fuck you. *Just take it off.* I have to see—what that bastard did to you, Eileen."

Her hands fell to her sides as she exhaled; the right hand twitched. Otherwise she didn't move.

"You *know*? After all these years I'm going to find out who did this to me?"

"I've got a good idea."

She made a sound deep in her throat of pain and sorrow, but didn't attempt to remove the mask. She shied when Peter impatiently put out a hand to her shrouded face.

"It's okay. You can trust me, Eileen." Inches from her body, feeling the heat of her, aware of a light perfume and arousing musk, he reached slowly behind her blond head and touched the little bow where her mask was tied as gently as if he were about to grasp a butterfly.

"I've only trusted one man in my life," she said dispiritedly. Then, unagressively but firmly, she snugged her groin against his, tamely laying her head on his shoulder so he could easily untie the mask.

He'd been expecting scars similar to those Anne Van Lier wore for life. But Eileen's were worse. Much of her face had burned, rendered almost to bone. The scar-gullies were slick and mahogany-colored, with glisters of purple. He could see a gleam of her back teeth on the left, most heavily-damaged side.

She flinched at his appalled examination, lowering her head, thrusting at him with her pelvis.

"All right," she said. "Now you're satisfied? Or are we just getting started?"

"I told you I didn't want to—"

"That's a lie. You're ready to explode in your pants." But she relented, stepping back from him, with a grin that was almost evil in the context of a ravaged face. "What's the matter? Your mommy told you to stay away from women like me? I'm clean. Cleaner than any little piece you're likely to pick up in a bar on Friday night. Huh? We're regulated in Nevada, in case you didn't know. The Board of Health dudes are here every week."

"I just want to talk. How did you get the face, Eileen?"

Her breath whistled painfully between her teeth.

"Fuck you mean? It's all in the case file."

"But I want to hear it from you."

Her face had little mobility, but her lovely eyes could sneer.

"Oh. Cops and their perversions. You all belong in a Dumpster. Give me back my mask."

She shied again when he tried to tie the mask on, then sighed, touching one of Peter's wrists, an exchange of intimacy.

"My face, my fortune," she said. "Would you believe how many men need a freakshow to get them up? God damn all of them. Present company excluded, I guess. You try to act tough but you've got a kind face." With the mask secure she felt bold enough to look him in the eye. "Your coffee must have cooled off by now," she said, suddenly the gracious hostess. "Would you like another cup?"

He nodded. She sat on the edge of a gilt and maroon-striped settee to pour coffee for them.

"So you want to hear it again. Why not?" She licked a sugar cube a couple of times before putting it into her cup. "I was alone in the lab, working on an experiment. Part of my Ph.D. requirement in O-chem." Peter sipped coffee from the cup she handed him as he remained standing close to the settee. Still encouraging the intimacy she seemed to crave. It wasn't just cop technique to get someone to spill their guts. He felt anguish for Eileen, as her eyes wandered in remembrance. "I, I was tired, you know, hadn't slept for thirty-six hours. Something like that. Didn't hear anyone come in. Didn't know he was there until he was breathing down my neck." She looked up. "Is this what turns you on?" she said, as if she'd lost track of who he was. Only another john to be entertained. She took Peter's free hand, raised it to her face, guided his ring finger beneath the mask and between her lips, touching it with the tip of her tongue. That was a new one on Peter, but the effect was disturbingly erotic.

"I started to turn on my stool," Eileen said, her voice close to a whisper as she looked up at Peter, lips caressing his captive finger, "and got a cup of H_2SO_4 in my face."

"But you didn't see—"

"All I saw was a gloved hand, an arm. Then—I was burning in hell." She bit down on his finger, at the base of the nail, laughed delightedly when he jerked his hand away.

"I can tell you who it was," Peter said angrily. "Because you're not the first woman who posed for John Ransome and got a face like yours."

He wasn't fully prepared for the ferocity with which she came at him, hissing like a feral cat, hands clawlike to ream out his eyes. He caught her wrists and forced her hands down.

"John Ransome? That's crazy! John loved me and I loved him!"

"Take it easy, Eileen! Did he come to see you after it happened?"

"No! So what? You think I wanted him to see me like this? Think I want anyone looking at me unless they're paying for it? Oh how I make them pay!"

"Eileen, I'm sorry." He had used as much force as he dared; she was strong in her fury and could inadvertantly break a wrist struggling with him. When she was off balance Peter pushed her hard away from him. "I'm sorry, but I'm not wrong." He moved laterally away from her, not wanting some of his face to wind up under her fingernails. But she had choked on her outrage and was having trouble getting her breath.

"F-Fuck you! What are you cops . . . trying to *do* to John? Did one of the others say something against him? Tell me, I'll tear her fucking heart out!"

"Were you that much in love with him?"

"I'm not talking to you any more! Some things are still sacred to me!"

Eileen backed up a few steps and sat down heavily, her body in a bind as if she wore a straitjacket, harrowing sounds of grief in her throat.

"Whatever happened to that Ph.D.?" he asked calmly, though the skin of his forearms was prickling.

"That was someone else. Get out of here, before I have you thrown out. The sheriff and I are old friends. We paint each other's toenails. The chain-link fence? The goddamn desert? Forget about it. This is my *home*, no matter what you think. I *own* the Rooster. John paid for it."

Saying his name she quaked as if an old, unendurable torment was about to erupt. She leaned forward and, one arm moving jerkily like a string puppet's, she began smashing teacups on the tray with her fist. Shards flew. When she stopped her hand was bleeding profusely. She put it in her lap and let it bleed.

"On your way, bud," Eileen said to Peter. "Would you mind asking Lourdes to come in? I think it may be time for my meds."

While he was waiting at the Las Vegas airport for his flight to Houston, delayed an hour and a half because of a storm out of the Gulf of Mexico, Peter composed a long e-mail to Echo, concluding with:

> So far I can't prove anything. There's at least two more of them I need to see, so I'm on my way to Texas. But I want you to get off the island *now*. No good-byes, don't bother to pack. Go to my Uncle Charlie's in Brookline. 3074 East Mather. Wait for me there, I'll only be a couple of days.

By the time he boarded his flight to Houston, there still was no acknowledgment from Echo. It was six thirty-six P.M. in the east.

John Ransome was still working in his aerie studio and Echo was taking a shower when the Woman in Black walked into Echo's bedroom without a knock and had a look around. Art books heaped on the writing desk. The blouse and skirt and pearls she'd laid out for a leisurely dinner with Ransome. Her silver rosary, her Bible, her laptop. There was an e-mail message on the screen from Rosemay, apparently only half-read. Taja scrolled past it to another e-mail from a girl whom she knew had been Echo's college roommate. She skipped that one too and came to Peter O'Neill's most recent message.

This one Taja read carefully. Obviously Echo hadn't seen it, or she wouldn't have been humming so contentedly in the slow-running shower. Washing her hair.

Taja deleted the message. But of course if Peter didn't hear from Echo soon, he'd just send another, more urgent e-mail. The weather was decent for now, the wi-fi signal steady.

She figured she had four or five minutes, at least, to disable the laptop skillfully enough so that Echo wouldn't catch on that it had been sabotaged.

But Peter O'Neill was the real problem—just as she had suspected and conveyed to John Ransome in the beginning, when Ransome was considering Echo as his next subject.

No matter how he rated as a detective, he wasn't going to learn anything useful in Texas. Taja could be certain of that.

And she had a good idea of where he would show up during the next forty-eight hours.

TEN

"Eventually they would have reconstructed her face," the late Nan McLaren's aunt Elisa said to Peter. "The plastic surgery group is the best in Houston. World-renowned, in fact."

He was sitting with the aging socialite, who still retained a certain gleam that diet and exercise afforded septuagenerians, in the orangerie of a very large estate home in Sherwood Forest. There was a slow drip of rain from two big magnolias outside that were strung with tiny twinkling holiday lights. The woman had finished a brandy and soda and wanted another; she signaled the black houseboy tending bar. Peter declined another ginger ale.

"Of course Nan would never have looked the same. What was indefinable yet unique about her youthful beauty—gone forever. Her nose demolished; facial bones not just broken but shattered. Such unexpected cruelty, so deadly to the soul, destroyed her optimism, her innocent ecstasy and *joie de vivre.* If you're familiar with the portraits that John Ransome painted, you know the Nan I'm speaking of."

"I saw them on the Internet."

"I only wish the family owned one. I understand all of his work has increased tremendously in value in the past few years." Elisa sighed and shifted the weight of the bichon frisé dog on her lap. She stared at a recessed gas log fire in one angle of the octagonal garden room. "Who would have thought that a single, unexpected blow from a man's fist could do such terrible damage?"

"In New York they're called 'sly-rappers,'" Peter said. "Sometimes they use a brick, or wear brass knuckles. They come up behind their intended victims, usually on a crowded sidewalk, tap them on a shoulder. And when they turn, totally defenseless, to see who's there—"

"Is it always a woman?"

"In my experience. Young and beautiful, like Nan was."

"Dreadful."

"I understand Houston PD didn't get anywhere trying to find the perp."

"'Perp?' Yes, that's how they kept referring to him. But it happened so quickly; there were only a couple of witnesses, and he disappeared while Nan was bleeding there on the sidewalk." She reached up for the drink that the houseboy brought her. "Her skull was fractured when she fell. She didn't regain consciousness for more than a week." Elisa looked at Peter while the bichon frisé eagerly lapped at the brimming drink she held on one knee. "But you haven't explained why the New York police department is interested in Nan's case."

"I can't say at this time, I'm sorry. Could you tell me when Nan started doing heroin?"

"Between, I think, her third and fourth surgeries. What she really needed was therapy, but she stopped seeing her psychiatrist when she took up with a rather dubious young man. He, I'm sure, was the one who—what is the expression? Got her hooked."

"Calvin Cotrona. A few busts, petty stuff. Yeah, he was a user."

Elisa took her brandy and soda away from the white dog with the large ruff of head; he scolded her with a sharp bark. "Can't give him any more," she explained to Peter. "He becomes obstreperous, and pees on the Aubusson. Rather like my third husband, who couldn't hold his liquor either. Quiet down, Richelieu, or mommy will become deeply annoyed." She studied Peter again. "You seem to know so much about Nan's tragedy and how she died. What is it you hoped to learn from me, Detective?"

Peter rubbed tired eyes. "I wanted to know if Nan saw or heard from John Ransome once she'd finished posing for him."

"Not to my knowledge. After she returned to Houston she was quite blue and unsociable for many months. I suspected at the time she was infatuated with the man. But I never asked. Is it important?" Elisa raised her glass but didn't drink; her hand trembled. She looked startled. "But you can't mean—you can't be thinking—"

"Mrs. McLaren, I've talked to two other of Ransome's models in the past few weeks. Both were disfigured. A knife in one case, sulphuric acid in the other. In a day or two, with luck, I'll be talking to another of the Ransome women, Valerie Angelus. And I hope to God that nothing has happened to *her* face. Because that's stretching coincidence way too far. And already it's scaring the hell out of me."

In his room at a Motel Six near Houston's major airport, named for one of the U.S. presidents who had bloomed and thrived where a stink of corruption was part of the land, Peter called his uncle Charlie in Brookline, Massachusetts. Thirty-six hours had passed since he'd e-mailed her from Vegas, but Echo hadn't showed up there. He tried Rosemay in New York; she hadn't heard from Echo either. He sent another e-mail that didn't go through. In exasperation he tried leaving a message on her pager, but it was turned off.

Frustrated, he stretched out on the bed with a cold washcloth over his eyes. Traveling always gave him a queasy stomach and a headache. He chewed a Pepcid and tried to convince himself he had nothing to seriously worry about. The other Ransome women he knew of or had already interviewed had been attacked months after their commitments to the artist, and, presumably, their love affairs, were over.

Violent psychopaths had consistent profiles. Pete couldn't see the urbane Mr. Ransome as a part-time stalker and slasher, no matter what the full moon could do to potentially unstable psyches. But there was another breed, and not so rare according to his readings of case studies in psychopathology, who, insulated by wealth and position and perverse beyond human ken, would pay handsomely to have others gratify their sick, secret urges.

There was no label he could pin on John Ransome yet. But the notion that Ransome had spent several weeks already carefully and unhurriedly manipulating Echo, first to seduce and finally to destroy her, detonated the fast-food meal that had been sitting undigested in his stomach like a bomb. He went into the bathroom to throw up, afterward sat on the floor exhausting himself in a helpless rage. Feeling Echo on his skin, allure of a supple body, her creases and small breast buds and tempting, half-awake eyes. Thinking of her desire to make love to him at the cottage in Bedford and his stiff-necked refusal of her. A defining instance of false pride that might have sent his life careening off in a direction he'd never intended it to go.

He wanted Echo now, desperately. But while he was savagely getting himself off what he felt was a whore's welcome in silk, what he saw was the rancor in Eileen's dark eyes.

John Ransome didn't show up at the house until a quarter of ten, still wearing his work clothes that retained the pungency of the studio. Oil paints. To Echo the most intoxicating of odors. She caught a whiff of the oils before she saw him reflected in the glass of one of the bookcases in the first-floor library where she had passed the time with a sketchbook and her Prismacolor pencils, copying an early Ransome seascape. Painting the sea gave her a lot of trouble; it changed with the swiftness of a dream.

"I am so sorry, Mary Catherine." He had the look of a man wearied but satisfied after a fulfilling day.

"Don't worry, John. But I don't know about dinner."

"Ciera's used to my lateness. I need twenty minutes. You could select the wine. Chateau Petrus."

"John?"

Yes?"

"I was looking at your self-portrait again—"

"Oh, that. An exercise in monomania. But I was sick of staring at myself before I finished. I don't know how Courbet could have done *eight* self-studies. Needless to say he was better looking than I am. I ought to take that blunder down and shove it in the closet under the stairs."

"Don't you dare! John, really, it's magnificent."

"Well, then. If you like it so much, Mary Catherine, it's yours."

"What? No," she protested, laughing. "I only wanted to ask you about the girl—the one who's reflected in the mirror behind your chair? So mysterious. Who is she?"

He came into the library and stood beside her, rubbed a cheekbone where his skin, sensitive to paint-thinner, was inflamed.

"My cousin Brigid. She was the first Ransome girl."

"No, really?"

"Years before I began to dedicate myself to portraits, I did a nude study of Brigid. After we were both satisfied with the work, we burned it together. In fact, we toasted marshmallows over the fire."

Echo smiled in patient disbelief.

"If the painting was so good . . ."

"Oh, I think it was. But Brigid wasn't of age when she posed."

"And you were?"

"Nineteen." He shrugged and made a palms-up gesture. "She

was very mature for her years. But it would have been a scandal. Very hard on Brigid, although I didn't care what anyone would think."

"Did you ever paint her again?"

"No. She died not long after our little bonfire. Contracted septicemia at her boarding school in Davos." He took a step closer to the portrait as if to examine the mirror-cameo more closely. "She had been dead almost two years when I attempted this painting. I missed Brigid. I included her as a—I suppose your term would be guardian angel. I did feel her spirit around me at the time, her wonderful, free spirit. I was tortured. I suppose even angels can lose hope for those they try to protect."

"Tortured? Why?"

"I said that she died of septicemia. The results of a classmate's foolhardy try at aborting Brigid's four-month-old fetus. And, yes, the child was mine. Does that disgust you?"

After a couple of blinks Echo said, "Nothing human disgusts me."

"We made love after we ate our marshmallows, shedding little flakes of burnt canvas as we undressed each other. It was a warm summer night." His eyes had closed, not peacefully. "Warm night, star bright. I remember how sticky our lips were from the marshmallows. And how beautifully composed Brigid seemed to me, kneeling. On that first night of the one brief idyll of our lives."

"Did you know about the baby?"

"Brigid wrote to me. She sounded almost casual about her pregnancy. She said she would take care of it, I shouldn't worry." For an instant his eyes seemed to turn ashen from self-loathing. "Women have always given me the benefit of the doubt, it seems."

"You're not convincing either of us that you deserve to suffer. You were immature, that's all. Pardon me, but shit happens. There's still hope for all of us, on either side of heaven."

While she was looking for a bottle of the Chateau Petrus '82 that Ransome had suggested they have with their dinner, Echo heard Ciera talking to someone. She opened another door between the rock-walled wine storage pantry and the kitchen and saw Taja sitting at the counter with a mug of coffee in her hands. Echo smiled but Taja only stared before deliberately looking away.

"Oh, she comes and goes," Ransome said of Taja after Ciera had served their bisque and returned to the kitchen.

"Why doesn't she have dinner with us?" Echo said.

"It's late. I assume she's already eaten."

"Is she staying here tonight?"

"She prefers being aboard the boat if we're not in for a blow."

Echo sampled her soup. "She chose me for you—didn't she? But I don't think she likes me at all."

"It isn't what you're thinking."

"I don't know what I'm thinking. I get that way sometimes."

"I'll have her stay away from the house while you're—"

"No, please! Then I really am at fault somehow." Echo sat back in her chair, trailing a finger along the tablecloth crewelwork. "You've known her longer than all of the Ransome women. Did you ever paint Taja? Or did you toast marshmallows over those ashes too?"

"It would be like trying to paint a mask within a mask," Ransome said regretfully. "I can't paint such a depth of solitude. Sometimes . . . she's like a dark ghost to me, sealed in a world of night I'm at a loss to imagine. Taja has always known that I can't paint her." He had bowed his head, as if to conceal a play of emotion in his eyes. "She understands."

ELEVEN

The Knowles-Rembar Clinic, an upscale facility for the treatment of well-heeled patients with a variety of addictions or emotional traumas, was located in a Boston suburb not far from the campus of Wellesley College. Knowles-Rembar had its own campus of gracefully rolling lawns, brick-paved walks, great oaks and hollies and cedars and old rhododendrons that would be bountifully ablaze by late spring. In mid December they were crusted with ice and snow. At one-twenty in the afternoon the sun was barely there, a mild buzz of light in layered gray clouds that promised more snow.

The staff psychiatrist Peter had come to see was a height-disadvantaged man who greatly resembled Barney Rubble with thick glasses. His name was Mark Gosden. He liked to eat his lunch outdoors, weather permitting. Peter accommodated him. He drank vending machine coffee and shared one of the oatmeal cookies Gosden's mother had baked for him. Peter didn't ask if the psychiatrist still lived with her.

"This is a voluntary facility," Gosden explained. "Valerie's most recent stay was for five months. Although I felt it was contrary to her best interests, she left us three weeks ago."

"Who was paying her bills?"

"I only know that they went to an address in New York, and checks were remitted promptly."

"How many times has Valerie been here?"

"The last was her fourth visit."

Peter was aware of a young woman slipping up on them from behind. She gave Peter a glance, put a finger to her lips, then pointed at Gosden and smiled mischievously. Mittens attached to the cuffs of her parka dangled. She had a superb small face and jug-handle ears. In spite of the smile he saw in her eyes the blankness of a saintly disorder.

"And you don't think much of her chances of surviving on the outside," Peter said to the psychiatrist, who grimaced slightly.

"I couldn't discuss that with you, Detective."

"Do you know where I can find Valerie?"

Gosden brushed bread crumbs from his lap and drank some consommé from his lunchbox thermos. "Well, again. That's highly confidential without, of course, a court order."

When he put the thermos down the young woman, probably still a teenager, Peter thought, put her chilly hands over Gosden's eyes. He flinched, then forced a smile.

"I wonder who this could be? I know! Britney Spears."

The girl took her hands away. "Ta-da!" She pirouetted for them, mittens flopping, and looked speculatively at Peter.

"How about that?" Gosden said. "It's Sydney Nova!" He glanced at his watch and said with a show of dismay, "Sydney, wouldn't you know it, I'm running late. 'Fraid I don't have time for a song today." He closed his lunchbox and got up from the bench, glancing at Peter. "If you'll excuse me, I do have a seminar with our psych-tech trainees. I'm sorry I can't be of more help."

"Thanks for your time, doctor."

Sydney Nova leaned on the back of the bench as Gosden walked away, giving her hair a couple of tosses like a frisky colt.

"You don't have to run off, do you?" she said to Peter. "I heard what, I mean who, you and Goz were talking about."

"Did you know Valerie Angelus?"

Sydney held up two joined fingers, indicating the closeness of their relationship. "When she's around, I mean. Do you have a cigarette I can bum?"

"Don't smoke."

"Got a name?"

"Peter."

"Cop, huh? You're yummy for a cop, Pete."

"Thanks. I guess."

Sydney had a way of whistling softly as a space filler. She continued to look Peter over.

"Yeah, Val and I talk a lot when she's here. She trusts me. We tell each other our dirty little secrets. Did you know she was a famous model before she threw a wheel the first time?"

"Yeah. I knew that."

"Say, dude. Do you like your father?"

"Sure. I like him a lot."

Sydney whistled again a little mournfully. She cocked her head this way and that, as if she were watching rats racing around her mental attic.

"Magazine covers when she was sixteen. Totally demento at eighteen. I guess fame isn't all that it's cracked up to be." Sydney cocked her head again, making a wry mouth. "But nothing beats it for bringing in the money." Whistling. "I haven't had my fifteen minutes yet. But I will. Keep getting sidetracked." She looked around the Knowles-Rembar campus, tight-lipped.

"Tell me more about Valerie."

"More? Well, she got like resurrected by that artist guy, spent a whole year with him on some island. Talk about head cases."

"You mean John Ransome?"

"You got it, delicious dude."

"What did he do to Valerie?"

"Some secrets you don't tell! I'll eat rat poison first. Oh, I forgot. Been there, done that. Hey, do you like *The Sound of Music*? I know all the songs."

As if she'd been asked to audition, Sydney stood on the bench with her little hands spread wide and sang some of "Climb Ev'ry Mountain." Peter smiled admiringly. Sydney did have a good voice. She basked in his attention, muffed a lyric, and stopped singing. She looked down at him.

"I bet I know where Val is. Most of the time."

"You do?"

"Help me down, Pete?"

He put his hands on her small waist. She contrived to collapse into his arms. In spite of the bulky parka and her boots she seemed to weigh next to nothing. Her parted lips were an inch from his.

"Val has a thing for cemeteries," Sydney said. "She can spend the whole day—you know, like it's Disneyland for dead people."

Peter set her down on the brick walk. "Cemeteries. For instance?"

"Oh, like that big one in Watertown? Mount Auburn, I think it is. Okay, your turn."

"For what, Sydney?"

"Whatever Gosden said about *voluntary*, it's total bullshit. I'm in here like forever. But I could go with you. In the trunk of your car? Get me out of this place and I'll be real sweet to you."

"Sorry, Sydney."

She looked at him awhile longer, working on her lower lip with little fox teeth. Her gaze earthbound. She began to whistle plaintively.

"Thanks, Sydney. You were a big help."

She didn't look up as he walked away on the path.

"I put *my* father's eyes out," Peter heard her say. "So he couldn't find me in the dark any more."

Peter spent a half hour in Mount Auburn cemetery, driving slowly in his rental car between groupings of very old mausoleums resembling grim little villages, before he came to a station wagon parked alongside the drive, its tailgate down. A woman in a dark veil was lifting an armload of flowers from the back of the wagon. He couldn't tell much about her by winter light, but the veil was an unfortunate clue. He parked twenty feet away and got out. She glanced his way. He didn't approach her.

"Valerie? Valerie Angelus?"

"What is it? I still have sites to visit, and I'm late today."

There were more floral tributes in the station wagon. But even from where he was the flowers didn't appear to be fresh; some were obviously withered.

"My name is Peter O'Neill. Okay if I talk to you, Valerie?"

"Could we just skip that, I'm very busy."

"I could help you while we talk."

She had started uphill in a swirl of large snowflakes toward a mausoleum of rust-red marble with a Greek porch. She paused and shifted the brass container of wilted sprays of flowers that she held in both arms and looked around.

"Oh. That would be very nice of you. What is the nature of your business?"

"I'm a New York City detective." He walked past the station wagon. She was waiting for him. "Are you in the floral business, Valerie?"

"No." She turned again to the mausoleum on the knoll. Peter caught up to her as she was laying the memorial flowers at the vault's entrance.

"Is this your family—"

"No," she said, kneeling to position the brass pot just so in front of barred doors, fussing with the floral arrangement. She stepped back for a critical look at her work, then glanced at the inscription tablet above the doors. The letters and numerals were worn, nearly unreadable. "I don't know who they were," she said. "It's a very old mausoleum, as you can see. I suppose there aren't many descendants who remember, or care." She exhaled, the mourning veil fluttering. The veil did a decent job of disguising the fact that her facial features were distorted. If the veil had been any darker or more closely woven, probably she wouldn't be able to see where she was going. "But we'll all want to be remembered, won't we?"

"That's why you're doing this?"

"Yes." She turned and walked past him down the knoll, boots crunching through snow crust. "You're a detective? I thought you might be another insurance investigator." The cold wind teased her veil. "Well, come on. We're doing that one next." She pointed to another vault across the drive from where she'd left her station wagon.

Peter helped her pull a white fan-shaped latticework filled with hothouse flowers onto the tailgate. The weather was too brutal for her not to be wearing gloves, but with her arm extended an inch or so of wrist was exposed. The multiple scars there were reminders of more than one suicide attempt.

They carried the lattice to the next mausoleum, large enough to enclose a family tree of Biblical proportions. A squirrel nickered at them from a pediment.

"They wouldn't pay, you know," Valerie said. "They claimed that because of my . . . history, I disabled my own car. Now that's just silly. I don't know anything about cars. How the brakes are supposed to work."

"Your brakes failed?"

"We'll put it here," Valerie said, sweeping away leaves collected in a niche. When she was satisfied that the tribute was properly displayed she looked uneasily around. "Next we're going to that sort of ugly one with the little fountain. But we need to hurry. They make me leave, you know, they're very strict about that. I can't come back until seven-thirty in the morning. So I . . . must spend the night by myself. That's always the hard part, isn't it? Getting through the night."

She didn't talk much while they finished unloading the flowers and dressing up the neglected mausoleums. Once she appeared to be pleased with her afternoon's work and at peace with herself, Peter asked, as if all along they'd been having a conversation about Ransome, "Did John come to see you after your accident?"

Valerie paused to run a gloved hand over a damaged marble plinth.

"Seventeen sixty-two. Wasn't *that* a long time ago."

"Valerie—"

"I don't know why you're asking me questions," she said crossly. "I'm cold. I want to go to my car." She began walking away, then hesitated. "John is . . . all right, isn't he?"

"Was the last time I saw him. By the way, he sends his warmest regards."

"Ohhh. Well, there's good news. I mean that he's all right. And still painting?" Peter nodded. "He's a genius, you know."

"I'm not one to judge."

Her tone changed as they walked on. "Let's just skip it. Talking about John. I can't get Silkie to shut up about him. He was always so generous to me. I don't know why Silkie is afraid of him. John wouldn't hurt her."

"Who's Silkie?"

"My friend. I mean she comes around. Says she's my friend."

"What does she say about John?"

Valerie closed the tailgate of her wagon. She crossed her arms, shuddering in spite of the fur-lined greatcoat she wore.

"That John wanted to—destroy all of us. So that only his paintings live. How ridiculous. The one thing I was always sure of was John's love for me. And I loved him. I'm able to say it now. *Loved* him. I was going to have his baby."

Peter took a few unhappy moments to absorb that. "Did he know?"

"Uh-uh. I found out after I left the island. I tried and tried to get in touch with John, but—*they* wouldn't let me. So I—"

Valerie faced Peter. In the twilight he could see her staring at him through the mesh over her face. She drew a horizontal line with a finger where her abdomen would be beneath the greatcoat.

"—Did this. And then I—" She held up an arm, exposing another scarred wrist above the fur cuff of the coat sleeve. "—did this. I was so . . . angry." She let her arm drop. "I don't know why I'm telling you this. But Dr. Gosden says 'Don't keep the bad things hidden, Valerie.' And you *are* a friend of John's. I would never want him to think poorly of me, as my mother used to say. Skip my mother. I never talk about her. Would you let John know I'm okay now? The anger is gone. I'll be just fine, no matter what Goz thinks." She lifted her face to the darkened sky, snowflakes spangling her veil. She swallowed nervously. "Do you have the time, Peter?"

"Ten to five." He stamped his feet; his toes were freezing.

"Gates close at five in winter. We'd better go."

"Valerie, when did Silkie pose for Ransome?"

"Oh, that was over with a year ago. I've never been jealous of her."

"Has Silkie had any accidents you know of?"

"No," Valerie said, sounding mildly perplexed. "But I told you, obsessing about John John *John* all the time has her in a state. What I think, she's just having a hard time getting over him, so she makes up stuff about how he wants to hurt her. When it's the other way around. Goz would say she's having neurotic displacements. Anyway, she uses different names and doesn't have a home of her own. Picks up guys and stays with them a couple of nights, week at the most, then moves on."

"Then you don't know how I can get hold of her."

"Well—she left me a phone number. If I ever needed her, she said." Valerie turned the key in the ignition and the engine rumbled.

She looked back at Peter. "I can try to find the humber for you, later." Her usually somber tone had lightened. "Why don't you come by, say, nine o'clock?"

"Where?"

"Four-fifteen West Churchill. I'm in six-A. I know I must seem old to you, Peter. Sometimes I feel—ancient. Like I'm living a whole lot of lives at the same time. Skip that. Truth is I'm only twenty-seven! You probably wouldn't have guessed. I'm not coming on to you or anything, but I could make dinner for us. Would you like that?"

"Very much. Thank you, Valerie."

"Call me Val, why don't you?" she said, and drove off.

Echo was rosy-fresh from a long hot soak, sitting at the foot of her bed with her hair bound up, frowning at the laptop computer she couldn't get to work. She looked up at a knock on her door; she was clearing her throat to speak when the door opened and John Ransome looked in.

"Oh, Mary Catherine. I'm sorry—"

"No, it's okay. I was about to get dressed. John, there's something wrong with my laptop, it isn't working at all."

He shook his head. "Wish I could help. I'm barely computer-literate; I've never even looked inside one of those things. There's a computer in my office you're welcome to use."

"Thank you."

He was closing the door when she said, "John?"

"Yes?"

It's going well for you, isn't it? Your painting. You know, you looked happy today—well, most of the time."

"Did I?" he smiled, almost reluctant to confirm this. "All I know is, the hours go by so quickly in good company. And the work—yes, I am pleased. I don't feel tired tonight. How about you? Posing doesn't seem to tire or bore you."

"Because I always have something interesting to think about or tell you. I try not to talk *too* much. I'm not tired either but I'm *star*ving."

"Then I'll see you downstairs." But he didn't leave or look away from her. He'd had his own bath. He wore corduroys and a thick sweater with a shawl collar. He had a glass of wine in his left hand. "Mary Catherine, I was thinking—but this really isn't the time, I'm intruding."

"What is it, John? You can come in, it's okay."

He smiled and opened the door wider. But he stayed in the doorway, drank some wine, looked fondly at her.

"I've been thinking of trying something new, for me. Painting you contrapposto, nothing else on the canvas, no background."

She nodded thoughtfully.

"Old dog, new tricks," he said with a shrug, still smiling.

"You'd want me to pose nude, then."

"Yes. Unless you have strong reservations. I'd understand. It's just an idea."

"But I think it's a good idea," she said quickly. "You know I'm in favor of whatever makes the work go more easily, inspires you. That's why I'm here."

"You don't have to decide impetuously," he cautioned. "There's plenty of time—"

Echo nodded again. "I'm fine with it, John. Believe me."

After a few moments she rose slowly from the bed, her lips lightly compressed, with a certain inwardness that distanced her from Ransome. She slowly and with pleasure let down her hair, arms held high, glistening by lamplight. She gave her abundant dark mane a full shakeout, then stared at the floor for a few seconds longer before turning away from him as she undid the towel.

Ransome's face was impassive as he stared at Echo, his creative eye absorbing motion, light, shadow, coloring, contour. In that part of his mind removed from her subtle eroticism there was a great cold weight of ocean, the tolling waves.

Having folded the towel and lain it on the counterpane, Echo was still, seeming not to breathe, a hand outstretched as if she were a nymph reaching toward her reflection on the surface of a pool.

When at last she faced him she was easeful in her beauty, strong in her trust of herself, her purpose, her value. Proud of what they were creating together.

"Will you excuse me now, John?" she said.

TWELVE

When Valerie finished dressing for her anticipated dinner date with Peter O'Neill, having selected a clingy rose cocktail dress she'd almost forgotten was in her closet and a veil from her drawerful of veils to match, she returned to the apartment kitchen to check on how dinner was coming along. They were having gingered braised pork with apple and winter squash kebobs. She'd marinated the pork and other ingredients for two hours. The skewers were ready to grill as soon as Peter arrived. There was a bowl of tossed salad in the refrigerator. For dessert—now what had she planned for dessert? Oh, yes. Lemon-mint frappes.

But as soon as she walked into the small neat kitchen Valerie saw that the glass dish on the counter was empty and clean. No pork cubes marinating in garlic, orange juice, allspice and olive oil. The unused metal skewers were to the left of the dish. The recipe book lay open.

She stared blankly at the untouched glass dish. Her scarred lips were pursed beneath her veil. She felt something let go in her mind and build momentum swiftly, like a roller-coaster on the downside of a bell curve with a 360-degree loop just ahead. She heard herself scream childishly on a distant day of fun and apprehension.

But I—

"There's nothing in the refrigerator either," she heard her mother say. "Just a carton of scummy old milk."

The roller-coaster plummeted into a pit of darkness. Valerie turned. Her mother was leaning in the kitchen doorway. The familiar sneer. Ida had compromised the ardor of numerous men (including Valerie's daddy), methodically breaking them on the wheel of her scorn. Now her once-lush body sagged; her potent beauty had turned, glistering like the scales of a dead fish.

"Hopeless. You're just hopeless, Valerie."

Valerie swallowed hurt feelings, knowing it was pointless to try to defend herself. She closed her eyes. The thunder of the roller-coaster had reached her heart. When she looked up again her mother was still hanging around with her wicked lip and punishing sarcasm. Giving it to little Val for possessing the beauty Ida had lost forever. Valerie could go deaf when she absolutely needed to. Now should she take a peek into the refrigerator? But she knew her mother had been right. Good intentions aside, Val accepted that she'd drifted off somewhere when she was supposed to be preparing a feast.

Okay, embarrassing. Skip all that.

Valerie returned to the dining nook where the table was set, the wine decanted, candles lit. Beautiful. At least she'd done that right. She was thirsty. She thought it would be okay if she had a glass of wine before John arrived.

No, wait—could he really be coming to see her after all this time? She glanced fearfully at her veiled reflection in the dark of the window behind the table. Then she picked up the carafe in both hands and managed to pour a glass nearly full without spilling a drop. As she drank the roller-coaster stopped its jolting spree, swooping from brains to heart and back again.

Her mother said, "You can't be in any more pageants if you're going to wet yourself onstage. We're all fed up, just fed up and disgusted with you, Val."

Valerie looked guiltily at the carpet between her feet where she was dripping urine. The roller-coaster gave a start-up lurch, pitching her sideways. And she wasn't securely locked in this time. She felt panic.

Her mother said, "For once have the guts to take what's coming to you."

Valerie said, "You're an evil bitch and I've always hated you."

Her mother said, "Fuck that. You hate yourself."

No use arguing with her when Ida was in high dander and fine acidic fettle. When she was death by a thousand tiny cuts.

Valerie felt the slow, heavy, ratcheting-up of the coaster toward the pinnacle that no longer seemed unobtainable to her. Her throat had swelled nearly closed from unshed tears.

She set her glass down and filled it again. Walked a little unsteadily with the motion of the roller-coaster inside her providing impetus through the furnished apartment that was bizarrely decorated with old putrid flowers she picked up for nickels and dimes at the wholesale market. She unlocked the door and walked out, leaving the door standing open.

When the elevator came she wasn't at all surprised to see John Ransome inside.

"Where're you going?" he asked her. "To the top this time?"

"Of course."

He pushed the button for the twentieth floor. Valerie sipped her wine and stared at him. He looked the same. The smile that went down like cream and had you purring in no time. But that was then.

"You did love me, didn't you?" she asked timidly, barely hearing herself for the racket the roller-coaster was making, all the screaming souls aboard.

"Don't make me deal with that now," he said, a hint of vexation souring his smile.

Valerie pushed the veil she'd been holding away from her face to the crown of her head, where it became tangled in her hair.

"You were always an insensitive selfish son of a bitch."

"Good for you, Valerie," her mother said. Coming from Ida it was like a benediction.

John Ransome acknowledged her human failings and with a ghostly nod forgave her.

"I believe this is your floor."

Valerie got off the elevator, kicked her shoes from her feet (no good for walking on walls) and proceeded to the steel door that led to the roof of her building. There she quailed.

"Isn't anyone coming with me?" she said.

When she turned around she saw that the elevator was empty, the doors silently closing.

Oh, well, Valerie thought. *Skip it.*

Peter arrived at four-fifteen West Churchill thirty seconds behind the fire department—a pumper truck and a paramedic bus—which had passed him on the way. Two police cars were just pulling up from different directions. Two couples with dogs on leashes were looking up at the roof of the high-rise building. The doorman apparently had just finished throwing up in shrubbery.

The night was windless. Snow fell straight down, thick as a theatre scrim. The dogs were agitated in the presence of death. The body lay on the walk about twenty feet outside the canopy at the building's entrance. Red dress contrasting with an icy, broken-off wing of an arbor vitae. Peter knew who it was, had to be, before he got out of the car.

He checked his watch automatically. Eight minutes to nine o'clock. His stomach churned from shock and rage as he walked across the street and stepped over a low snowbank, shield in hand.

One of the cops was taking a tarp and body bag out of the trunk of his unit. The other one was talking to the severely shaken doorman.

"She just missed me." He looked at the front of his coat as if afraid of finding traces of spattered gore. "Hit that tree first and bounced." He looked around, face white as snails. "Aw Jesus."

"Any idea who she is?"

"Well, the veil. She always wore veils, you know, she was in an accident, went head-first through the windshield. Valerie Angelus. Used to be a model. Big-time, I mean."

Peter kneeled beside Valerie's body, lying all wrong in its heaped brokenness. Twenty-one stories including the roof, a minimum of two hundred twenty feet. Her blood black on the recently cleared walk, absorbing snowflakes. The cop put his light on Valerie's head for a few seconds; fortunately not much of her face was showing. Peter told him to turn the flashlight off. He crossed himself and stood.

"Want I should check the roof?" the uniform asked him. "Before CSI gets here?"

Peter nodded. He was a couple of states outside of his jurisdiction and still on autopilot, trying to deal with another dead end of a long-running tragedy.

The paramedics had come over. Peter didn't want to explain his presence or interest in Valerie to the detectives who would be showing up along with CSI. Time to go.

When Peter turned away he saw a familiar face through the fall of snow. She was about a hundred feet away. She had stepped out of a Cadillac Escalade on the driver's side that was idling at an intersection. He knew her, but he couldn't place her.

She was tall, a black woman, well-dressed. Even at the distance an expression of horror was vivid on her face. He wondered how long she'd been there. He stared at her, but nothing clicked right away. Nevertheless he began walking briskly toward the woman.

His interest startled her. She slipped back into the Escalade.

Glimpsing her from a different angle, he remembered. She had been John Ransome's model before Echo. And as far as he could tell, although the snow obscured his vision, there was nothing wrong with her face.

Then she had to be Silkie, Valerie's friend. Who, Valerie had claimed, was afraid—very afraid—of John Ransome.

He began running toward the Escalade, shield in hand. But Silkie, after staring at him for a couple of moments through the windshield, looked back and threw the SUV into reverse. Hell-bent to get out of there. As if the shock of Valerie's death had been replaced by fear of being detained by cops and questioned.

Of all the Ransome women, she just might be the one who could help him nail John Ransome's ass. He ran. She couldn't drive backwards forever, even though she was pulling away from him.

At the next intersection she swerved around a car that had jammed on its brakes and slid to the curb. Obviously the Escalade was in four-wheel drive; no handling problems. She straightened out the SUV and gunned it. But Peter got a break as the headlights of the car she had nearly run up on the sidewalk shone on the license plate. Long enough for him to pick up most of the plate number. He stopped running and watched the SUV disappear down a divided street. He took out his ballpoint pen and jotted down the number of the Escalade. Missing a digit, probably, but that wouldn't be a problem.

He had Silkie. Unless, of course, the SUV was stolen.

The wind was high. Echo dreamed uneasily. She was naked in the cottage in Bedford. Going from room to room, desperate to talk to Peter. He wasn't there. None of the phones she tried were working. Forget about e-mail; her laptop was still down.

John Ransome was calling her. Angry that she'd left him before she finished posing. But she didn't want to be with him. His studio was filled with ugly birds. She'd never liked birds since a pigeon pecked her once while she was sitting on a bench at the Central Park Zoo. These were all black, like the Woman in Black. They screeched at her from their perches in the cage John had put her in. He painted her from outside the cage, using a long brush with a sable tip that stroked over her body like waves. She wasn't afraid of these waves, but she felt guilty because she liked it so much, trembling at the onset of that great rogue wave that was rolling erotically through her body. She tried to twist and turn away from the insidious strokes of his brush.

"No! What are you trying to do to us? You're not going anywhere!"

Echo sat straight up in bed, breathing hard at the crest of her sex dream. Then she sagged to one side, weak from vertigo. All but helpless. Her mouth and throat were dry. She lay quietly for a minute or so until her heartbeat subsided and strength crept back into her hands. Her reading lamp was on. She'd fallen asleep while reading *Villette*.

The wind outside moaned and that shutter was loose again. When she moved her body beneath the covers she could tell her sap had been running at the climax of her dream. She sighed and yawned, still spikey with nerves, turned to reach for a bottle of water on the night table and discovered John Ransome standing in the doorway of her bedroom.

He was unsteady on his feet, head nodding a little, eyes glass. Dead drunk, she thought, with a jolt of fear.

"John—"

His lips moved but he didn't make a sound.

"You can't be here," she said. "Please go away."

He leaned against the jamb momentarily, then walked as if he were wearing dungeon irons toward the bed.

"No, John," she said. Prepared to fight him off.

He gestured as if waving away her objection. "Couldn't stop her," he mumbled. "Hit me. Gone. This is—"

Three feet from Echo he lost what little control he had of his body, pitched forward onto the bed, held onto the comforter for a few moments, eyes rolling up meekly in his head; then he slowly crumpled to the floor.

Echo jumped off the bed to kneel beside him. She saw the swelling lump as large as her fist through the hair on the left side of his head. There was a little blood—in his hair, sprinkled on his shirt collar. Not a gusher. She didn't mind the sight of blood but she knew she might have lost it if he was critically injured. Didn't look so bad on the outside but the fragile brain had taken a beating. That was her biggest worry. There was no doctor on the island. Three men and a woman were certified as EMTs, but Echo didn't know who they were or where they lived.

She was able to lift him up onto the bed. Déjà vu all again, without the threat of hypothermia this time. He wasn't unconscious. She rolled him onto his stomach and turned his head aside so he would be less likely to aspirate his own vomit if he became nauseous. Ciera, she knew, sometimes got the vapors over a hot stove and kept ammonium carbonate on hand. Echo fled downstairs to the kitchen, found the smelling salts, twisted ice in a towel and ran back to her room.

She heard him snoring gently. It had to be a good sign. She carefully packed the swelling in ice.

What a crack on the head. Let him sleep or keep him awake? She wiped at tears that wouldn't stop. Go down the road and knock on doors until she found an EMT? But she was afraid to go out into freezing wind and dark, afraid of Taja.

Taja, she thought, as the shutter slammed and her backbone iced up to the roots of her hair. Couldn't stop her, John had said. *Gone.* But why had she done this to him, what were they fighting about?

Echo slid the hammer from under the bed. She went to the door. There was no lock. She put a straight-back chair against it, jammed under the doorknob, then climbed back onto her bed beside John Ransome.

She counted his pulse, wrote it down, noted the time. Every fifteen minutes. Keep doing it, all night. While watching over him. Until he woke up, or—but she refused to think about the alternative.

At dawn he stirred and opened his eyes. Looked at her without comprehension.

"Brigid?"

"I'm Ec—Mary Catherine, John."

"Oh." His eyes cleared a little. "Happened to me?"

"I think Taja hit you with something. No, don't touch that lump." She had him by the wrist.

"Wha? Never did that before." An expression close to terror crossed his face. "Where she?"

"I don't know, John."

"Bathroom."

"You're going to throw up?"

"No. Don't think so. Pee."

She helped him to her bathroom and waited outside in case he lost consciousness again and fell. She heard him splash water in his face, moaning softly. When he came out again he was steadier on his feet. He glanced at her.

"Did I call you Brigid?"

"Yes."

"Would've been like you, if she'd lived."

"Lie down again, John."

"Have to—"

"Do what?"

He shook his head, and regretted it. She guided him to her bed and he stretched out on his back, eyes closing.

"Stay with me?"

"I will, John." She touched her lips to his dry lips. Not exactly a kiss. And lay down beside him, staring at the first flush of sun through the window with the broken shutter. She felt anxious, a little demoralized, but immensely grateful that he seemed to be okay.

As for Taja, when he was ready they were going to have a serious talk. Because she understood now just how deeply afraid John Ransome was of the Woman in Black.

And his fear had become hers.

Thirteen

The SUV Silkie had been driving belonged to a thirty-two-year-old architect named Milgren who lived a few blocks from MIT in Cambridge. Peter called Milgren's firm and was told he was attending a friend's wedding in the Bahamas and would be away for a few days. Was there a Mrs. Milgren? No.

Eight inches of fresh snow had fallen overnight; the street in front of the building where Milgren lived was being plowed. Peter had a late breakfast, then returned. The address was a recently renovated older building with a gated drive on one side and tenant parking behind it. He left his rental car in the street behind a painter's van. The day was sharply blue, with a lot of ice-sparkle in the leafless trees. The snow had moved west.

The gate of the parking drive was opening for a Volvo wagon. He went in that way and around to the parking lot, found the Cadillac Escalade in its assigned space. Apartment 4-C.

Four apartments on the fourth floor, two at each end of a wide well-lit marble-floored hallway. There was a skylight above the central foyer: elevator on one side, staircase on the other.

The painter or painters had been working on the floor, but the scaffold that had been erected to make it easier to get at the fifteen-foot-high tray ceiling was unoccupied. On the scaffold a five-gallon can of paint was overturned. A pool of it like melted pistachio ice cream was spreading along the marble floor. The can still dripped.

Peter looked from the spilled paint to the door of 4-C, which stood open a couple of feet. There was a TV on inside, loudly showing a rerun of *Hollywood Squares*.

He walked to the door and looked in. An egg-crate set filled with decommissioned celebrities was on the LCD television screen at one end of a long living room. Peter edged the door half open. A man wearing a painter's cap occupied a recliner twenty feet from the TV. All Peter could see of him was the cap, and one hand gripping an arm of the chair as if he were about to be catapulted into space.

Peter rapped softly and spoke to him but the man didn't look around. There was a lull in the hilarity on TV as they went to commercials. Peter could hear the man breathing. Shallow, distressed breaths. Peter walked in and across the short hall, to the living room. Plantation-style shutters were closed. Only a couple of low-wattage bulbs glowed in widely separated wall sconces. All of the apartment was quite dark in contrast to the brilliant day outside.

"I'm looking for Silkie," he said to the man. "She's staying here, isn't she?"

No response. Peter paused a few feet to the left of the man in the leather recliner. His feet were up. His paint-stained coveralls had the look of impressionistic masterpieces. By TV light his jowly face looked sweaty. His chest rose and fell as he tried to drag more air into his lungs.

"You okay?"

The man rolled his eyes at Peter. The fingers of his left hand had left raw scratch marks all over the red leather armrest. His other hand was nearly buried in the pulpy mass above his belt. Peter smelled the blood.

"She—made me do it—talk to the lady—get her to—unlock the door. Help me. Can't move. Guts are—falling out. My daughter's coming home—for the holidays. Now I won't be here."

Peter's gun was in his hand before the man had said ten words. "Where are they?"

The painter had run out of time. He sagged a little as his life ebbed away. His eyes remained open. There was a burst of laughter from the TV.

"Jesus and Mary," Peter whispered, then raised his voice to a shout. "Silkie, you okay? It's the police!"

With his other hand he dug out his cell phone, dialed without looking, identified himself.

"Do you want police, fire, or medical emergency?"

"Cops. Paramedics. I've got a dying man here."

He began his sweep of the apartment while he was still on the phone.

"Please stay on the line, Detective," the dispatcher said. "Help is on the way."

"I may need both hands," Peter said, and dropped the cell phone back into his pocket.

He kicked open a door to what appeared to be the architect's study and workroom. Enough light coming in here to show him at a glance the room was empty.

"Silkie!"

The master bed- and sitting room was at the end of the hall. Double doors, one standing open. As he approached along one wall, Glock held high in both hands, he made out the shapes of furnishings because of a bathroom light shining beyond a four-poster bed draped with a gauzelike material.

Furniture was overturned in the sitting room. A fish tank had been shattered.

Peter edged around the foot of the Victorian bedstead and had a partial view of a seminude body face down on the tiles. Black girl. There was broken glass from a mirror and a ribbon of blood.

"Silkie, answer me, what happened here?"

He was almost to the bathroom door when Silkie stirred, looked around blank-eyed, then tried to push herself up with both hands as she flooded with terror. Blood dripped from a long cut that started below her right eye and ran almost to the jawline.

"Is she gone?" Silkie gasped.

Peter read the shock in her widening eyes but was a split second late turning as Taja came off the bed, where she'd been lying amid a pile of pillows he hadn't paid enough attention to, and slashed at him with her stiletto.

He turned his wrist just enough so veins weren't severed but lost his automatic. He backhanded her in the face with his other hand. Taja went down in a sprawl that she corrected almost instantly, cat-quick, and rushed him again with her knife ready to thrust, held close to her side. Her face looked as wooden as a ceremonial mask. She knew her business. He blocked an attempt she made to slash upward near his groin and across the femoral artery. She knew where he was most vulnerable and didn't try for the chest, where her blade could get hung up on the zipper of his leather jacket, or his throat, which was partially protected by a scarf. And she was in no hurry, she was between him and his only way out. Acrobatic in her moves, she feinted him in the direction she wanted him to go—which was back against the bed and into the mass of sheer drapery hanging there.

Peter heard Silkie scream but he was too busy to pay attention to her. The bed drapery clung to him like spiderweb as he struggled to free himself and avoid Taja. She slashed away methodically, the material beginning to glow red from his blood.

His gun fired. Deafening.

Taja flinched momentarily, then went into a crouch, turning away from Peter, finding Silkie. She was standing just inside the bathroom, Peter's Glock 9 in both hands.

"Bitch." She fired again, range about eight feet. Taja jerked to one side; hesitated a second, glanced at Peter, who had fought his way out of the drapery. Then she sprang to the bedroom doors and vanished.

Peter slipped a hand inside his jacket where his side stung from a long caress of Taja's stiletto. A lot of blood on the hand when he looked at it. Holy Jesus. He looked at Silkie, who hadn't budged from the threshold of the bathroom nor lowered his gun. When he moved toward her she gave him a deeply suspicious look. She was nude to well below her navel. Blood dripped from her chin. She had beautifully modeled features even Echo might have envied. Peter coughed, waited suspensefully, but no blood had come up. He saw that the cut on Silkie's face could've been a lot worse, the flesh laid open. Part of it was just a scratch down across the cheekbone. A little deeper in the soft flesh near her mouth.

He had to pry his gun from Silkie's hands. His own hands were so bloody he nearly dropped the Glock. He no longer considered going after Taja. Shock had him by the back of the neck. He heard sirens before a rising teakettle hiss in his ears shut out the sound. His face dripped perspiration, but his skin was turning cold. He had to lean against the jamb, his face a few inches from the tall girl's breasts. My God but they were something.

"What's your name?" he asked Silkie.

She had the hiccups. "Ma-MacKENzie."

"I'm Peter. Peter O'Neill. We're old friends, Silkie. We dated in New York. I came up here for a visit. Can you remember that?"

"Y-yes. P-P-PETEr O'Neill. From New York."

"And you don't know who attacked you. Never saw her before. Got that?"

He looked her in the eye, wondering if they had a chance in hell of selling it. She looked back at him with a slight twitch of her head.

"Why?"

"Because Valerie Angelus is dead and you came close and that, *that* he does not get away with, don't care how much money. I want John Ransome. Want his ass all to myself until I'm ready to hand him over."

"But Taja—"

"Taja's just been doing the devil's work. That's what I believe now. *Help me*, Silkie."

She touched a finger to her chin, wiped a drop of blood away. The wound had nearly stopped oozing.

"All right," she said, beginning to cry. "How bad am I?"

"Cut's not deep. You'll always be beautiful. Listen. Hear that? Medics. On the way up. Now I need to—" He began to slide to the floor at her feet. Shuddering. His tongue getting a little thick in his mouth. "Sit down before I uh pass out. Silkie, put something on. Now listen to me. Way you talk to cops is, keep it simple. Say it the same way every time. 'We met at a party. He's only a friend.' No details. It's details that trip you up if you're lying."

"You are—a friend," she said, kneeling, putting an arm around him for a few moments. Then she stood and reached for a robe hanging up behind the bathroom door.

"We'll get him, Silkie. You'll never be hurt again. Promise." Finding it hard to breathe now. He made himself smile at her. "We'll get the bastard."

———

When Echo woke up half the day was gone. So was John Ransome, from her bed.

She looked for him first in his own room. He'd been there, changed his clothes. She found Ciera in Ransome's study, straightening up after what appeared to have been a donnybrook. A lamp was broken. Dented metal shade; had Taja hit him with it? Ciera stared at Echo and shook her head worriedly.

"Do you know where John is?"

"No," Ciera said, talkative as ever.

The day had started clear but very cold; now thick clouds were moving in and the seas looked wild as Echo struggled to keep her balance on the long path to the lighthouse studio.

The shutters inside the studio were closed. Looking up as she drew closer, Echo couldn't tell if Ransome was up there.

She skipped the circular stairs and took the cabinet-size birdcage elevator that rose through a shaft of opaque glass to the studio seventy-five feet above ground level.

Inside some lights were on. John Ransome was leaning over his worktable, knotting twine on a wrapped canvas. Echo glanced at her portrait that remained unfinished on the large easel. How serene she looked. In contrast to the turmoil she was feeling now.

He'd heard the elevator. Knew she was there.

"John."

When he looked back he winced at the pain even that slow movement of his head caused him. The goose egg, what she could see of it, was a shocking violet color. She recognized raw anger in conjunction with his pain, although he didn't seem to be angry at her.

"Are you all right? Why didn't you wake me up?"

"You needed your sleep, Mary Catherine."

"What are you doing?" The teakettle on the hot plate had begun to wheeze. She took it off, looking at him, and prepared tea for both of them.

"Tying up some loose ends," he said. He cut twine with a pair of scissors. Then his hand lashed out as if the stifled anger had found a vent; a tall metal container of brushes was swept off his work table. She couldn't be sure he'd done it on purpose. His movements were haphazard, they mimicked drunkenness although she saw no evidence in the studio that he'd been drinking.

"John, why don't you—I've made tea—"

"No, I have to get this down to the dock, make sure it's on the late boat."

"All right. But there's time, and I could do that for you."

He backed into his stool, sat down uneasily. She put his tea within reach, then stooped to gather up the scattered brushes.

"Don't do that!" he said. "Don't pick up after me."

She straightened, a few brushes in hand, and looked at him, lower lip folded between her teeth.

"I'm afraid," he said tautly, "that I've reached the point of diminished returns. I won't be painting any more."

"We haven't finished!"

"And I want you to leave the island. Be on that boat too, Mary Catherine."

"Why? What have I— you can't mean that, John!"

He glanced at her with an intake hiss of breath that scared her. His eyes looked feverish. "Exactly that. Leave. For your safety."

"My—? What has Taja done? Why were you fighting with her last night? Why are you afraid of her?"

"Done? Why, she's spent the past few years hunting seven beautiful women after I had finished painting them."

"Hunting—?"

"Then she slashed, burned, maimed—*killed*, for all I know! And always she returned to me after the hunt, silently gloating. Now she's out there again, searching for Silkie MacKenzie."

"Dear *God*. Why?"

"Don't you understand? To make them pay, for all they've meant to me."

Echo had the odd feeling that she wasn't fully awake after all, that she just wanted to sink to the floor, curl up and go back to sleep. She couldn't look at his face another moment. She went hesitantly to a curved window, opened the shutters there and rested her cheek on insulated safety glass that could withstand hurricane winds. She stared at the brute pounding of the sea below, feeling the force of the waves in the shiver of glass, repeating the surge of her own heartbeats.

"How long have you known?"

"More than two years ago I became suspicious of what she might be doing during prolonged absences. I hired the Blackwelder Organization to investigate. What they came up with was horrifying, but still circumstantial."

"Did you really *want* proof?" Echo cried.

"Of course I did! And last night I finally received it, an e-mail from Australia. Where one of my former models—"

"Another victim?"

"Yes," Ransome said, his head down. "Her name is Aurora Leigh. She'd been in seclusion. But she was in adequate shape emotionally to identify Taja as her attacker from sketches I provided."

"Adequate shape emotionally," Echo repeated numbly. "Why did Taja hit you last night?"

"I confronted her with what I knew."

"Was she trying to kill you?"

"No. I don't think so. Just letting me know her business isn't finished yet."

"Oh Jesus and Mary! The police—did you call—"

"I called my lawyers this morning. They'll handle it. Taja will be stopped."

"But what if Taja's still here? You'll need—"

"Her boat's gone. She's not on the island."

"There are dozens of islands where she could be hiding!"

"I can take care of myself."

"Oh, *sure*," Echo said, bouncing the heel of her hand off her forehead as she began to pace.

"Don't be frightened. Just go back to New York. If there's even a remote possibility Taja will be free long enough to return to Kincairn—well then, Taja is, she's always been, my responsibility."

Echo paused, stared, caught her breath, alarmed by something ominous hanging around behind his words. "Why do you say that? You didn't make her what she is. That must have happened long before you met her, where—?"

"In Budapest."

"Doing what, mugging tourists?"

"When I first saw Taja," he said, his voice laboring, "she was drawing with chalk on the paving stones near the Karoly Kert gate. For what little money passersby were willing to throw her way." He raised his head slowly. "I don't know how old she was then; I don't know her age now. As I told you once, terrible things had been done to her. She was barefoot, her hair wild, her dress shabby." He smiled faintly at Echo. His lips were nearly bloodless. "Yes, I should have walked on by. But I was astounded by her talent. She drew wonderful, suffering, religious faces. They burned with fevers, the hungers of martyrdom. All of the faces washing away each time it rained, or scuffed underfoot by the heedless. But every day she would draw them again. Her knees, her elbows were scabbed. For hours she barely paused to look up from her work. Yet she knew I was there. And after a while it was my face she sought, my approval. Then, late one afternoon when it didn't rain, I—I followed her. Sensing that she was dangerous. But I've never wanted a tame affair. It's immolation I always seem to be after."

His smile showed a slightly crooked eye tooth Echo was more or less enamored with, a sly imperfection.

"Just how dangerous she was at that time became a matter of no great importance. You see, we may all be dangerous, Mary Catherine, depending on what is done to us."

"Oh, was the sex that good?" Echo said harshly, her face flaming.

"Sometimes sex isn't the necessary thing, depending on the nature of one's obsession."

Echo began, furiously, to sob. She turned again to the horizon, the darkening sea.

After a couple of minutes he said, "Mary Catherine—"

"You know I'm not going! I won't let you give up painting because of what Taja did! You're not going to send me away, John, you need me!"

"It's not in your power to get me to paint again."

"Oh, isn't it?" She wiped her leaky nose on the sleeve of her fisherman's sweater; hadn't done that in quite a few years. Then she pulled off the sweater, gave her head a shake, swirling her abundant hair. Ransome smiled cautiously when she looked at him again, began to stare him down. A look as old, as eternal as the sea below.

"We have to complete what we've started," Echo said reasonably. She moved closer to him, the better for him to see the fierceness of eye, the high flame of her own obsession. She swept a hand in the direction of her portrait on his easel. "Look, John. And look again! I'm not just a face on a sidewalk. I *matter*!"

She seized and kissed him, knowing that the pain in his sore head made it not particularly enjoyable; but that wasn't her reason just then for doing it.

"Okay?" she said mildly and took a step back, clasping hands at her waist. The pupil. The teacher. Who was who awaited clarification, perhaps the tumult and desperation of an affair now investing the air they breathed with the power of a blood oath.

"Oh, Mary Catherine—" he said despairingly.

"I asked you, *is it okay*? Do we go on from here? Where? When? What do we do now, John?"

He sighed, nodded slightly. That hurt too. He put a hand lightly to the bump on his head.

"You're a tough, wonderful kid. Your heart . . . is just so different than mine. That's what makes you valuable to me, Mary Catherine." He gravely touched her shoulder, tapping it twice, dropped his hand. "And now you've been warned."

She liked the touch, ignored his warning. "Shall I pick up the rest of those brushes that were spilled?"

After a long silence Ransome said, "I've always found salvation in my work. As you must know. I wonder, could that be why your god sent you to me?"

"We'll find out," Echo said.

Peter heard one of the detectives ask, "How close did she come to his liver?"

A woman, probably the ER doc who had been stitching him up, replied, "Too close to measure."

The other detective on the team, who had the flattened Southie nasal tone, said, "Irish luck. Okay if we talk to him now?"

"He's awake. The Demerol has him groggy."

They came into Peter's cubicle. The older detective, probably nudging retirement, had a paunch and an archaic crook of nose like an old Roman in marble. The young one, but not that young—close to forty, Peter guessed—had red hair in cheerful disarray and hard-ass good looks the women probably went for like a guilty pleasure. Cynicism was a fixture in his face, like the indentations from long-ago acne.

He grinned at Peter. "How you doin', you lucky baastud?"

"Okay, I guess."

"Frank Tillery, Cambridge PD. This here is my Fathah Superior, Sal Tranca."

"Hiya."

"Hiya."

Peter wasn't taken in by their show of camaraderie. They didn't like what they had seen in the architect's apartment and they didn't like what they'd heard so far from Silkie. They didn't like him, either.

"Find the perp yet?" he said, taking the initiative.

Sal said, "Hasn't turned up. Found her blade in a can of paint. Seven inches, thin, what they call a stiletto in the old country."

Tillery leaned against a wall with folded arms and a lemon twist of a grin and said, "Pete, you mind tellin' us why you was trackin' a homicidal maniac in our town without so much as a courtesy call to us?"

"I'm not on the job. I was—looking for Silkie MacKenzie. Walked right into the play."

"What did you want with MacKenzie? I mean, if I'm not bein' too subtle here."

"Met her—in New York." His ribs were taped, and it was hard for him to breathe. "Like I told you at the scene, had some time off so I thought I'd look her up."

"Apparently she was already shacked up with one guy, owns the apartment," Sal said. "Airline ticket in your coat pocket tells us you flew in from Houston yesterday morning."

Peter said, "I got friends all over. On vacation, just hangin' out."

"Hell of a note," Tillery said. "Lookin' to chill, relax with some good-lookin' pussy, next thing you know you're in Mass General with eighty-four stitches."

"She was real good with that, what'a'ya call it, stiletto?"

Sal said, "So, Pete. Want to do your statement now, or later we come around after your nap? As a courtesy to a fellow shield. Who seems to be goddamn well connected where he comes from." Sal looked around as if for a place to spit.

"I'll come to you. How's Silkie?"

"Plastic surgeon looked at her already. There's gonna be some scarring they can clean up easy."

"She say she knew the perp?"

Tillery and Tranca exchanged jaundiced glances. "About as well as you did," Sal said.

"Well, you enjoy that dark meat," Tillery said. He was on the way out when something occurred to him to ask. He turned to Peter with his cynical grin.

"How long you had your gold, Pete?"

"Nine months."

"Hey, congrats. Sal here, he's got twenty-one years on the job. Me, I got eleven."

"Yeah?" Peter said, closing his eyes.

"What Frank is gettin' at," Sal said dourly, "we can smell a crock of shit when it's right under our noses."

FOURTEEN

Echo was putting her clothes back on inside the privacy cubicle in John Ransome's studio when she heard the door close, heard him locking her in.

"John!"

The door was thick tempered glass. He looked back at her tiredly as she emerged holding the sweater to her bare breasts and tugged at the door handle, not believing this.

"I'm sorry," he said. His voice was muffled by the thickness of the door. "When it's done—if it's done tonight—I'll be back for you."

"No! Let me out *now*!"

He shook his head slightly, then clattered down the iron staircase like a man in search of a nervous breakdown while Echo battled the door; still unwilling to believe that she was locked up until Ransome decided otherwise.

She glanced at the nude study he had begun, only a free-flowing sketch at this point but unmistakably Echo. She then demonstrated, at the top of her voice, how many obscene street oaths she'd picked up over the years.

But the harsh wind off a tumbled sea that caused her glass jail to shimmy on its high perch wailed louder than she could hope to.

Peter woke up with a start when Silkie MacKenzie put a hand on his shoulder. He felt sharp pain, then nausea before he could focus on her.

"Hello, Peter. It's Silkie."

He swallowed his distress, attempted a smile. The right side of her face was neatly bandaged. "How you doin'?"

"I'll be all right."

"What time is it, Silkie?"

She looked at her gold Piaget. "Twenty past three."

"Oh, Jesus." He licked dry lips. There was an IV hookup in the back of his left hand for fluids and antibiotics. But his mouth was parched. With his heavily-wrapped right hand—how many times had Taja cut him?—he motioned for Silkie to lean her face close to his. "Talk to you," he whispered. "Not here. They may have left a device. Couldn't watch both of them all the time."

"Isn't that illegal?"

"Wouldn't be admissable in a courtroom. But they don't trust either of us, so they could be fishing—for an angle to use during an interrogation. Walk me to the bathroom."

She got him out of bed and supported him, rolling the IV pole with her other hand. He had Silkie come inside the bathroom with him. All the fluids they'd dripped into Peter had him desperate to pee. Silkie continued to hold his elbow for support and looked at a wall.

"Today wasn't the first time Taja came after you," Peter said.

"No. Five months ago I was in Los Angeles. I had a commercial, the first work my agent was able to get for me after I'd finished my assignment with John. But John didn't want me working, you see. My face all over telly. That would have destroyed the—the allure, the fascination, the mystery he works so hard to create and maintain."

"So keep the paintings, destroy the model. I've seen Anne Van Lier and Eileen Wendkos."

Silkie looked around at him; she was close enough for Peter to feel the tremor that ran through her body.

"Then I had a glimpse of Taja, at a restaurant opposite Sunset Plaza. She pretended not to notice me. But I—all of my life I've had premonitions. There was suddenly the darkest, angriest cloud I'd ever seen pressing down on Sunset Boulevard. So I ran for my life. Later I hired private detectives. I was very curious to know what had happened to my—my predecessors? I found out, as you did. And once I talked to Valerie, I understood what my sixth sense had always told me about John. I believe he may be insane."

"We have to get out of here. Now. I have a rental car if Cambridge PD didn't impound it. But I'm not sure how much driving I can do." He bumped her as he turned in their small space; weakness followed pain, and it worried him. "Silkie, help me pull this IV out of my hand, then bring the rest of my clothes to me."

"Where are we going?"

"The nearest airport to Kincairn Island is in Bangor, Maine."

"I don't think the weather is good up there."

"Then the sooner we leave, the better. Get my wallet and watch from the lockbox. Use my credit card to reserve two seats on the next flight Boston to Bangor."

"I'm not so sure I want to do that. I mean, go back there. I'm afraid, Peter."

"Please, Silkie! You gotta help me. My girl's on that island with that sick son of a bitch Ransome!"

The owner and chief pilot of Lola's Flying Service at Bangor airport was going over accounts in her office when Peter and Silkie walked in at ten minutes to eight. Snow particles were flying outside the hangar, and they had felt sharp enough to etch glass.

Lola was a large cockeyed jalopy of a woman, salty as Lot's wife. Peter explained his needs.

"Chopper the two a ya's down to Kincairn in this freakin' weather? Not if I hope to achieve my average life expectancy."

Peter produced his shield. Lola greeted that show of authority with a lopsided smile.

"I'm Born Again, honeybunch; and I surely would hate to miss the Rapture. Otherwise what's Born Again good for?"

Silkie said, "Please listen to me. We must get there. Something very bad is going to happen on the island tonight. I have a premonition."

Lola, looking vastly amused, said, "Bullshit."

"Her premonitions are very accurate," Peter said.

Lola looked them over again. The bandages and bruises.

"I had my tea leaves read once. They said I shouldn't get involved with people who show up looking like the losers in a domestic disturbance competition." She picked up the remains of a ham on whole wheat from a takeout carton and polished it off in two bites.

Silkie patiently opened her tote and took out a very large roll of bills, half of which, she made it plain to Lola, were hundreds.

"On the other hand," Lola said, "you have any premonitions about what this little jaunt is gonna cost you?"

"Name your price," Silkie said calmly, and she began laying C-notes in the carton on top of a wilted lettuce leaf.

Echo's immediate needs were met by a chemical toilet; a small refrigerator that contained milk, a wedge of Jarlsburg, bottled water and white wine; and an electric heater that dispelled the worst of the cold after sundown. There was also a large sheepskin throw to wrap up in while she rocked herself in the only chair in John Ransome's studio. Physically she was fine. She had drunk the rest of an already-opened bottle of Cabernet Sauvignon, ordinarily enough wine to put her soundly to sleep. But the wind that was hitting forty knots according to the gauge outside and her circumstances kept her alert and sober, with an aching heart and a sense of impending tragedy.

If it's done tonight, Ransome had said forebodingly. What did he know about Taja, and what was he planning?

Every few minutes, between decades of the rosary that went everywhere with her, Echo jumped up restlessly to pace the inner circumference of the studio, then stop to peer through the shutters in the direction of the stone house three hundred yards away. She could make out only blurred lights through horizontal lashings of snow. She'd seen nothing of Ransome since his head had disappeared down the circular lighthouse stairs. She hadn't seen anyone except Ciera, who had left the house early, perhaps dismissed by Ransome. In twilight, on her way across the island, Ciera's path had brought her within two hundred feet of the Kincairn light. Echo had pounded on the glass, screamed at her, but Ciera never looked up.

She'd turned off the studio lights. After the wine she had a lingering headache, more from stress than from drinking. The light hurt her eyes and made it more difficult to see anything outside. At full dark she relied on the glow from the heater and the red warning strobe atop the studio for illumination.

When she tired of walking in circles and trying to see through the fulminating storm, she slumped in the rocking chair with her feet tucked under her. She was past sulking, brooding, and prayer. It was time to get tough with herself. *You have a little problem, Mary C.? Solve it.*

That was when the pulse of the strobe overhead gave her an idea of how to begin.

On the way down from Bangor in the three-passenger Eurocopter that had become surplus when Manuel Noriega fell out of favor with the CIA, Peter had plenty of time to reflect on the reasons why he'd never taken up flying as a hobby.

It was a strange night, clearing up in places on the coast but still with force eight winds. The sea from twelve hundred feet was visible to the horizon; beneath them it was a scumble of whitecaps going every which way. The sky overhead was tarnished silver in the light from the moon. Lola, dealing with the complexities of flying through the gauntlet of a gale that had the chopper rattling and vibrating, looked unperturbed, confident of her skills, although she was having a hard chew on the wad of grape-flavored gum in her right cheek.

"Should've calmed down some by now," she groused. "That's why we waited."

Silkie had become sick to her stomach two minutes after they lifted off at twelve-thirty in the morning, and she'd stayed sick and moaning all the way. Peter, whose father and uncles had always owned boats, was a competent sailor himself and used to rough weather, although this was something special even for him. The knife wounds Taja had inflicted were throbbing; at each jolt they took he hoped the stitches would hold.

Lola and Peter wore headphones. Silkie had taken hers off to get a better grip on her head with both hands.

"Where are we now?" Peter asked Lola.

"Over Blue Hill Bay. See that light down to our left?"

"Uh-huh," he said, his teeth clicking together.

"That's Bass Harbor head. Uh-oh. That's a Coast Guard cutter down there, steaming southwest. Somebody's got trouble. Take a dip in those waters tonight, you've got about twelve minutes. Okay, southwest is where we're heading now; right two-four-zero and closer to the deck. It's gonna get rougher, kids."

Peter checked the action of the old Colt Pocket Nine he'd borrowed from his uncle Charlie in Brookline before heading up to Maine. Then he looked at islands appearing below. A lot of islands, some just specks on the IR.

"How are you going to find—"

"I know Kincairn by its light. Problem is, I don't think anyone's tried to land a helicopter there. Not a level spot on the island. Wind shear around a rock pile like Kincairn, conditions are just about perfect for an SOL funeral."

"SOL?" Silkie said. She'd put her headphones back on.

"Shit outa luck," Lola said, and laughed uproariously.

From a window of his study John Ransome observed through binoculars the lights in the studio flashing. A familiar sequence. Morse Code distress signal. Mary Catherine's ingenuity made him smile. Of course he wouldn't have expected less of her. She was the last and the best of the Ransome women.

When he looked at the base of the Kincairn light, then down the road to the town, he saw one of the two Land Rovers he kept on the island coming up from the cove. When it stopped near the lighthouse, he wasn't surprised to see Taja get out.

Mary Catherine's face appeared behind salt-bleared glass, then vanished quickly, as if she'd seen Taja.

When the Woman in Black started toward the lighthouse, she walked slowly and stiffly, head lowered against the blasts of wind. She held her right side as if she'd been thrown around and injured while bringing the boat in through rough seas. Watching her, Ransome felt neither pity not regret. She was just a blight on his soul, as he had tried to explain to Mary Catherine. The time had come to remove it.

He put the binoculars down on his desk and unlocked a drawer. He kept an S & W police model .38 there. Hadn't fired the revolver in years but the bore was clean when he checked it.

Afterward a couple of phone calls and everything would be taken care of for him. As it always was. No messy publicity.

He felt deep empathy for Mary Catherine. It was unfortunate she had to be a part of the cleansing. But he would take care of her afterward, as he had all of the Ransome women. He had never used his genius as an excuse for poor behavior. When her own god failed her—as He would tonight—John Ransome would provide.

He was putting on his coat when he heard, above the wind, a helicopter fly low over the house.

"Peter, it's Taja!" Silkie yelled.

He saw the Woman in Black, looking up at the helicopter a hundred yards away. She had opened the door at the base of the lighthouse.

The studio lights were blinking again. Then Echo rushed to the windows, frantically signaling the helicopter.

"Who is that?" Silkie said.

"It's Echo," Peter said happily. Then, as Taja entered the lighthouse his momentary elation vanished. "Put us down!" he said to Lola.

"Not here! Maybe in the cove, on the dock!"

"How far's that?"

"Three miles south, I think."

"No! Can you drop me off here? Next to the lighthouse?"

"What are you doing?" Silkie asked anxiously.

"I can't maintain a hover more than three-four seconds," Lola advised him. "And not closer than ten feet off the ground!"

"Close enough!" Peter said. "Silkie! Go back with Lola. There's an APB out on Taja. Call the state cops, tell them she's on Kincairn!"

He opened the door on his side, looked at the rocks below in the undercarriage floodlight. The danger of it chilled him more than the wind in his face. If he landed wrong, a ten-foot jump onto frozen stony ground was going to feel like fifty.

In John Ransome's studio, Echo saw Taja get off the small elevator outside. They looked at each other for a few moments until Echo turned to the windows, seeing the helicopter fly away.

When she turned again Taja had unlocked the glass door and walked inside.

With the door open Echo's only thought was to get the hell out of there. But she couldn't get past Taja, who was quick and strong. An image of the PR boy in the subway repeated in Echo's mind as she was caught by one arm and pushed back. All the way to the easel that still held Ransome's beginning nude study of her. The portrait seemed to distract Taja as Echo struggled in her grip, swearing, swinging a wild left hand at the Woman in Black.

Taja's free hand came away from her side. The glove was sticky with blood. She groped behind her on the worktable. Her fingers closed on the handle of the knife that Ransome honed daily before trimming his brushes.

And Echo screamed.

Peter was halfway up the circular iron stairs, hobbling on a sprained ankle, when he heard the scream. Knew what it meant. But he was too slow and far from Echo to do her any good.

Taja struck once at Echo, slashing her across the heel of the hand Echo flung up to protect her face.

Then, instead of a lethal follow-up, Taja took the time to drive the knife into the canvas on the easel, ripping it in a gesture of fury.

Taja's body was momentarily at an angle to Echo, and vulnerable. Echo braced herself against the worktable and drove a knee high to the rib cage where Silkie had shot her in the Cambridge apartment.

Taja went down with a hoarse scream, dropped the knife. She was groping for it when Peter barreled into the studio and lunged at her.

"No, goddamn it, no!"

He grabbed her knife hand as she tried to come up off the floor at him. His free hand went to Taja's face, street-fighter style. He missed her eyes, tried to get a grip as she jerked her head aside.

Part of her flesh seemed to come loose in his hand. But it was only latex.

The face beneath her second skin was pocked with random, circular scars, as if from a dozen cigarette burns.

They were both hurt but Peter couldn't hold her. He knew the knife was coming. Then Echo got an armlock on Taja's neck and pulled her back; Peter stepped in with a short hook to Taja's jaw that dropped her instantly. He wrenched the knife away and pulled her back onto her feet. She wasn't unconscious but her eyes were crossing, no fight left in her.

"Let her go, Peter," John Ransome said behind them. "It's finished."

Peter shot a look behind him. "Not yet!" He looked again into Taja's eyes. "Tell me one thing! Was it Ransome? Did he send you after those women? Tell me!"

"Peter, she can't talk!" Echo said.

Taja still wasn't focusing. There was a trickle of blood at one corner of her mouth.

"Find a way to talk to me! I want to know!"

"Peter," John Ransome said, "please let her go." His tone weary. "It's up to me to deal with Taja. She's my—"

"Was it Ransome!" Peter screamed in Taja's face, as she blinked, stared at him.

She nodded. Her eyes closed. A second later Ransome shot her. Blood and bits of bone from the hole in her forehead splattered Peter's face. She hung in his grip as Echo screamed. Still holding Taja up, Peter turned to Ransome, speechless with rage.

Ransome lowered his .38, taking a deep breath. "My responsibility. Sorry. Now will you put her down?"

Peter let Taja fall and went for his own gun, brought it up in both hands inches from Ransome's face.

"Drop your piece! So help me God I'll cap you right here!"

"Peter, no—!"

Ransome took another breath, his gun hand moving slowly toward the worktable, his finger off the trigger. "It's all right." He sounded eerily calm. I'm putting the gun down. Just don't let your emotions get the best of you. No accidents, Peter." The .38 was on the table. He lifted his hand slowly away from it, looked at Taja's body between them. Peter moved him at gunpoint back from the table.

"You're under arrest for murder! You have the right to remain silent. You have the right to be represented by an attorney. Anything you say can and will be used against you in a court of law. Do you understand what I've just said to you?"

Ransome nodded. "Peter, it was self-defense."

"Shut up, damn you! You don't get away with that!"

"You're out of your jurisdiction here. One more thing. I *own* this island."

"On your knees, hands behind your head."

"I think we need to talk when you're in a more rational—"

Peter took his finger off the trigger of the 9mm Colt and bounced it off the top of Ransome's head. Ransome staggered and dropped to one knee. He slowly raised his hands.

Peter glanced at Echo, who had pulled the sleeve of her sweater down over the hand that Taja had slashed. She'd made a fist to try to stop the bleeding. She shook from fear.

"Oh Peter, oh God! What are you going to do?"

"You own the island?" Peter said to Ransome. "Who cares? This is where we get off."

FIFTEEN

The boat Taja had used getting back and forth was a twenty-eight-foot Rockport-built island cruiser. Peter had John Ransome in the wheelhouse attached to a safety line with his hands lashed together in front of him. Echo was trying to hold the muzzle of the Colt 9mm on him while Peter battled wind gusts up to fifty knots and heavy seas once they left the shelter of Kincairn cove. In addition to the safety lines they all wore life vests. They were bucked all over the place. Peter found he could get only about eighteen knots from the Volvo diesel, and that it was nearly impossible to keep the wind on his stern unless he wanted to sail to Portugal. The wind chill was near zero. They were shipping a lot of water with a temperature of only a few degrees above freezing. The pounding went on without letup. Under reasonably good conditions it was thirty minutes to the mainland. Peter wasn't at all sure he had half an hour before hypothermia rendered him helpless.

John Ransome knew it. Watching Peter try to steer with one good hand, seeing Echo shaking with vomit on the front of her life vest, he said, "We won't make it. Breathe through your nose, Mary Catherine, or you'll freeze your lungs. You know I don't want you to die like this! Talk sense to Peter! Best of times it's like threading a needle through all the little islands. In a blow you can lose your boat on the rocks."

"Peter's s-sailed b-boats all his life!"

Ransome shook his head. "Not under these conditions."

A vicious gust heeled them to port; the bow was buried in a cornering wave. Water cascaded off the back of the overhead as the cruiser righted itself sluggishly.

"Peter!"

"We're okay!" he yelled, leaning on the helm.

Ransome smiled in sympathy with Echo's terror.

"We're not okay." He turned to Peter. "There is a way out of this dilemma, Peter! If you'd only give me a chance to make things right for all of us! But you must turn back *now*!"

"I told you, I don't have dilemmas! Echo, keep that gun on him!"

Ransome said, his eyes on the shivering girl, "I don't think Peter knows you as well as I've come to know you, Mary Catherine! You couldn't shoot me. No matter what you think I've done."

Echo, her eyes red from salt, raised the muzzle of the Colt unsteadily as she tried to keep from slipping off the bench opposite Ransome.

"Which one—are you tonight?" she said bitterly. "The g-god who creates, or the god who destroys?"

They were taking on water faster than the pump could empty the boat. The cruiser wallowed, nearly directionless.

"Remember the rogue wave, Mary Catherine? You saved me then. Am I worth saving now?"

"Don't listen to him!" Peter rubbed his eyes, trying to focus through the spume on the wheelhouse window. What he saw momentarily and some distance away were the running lights of a large yacht or even a cutter. Because of the cold he had only limited use of his left hand. His wrist had begun bleeding again during his fight with Taja at the lighthouse. With numbed fingers he was able to open a locker in front of him. "Echo, this guy has fucked up every life he ever touched!"

"There's no truth in that! It was Taja, no matter what she wanted you to believe. Her revenge on me. And I was the only one who ever cared about her! Mary Catherine, last night I tried to stop her from going after Silkie MacKenzie! You know what happened. But the story of Taja and myself is not easy to explain. You understand, though, don't you?"

"You should have seen what I've seen the last forty-eight hours, Echo! The faces of Ransome's women. Slashed, burned, broken! Two that I know of are dead! Nan McLaren O.D.'d, Ransome—you hear about that?"

"Yes. Poor Nan—but I—"

"Last night Valerie Angelus went off the roof of her building! You set her up for that, you son of a bitch!"

Ransome lifted his head.

"But you could've stopped her. A year, two years ago, it wouldn't have been too late for Valerie! You didn't want her. Don't talk about caring, it makes me sick!"

Ransome lunged off his bench toward Echo and easily took the automatic from her half-frozen hands. He turned toward Peter with it but lost his footing. Peter abandoned the helm, kicked the Colt into the stern of the boat, then pointed a Kilgore flare pistol, loaded with a twenty-thousand-candlepower parachute flare, at Ransome's head.

"I think the Coast Guard's out there to starboard," Peter said. "If you make a big enough bonfire they'll see it."

"The flare will only destroy my face," Ransome said calmly. "I suppose you would consider that to be justice." On his knees, Ransome held up his bound hands suppliantly. "We could have settled this among ourselves. Now it's too late." He looked at Echo. "*Is* it too late, Mary Catherine?"

She was sitting in a foot of water on the deck, exhausted, just trying to hold on as the boat rolled violently. She looked at him, and looked away. "Oh God, John."

Ransome struggled to his feet. "Take the helm, Peter, or she'll roll over! And the two of you may still have a life together."

"Just shut up, Ransome!"

He smiled. "You're both very young. Some day I hope you will learn that the greater part of wisdom is . . . forgiveness."

He unclipped his safety line from the vest as the bow of the cruiser rose, letting the motion carry him backwards to the transom railing. Where he threw himself overboard, vanishing into the pitch-dark water.

Echo cried out, a wail of despair, then sobbed. Peter felt nothing other than a cold indifference to the fate the artist had chosen. He raised the flare pistol and fired it, then returned to the helm as the flare shed its light upon the water, bringing nearby islands into jagged relief. A few moments later they heard siren through the low scream of wind; a searchlight probed the darkness and found them. Peter closed his eyes in the glare and leaned against the helm with Echo laid against his back, arms around him.

Below decks of the Coast Guard cutter as it returned to the station on Mount Desert Island with the cruiser in tow, a change in pitch in the cutter's engine and a shudder that ran through the vessel caused Echo to wake up in a cocoon of blankets. She jerked violently.

"Easy," Peter said. He was sitting beside her on the sick bay rack, holding her hand.

"Where are we?"

"Coming in, I guess. You okay?"

She licked her chapped lips. "I think so. Peter, are we in trouble?"

"No. I mean, there's gonna be a hell of an inquiry. We'll take what comes and say what is. Want coffee?"

"No. Just want to sleep."

"Echo, I have to know—"

"Can't talk now," she protested wanly.

"Maybe we should. Get it out of the way, you know? Just say what is. Either way, I promise I can deal with it."

She blinked, looked at him with ghostly eyes, raised her other hand to gently touch his face.

"I posed for him—well, you saw the work Taja took a knife to."

"Yeah."

She took a deep breath. Peter was like stone.

"I didn't sleep with him, Peter."

After a few moments he shrugged. "Okay."

"But—no—I want to tell you all of it. Peter, I was getting ready to. Another couple of days, a week—it would've happened."

"Oh, Jesus."

"I just needed to be with him. But I didn't love him. It's something I—I don't think I'll ever understand about myself. I'm sorry."

Peter shook his head, perplexed, dismayed. She waited tensely for the anger. Instead he put his arms around her.

"You don't have to be sorry. I know what he was. And I know what I saw—in the eyes of those other women. I don't see it in your eyes." He kissed her. "He's gone. And that's all I care about."

A second kiss, and her glum face lost its anxiety, she began to lighten up.

"I do love you. Infinity."

"Infinity," he repeated solemnly. "Echo?"

"Yes?"

"I looked at a sublet before I left the city a few days ago. Fully furnished loft in Williamsburg. Probably still available. Fifteen hundred a month. We can move in by Christmas."

"Hey. Fifteen? We can swing that." She smiled slightly, teasing. "Live in sin for a little while, that what you mean?"

"Just live," he said.

On a Sunday in mid April, four weeks before their wedding, Peter and Echo, enjoying each other's company and one of life's minor enchantments, which was to laze with no purpose, heard the elevator in their building start up.

"Company?" Peter said. He was watching the Knicks on TV.

"Mom and Julia aren't coming until four," Echo said. She was doing tai chi exercises on a floor mat, barefoot, wearing only gym shorts. The weather in Brooklyn was unseasonably warm.

"Then it's nobody, Peter said. "But maybe you should pull on a top anyhow."

He walked across the painted floor of the loft they shared and watched the elevator rising toward them. In the dimness of the shaft he couldn't make out anyone in the cage.

When it stopped he pulled up the gate and looked inside. A wrapped package leaned against one side of the elevator. About three feet by five. Brown paper, tape, twine.

"Hey, Echo?"

She wriggled into a halter top and came over to look. Her lips parted in astonishment.

"It's a painting. Omigod!"

"What?"

"Get it! Open it!"

Peter lugged the wrapped painting, which seemed to be framed, to the table in their kitchen. Echo followed with scissors and cut the twine.

"But it can't be! There's no way—! No, be careful, let me do this!"

She removed the thick paper and laid the painting flat on the table.

"Oh no," Peter groaned. "I don't believe this. He's back."

The painting was John Ransome's self-portrait that had been hanging in the artist's library on Kincairn when Echo had last seen it.

Echo turned it over. On the back Ransome had inscribed, "Given to Mary Catherine Halloran as a remembrance of our friendship." It was signed and dated two days before Ransome's disappearance.

She turned suddenly, shoving Peter aside, and ran to the loft windows that overlooked a cobbled mews and afforded a partial view of the Brooklyn Bridge, with lower Manhattan beyond.

"Peterrrr!"

He caught up to her, looked over her shoulder and down at the mews. There were kids playing, a couple of women with strollers. And a man in a black topcoat getting into a cab on the corner where the fruit and vegetable stand was doing brisk business. The man had shoulder-length gray hair and wore dark glasses. That was all they could see of him.

Peter looked at Echo as the cab drove away. Touched her shoulder until she focused on him, on the here and now.

"He drowned, Echo."

She turned with a broad gesture in the direction of the portrait. "But—"

"Maybe his body never turned up, but the water—we nearly froze ourselves on the boat. His hands were tied. Telling you, no way he survived."

"John told me he swam the Hellespont once. The Dardanelles Strait. That's at least a couple miles across. And hypothermia—everybody's tolerance of cold is different. Sailors have survived for hours in seas that probably would kill you or me in fifteen minutes." She gestured again, excited. "Peter—who else?"

"Maybe it was somebody works for Cy Mellichamp. That slick son of a bitch. Just having his little joke. Listen, I don't want the damn picture in our house. I don't want to be reminded, Echo. How you got short-changed on your contract. None of it." He waited. "Do you?"

"Well—" She looked around their loft. Shrugged. "I guess it wouldn't be, uh, appropriate. But obviously—it was meant as a wedding gift." She smiled strangely. "All I did was say how much I admired his self-portrait. John told me all about it. There's quite a story goes with it, which would make the painting especially valuable to a collector. It's unique in the Ransome canon."

"Yeah? How valuable?"

"Hard to say. I know a Ransome was knocked down recently at Christie's for just under five million dollars."

Peter didn't say anything.

"The fact that his body hasn't been recovered complicated matters for his estate. But," Echo said judiciously, "as Stefan put it, 'it certainly has done no harm to the value of his art.' "

"You want a beer?"

"I would love a beer."

Echo remained by the windows looking out while Peter went to the refrigerator. While he was popping tops he said, "So—figure we just put the portrait away in a closet a couple years, then it could be worth a shitload?"

"Oh baby," Echo replied.

"Then, also in a couple years," Peter said, coming back to her and carefully fitting a can of Heineken into her hand, "when Ransome's estate gets settled, that cottage in Bedford, which looks like a pretty nice investment, will go on the market?"

"Might." Echo took a long drink of the beer and began laughing softly, ironically, to herself.

"All this could depend on, you know, he doesn't turn up." Peter looked out the window. "Again."

The last Ransome woman was silent. Wondering, lost in a private rapture.

Peter said, "You want to order in Chinese for Rosemay and Julia tonight? I've still got a few bucks left on my MasterCard."

"Yeah," Echo said, and leaned her head on his shoulder. "Chinese. Sounds good."

Jeffery Deaver

Jeffery Deaver has had a rapid and much-deserved rise to the top of the bestseller lists. His novels have always been riveting reads, especially those he wrote about Rune, a woman living and working in New York City. Seen through her eyes, the urban landscape is a wondrous—and sometimes frightening—place indeed. Fans of his work know that this is to be expected, or he can take the most commonplace career or event—news reporting, marriage—and turn it upside down with one of the surprising plot twists that have become his trademark. These days, he writes such bestsellers as *Praying for Sleep*, *A Maiden's Grave*, *Hard News*, and *The Bone Collector*, featuring the brilliant quadriplegic detective Lincoln Rhyme and his assistant Amelia Sachs. *The Bone Collector* was the basis for the successful movie of the same name starring Denzel Washington and Angelina Jolie. His readership expands with each new novel, and with each new short story he writes. His most recent novel is *Garden of Beasts*, and a new collection of short stories, *Twisted*, came out in November 2004.

FOREVER

Jeffery Deaver

Mathematics is not a careful march down a well-cleared highway, but a journey into a strange wilderness, where the explorers often get lost.

—W. S. ANGLIN, "Mathematics and History"

∞

An old couple like that, the man thought, acting like kids.

Didn't have a clue how crazy they looked.

Peering over the boxwood hedge he was trimming, the gardener was looking at Sy and Donald Benson on the wide, back deck of their house, sitting in a rocking love seat and drinking champagne. Which they'd had plenty of. That was for sure.

Giggling, laughing, loud.

Like kids, he thought contemptuously.

But enviously too a little. Not at their wealth—oh, he didn't resent that; he made a good living tending the grounds of the Bensons' neighbors, who were just as rich.

No, the envy was simply that even at this age they looked like they were way in love and happy.

The gardener tried to remember when he'd laughed like that with his wife. Must've been ten years. And holding hands like the Bensons were doing? Hardly ever since their first year together.

The electric hedge trimmer beckoned but the man lit a cigarette and continued to watch them. They poured the last of the champagne into their glasses and finished it. Then Donald leaned forward, whispering something in the woman's ear and she laughed again. She said something back and kissed his cheek.

Gross. And here they were, totally ancient. Sixties, probably. It was like seeing his own parents making out. Christ . . .

They stood up and walked to a metal table on the edge of the patio and piled dishes from their lunch on a tray, still laughing, still talking. With the old guy carrying the tray, they both headed into the kitchen, the gardener wondering if he'd drop it, he was weaving so much. But, no, they made it inside all right and shut the door.

The man flicked the butt into the grass and turned back to examine the boxwood hedge.

A bird trilled nearby, a pretty whistle. The gardener knew a lot about plants but not so much about wildlife and he wasn't sure what kind of bird this was.

But there was no mistaking the sound that cut through the air a few seconds later and made the gardener freeze where he stood, between a crimson azalea and a purple. The gunshot, coming from inside the Bensons' house, was quite distinctive. Only a moment later he heard a second shot.

The gardener stared at the huge Tudor house for three heartbeats, then, as the bird resumed its song, he dropped the hedge trimmer and sprinted back to his truck where he'd left his cell phone.

The county of Westbrook, New York, is a large trapezoid of suburbs elegant and suburbs mean, parks, corporate headquarters and light industry—a place where the majority of residents earn their keep by commuting into Manhattan, some miles to the south.

Last year this generally benign-looking county of nearly 900,000 had been the site of 31 murders, 107 rapes, 1,423 robberies, 1,575 aggravated assaults, 4,360 burglaries, 16,955 larcenies, and 4,130 automobile thefts, resulting in a crime rate of 3,223.3 per 100,000 population, or 3.22 percent for these so-called "index crimes," a standardized list of offenses used nationwide by statisticians to compare one community to another, and each community to its own past. This year Westbrook County was faring poorly compared with last. Its year-to-date index crime rate was already hovering near 4.5 percent and the temper-inflaming months of summer were still to come.

These facts—and thousands of others about the pulse of the

county—were readily available to whoever might want them, thanks largely to a slim young man, eyes as dark as his neatly cut and combed hair, who was presently sitting in a small office on the third floor of the Westbrook County Sheriff's Department, the Detective Division. On his door were two signs. One said, DET. TALBOT SIMMS. The other read, FINANCIAL CRIMES/STATISTICAL SERVICES.

The Detective Division was a large open space, surrounded by a U of offices. Tal and the support services were on one ascending stroke of the letter, dubbed the "Unreal Crimes Department" by everybody on the other arm (yes, the "Real Crimes Department," though the latter was officially labeled Major Crimes and Tactical Services).

This April morning Tal Simms sat in his immaculate office, studying one of the few items spoiling the smooth landscape of his desktop: a spreadsheet—evidence in a stock scam perpetrated in Manhattan. The Justice Department and the SEC were jointly running the case but there was a small local angle that required Tal's attention.

Absently adjusting his burgundy-and-black striped tie, Tal jotted some notes in his minuscule, precise handwriting as he observed a few inconsistencies in the numbers on the spreadsheet. Hmm, he was thinking, a .588 that should've been a .743. Small but extremely incriminating. He'd have to—

His hand jerked suddenly as a deep voice boomed outside his door, "It was a goddamn suicide. Waste of time."

Erasing the errant pencil tail from the margins of the spreadsheet, Tal saw the bulky form of the head of Homicide—Detective Greg LaTour—stride through the middle of the pen, past secretaries and communications techs, and push into his own office, directly across from Tal's. With a loud clunk the detective dropped a backpack on his desk.

"What?" somebody called. "The Bensons?"

"Yeah, that was them," LaTour called. "On Meadowridge in Greeley."

"Came in as a homicide."

"Well, it fucking wasn't."

Technically, it *was* a homicide—all non-accidental deaths were, even suicides, reflected Tal Simms, whose life was devoted to making the finest of distinctions. But to correct the temperamental Greg LaTour you had to either be a good friend or have a good reason and Tal fell into none of these categories.

"Gardener working next door heard a coupla shots, called it in," LaTour grumbled. "Some blind rookie from Greeley P.D. responded."

"Blind?"

"Had to be. Looked at the scene and thought they'd been murdered. Why don't the local boys stick to traffic?"

Like everyone else in the department Tal had been curious about the twin deaths. Greeley was an exclusive enclave in Westbrook and—Tal had looked it up—had never been the scene of a double murder. He wondered if the fact that the incident was a double *suicide* would bring the event slightly back toward the statistical norm.

Tal straightened the spreadsheet and his notepad, set his pencil in its holder, then walked over to the Real Crimes portion of the room. He stepped through LaTour's doorway.

"So, suicide?" Tal asked.

The hulking homicide detective, sporting a goatee and weighing nearly twice what Tal did, said, "Yeah. It was so fucking obvious to me. . . . But we got the crime scene boys in to make sure. They found GSR on—"

"Global—?" Tal interrupted.

"GSR. Gunshot residue. On both their hands. Her first, then him."

"How do you know?"

LaTour looked at Tal with a well, duh blink. "He was lying on top of her."

"Oh. Sure."

LaTour continued. "There was a note too. And the gardener said they were acting like teenagers—drunk on their asses, staggering around."

"Staggering."

"Old folks. Geezers, he said. Acting like kids."

Tal nodded. "Say, I was wondering. You happen to do a questionnaire?"

"Questionnaire?" he asked. "Oh, your questionnaire. Right. You know, Tal, it was just a suicide."

Tal nodded. "Still, I'd like to get that data."

"Data plural," LaTour said, pointing a finger at him and flashing a big, phony grin. Tal had once sent around a memo that included the sentence "The data were very helpful." When another cop corrected him Tal had said, "Oh, *data*'s plural; *datum*'s singular." The ensuing ragging taught him a pointed lesson about correcting fellow cops' grammar.

"Right," Tal said wearily. "Plural. It'd—"

LaTour's phone rang and he grabbed it. " 'Lo? . . . I don't know, couple days we'll have the location . . . Naw, I'll go in with SWAT. I wanta piece of him personal. . . ."

Tal looked around the office. A Harley poster. Another, of a rearing grizzly—"Bear" was LaTour's nickname. A couple of flyblown certificates from continuing education courses. No other decorations. The desk, credenza, and chairs were filled with an irritating mass of papers, dirty coffee cups, magazines, boxes of ammunition, bullet-riddled targets, depositions, crime lab reports, a scabby billy club. The big detective continued into the phone, "When? . . . Yeah, I'll let you know." He slammed the phone down and glanced back at Tal. "Anyway. I didn't think you'd want it, being a suicide. The questionnaire, you know. Not like a murder."

"Well, it'd still be pretty helpful."

LaTour was wearing what he usually did, a black leather jacket cut like a sport coat and blue jeans. He patted the many pockets involved in the outfit. "Shit, Tal. Think I lost it. The questionnaire, I mean. Sorry. You have another one?" He grabbed the phone, made another call.

"I'll get you one," Tal said. He returned to his office, picked up a questionnaire from a neat pile on his credenza and returned to LaTour. The cop was still on the phone, speaking in muted but gruff tones. He glanced up and nodded at Tal, who set the sheet on his desk.

LaTour mouthed, Thank you.

Tal waited a moment and asked, "Who else was there?"

"What?" LaTour frowned, irritated at being interrupted. He clapped his hand over the mouthpiece.

"Who else was at the scene?"

"Where the Bensons offed themselves? Fuck, I don't know. Fire and Rescue. That Greeley P.D. kid." A look of concentration that Tal didn't believe. "A few other guys. Can't remember." The detective returned to his conversation.

Tal walked back to his office, certain that the questionnaire was presently being slam-dunked into LaTour's wastebasket.

He called the Fire and Rescue Department but couldn't track down anybody who'd responded to the suicide. He gave up for the time being and continued working on the spreadsheet.

After a half hour he paused and stretched. His eyes slipped from the spreadsheet to the pile of blank questionnaires. A Xeroxed note was stapled neatly to each one, asking the responding or case officer to fill it out in full and explaining how helpful the information would be. He'd agonized over writing that letter (numbers came easy to Talbot Simms, words hard). Still, he knew the officers didn't take the questionnaire seriously. They joked about it. They joked about *him* too, calling him "Einstein" or "Mr. Wizard" behind his back.

1. Please state nature of incident:

He found himself agitated, then angry, tapping his mechanical pencil on the spreadsheet like a drumstick. Anything not filled out properly rankled Talbot Simms; that was his nature. But an unanswered questionnaire was particularly irritating. The information the forms harvested was important. The art and science of statistics not only compiles existing information but is used to make vital decisions and predict trends. Maybe a questionnaire in this case would reveal some fact, some *datum*, that would help the county better understand elderly suicides and save lives.

4. Please indicate the sex, approximate age, and apparent nationality and/or race of each victim:

The empty lines on the questions were like an itch—aggravated by hot-shot LaTour's condescending attitude.

"Hey, there, Boss." Shellee, Tal's firecracker of a secretary, stepped into his office. "*Finally* got the Templeton files. Sent 'em by mule train from Albany's my guess." With massive blonde ringlets and the feistiness of a truck-stop waitress compressed into a five-foot, hundred-pound frame, Shellee looked as if she'd sling out words with a twangy Alabaman accent but her intonation was pure Hahvahd Square Bostonian.

"Thanks." He took the dozen folders she handed off, examined the numbers on the front of each and rearranged them in ascending order on the credenza behind his desk.

"Called the SEC again and they promise, promise, promise they'll have us the—Hey, you leaving early?" She was frowning, looking at her watch, as Tal stood, straightened his tie and pulled on the thin, navy-blue raincoat he wore to and from the office.

"Have an errand."

A frown of curiosity filled her round face, which was deceptively girlish (Tal knew she had a twenty-one year-old-daughter and a husband who'd just retired from the phone company). "Sure. You do? Didn't see anything on your calender."

The surprise was understandable. Tal had meetings out of the office once or twice a month at the most. He was virtually always at his desk, except when he went out for lunch, which he did at twelve-thirty every day, joining two or three friends from a local university at the Corner Tap Room up the street.

"Just came up."

"Be back?" Shellee asked.

He paused. "You know, I'm not really sure." He headed for the elevator.

The white-columned Colonial on Meadowridge had to be worth six, seven million. Tal pulled his Honda Accord into the circular drive, behind a black sedan, which he hoped belonged to a Greeley P.D. officer, somebody who might have the information he needed. Tal took the questionnaire and two pens from his briefcase, made sure the tips were retracted then slipped them into his shirt pocket. He walked up the flagstone path to the house, the door to which was unlocked. He stepped inside and identified himself to a man in jeans and work shirt, carrying a clipboard. It was his car in the drive, he explained. He was here to meet the Bensons' lawyer about liquidating their estate and knew nothing about the Bensons or their death, other than what he'd heard about the suicides.

He stepped outside, leaving Tal alone in the house.

As he walked through the entry foyer and into the spacious first floor a feeling of disquiet came over him. It wasn't the queasy sense that somebody'd just died here; it was that the house was such an unlikely setting for death. He looked over the yellow-and-pink floral upholstery, the boldly colorful abstracts on the walls, the gold-edged china and prismatic glasses awaiting parties, the collection of crystal animals, the Moroccan pottery, shelves of well-thumbed books, framed snapshots on the walls and mantle. Two pairs of well-worn slippers—a man's size and a woman's—sat poignantly together by the back door. Tal imagined the couple taking turns to be the first to rise, make coffee and brave the dewy cold to collect *The New York Times* or the Westbrook *Ledger*.

The word that came to him was "home." The idea of the owners here shooting themselves was not only disconcerting, it was downright eerie.

Tal noticed a sheet of paper weighted down by a crystal vase and blinked in surprise as he read it.

> To our friends:
> We're making this decison with great contenment in hearts, joyous in the knowldge that we'll be together forever.

Both Sy and Don Benson had signed it. He stared at the words for a moment then wandered to the den, which was cordoned off with crime scene tape. He stopped cold, gasping faintly.

Blood.

On the couch, on the carpet, on the wall.

He could clearly see where the couple had been when they'd died; the blood explained the whole scenario to him. Brown, opaque, dull. He found himself breathing shallowly, as if the stains were giving off toxic fumes.

Tal stepped back into the living room and decided to fill out as much of the questionnaire as he could. Sitting on a couch he clicked a pen point out and picked up a book from the coffee table to use as a writing surface. He read the title: *Making the Final Journey: The Complete Guide to Suicide and Euthanasia.*

Okay . . . I don't think so. He replaced the book and made a less troubling lap desk from a pile of magazines. He filled out some of the details, then he paused, aware of the front door opening. Footsteps sounded on the foyer tile and a moment later a stocky man in an expensive suit walked into the den. He frowned.

"Sheriff's Department," Tal said and showed his ID, which the man looked at carefully.

"I'm their lawyer. George Metzer," he said slowly, visibly

shaken. "Oh, this is terrible. Just terrible. I got a call from somebody in your department. My secretary did, I mean. . . . You want to see some ID?"

Tal realized that a Real Cop would have asked for it right up front. "Please."

He looked over the driver's license and nodded, then gazed past the man's pudgy hand and looked again into the den. The blood stains were like brown laminate on cheap furniture.

"Was there a note?" the lawyer asked, putting his wallet away.

Tal walked into the dining room. He nodded toward the note.

Together forever . . .

The lawyer looked it over, shook his head again. He glanced into the den and blinked, seeing the blood. Turned away.

Tal showed Metzer the questionnaire. "Can I ask you a few questions? For our statistics department? It's anonymous. We don't use names."

"Sure, I guess."

Tal began querying the man about the couple. He was surprised to learn they were only in their mid sixties, he'd assumed LaTour's assessment had been wrong and the Bensons were older.

"Any children?"

"No. No close relatives at all. A few cousins they never see. . . . Never *saw*, I mean. They had a lot of friends, though. They'll be devastated."

He got some more information, and finally felt he had nearly enough to process the data, but one more question needed an answer.

9. Apparent motives for the incident:

"You have any idea why they'd do this?" Tal asked.

"I know exactly," Metzer said. "Don was ill."

Tal glanced down at the note again and noticed that the writing was unsteady and a few of the words were misspelled. LaTour'd said something about them drinking but Tal remembered seeing a wicker basket full of medicine bottles sitting on the island in the kitchen. He mentioned this then asked, "Did one of them have some kind of palsy? Nerve disease?"

The lawyer said, "No, it was heart problems. Bad ones."

In space number nine Tal wrote: *Illness*. Then he asked, "And his wife?"

"No, Sy was in good health. But they were very devoted to each other. Totally in love. She must've decided she didn't want to go on without him."

"Was it terminal?"

"Not the way he described it to me," the lawyer said. "But he could've been bedridden for the rest of his life. I doubt Don could've handled that. He was so active, you know."

Tal signed the questionnaire, folded and slipped it into his pocket.

The round man gave a sigh. "I should've guessed something was up. They came to my office a couple of weeks ago and made a few changes to the will and they gave me instructions for their memorial service. I thought it was just because Don was going to have the surgery, you know, thinking about what would happen *if*. . . . But I should've read between the lines. They were planning it then, I'll bet."

He gave a sad laugh. "You know what they wanted for their memorial service? See, they weren't religious so they wanted to be cremated then have their friends throw a big party at their country club and scatter their ashes on the green at the eighteenth hole." He grew somber again. "It never occurred to me they had something like this in mind. They seemed so happy, you know? . . . Crazy fucked-up life sometimes, huh? Anyway, I've got to meet with this guy outside. Here's my card. Call me, you got any other questions, Detective."

Tal walked around the house one more time. He glanced at the calendar stuck to the refrigerator with two magnets in the shape of lobsters. *Newport Rhode Island* was written in white across the bright red tails. In the calendar box for yesterday there was a note to take the car in to have the oil changed. Two days before that Sy'd had a hair appointment.

Today's box was empty. And there was nothing in any of the future dates for the rest of April. Tal looked through the remaining months. No notations. He made a circuit of the first floor, finding nothing out of the ordinary.

Except, someone might suggest, maybe the troubled spirits left behind by two people alive that morning and now no longer so.

Tal Simms, mathematician, empirical scientist, statistician, couldn't accept any such presence. But he hardly needed to, in order to feel a churning disquiet. The stains of dark blood that had spoiled the reassuring comfort of this homey place were as chilling as any ghost could be.

When he was studying math at Cornell ten years earlier Talbot Simms dreamed of being a John Nash, a Pierre de Fermat, a Euler, a Bernoulli. By the time he hit grad school and looked around him, at the other students who wanted to be the same, he realized two things: one, that his love of the beauty of mathematics was no less than it had ever been but, two, he was utterly sick of academics.

What was the point? he wondered. Writing articles that a handful of people would read? Becoming a professor? He could have done so easily thanks to his virtually perfect test scores and grades but to him that life was like a Mobius strip—the twisted ribbon with a single surface that never ends. Teaching more teachers to teach . . .

No, he wanted a practical use for his skills and so he dropped out of graduate school. At the time there was a huge demand for statisticians and analysts on Wall Street, and Tal joined up. In theory the job seemed a perfect fit—numbers, numbers and more numbers, and a practical use for them. But he soon found something else: Wall Street mathematics was a fishy math. Tal felt pressured to skew his statistical analysis of certain companies to help his bank sell financial products to the clients. To Tal, 3 was no more nor less than 3. Yet his bosses sometimes wanted 3 to *appear* to be 2.9999 or 3.12111. There was nothing illegal about this—all the qualifications were disclosed to customers. But statistics, to Tal, helped us understand life; they weren't smoke screens to let predators sneak up on the unwary. Numbers were pure. And the glorious compensation he received didn't take the shame out of his prostitution.

On the very day he was going to quit, though, the FBI arrived in Tal's office—not for anything he or the bank had done—but to serve a warrant to examine the accounts of a client who'd been indicted in a stock scam. It turned out the agent looking over the figures was a mathematician and accountant. He and Tal had some fascinating discussions while the man pored over the records, armed with handcuffs, a large automatic pistol, and a Texas Instruments calculator.

Here at last was a logical outlet for his love of numbers. He'd always been interested in police work. As a slight, reclusive only child he'd read not only books on logarithms and trigonometry and Einstein's theories but murder mysteries as well, Agatha Christie and A. Conan Doyle. His analytical mind would often spot the surprise villain early in the story. After he'd met with the agent, he called the Bureau's personnel department. He was disappointed to learn that there was a federal government hiring freeze in effect. But, undeterred, he called the NYPD and other police departments in the metro area—including Westbrook County, where he'd lived with his family for several years before his widower father got a job teaching math at UCLA.

Westbrook, it turned out, needed someone to take over their financial crimes investigations. The only problem, the head of county personnel admitted, was that the officer would also have to be in charge of gathering and compiling statistics. But, to Tal Simms, numbers were numbers and he had no problem with the piggy-backed assignments.

One month later, Tal kissed Wall Street good-bye and moved into a tiny though pristine Tudor house in Bedford Plains, the county seat.

There was one other glitch, however, which the Westbrook County personnel office had neglected to mention, probably because it was so obvious: To be a member of the sheriff's department financial crimes unit he had to become a cop.

The four-month training was rough. Oh, the academic part about criminal law and procedure went fine. The challenge was the physical curriculum at the academy, which was a little like army basic training. Tal Simms, who was five-foot-nine and had hovered around 153 pounds since high school, had fiercely avoided all sports except volleyball, tennis, and the rifle team, none of which had buffed him up for the Suspect Takedown and Restraint course. Still, he got through it all and graduated in the top 1.4 percent of his class. The swearing-in ceremony was attended by a dozen friends from local colleges and Wall Street, as well as his father, who'd flown in from the Midwest where he was a professor of advanced mathematics at the University of Chicago. The stern man was unable to fathom why his son had taken this route but, having largely abandoned the boy for the world of numbers in his early years, Simms senior had forfeited all rights to nudge Tal's career in one direction or another.

As soon as he started work Tal learned that financial crimes were rare in Westbrook. Or, more accurately, they tended to be adjunct to federal prosecutions and Tal found himself sidelined as an investigator. He was, however, in great demand as a statistician.

Finding and analyzing data are more vital than the public thinks. Certainly crime statistics determine budget and staff hiring strategies. But, more than that, statistics can diagnose a community's ills. If the national monthly average for murders of teenagers by other teenagers in neighborhoods with a mean income of $26,000 annual is .03, and Kendall Heights in southern Westbrook was home to 1.1 such killings per month, why? And what could be done to fix the problem?

Hence, the infamous questionnaire.

Now, 6:30 P.M., armed with the one he'd just completed, Tal returned to his office from the Benson house. He inputted the information from the form into his database and placed the questionnaire itself into his to-be-filed basket. He stared at the information on the screen for a moment then began to log off. But he changed his mind and went online to the Internet and searched some databases. Then he read the brief official report on the Bensons' suicides.

He jumped when someone walked into his office. "Hey, Boss." Shellee blinked. "Thought you were gone."

"Just wanted to finish up a few things here."

"I've got that stuff you wanted."

He glanced at it. The title was, "Supplemental reports. SEC case 04-5432."

"Thanks," he said absently, staring at his printouts.

"Sure." She eyed him carefully. "You need anything else?"

"No, go on home. . . . 'Night." When she turned away, though, he glanced at the computer screen once more and said, "Wait, Shell. You ever work in Crime Scene?"

"Never did. Bill watches that TV show. It's icky."

"You know what I'd have to do to get Crime Scene to look over the house?"

"House?"

"Where the suicide happened. The Benson house in Greeley."

"The—"

"Suicides. I want Crime Scene to check it out. All they did was test for gunshot residue and take some pictures. I want a complete search. But I don't know what to do."

"Something funny about it?"

He explained, "Just looked up a few things. The incident profile was out of range. I think something weird was going on there."

"I'll make a call. Ingrid's still down there, I think."

She returned to her desk and Tal rocked back in his chair.

The low April sun shot bars of ruddy light into his office, hitting the large, blank wall and leaving a geometric pattern on the white paint. The image put in mind the blood on the walls and couch and carpet of the Bensons' house. He pictured too the shaky lettering of their note.

Together forever . . .

Shellee appeared in the doorway. "Sorry, Boss. They said it's too late to twenty-one-twenty-four it."

"To?—"

"That's what they said. They said you need to declare a twenty-one-twenty-four to get Crime Scene in. But you can't do it now."

"Oh. Why?"

"Something about it being too contaminated now. You have to do it right away or get some special order from the sheriff himself. Anyway, that's what they told me, Boss."

Even though Shellee worked for three other detectives Tal was the only one who received this title—a true endearment, coming from her. She was formal, or chill, with the other cops in direct proportion to the number of times they asked her to fetch coffee or snuck peeks at her ample breasts.

Outside, a voice from the Real Crimes side of the room called out, "Hey, Bear, you get your questionnaire done?" A chortle followed.

Greg LaTour called back, "Naw, I'm taking mine home. Had front-row Knicks tickets but I figured, fuck, it'd be more fun to fill out paperwork all night."

More laughter.

Shellee's face hardened into a furious mask. She started to turn but Tal motioned her to stop.

"Hey, guys, tone it down." The voice was Captain Dempsey's. "He'll hear you."

"Naw," LaTour called, "Einstein left already. He's probably home humping his calculator. Who's up for Sal's?"

"I'm for that, Bear."

"Let's do it. . . ."

Laughter and receding footsteps.

Shellee muttered, "It just frosts me when they talk like that. They're like kids in the schoolyard."

True, they were, Tal thought. Math whizzes know a lot about bullies on playgrounds.

But he said, "It's okay."

"No, Boss, it's *not* okay."

"They live in a different world," Tal said. "I understand."

"Understand how people can be cruel like that? Well, I surely don't."

"You know that thirty-four percent of homicide detectives suffer from depression? Sixty-four percent get divorced. Twenty-eight percent are substance abusers."

"You're using those numbers to excuse 'em, Boss. Don't do it. Don't let 'em get away with it." She slung her purse over her shoulder and started down the hall, calling "Have a nice weekend, Boss. See you Monday."

"And," Tal continued, "six point three percent kill themselves before retirement." Though he doubted she could hear.

The residents of Hamilton, New York, were educated, pleasant, reserved and active in politics and the arts. In business too; they'd chosen to live here because the enclave was the closest exclusive Westbrook community to Manhattan. Industrious bankers and lawyers could be at their desks easily by eight o'clock in the morning.

The cul-de-sac of Montgomery Way, one of the nicest streets in Hamilton, was in fact home to two bankers and one lawyer, as well as one retired couple. These older residents, at number 205, had lived in their house for twenty-four years. It was a six thousand-square-foot stone Tudor with leaded-glass windows and a shale roof, surrounded by five acres of clever landscaping.

Samuel Ellicott Whitley had attended law school while his wife worked in the advertising department of Gimbel's, the department store near the harrowing intersection of Broadway, Sixth Avenue, and Thirty-Fourth Street. He'd finished school in '57 and joined Brown, Lathrop & Soames on Broad Street. The week after he was named partner, Elizabeth gave birth to a daughter, and after a brief hiatus, resumed classes at Columbia's graduate business school. She later took a job at one of the country's largest cosmetics companies and rose to be a senior vice president.

But the lives of law and business were behind the Whitleys now and they'd moved into the life of retirement as gracefully and comfortably as she stepped into her Dior gowns and he into his Tripler's tux.

Tonight, a cool, beautiful April Sunday, Elizabeth hung up the phone after a conversation with her daughter, Sandra, and piled the dinner dishes in the sink. She poured herself another vodka and tonic. She stepped outside onto the back patio, looking out over the azure dusk crowning the hemlocks and pine. She stretched and sipped her drink, feeling tipsy and completely content.

She wondered what Sam was up to. Just after they'd finished dinner he'd said that he'd had to pick up something. Normally she would have gone with him. She worried because of his illness. Afraid not only that his undependable heart would give out but that he might faint at the wheel or drive off the road because of the medication. But he'd insisted that she stay home; he was only going a few miles.

Taking a long sip of her drink, she cocked her head, hearing an automobile engine and the hiss of tires on the asphalt. She looked toward the driveway. But she couldn't see anything. Was it Sam? The car, though, had not come up the main drive but had turned off the road at the service entrance and eased through the side yard, out of sight of the house. She squinted but with the foliage and the dim light of dusk she couldn't see who it was.

Logic told her she should be concerned. But Elizabeth was comfortable sitting here with her glass in hand, under a deep blue evening sky. Feeling the touch of cashmere on her skin, happy, warm . . . No, life was perfect. What could there possibly be to worry about?

Three nights of the week—or as Tal would sometimes phrase it, 42.8751 percent of his evenings—he'd go out. Maybe on a date, maybe to have drinks and dinner with friends, maybe to his regular poker game (the others in the quintet enjoyed his company, though they'd learned it could be disastrous to play with a man who could remember cards photographically and calculate the odds of drawing to a full house like a computer).

The remaining 57.1249 percent of his nights he'd stay home and lose himself in the world of mathematics.

This Sunday, nearly 7:00 P.M., Tal was in his small library, which was packed with books but was as ordered and neat as his office at work. He'd spent the weekend running errands, cleaning the house, washing the car, making the obligatory—and ever awkward—call to his father in Chicago, dining with a couple up the road who'd made good their threat to set him up with a cousin (e-mail addresses had been unenthusiastically exchanged over empty mousse dishes). Now, classical music playing on the radio, Tal had put the rest of the world aside and was working on a proof.

This is the gold ring that mathematicians constantly seek. One might have a brilliant insight about numbers but without completing the proof—the formal argument that verifies the premise—that insight remains merely a theorem; it's pure speculation.

The proof that had obsessed him for months involved perfect numbers. These are positive numbers whose divisors (excluding the number itself) add up to that number. The number 6, for instance, is perfect because it's divisible only by 1, 2, and 3 (not counting 6), and 1, 2, and 3 also add up to 6.

The questions Tal had been trying to answer: How many even perfect numbers are there? And, more intriguing, are there any *odd* perfect numbers? In the entire history of mathematics no one has been able to offer a proof that an odd perfect number exists (or that it can't exist).

Perfect numbers have always intrigued mathematicians—theologians too. St. Augustine felt that God intentionally chose a perfect number of days—six—to create the world. Rabbis attach great mystical significance to the number 28, the days in the moon's cycle. Tal didn't consider perfect numbers in such a spiritual or philosophical way. For him they were simply a curious mathematical construct. But this didn't minimize their importance to him; proving theorems about perfect numbers (or any other mathematical enigmas) might lead other insights about math and science . . . and perhaps life in general.

He now hunched over his pages of neat calculations, wondering if the odd perfect number was merely a myth or if it was real and waiting to be discovered, hiding somewhere in the dim distance of numbers approaching infinity.

Something about this thought troubled him and he leaned back in his chair. It took a moment to realize why. Thinking of infinity reminded him of the suicide note Don and Sy Benson had left.

Together forever . . .

He pictured the room where they'd died, the blood, the chilling sight of the grim how-to guide they'd bought. *Making the Final Journey.*

Tal stood and paced. Something definitely wasn't right. For the first time in years he decided to return to the office on a Sunday night. He wanted to look up some background on suicides of this sort.

A half hour later he was walking past the surprised desk sergeant who had to think for a moment or two before he recognized him.

"Officer . . ."

"Detective Simms."

"Right. Yessir."

Ten minutes later he was in his office, tapping on the keyboard, perusing information about suicides in Westbrook County. At first irritated that the curious events of today had taken him away from his mathematical evening, he soon found himself lost in a very different world of numbers—those that defined the loss of life by one's own hand in Westbrook County.

Sam Whitley emerged from the kitchen with a bottle of old Armagnac and joined his wife in the den.

It had been her husband arriving fifteen minutes ago, after all, driving up the back driveway for reasons he still hadn't explained.

Elizabeth now pulled her cashmere sweater around her shoulders and lit a vanilla-scented candle, which sat on the table in front of her. She glanced at the bottle in his hand and laughed.

"What?" her husband asked.

"I was reading some of the printouts your doctor gave you."

He nodded.

"And it said that some wine is good for you."

"I read that too." He wiped dust off the bottle, examined the label.

"That you should have a glass or two every day. But cognac wasn't on the list. I don't know how good *that* is for your health."

Sam laughed too. "I feel like living dangerously."

He expertly opened the bottle, whose cork stopper was close to disintegrating.

"You were always good at that," his wife said.

"I never had many talents—only the important skills." He handed her a glass of the honey-colored liquor and then he filled his. They downed the drink. He poured more.

"So what've you got there?" she asked, feeling even warmer now, giddier, happier. She was nodding toward a bulge in the side pocket of his camel-hair sport coat, the jacket he always wore on Sundays.

"A surprise."

"Really? What?"

He tapped her glass and they drank again. He said, "Close your eyes."

She did. "You're a tease, Samuel." She felt him sit next to her, sensed his body close. There was a click of metal.

"You know I love you." His tone overflowed with emotion. Sam occasionally got quite maudlin. Elizabeth had long ago learned, though, that among the long list of offenses in the catalog of masculine sins sentiment was the least troublesome.

"And I love you, dear," she said.

"Ready?"

"Yes, I'm ready."

"Okay. . . . Here."

Another click of metal . . .

Then Elizabeth felt something in her hand. She opened her eyes and laughed again.

"What . . . Oh, my God, is this—?" She examined the key ring he'd placed in her palm. It held two keys and bore the distinctive logo of a British MG sports car. "You . . . you found one?" she stammered. "Where?"

"That import dealer up the road, believe it or not. Two miles from here! It's a nineteen-fifty-four. He called a month ago but it needed some work to get in shape."

"So that's what those mysterious calls were about. I was beginning to suspect another woman," she joked.

"It's not the same color. It's more burgundy."

"As if that matters, honey."

The first car they'd bought as a married couple had been a red MG, which they'd driven for ten years until the poor thing had finally given out. While Liz's friends were buying Lexuses or Mercedes she refused to join the pack and continued to drive her ancient Cadillac, holding out for an old MG like their original car.

She flung her arms around his shoulders and leaned up to kiss him.

Lights from an approaching car flashed into the window, startling them.

"Caught," she whispered, "just like when my father came home early on our first date. Remember?" She laughed flirtatiously, feeling just like a carefree, rebellious Sarah Lawrence sophomore in a pleated skirt and Peter-Pan collared blouse—exactly who she'd been forty-two years ago when she met this man, the one she would share her life with.

Tal Simms was hunched forward, jotting notes, when the dispatcher's voice clattered thought the audio monitor, which was linked to the 911 system, in the darkened detective pen. "All units in the vicinity of Hamilton. Reports of a possible suicide in progress."

Tal froze. He pushed back from his computer monitor and rose to his feet, staring at the speaker, as the electronic voice continued. "Neighbor reports a car engine running in the closed garage at two-oh-five Montgomery Way. Any units in the vicinity, respond."

Tal Simms looked up at the speaker and hesitated only a moment. Soon, he was sprinting out of the building. He was halfway out of the parking lot, doing seventy in his Toyota, when he realized that he'd neglected to put his seat belt on. He reached for it but lost the car to a skid and gave up and sped toward the suburb of Hamilton on the Hudson, five miles away from the office.

You couldn't exactly call any of Westbrook County desolate but Hamilton and environs were surrounded by native-wood parks and the estates of very wealthy men and women who liked their privacy; most of the land here was zoned five or ten acres and some homes were on much larger tracts. The land Tal was now speeding past was a deserted mess of old forest, vines, brambles, jutting rocks. It was not far from here, he reflected, that Washington Irving had thought up the macabre tale of the Headless Horseman.

Normally a cautious, patient driver, Tal wove madly from lane to lane, laying on the horn often. But he didn't consider the illogic of what he was doing. He pictured chocolate-brown blood in the Bensons' den, pictured the unsteady handwriting of their last note.

We'll be together forever . . .

He raced through downtown Hamilton at nearly three times the speed limit. As if the Headless Horseman himself were galloping close behind.

∞

His gray sedan swerved down the long driveway leading to the Whitley house, bounding off the asphalt and taking out a bed of blooming white azaleas.

He grimaced at the damage as he skidded to a stop in front of the doorway.

Leaping from his car, he noticed a Hamilton Village police car and a boxy county ambulance pull up. Two officers and two medical technicians jogged to meet him and they all sprinted to the garage door. He smelled fumes and could hear the rattle of a car engine inside.

As a uniformed cop banged on the door, Tal noticed a handwritten note taped to the front.

> WARNING: The garage is filled with dangrous fumes. We've left the remote control on the groun in front of the flower pot. Please use it to the door and let it air out before entring.

"No!" Tal dropped the note and began tugging futilely at the door, which was locked from the inside. In the dark they couldn't immediately find the remote so a fireman with an axe ran to the side door and broke it open with one swing.

But they were too late.

To save either of them.

Once again it was a multiple suicide. Another husband and wife.

Samuel and Elizabeth Whitley were in the garage, reclining in an open convertible, a old-fashioned MG sports car. While one officer had shut off the engine and firemen rigged a vent fan, the medical techs had pulled them out of the car and rested them on the driveway. They'd attempted to revive them but the efforts were futile. The couple had been very efficient in their planning; they'd sealed the doors, vents, and windows of the garage with duct tape. Shades had been drawn, so no one could look inside and interrupt their deaths. Only the unusual rattle of the engine had alerted a dog-walking neighbor that something was wrong.

Talbot Simms stared at them, numb. No blood this time but the deaths were just as horrible to him—seeing the bodies and noting the detachment in their planning: the thoughtfulness of the warning note, its cordial tone, the care in sealing the garage. And the underlying uneasiness; like the Bensons' note, this one was written in unsteady writing and there were misspellings—"dangrous"—and a missing word or two: "use it to the door . . ."

The uniformed officers made a circuit of the house, to make certain nobody else was inside and had been affected by the carbon monoxide. Tal too entered but hesitated at first when he smelled a strong odor of fumes. But then he realized that the scent wasn't auto exhaust but smoke from the fireplace. Brandy glasses and a dusty bottle sat on the table in front of a small couch. They'd had a final romantic drink together in front of a fire—and then died.

"Anybody else here?" Tal asked the cops as they returned to the main floor.

"No, it's clean. Neatest house I've ever seen. Looks like it was just scrubbed. Weird, cleaning the house to kill yourself."

In the kitchen they found another note, the handwriting just as unsteady as the warning about the gas.

> To our friends and family:
> We do this with great joy in hearts and with love for
> everone in our family and everyone we've known.
> Don't feel any sorrow; weve never been happier.

The letter ended with the name, address, and phone number of their attorney. Tal lifted his mobile phone from his pocket and called the number.

"Hello."

"Mr. Wells, please. This is Detective Simms with the county police."

A hesitation. "Yes, sir?" the voice asked.

The pause was now on Tal's part. "Mr. Wells?"

"That's right."

"You're the Whitleys' attorney?"

"That's right. What's this about?"

Tal took a deep breath. "I'm sorry to tell you that they've . . . passed away. It was a suicide. We found your name in their note."

"My, God, no. . . . What happened?"

"How, you mean? In their garage. Their car exhaust."

"When?"

"Tonight. A little while ago."

"No! . . . Both of them? Not both of them?"

"I'm afraid so," Tal replied.

There was a long pause. Finally the lawyer, clearly shaken, whispered, "I should've guessed."

"How's that? Had they talked about it?"

"No, no. But Sam was sick."

"Sick?"

"His heart. It was pretty serious."

Just like Don Benson.

More common denominators.

"His wife? Was she sick too?"

"Oh, Elizabeth. No. She was in pretty good health. . . . Does the daughter know?"

"They have a daughter?" This news instantly made the deaths exponentially more tragic.

"She lives in the area. I'll call her." He sighed. "That's what they pay me for. . . . Well, thank you, Officer. . . . What was your name again?"

"Simms."

"Thank you."

Tal put his phone away and started slowly through the house. It reminded him of the Bensons'. Tastefully opulent. Only more so. The Whitleys were, he guessed, much richer.

Glancing at the pictures on the wall, many of which showed a cute little girl who'd grown into a beautiful young woman.

He was grateful that the lawyer would be making the call to their daughter.

Tal walked into the kitchen. No calendars here.

He looked again at the note.

Joy . . . Never been happier.

Nearby was another document. He looked it over and frowned. Curious. It was a receipt for the purchase of a restored MG automobile. Whitley'd paid for a deposit on the car earlier but had given the dealer the balance today.

Tal walked to the garage and hesitated before entering. But he steeled up his courage and stepped inside, glanced at the tarps covering the bodies. He located the vehicle identification number. Yes, this was the same car as on the receipt.

Whitley had bought an expensive restored antique vehicle today, driven it home and then killed himself and his wife.

Why?

There was motion in the driveway. Tal watched a long, dark-gray van pull up outside. LEIGHEY'S FUNERAL HOME was printed on the side. Already? Had the officers called or the lawyer? Two men got out of the hearse and walked up to a uniformed officer. They seemed to know each other.

Then Tal paused. He noticed something familiar. He picked up a book on a table in the den. *Making the Final Journey.*

The same book the Bensons had.

Too many common denominators. The suicide book, the heart diseases, spouses also dying.

Tal walked into the living room and found the older trooper filling out a form—not *his* questionnaire, Tal noticed. He asked one of the men from the funeral home, "What're you doing with the bodies?"

"Instructions were cremation as soon as possible."

"Can we hold off on that?"

"Hold off?" he asked and glanced at the Hamilton officer. "How do you mean, Detective?"

Tal said, "Get an autopsy?"

"Why?"

"Just wondering if we can."

"You're county," the heavy-set cop said. "You're the boss. Only, I mean, you know—you can't do it halfway. Either you declare a twenty-one-twenty-four or you don't."

Oh, *that.* He wondered what exactly it was.

A glance at the sports car. "Okay, I'll do that. I'm declaring a twenty-four-twenty-one."

"You mean twenty-one-twenty-four. . . . You sure about this?" the officer asked, looking uncertainly toward the funeral home assistant, who was frowning; even he apparently knew more about the mysterious 2124 than Tal did.

The statistician looked outside and saw the other man from the funeral home pull a stretcher out of the back of the hearse and walk toward the bodies.

"Yes," he said firmly. "I'm sure." And tapped loudly on the window, gesturing for the man to stop.

The next morning, Monday, Tal saw the head of the Crime Scene Unit walk into the Detective pen and head straight toward LaTour's office. He was carrying a half dozen folders.

He had a gut feeling that this was the Whitley scene report and was out of his office fast to intercept him. "Hey, how you doing? That about the Whitley case?"

"Yeah. It's just the preliminary. But there was an expedite on it. Is Greg in? LaTour?"

"I think it's for me."

"You're . . ."

"Simms."

"Oh, yeah," the man said, looking at the request attached to the report. "I didn't notice. I figured it was LaTour. Being head of Homicide, you know." He handed the files to Tal.

A 2124, it turned out, was a declaration that a death was suspicious. Like hitting a fire alarm button, it set all kinds of activities in motion—getting Crime Scene to search the house, collect evidence, record friction-ridge prints and extensively photograph and video the scene; scheduling autopsies, and alerting the prosecutor's office that a homicide investigation case file had been started. In his five years on the job Tal had never gotten so many calls before 10:00 as he had this morning.

Tal glanced into the captain's office then LaTour's. Nobody seemed to notice that a statistician who'd never issued a parking ticket in his life was clutching crime scene files.

Except Shellee, who subtly blessed herself and winked.

Tal asked the Crime Scene detective, "Preliminary, you said. What else're you waiting for?"

"Phone records, handwriting confirmation of the note and autopsy results. Hey, I'm really curious. What'd you find that made you think this was suspicious? Fits the classic profile of every suicide I've ever worked."

"Some things."

"Things," the seasoned cop said, nodding slowly. "Things. Ah. Got a suspect?"

"Not yet."

"Ah. Well, good luck. You'll need it."

Back in his office Tal carefully filed away the spreadsheet he'd been working on then opened the CSU files. He spread the contents out on his desk.

We begin with inspiration, a theorem, an untested idea: There is a perfect odd number. There is a point at which pi repeats. The universe is infinite.

A mathematician then attempts to construct a proof that shows irrefutably that his position either is correct or cannot be correct.

Tal Simms knew how to create such proofs with numbers. But to prove the theorem that there was something suspicious about the deaths of the Bensons and the Whitleys? He had no idea how to do this and stared at the hieroglyphics of the crime scene reports, increasingly discouraged. He had basic academy training, of course, but, beyond that, no investigation skills or experience.

But then he realized that perhaps this wasn't quite accurate. He did have one talent that might help: the cornerstone of his profession as a mathematician—logic.

He turned his analytical mind to the materials on his desk as he examined each item carefully. He first picked the photos of the Whitleys' bodies. All in graphic, colorful detail. They troubled him a great deal. Still, he forced himself to examine them carefully, every inch. After some time he concluded that nothing suggested that the Whitleys had been forced into the car or had struggled with any assailants.

He set the photos aside and read the documents in the reports themselves. There were no signs of any break-in, though the front and back doors weren't locked, so someone might have simply walked in. But with the absence of signs of physical assault an intrusion seemed unlikely. And their jewelry, cash, and other valuables were untouched.

One clue, though, suggested that all was not as it seemed. The Latents team found that both notes contained, in addition to Sam Whitley's, Tal's and the police officers' prints, smudges that were probably from gloved hands or fingers protected by a cloth or tissue. The team had also found glove prints in the den where the couple had had their last drink, in the room where the note had been found, and in the garage.

Gloves? Tal wondered. Curious.

The team had also found fresh tire prints on the driveway. The prints didn't match the MG, the other cars owned by the victims or the vehicles driven by the police, medical team, or the funeral home. The report concluded that the car had been there within the three hours prior to death. The tread marks were indistinct, so that the brand of tire couldn't be determined, but the wheelbase meant the vehicle was a small one.

A search of the trace evidence revealed several off-white cotton fibers—one on the body of Elizabeth Whitley and one on the living room couch—that didn't appear to match what the victims were wearing or any of the clothes in their closets. An inventory of drugs in the medicine cabinets and kitchen revealed no antidepressants, which suggested, even if tenuously, that mood problems and thoughts of suicide might not have occurred in the Whitley house recently.

He rose, walked to his doorway and called Shellee in.

"Hi, Boss. Havin' an exciting morning, are we?"

He rolled his eyes. "I need you to do something for me."

"Are you . . . ? I mean, you look tired."

"Yes, yes, I'm fine. It's just about this case."

"What case?"

"The suicide."

"Oh."

"I need to find out if anybody's bought a book called *Making the Final Journey.* Then a subhead—something about suicide and euthanasia."

"A book. Sure."

"I don't remember exactly. But *Making the Journey* or *Making the Final Journey* is the start of the title."

"Okay. And I'm supposed to check on—?"

"If anybody bought it."

"I mean, everywhere? There're probably a lot of—"

"For now, just in Westbrook County. In the last couple of weeks. Bookstores. And that online place, the big one, Booksource dot com."

"Hey, when I call, is it okay to play cop?"

Tal hesitated. But then he said, "Oh, hell, sure. You want, you can be a detective."

"Yippee," she said. "Detective Shellee Bingham."

"And if they *haven't* sold any, give them my name and tell them if they *do*, call us right away."

"We need a warrant or anything?" Detective Shellee asked, thoughtful now.

Did they? he wondered.

"Hmm. I don't know. Let's just try it without and see what they say."

Five minutes later Tal felt a shadow over him and he looked up to see Captain Ronald Dempsey's six-foot-three form fill the doorway in his ubiquitous striped shirt, his sleeves ubiquitously rolled up.

The man's round face smiled pleasantly. But Tal thought immediately: I'm busted.

"Captain."

"Hey, Tal." Dempsey leaned against the doorjamb, looking over the desktop. "Got a minute?"

"Sure do."

Tal had known that the brass would find out about the 2124, of course, and he'd planned to talk to Dempsey about it soon; but he'd hoped to wait until his proof about the suspicious suicide was somewhat further developed.

"Heard about the twenty-one-twenty-four at the Whitleys'."

"Sure."

"What's up with *that*?"

Tal explained about the two suicides, the common denominators.

Dempsey nodded. "Kind of a coincidence, sure. But you know, Tal, we don't have a lot of resources for full investigations. Like, we've only got one dedicated homicide crime scene unit."

"Didn't know that."

"And there was a shooting in Rolling Hills Estates last night. Two people shot up bad, one died. The unit was late running that scene 'cause you had them in Hamilton."

"I'm sorry about that, Captain."

"It's also expensive. Sending out CS."

"Expensive? I didn't think about that."

"Thousands, I'm talking. Crime scene bills everything back to us. Every time they go out. Then there're lab tests and autopsies and everything. The M.E. too. You know what an autopsy costs?"

"They *bill* us?" Tal asked.

"It's just the more we save for the county the better we look, you know."

"Right. I guess it would be expensive."

"You bet." No longer smiling, the captain adjusted his sleeves. "Other thing is, the way I found out: I heard from their daughter. Sandra Whitley. She was going to make funeral arrangements and then she hears about the M.E. autopsy. Phew . . . she's pissed off. Threatening to sue. . . . I'm going to have to answer questions. So. Now, what *exactly* made you twenty-one-twenty-four the scene, Tal?"

He scanned the papers on his desk, uneasy, wondering where to start. "Well, a couple of things. They'd just bought—"

"Hold on there a minute," the captain said, holding up a finger.

Dempsey leaned out the door and shouted, "LaTour! . . . Hey, LaTour?"

"What?" came the grumbling baritone.

"Come over here. I'm with Simms."

Tal heard the big man make his way toward the Unreal Crimes side of the detective pen. The ruddy, goateed face appeared in the office. Ignoring Tal, he listened as the captain explained about the Whitleys' suicide.

"Another one, huh?"

"Tal declared a twenty-one-twenty-four."

The homicide cop nodded noncommitally. "Uh-huh. Why?"

The question was directed toward Dempsey, who turned toward Tal.

"Well, I was looking at the Bensons' deaths and I pulled up the standard statistical profile on suicides in Westbrook County. Now, when you look at all the attributes—"

"Attributes?" LaTour asked, frowning, as if tasting sand.

"Right. The attributes of the Bensons' death—and the Whitleys' too now—they're way out of the standard range. Their deaths are outliers."

"Out-liars? The fuck's that?"

Tal explained. In statistics an outlier was an event significantly different from a group of similar events. He gave a concrete example. "Say you're analyzing five murderers. Three perps killed a single victim each, one of them killed two victims, and the final man was a serial killer who'd murdered twenty people. To draw any meaningful conclusions from that, you need to treat the last one as an outlier and analyze him separately. Otherwise, your analysis'll be mathematically correct but misleading. Running the numbers, the mean—the average—number of victims killed by each suspect is five. But that exaggerates the homicidal nature of the first four men and underplays the last one. See what I mean?"

The frown on LaTour's face suggested he didn't. But he said, "So you're saying these two suicides're different from most of the others in Westbrook."

"*Significantly* different. Fewer than six percent of the population kill themselves when they're facing a possibly terminal illness. That number drops to two point six percent when the victim has medical insurance and down to point nine when the net worth of the victim is over one million dollars. It drops even further when the victims are married and are in the relatively young category of sixty-five to seventy-five, like these folks. And love-pact deaths are only two percent of suicides nationwide and ninety-one percent of those involve victims under the age of twenty-one. . . . Now, what do you think the odds are that two heart patients would take their own lives, and their wives', in the space of two days?"

"I don't really know, Tal," LaTour said, clearly uninterested. "What else you got? Suspicious, I mean."

"Okay, the Whitleys'd just bought a car earlier that day. Rare, antique MG. Why do that if you're going to kill yourself?"

LaTour offered, "They needed a murder weapon. Didn't want a gun. Probably there was something about the MG that meant something to them. From when they were younger, you know. They wanted to go out that way."

"Makes sense," Dempsey said, tugging at a sleeve.

"There's more," Tal said and explained about the gloves, the fiber, the smudges on the note. And the recent visitor's tire prints.

"Somebody else was there around the time they killed themselves. Or just after."

LaTour said, "Lemme take a look."

Tal pushed the reports toward him. The big cop examined everything closely. Then shook his head. "I just don't see it," he said to the captain. "No evidence of a break-in or struggle . . . The note?" He shrugged. "Looks authentic. I mean, Documents'll tell us for sure but look—" he held up the Whitleys' checkbook ledger and the suicide note, side by side. The script was virtually identical. "Smudges from gloves on paper? We see that on every piece of paper we find at a scene. Hell, half the pieces of paper *here* have smudges on them that look like smeared FRs—"

"FRs?"

"Friction ridges," LaTour muttered. "*Fingerprints.* Smudges—from the manufacturer, stockers, browsing customers."

"The fiber?" He leaned forward and lifted a tiny white strand off Tal's suit jacket. "This's the same type the Crime Scene found. Cotton worsted. See it all the time. The fibers at the Whitleys' could've come from anywhere. It might've come from you." Shuffling sloppily through the files with his massive paws. "Okay, the gloves and the tread marks? Those're Playtex kitchen gloves; I recognize the ridges. No perps ever use them because the wear patterns can be traced. . . ." He held up the checkbook ledger again. "Lookit the check the wife wrote today. To Esmerelda Constanzo 'For cleaning services.' The housekeeper was in yesterday, cleaned the house wearing the gloves—maybe she even straightened up the stack of paper they used later for the suicide note, left the smudges then. The tread marks? That's about the size of a small import. Just the sort that a cleaning woman'd be driving. They were hers. Bet you any money."

Though he didn't like the man's message, Tal was impressed at the way his mind worked. He'd made all those deductions—extremely *logical* deductions—based on a three-minute examination of the data.

"Got a case needs lookin' at," LaTour grumbled and tossed the report onto Tal's desk. He clomped back to his office.

Breaking the silence that followed, Dempsey said, "Hey, I know you don't get out into the field much. Must get frustrating to sit in the office all day long, not doing . . . you know . . ."

Real police work? Tal wondered if that's what the captain was hesitating to say.

"More active stuff" turned out to be the captain's euphemism. "You probably feel sometimes like you don't fit in."

He's probably home humping his calculator. . . .

"We've all felt that way sometimes. Honest. But being out in the field's not what it's cracked up to be. Not like TV, you know. And you're the best at what you do, Tal. Statistician. Man, that's a hard job. An *important* job. Let's face it—" Lowering his voice. "—guys like Greg wouldn't know a number if it jumped out and bit 'em on the ass. You've got a real special talent."

Tal weathered the condescension with a faint smile, which obscured the anger beneath his flushed face. The speech was clearly out of a personnel management training manual. Dempsey had just plugged in "statistician" for "traffic detail" or "receptionist."

"Okay, now, don't you have some numbers to crunch? We've got that midyear assignment meeting coming up and nobody can put together a report like you, my friend."

Monday evening's drive to the Whitleys' house took considerably longer than his Headless Horseman race night before, since he drove the way he usually did: within the speed limit and perfectly centered in his lane (and with the belt firmly clasped this time).

Noting with a grimace how completely he'd destroyed the shrubs last night, Tal parked in front of the door and ducked under the crime scene tape. He stepped inside, smelling again the sweet, poignant scent of the woodsmoke from the couple's last cocktail hour.

Inside their house, he pulled on latex gloves he'd bought at a drugstore on the way here (thinking only when he got to the checkout lane: Damn, they probably have hundreds of these back in the Detective pen). Then he began working his way though the house, picking up anything that Crime Scene had missed that might shed some light on the mystery of the Whitleys' deaths.

Greg LaTour's bluntness and Captain Dempsey's pep talk, in other words, had no effect on him. All intellectually honest mathematicians welcome the disproving of their theorems as much as the proving. But the more LaTour had laid out the evidence that the 2124 was wrong, the more Tal's resolve grew to get to the bottom of the deaths.

There *was* an odd perfect number out there, and there *was* something unusual about the deaths of the Bensons and the Whitleys; Tal was determined to write the proof.

Address books, DayTimers, receipts, letters, stacks of papers, piles of business cards for lawyers, repairmen, restaurants, investment advisors, accountants. He felt a chill as he read one for some new age organization, the Lotus Research Foundation for Alternative Treatment, tucked in with all the practical and mundane cards—evidence of the desperation of rational people frightened by impending death.

A snap of floorboard, a faint clunk. A metallic sound. It startled him and he felt uneasy—vulnerable. He'd parked in the front of the house; whoever'd arrived would know he was here. The police tape and crime scene notice were clear about forbidding entry; he doubted that the visitor was a cop.

And, alarmed, he realized that a corollary of his theorem that the Whitleys had been murdered was, of course, that there had to be a murderer.

He reached for his hip and realized, to his dismay, that he'd left his pistol in his desk at the office. The only suspects Tal had ever met face to face were benign accountants or investment bankers and even then the confrontation was usually in court. He never carried the gun—about the only regulation he ever broke. Palms sweating, Tal looked around for something he could use to protect himself. He was in the bedroom, surrounded by books, clothes, furniture. Nothing he could use as a weapon.

He looked out the window.

A twenty-foot drop to the flagstone patio.

Was he too proud to hide under the bed?

Footsteps sounded closer, walking up the stairs. The carpet muted them but the old floorboards creaked as the intruder got closer.

No, he decided, he wasn't too proud for the bed. But that didn't seem to be the wisest choice. Escape was better.

Out the window.

Tal opened it, swung the leaded-glass panes outward. No grass below; just a flagstone deck dotted with booby traps of patio furniture.

He heard the metallic click of a gun. The steps grew closer, making directly for the bedroom.

Okay, jump. He glanced down. Aim for the padded lawn divan. You'll sprain your ankle but you won't get shot.

He put his hand on the windowsill, was about to boost himself over when a voice filled the room, a woman's voice. "Who the hell're you?"

Tal turned fast, observing a slim blonde in her mid or late thirties, eyes narrow. She was smoking a cigarette and putting a gold lighter back into her purse—the metallic sound he'd assumed was a gun. There was something familiar—and troubling—about her and he realized that, yes, he'd seen her face—in the snapshots on the walls. "You're their daughter."

"Who are you?" she repeated in a gravelly voice.

"You shouldn't be in here. It's a crime scene."

"You're a cop? Let me see some ID." She glanced at his latex-gloved hand on the window, undoubtedly wondering what he'd been about to do.

He offered her the badge and identification card.

She glanced at them carefully. "You're the one who did it?"

"What?"

"You had them taken to the morgue? Had them goddamn *butchered*?"

"I had some questions about their deaths. I followed procedures."

More or less.

"So you *were* the one. Detective Talbot Simms." She'd memorized his name from the brief look at his ID. "I'll want to be sure you're personally named in the suit."

"You're not supposed to be here," Tal repeated. "The scene hasn't been released yet."

He remembered this from a cop show on TV.

"Fuck your scene."

A different response than on the TV show.

"Let me see some ID," Tal said stepping forward, feeling more confident now.

The staring match began.

He added cheerfully, "I'm happy to call some officers to take you downtown." This—from another show—was a bit inaccurate; the Westbrook Sheriff's Department wasn't downtown at all. It was in a strip mall next to a large Stop 'N' Shop grocery.

She reluctantly showed him her driver's license. Sandra Kaye

Whitley, thirty-six. He recognized the address, a very exclusive part of the county.

"What was so fucking mysterious about their deaths? They killed themselves."

Tal observed something interesting about her. Yes, she was angry. But she wasn't sad.

"We can't talk about an open case."

"What *case*?" Sandra snapped. "You keep saying that."

"Well, it was a murder, you know."

Her hand paused then continued carrying her cigarette to her lips. She asked coolly, "Murder?"

Tal said, "Your father turned the car ignition on. Technically he murdered your mother."

"That's bullshit."

Probably it was. But he sidestepped the issue. "Had they ever had a history of depression?"

She debated for a moment then answered. "My father's disease was serious. And my mother didn't want to live without him."

"But his illness wasn't terminal, was it?"

"Not exactly. But he *was* going to die. And he wanted to do it with dignity."

Tal felt he was losing this contest; she kept him on the defensive. He tried to think more like Greg LaTour. "What exactly're you doing here?"

"It's my family's house," she snapped. "*My* house. I grew up here. I wanted to see it. They *were* my parents, you know."

He nodded. "Of course. . . . I'm sorry for your loss. I just want to make sure that everything's what it seems to be. Just doing my job."

She shrugged and stubbed the cigarette out in a heavy crystal ashtray on the dresser. She noticed, sitting next to it, a picture of her with her parents. For a long moment she stared at it then looked away, hiding tears from him. She wiped her face then turned back. "I'm an attorney, you know. I'm going to have one of my litigation partners look at this situation through a microscope, Detective."

"That's fine, Ms. Whitley," Tal said. "Can I ask what you put in your purse earlier?"

She blinked. "Purse?"

"When you were downstairs."

A hesitation. "It's nothing important."

"This is a crime scene. You can't take anything. That's a felony. Which I'm sure you knew. Being an attorney, as you say."

Was it a felony? he wondered.

At least Sandra didn't seem to know it *wasn't.*

"You can give it to me now and I'll forget about the incident. Or we can take that trip downtown."

She held his eye for a moment, slicing him into tiny pieces, as she debated. Then she opened her purse. She handed him a small stack of mail. "It was in the mailbox to be picked up. But with that yellow tape all over the place the mailman couldn't come by. I was just going to mail it."

"I'll take it."

She held the envelopes out to him with a hand that seemed to be quivering slightly. He took them in his gloved hands.

In fact, he'd had no idea that she'd put anything in her purse; he'd had a flash of intuition. Talbot Simms suddenly felt a rush of excitement; statisticians never bluff.

Sandra looked around the room and her eyes seemed mournful again. But he decided it was in fact anger. She said icily, "You *will* be hearing from my litigation partner, Detective Simms. Shut the lights out when you leave, unless the county's going to be paying the electric bill."

∞

"I'm getting coffee, Boss. You want some?"

"Sure, thanks," he told Shellee.

It was the next morning and Tal was continuing to pore over the material he'd collected. Some new information had just arrived: the Whitleys' phone records for the past month, the autopsy results, and the handwriting analysis of the suicide note.

He found nothing immediately helpful about the phone records and set them aside, grimacing as he looked for someplace to rest them. There wasn't any free space on his desk and so he stacked them, as orderly as he could, on top of another stack. It made him feel edgy, the mess, but there wasn't anything else he could do, short of moving a table or another desk into his office—and he could imagine the ribbing he'd take for that.

Data plural . . . humping his calculator . . .

Tal looked over the handwriting expert's report first. The woman said that she could state with 98 percent certainty that Sam Whitley had written the note, though the handwriting had been unsteady and the spelling flawed, which was unusual for a man of his education.

The garage is filled with dangrous fumes.

This suggested some impairment, possible severe, she concluded.

Tal turned to the autopsy results. Death was, as they'd thought, due to carbon monoxide poisoning. There were no contusions, tissue damage, or ligature marks to suggest they'd been forced into the car. There was alcohol in the blood, .010 percent in Sam's system, 0.019 in Elizabeth's, neither particularly high. But they both had medication in their bloodstreams too.

> Present in both victims were unusually large quantities of 9-fluoro, 7-chloro-1, 3-dihydro-1-methyl-5-phenyl-2H-1,4-benzodiazepin, 5-hydroxytryptamine and N-(1-phenethyl-4-piperidyl) propionanilide citrate.

This was, the M.E.'s report continued, an analgesic/anti-anxiety drug sold under the trade name Luminux. The amount in their blood meant that the couple had recently taken nearly three times the normally prescribed strength of the drug, though, it did not, the M.E. concluded, make them more susceptible to carbon monoxide poisoning or otherwise directly contribute to their deaths.

Looking over his desk—too goddamn many papers!—he finally found another document and carefully read the inventory of the house, which the Crime Scene Unit had prepared. The Whitleys had plenty of medicine—for Sam's heart problem, as well as for Elizabeth's arthritis and other maladies—but no Luminux.

Shellee brought him the coffee. Her eyes cautiously took in the cluttered desktop.

"Thanks," he muttered.

"Still lookin' tired, Boss."

"Didn't sleep well." Instinctively he pulled his striped tie straight, kneaded the knot to make sure it was tight.

"It's fine, Boss," she whispered, nodding at his shirt. Meaning: Quit fussing.

He winked at her.

Thinking about common denominators . . .

The Bensons' suicide note too had been sloppy, Tal recalled. He rummaged though the piles on his desk and found their lawyer's card then dialed the man's office and was put through to him.

"Mr. Metzer, this's Detective Simms. I met you at the Bensons' a few days ago."

"Right. I remember."

"This is a little unusual but I'd like permission to take a blood sample."

"From me?" he asked in a startled voice.

"No, no, from the Bensons."

"Why?"

He hesitated, then decided to go ahead with the lie. "I'd like to update our database about medicines and diseases of recent suicides. It'll be completely anonymous."

"Oh. Well, sorry, but they were cremated this morning."

"They were? That was fast."

"I don't know if it was fast or it was slow. But that's what they wanted. It was in their instructions to me. They wanted to be cremated as soon as possible and the contents of the house sold—"

"Wait. You're telling me—"

"—the contents of the house sold immediately."

"When's that going to happen?"

"It's probably already done. We've had dealers in the house since Sunday morning. I don't think there's much left."

Tal remembered the man at the Whitleys' house—there to arrange for the liquidation of the estate. He wished he'd known about declaring 2124s when he'd been to the Bensons' house.

Common denominators . . .

"Do you still have the suicide note?"

"I didn't take it. I imagine it was thrown out when the service cleaned the house."

This's all way too fast, Tal thought. He looked over the papers on his desk. "Do you know if either of them was taking a drug called Luminux?"

"I don't have a clue."

"Can you give me Mr. Benson's cardiologist's name?"

A pause then the lawyer said, "I suppose it's okay. Yeah. Dr. Peter Brody. Over in Glenstead."

Tal was about to hang up but then a thought occurred to him. "Mr. Metzer, when I met you on Friday, didn't you tell me the Bensons weren't religious?"

"That's right. They were atheists. . . . What's this all about, Detective?"

"Like I say—just getting some statistics together. That's all. Thanks for your time."

He got Dr. Brody's number and called the doctor's office. The man was on vacation and his head nurse was reluctant to talk about patients, even deceased ones. She did admit, though, that Brody had not prescribed Luminux for them.

Tal then called the head of Crime Scene and learned that the gun the Bensons had killed themselves with was in an evidence locker. He asked that Latents look it over for prints. "Can you do a rush on it?"

"Happy to. It's comin' outa your budget, Detective," the man said cheerfully. "Be about ten, fifteen minutes."

"Thanks."

As he waited for the results on the gun, Tal opened his briefcase and noticed the three letters Sandra Whitley had in her purse at her parents' house. Putting on a pair of latex gloves once again, he ripped open the three envelopes and examined the contents.

The first one contained a bill from their lawyer for four hours of legal work, performed that month. The project, the bill summarized, was for "estate planning services."

Did he mean redoing the will? Was this another common denominator? Metzer had said that the Bensons had just redone theirs.

The second letter was an insurance form destined for the Cardiac Support Center at Westbrook Hospital, where Sam had been a patient.

Nothing unusual here.

But then he opened the third letter.

He sat back in his chair, looking at the ceiling then down at the letter once more.

Debating.

Then deciding that he didn't have any choice. When you're writing a mathematical proof you go anywhere the numbers take you. Tal rose and walked across the office, to the Real Crimes side of the pen. He leaned into an open door and knocked on the jamb. Greg LaTour was sitting back in his chair, boots up. He was reading a document. "Fucking liar," he muttered and put a large check mark next to one of the paragraphs. Looking up, he cocked an eyebrow.

Humping his calculator . . .

Tal tried to be pleasant. "Greg. You got a minute?"

"Just."

"I want to talk to you about the case."

"Case?" The man frowned. "Which case?"

"The Whitleys."

"Who?"

"The suicides."

"From Sunday? Yeah, okay. Drew a blank. I don't think of suicides as cases." LaTour's meaty hand grabbed another piece of paper. He looked down at it.

"You said that the cleaning lady'd probably been there? She'd left the glove prints? And the tire treads."

It didn't seem that he remembered at first. Then he nodded. "And?"

"Look." He showed LaTour the third letter he'd found at the Whitleys. It was a note to Esmerelda Constanzo, the Whitleys' cleaning lady, thanking her for her years of help and saying they wouldn't be needing her services any longer. They'd enclosed the check that LaTour had spotted in the register.

"They'd put the check in the mail," Tal pointed out. "That means she wasn't there the day they died. Somebody else wore the gloves. And I got to thinking about it? Why would a cleaning lady wear kitchen gloves to clean the rest of the house? Doesn't make sense."

LaTour shrugged. His eyes dipped to the document on his desk and then returned once more to the letter Tal held.

The statistician added, "And that means the car wasn't hers either. The tread marks. Somebody else was there around the time they died."

"Well, Tal—"

"Couple other things," he said quickly. "Both the Whitleys had high amounts of a prescription drug in their bloodstream. Some kind of narcotic. Luminux. But there were no prescription bottles for it in their house. And their lawyer'd just done some estate work for them. Maybe revising their wills."

"You gonna kill yourself, you gonna revise your will. That ain't very suspicious."

"But then I met the daughter."

"Their daughter?"

"She broke into the house, looking for something. She'd pocketed the mail but she might've been looking for something else. Maybe she got scared when she heard we didn't buy the suicide—"

"*You.* Not we."

Tal continued, "And she wanted to get rid of any evidence about the Luminux. I didn't search her. I didn't think about it at the time."

"What's this with the drugs? They didn't OD."

"Well, maybe she got them doped up, had them change their will and talked them into killing themselves."

"Yeah, right," LaTour muttered. "That's outa some bad movie."

Tal shrugged. "When I mentioned murder she freaked out."

"Murder? Why'd you mention murder?" He scratched his huge belly, looking for the moment just like his nickname.

"I meant murder-suicide. The husband turning the engine on."

LaTour gave a grunt—Tal hadn't realized that you could make a sound like that condescending.

"And, you know, she had this attitude."

"Well, now, Tal, you *did* send her parents to the county morgue. You know what they do to you there, don'tcha? Knives and saws. That's gotta piss the kid off a little, you know."

"Yes, she was pissed. But mostly, I think, 'cause I was there, checking out what'd happened. And you know what she didn't seem upset about?"

"What's that?"

"Her parents. Them dying. She *seemed* to be crying. But I couldn't tell. It could've been an act."

"She was in shock. Skirts get that way."

Tal persisted, "Then I checked on the first couple. The Bensons? They were cremated right after they died and their estate liquidated in a day or two."

"Liquidated?" LaTour lifted an eyebrow and finally delivered a comment that was neither condescending nor sarcastic. "And cremated that fast, hm? Seems odd, yeah. I'll give you that."

"And the Bensons' lawyer told me something else. They were atheists, both of them. But their suicide note said they'd be together forever or something like that. Atheists aren't going to say that. I'm thinking maybe *they* might've been drugged too. With that Luminux."

"What does their doctor?—"

"No, he didn't prescribed it. But maybe somebody slipped it to them. Their suicide note was unsteady too, sloppy, just like the Whitleys'."

"What's the story on *their* doctor?"

"I haven't got that far yet."

"Maybe, maybe, maybe." LaTour squinted. "But that gardener we talked to at the Benson place? He said they'd been boozing it up. You did the blood work on the Whitleys. They been drinking?"

"Not too much. . . . Oh, one other thing. I called their cell phone company and checked the phone records—the Whitleys'. They received a call from a pay phone forty minutes before they died. Two minutes long. Just enough time to see if they're home and say you're going to stop by. And who calls from pay phones anymore? Everybody's got cells, right?"

Reluctantly LaTour agreed with this.

"Look at it, Greg: Two couples, both rich, live five miles from each other. Both of 'em in the country club set. Both husbands have heart disease. Two murder-suicides a few days apart. What do you think about that?"

In a weary voice LaTour asked, "Outliers, right?"

"Exactly.

"You're thinking the bitch—"

"Who?" Tal asked.

"The daughter."

"I didn't say that."

"I'm not gonna quote you in the press, Tal."

"Okay," he conceded, "she's a bitch."

"You're thinking she's got access to her folks, there's money involved. She's doing something funky with the will or insurance."

"It's a theorem."

"A what?" LaTour screwed up his face.

"It's a hunch is what I'm saying."

"Hunch. Okay. But you brought up the Bensons. The Whitley

daughter isn't going to off *them* now, is she? I mean, why would she?"

Tal shrugged. "I don't know. Maybe she's the Bensons' goddaughter and she was in their will too. Or maybe her father was going into some deal with Benson that'd tie up all the estate money so the daughter'd lose out and she had to kill them both."

"Maybe, maybe, maybe," LaTour repeated.

Shellee appeared in the doorway and, ignoring LaTour, said, "Latents called. They said the only prints on the gun were the Bensons' and a few smears from cloth or paper."

"What fucking gun?" he asked.

"I will thank you not to use that language to me," Shellee said icily.

"I was talking to *him*," LaTour snapped and cocked an eyebrow at Tal.

Tal said, "The gun the Bensons killed themselves with. Smears—like on the Whitleys' suicide note."

Shellee glanced at the wall poster behind the desk then back to the detective. Tal couldn't tell whether the distasteful look was directed at LaTour himself or the blonde in a red-white-and-blue bikini lying provocatively across the seat and teardrop gas tank of the Harley. She turned and walked back to her desk quickly, as if she'd been holding her breath while she was inside the cop's office.

"Okay. . . . This's getting marginally fucking interesting." LaTour glanced at the huge gold watch on his wrist. "I gotta go. I got some time booked at the range. Come with me. Let's go waste some ammunition, talk about the case after."

"Think I'll stay here."

LaTour frowned, apparently unable to understand why somebody wouldn't jump at the chance to spend an hour punching holes in a piece of paper with a deadly weapon. "You don't shoot?"

"It's just I'd rather work on this."

Then enlightenment dawned. Tal's office was, after all on the Unreal Crimes side of the pen. He had no interest in cop toys.

You're the best at what you do, statistician. Man, that's a hard job. . . .

"Okay," LaTour said. "I'll check out the wills and the insurance policies. Gimme the name of the icees."

"The?—"

"The corpses, the stiffs . . . the losers who killed 'emselves, Tal. And their lawyers."

Tal wrote down the information and handed the neat note to LaTour, who stuffed it into his plaid shirt pocket behind two large cigars. He ripped open a desk drawer and took out a big, chrome automatic pistol.

Tal asked, "What should I do?"

"Get a P-I-I team and—"

"A what?"

"You go to the same academy as me, Tal? Post-Incident Interviewing team," he said as if he was talking to a three-year-old. "Use my name and Doherty'll put one together for you. Have 'em talk to all the neighbors around the Bensons' and the Whitleys' houses. See if they saw anybody around just before or after the TOD. Oh, that's—"

"Time of death."

LaTour gave him a thumbs up. "We'll talk this afternoon. I'll see you back here, how's four?"

"Sure. Oh, and maybe we should find out what kind of car the Whitleys' daughter drove. See if the wheelbase data match."

"That's good thinking, Tal," he said, looking honestly impressed. Grabbing some boxes of 9mm cartridges, LaTour walked heavily out of the Detective Division.

Tal returned to his desk and arranged for the P-I-I team. Then he called DMV, requesting information on Sandra Whitley's car. He glanced at his watch. One P.M. He realized he was hungry; he'd missed his regular lunch with his buddies from the university. He walked down to the small canteen on the second floor, bought a cheese sandwich and a diet soda and returned to his desk. As he ate he continued to pore over the pages of the crime scene report and the documents and other evidence he himself had collected at the house.

Shellee walked past his office, then stopped fast and returned. She stared at him then barked a laugh.

"What?" he asked.

"This is too weird, you eating at your desk."

Hadn't he ever done that? he wondered. He asked her.

"No. Not once. Ever. . . . And here you are, going to crime scenes, cluttering up your desk. . . . Listen, Boss, on your way home?"

"Yes?"

"Watch out for flying pigs. The sky's gotta be full of 'em today."

"Hi," Tal said to the receptionist.

Offering her a big smile. Why not? She had sultry, doe eyes, a heart-shaped face and the slim, athletic figure of a Riverdance performer.

Margaret Ludlum—according to the name plate—glanced up and cocked a pale, red eyebrow. "Yes?"

"It's Maggie, right?"

"Can I help you?" she asked in a polite but detached tone. Tal offered a second assault of a smile then displayed his badge and ID, which resulted in a cautious frown on her freckled face.

"I'm here to see Dr. Sheldon." This was Sam Whitley's cardiologist, whose card he'd found in the couple's bedroom last night.

"It's . . ." She squinted at the ID card.

"Detective Simms."

"Sure. Just hold on. Do you have—"

"No. An appointment? No. But I need to talk to him. It's important. About a patient. A former patient. Sam Whitley."

She nodded knowingly and gave a slight wince. Word of the deaths would have spread fast, he assumed.

"Hold on, please."

She made a call and a few minutes later a balding man in his fifties stepped out into the waiting room and greeted him. Dr. Anthony Sheldon led Tal back into a large office, whose walls were filled with dozens of diplomas and citations. The office was large and beautifully decorated, as one would expect for a man who probably made a few thousand dollars an hour.

Gesturing for Tal to sit across the desk, Sheldon dropped into his own high-backed chair.

"We're looking into their deaths," Tal said. "I'd like to ask you a few questions if I could."

"Yeah, sure. Anything I can do. It was . . . I mean, we heard it was a suicide, is that right?"

"It appeared to be. We just have a few unanswered questions. How long had you treated them?"

"Well, first, not *them*. Only Sam Whitley. He'd been referred to me by his personal GP."

"That's Ronald Weinstein," Tal said. Another nugget from the boxes of evidence that'd kept him up until three A.M. "I just spoke to him."

Tal had learned a few facts from the doctor, though nothing particularly helpful, except that Weinstein had not prescribed Luminux to either of the Whitleys, nor had he ever met the Bensons. Tal continued to Sheldon, "How serious was Sam's cardiac condition?"

"Fairly serious. Hold on—let me make sure I don't misstate anything."

Sheldon pressed a buzzer on his phone.

"Yes, Doctor?"

"Margaret, bring me the Whitley file, please."

So, not Maggie.

"Right away."

A moment later the woman walked briskly into the room, coolly ignoring Tal.

He decided that he liked the Celtic dancer part. He liked "Margaret" better than "Maggie."

The tough-as-nails part gave him some pause.

"Thanks."

Sheldon looked over the file. "His heart was only working at about fifty per cent efficiency. He should've had a transplant but wasn't a good candidate for one. We were going to replace valves and several major vessels."

"Would he have survived?"

"You mean the procedures? Or afterward?"

"Both."

"The odds weren't good for either. The surgeries themselves were the riskiest. Sam wasn't a young man and he had severe deterioration in his blood vessels. If he'd survived that, he'd have a fifty-fifty chance for six months. After that, the odds would've improved somewhat."

"So it wasn't hopeless."

"Not necessarily. But, like I told him, there was also a very good chance that even if he survived he'd be bedridden for the rest of his life."

Tal said, "So you weren't surprised to hear that he'd killed himself?"

"Well, I'm a doctor. Suicide doesn't make sense to most of us. But he was facing a very risky procedure and a difficult, painful recovery with an uncertain outcome. When I heard that he'd died, naturally I was troubled, and guilty too—thinking maybe I didn't explain things properly to him. But I have to say that I wasn't utterly shocked."

"Did you know his wife?"

"She came to most of his appointments."

"But she was in good health?"

"I don't know. But she seemed healthy."

"They were close?"

"Oh, very devoted to each other."

Tal looked up. "Doctor, what's Luminux?"

"Luminux? A combination antidepressant, pain-killer and antianxiety medication. I'm not too familiar with it."

"Then you didn't prescribe it to Sam or his wife?"

"No—and I'd never prescribe anything to a spouse of a patient unless she was a patient of mine too. Why?"

"They both had unusually high levels of the drug in their bloodstreams when they died."

"Both of them?"

"Right."

Dr. Sheldon shook his head. "That's odd. . . . Was that the cause of death?"

"No, it was carbon monoxide."

"Oh. Their car?"

"In the garage, right."

The doctor shook his head. "Better way to go than some, I suppose. But still . . ."

Another look at the notes he'd made from his investigation. "At their house I found an insurance form for the Cardiac Support Center here at the hospital. What's that?"

"I suggested he and Liz see someone there. They work with terminal and high-risk patients, transplant candidates. Counseling and therapy mostly."

"Could they have prescribed the drug?"

"Maybe. They have MDs on staff."

"I'd like to talk to them. Who should I see?"

"Dr. Peter Dehoeven is the director. They're in building J. Go back to the main lobby, take the elevator to three, turn left and keep going."

He thanked the doctor and stepped back into the lobby. Cell phone calls weren't allowed in the hospital so he asked Margaret if he could use one of the phones on her desk. She gestured toward it distractedly and turned back to her computer. It was 3:45 and Tal had to meet Greg LaTour in fifteen minutes.

One of the Homicide Division secretaries came on the line and he asked her to tell LaTour that he'd be a little late.

But she said, "Oh, he's gone for the day."

"Gone? We had a meeting."

"Didn't say anything about it."

He hung up, angry. Had LaTour just been humoring him, agreeing to help with the case to get Tal out of his hair?

He made another call—to the Cardiac Support Center. Dr. Dehoeven was out but Tal made an appointment to see him at eight-thirty in the morning. He hung up and nearly asked Margaret to clarify the way to the Cardiac Support Center. But Sheldon's directions were solidly implanted in his memory and he'd only bring up the subject to give it one more shot with sweet Molly Malone. But why bother? He knew to a statistical certainty that he and this red-haired lass would never be step-dancing the night away then lying in bed till dawn discussing the finer point of perfect numbers.

"All the valves?" Seventy-two-year-old Robert Covey asked his cardiologist, who was sitting across from him. The name on the white jacket read *Dr. Lansdowne* in scripty stitching, but with her frosted blonde hair in a Gwyneth Paltrow bun and sly red lipstick, he thought of her only as "Dr. Jenny."

"That's right." She leaned forward. "And there's more."

For the next ten minutes she proceeded to give him the low-down on the absurd medical extremes he'd have to endure to have a chance of seeing his seventy-third birthday.

Unfair, Covey thought. Goddamn unfair to've been singled out this way. His weight, on a six-foot-one frame, was around 180, had been all his adult life. He gave up smoking forty years ago. He'd taken weekend hikes every few months with Veronica until he lost her and then had joined a hiking club where he got even more exercise than he had with his wife, outdistancing the widows who'd try to keep up with him as they flirted relentlessly.

Dr. Jenny asked, "Are you married?"

"Widower."

"Children?"

"I have a son."

"He live nearby?"

"No, but we see a lot of each other."

"Anybody else in the area?" she asked.

"Not really, no."

The doctor regarded him carefully. "It's tough, hearing everything I've told you today. And it's going to get tougher. I'd like you to talk to somebody over at Westbrook Hospital. They have a social services department there just for heart patients. The Cardiac Support Center."

"Shrink?"

"Counselor/nurses, they're called."

"They wear short skirts?" Covey asked.

"The men don't," the doctor said, deadpan.

"Touché. Well, thanks, but I don't think that's for me."

"Take the number anyway. If nothing else, they're somebody to talk to."

She took out a card and set it on the desk. He noticed that she had perfect fingernails, opalescent pink, though they were very short—as befit someone who cracked open human chests on occasion.

Covey asked her a number of questions about the procedures and what he could expect, sizing up his odds. Initially she seemed reluctant to quantify his chances but she sensed finally that he could indeed handle the numbers and told him. "Sixty-forty against."

"Is that optimistic or pessimistic?"

"Neither. It's realistic."

He liked that.

There were more tests that needed to be done, the doctor explained, before any procedures could be scheduled. "You can make the appointment with Janice."

"Sooner rather than later?"

The doctor didn't smile when she said, "That would be the wise choice."

He rose. Then paused. "Does this mean I should stop having strenuous sex?"

Dr. Jenny blinked and a moment later they both laughed.

"Ain't it grand being old? All the crap you can get away with."

"Make that appointment, Mr. Covey."

He walked toward the door. She joined him. He thought she was seeing him out but she held out her hand; he'd neglected to take the card containing the name and number of the Cardiac Support Center at Westbrook Hospital.

"Can I blame my memory?"

"No way. You're sharper than me." The doctor winked and turned back to her desk.

He made the appointment with the receptionist and left the building. Outside, still clutching the Cardiac Support Center card, he noticed a trash container on the sidewalk. He veered toward it and lifted the card like a Frisbee, about to sail the tiny rectangle into the pile of soda empties and limp newspapers. But then he paused.

Up the street he found a pay phone. Worth more than fifty million dollars, Robert Covey believed that cell phones were unnecessary luxuries. He set the card on the ledge, donned his reading glasses and began fishing in his leather change pouch for some coins.

∞

Dr. Peter Dehoeven was a tall blond man who spoke with an accent that Tal couldn't quite place.

European—Scandinavian or German maybe. It was quite thick at times and that, coupled with his oddly barren office suggested that he'd come to the U.S. recently. Not only was it far sparser than the cardiologist Dr. Anthony Sheldon's but the walls featured not a single framed testament to his education and training.

It was early the next morning and Dehoeven was elaborating on the mission of his Cardiac Support Center. He told Tal that the CSC counselors helped seriously ill patients change their diets, create exercise regimens, understand the nature of heart disease, deal with depression and anxiety, find care-givers, and counsel family members. They also helped with death and dying issues—funeral plans, insurance, wills. "We live to be older nowadays, yes?" Dehoeven explained, drifting in and out of his accent. "So we are having longer to experience our bodies' failing than we used to. That means, yes, we must confront our mortality for a longer time too. That is a difficult thing to do. So we need to help our patients prepare for the end of life."

When the doctor was through explaining CSC's mission Tal told him that he'd come about the Whitleys. "Were you surprised when they killed themselves?" Tal found his hand at his collar, absently adjusting his tie knot; the doctor's hung down an irritating two inches from his buttoned collar.

"Surprised?" Dehoeven hesitated. Maybe the question confused him. "I didn't think about being surprised or not. I didn't know Sam personal, yes? So I can't say—"

"You never met him?" Tal was surprised.

"Oh, we're a very big organization. Our counselors work with the patients. Me?" He laughed sadly. "My life is budget and planning and building our new facility up the street. That is taking most of my time now. We're greatly expanding, yes? But I will find out who was assigned to Sam and his wife." He called his secretary for this information.

The counselor turned out to be Claire McCaffrey, who, Dehoeven explained, was both a registered nurse and a social worker/counselor. She'd been at the CSC for a little over a year. "She's good. One of the new generation of counselors, experts in aging, yes? She has her degree in that."

"I'd like to speak to her."

Another hesitation. "I suppose this is all right. Can I ask why?"

Tal pulled a questionnaire out of his briefcase and showed it to the doctor. "I'm the department statistician. I track all the deaths in the county and collect information about them. Just routine."

"Ah, routine, yes? And yet we get a personal visit." He lifted an eyebrow in curiosity.

"Details have to be attended to."

"Yes, of course." Though he didn't seem quite convinced that Tal's presence here was completely innocuous.

He called the nurse. It seemed that Claire McCaffrey was about to leave to meet a new patient but she could give him fifteen or twenty minutes.

Dehoeven explained where her office was. Tal asked, "Just a couple more questions."

"Yessir?"

"Do you prescribe Luminux here?"

"Yes, we do often."

"Did Sam have a prescription? We couldn't find a bottle at their house."

He typed on his computer. "Yes. Our doctors wrote several prescriptions for him. He started on it a month ago."

Tal then told Dehoeven how much drugs the Whitleys had in their blood. "What do you make of that?"

"Three times the usual dosage?" He shook his head. "I couldn't tell you."

"They'd also been drinking a little. But I'm told the drug didn't directly contribute to their death. Would you agree?"

"Yes, yes," he said quickly. "It's not dangerous. It makes you drowsy and giddy. That's all."

"Drowsy *and* giddy both?" Tal asked. "Is that unusual?" The only drugs he'd taken recently were aspirin and an antiseasickness medicine that didn't work for him, as a disastrous afternoon date on a tiny sailboat on Long Island Sound had proven.

"No, not unusual. Luminux is our anti-anxiety and mood-control drug of choice here at the Center. It was just approved by the FDA. We were very glad to learn that, yes? Cardiac patients can take it without fear of aggravating their heart problems."

"Who makes it?"

He pulled a thick book off his shelf and read through it. "Montrose Pharmaceuticals in Paramus, New Jersey."

Tal wrote this down. "Doctor," he asked, "did you have another patient here . . . Don Benson?"

"I'm not knowing the name but I know very little of the patients here, as I was saying to you, yes?" He nodded out the window through which they could hear the sound of construction—the new CSC facility that was taking all his time, Tal assumed. Dehoeven typed on the computer keyboard. "No, we are not having any patients named Benson."

"In the past?"

"This is for the year, going back." A nod at the screen. "Why is it you are asking?"

Tal tapped the questionnaire. "Statistics." He put the paper away, rose and shook the doctor's hand. He was directed to the nurse's office, four doors up the hall from Dehoeven's.

Claire McCaffrey was about his age, with wavy brunette hair pulled back in a ponytail. She had a freckled, pretty face—girl next door—but seemed haggard.

"You're the one Dr. Dehoeven called about? Officer—?"

"Simms. But call me Tal."

"I go by Mac," she said. She extended her hand and a charm bracelet jangled on her right wrist as he gripped her strong fingers. He noticed a small gold ring in the shape of an ancient coin on her right hand. There was no jewelry at all on her left, he observed. "Mac," he reflected. A Celtic theme today, recalling Margaret, Dr. Sheldon's somber step-dancer.

She motioned him to sit. Her office was spacious—a desk and a sitting area with a couch and two armchairs around a coffee table. It seemed more lived-in than her boss's, he noted, comfortable. The decor was soothing—crystals, glass globes, and reproductions of Native American artifacts, plants and fresh flowers, posters and paintings of seashores and deserts and forests.

"This is about Sam Whitley, right?" she asked in a troubled monotone.

"That's right. And his wife."

She nodded, distraught. "I was up all night about it. Oh, it's so sad. I couldn't believe it." Her voice faded.

"I just have a few questions. I hope you don't mind."

"No, go ahead."

"Did you see them the day they died?" Tal asked.

"Yes, I did. We had our regular appointment."

"What exactly did you do for them?"

"What we do with most patients. Making sure they're on a heart-friendly diet, helping with insurance forms, making sure their medication's working, arranging for help in doing heavy work around the house. . . . Is there some problem? I mean, official problem?"

Looking into her troubled eyes, he chose not to use the excuse of the questionnaire as a front. "It was unusual, their deaths. They didn't fit the standard profile of most suicides. Did they say anything that'd suggest they were thinking about killing themselves?"

"No, of course not," she said quickly. "I would've intervened. Naturally."

"But?" He sensed there was something more she wanted to say.

She looked down, organized some papers, closed a folder.

"It's just . . . See, there was one thing. I spent the last couple of days going over what they said to me, looking for clues. And I remember they said how much they'd enjoyed working with me."

"That was odd?"

"It was the way they put it. It was the past tense, you know. Not *enjoy* working with me. It was *enjoyed* working with me. It didn't strike me as odd or anything at the time. But now we know . . ." A sigh. "I should've listened to what they were saying."

Recrimination. Like the couples' lawyers, like the doctors, Nurse McCaffrey would probably live with these deaths for a long, long time.

Perhaps forever . . .

"Did you know," he asked, "they just bought a book about suicide? *Making the Final Journey*."

"No, I didn't know that," she said, frowning.

Behind her desk Nurse McCaffrey—Mac—had a picture of an older couple with their arms around each other, two snapshots of big, goofy black labs, and one picture of her with the dogs. No snaps of boyfriends or husbands—or girlfriends. In Westbrook County, married or cohabitating couples comprised 74 percent of the adult population, widows 7 percent, widowers 2 percent and unmarried/divorced/noncohabitating were 17 percent. Of that latter category only 4 percent were between the ages of twenty-eight and thirty-five.

He and Mac had at least one thing in common; they were both members of the Four Percent Club.

She glanced at her watch and he focused on her again. "They were taking Luminux, right?"

She nodded. "It's a good anti-anxiety drug. We make sure the patients have it available and take it if they have a panic attack or're depressed."

"Both Sam and his wife had an unusually large amount in their bloodstreams when they died."

"Really?"

"We're trying to find what happened to the prescription, the bottle. We couldn't find it at their house."

"They had it the other day, I know."

"Are you sure?"

"Pretty sure. I don't know how much they had left on the prescription. Maybe it was gone and they threw the bottle out."

Raw data, Tal thought. Wondering what to make of these facts. Was he asking the right questions? Greg LaTour would know.

But LaTour was not here. The mathematician was on his own. He asked, "Did the Whitleys ever mention Don and Sy Benson?"

"Benson?"

"In Greeley."

"Well, no. I've never heard of them."

Tal asked, "Had anybody else been to the house that day?"

"I don't know. We were alone when I was there."

"Did you happen to call them from a pay phone that afternoon?"

"No."

"Did they mention they were expecting anyone else?"

She shook her head.

"And you left when?"

"At four. A little before."

"You sure of the time?"

"Yep. I know because I was listening to my favorite radio program in the car on my way home. The Opera Hour on NPR." A sad laugh. "It was highlights from *Madame Butterfly*."

"Isn't that about the Japanese woman who . . ." His voice faded.

"Kills herself." Mac looked up at a poster of the Grand Tetons, then one of the surf in Hawaii. "My whole life's been devoted to prolonging people's lives. This just shattered me, hearing about Sam and Liz." She seemed close to tears then controlled herself. "I was talking to Dr. Dehoeven. He just came over here from Holland. They look at death differently over there. Euthanasia and suicide are a lot more acceptable. . . . He heard about their deaths and kind of shrugged. Like it wasn't any big deal. But I can't get them out of my mind."

Silence for a moment. Then she blinked and looked at her watch again. "I've got a new patient to meet. But if there's anything I can do to help, let me know." She rose, then paused. "Are you . . . what *are* you exactly? A homicide detective?"

He laughed. "Actually, I'm a mathematician."

"A—"

But before he could explain his curious pedigree his pager went off, a sound Tal was so unaccustomed to that he dropped his briefcase then knocked several files off the nurse's desk as he bent to retrieve it. Thinking: Good job, Simms, way to impress a fellow member of the Westbrook County Four Percent Club.

"He's in there and I couldn't get him out. I'm spitting nails, Boss."

In a flash of panic Tal thought that Shellee, fuming as she pointed at his office, was referring to the sheriff himself, who'd descended from the top floor of the county building to fire Tal personally for the 2124.

But, no, she was referring to someone else.

Tal stepped inside and lifted an eyebrow to Greg LaTour. "Thought we had an appointment yester—"

"So where you been?" LaTour grumbled. "Sleepin' in?" The huge man was finishing Tal's cheese sandwich from yesterday, sending a cascade of bread crumbs everywhere.

And resting his boots on Tal's desk.

It had been LaTour's page that caught him with Mac McCaffrey. The message: "Office twenty minutes. LaTour."

The slim cop looked unhappily at the scuff marks on the desktop.

LaTour noticed but ignored him. "Here's the thing. I got the information on the wills. And, yeah, they were both changed—"

"Okay, that's suspicious—"

"Lemme finish. No, it's *not* suspicious. The beneficiaries weren't any crazy housekeepers or Moonie guru assholes controlling their minds. The Bensons didn't have any kids so all they did was add a few charities and create a trust for some nieces and nephews—for college. A hundred thousand each. Small potatoes. The Whitley girl didn't get diddly-squat from them.

"Now, the Whitleys gave their daughter—bitch or not—a third of the estate in the first version of the will. She still gets the same for herself in the new version but she also gets a little more so she can set up a Whitley family library." LaTour looked up. "Now *there's* gonna be a fucking fun place to spend Sunday afternoons. . . . Then they added some new chartites too and got rid of some other ones. . . . Oh, and if you were going to ask, they were *different* charities from the ones in the Bensons' will."

"I wasn't."

"Well, you should have. Always look for connections, Tal. That's the key in homicide. Connections between facts."

"Just like—"

"—don't say fucking statistics."

"Mathematics. Common denominators."

"Whatever," LaTour muttered. "So, the wills're out as motives. Same with—"

"The insurance polices."

"I was going to say. Small policies and most of the Bensons' goes to paying off a few small debts and giving some bucks to retired employees of the husband's companies. It's like twenty, thirty grand. Nothing suspicious there . . . Now, what'd you find?"

Tal explained about Dr. Sheldon, the cardiologist, then about Dehoeven, Mac, and the Cardiac Support Center.

LaTour asked immediately, "Both Benson and Whitley, patients of Sheldon?"

"No, only Whitley. Same for the Cardiac Support Center."

"Fuck. We . . . what'sa matter?"

"You want to get your boots off my desk."

Irritated, LaTour swung his feet around to the floor. "We need a connection, I was saying. Something—"

"I might have one," Tal said quickly. "Drugs."

"What, the old folks were dealing?" The sarcasm had returned. He added, "You still harping on that Lumicrap?"

"Lumi*nux*." Makes you drowsy *and* happy. Could mess up your judgment. Make you susceptible to suggestions."

"That you blow your fucking brains out? One hell of a suggestion."

"Maybe not—if you were taking three times the normal dosage . . ."

"You think somebody slipped it to 'em?"

"Maybe." Tal nodded. "The counselor from the Cardiac Support unit left the Whitleys' at four. They died around eight. Plenty of time for somebody to stop by, put some stuff in their drinks. Whoever called them from that pay phone."

"Okay, the Whitleys were taking it. What about the Bensons?"

"They were cremated the day after they died, remember? We'll never know."

LaTour finished the sandwich. "You don't mind, do you? It was just sitting there."

He glanced at the desktop. "You got crumbs everywhere."

The cop leaned forward and blew them to the floor. He sipped coffee from a mug that'd left a sticky ring on an evidence report file. "Okay, your—what the fuck do you call it? Theory?"

"Theorem."

"Is that somebody slipped 'em that shit? But who? And why?"

"I don't know that part yet."

"Those *parts*," LaTour corrected. "Who and why. Parts plural."

Tal sighed.

"You think you could really give somebody a drug and tell 'em to kill themselves and they will?"

"Let's go find out," Tal said.

"Huh?"

The statistician flipped through his notes. "The company that makes the drug? It's over in Paramus. Off the Parkway. Let's go talk to 'em."

"Shit. All the way to Jersey."

"You have a better idea?"

"I don't need any fucking ideas. This's your case, remember?"

"Maybe *I* twenty-one-twenty-foured it. But it's *everybody's* case now. Let's go."

She would've looked pretty good in a short skirt, Robert Covey thought, but unfortunately she was wearing slacks.

"Mr. Covey, I'm from the Cardiac Support Center."

"Call me Bob. Or you'll make me feel as old as your older brother."

She was a little short for his taste but then he had to remind himself that she was here to help him get some pig parts stuck into his chest and rebuild a bunch of leaking veins and arteries—or else die with as little mess as he could. Besides, he claimed that he had a rule he'd never date a woman a third his age. (When the truth was that after Veronica maybe he joked and maybe he flirted but in his heart he was content never to date at all.)

He held the door for her and gestured her inside with a slight bow. He could see her defenses lower a bit. She was probably used to dealing with all sorts of pricks in this line of work and was wary during their initial meeting, but Covey limited his grousing to surly repairmen and clerks and waitresses who thought because he was old he was stupid.

There was, he felt, no need for impending death to skew his manners. He invited her in and directed her to the couch in his den.

"Welcome, Ms. McCaffrey—"

"How 'bout Mac? That's what my mother used to call me when I was good."

"What'd she call you when you were bad?"

"Mac then too. Though she managed to get two syllables out of it. So, go ahead."

He lifted an eyebrow. "With what?"

"With what you were going to tell me. That you don't need me here. That you don't need any help, that you're only seeing me to humor your cardiologist, that you don't want any hand-holding, that you don't want to be coddled, that you don't want to change your diet, you don't want to exercise, you don't want to give up smoking and you don't want to stop drinking your—" She glanced at the bar and eyed the bottles. "—your port. So here're the ground rules. Fair enough, no hand-holding, no coddling. That's my part of the deal. But, yes, you'll give up smoking—"

"Did before you were born, thank you very much."

"Good. And you will be exercising and eating a cardio-friendly diet. And about the port—"

"Hold on—"

"I think we'll limit you to three a night."

"Four," he said quickly.

"Three. And I suspect on most nights you only have two."

"I can live with three," he grumbled. She'd been right about the two (though, okay, sometimes a little bourbon joined the party).

Damn, he liked her. He always had liked strong women. Like Veronica.

Then she was on to other topics. Practical things about what the Cardiac Support Center did and what it didn't do, about care givers, about home care, about insurance.

"Now, I understand you're a widower. How long were you married?"

"Forty-nine years."

"Well, now, that's wonderful."

"Ver and I had a very nice life together. Pissed me off we missed the fiftieth. I had a party planned. Complete with a harpist and open bar." He raised an eyebrow. "Vintage port included."

"And you have a son?"

"That's right. Randall. He lives in California. Runs a computer company. But one that actually makes money. Imagine that! Wears his hair too long and lives with a woman—he oughta get married—but he's a good boy."

"You see him much?"

"All the time."

"When did you talk to him last?"

"The other day."

"And you've told him all about your condition?"

"You bet."

"Good. Is he going to get out here?"

"In a week or so. He's traveling. Got a big deal he's putting together."

She was taking something out of her purse. "Our doctor at the clinic prescribed this." She handed him a bottle. "Luminux. It's an anti-anxiety agent."

"I say no to drugs."

"This's a new generation. You're going through a lot of stuff right now. It'll make you feel better. Virtually no side effects—"

"You mean it won't take me back to my days as a beatnik in the Village?" She laughed and he added, "Actually, think I'll pass."

"It's good for you." She shook out two pills into a small cup and handed them to him. She walked to the bar and poured a glass of water.

Watching her, acting like she lived here, Covey scoffed, "You ever negotiate?"

"Not when I know I'm right."

"Tough lady." He glanced down at the pills in his hand. "I take these, that means I can't have my port, right?"

"Sure you can. You know, moderation's the key to everything."

"You don't seem like a moderate woman."

"Oh, hell no, I'm not. But I don't practice what I preach." And she passed him the glass of water.

Late afternoon, driving to Jersey.

Tal fiddled with the radio trying to find the Opera Hour program that Nurse Mac had mentioned.

LaTour looked at the dash as if he was surprised the car even had a radio.

Moving up and down the dial, through the several National Public Radio bands, he couldn't find the show. What time had she'd said it came on? He couldn't remember. He wondered why he cared what she listened to. He didn't even like opera that much. He gave up and settled on all news, all the time. LaTour stood that for five minutes then put the game on.

The homicide cop was either preoccupied or just a natural-born bad driver. Weaving, speeding well over the limit, then braking to a crawl. Occasionally he'd lift his middle finger to other drivers in a way that was almost endearing.

Probably happier on a motorcycle, Tal reflected.

LaTour tuned in the game on the radio. They listened for a while, neither speaking.

"So," Tal tried. "Where you live?"

"Near the station house."

Nothing more.

"Been on the force long?"

"A while."

New York seven, Boston three. . . .

"You married?" Tal had noticed that he wore no wedding band.

More silence.

Tal turned down the volume and repeated the question.

After a long moment LaTour grumbled, "That's something else."

"Oh." Having no idea what the cop meant.

He supposed there was a story here—a hard divorce, lost children.

And six point three percent kill themselves before retirement . . .

But whatever the sad story might be, it was only for Bear's friends in the Department, those on the Real Crimes side of the pen.

Not for Einstein, the calculator humper.

They fell silent and drove on amid the white noise of the sportscasters.

Ten minutes later LaTour skidded off the parkway and turned down a winding side road.

Montrose Pharmaceuticals was a small series of glass and chrome buildings in a landscaped industrial park. Far smaller than Pfizer and the other major drug companies in the Garden State, it nonetheless must've done pretty well in sales—to judge from the number of Mercedes, Jaguars, and Porsches in the employee parking lot.

Inside the elegant reception area, Westbrook County Sheriff's Department badges raised some eyebrows. But, Tal concluded, it was LaTour's bulk and hostile gaze that cut through whatever barriers existed here to gaining access to the inner sanctum of the company's president.

In five minutes they were sitting in the office of Daniel Montrose, an earnest, balding man in his late forties. His eyes were as quick as his appearance was rumpled and Tal concluded that he was a kindred soul; a scientist, rather than a salesperson. The man rocked back and forth in his chair, peering at them through stylish glasses with a certain distraction. Uneasiness too.

Nobody said anything for a moment and Tal felt the tension in the office rise appreciably. He glanced at LaTour, who simply sat in the leather-and-chrome chair, looking around the opulent space. Maybe stonewalling was a technique that real cops used to get people to start talking.

"We've been getting ready for our sales conference," Montrose suddenly volunteered. "It's going to be a good one."

"Is it?" Tal asked.

"That's right. Our biggest. Las Vegas this year." Then he clammed up again.

Tal wanted to echo, "Vegas?" for some reason. But he didn't.

Finally LaTour said, "Tell us about Luminux."

"Luminux. Right, Luminux . . . I'd really like to know, I mean, if it's not against any rules or anything, what you want to know for. I mean, and what are you doing here? You haven't really said."

"We're investigating some suicides."

"Suicides?" he asked, frowning. "And Luminux is involved?"

"Yes indeedy," LaTour said with all the cheer that the word required.

"But . . . it's based on a mild diazepam derivative. It'd be very difficult to fatally overdose on it."

"No, they died from other causes. But we found—"

The door swung open and a strikingly beautiful woman walked into the office. She blinked at the visitors and said a very unsorrowful, "Sorry. Thought you were alone." She set a stack of folders on Montrose's desk.

"These are some police officers from Westbrook County," the president told her.

She looked at them more carefully. "Police. Is something wrong?"

Tal put her at forty. Long, serpentine face with cool eyes, very beautiful in a European fashion-model way. Slim legs with runner's calves. Tal decided that she was like Sheldon's Gaelic assistant, an example of some predatory genus very different from Mac McCaffrey's.

Neither Tal nor LaTour answered her question. Montrose introduced her—Karen Billings. Her title was a mouthful but it had something to do with product support and patient relations.

"They were just asking about Luminux. There've been some problems, they're claiming."

"Problems?"

"They were just saying . . ." Montrose pushed his glasses higher on his nose. "Well, what *were* you saying?"

Tal continued, "A couple of people who killed themselves had three times the normal amount of Luminux in their systems."

"But that can't kill them. It couldn't have. I don't see why . . ." Her voice faded and she looked toward Montrose. They eyed each other, poker-faced. She then said coolly to LaTour, "What exactly would you like to know?"

"First of all, how could they get it into their bloodstream?" LaTour sat back, the chair creaking alarmingly. Tal wondered if he'd put his feet up on Montrose's desk.

"You mean how could it be administered?"

"Yeah."

"Orally's the only way. It's not available in an IV form yet."

"But could it be mixed in food or a drink?"

"You think somebody did that?" Montrose asked. Billings remained silent, looking from Tal to LaTour and back again with her cautious, swept-wing eyes.

"Could it be done?" Tal asked.

"Of course," the president said. "Sure. It's water soluble. The vehicle's bitter—"

"The—?"

"The inert base we mix it with. The drug itself is tasteless but we add a compound to make it bitter so kids'll spit it out if they eat it by mistake. But you can mask that with sugar or—"

"Alcohol?"

Billings snapped, "Drinking isn't recommended when taking—"

LaTour grumbled, "I'm not talking about the fucking fine print on the label. I'm talking about could you hide the flavor by mixing it in a drink?"

She hesitated. Then finally answered, "One could." She clicked her nails together in impatience or anger.

"So what's it do to you?"

Montrose said, "It's essentially an anti-anxiety and mood-elevating agent, not a sleeping pill. It makes you relaxed. You get happier."

"Does it mess with your thinking?"

"There's some cognitive dimunition."

"English?" LaTour grumbled.

"They'd feel slightly disoriented—but in a happy way."

Tal recalled the misspellings in the note. "Would it affect their handwriting and spelling?"

Dangrous . . .

"It could, yes."

Tal said. "Would their judgment be affected?"

"Judgment?" Billings asked harshly. "That's subjective."

"Whatta you mean?"

"There's no quantifiable measure for one's ability to judge something."

"No? How 'bout if *one* puts a gun to *one*'s head and pulls the trigger?" LaTour said. "I call that *bad* judgment. Any chance we agree on that?"

"What the fuck're you getting at?" Billings snapped.

"Karen," Montrose said, pulling off his designer glasses and rubbing his eyes.

She ignored her boss. "You think they took our drug and decided to kill themselves? You think we're to blame for that? This drug—"

"This drug that a couple of people popped—maybe *four* people—and then killed themselves. Whatta we say about that from a statistical point of view?" LaTour turned to Tal.

"Well within the percentile of probability for establishing a causal relationship between the two events."

"There you go. Science has spoken."

Tal wondered if they were playing the good-cop/bad-cop routine you see in movies. He tried again. "Could an overdose of Luminux have impaired their judgment?"

"Not enough so that they'd decide to kill themselves," she said firmly. Montrose said nothing.

"That your opinion too?" LaTour muttered to him.

The president said, "Yes, it is."

Tal persisted, "How about making them susceptible?"

Billings leapt in with, "I don't know what you mean. . . . This is all crazy."

Tal ignored her and said levelly to Montrose, "Could somebody persuade a person taking an overdose of Luminux to kill themselves?"

Silence filled the office.

Billings said, "I strongly doubt it."

"But you ain't saying no." LaTour grumbled.

A glance between Billings and Montrose. Finally he pulled his wire-rims back on, looked away and said, "We're not saying no."

∞

They next morning Tal and LaTour arrived at the station house at the same time, and the odd couple walked together through the Detective Division pen into Tal's office.

They looked over the case so far and found no firm leads.

"Still no who," LaTour grumbled. "Still no why."

"But we've got a how," Tal pointed out. Meaning the concession about Luminux making one suggestible.

"Fuck *how*. I want *who*."

At just that moment they received a possible answer.

Shellee stepped into Tal's office. Pointedly ignoring the homicide cop, she said, "You're back. Good. Got a call from the P-I-I team in Greeley. They said a neighbor saw a woman in a small, dark car arrive at the Bensons' house about an hour before they died. She was wearing sunglasses and a tan or beige baseball cap. The neighbor didn't recognize her."

"Car?" LaTour snapped.

It's hard to ignore an armed, 250-pound, goateed man named Bear but Shellee was just the woman for the job.

Continuing to speak to her boss, she said, "They weren't sure what time she got there but it was before lunch. She stayed maybe forty minutes then left. That'd be an hour or so before they killed themselves." A pause. "The car was a small sedan. The witness didn't remember the color."

"Did you ask about the—" LaTour began.

"They didn't see the tag number," she told Tal. "Now, that's not all. DMV finally calls back and tells me that Sandra Whitley drives a blue BMW 325."

"Small wheelbase," Tal said.

"And, getting better 'n' better, Boss. Guess who's leaving town before her parents' memorial service."

"Sandra?"

"How the hell d'you find that out?" LaTour asked.

She turned coldly to him. "Detective Simms asked to me organize all the evidence from the Whitley crime scene. Because, like he says, having facts and files out of order is as bad as not having them at all. I found a note in the Whitley evidence file with an airline locator number. It was for a flight from Newark today to San Francisco, continuing on to Hawaii. I called and they told me it was a confirmed ticket for Sandra Whitley. Return is open."

"Meaning the bitch might not be coming back at all," LaTour said. "Going on vacation without saying goodbye to the folks? That's fucking harsh."

"Good job," Tal told Shellee.

Eyes down, a faint smile of acknowledgment.

LaTour dropped into one of Tal's chairs, belched softly and said, "You're doing such a good job, Sherry, here, look up whatever you can about this shit." He offered her the notes on Luminux.

"It's Shellee," she snapped and glanced at Tal, who mouthed, "Please."

She snatched them from LaTour's hand and clattered down the hall on her dangerous heels.

LaTour looked over the handwritten notes she'd given them and growled, "So what about the why? A motive?"

Tal spread the files out of his desk—all the crime scene information, the photos, the notes he'd taken.

What were the common denominators? The deaths of two couples. Extremely wealthy. The husbands ill, yes, but not hopelessly so. Drugs that make you suggestible.

A giddy lunch then suicide, a drink beside a romantic fire then suicide . . .

Romantic . . .

"Hmm," Tal mused, thinking back to the Whitleys'.

"What hmm?"

"Let's think about the wills again."

"We tried that," LaTour said.

"But what if they were *about* to be changed?"

"Whatta you mean?"

"Try this for an assumption: Say the Whitleys and their daughter had some big fight in the past week. They were going to change their will again—this time to cut her out completely."

"Yeah, but their lawyer'd know that."

"Not if she killed them before they talked to him. I remember smelling smoke from the fire when I walked into the Whitley house. I thought they'd built this romantic fire just before they killed themselves. But maybe they hadn't. Maybe Sandra burned some evidence—something about changing the will, memos to the lawyer, estate planning stuff. Remember, she snatched the mail at the house. One was to the lawyer. Maybe that was why she came back—to make sure there was no evidence left. Hell, wished I'd searched her purse. I just didn't think about it."

"Yeah, but offing her own *parents*?" LaTour asked skeptically.

"Seventeen point two percent of murderers are related to their victims." Tal added pointedly, "I know that because of my questionnaires, by the way."

LaTour rolled his eyes. "What about the Bensons?"

"Maybe they met in some cardiac support group, maybe they were in the same country club. Whitley might've mentioned something about the will to them. Sandra found out and had to take them out too."

"Jesus, you say 'maybe' a lot."

"It's a theorem, I keep saying. Let's go prove it or disprove it. See if she's got an alibi. And we'll have forensics go through the fireplace."

"If the ash is intact," LaTour said, "they can image the printing on the sheet. Those techs're fucking geniuses."

Tal called Crime Scene again and arranged to have a team return to the Whitleys' house. Then he said, "Okay, let's go visit our suspect."

"Hold on there."

When Greg LaTour charged up to you, muttering the way he'd just done, you held on there.

Even tough Sandra Whitley.

She'd been about to climb into the BMW sitting outside her luxurious house. Suitcases sat next to her.

"Step away from the car," LaTour said, flashing his badge.

Tal said, "We'd like to ask you a few questions, ma'am."

"You again! What the hell're you talking about?" Her voice was angry but she did as she was told.

"You're on your way out of town?" LaTour took her purse off her shoulder. "Just keep your hands at your sides."

"I've got a meeting I can't miss."

"In Hawaii?"

Sandra was regaining the initiative. "I'm an attorney, like I told you. I *will* find out how you got that information and for your sake there better've been a warrant involved."

Did they *need* a warrant? Tal wondered.

"Meeting in Hawaii?" LaTour repeated. "With an open return?"

"What're you implying?"

"It's a little odd, don't you think. Flying off to the South Seas a few days after your parents die? Not going to the funeral?"

"Funerals're for the survivors. I've made peace with my parents and their deaths. They wouldn't've wanted me to blow off an important meeting. Dad was as much a businessman as a father. I'm as much a businesswoman as a daughter."

Her eyes slipped to Tal and she gave a sour laugh. "Okay, you got me, Simms." Emphasizing the name was presumably to remind him again that his name would be prominently included in the court documents she filed. She nodded to the purse. "It's all in there. The evidence about me escaping the country after—what?—stealing my parents' money? What *exactly* do you think I've done?"

"We're not accusing you of anything. We just want to—"

"—ask you a few questions."

"So ask, goddamn it."

LaTour was reading a lengthy document he'd found in her purse.

He frowned and handed it to Tal, then asked her, "Can you tell me where you were the night your parents died?"

"Why?"

"Look, lady, you can cooperate or you can clam up and we'll—"

"Go downtown. Yadda, yadda, yadda. I've heard this before."

LaTour frowned at Tal and mouthed, "What's downtown?" Tal shrugged and returned to the document. It was a business plan for a company that was setting up an energy joint venture in Hawaii. Her law firm was representing it. The preliminary meeting seemed to be scheduled for two days from now in Hawaii. There was a memo saying that the meetings could go on for weeks and recommended that the participants get open-return tickets.

Oh.

"Since I have to get to the airport now," she snapped, "and I don't have time for any bullshit, okay, I'll tell you where I was on the night of the quote crime. On an airplane. I flew back on United Airlines from San Francisco, the flight that got in about 11 P.M. My boarding pass is probably in there—" A contemptuous nod at the purse LaTour held. "And if it isn't, I'm sure there's a record of the flight at the airline. With security being what it is nowadays, picture IDs and everything, that's probably a pretty solid alibi, don't you think?"

Did seem to be, Tal agreed silently. And it got even more solid when LaTour found the boarding pass and ticket receipt in her purse.

Tal's phone began ringing and he was happy for the chance to escape from Sandra's searing fury. He heard Shellee speak from the receiver. "Hey, Boss, 's'me."

"What's up?"

"Crime Scene called. They went through all the ash in the Whitleys' fireplace, looking for a letter or something about changing the will. They didn't find anything about that at all. Something had been burned but it was all just a bunch of information on companies—computer and biotech companies. The Crime Scene guy was thinking Mr. Whitley might've just used some old junk mail or something to start the fire."

Once again: Oh.

Then: Damn.

"Thanks."

He nodded LaTour aside and told him what Crime Scene had reported.

"Shit on the street," he whispered. "Jumped a little fast here . . . Okay, let's go kiss some ass. Brother."

The groveling time was quite limited—Sandra was adamant about catching her plane. She sped out of the driveway, leaving behind a blue cloud of tire smoke.

"Aw, she'll forget about it," LaTour said.

"You think?" Tal asked.

A pause. "Nope. We're way fucked." He added, "We still gotta find the mysterious babe in the sunglasses and hat." They climbed into the car and LaTour pulled into traffic.

Tal wondered if Mac McCaffrey might've seen someone like that around the Whitleys' place. Besides, it'd be a good excuse to see her again. Tal said, "I'll look into that one."

"You?" LaTour laughed.

"Yeah. Me. What's so funny about that?"

"I don't know. Just you never investigated a case before."

"So? You think I can't interview witnesses on my own? You think I should just go back home and hump my calculator?"

Silence. Tal hadn't meant to say it.

"You heard that?" LaTour finally asked, no longer laughing.

"I heard."

"Hey, I didn't mean it, you know."

"Didn't mean it?" Tal asked, giving an exaggerated squint. "As in you didn't mean for me to hear you? Or as in you don't actually believe I have sex with adding machines?"

"I'm sorry, okay? . . . I bust people's chops sometimes. It's the way I am. I do it to everybody. Fuck, people do it to me. They call me Bear 'causa my gut. They call you Einstein 'cause you're smart."

"Not to my face."

LaTour hesitated. "You're right. Not to your face. . . . You know, you're too polite, Tal. You can give me a lot more shit. I wouldn't mind. You're too uptight. Loosen up."

"So it's *my* fault that I'm pissed 'cause you dump on me?"

"It was . . ." He began defensively but then he stopped. "Okay, I'm sorry. I am. . . . Hey, I don't apologize a lot, you know. I'm not very good at it."

"That's an apology?"

"I'm doing the best I can . . . Whatta you want?"

Silence.

"All right," Tal said finally.

LaTour sped the car around a corner and wove frighteningly through the heavy traffic. Finally he said, "It's okay, though, you know."

"What's okay?"

"If you want to."

"Want to what?" Tal asked.

"You know, you and your calculator. . . . Lot safer than some of the weird shit you see nowadays."

"LaTour," Tal said, "you can—"

"You just seemed defensive about it, you know. Figure I probably hit close to home, you know what I'm saying?"

"You can go fuck yourself."

The huge cop was laughing hard. "Shit, don'tcha feel like we're finally breaking the ice here? I think we are. Now, I'll drop you off back at your car, Einstein, and you can go on this secret mission all by your lonesome."

His stated purpose was to ask her if she'd ever seen the mysterious woman in the baseball cap and sunglasses, driving a small car, at the Whitleys' house.

Lame, Tal thought.

Lame *and* transparent—since he could've asked her that on the phone. He was sure the true mission here was so obvious that it was laughable: To get a feel for what would happen if he asked Mac McCaffrey out to dinner. Not to actually *invite* her out at this point, of course; she was, after all, a potential witness. No, he just wanted to test the waters.

Tal parked along Elm Street and climbed out of the car, enjoying the complicated smells of the April air, the skin-temperature breeze, the golden snowflakes of fallen forsythia petals covering the lawn.

Walking toward the park where he'd arranged to meet her, Tal reflected on his recent romantic life.

Fine, he concluded. It was fine.

He dated 2.66 women a month. The median age of his dates in

the past 12 months was approximately 31 (a number skewed somewhat by the embarrassing—but highly memorable—outlier of a Columbia University senior). And the mean IQ of the women was around 140 or up—and that latter statistic was a very sharp bell curve with a very narrow standard deviation; Talbot Simms went for intellect before anything else.

It was this latter criteria, though, he'd come to believe lately, that led to the tepid adjective "fine."

Yes, he'd had many interesting evenings with his 2⅔ dates every month. He'd discussed with them Cartesian hyperbolic doubt. He'd argue about the validity of analyzing objects in terms of their primary qualities ("No way! *I'm* suspicious of secondary qualities too. . . . I mean, how 'bout that? We have a lot in common!") They'd draft mathematical formulae in crayon on the paper table coverings at the Crab House. They'd discuss Fermat's Last Theorem until 2:00 or 3:00 A.M. (These were not wholly academic encounters, of course; Tal Simms happened to have a full-size chalkboard in his bedroom).

He was intellectually stimulated by most of these women. He even learned things from them.

But he didn't really have a lot of fun.

Mac McCaffrey, he believed, would be fun.

She'd sounded surprised when he'd called. Cautious too at first. But after a minute or two she'd relaxed and had seemed almost pleased at the idea that he wanted to meet with her.

He now spotted her in the park next to the Knickerbocker Home, which appeared to be a nursing facility, where she suggested they get together.

"Hey," he said.

"Hi there. Hope you don't mind meeting outside. I hate to be cooped up."

He recalled the Sierra Club posters in her office. "No, it's beautiful here."

Her sharp green eyes, set in her freckled face, looked away and took in the sights of the park. Tal sat down and they made small talk for five minutes or so. Finally she asked, "You started to tell me that you're, what, a mathematician?"

"That's right."

She smiled. There was crookedness to her mouth, an asymmetry, which he found charming. "That's pretty cool. You could be on a TV series. Like *CSI* or *Law and Order*, you know. Call it *Math Cop*."

They laughed. He glanced down at her shoes, old black Reeboks, and saw they were nearly worn out. He noticed too a bare spot on the knee of her jeans. It'd been rewoven. He thought of cardiologist Anthony Sheldon's designer wardrobe and huge office, and reflected that Mac worked in an entirely different part of the health care universe.

"So I was wondering," she asked. "Why this interest in the Whitleys' deaths?"

"Like I said. They were out of the ordinary."

"I guess I mean, why are *you* interested? Did you lose somebody? To suicide, I mean."

"Oh, no. My father's alive. My mother passed away a while ago. A stroke."

"I'm sorry. She must've been young."

"Was, yes."

She waved a bee away. "Is your dad in the area?"

"Nope. Professor in Chicago."

"Math?"

"Naturally. Runs in the family." He told her about Wall Street, the financial crimes, statistics.

"All that adding and subtracting. Doesn't it get, I don't know, boring?"

"Oh, no, just the opposite. Numbers go on forever. Infinite questions, challenges. And remember, math is a lot more than just calculations. What excites me is that numbers let us understand the world. And when you understand something you have control over it."

"Control?" she asked, serious suddenly. "Numbers won't keep you from getting hurt. From dying."

"Sure they can," he replied. "Numbers make car brakes work and keep airplanes in the air and let you call the fire department. Medicine, science."

"I guess so. Never thought about it." Another crooked smile. "You're pretty enthusiastic about the subject."

Tal asked, "Pascal?"

"Heard of him."

"A philosopher. He was a prodigy at math but he gave it up completely. He said math was so enjoyable it had to be related to sex. It was sinful."

"Hold on, mister," she said, laughing. "You got some math porn you want to show me?"

Tal decided that the preliminary groundwork for the date was going pretty well. But, apropos of which, enough about himself. He asked, "How'd you get into your field?"

"I always liked taking care of people . . . or animals," she explained. "Somebody's pet'd get hurt, I'd be the one to try to help it. I hate seeing anybody in pain. I was going to go to med school but my mom got sick and, without a father around, I had to put that on hold—where it's been for. . . . well, for a few years."

No explanation about the missing father. But he sensed that, like him, she didn't want to discuss dad. A common denominator among these particular members of the Four Percent Club.

She continued, looking at the nursing home door. "Why I'm doing *this* particularly? My mother, I guess. Her exit was pretty tough. Nobody really helped her. Except me, and I didn't know very much. The hospital she was in didn't give her any support. So after she passed I decided I'd go into the field myself. Make sure patients have a comfortable time at the end."

"It doesn't get you down?"

"Some times are tougher than others. But I'm lucky. I'm not all that religious but I do think there's something there after we die."

Tal nodded but he said nothing. He'd always wanted to believe in that *something* too but religion wasn't allowed in the Simms household—nothing, that is, except the cold deity of numbers his father worshiped—and it seemed to Tal that if you don't get hooked early by some kind of spiritualism, you'll rarely get the bug later. Still, people do change. He recalled that the Bensons had been atheists but apparently toward the end had come to believe differently.

Together forever . . .

Mac was continuing, speaking of her job at the Cardiac Support Center. "I like working with the patients. And I'm good, if I do say so myself. I stay away from the sentiment, the maudlin crap. I knock back some scotch or wine with them. Watch movies, pig out on low-fat chips and popcorn, tell some good death and dying jokes."

"No," Tal said, frowning. "Jokes?"

"You bet. Here's one: When I die, I want to go peacefully in my sleep, like my grandfather. . . . Not screaming like the passengers in the car with him."

Tal blinked then laughed hard. She was pleased he'd enjoyed it, he could tell. He said, "Hey, there's a statistician joke. Want to hear it?"

"Sure."

"Statistics show that a person gets robbed every four minutes. And, man, is he getting tired of it."

She smiled. "That really sucks."

"Best we can do," Tal said. Then after a moment he added, "But Dr. Dehoeven said that your support center isn't all death and dying. There's a lot of things you do to help before and after surgery."

"Oh, sure," she said. "Didn't mean to neglect that. Exercise, diet, care giving, getting the family involved, psychotherapy."

Silence for a moment, a silence that, he felt, was suddenly asking: what exactly was he doing here?

He said, "I have a question about the suicides. Some witnesses said they saw a woman in sunglasses and a beige baseball cap, driving a small car, at the Bensons' house just before they killed themselves. I was wondering if you ever saw anyone like that around their house."

A pause. "Me?" she asked, frowning. "I wasn't seeing the Bensons, remember?"

"No, I mean at the Whitleys."

"Oh." She thought for a moment. "Their daughter came by a couple of times."

"No, it wasn't her."

"They had a cleaning lady. But she drove a van. And I never saw her in a hat."

Her voice had grown weaker and Tal knew that her mood had changed quickly. Probably the subject of the Whitleys had done it—raised the issue of whether there was anything else she might've done to keep them from dying.

Silence surrounded them, as dense as the humid April air, redolent with the scent of lilac. He began to think that it was a bad idea to mix a personal matter with a professional one—especially when it involved patients who had just died. Conversation resumed but it was now different, superficial, and, as if by mutual decision, they both glanced at their watches, said goodbye, then rose and headed down the same sidewalk in different directions.

Shellee appeared in the doorway of Tal's office, where the statistician and LaTour were parked. "Found something," she said in her Beantown accent.

"Yeah, whatsat?" LaTour asked, looking over a pile of documents that she was handing her boss.

She leaned close to Tal and whispered, "He just gonna move in here?"

Tal smiled and said to her, "Thanks, Detective."

An eye-roll was her response.

"Where'd you get all that?" LaTour asked, pointing at the papers but glancing at her chest.

"The Internet," Shellee snapped as she left. "Where else?"

"She got all that information from there?" the big cop asked, taking the stack and flipping through it.

Tal saw a chance for a bit of cop-cop jibe, now that, yeah, the ice was broken, and he nearly said to LaTour, you'd be surprised, there's a lot more on line than wicked-sluts.com that you browse through in the wee hours. But then he recalled the silence when he asked about the cop's family life.

That's something else . . .

And he decided a reference to lonely nights at home was out of line. He kept the joke to himself.

LaTour handed the sheets to Tal. "I'm not gonna read all this crap. It's got fucking numbers in it. Gimme the bottom line."

Tal skimmed the information, much of which might have contained numbers but was still impossible for him to understand. It was mostly chemical jargon and medical formulae. But toward the end he found a summary. He frowned and read it again.

"Jesus."

"What?"

"We maybe have our perps."

"No shit."

The documents Shellee had found were from a consumer protection Web site devoted to medicine. They reported that the FDA was having doubts about Luminux because the drug trials showed that it had hallucinogenic properties. Several people in the trials had had psychotic episodes believed to have been caused by the drug. Others reported violent mood swings. Those with serious problems were a small minority of those in the trials, less than a tenth of one percent. But the reactions were so severe that the FDA was very doubtful about approving it.

But Shellee also found that the agency had approved Luminux a year ago, despite the dangers.

"Okay, got it," LaTour said. "How's this for a maybe, Einstein? Montrose slipped some money to somebody to get the drug approved and then kept an eye on the patients taking it, looking for anybody who had bad reactions."

The cops speculated that he'd have those patients killed—making it look like suicide—so that no problems with Luminux ever surfaced. LaTour wondered if this was a realistic motive—until Tal found a printout that revealed that Luminux was Montrose's only money-maker, to the tune of $78 million a year.

Their other postulate was that it had been Karen Billings—as patient relations director—who might have been the woman in the hat and sunglasses at the Bensons and who'd left the tire tracks and worn the gloves at the Whitleys. She'd spent time with them, given them overdoses, talked them into buying the suicide manual and helped them—what had Mac said? That was it: Helped them "exit."

"Some fucking patient relations," LaTour said. "That's harsh." Using his favorite adjective. "Let's go see 'em."

Ignoring—with difficulty—the clutter on his desk, Tal opened the top drawer of his desk and pulled out his pistol. He started to mount it to his belt but the holster clip slipped and the weapon dropped to the floor. He winced as it hit. Grimacing, Tal bent down and retrieved then hooked it on successfully.

As he glanced up he saw LaTour watching him with a faint smile on his face. "Do me a favor. It probably won't come to it but if it does, lemme do the shooting, okay?"

Nurse McCaffrey would be arriving soon.

No, "Mac" was her preferred name, Robert Covey reminded himself.

He stood in front of his liquor cabinet and finally selected a nice vintage port, a 1977. He thought it would go well with the Saga blue cheese and shrimp he'd had laid out for her, and the water crackers and nonfat dip for himself. He'd driven to the Stop 'N' Shop that morning to pick up the groceries.

Covey arranged the food, bottle and glasses on a silver tray. Oh, napkins. Forgot the napkins. He found some under the counter and set them out on the tray, which he carried into the living room. Next to it were some old scrapbooks he'd unearthed from the basement. He wanted to show her pictures—snapshots of his brother, now long gone, and his nieces, and his wife, of course. He also had many pictures of his son.

Oh, Randall . . .

Yep, he liked Mac a lot. It was scary how in minutes she saw right into him, perfectly.

It was irritating. It was good.

But one thing she couldn't see through was the lie he'd told her.

"You see him much?"

"All the time."

"When did you talk to him last?"

"The other day."

"And you've told him all about your condition?"

"You bet."

Covey called his son regularly, left messages on his phone at work and at home. But Randy never returned the calls. Occasionally he'd pick up, but it was always when Covey was calling from a different phone, so that the son didn't recognize the number (Covey even wondered in horror if the man bought a caller ID phone mostly to avoid his father).

In the past week he'd left two messages at his son's house. He'd never seen the place but pictured it being a beautiful high-rise somewhere in L.A., though Covey hadn't been to California in years and didn't even know if they had real high-rises there, the City of Angels being to earthquakes what trailer parks in the Midwest are to twisters.

In any case, whether his home was high-rise, low- or a hovel, his son had not returned a single call.

Why? he often wondered in despair. *Why?*

He looked back on his days as a young father. He'd spent much time at the office and traveling, yes, but he'd also devoted many, many hours to the boy, taking him to the Yankees games and movies, attending Randy's recitals and Little League.

Something had happened, though, and in his twenties he'd drifted away. Covey had thought maybe he'd gone gay, since he'd never married, but when Randy came home for Ver's funeral he brought a beautiful young woman with him. Randy had been polite but distant and a few days afterward he'd headed back to the coast. It had been some months before they'd spoken again.

Why? . . .

Covey now sat down on the couch, poured himself a glass of the port, slowly to avoid the sediment, and sipped it. He picked up another scrapbook and began flipping through it.

He felt sentimental. And then sad and anxious. He rose slowly from the couch, walked into the kitchen and took two of his Luminux pills.

In a short while the drugs kicked in and he felt better, giddy. Almost carefree.

The book sagged in his hands. He reflected on the big question: Should he tell Randy about his illness and the impending surgery? Nurse Mac would want him to, he knew. But Covey wouldn't do that. He wanted the young man to come back on his own or not at all. He wasn't going to use sympathy as a weapon to force a reconciliation.

A glance at the clock on the stove. Mac would be here in fifteen minutes.

He decided to use the time productively and return phone calls. He confirmed his next appointment with Dr. Jenny and left a message with Charley Hanlon, a widower up the road, about going to the movies next weekend. He also made an appointment for tomorrow about some alternative treatments the hospital had suggested he look into. "Long as it doesn't involve colonics, I'll think about it," Covey grumbled to the soft-spoken director of the program, who'd laughed and assured him that it did not.

He hung up. Despite the silky calm from the drug Covey had a moment's panic. Nothing to do with his heart, his surgery, his mortality, his estranged son, tomorrow's non-colonic treatment.

No, what troubled him: What if Mac didn't like blue cheese?

Covey rose and headed into the kitchen, opened the refrigerator and began to forage for some other snacks.

"You can't go in there."

But in there they went.

LaTour and Tal pushed past the receptionist into the office of Daniel Montrose.

At the circular glass table sat the president of the company and the other suspect, Karen Billings.

Montrose leaned forward, eyes wide in shock. He stood up slowly. The woman too pushed back from the table. The head of the company was as rumpled as before; Billings was in a fierce crimson dress.

"You, don't move!" LaTour snapped.

The red-dress woman blinked, unable to keep the anger out of her face. Tal could hear the tacit rejoinder: Nobody talks to me that way.

"Why didn't you tell us about the problems with Luminux?"

The president exchanged a look with Billings.

He cleared his throat. "Problems?"

Tal dropped the downloaded material about the FDA issues with Luminux on Montrose's desk. The president scooped it up and read.

LaTour had told Tal to watch the man's eyes. The eyes tell if someone's lying, the homicide cop had lectured. Tal squinted and studied them. He didn't have a clue what was going on behind his expensive glasses.

LaTour said to Billings, "Can you tell me where you were on April seventh and the ninth?"

"What the fuck are you talking about?"

"Simple question, lady. Where were you?"

"I'm not answering any goddamn questions without our lawyer." She crossed her arms, sat back and contentedly began a staring contest with LaTour.

"Why didn't you tell us about this?" Tal nodded at the documents.

Montrose said to Billings, "The dimethylamino."

"They found out about that?" she asked.

"Yeah, we found out about it," LaTour snapped. "Surprise."

Montrose turned to Tal. "What exactly did you find in the victims' blood?"

Unprepared for the question, he frowned. "Well, Luminux."

"You have the coroner's report?"

Tal pulled it out of his briefcase and put it on the table. "There."

Montrose frowned in an exaggerated way. "Actually, it doesn't say 'Luminux.'"

"The fuck you talking about? It's—"

Montrose said, "I quote: '9-fluoro, 7-chloro-1,3-dihydro-1-methyl-5-phenyl-2H-1, 4-benzodiazepin, 5-hydroxytryptamine and N-(1-phenethyl-4-piperidyl) propionanilide citrate.'"

"Whatever," LaTour snapped, rolling his eyes. "That *is* Luminux. The medical examiner said so."

"That's right," Karen snapped right back. "That's the approved version of the drug."

LaTour started to say something but fell silent.

"Approved?" Tal asked uncertainly.

Montrose said, "Look at the formula for the early version."

"Early?"

"The one the FDA rejected. It's in that printout of yours."

Tal was beginning to see where this was headed and he didn't like the destination. He found the sheet in the printout and compared it to the formula in the medical examiner's report. They were the same except that the earlier version of the Luminux contained another substance, dimethylamino ethyl phosphate ester.

"What's—"

"A mild antipsychotic agent known as DEP. That's what caused the problems in the first version. In combination it had a slight psychedelic effect. As soon as we took it out the FDA approved the drug. That was a year ago. You didn't find any DEP in the bodies. The victims were taking the approved version of the drug. No DEP-enhanced Luminux was every released to the public."

Billings muttered, "And we've never had a single incidence of suicide among the six million people worldwide on the drug—a lot of whom are probably alive today because they were taking Luminux and *didn't* kill themselves."

Montrose pulled a large binder off his desk and dropped it on his desk. "The complete study and FDA approval. No detrimental side effects. It's even safe with alcohol in moderation."

"Though we don't recommend it," Billings snapped, just as icily as she had at their first meeting.

"Why didn't you tell us before?" LaTour grumbled.

"You didn't ask. All drugs go through a trial period while we make them safe." Montrose wrote a number on a memo pad. "If you still don't believe us—this's the FDA's number. Call them."

Billings's farewell was "You found your way in here. You can find your way out."

Tal slouched in his office chair. LaTour was across from him with his feet up on Tal's desk again.

"Got a question," Tal asked. "You ever wear spurs?"

"Spurs? Oh, you mean like for horses? Why would I wear spurs? Or is that some kind of math nerd joke about putting my feet on your fucking desk?"

"You figure it out," Tal muttered as the cop swung his feet to the floor. "So where do we go from here? No greedy daughters, no evil drug maker. And we've pretty much humiliated ourselves in front of two *harsh* women. We're batting oh for two." The statistician sighed. Maybe they *did* kill themselves. Hell, sometimes life is just too much for some people."

"You don't think that, though."

"I don't *feel* it but I do *think* it and I do better thinking. When I start feeling I get into trouble."

"And the world goes round and round," LaTour said. "Shit. It time for a beer yet?"

But a beer was the last thing on Tal's mind. He stared at the glacier of paper on his desk, the printouts, the charts, the lists, the photographs, hoping that he'd spot one fact, one *datum*, that might help them.

Tal's phone rang. He grabbed it. " 'Lo?"

"Is this Detective Simms?" a meek voice asked.

"That's right."

"I'm Bill Fendler, with Oak Creek Books in Barlow Heights. Somebody from your office called and asked to let you know if we sold any copies of *Making the Final Journey: The Complete Guide to Suicide and Euthanasia.*"

Tal sat up. "That's right. Have you?"

"I just noticed the inventory showed one book sold in the last couple of days."

LaTour frowned. Tal held up a wait-a-minute finger.

"Can you tell me who bought it"

"That's what I've been debating. . . . I'm not sure it's ethical. I was thinking if you had a court order it might be better."

"We have reason to believe that somebody might be using that book to cover up a series of murders. That's why we're asking about it. Maybe it's not ethical. But I'm asking you, please, give me the name of the person who bought it."

A pause. The man said, "Okay. Got a pencil."

Tal found one. "Go ahead."

The mathematician started to write the name. Stunned, he paused. "Are you sure?" he asked.

"Positive, Detective. The receipt's right here in front of me."

The phone sagged in Tal's hand. He finished jotting the name, showed it to LaTour. "What do we do now?" he asked.

LaTour lifted a surprised eyebrow. "Search warrant," he said. "That's what we do."

The warrant was pretty easy, especially since LaTour was on good terms with nearly every judge and magistrate in Westbrook County personally, and a short time later they were halfway through their search of the modest bungalow located in even more modest Harrison Village. Tal and LaTour were in the bedroom, three uniformed county troopers were downstairs.

Drawers, closets, beneath the bed . . .

Tal wasn't exactly sure what they were looking for. He followed LaTour's lead. The big cop had considerable experience sniffing out hiding places, it seemed, but it was Tal who found the jacket, which was shedding off-white fibers that appeared to match the one they'd found at the Whitleys' death scene.

This was *some* connection, though a tenuous one.

"Sir, I found something outside!" a cop called up the stairs.

They went out to the garage, where the officer was standing over a suitcase, hidden under stacks of boxes. Inside were two large bottles of Luminux, with only a few pills remaining in each. There were no personal prescription labels attached but they seemed to be the containers that were sold directly to hospitals. This one had been sold to the Cardiac Support Center. Also in the suitcase were articles cut from magazines and newspapers—one was from several years ago. It was about a nurse who'd killed elderly patients in a nursing home in Ohio with lethal drugs. The woman was quoted as saying, "I did a good thing, helping those people die with dignity. I never got a penny from their deaths. I only wanted them to be at peace. My worst crime is I'm an Angel of Mercy." There were a half-dozen others, too, the theme being the kindness of euthanasia. Some actually gave practical advice on "transitioning" people from life.

Tal stepped back, arms crossed, staring numbly at the find.

Another officer walked outside. "Found these hidden behind the desk downstairs."

In his latex-gloved hands Tal took the documents. They were the Bensons' files from the Cardiac Support Center. He opened and read through the first pages.

LaTour said something but the statistician didn't hear. He'd hoped up until now that the facts were wrong, that this was all a huge misunderstanding. But true mathematicians will always accept where the truth leads, even if it shatters their most heart-felt theorem.

There was no doubt that Mac McCaffrey was the killer.

She'd been the person who'd just bought the suicide book. And it was here, in her house, that they'd found the jacket, the Luminux bottles and the euthanasia articles. As for the Bensons' files, her name was prominently given as the couple's nurse/counselor. She'd lied about working with them.

The homicide cop spoke again.

"What'd you say?" Tal muttered.

"Where is she, you think?"

"At the hospital, I'd guess. The Cardiac Support Center."

"So you ready?" LaTour asked.

"For what?"

"To make your first collar."

The blue cheese, in fact, turned out to be a bust.

But Nurse Mac—the only way Robert Covey could think of her now—seemed to enjoy the other food he'd laid out.

"Nobody's ever made appetizers for me," she said, touched.

"They don't make gentlemen like me anymore."

And bless her, here was a woman who didn't whine about her weight. She smeared a big slab of paté on a cracker and ate it right down, then went for the shrimp.

Covey sat back on the couch in the den, a bit perplexed. He recalled her feistiness from their first meeting and was anticipating—and looking forward to—a fight about diet and exercise. But she made only one exercise comment—after she'd opened the back door.

"Beautiful yard."

"Thanks. Ver was the landscaper."

"That's a nice pool. You like to swim?"

He told her he loved to, though since he'd been diagnosed with the heart problem he didn't swim alone, worried he'd faint or have a heart attack and drown.

Nurse Mac had nodded. But there was something else on her mind. She finally turned away from the pool. "You're probably wondering what's on the agenda for this session?"

"Yes'm, I am."

"Well, I'll be right up front. I'm here to talk you into doing something you might not want to do."

"Ah, negotiating, are we? This involve the fourth glass of port?"

She smiled. "It's a little more important than that. But now that you've brought it up . . ." She rose and walked to the bar. "You don't mind, do you?" She picked up a bottle of old Taylor-Fladgate, lifted an eyebrow.

"I'll mind if you pour it down the drain. I don't mind if we drink some."

"Why don't you refill the food," she said. "I'll play bartender."

When Covey returned from the kitchen Nurse Mac had poured him a large glass of port. She handed it to him then poured one for herself. She lifted hers. He did too and the crystal rang.

They both sipped.

"So what's this all about, you acting so mysterious?"

"What's it about?" she mused. "It's about eliminating pain, finding peace. And sometimes you just can't do that alone. Sometimes you need somebody to help you."

"Can't argue with the sentiment. What've you got in mind? Specific, I mean."

Mac leaned forward, tapped her glass to his. "Drink up." They downed the ruby-colored liquor.

"Go, go, go!"

"You wanna drive?" LaTour shouted over the roar of the engine. They skidded sharply around the parkway, over the curb and onto the grass, nearly scraping the side of the unmarked car against a jutting rock.

"At least I know *how* to drive," Tal called. Then: "Step on it!"

"Shut the fuck up. Let me concentrate."

As the wheel grated against another curb Tal decided that shutting up was a wise idea and fell silent.

Another squad car was behind them.

"There, that's the turn-off." Tal pointed.

LaTour controlled the skid and somehow managed to keep them out of the oncoming traffic lane.

Another three hundred yards. Tal directed the homicide cop down the winding road then up a long driveway, at the end of which was a small, dark-blue sedan. The same car the witnesses had seen outside the Bensons' house, the same car that had left the tread marks at the Whitley's the day they died.

Killing the siren, LaTour skidded to a stop in front of the car. The squad car parked close behind, blocking the sedan in.

All four officers leapt out. As they ran past the vehicle Tal glanced in the backseat and saw the tan baseball cap that the driver of the car, Mac McCaffrey, had worn outside the Bensons' house, the day she'd engineered their deaths.

In a movement quite smooth for such a big man LaTour unlatched the door and shoved inside, not even breaking stride. He pulled his gun from his holster.

They and the uniformed officers charged into the living room and then the den.

They stopped, looking at the two astonished people on the couch.

One was Robert Covey, who was unharmed.

The other, the woman who'd been about to kill him, was standing over him, eyes wide. Mac was just offering the old man one of the tools of her murderous trade: a glass undoubtedly laced with enough Luminux to render him half conscious and suggestible to suicide. Tal noticed that the back door was open, revealing a large swimming pool. So, not a gun or carbon monoxide. Death by drowning this time.

"Tal!" she gasped.

But he said nothing. He let LaTour step forward to cuff her and arrest her. The homicide cop was, of course, much better versed in such matters of protocol.

The homicide detective looked through her purse and found the suicide book inside.

Robert Covey was in the ambulance outside, being checked out by the medics. He'd seemed okay but they were taking their time, just to make sure.

After they found the evidence at Mac's house, Tal and LaTour had sped to the hospital. She was out but Dr. Dehoeven at the CRC had pulled her client list and they'd gone through her calendar, learning that she was meeting with Covey at that moment. He hadn't answered the phone, and they'd raced to the elderly man's house.

LaTour would've been content to ship Mac off to Central Booking but Tal was a bit out of control; he couldn't help confronting her. "You *did* know Don and Sy Benson. Don was your client. You lied to me."

Mac started to speak then looked down, her tearful eyes on the floor.

"We found Benson's files in your house. And the computer logs at CSC showed you erased his records. You *were* at their house the day they died. It was you the witness saw in the hat and sunglasses. And the Whitleys? You killed them too."

"I didn't kill anybody!"

"Okay, fine—you *helped* them kill themselves. You drugged them and talked them into it. And then cleaned up after." He turned to the uniformed deputy. "Take her to Booking."

And she was led away, calling, "I didn't do anything wrong!"

"Bullshit," LaTour muttered.

Though, staring after her as the car eased down the long drive, Tal reflected that in a way—some abstract, moral sense—she truly *did* believe she hadn't done anything wrong.

But to the people of the state of New York, the evidence was irrefutable. Nurse Claire "Mac" McCaffrey had murdered four people and undoubtedly intended to murder scores of others. She'd gotten the Bensons doped up on Friday and helped them kill themselves. Then on

Sunday she'd called the Whitleys from a pay phone, made sure they were home then went over there and arranged for their suicides too. She'd cleaned up the place, taken the Luminux and hadn't left until *after* they died: (Tal had learned that the opera show she listened to wasn't on until 7:00 P.M. Not 4:00, as she'd told him. That's why he hadn't been able to find it when he'd surfed the frequencies in LaTour's car.)

She'd gone into this business to ease the suffering of patients—because her own mother had had such a difficult time dying. But what she'd meant by "easing suffering" was putting them down like dogs.

Robert Covey returned to his den. He was badly shaken but physically fine. He had some Luminux in his system but not a dangerously high dosage. "She seemed so nice, so normal," he whispered.

Oh, you bet, Tal thought bitterly. A goddamn perfect member of the Four Percent Club.

He and LaTour did some paperwork—Tal so upset that he didn't even think about his own questionnaire—and they walked back to LaTour's car. Tal sat heavily in the front seat, staring straight ahead. The homicide cop didn't start the engine. He said, "Sometimes closing a case is harder than not closing it. That's something they don't teach you at the academy. But you did what you had to. People'll be alive now because of what you did."

"I guess," he said sullenly. He was picturing Mac's office. Her crooked smile when she'd look over the park. Her laugh.

"Let's file the papers. Then we'll go get a beer. Hey, you do drink beer, don'tcha?"

"Yeah, I drink beer," Tal said.

"We'll make a cop outta you yet, Einstein."

Tal clipped his seatbelt on, deciding that being a real cop was the last thing in the world he wanted.

∞

A beep on the intercom. "Mr. Covey's here, sir."

"I'll be right there." Dr. William Farley rose from his desk, a glass-sheet-covered Victorian piece his business partner had bought for him in New England on one of the man's buying sprees. Farley would have been content to have a metal desk or even a card table.

But in the *business* of medicine, not the *practice*, appearances count. The offices of the Lotus Research Foundation, near the mall containing Neiman Marcus and Saks Fifth Avenue, were filled with many antiques. Farley had been amused when they'd moved here three years ago to see the fancy furniture, paintings, objets d'art. Now, they were virtually invisible to him. What he greatly preferred was the huge medical facility itself behind the offices. As a doctor and researcher, that was the only place he felt truly at home.

Forty-eight, slim to the point of being scrawny, hair with a mind of its own, Farley had nonetheless worked hard to rid himself of his backroom medical researcher's image. He now pulled on his thousand-dollar suit jacket and applied a comb. He paused at the door, took a deep breath, exhaled and stepped into a lengthy corridor to the foundation's main lobby. It was deserted except for the receptionist and one elderly man, sitting in a deep plush couch.

"Mr. Covey?" the doctor asked, extending his hand.

The man set down the coffee cup he'd been given by the receptionist and they shook hands.

"Dr. Farley?"

A nod.

"Come on into my office."

They chatted about the weather as Farley led him down the narrow corridor to his office. Sometimes the patients here talked about sports, about their families, about the paintings on the walls.

Sometimes they were so nervous they said nothing at all.

Entering the office, Farley gestured toward a chair and then sat behind the massive desk. Covey glanced at it, unimpressed. Farley looked him over. He didn't appear particularly wealthy—an off-the-rack suit, a tie with stripes that went one way while those on his shirt went another. Still, the director of the Lotus Foundation had learned enough about rich people to know that the wealthiest were those who drove hybrid Toyota gas-savers and wore raincoats until they were threadbare.

Farley poured more coffee and offered Covey a cup.

"Like I said on the phone yesterday, I know a little about your condition. Your cardiologist is Jennifer Lansdowne, right?"

"That's right."

"And you're seeing someone from the Cardiac Support Center at the hospital."

Covey frowned. "I *was*."

"You're not any longer?"

"A problem with the nurse they sent me. I haven't decided if I'm going back. But that's a whole 'nother story."

"Well, we think you might be a good candidate for our services here, Mr. Covey. We offer a special program to patients in certain cases."

"What kind of cases?"

"Serious cases."

"The Lotus Research Foundation for *Alternative* Treatment," Covey recited. "Correct me if I'm wrong but I don't think ginseng and acupuncture work for serious cases."

"That's not what we're about." Farley looked him over carefully. "You a businessman, sir?"

"Was. For half a century."

"What line?"

"Manufacturing. Then venture capital."

"Then I imagine you generally like to get straight to the point."

"You got that right."

"Well, then let me ask you this, Mr. Covey. How would you like to live forever?"

"How's that?"

In the same way that he'd learned to polish his shoes and speak in words of fewer than four syllables, Farley had learned how to play potential patients like trout. He knew how to pace the pitch. "I'd like to tell you about the foundation. But first would you mind signing this?" He opened the drawer of his desk and passed a document to Covey.

He read it. "A nondisclosure agreement."

"It's pretty standard."

"I know it is," the old man said. "I've written 'em. Why do you want me to sign it?"

"Because what I'm going to tell you can't be made public."

He was intrigued now, the doctor could tell, though trying not to show it.

"If you don't want to, I understand. But then I'm afraid we won't be able to pursue our conversation further."

Covey read the sheet again. "Got a pen?"

Farley handed him a Mont Blanc; Covey took the heavy barrel with a laugh suggesting he didn't like ostentation very much. He signed and pushed the document back.

Farley put it into his desk. "Now, Dr. Lansdowne's a good woman. And she'll do whatever's humanly possible to fix your heart and give you a few more years. But there're limits to what medical science can do. After all, Mr. Covey, we all die. You, me, the children being born at this minute. Saints and sinners . . . we're all going to die."

"You got an interesting approach to medical services, Doctor. You cheer up all your patients this way?"

Dr. Farley smiled. "We hear a lot about aging nowadays."

"Can't turn on the TV without it."

"And about people trying to stay young forever."

"Second time you used that word. Keep going."

"Mr. Covey, you ever hear about the Hayflick rule?"

"Nope. Never have."

"Named after the man who discovered that human cells can reproduce themselves a limited number of times. At first, they make perfect reproductions of themselves. But after a while they can't keep up that level of quality control, you could say; they become more and more inefficient."

"Why?"

Covey, he reflected, was a sharp one. Most people sat there and nodded with stupid smiles on their faces. He continued. "There's an important strand of DNA that gets shorter and shorter each time the cells reproduce. When it gets too short, the cells go haywire and they don't duplicate properly. Sometimes they stop altogether."

"I'm following you in general. But go light on the biology bullshit. Wasn't my strong suit."

"Fair enough, Mr. Covey. Now, there're some ways to cheat the Hayflick limit. In the future it may be possible to extend life span significantly, dozens, maybe hundreds of years."

"That ain't forever."

"No, it's not."

"So cut to the chase."

"We'll never be able to construct a human body that will last more than a few hundred years at the outside. The laws of physics and nature just don't allow it. And even if we could we'd still have disease and illness and accidents that shorten life spans."

"This's getting cheerier and cheerier."

"Now, Dr. Lansdowne'll do what she can medically and the Cardiac Support Center will give you plenty of help."

"Depending on the nurse," Covey muttered. "Go on."

"And you might have another five, ten, fifteen years. . . . Or you can consider our program." Farley handed Covey a business card and tapped the logo of the Lotus Foundation, a golden flower. "You know what the lotus signifies in mythology?"

"Not a clue."

"Immortality."

"Does it now?"

"Primitive people'd see lotuses grow up out of the water in riverbeds that'd been dry for years. They assumed the plants were immortal."

"You said you can't keep people from dying."

"We can't. You will die. What we offer is what you might call a type of reincarnation."

Covey sneered. "I stopped going to church thirty years ago."

"Well, Mr. Covey. I've never gone to church. I'm not talking about spiritual reincarnation. No, I mean scientific, provable reincarnation."

The old man grunted. "This's about the time you start losing people, right?"

Farley laughed hard. "That's right. Pretty much at that sentence."

"Well, you ain't lost me yet. Keep going."

"It's very complex but I'll give it to you in a nutshell—just a little biology."

The old man sipped more coffee and waved his hand for the doctor to continue.

"The foundation holds the patent on a process that's known as neuro stem cell regenerative replication. . . . I know, it's a mouthful. Around here we just call it consciousness cloning."

"Explain that."

"What is consciousness?" Farley asked. "You look around the room, you see things, smell them, have reactions. Have thoughts. I sit in the same room, focus on different things, or focus on the same things, and have different reactions. Why? Because our brains are unique."

A slow nod. This fish was getting close to the fly.

"The foundation's developed a way to genetically map your brain and then program embryonic cells to grow in a way that duplicates it perfectly. After you die your identical consciousness is recreated in a fetus. You're—" A slight smile. "—born again. In a secular, biological sense, of course. The sensation you have is as if your brain were transplanted into another body."

Farley poured more coffee, handed it to Covey, who was shaking his head.

"How the hell do you do this?" Covey whispered.

"It's a three-step process." The doctor was always delighted to talk about his work. "First, we plot the exact structure of your brain as it exists now—the parts where the consciousness resides. We use supercomputers and micro-MRI machines."

"MRI. . . . that's like a fancy X-ray, right?"

"Magnetic resonance. We do a perfect schematic of your consciousness. Then step two: you know about genes, right? They're the blueprints for our bodies, every cell in your body contains them. Well, genes decide not only what your hair color is and your height and susceptibility to certain diseases but also how your brain develops. After a certain age the brain development gene shuts off; your brain's structure is determined and doesn't change—that's why brain tissue doesn't regenerate if it's destroyed. The second step is to extract and reactivate the development gene. Then we implant it into a fetus."

"You clone me?"

"No, not your body. We use donor sperm and egg and a surrogate mother. There's an in vitro clinic attached to the foundation. You're 'placed,' we call it, with a good family from the same social-economic class as you live in now."

Covey wanted to be skeptical, it seemed, but he was still receptive.

"The final part is to use chemical and electromagnetic intervention to make sure the brain develops identically to the map we made of your present one. Stimulate some cells' growth, inhibit others'. When you're born again, your perceptions will be exactly what they are from your point of view now. Your sensibilities, interests, desires."

Covey blinked.

"You won't look like you. Your body type will be different.

Though you will be male. We insist on that. It's not our job to work out gender-identity issues."

"Not a problem," he said shortly, frowning at the absurdity of the idea. Then: "Can you eliminate health problems? I had skin cancer. And the heart thing, of course."

"We don't do that. We don't make supermen or superwomen. We simply boost your consciousness into another generation, exactly as you are now."

Covey considered this for a moment. "Will I remember meeting you, will I have images of this life?"

"Ah, memories . . . We didn't quite know about those at first. But it seems that, yes, you will remember, to some extent—because memories are hard-wired into some portions of the brain. We aren't sure how many yet, since our first clients are only three or four years old now—in their second lives, of course—and we haven't had a chance to fully interview them yet."

"You've actually *done* this?" he whispered.

Farley nodded. "Oh, yes, Mr. Covey. We're up and running."

"What about will I go wacko or anything? That sheep they cloned died? She was a mess, I heard."

"No, that can't happen because we control development, like I was explaining. Every step of the way."

"Jesus," he whispered. "This isn't a joke?"

"Oh, no, not at all."

"You said, 'Forever.' So, how does it work—we do the same thing in seventy years or whatever?"

"It's literally a lifetime guarantee, even if that lifetime lasts ten thousand years. The Lotus Foundation will stay in touch with all our clients over the years. You can keep going for as many generations as you want."

"How do I know you'll still be in business?"

A slight chuckle. "Because we sell a product there's an infinite demand for. Companies that provide that don't ever go out of business."

Covey eyed Farley and the old man said coyly, "Which brings up your fee."

"As you can imagine . . ."

"Forever don't come cheap. Gimme a number."

"One half of your estate with a minimum of ten million dollars."

"One half? That's about twenty-eight million. But it's not liquid. Real estate, stocks, bonds. I can't just write you a check for it."

"We don't want you to. We're keeping this procedure very low-key. In the future we hope to offer our services to more people but now our costs are so high we can work only with the ones who can cover the expenses. . . . And, let's be realistic, we prefer people like you in the program."

"Like me?"

"Let's say higher in the gene pool than others."

Covey grunted. "Well, how *do* you get paid?"

"You leave the money to one of our charities in your will."

"Charities?"

"The foundation owns dozens of them. The money gets to us eventually."

"So you don't get paid until I die."

"That's right. Some clients wait until they actually die of their disease. Most, though, do the paperwork and then transition themselves."

"Transition?"

"They end their own life. That way they avoid a painful end. And, of course, the sooner they leave, the sooner they come back."

"How many people've done this?"

"Eight."

Covey looked out the window for a moment, at the trees in Central Park, waving slowly in a sharp breeze. "This's crazy. The whole thing's nuts."

Farley laughed. "*You'd* be nuts if you didn't think that at first. . . . Come on, I'll give you a tour of the facility."

Setting down his coffee, Covey followed the doctor out of the office. They walked down the hallway through an impressive-looking security door into the laboratory portion of the foundation. Farley pointed out first the massive supercomputers used for brain mapping and then the genetics lab and cryogenic facility itself, which they couldn't enter but could see from windows in the corridor. A half dozen white-coated employees dipped pipettes into tubes, grew cultures in petri dishes and hunched over microscopes.

Covey was intrigued but not yet sold, Farley noted.

"Let's go back to the office."

When they'd sat again the old man finally said, "Well, I'll think about it."

Sheldon nodded with a smile and said, "You bet. A decision like this . . . Some people just can't bring themselves to sign on. You take your time." He handed Covey a huge binder. "Those're case studies, genetic data for comparison with the transitioning clients and their next-life selves, interviews with them. There's nothing identifying them but you can read about the children and the process itself." Farley paused and let Covey flip through the material. He seemed to be reading it carefully. The doctor added, "What's so nice about this is that you never have to say good-bye to your loved ones. Say you've got a son or daughter . . . we could contact them when they're older and propose our services to them. You could reconnect with them a hundred years from now."

At the words *son or daughter*, Covey had looked up, blinking. His eyes drifted off and finally he said, "I don't know. . . ."

"Mr. Covey," Farley said, "let me just add one thing. I understand your skepticism. But you tell me you're a businessman? Well, I'm going to treat you like one. Sure, you've got doubts. Who wouldn't? But even if you're not one hundred percent sure, even if you think I'm trying to sell you a load of hooey, what've you got to lose? You're going to die anyway. Why don't you just roll the dice and take the chance?"

He let this sink in for a minute and saw that the words—as so often—were having an effect. Time to back off. He said, "Now, I've got some phone calls to make, if you'll excuse me. There's a lounge through that door. Take your time and read through those things."

Covey picked up the files and stepped into the room the doctor indicated. The door closed.

Farley had pegged the old man as shrewd and deliberate. And accordingly the doctor gave him a full forty-five minutes to examine the materials. Finally he rose and walked to the doorway. Before he could say anything Covey looked up from the leather couch he was sitting in and said, "I'll do it. I want to do it."

"I'm very happy for you," Farley said sincerely.

"What do I need to do now?"

"All you do is an MRI scan and then give us a blood sample for the genetic material."

"You don't need part of my brain?"

"That's what's so amazing about genes. All of us is contained in a cell of our own blood."

Covey nodded.

"Then you change your will and we take it from there." He looked in a file and pulled out a list of the charities the foundation had set up recently.

"Any of these appeal? You should pick three or four. And they ought to be something in line with interests or causes you had when you were alive."

"There." Covey circled three of them. "I'll leave most to the Metropolitan Arts Assistance Association." He looked up. "Veronica, my wife, was an artist. That okay?"

"It's fine." Farley copied down the names and some other information and then handed a card to Covey. "Just take that to your lawyer."

The old man nodded. "His office is only a few miles from here. I could see him today."

"Just bring us a copy of the will." He didn't add what Covey, of course, a savvy businessman, knew. That if the will was not altered, or if he changed it later, the foundation wouldn't do the cloning. They had the final say.

"What about the . . . transition?"

Farley said, "That's your choice. Entirely up to you. Tomorrow or next year. Whatever you're comfortable with."

At the door Covey paused and turned back, shook Farley's hand. He gave a faint laugh. "Who would've thought? Forever."

In Greek mythology Eos was the goddess of dawn and she was captivated with the idea of having human lovers. She fell deeply in love with a mortal, Tithonos, the son of the king of Troy, and convinced Zeus to let him live forever.

The god of gods agreed. But he neglected one small detail: granting him youth as well as immortality. While Eos remained unchanged Tithonos grew older and more decrepit with each passing year until he was so old he was unable to move or speak. Horrified, Eos turned him into an insect and moved on to more suitable paramours.

Dr. William Farley thought of this myth now, sitting at his desk in the Lotus Research Foundation. The search for immortality's always been tough on us poor humans, he reflected. But how doggedly we ignore the warning in Tithonos's myth—and the logic of science—and continue to look for ways to cheat death.

Farley glanced at a picture on his desk. It showed a couple, arm in arm—younger versions of those in a second picture on his credenza. His parents, who'd died in an auto accident when Farley was in medical school.

An only child, desperately close to them, he took months to recover from the shock. When he was able to resume his studies, he decided he'd specialize in emergency medicine—devoting his to saving lives threatened by trauma.

But the young man was brilliant—too smart for the repetitious mechanics of ER work. Lying awake nights he would reflect about his parents' deaths and he took some reassurance that they were, in a biochemical way, still alive within him. He developed an interest in genetics, and that was the subject he began to pursue in earnest.

Months, then years, of manic twelve-hour days doing research in the field resulted in many legitimate discoveries. But this also led to some ideas that were less conventional, even bizarre—consciousness cloning, for instance.

Not surprisingly, he was either ignored or ridiculed by his peers. His papers were rejected by professional journals, his grant requests turned down. The rejection didn't discourage him, though he grew more and more desperate to find the millions of dollars needed to research his theory. One day—about seven years ago—nearly penniless and living in a walk-up beside one of Westbrook's commuter train lines, he'd gotten a call from an old acquaintance. The man had heard about Farley's plight and had an idea.

"You want to raise money for your research?" he'd asked the impoverished medico. "It's easy. Find really sick, really wealthy patients and sell them immortality."

"What?"

"Listen," the man had continued. "Find patients who're about to die anyway. They'll be desperate. You package it right, they'll buy it."

"I can't sell them anything yet," Farley had replied. "I *believe* I can make this work. But it could take years."

"Well, sometimes sacrifices have to be made. You can pick up ten million overnight, twenty. That'd buy some pretty damn nice research facilities."

Farley had been quiet, considering those words. Then he'd said, "I *could* keep tissue samples, I suppose, and then when we actually can do the cloning, I could bring them back then."

"Hey, there you go," said the doctor. Something in the tone suggested to Farley that he didn't think the process would ever work. But the man's disbelief was irrelevant if he could help Farley get the money he needed for research.

"Well, all right," Farley said to his colleague—whose name was Anthony Sheldon, of the cardiology department at Westbrook Hospital, a man who was as talented an entrepreneur as he was a cardiovascular surgeon.

Six years ago they'd set up the Lotus Research Foundation, an in vitro clinic and a network of bogus charities. Dr. Sheldon, whose office was near the Cardiac Support Center, would finagle a look at the files of patients there and would find the richest and sickest. Then he'd arrange for them to be contacted by the Lotus Foundation and Farley would sell them the program.

Farley had truly doubted that anybody would buy the pitch but Sheldon had coached him well. The man had thought of everything. He found unique appeals for each potential client and gave Farley this information to snare them. In the case of the Bensons, for instance, Sheldon had learned how much they loved each other. His pitch to them was that this was the chance to be together forever, as they so poignantly noted in their suicide note. With Robert Covey, Sheldon had learned about his estranged son, so Farley added the tactical mention that a client could have a second chance to connect with children.

Sheldon had also come up with one vital part of the selling process. He made sure the patients got high doses of Luminux (even the coffee that Covey had just been drinking, for instance, was laced with the drug). Neither doctor believed that anyone would sign up for such a far-fetched idea without the benefit of some mind-numbing Mickey Finn.

The final selling point was, of course, the desperate desire of people facing death to believe what Farley promised them.

And that turned out to be one hell of a hook. The Lotus Research Foundation had earned almost 93 million in the past six years.

Everything had gone fine—until recently, when their greed got the better of them. Well, got the better of Sheldon. They'd decided that the cardiologist would never refer his own patients to the foundation—and would wait six months or a year between clients. But Tony Sheldon apparently had a mistress with very expensive taste and had lost some serious money in the stock market recently. Just after the Bensons signed up, the Whitleys presented themselves. Although Sam Whitley was a patient, they were far too wealthy to pass up and so Farley reluctantly yielded to Sheldon's pressure to go ahead with the plan.

But they learned that, though eager to proceed, Sam Whitley had wanted to reassure himself that this wasn't pure quackery and he'd tracked down some technical literature about the computers used in the technique and genetics in general. After the patients had died, Farley and Sheldon had to find this information in his house, burn it and scour the place for any other evidence that might lead back to the foundation.

The intrusion, though, must've alerted the police to the possibility that the families' deaths were suspicious. Officers had actually interviewed Sheldon, sending a jolt of panic through Farley. But then a scapegoat stumbled into the picture: Mac McCaffrey, a young nurse/counselor at the Cardiac Support Center. She was seeing their latest recent prospect—Robert Covey—as she'd been working with the Bensons and the Whitleys. This made her suspect to start with. Even better was her reluctance to admit she'd seen the Bensons; after their suicide the nurse had apparently lied about them and had stolen their files from the CSC. A perfect setup. Sheldon had used his ample resources to bribe a pharmacist at the CSC to doctor the logs and give him a couple of wholesale bottles containing a few Luminux tablets, to make it look like she'd been drugging patients for some time. Farley, obsessed with death and dying, had a vast library of articles on euthanasia and suicide. He copied several dozen of these. The drugs and the articles they planted in the nurse's garage—insurance in case they needed somebody to take the fall.

Which they had. And now the McCaffrey woman had just been hauled off to jail.

A whole 'nother story, as Covey had said.

The nurse's arrest had troubled Farley. He'd speculated out loud about telling the police that she was innocent. But Sheldon reminded him coolly what would happen to them and the foundation if Farley did that and he relented.

Sheldon had said, "Look, we'll do one more—this Covey—and then take a break. A year. Two years."

"No. Let's wait."

"I checked him out," Sheldon said, "He's worth over fifty million."

"I think it's too risky."

"I've thought about that." With the police still looking into the Benson and Whitley suicides, Sheldon explained, it'd be better to have the old man die in a mugging or hit and run, rather than killing himself.

"But," Farley had whispered, "you mean murder?"

"A suicide'll be way too suspicious."

"We can't."

But Sheldon had snapped, "Too late for morality, Doctor. You made your deal with the devil. You can't renegotiate now." And hung up.

Farley stewed for a while but finally realized the man was right; there was no going back. And, my, what he could do with another $25 million. . . .

His secretary buzzed him on the intercom.

"Mr. Covey's back, sir."

"Show him in."

Covey walked into the office. They shook hands again and Covey sat. As cheerful and blinky as most patients on seventy-five milligrams of Luminux. He happily took another cup of special brew then reached into his jacket pocket and displayed a copy of the codicil to the will. "Here you go."

Though Farley wasn't a lawyer he knew what to look for; the document was in proper form.

They shook hands formally.

Covey finished his coffee and Farley escorted him to the lab, where he would undergo the MRI and give a blood sample, making the nervous small talk that the clients always made at this point in the process.

The geneticist shook his hand and told him he'd made the right decision. Covey thanked Farley sincerely, with a hopeful smile on his face that was, Farley knew, only partly from the drug. He returned to his office and the doctor picked up the phone, called Anthony Sheldon. "Covey's changed the will. He'll be leaving here in about fifteen minutes."

"I'll take care of him now," Sheldon said and hung up.

Farley sighed and dropped the received into the cradle. He stripped off his suit jacket then pulled on a white lab coat. He left his office and fled up the hall to the research lab, where he knew he would find solace in the honest world of science, safe from all his guilt and sins, as if they were barred entry by the double-sealed doors of the airlock.

Robert Covey was walking down the street, feeling pretty giddy, odd thoughts going through his head.

Thinking of his life—the way he'd lived it. And the people who'd touched him and whom he'd touched. A foreman in the Bedford plant, who'd worked for the company for forty years . . . The men in his golfing foursome . . . Veronica . . . His brother . . .

His son, of course.

Still no call from Randy. And for the first time it occurred to him that maybe there *was* a reason the boy—well, young man—had been ignoring him. He'd always assumed he'd been such a good father. But maybe not.

Nothing makes you question your life more closely than when somebody's trying to sell you immortality.

Walking toward the main parking garage, Covey noted that the area was largely deserted. He saw only a few grungy kids on skateboards, a pretty redhead across the street, two men getting out of a white van parked near an alley.

He paid attention only to the men, because they were large, dressed in what looked like cheap suits and, with a glance up and down, started in his direction.

Covey soon forgot them, though, and concentrated again on his son. Thinking about his decision not to tell the boy about his illness. Maybe withholding things like this had been a pattern in Covey's life. Maybe the boy had felt excluded.

He laughed to himself. Maybe he should leave a message about what he and Farley had just been talking about. Lord have mercy, what he wouldn't give to see Randy's reaction when he listened to that! He could—

Covey slowed, frowning.

What was this?

The two men from the van were now jogging—directly toward him. He hesitated and shied back. Suddenly the men split up. One stopped and turned his back to Covey, scanning the sidewalk, while the other sped up, springing directly toward the old man. Then simultaneously they both pulled guns from under their coats.

No!

He turned to run, thinking that sprinting would probably kill him faster than the bullets. Not that it mattered. The man approaching him was fast and before Covey had a chance to take more than a few steps he was being pulled roughly into the alleyway behind him.

"No, what are you doing? Who are—"

"Quiet!"

The man pressed Covey against the wall.

The other joined them but continued to gaze out over the street as he spoke into a walkie-talkie. "We've got him. No sign of hostiles. Move in, all units, move in!"

From out on the street came the rushing sound of car engines and the bleats of siren.

"Sorry, Mr. Covey. We had a little change of plans." The man speaking was the one who'd pulled him into the alley. They both produced badges and ID cards of the Westbrook County Sheriff's Department. "We work with Greg LaTour."

Oh, LaTour . . . He was the burly officer who, along with that skinny young officer named Talbot Simms, had come to his house early this morning with a truly bizarre story. This outfit called the Lotus Research Foundation might be running some kind of scam, targeting sick people, but the police weren't quite sure how it worked. Had he been contacted by anyone there? When Covey had told them, yes, and that he was in fact meeting with its director, Farley, that afternoon they wondered if he'd be willing to wear a wire to find out what it was all about.

Well, what it was all about was immortality . . . and it *had* been one hell of a scam.

The plan was that after he stopped at Farley's office and dropped off the fake codicil to his will (he executed a second one at the same time, voiding the one he'd given Farley), he was going to meet LaTour and Simms at a Starbucks not far away.

But now the cops had something else in mind.

"Who're you?" Covey now asked. "Where're Laurel and Hardy?" Meaning Simms and LaTour.

The young officer who'd shoved him into the alley had blinked, not understanding the reference. He said, "Well, sir, what happened was we had a tap on the phone in Farley's office. He called Sheldon to tell him about you and it seems they weren't going to wait to try to talk you into killing yourself. Sheldon was going to kill you right away—make it look like a mugging or hit and run, we think."

Covey muttered, "You might've thought about that possibility up front."

There was a crackle in the mike/speaker of one of the officers. Covey couldn't hear too well but the gist of it was that they'd arrested Dr. Anthony Sheldon just outside his office. They now stepped out of the alley and Covey observed a half dozen police officers escorting William Farley and three men in lab coats out of the Lotus Foundation offices in handcuffs.

Covey observed the procession coolly, feeling contempt for the depravity of the foundation's immortality scam, though also with a grudging admiration. A businessman to his soul, Robert Covey couldn't help be impressed by someone who'd identified an inexhaustible market demand. Even if that product he sold was completely bogus.

The itch had yet to be scratched. Tal's office was still as sloppy as LaTour's. The mess was driving him crazy, though Shellee seemed to think it was a step up on the evolutionary chain—for him to have digs that looked like everyone else's.

Captain Dempsey was sitting in the office, playing with one rolled-up sleeve, then the other. Greg LaTour too, his booted feet on the floor for a change, though the reason for this propriety seemed to be that Tal's desk was piled too high with paper to find a place to rest them.

"How'd you tip to this scam of theirs?" the captain asked. "The Lotus Foundation?"

Tal said, "Some things just didn't add up."

"Haw." From LaTour.

Both the captain and Tal glanced at him.

LaTour stopped smiling. "He's the math guy. He says something didn't *add* up. I thought it was a joke." He grumbled, "Go on."

Tal explained that after he'd returned to the office following Mac's arrest, he couldn't get her out of his head.

"Women do that," LaTour said.

"No, I mean there was something odd about the whole case," he continued. "Issues I couldn't reconcile. So I checked with Crime Scene—there *was* no Luminux in the port Mac was giving Covey. Then I went to see her in the lockup. She admitted she'd lied about not being the Bensons' nurse. She said she destroyed their records at the Cardiac Support Center and that she was the one that the witnesses had seen the day they died. But she lied because she was afraid she'd lose her job—two of her patients killing themselves? When, to her, they seemed to be doing fine? It shook her up bad. That's why she bought the suicide book. She bought it *after* I told her about it—she got the title from me. She wanted to know what to look for, to make sure nobody else died."

"And you believed her?" the captain asked.

"Yes, I did. I asked Covey if she'd ever brought up suicide. Did he have any sense that she was trying to get him to kill himself. But he said, no. All she'd talked about at that meeting—when we arrested her—was how painful and hard it is to go through a tough illness alone. She'd figured that he hadn't called his son, Randall, and told him, like he'd said. She gave him some port, got him relaxed and was trying to talk him into calling the boy."

"You said something about an opera show?" Dempsey continued, examining both sleeves and making sure they were rolled up to within a quarter inch of each other. Tal promised himself never to compulsively play with his tie knot again. His boss continued, "You said she lied about the time it was on."

"Oh. Right. Oops."

"Oops?"

"The Whitleys died on Sunday. The show's on at four then. But it's on at *seven* during the week, just after the business report. I checked the NPR program guide."

The captain asked, "And the articles about euthanasia? The ones they found in her house?"

"Planted. Her fingerprints weren't on them. Only glove-print smudges. The stolen Luminux bottle too. No prints. And, according to the inventory, those drugs disappeared from the clinic when Mac was out of town. Naw, she didn't have anything to do with the scam. It was Farley and Sheldon."

LaTour continued, "Quite a plan. Slipping the patients drugs, getting them to change their wills, then kill themselves and clean up afterwards.

"They did it all themselves? Farley and Sheldon?"

LaTour shook his head. "They must've hired muscle or used somebody in the foundation for the dirty work. We got four of 'em in custody. But they clammed up. Nobody's saying anything." LaTour sighed. "And they got the best lawyers in town. Big surprise, with all the fucking money they've got."

Tal said, "So, anyway, I knew Mac was being set up. But we still couldn't figure what was going on. You know, in solving an algebra problem you look for common denominators and—"

"Again with the fucking math," LaTour grumbled.

"Well, what was the denominator? We had two couples committing suicide and leaving huge sums of money to charities—more than half their estates. I looked up the statistics from the NAEPP."

"The—"

"The National Association of Estate Planning Professionals. When people have children, only two percent leave that much of their estate to charities. And even when they're childless, only twelve percent leave significant estates—that's over ten million dollars—to charities. So that made me wonder what was up with these nonprofits. I called the guy at the SEC I've been working with and he put me in touch with the people in charge of registering charities in New York, New Jersey, Massachusetts, and Delaware. I followed the trail of the nonprofits and found they were all owned ultimately by the Lotus Research Foundation. It's controlled by Farley and Sheldon. I checked them out. Sheldon was a rich cardiologist who'd been sued for malpractice a couple of times and been investigated for some securities fraud and insider trading. Farley? . . . Okay, now *he* was interesting. A crackpot. Trying to get funding for some weird cloning theory. I'd found his name on a card for the Lotus Foundation at the Whitleys'. It had something to do with alternative medical treatment but it didn't say what specifically."

LaTour explained about checking with Mac and the other Cardiac Support Center patients to see if they'd heard from the foundation. That led them to Covey.

"Immortality," Dempsey said slowly. "And people fell for it."

Together forever. . . .

"Well, they were pretty doped up on Luminux, remember," Tal said.

But LaTour offered what was perhaps the more insightful answer. "People always fall for shit they wanta fall for."

"That McCaffrey woman been released yet?" Dempsey asked uneasily. Arresting the wrong person was probably as embarrassing as declaring a bum 2124 (and as expensive; Sandra Whitley's lawyer—a guy as harsh as she was—had already contacted the Sheriff's Department, threatening suit).

"Oh, yeah. Dropped all charges," Tal said. Then he looked over his desk. "I'm going to finish up the paperwork and ship it off to the prosecutor. Then I've got some spreadsheets to get back to."

He glanced up to see a cryptic look pass between LaTour and the captain. He wondered what it meant.

Naiveté.

The tacit exchange in Tal's office between the two older cops was a comment on Tal's naiveté. The paperwork didn't get "finished up" at all. Over the next few days it just grew and grew and grew.

As did his hours. His working day expanded from an average 8.3 hours to 12 plus.

LaTour happily pointed out, "You call a twenty-one-twenty-four, you're the case officer. You stay with it all the way till the end. Ain't life sweet?"

And the end was nowhere in sight. Analyzing the evidence—the hundreds of cartons removed from the Lotus Foundation and from Sheldon's office—Tal learned that the Bensons hadn't been the first victims. Farley and Sheldon had engineered other suicides, going back several years, and had stolen tens of millions of dollars. The prior suicides were like the Bensons and the Whitleys—upper class and quite ill, though not necessarily terminally. Tal was shocked to find that he was familiar with one of the earlier victims: Mary Stemple, a physicist who'd taught at the Princeton Institute for Advanced Study, the famed think-tank where Einstein had worked. Tal had read some of her papers. A trained mathematician, she'd done most of her work in physics and astronomy and made important discoveries about the size and nature of the universe. It was a true shame that she'd been tricked into taking her life; she might have had years of important discoveries ahead of her.

He was troubled by the deaths, yes, but he was even more shocked to find that the foundation had actually supervised the in vitro fertilization of six eggs, which had been implanted in surrogate mothers, three of whom had already given birth to children. They were ultimately placed with parents who could not otherwise conceive.

This had been done, Tal, LaTour, and the district attorney concluded, so that Farley and Sheldon could prove to potential clients that they were actually doing the cloning (though another reason, it appeared, was to make an additional fee from childless couples).

The main concern was for the health of the children and the county hired several legitimate genetics doctors and pediatricians to see if the three children who'd been born and the three fetuses within the surrogate mothers were healthy. They were examined and found to be fine and, despite the immortality scam, the surrogate births and the adoption placements were completely legal, the attorney general concluded.

One of the geneticists Tal and LaTour had consulted said, "So Bill Farley was behind this?" The man had shaken his head. "We've been hearing about his crazy ideas for years. A wacko."

"There any chance," Tal wondered, "that someday somebody'll actually be able to do what he was talking about?"

"Cloning consciousness?" The doctor laughed. "You said you're a statistician, right?"

"That's right."

"You know what the odds are of being able to perfectly duplicate the structure of any given human brain?"

"Small as a germ's ass?" LaTour suggested.

The doctor considered this and said, "That sums it up pretty well."

The day was too nice to be inside so Mac McCaffrey and Robert Covey were in the park. Tal spotted them on a bench overlooking a duck pond. He waved and veered toward them.

She appeared to be totally immersed in the sunlight and the soft breeze; Tal remembered how much this member of the Four Percent Club loved the out-of-doors.

Covey, Mac had confided to Tal, was doing pretty well. His blood pressure was down and he was in good spirits as he approached his surgery. She was breaching confidentiality rules by telling Tal this but she justified it on the grounds that Tal was a police officer investigating a case involving her patient. Another reason was simply that Tal liked the old guy and was concerned about him.

Mac also told him that Covey had finally called his son and left a message about his condition and the impending surgery. There'd been no reply, though Covey'd gotten a hang-up on his voice mail, the caller ID on the phone indicating "Out of Area." Mac took the optimistic position that it had indeed been his son on the other end of the line and the man hadn't left a message because he preferred to talk to his father in person. Time would tell.

In his office an hour ago, on the phone, Tal had been distracted as he listened to Mac's breathy, enthusiastic report about her patient. He'd listened attentively but was mostly waiting for an appropriate lull in the conversation to leap in with a dinner invitation. None had presented itself, though, before she explained she had to get to a meeting. He'd hurriedly made plans to meet here.

Tal now joined them and she looked up with that charming crooked smile that he really liked (and was more than just a little sexy).

"Hey," he said.

"Officer," Robert Covey said. They warmly shook hands. Tal hesitated for a moment in greeting Mac but then thought, hell with it, bent down and kissed her on the cheek. This seemed unprofessional on several levels—his as well as hers—but she didn't seem to care; he knew *he* certainly didn't have a problem with the lapse.

Tal proceeded to explain to Covey that since he was the only victim who'd survived the Lotus Foundation scam the police needed a signed and notarized copy of his statement.

"In case I croak when I'm under the knife you'll still have the evidence to put the pricks away."

That was it exactly. Tal shrugged. "Well . . ."

"Don'tcha worry," the old man said. "I'm happy to."

Tal handed him the statement. "Look it over, make any changes you want. I'll print out a final version and we'll get it notarized."

"Will do." Covey skimmed it and then looked up. "How 'bout something to drink? There's a bar—"

"Coffee, tea or soda," Mac said ominously. "It's not even noon yet."

"She claims she negotiates," Covey muttered to Tal. "But she don't."

The old man pointed toward the park's concession stand at the top of a hill some distance away. "Coffee's not bad there—for an outfit that's not named for a whaler."

"I'll get it."

"I'll have a large with cream."

"He'll have a medium, skim milk," Mac said. "Tea for me, please. Sugar." She fired a crooked smile Tal's way.

About a hundred yards from the bench where the old man sat chatting away with his friend, a young woman walked along the park path. The redhead was short, busty, attractive, wearing a beautiful tennis bracelet and a diamond/emerald ring, off which the sunlight glinted fiercely.

She kept her eyes down as she walked, so nobody could see her abundant tears.

Margaret Ludlum had been crying on and off for several days. Ever since her boss and lover, Dr. Anthony Sheldon, had been arrested.

Margaret had greeted the news of his arrest—and Farley's too—with horror, knowing that she'd probably be the next to be picked up. After all, she'd been the one that Sheldon and Farley had sent as a representative of the Lotus Research Foundation to the couples who were planning to kill themselves. It was she who'd slipped them plenty of Luminux during their last few weeks on earth, then suggested they buy the blueprint for their deaths—the suicide books—and coerced them into killing themselves and afterwards cleaned up any evidence linking them to the Foundation or its two principals.

But the police had taken her statement—denying everything, of course—and let her go. It was clear they suspected Sheldon and Farley had an accomplice but seemed to think that it was one of Farley's research assistants. Maybe they thought that only a man was capable of killing defenseless people.

Wrong. Margaret had been completely comfortable with assisted suicide. And more: She'd been only a minute away from murdering Robert Covey the other day as he walked down the street after leaving the Lotus Research Foundation. But just as she started toward him a van stopped nearby and two men jumped out, pulling him to safety. Other officers had raided the foundation. She'd veered down a side street and called Sheldon to warn him. But it was too late. They got him outside his office at the hospital as he'd tried to flee.

Oh, yes, she'd been perfectly willing to kill Covey then.

And was perfectly willing to kill him now.

She watched that detective who'd initially come to interview Tony Sheldon walk away from the bench and up the path toward the refreshment stand. It didn't matter that he was leaving; he wasn't her target.

Only Covey. With the old man gone it would be much harder to get a conviction, Sheldon explained. He might get off altogether or serve only a few years—that's what they doled out in most cases of assisted suicides. The cardiologist promised he'd finally get divorced and he and Margaret would move to Europe. . . . They'd taken some great trips to the south of France and the weeks there had been wonderful. Oh, how she missed him.

Missed the money too, of course. That was the other reason she had to get Tony out of jail, of course. The doctor had been meaning to set up an account for her but hadn't gotten around to it. She'd let it slide for too long and the paperwork never materialized.

In her purse, banging against her hip, she felt the heavy pistol, the one she'd been planning to use on Covey several days ago. She was familiar with guns—she'd helped several of the other foundation clients "transition" by shooting themselves. And though she'd never actually pulled the trigger and murdered someone, she knew she could do it.

The tears were gone now. She was thinking of how best to handle the shooting. Studying the old man and that woman—who'd have to die too, of course; she'd be a witness against Margaret herself for the murder today. Anyway, the double murder would make the scenario more realistic. It would look like a mugging. Margaret would demand the wallet and the woman's purse and when they handed the items over, she'd shoot them both in the head.

Pausing now, next to a tree, Margaret looked over the park. A few passersby, but no one was near Covey and the woman. The detective—Simms, she recalled—was still hiking up the hill to the concession stand. He was two hundred yards from the bench; she could kill them both and be in her car speeding away before he could sprint back to the bench.

She waited until he disappeared into a stand of trees then reached into her purse, cocking the pistol. Margaret stepped out from behind the tree and moved quickly down the path that led to the bench. A glance around her. Nobody was present.

Closer now, closer. Along the asphalt path, damp from an earlier rain and the humid spring air.

She was twenty feet away . . . ten . . .

She stepped quickly up behind them. They looked up. The woman gave a faint smile in greeting—a smile that faded as she noted Margaret's cold eyes.

"Who are you?" the woman asked, alarm in her voice.

Margaret Ludlum said nothing. She pulled the gun from her purse.

∞

"Wallet!" Pointing the pistol directly at the old man's face.

"What?"

"Give me your wallet!" Then turning to the woman, "And the purse! Now!"

"You want—?"

They were confused, being mugged by someone outfitted by Neiman Marcus.

"Now!" Margaret screamed.

The woman thrust the purse forward and stood, holding her hands out. "Look, just calm down."

The old man was frantically pulling his wallet from his pocket and holding it out unsteadily.

Margaret grabbed the items and shoved them into her shoulder bag. Then she looked at the man's eyes and—rather than feel any sympathy, she felt that stillness she always did when slipping someone drugs or showing them how to grip the gun or seal the garage with duct tape to make the most efficient use of the carbon monoxide.

The woman was saying, "Please, don't do anything stupid. Just take everything and leave!"

Then Robert Covey squinted. He was looking at Margaret with certain understanding. He knew what this was about. "Leave her alone," he said. "Me, it's okay. It's all right. Just let her go."

But she thrust the gun forward at Covey as the woman with him screamed and dropped to the ground. Margaret began to pull the trigger, whispering the phrase she always did when helping transition the foundation's clients, offering a prayer for a safe journey. "God be with—"

A flash of muddy light filled her vision as she felt, for a tiny fragment of a second, a fist or rock slam into her chest.

"But . . . what . . ."

Then nothing but numb silence.

A thousand yards away, it seemed.

If not miles.

Talbot Simms squinted toward the bench, where he could see the forms of Robert Covey and Mac on their feet, backing away from the body of the woman he'd just shot. Mac was pulling out her cell phone, dropping it, picking it up again, looking around in panic.

Tal lowered the gun and stared.

A moment before, Tal had paid the vendor and was turning from the concession stand, holding the tray of drinks. Frowning, he saw a woman standing beside the bench, pointing something toward Mac and Covey, Mac rearing away then handing her purse over, the old man giving her something, his wallet, it seemed.

And then Tal had noticed that what she held was a gun.

He knew that she was in some way connected to Sheldon or Farley and the Lotus Foundation. The red hair . . . Yes! Sheldon's secretary, unsmiling Celtic Margaret. He'd known too that she'd come here to shoot the only living eyewitness to the scam—and probably Mac too.

Dropping the tray of tea and coffee, he'd drawn his revolver. He'd intended to sprint back toward them, calling for her to stop, threatening her. But when he saw Mac fall to the ground, futilely covering her face, and Margaret shoving the pistol forward, he'd known she was going to shoot.

Tal had cocked his own revolver to single-action and stepped into a combat firing stance, left hand curled under and around his right, weight evenly distributed on both feet, aiming high and slightly to the left, compensating for gravity and a faint breeze.

He'd fired, felt the kick of the recoil and heard the sharp report, followed by screams behind him of bystanders diving for cover.

Remaining motionless, he'd cocked the gun again and prepared to fire a second time in case he'd missed.

But he saw immediately that another shot wouldn't be necessary.

Tal Simms carefully lowered the hammer of his weapon, replaced it in his holster and began running down the path.

"Excuse me, you were standing *where*?"

Tal ignored Greg LaTour's question and asked them both one more time, "You're okay? You're sure?"

The bearded cop persisted. "You were on *that* hill. Way the fuck up *there*?"

Mac told Tal that she was fine. He instinctively put his arm around her. Covey too said that he was unhurt, though he added that, as a heart patient, he could do without scares like that one.

Margaret Ludlum's gun had fired but it was merely a reflex after Tal's bullet had struck her squarely in the chest. The slug from her pistol had buried itself harmlessly in the ground.

Tal glanced at her body, now covered with a green tarp from the Medical Examiner's Office. He waited to feel upset, or shocked or guilty, but he was only numb. Those feelings would come later, he supposed. At the moment he was just relieved to find that Mac and Robert Covey were all right—and that the final itch in the case had been alleviated: The tough Irish girl, Margaret, was the missing link.

They must've hired muscle or used somebody in the foundation for the dirty work.

As the Crime Scene techs picked up evidence around the body and looked through the woman's purse, LaTour persisted. "That hill up there? No fucking way."

Tal glanced up. "Yeah. Up there by the concession stand. Why?"

The bearded cop glanced at Mac. "He's kidding. He's jerking my chain, right?"

"No, that's where he was."

"That's a fucking long shot. Wait . . . how big's your barrel?"

"What?"

"On your service piece."

"Three inch."

LaTour said. "You made that shot with a three-inch barrel?"

"We've pretty much established that, Greg. Can we move on?" Tal turned back to Mac and smiled, feeling weak, he was so relieved to see her safe.

But LaTour said, "You told me you don't shoot."

"I didn't say that at all. You *assumed* I don't shoot. I just didn't want to go the range the other day. I've shot all my life. I was captain of the rifle team at school."

LaTour squinted at the distant concession stand. He shook his head. "No way."

Tal glanced at him and asked, "Okay, you want to know how I did it? There's a trick."

"What?" the big cop asked eagerly.

"Easy. Just calculate the correlation between gravity as a constant and the estimated mean velocity of the wind over the time it takes the bullet to travel from points A to B—that's the muzzle to the target. Got that? Then you just multiply distance times that correlated factor divided by the mass of the bullet times its velocity squared."

"You—" The big cop squinted again. "Wait, you—"

"It's a joke, Greg."

"You son of a bitch. You had me."

"Haven't you noticed it's not that hard to do?"

The cop mouthed words that Mac couldn't see but Tal had no trouble deciphering.

LaTour squinted one last time toward the knoll and exhaled a laugh. "Let's get statements." He nodded to Robert Covey and escorted him toward his car, calling back to Tal, "You get hers. That okay with you, Einstein?"

"Sure."

Tal led Mac to a park bench out of sight of Margaret's body and listened to what she had to say about the incident, jotting down the facts in his precise handwriting. An officer drove Covey home and Tal found himself alone with Mac. There was silence for a moment and he asked, "Say, one thing? Could you help me fill out this questionnaire?"

"I'd be happy to."

He pulled one out of his briefcase, looked at it, then back to her. "How 'bout dinner tonight?"

"Is that one of the questions?"

"It's one of *my* questions. Not a police question."

"Well, the thing is I've got a date tonight. Sorry."

He nodded. "Oh, sure." Couldn't think of anything to follow up with. He pulled out his pen and smoothed the questionnaire, thinking: Of *course* she had a date. Women like her, high-ranking members of the Four Percent Club, always had dates. He wondered if it'd been the Pascal-sex comment that had knocked him out of the running. Note for the future: Don't bring that one up too soon.

Mac continued, "Yeah, tonight I'm going to help Mr. Covey find a health club with a pool. He likes to swim but he shouldn't do it alone. So we're going to find a place that's got a lifeguard."

"Really? Good for him." He looked up from Question 1.

"But I'm free Saturday," Mac said.

"Saturday? Well, I am too."

Silence. "Then how's Saturday?" she asked.

"I think it's great . . . Now how 'bout those questions?"

A week later the Lotus Research Foundation case was nearly tidied up—as was Tal's office, much to his relief—and he was beginning to think about the other tasks awaiting him: the SEC investigation, the statistical analysis for next year's personnel assignments and, of course, hounding fellow officers to get their questionnaires in on time.

The prosecutor still wanted some final statements for the Farley and Sheldon trials, though, and he'd asked Tal to interview the parents who'd adopted the three children born following the in vitro fertilization at the foundation.

Two of the three couples lived nearby and he spent one afternoon taking their statements. The last couple was in Warwick, a small town outside of Albany, over an hour away. Tal made the drive on a Sunday afternoon, zipping down the picturesque roadway along the Hudson River, the landscape punctuated with blooming azaleas, forsythia, and a billion spring flowers, the car filling with the scent of mulch and hot loam and sweet asphalt.

He found both Warwick and the couple's bungalow with no difficulty. The husband and wife, in their late twenties, were identically pudgy and rosy skinned. Uneasy too, until Tal explained that his mission there had nothing to do with any challenges to the adoption. It was merely a formality for a criminal case.

Like the other parents they provided good information that would be helpful in prosecuting Farley and Sheldon. For a half hour Tal jotted careful notes and then thanked them for their time. As he was leaving he walked past a small, cheery room decorated in a circus motif.

A little girl, about four, stood in the doorway. It was the youngster the couple had adopted from the foundation. She was adorable—blond, gray-eyed, with a heart-shaped face.

"This is Amy," the mother said.

"Hello, Amy," Tal offered.

She nodded shyly.

Amy was clutching a piece of paper and some crayons. "Did you draw that?" he asked.

"Uh-huh. I like to draw."

"I can tell. You've got lots of pictures." He nodded at the girl's walls.

"Here," she said, holding the sheet out. "You can have this. I just drew it."

"For me?" Tal asked. He glanced at her mother, who nodded her approval. He studied the picture for a moment. "Thank you, Amy. I love it. I'll put it up on my wall at work."

The girl's face broke into a beaming smile.

Tal said good-bye to her parents and ten minutes later he was cruising south on the parkway. When he came to the turnoff that would take him to his house and his Sunday retreat into the world of mathematics, though, Tal continued on. He drove instead to his office at the County Building.

A half hour later he was on the road again. En route to an address in Chesterton, a few miles away.

He pulled up in front of a split-level house surrounded by a small but immaculately trimmed yard. Two plastic tricycles and other assorted toys sat in the driveway.

But this wasn't the right place, he concluded with irritation. Damn. He must've written the address down wrong.

The house he was looking for had to be nearby and Tal decided to ask the owner here where it was. Walking to the door, Tal pushed the bell then stood back.

A pretty blonde in her thirties greeted him with a cheerful, "Hi. Help you?"

"I'm looking for Greg LaTour's house."

"Well, you found it. Hi, I'm his wife, Joan."

"He lives *here*?" Tal asked, glancing past her into a suburban home right out of a Hollywood sitcom. Thinking too: *And he's married?*

She laughed. "Hold on. I'll get him."

A moment later Greg LaTour came to the door, wearing shorts, sandals, and a green Izod shirt. He blinked in surprise and looked back over his shoulder into the house. Then he stepped outside and pulled the door shut after him. "What're you doing here?"

"Needed to tell you something about the case. . . ." But Tal's voice faded. He was staring at two cute blond girls, twins, about eight years old, who'd come around the side of the house and were looking at Tal curiously.

One said, "Daddy, the ball's in the bushes. We can't get it."

"Honey, I've got to talk to my friend here," he said in a singsong, fatherly voice. "I'll be there in a minute."

"Okay." They disappeared.

"You've got two kids?"

"*Four* kids."

"How long you been married?"

"Eighteen years."

"But I thought you were single. You never mentioned family. You didn't wear a ring. Your office, the biker posters, the bars after work . . ."

"That's who I need to be to do my job," LaTour said in a low voice. "That life—" He nodded vaguely in the direction of the Sheriff's Department. "—and this life I keep separate. Completely."

That's something else . . .

Tal now understood the meaning of the phrase. It wasn't about tragedies in his life, marital breakups, alienated children. And there was nothing LaTour was hiding from Tal. This was a life kept separate from everybody in the department.

"So you're mad I'm here," Tal said.

A shrug. "Just wish you'd called first."

"Sorry."

LaTour shrugged. "You go to church today?"

"I don't go to church. Why?"

"Why're you wearing a tie on Sunday?"

"I don't know. I just do. Is it crooked?"

The big cop said, "No it's not crooked. So. What're you doing here?"

"Hold on a minute."

Tal got his briefcase out of the car and returned to the porch. "I stopped by the office and checked up on the earlier suicides Sheldon and Farley arranged."

"You mean from a few years ago?"

"Right. Well, one of them was a professor named Mary Stemple. I'd heard of her—she was a physicist at Princeton. I read some of her work a while ago. She was brilliant. She spent the last three years of her life working on this analysis of the luminosity of stars and measuring blackbody radiation—"

"I've got burgers about to go on the grill," LaTour grumbled.

"Okay. Got it. Well, this was published just before she killed herself." He handed LaTour what he'd downloaded from the *Journal of Advanced Astrophysics* Web site:

THE INFINITE JOURNEY OF LIGHT:
A NEW APPROACH TO MEASURING
DISTANT STELLAR RADIATION
BY PROF. MARY STEMPLE, PH.D.

He flipped to the end of the article, which consisted of several pages of complicated formulae. They involved hundreds of numbers and Greek and English letters and mathematical symbols. The one that occurred most frequently was the sign for infinity: ∞

LaTour looked up. "There a punch line to all this?"

"Oh, you bet there is." He explained about his drive to Warwick to interview the adoptive couple.

And then he held up the picture that their daughter, Amy, had given him. It was a drawing of the earth and the moon and a spaceship—and all around them, filling the sky, were infinity symbols, growing smaller and smaller as they receded into space.

Forever . . .

Tal added, "And this wasn't the only one. Her walls were *covered* with pictures she'd done that had infinity signs in them. When I saw this I remembered Stemple's work. I went back to the office and I looked up her paper."

"What're you saying?" LaTour frowned.

"Mary Stemple killed herself five years ago. The girl who drew this was conceived at the foundation's clinic a month after she died."

"Jesus . . ." The big cop stared at the picture. "You don't think . . . Hell, it can't be real, that cloning stuff. That doctor we talked to, he said it was impossible."

Tal said nothing, continued to stare at the picture.

LaTour shook his head. "Naw, naw. You know what they did, Sheldon or that girl of his? Or Farley? They showed the kid pictures of that symbol. You know, so they could prove to other clients that the cloning worked. That's all."

"Sure," Tal said. "That's what happened. . . . Probably."

Still, they stood in silence for a long moment, this trained mathematician and this hardened cop, staring, captivated, at a clumsy, crayon picture drawn by a cute four-year-old.

"It can't be," LaTour muttered. "Germ's ass, remember?"

"Yeah, it's impossible," Tal said, staring at the symbol. He repeated: "Probably."

"Daddy!" Came a voice from the backyard.

LaTour called, "Be there in a minute, honey!" Then he looked up at Tal and said, "Hell, as long as you're here, come on in. Have dinner. I make great burgers."

Tal considered the invitation but his eyes were drawn back to the picture, the stars, the moon, the infinity signs. "Thanks but think I'll pass. I'm going back to the office for a while. All that evidence we took out of the foundation? I wanta look over the data a little more."

"Suit yourself, Einstein," the homicide cop said. He started back into the house but paused and turned back. "Data plural," he said, pointing a huge finger at Tal's chest.

"Data plural," Tal agreed.

LaTour vanished inside, the screen door swinging shut behind him with a bang.

Lawrence Block

There are two kinds of stylists: the show-off who wants to be congratulated every time he turns a nice phrase and the kind who quietly turns a nice phrase but just gets on with the story. **Lawrence Block** is one of the latter. Even at the outset of his career, when he was turning out books at a furious pace, he managed to bring elegance and taste to even minor assignments, particularly with a knowing, wry take on the relationships and interactions between his characters: men with women, men with men, fathers and sons, husbands and wives. His hard work paid off. Not only is he one of the premier crime novelists of our time—with two bestselling series: the Matt Scudder novels (dark), including *Eight Million Ways to Die*, *The Devil Knows You're Dead*, and the Edgar-winning *A Dance at the Slaughterhouse*; and the Bernie Rhodenbarr mysteries (humorous), including *The Burglar Who Thought He Was Bogart* and *The Burglar Who Traded Ted Williams*—he is also one of our most accomplished short story writers. No wonder the Mystery Writers of America hailed him as one of the Grand Masters. Recently he turned to editing books, with seven stellar anthologies published: *Master's Choice, Vol. 1 and 2*, *Opening Shots, Vol. 1 and 2*, *Speaking of Lust* and *Speaking of Greed*, and the MWA anthology *Blood on Their Hands*. His latest novels are the acclaimed ode to New York City after 9/11, *Small Town*, and another Bernie Rhodenbarr mystery, *The Burglar on the Prowl*.

KELLER'S ADJUSTMENT

Lawrence Block

Keller, waiting for the traffic light to turn from red to green, wondered what had happened to the world. The traffic light wasn't the problem. There'd been traffic lights for longer than he could remember, longer than he'd been alive. For almost as long as there had been automobiles, he supposed, although the automobile had clearly come first, and would in fact have necessitated the traffic light. At first they'd have made do without them, he supposed, and then, when there were enough cars around for them to start slamming into one another, someone would have figured out that some form of control was necessary, some device to stop east-west traffic while allowing north-south traffic to proceed, and then switching.

He could imagine an early motorist fulminating against the new regimen. *Whole world's going to hell. They're taking our rights away one after another. Light turns red because some damn timer tells it to turn red, a man's supposed to stop what he's doing and hit the brakes. Don't matter if there ain't another car around for fifty miles, he's gotta stop and stand there like a goddam fool until the light turns green and tells him he can go again. Who wants to live in a country like that? Who wants to bring children into a world where that kind of crap goes on?*

A horn sounded, jarring Keller abruptly from the early days of the twentieth century to the early days of the twenty-first. The light, he noted, had turned from red to green, and the fellow in the SUV just behind him felt a need to bring this fact to Keller's attention. Keller, without feeling much in the way of actual irritation or anger, allowed himself a moment of imagination in which he shifted into park, engaged the emergency brake, got out of the car and walked back to the SUV, whose driver would already have begun to regret leaning on the horn. Even as the man (pig-faced and jowly in Keller's fantasy) was reaching for the button to lock the door, Keller was opening the door, taking hold of the man (sweating now, stammering, making simultaneous threats and excuses) by the shirtfront, yanking him out of the car, sending him sprawling on the pavement. Then, while the man's child (no, make it his wife, a fat shrew with dyed hair and rheumy eyes) watched in horror, Keller bent from the waist and dispatched the man with a movement learned from the Burmese master U Minh U, one in which the adept's hands barely appeared to touch the subject, but death, while indescribably painful, was virtually instantaneous.

Keller, satisfied by the fantasy, drove on. Behind him, the driver of the SUV—an unaccompanied young woman, Keller now noted, her hair secured by a bandana, and a sack of groceries on the seat beside her—followed along for half a block, then turned off to the right, seemingly unaware of her close brush with death.

How you do go on, he thought.

It was all the damned driving. Before everything went to hell, he wouldn't have had to drive clear across the country. He'd have taken a cab to JFK and caught a flight to Phoenix, where he'd have rented a car, driven it around for the day or two it would take to do the job, then turned it in and flown back to New York. In and out, case closed, and he could get on with his life.

And leave no traces behind, either. They made you show ID to get on the plane, they'd been doing that for a few years now, but it didn't have to be terribly good ID. Now they all but fingerprinted you before they let you board, and they went through your checked baggage and gave your carry-on luggage a lethal dose of radiation. God help you if you had a nail clipper on your key ring.

He hadn't flown at all since the new security procedures had gone into effect, and he didn't know that he'd ever get on a plane again. Business travel was greatly reduced, he'd read, and he could understand why. A business traveler would rather hop in his car and drive five hundred miles than get to the airport two hours early and go through all the hassles the new system imposed. It was bad enough if your business consisted of meeting with groups of salesmen and giving them pep talks. If you were in Keller's line of work, well, it was out of the question.

Keller rarely traveled other than for business, but sometimes he'd go somewhere for a stamp auction, or because it was the middle of a New York winter and he felt the urge to lie in the sun somewhere. He supposed he could still fly on such occasions, showing valid ID and clipping his nails before departure, but would he want to? Would it still be pleasure travel if you had to go through all that in order to get there?

He felt like that imagined motorist, griping about red lights. *Hell, if that's what they're gonna make me do, I'll just walk. Or I'll stay home. That'll show them!*

It all changed, of course, on a September morning, when a pair of airliners flew into the twin towers of the World Trade Center. Keller, who lived on First Avenue not far from the UN building, had not been home at the time. He was in Miami, where he had already spent a week, getting ready to kill a man named Rubén Olivares. Olivares was a Cuban, and an important figure in one of the Cuban exile groups, but Keller wasn't sure that was why someone had been willing to spend a substantial amount of money to have him killed. It was possible, certainly, that he was a thorn in the side of the Castro government, and that someone had decided it would be safer and more cost-effective to hire the work done than to send a team of agents from Havana. It was also possible that Olivares had turned out to be a spy for Havana, and it was his fellow exiles who had it in for him.

Then too, he might be sleeping with the wrong person's wife, or muscling in on the wrong person's drug trade. With a little investigative work, Keller might have managed to find out who wanted Olivares dead, and why, but he'd long since determined that such considerations were none of his business. What difference did it make? He had a job to do, and all he had to do was do it.

Monday night, he'd followed Olivares around, watched him eat dinner at a steakhouse in Coral Gables, then tagged along when Olivares and two of his dinner companions hit a couple of titty bars in Miami Beach. Olivares left with one of the dancers, and Keller tailed him to the woman's apartment and waited for him to come out. After an hour and a half, Keller decided the man was spending the night. Keller, who'd watched lights go on and off in the apartment house, was reasonably certain he knew which apartment the couple was occupying, and didn't think it would prove difficult to get into the building. He thought about going in and getting it over with. It was too late to catch a flight to New York, it was the middle of the night, but he could get the work done and stop at his motel to shower and collect his luggage, then go straight to the airport and catch an early morning flight to New York.

Or he could sleep late and fly home sometime in the early afternoon. Several airlines flew from New York to Florida, and there were flights all day long. Miami International was not his favorite airport—it was not anybody's favorite airport—but he could skip it if he wanted, turning in his rental car at Fort Lauderdale or West Palm Beach and flying home from there.

No end of options, once the work was done.

But he'd have to kill the woman, the topless dancer.

He'd do that if he had to, but he didn't like the idea of killing people just because they were in the way. A higher body count drew more police and media attention, but that wasn't it, nor was the notion of slaughtering the innocent. How did he know the woman was innocent? For that matter, who was to say Olivares was guilty of anything?

Later, when he thought about it, it seemed to him that the deciding factor was purely physical. He'd slept poorly the night before, rising early and spending the whole day driving around unfamiliar streets. He was tired, and he didn't much feel like forcing a door and climbing a flight of stairs and killing one person, let alone two. And suppose she had a roommate, and suppose the roommate had a boyfriend, and—

He went back to his motel, took a long hot shower, and went to bed.

When he woke up he didn't turn on the TV, but went across the street to the place where he'd been having his breakfast every morning. He walked in the door and saw that something was different. They had a television set on the back counter, and everybody was staring at it. He watched for a few minutes, then picked up a container of coffee and took it back to his room. He sat in front of his own TV and watched the same scenes, over and over and over.

If he'd done his work the night before, he realized, he might have been in the air when it happened. Or maybe not, because he'd probably have decided to get some sleep instead, so he'd be right where he was, in his motel room, watching the plane fly into the building. The only certain difference was that Rubén Olivares, who as things stood was probably watching the same footage everybody else in America was watching (except that he might well be watching it on a Spanish-language station)—well, Olivares wouldn't be watching TV. Nor would he be on it. A garden-variety Miami homicide wasn't worth airtime on a day like this, not even if the deceased was of some importance in the Cuban exile community, not even if he'd been murdered in the apartment of a topless dancer, with her own death a part of the package. A newsworthy item any other day, but not on this day. There was only one sort of news today, one topic with endless permutations, and Keller watched it all day long.

It was Wednesday before it even occurred to him to call Dot, and late Thursday before he finally got a call through to her in White Plains. "I've been wondering about you, Keller," she said. "There are all these planes on the ground in Newfoundland, they were in the air when it happened and got rerouted there, and God knows when they're gonna let them come home. I had the feeling you might be there."

"In Newfoundland?"

"The local people are taking the stranded passengers into their homes," she said. "Making them welcome, giving them cups of beef bouillon and ostrich sandwiches, and—"

"Ostrich sandwiches?"

"Whatever. I just pictured you there, Keller, making the best of a bad situation, which I guess is what you're doing in Miami. God knows when they're going to let you fly home. Have you got a car?"

"A rental."

"Well, hang on to it," she said. "Don't give it back, because the car rental agencies are emptied out, with so many people stranded and trying to drive home. Maybe that's what you ought to do."

"I was thinking about it," he said. "But I was also thinking about, you know. The guy."

"Oh, him."

"I don't want to say his name, but—"

"No, don't."

"The thing is, he's still, uh . . ."

"Doing what he always did."

"Right."

"Instead of doing like John Brown."

"Huh?"

"Or John Brown's body," Dot said. "Moldering in the grave, as I recall."

"Whatever *moldering* means."

"We can probably guess, Keller, if we put our minds to it. You're wondering is it still on, right?"

"It seems ridiculous even thinking about it," he said. "But on the other hand—"

"On the other hand," she said, "they sent half the money. I'd just as soon not have to give it back."

"No."

"In fact," she said, "I'd just as soon have them send the other half. If they're the ones to call it off, we keep what they sent. And if they say it's still on, well, you're already in Miami, aren't you? Sit tight, Keller, while I make a phone call."

Whoever had wanted Olivares dead had not changed his mind as a result of several thousand deaths fifteen hundred miles away. Keller, thinking about it, couldn't see why he should be any less sanguine about the prospect of killing Olivares than he had been Monday night. On the television news, there was a certain amount of talk about the possible positive effects of the tragedy. New Yorkers, someone suggested, would be brought closer together, aware as never before of the bonds created by their common humanity.

Did Keller feel a bond with Rubén Olivares of which he'd been previously unaware? He thought about it and decided he did not. If anything, he was faintly aware of a grudging resentment against the man. If Olivares had spent less time over dinner and hurried through the foreplay of the titty bar, if he'd gone directly to the topless dancer's apartment and left the premises in the throes of post-coital bliss, Keller could have taken him out in time to catch the last flight back to the city. He might have been in his own apartment when the attack came.

And what earthly difference would that have made? None, he

had to concede. He'd have watched the hideous drama unfold on his own television set, just as he'd watched on the motel's unit, and he'd have been no more capable of influencing events whatever set he watched.

Olivares, with his steak dinners and topless dancers, made a poor surrogate for the heroic cops and firemen, the doomed office workers. He was, Keller conceded, a fellow member of the human race. If all men were brothers, a possibility Keller, an only child, was willing to entertain, well, brothers had been killing one another for a good deal longer than Keller had been on the job. If Olivares was Abel, Keller was willing to be Cain.

If nothing else, he was grateful for something to do.

And Olivares made it easy. All over America, people were writing checks and inundating blood banks, trying to do something for the victims in New York. Cops and firemen and ordinary citizens were piling into cars and heading north and east, eager to join in the rescue efforts. Olivares, on the other hand, went on leading his life of self-indulgence, going to an office in the morning, making a circuit of bars and restaurants in the afternoon and early evening, and finishing up with rum drinks in a room full of bare breasts.

Keller tagged him for three days and three nights, and by the third night he'd decided not to be squeamish about the topless dancer. He waited outside the titty bar, until a call of nature led him into the bar, past Olivares's table (where the man was chatting up three silicone-enhanced young ladies) and on to the men's room. Standing at the urinal, Keller wondered what he'd do if the Cuban took all three of them home.

He washed his hands, left the restroom, and saw Olivares counting out bills to settle his tab. All three women were still at the table, and playing up to him, one clutching his arm and leaning her breasts against it, the others just as coquettish. Keller, who'd been ready to sacrifice one bystander, found himself drawing the line at three.

But wait—Olivares was on his feet, his body language suggesting he was excusing himself for a moment. And yes, he was on his way to the men's room, clearly aware of the disadvantage of attempting a night of love on a full bladder.

Keller slipped into the room ahead of him, ducked into an empty stall. There was an elderly gentleman at the urinal, talking soothingly in Spanish to himself, or perhaps to his prostate. Olivares entered the room, stood at the adjoining urinal, and began chattering in Spanish to the older man, who spoke slow sad sentences in response.

Shortly after arriving in Miami, Keller had gotten hold of a gun, a .22-caliber revolver. It was a small gun with a short barrel, and fit easily in his pocket. He took it out now, wondering if the noise would carry.

If the older gentleman left first, Keller might not need the gun. But if Olivares finished first, Keller couldn't let him leave, and would have to do them both, and that would mean using the gun, and a minimum of two shots. He watched them over the top of the stall, wishing that something would happen before some other drunken voyeur felt a need to pee. Then the older man finished up, tucked himself in, and headed for the door.

And paused at the threshold, returning to wash his hands, and saying something to Olivares, who laughed heartily at it, whatever it was. Keller, who'd returned the gun to his pocket, took it out again, and replaced it a moment later when the older gentleman left. Olivares waited until the door closed after him, then produced a little blue glass bottle and a tiny spoon. He treated each of his cavernous nostrils to two quick hits of what Keller could only presume to be cocaine, then returned the bottle and spoon to his pocket and turned to face the sink.

Keller burst out of the stall. Olivares, washing his hands, evidently couldn't hear him with the water running; in any event he didn't react before Keller reached him, one hand cupping his jowly chin, the other taking hold of his greasy mop of hair. Keller had never studied the martial arts, not even from a Burmese with an improbable name, but he'd been doing this sort of thing long enough to have learned a trick or two. He broke Olivares's neck and was dragging him across the floor to the stall he'd just vacated when, damn it to hell, the door burst open and a little man in shirtsleeves got halfway to the urinal before he suddenly realized what he'd just seen. His eyes widened, his jaw dropped, and Keller got him before he could make a sound.

The little man's bladder, unable to relieve itself in life, could not be denied in death. Olivares, having emptied his bladder in his last moments of life, voided his bowels. The men's room, no garden spot to begin with, stank to the heavens. Keller stuffed both bodies into one stall and got out of there in a hurry, before some other son of a bitch could rush in and join the party.

Half an hour later he was heading north on I-95. Somewhere north of Stuart he stopped for gas, and in the men's room—empty, spotless, smelling of nothing but pine-scented disinfectant—he put his hands against the smooth white tiles and vomited. Hours later, at a rest area just across the Georgia line, he did so again.

He couldn't blame it on the killing. It had been a bad idea, lurking in the men's room. The traffic was too heavy, with all those drinkers and cocaine-sniffers. The stench of the corpses he'd left there, on top of the reek that had permeated the room to start with, could well have turned his stomach, but it would have done so then, not a hundred miles away when it no longer existed outside of his memory.

Some members of his profession, he knew, typically threw up after a piece of work, just as some veteran actors never failed to vomit before a performance. Keller had known a man once, a cheerfully cold-blooded little murderer with dainty little-girl wrists and a way of holding a cigarette between his thumb and forefinger. The man would chatter about his work, excuse himself, throw up discreetly into a basin, and resume his conversation in midsentence.

A shrink would probably argue that the body was expressing a revulsion which the mind was unwilling to acknowledge, and that sounded about right to Keller. But it didn't apply to him, because he'd never been one for puking. Even early on, when he was new to the game and hadn't found ways to deal with it, his stomach had remained serene.

This particular incident had been unpleasant, even chaotic, but he could if pressed recall others that had been worse.

But there was a more conclusive argument, it seemed to him. Yes, he'd thrown up outside of Stuart, and again in Georgia, and he'd very likely do so a few more times before he reached New York. But it hadn't begun with the killings.

He'd thrown up every couple of hours ever since he sat in front of his television set and watched the towers fall.

A week or so after he got back, there was a message on his answering machine. Dot, wanting him to call. He checked his watch, decided it was too early. He made himself a cup of coffee, and when he'd finished it he dialed the number in White Plains.

"Keller," she said. "When you didn't call back, I figured you were out late. And now you're up early."

"Well," he said.

"Why don't you get on a train, Keller? My eyes are sore, and I figure you're a sight for them."

"What's the matter with your eyes?"

"Nothing," she said. "I was trying to express myself in an original fashion, and it's a mistake I won't make again in a hurry. Come see me, why don't you?"

"Now?"

"Why not?"

"I'm beat," he said. "I was up all night, I need to get to sleep."

"What were you . . . never mind, I don't need to know. All right, I'll tell you what. Sleep all you want and come out for dinner. I'll order something from the Chinese. Keller? You're not answering me."

"I'll come out sometime this afternoon," he said.

He went to bed, and early that afternoon he caught a train to White Plains and a cab from the station. She was on the porch of the big old Victorian on Taunton Place, with a pitcher of iced tea and two glasses on the tin-topped table. "Look," she said, pointing to the lawn. "I swear the trees are dropping their leaves earlier than usual this year. What's it like in New York?"

"I haven't really been paying attention."

"There was a kid who used to come around to rake them, but I guess he must have gone to college or something. What happens if you don't rake the leaves, Keller? You happen to know?"

He didn't.

"And you're not hugely interested, I can see that. There's something different about you, Keller, and I've got a horrible feeling I know what it is. You're not in love, are you?"

"In love?"

"Well, are you? Out all night, and then when you get home all you can do is sleep. Who's the lucky girl, Keller?"

He shook his head. "No girl," he said. "I've been working nights."

"Working? What the hell do you mean, working?"

He let her drag it out of him. A day or two after he got back to the city and turned in his rental car, he'd heard something on the news and went to one of the Hudson River piers, where they were enlisting volunteers to serve food for the rescue workers at Ground Zero. Around ten every evening they'd all get together at the pier, then sail down the river and board another ship anchored near the site. Top chefs supplied the food, and Keller and his fellows dished it out to men who'd worked up prodigious appetites laboring at the smoldering wreckage.

"My God," Dot said. "Keller, I'm trying to picture this. You stand there with a big spoon and fill their plates for them? Do you wear an apron?"

"Everybody wears an apron."

"I bet you look cute in yours. I don't mean to make fun, Keller. What you're doing's a good thing, and of course you'd wear an apron. You wouldn't want to get marinara sauce all over your shirt. But it seems strange to me, that's all."

"It's something to do," he said.

"It's heroic."

He shook his head. "There's nothing heroic about it. It's like working in a diner, dishing out food. The men we feed, they work long shifts doing hard physical work and breathing in all that smoke. That's heroic, if anything is. Though I'm not sure there's any point to it."

"What do you mean?"

"Well, they call them rescue workers," he said, "but they're not rescuing anybody, because there's nobody to rescue. Everybody's dead."

She said something in response but he didn't hear it. "It's the same as with the blood," he said. "The first day, everybody mobbed the hospitals, donating blood for the wounded. But it turned out there weren't any wounded. People either got out of the buildings or they didn't. If they got out, they were okay. If they didn't, they're dead. All that blood people donated? They've been throwing it out."

"It seems like a waste."

"It's all a waste," he said, and frowned. "Anyway, that's what I do every night. I dish out food, and they try to rescue dead people. That way we all keep busy."

"The longer I know you," Dot said, "the more I realize I don't."

"Don't what?"

"Know you, Keller. You never cease to amaze me. Somehow I never pictured you as Florence Nightingale."

"I'm not nursing anybody. All I do is feed them."

"Betty Crocker, then. Either way, it seems like a strange role for a sociopath."

"You think I'm a sociopath?"

"Well, isn't that part of the job description, Keller? You're a hit man, a contract killer. You leave town and kill strangers and get paid for it. How can you do that without being a sociopath?"

He thought about it.

"Look," she said, "I didn't mean to bring it up. It's just a word, and who even knows what it means? Let's talk about something else, like why I called you and got you to come out here."

"Okay."

"Actually," she said, "there's two reasons. First of all, you've got money coming. Miami, remember?"

"Oh, right."

She handed him an envelope. "I thought you'd want this," she said, "although it couldn't have been weighing on your mind, because you never asked about it."

"I hardly thought about it."

"Well, why would you want to think about blood money while you were busy doing good works? But you can probably find a use for it."

"No question."

"You can always buy stamps with it. For your collection."

"Sure."

"It must be quite a collection by now."

"It's coming along."

"I'll bet it is. The other reason I called, Keller, is somebody called me."

"Oh?"

She poured herself some more iced tea, took a sip. "There's work," she said. "If you want it. In Portland, something to do with labor unions."

"Which Portland?"

"You know," she said, "I keep forgetting there's one in Maine, but there is, and I suppose they've got their share of labor problems there, too. But this is Portland, Oregon. As a matter of fact, it's Beaverton, but I think it's a suburb. The area code's the same as Portland."

"Clear across the country," he said.

"Just a few hours in a plane."

They looked at each other. "I can remember," he said, "when all you did was step up to the counter and tell them where you wanted to go. You counted out bills, and they were perfectly happy to be paid in cash. You had to give them a name, but you could make it up on the spot, and the only way they asked for identification was if you tried to pay them by check."

"The world's a different place now, Keller."

"They didn't even have metal detectors," he remembered, "or scanners. Then they brought in metal detectors, but the early ones didn't work all the way down to the ground. I knew a man who used to stick a gun into his sock and walk right onto the plane with it. If they ever caught him at it, I never heard about it."

"I suppose you could take a train."

"Or a clipper ship," he said. "Around the Horn."

"What's the matter with the Panama Canal? Metal detectors?" She finished the tea in her glass, heaved a sigh. "I think you answered my question. I'll tell Portland we have to pass."

After dinner she gave him a lift to the station and joined him on the platform to wait for his train. He broke the silence to ask her if she really thought he was a sociopath.

"Keller," she said, "it was just an idle remark, and I didn't mean anything by it. Anyway, I'm no psychologist. I'm not even sure what the word means."

"Someone who lacks a sense of right and wrong," he said. "He understands the difference but doesn't see how it applies to him personally. He lacks empathy, doesn't have any feeling for other people."

She considered the matter. "It doesn't sound like you," she said, "except when you're working. Is it possible to be a part-time sociopath?"

"I don't think so. I've done some reading on the subject. Case histories, that sort of thing. The sociopaths they write about, almost all of them have the same three things in their childhood background. Setting fires, torturing animals, and wetting the bed."

"You know, I heard that somewhere. Some TV program about FBI profilers and serial killers. Do you remember your childhood, Keller?"

"Most of it," he said. "I knew a woman once who claimed she could remember being born. I don't go back that far, and some of it's spotty, but I remember it pretty well. And I didn't do any of those three things. Torture animals? God, I loved animals. I told you about the dog I had."

"Nelson. No, sorry, that was the one you had a couple of years ago. You told me the name of the other one, but I can't remember it."

"Soldier."

"Soldier, right."

"I loved that dog," he said. "And I had other pets from time to time, the ways kids do. Goldfish, baby turtles. They all died."

"They always do, don't they?"

"I suppose so. I used to cry."

"When they died."

"When I was little. When I got older I took it more in stride, but it still made me sad. But torture them?"

"How about fires?"

"You know," he said, "when you talked about the leaves, and what happens if you don't rake them, I remembered raking leaves when I was a kid. It was one of the things I did to make money."

"You want to make twenty bucks here and now, there's a rake in the garage."

"What we used to do," he remembered, "was rake them into a pile at the curb, and then burn them. It's illegal nowadays, because of fire laws and air pollution, but back then it's what you were supposed to do."

"It was nice, the smell of burning leaves on the autumn air."

"And it was satisfying," he said. "You raked them up and put a match to them and they were gone. Those were the only fires I remember setting."

"I'd say you're oh-for-two. How'd you do at wetting the bed?"

"I never did, as far as I can recall."

"Oh-for-three. Keller, you're about as much of a sociopath as Albert Schweitzer. But if that's the case, how come you do what you do? Never mind, here's your train. Have fun dishing out the lasagna tonight. And don't torture any animals, you hear?"

Two weeks later he picked up the phone on his own and told her not to turn down jobs automatically. "Now you tell me," she said. "You at home? Don't go anywhere, I'll make a call and get back to you."

He sat by the phone, and picked it up when it rang. "I was afraid they'd found somebody by now," she said, "but we're in luck, if you want to call it that. They're sending us something by Airborne Express, which always sounds to me like paratroopers ready for battle. They swear I'll have it by nine tomorrow morning, but you'll just be getting home around then, won't you? Do you figure you can make the 2:04 from Grand Central? I'll pick you up at the station."

"There's a 10:08," he said. "Gets to White Plains a few minutes before eleven. If you're not there I'll figure you had to wait for the paratroopers, and I'll get a cab."

It was a cold, dreary day, with enough rain so that she needed to use the windshield wipers but not enough to keep the blades from squeaking. She put him at the kitchen table, poured him a cup of coffee, and let him read the notes she'd made and study the Polaroids that had come in the Airborne Express envelope, along with the initial payment in cash. He held up one of the pictures, which showed a man in his seventies, with a round face and a small white mustache, holding up a golf club as if in the hope that someone would take it from him.

He said the fellow didn't look much like a labor leader, and Dot shook her head. "That was Portland," she said. "This is Phoenix. Well, Scottsdale, and I bet it's nicer there today than it is here. Nicer than Portland, too, because I understand it always rains there. In Portland, I mean. It never rains in Scottsdale. I don't know what's the matter with me, I'm starting to sound like the Weather Channel. You could fly, you know. Not all the way, but to Denver, say."

"Maybe."

She tapped the photo with her fingernail. "Now according to them," she said, "the man's not expecting anything, and not taking any security precautions. Other hand, his life is a security precaution. He lives in a gated community."

"Sundowner Estates, it says here."

"There's an eighteen-hole golf course, with individual homes ranged around it. And each of them has a state-of-the-art home security system, but the only thing that ever triggers an alarm is when some clown hooks his tee shot through your living room picture window, because the only way into the compound is past a guard. No metal detector, and they don't confiscate your nail clippers, but you have to belong there for him to let you in."

"Does Mr. Egmont ever leave the property?"

"He plays golf every day. Unless it rains, and we've already established that it never does. He generally eats lunch at the clubhouse, they've got their own restaurant. He has a housekeeper who comes in a couple of times a week—they know her at the guard shack, I guess. Aside from that, he's all alone in his house. He probably gets invited out to dinner a lot. He's unattached, and there's always six women for every man in those Geezer Leisure communities. You're staring at his picture, and I bet I know why. He looks familiar, doesn't he?"

"Yes, and I can't think why."

"You ever play Monopoly?"

"By God, that's it," he said. "He looks like the drawing of the banker in Monopoly."

"It's the mustache," she said, "and the round face. Don't forget to pass Go, Keller. And collect two hundred dollars."

She drove him back to the train station, and because of the rain they waited in her car instead of on the platform. He said he'd pretty much stopped working on the food ship. She said she hadn't figured it was something he'd be doing for the rest of his life.

"They changed it," he said. "The Red Cross took it over. They do this all the time, their specialty's disaster relief, and they're pros at it, but it transformed the whole thing from a spontaneous New York affair into something impersonal. I mean, when we started we had name chefs knocking themselves out to feed these guys something they'd enjoy eating, and then the Red Cross took over and we were filling their plates with macaroni and cheese and chipped beef on toast. Overnight we went from Bobby Flay to Chef Boy-Ar-Dee."

"Took the joy out of it, did it?"

"Well, would you like to spend ten hours shifting scrap metal and collecting body parts and then tuck into something you'd expect to find in an army chow line? I got so I couldn't look them in the eye when I ladled the slop onto their plates. I skipped a night and felt guilty about it, and I went in the next night and felt worse, and I haven't been back since."

"You were probably ready to give it up, Keller."

"I don't know. I still felt good doing it, until the Red Cross showed up."

"But that's why you were there," she said. "To feel good."

"To help out."

She shook her head. "You felt good because you were helping out," she said, "but you kept coming back and doing it because it made you feel good."

"Well, I suppose so."

"I'm not impugning your motive, Keller. You're still a hero, as far as I'm concerned. All I'm saying is that volunteerism only goes so far. When it stops feeling good, it tends to run out of steam. That's when you need the professionals. They do their job because it's their job, and it doesn't matter whether they feel good about it or not. They buckle down and get it done. It may be macaroni and cheese, and the cheese may be Velveeta, but nobody winds up holding an empty plate. You see what I mean?"

"I guess so," Keller said.

Back in the city, he called one of the airlines, thinking he'd take Dot's suggestion and fly to Denver. He worked his way through their automated answering system, pressing numbers when prompted, and wound up on hold, because all of their agents were busy serving other customers. The music they played to pass the time was bad enough all by itself, but they kept interrupting it every fifteen seconds to tell him how much better off he'd be using their Web site. After a few minutes of this he called Hertz, and the phone was answered right away by a human being.

He picked up a Ford Taurus first thing the next morning and beat the rush hour traffic through the tunnel and onto the New Jersey Turnpike. He'd rented the car under his own name, showing his own driver's license and using his own American Express card, but he had a cloned card in another name that Dot had provided, and he used it in the motels where he stopped along the way.

It took him four long days to drive to Tucson. He would drive until he was hungry, or the car needed gas, or he needed a restroom, then get behind the wheel again and drive some more. When he got tired he'd find a motel and register under the name on his fake credit card, take a shower, watch a little TV, and go to bed. He'd sleep until he woke up, and then he'd take another shower and get dressed and look for someplace to have breakfast. And so on.

While he drove he played the radio until he couldn't stand it, then turned it off until he couldn't stand the silence. By the third day the solitude was getting to him, and he couldn't figure out why. He was used to being alone, he lived his whole life alone, and he certainly never had or wanted company while he was working. He seemed to want it now, though, and at one point turned the car's radio to a talk show on a clear-channel station in Omaha. People called in and disagreed with the host, or a previous caller, or some schoolteacher who'd given them a hard time in the fifth grade. Gun control was the announced topic for the day, but the real theme, as far as Keller could tell, was resentment, and there was plenty of it to go around.

Keller listened, fascinated at first, and before very long he reached the point where he couldn't stand another minute of it. If he'd had a gun handy, he might have put a bullet in the radio, but all he did was switch it off.

The last thing he wanted, it turned out, was someone talking to him. He had the thought, and realized a moment later that he'd not only thought it but had actually spoken the words aloud. He was talking to himself, and wondered—wondered in silence, thank God—if this was something new. It was like snoring, he thought. If you slept alone, how would you know if you did it? You wouldn't, not unless you snored so loudly that you woke yourself up.

He started to reach for the radio, stopped himself before he could turn it on again. He checked the speedometer, saw that the cruise control was keeping the car at three miles an hour over the posted speed limit. Without cruise control you found yourself going faster or slower than you wanted to, wasting time or risking a ticket. With it, you didn't have to think about how fast you were going. The car did the thinking for you.

The next step, he thought, would be steering control. You got in the car, keyed the ignition, set the controls, and leaned back and closed your eyes. The car followed the turns in the road, and a system of sensors worked the brake when another car loomed in front of you, swung out to pass when such action was warranted, and knew to take the next exit when the gas gauge dropped below a certain level.

It sounded like science fiction, but no less so in Keller's boyhood than cruise control, or auto-response telephone answering systems, or a good ninety-five percent of the things he nowadays took for granted. Keller didn't doubt for a minute that right this minute some bright young man in Detroit or Osaka or Bremen was working on steering control. There'd be some spectacular head-on collisions before they got the bugs out of the system, but before long every car would have it, and the accident rate would plummet and the state troopers wouldn't have anybody to give tickets to, and everybody would be crazy about technology's newest breakthrough, except for a handful of cranks in England who were convinced you had more control and got better mileage the old-fashioned way.

Meanwhile, Keller kept both hands on the steering wheel.

Sundowner Estates, home of William Wallis Egmont, was in Scottsdale, an upscale suburb of Phoenix. Tucson, a couple hundred miles to the east, was as close as Keller wanted to bring the Taurus. He followed the signs to the airport and left the car in long-term parking. Over the years he'd left other cars in long-term parking, but they'd been other men's cars, with their owners stuffed in the trunk, and Keller, having no need to find the cars again, had gotten rid of the claim checks at the first opportunity. This time was different, and he found a place in his wallet for the check the gate attendant had supplied, and noted the lot section and the number of the parking space.

He went into the terminal, found the car rental counters, and picked up a Toyota Camry from Avis, using his fake credit card and a matching Pennsylvania driver's license. It took him a few minutes to figure out the cruise control. That was the trouble with renting cars, you had to learn a new system with every car, from lights and windshield wipers to cruise control and seat adjustment. Maybe he should have gone to the Hertz counter and picked up another Taurus. Was there an advantage in driving the same model car throughout? Was there a disadvantage that offset it, and was some intuitive recognition of that disadvantage what had led him to the Avis counter?

"You're thinking too much," he said, and realized he'd spoken the words aloud. He shook his head, not so much annoyed as amused, and a few miles down the road realized that what he wanted, what he'd been wanting all along, was not someone to talk to him but someone to listen.

A little ways past an exit ramp, a kid with a duffel bag had his thumb out, trying to hitch a ride. For the first time that he could recall, Keller had the impulse to stop for him. It was just a passing thought; if he'd had his foot on the gas, he'd have barely begun to ease up on the gas pedal before he'd overruled the thought and sped onward. Since he was running on cruise control, his foot didn't even move, and the hitchhiker slipped out of sight in the rearview mirror, unaware what a narrow escape he'd just had.

Because the only reason to pick him up was for someone to talk to, and Keller would have told him everything. And, once he'd done that, what choice would he have?

Keller could picture the kid, listening wide-eyed to everything Keller had to tell him. He pictured himself, his soul unburdened, grateful to the youth for listening, but compelled by circumstance to cover his tracks. He imagined the car gliding to a stop, imagined the brief struggle, imagined the body left in a roadside ditch, the Camry heading west at a thoughtful three miles an hour above the speed limit.

The motel Keller picked was an independent mom-and-pop operation in Tempe, which was another suburb of Phoenix. He counted out cash and paid a week in advance, plus a twenty-dollar deposit for phone calls. He didn't plan to make any calls, but if he needed to use the phone he wanted it to work.

He registered as David Miller of San Francisco, and fabricated an address and zip code. You were supposed to include your license plate number, and he mixed up a couple of digits and put CA for the state instead of AZ. It was hardly worth the trouble, nobody was going to look at the registration card, but there were certain things he did out of habit, and this was one of them.

He always traveled light, never took along more than a small carry-on bag with a shirt or two and a couple changes of socks and underwear. That made sense when you were flying, and less sense when you had a car with an empty trunk and back seat at your disposal. By the time he got to Phoenix, he'd run through his socks and underwear. He picked up two three-packs of briefs and a six-pack of socks at a strip mall, and was looking for a trash bin for his dirty clothes when he spotted a Goodwill Industries collection box. He felt good dropping his soiled socks and underwear in the box, though not quite as good as he'd felt dishing out designer food to the smoke-stained rescue workers at Ground Zero.

Back at his motel, he called Dot on the prepaid cell phone he'd picked up on 23rd Street. He'd paid cash for it, and hadn't even been asked his name, so as far as he could tell it was completely untraceable. At best someone could identify calls made from it as originating with a phone manufactured in Finland and sold at Radio Shack. Even if they managed to pin down the specific Radio Shack outlet, so what? There was nothing to tie it to Keller, or to Phoenix.

On the other hand, cell phone communications were about as secure as shouting. Any number of listening devices could pick up your conversation, and whatever you said was very likely being heard by half a dozen people on their car radios and one old fart who was catching every word on the fillings in his teeth. That didn't bother Keller, who figured every phone was tapped, and acted accordingly.

He phoned Dot, and the phone rang seven or eight times, and he broke the connection. She was probably out, he decided, or in the shower. Or had he misdialed? Always a chance, he thought, and pressed Redial, then caught himself and realized that, if he had in fact misdialed, redialing would just repeat the mistake. He broke the connection again in midring and punched in the number afresh, and this time he got a busy signal.

He tried it again, got another busy signal, frowned, waited, and tried again. It had barely begun to ring when she picked up, barking "Yes?" into the phone, and somehow fitting a full measure of irritation into the single syllable.

"It's me," he said.

"What a surprise."

"Is something wrong?"

"I had somebody at the door," she said, "and the teakettle was whistling, and I finally got to the phone and picked it up in time to listen to the dial tone."

"I let it ring a long time."

"That's nice. So I put it down and turned away, and it rang again, and I picked it up in the middle of the first ring, and I was just in time to hear you hang up."

He explained about pressing redial, and realizing that wouldn't work.

"Except it worked just fine," she said, "since you hadn't misdialed in the first place. I figured it had to be you, so I pressed star sixty-nine. But whatever phone you're on, star sixty-nine doesn't work. I got one of those weird tones and a canned message saying return calls to your number were blocked."

"It's a cell phone."

"Say no more. Hello? Where'd you go?"

"I'm here. You said *Say no more*, and . . ."

"It's an expression. Tell me it's all wrapped up and you're heading for home."

"I just got here."

"That's what I was afraid of. How's the weather?"

"Hot."

"Not here. They say it might snow, but then again it might not. You're just calling to check in, right?"

"Right."

"Well, it's good to hear your voice, and I'd love to chat, but you're on a cell phone."

"Right."

"Call anytime," she said. "It's always a treat to hear from you."

Keller didn't know the population or acreage of Sundowner Estates, although he had a hunch neither figure would be hard to come by. But what good would the information do him? The compound was large enough to contain a full-size eighteen-hole golf course, and enough homes adjacent to it to support the operation.

And there was a ten-foot adobe wall encircling the entire affair. Keller supposed it was easier to sell homes if you called it Sundowner Estates, but Fort Apache would have better conveyed the stockadelike feel of the place.

He drove around the compound a couple of times, establishing that there were in fact two gates, one at the east and the other not quite opposite, at the southwest corner. He parked where he could keep an eye on the southwest gate, and couldn't tell much beyond the fact that every vehicle entering or leaving the compound had to stop for some sort of exchange with the uniformed guard. Maybe you flashed a pass at him, maybe he called to make sure you were expected, maybe they wanted a thumbprint and a semen sample. No way to tell, not from where Keller was watching, but he was pretty sure he couldn't just drive up and bluff his way through. People who willingly lived behind a thick wall almost twice their own height probably expected a high level of security, and a guard who failed to provide that would be looking for a new job.

He drove back to his motel, sat in front of the TV and watched a special on the Discovery Channel about scuba diving at Australia's Great Barrier Reef. Keller didn't think it looked like something he wanted to do. He'd tried snorkeling once, on a vacation in Aruba, and kept having to stop because he was getting water in his snorkel, and under his mask. And he hadn't been able to see much of anything, anyhow.

The divers on the Discovery Channel were having much better luck, and there were plenty of colorful fish for them (and Keller) to look at. After fifteen minutes, though, he'd seen as much as he wanted to, and was ready to change the channel. It seemed like a lot of trouble to go through, flying all the way to Australia, then getting in the water with a mask and fins. Couldn't you get pretty much the same effect staring into a fish tank at a pet shop, or a Chinese restaurant?

"I'll tell you this," the woman said. "If you do make a decision to buy at Sundowner, you won't regret it. Nobody ever has."

"That's quite a recommendation," Keller said.

"Well, it's quite an operation, Mr. Miller. I don't suppose I have to ask if you play golf."

"It's somewhere between a pastime and an addiction," he said.

"I hope you brought your clubs. Sundowner's a championship course, you know. Robert Walker Wilson designed it, and Clay Bunis was a consultant. We're in the middle of the desert, but you wouldn't know it inside the walls at Sundowner. The course is as green as a pasture in the Irish midlands."

Her name, Keller learned, was Michelle Prentice, but everyone called her Mitzi. And what about him? Did he prefer Dave or David?

That was a stumper, and Keller realized he was taking too long to answer it. "It depends," he said, finally. "I answer to either one."

"I'll bet business associates call you Dave," she said, "and really close friends call you David."

"How on earth did you know that?"

She smiled broadly, delighted to be right. "Just a guess," she said. "Just a lucky guess, David."

So they were going to be close friends, he thought. Toward that end she proceeded to tell him a few things about herself, and by the time they reached the guard shack at the east gate of Sundowner Estates, he learned that she was thirty-nine years old, that she'd divorced her rat bastard of a husband three years ago and moved out here from Frankfort, Kentucky, which happened to be the state capital, although most people would guess it was Louisville. She'd sold houses in Frankfort, so she'd picked up an Arizona Realtor's license first chance she got, and it was a lot better selling houses here than it had ever been in Kentucky, because they just about sold themselves. The entire Phoenix area was growing like a house on fire, she assured him, and she was just plain excited to be a part of it all.

At the east gate she moved her sunglasses up onto her forehead and gave the guard a big smile. "Hi, Harry," she said. "Mitzi Prentice, and this here's Mr. Miller, come for a look at the Lattimore house on Saguaro Circle."

"Miz Prentice," he said, returning her smile and nodding at Keller. He consulted a clipboard, then slipped into the shack and picked up a telephone. After a moment he emerged and told Mitzi she could go ahead. "I guess you know how to get there," he said.

"I guess I ought to," she told Keller, after they'd driven away from the entrance. "I showed the house two days ago, and he was there to let me by. But he's got his job to do, and they take it seriously, let me tell you. I know not to joke with him, or with any of them, because they won't joke back. They can't, because it might not look good on camera."

"There are security cameras running?"

"Twenty-four hours a day. You don't get in unless your name's on the list, and the camera's got a record of when you came and went, and what car you were driving, license plate number and all."

"Really."

"There are some very affluent people at Sundowner," she said, "and some of them are getting along in years. That's not to say you won't find plenty of people your age here, especially on the golf course and around the pool, but you do get some older folks, too, and they tend to be a little more concerned about security. Now just look, David. Isn't that a beautiful sight?"

She pointed out her window at the golf course, and it looked like a golf course to him. He agreed it sure looked gorgeous.

The living room of the Lattimore house had a cathedral ceiling and a walk-in fireplace. Keller thought the fireplace looked nice, but he didn't quite get it. A walk-in closet was one thing, you could walk into it and pick what you wanted to wear, but why would anybody want to walk into a fireplace?

For that matter, who'd want to hold a prayer service in the living room?

He thought of raising the point with Mitzi. She might find either question provocative, but would it fit the Serious Buyer image he was trying to project? So he asked instead what he figured were more typical questions, about heating and cooling systems and financing, good basic home-buyer questions.

There was, predictably enough, a big picture window in the living room, and it afforded the predictable view of the golf course, overlooking what Mitzi told him were the fifth green and the sixth tee. There was a man taking practice swings who might have been W. W. Egmont himself, although from this distance and angle it was hard to say one way or the other. But if the guy turned a little to his left, and if Keller could look at him not with his naked eye but through a pair of binoculars—

Or, he thought, a telescopic sight. That would be quick and easy, wouldn't it? All he had to do was buy the place and set up in the living room with a high-powered rifle, and Egmont's state-of-the-art home burglar alarm wouldn't do him a bit of good. Keller could just perch there like a vulture, and sooner or later Egmont would finish up the fifth hole by four-putting for a triple bogey, and Keller could take him right there and save the poor duffer a stroke or wait until he came even closer and teed up his ball for the sixth hole (525 yards, par 5). Keller was no great shakes as a marksman, but how hard could it be to center the crosshairs on a target and squeeze the trigger?

"I bet you're picturing yourself on that golf course right now," Mitzi said, and he grinned and told her she got that one right.

From the bedroom window in the back of the house, you could look out at a desert garden, with cacti and succulents growing in sand. The plantings, like the bright green lawn in front, were all the responsibility of the Sundowners Estates association, who took care of all maintenance. They kept it beautiful year-round, she told him, and you never had to lift a finger.

"A lot of people think they want to garden when they retire," she said, "and then they find out how much work it can be. And what happens when you want to take off for a couple of weeks in Maui? At Sundowner, you can walk out the door and know everything's going to be beautiful when you come back."

He said he could see how that would be a comfort. "I can't see the fence from here," he said. "I was wondering about that, if you'd feel like you were walled in. I mean, it's nice looking, being adobe and earth-colored and all, but it's a pretty high fence."

"Close to twelve feet," she said.

Even higher than he'd thought. He said he wondered what it would be like living next to it, and she said none of the houses were close enough to the fence for it to be a factor.

"The design was very well thought out," she said. "There's the twelve-foot fence, and then there's a big space, anywhere from ten to twenty yards, and then there's an inner fence, also of adobe, that stands about five feet tall, and there's cactus and vines in front of it for landscaping, so it looks nice and decorative."

"That's a great idea," he said. And he liked it; all he had to do was clear the first fence and follow the stretch of no-man's-land around to wherever he felt like vaulting the shorter wall. "About the taller fence, though. I mean, it's not really terribly secure, is it?"

"What makes you say that?"

"Well, I don't know. I guess it's because I'm used to the Northeast, where security's pretty up front and obvious, but it's just a plain old mud fence, isn't it? No razor wire on top, no electrified fencing. It looks as though all a person would have to do is lean a long ladder up against it and he'd be over the top in a matter of seconds."

She laid a hand on his arm. "David," she said, "you asked that very casually, but I have the sense that security's a real concern of yours."

"I have a stamp collection," he said. "It's not worth a fortune, and collections are hard to sell, but the point is I've been collecting since I was a kid and I'd hate to lose it."

"I can understand that."

"So security's a consideration, yes. And the fellow at the gate's enough to put anybody's mind at rest, but if any jerk with a ladder can just pop right over the fence—"

It was, she told him, a little more complicated than that. There was no razor or concertina wire, because that made a place look like a concentration camp, but there were sensors that set up some kind of force field, and no one could begin to climb the fence without setting off all kinds of alarms. Nor were you home free once you cleared the fence, because there were dogs that patrolled the belt of no-man's-land, Dobermans, swift and silent.

"And there's an unmarked patrol car that circles the perimeter at regular intervals twenty-four hours a day," she said, "so if they spotted you on your way to the fence with a ladder under your arm—"

"It wouldn't be me," he assured her. "I like dogs okay, but I'd just as soon not meet those Dobermans you just mentioned."

It was, he decided, a good thing he'd asked. Earlier, he'd found a place to buy an aluminum extension ladder. He could have been over the fence in a matter of seconds, just in time to keep a date with Mr. Swift and Mr. Silent.

In the Lattimore kitchen, they sat across a table topped with butcher block and Mitzi went over the fine points with him. The furniture was all included, she told him, and as he could see it was in excellent condition. He might want to make some changes, of course, as a matter of personal taste, but the place was in turnkey condition. He could buy it today and move in tomorrow.

"In a manner of speaking," she said, and touched his arm again. "Financing takes a little time, and even if you were to pay cash it would take a few days to push the paperwork through. Were you thinking in terms of cash?"

"It's always simpler," he said.

"It is, but I'm sure you wouldn't have trouble with a mortgage. The banks love to write mortgages on Sundowner properties, because the prices only go up." Her fingers encircled his wrist. "I'm not sure I should tell you this, David, but now's a particularly good time to make an offer."

"Mr. Lattimore's eager to sell?"

"Mr. Lattimore couldn't care less," she said. "About selling or anything else. It's his daughter who'd like to sell. She had an offer of ten percent under the asking price, but she'd just listed the property and she turned it down, thinking the buyer'd boost it a little, but instead the buyer went and bought something else, and that woman's been kicking herself ever since. What *I* would do, I'd offer fifteen percent under what she's asking. You might not get it for that, but the worst you'd do is get it for ten percent under, and that's a bargain in this market."

He nodded thoughtfully, and asked what happened to Lattimore. "It was very sad," she said, "although in another sense it wasn't, because he died doing what he loved."

"Playing golf," Keller guessed.

"He hit a very nice tee shot on the thirteenth hole," she said, "which is a par four with a dogleg to the right. 'That's a sweet shot,' his partner said, and Mr. Lattimore said, 'Well, I guess I can still hit one now and then, can't I?' And then he just went and dropped dead."

"If you've got to go . . ."

"That's what everyone said, David. The body was cremated, and then they had a nice nondenominational service in the clubhouse, and afterward his daughter and son-in-law rode golf carts to the sixteenth hole and put his ashes in the water hazard." She laughed involuntarily, and let go of his wrist to cover her mouth with her hand. "Pardon me for laughing, but I was thinking what somebody said. How his balls were already there, and now he could go look for them."

Her hand returned to his wrist. He looked at her, and her eyes were looking back at him. "Well," he said. "My car's at your office, so you'd better run me back there. And then I'll want to get back to where I'm staying and freshen up, but after that I'd love to take you to dinner."

"Oh, I wish," she said.

"You have plans?"

"My daughter lives with me," she said, "and I like to be home with her on school nights, and especially tonight because there's a program on television we never miss."

"I see."

"So you're on your own for dinner," she said, "but what do you and I care about dinner, David? Why don't you just take me into old Mr. Lattimore's bedroom and fuck me senseless?"

She had a nice body and used it eagerly and imaginatively. Keller, his mind on his work, had been only vaguely aware of the sexual possibilities, and had in fact surprised himself by asking her to dinner. In the Lattimore bedroom he surprised himself further.

Afterward she said, "Well, I had high expectations, but I have to say they were exceeded. Isn't it a good thing I'm busy tonight? Otherwise it'd be a couple of hours before we even got to the restaurant, and ages before we got to bed. I mean, why waste all that time?"

He tried to think of something to say, but she didn't seem to require comment. "For all those years," she said, "I was the most faithful wife since Penelope. And it's not like nobody was interested. Men used to hit on me all the time. David, I even had girls hitting on me."

"Really."

"But I was never interested, and if I was, if I felt a little itch, a little tickle, well, I just pushed it away and put it out of my mind. Because of a little thing called marriage. I'd made some vows, and I took them seriously.

"And then I found out the son of a bitch was cheating on me, and it turned out it was nothing new. On our wedding day? It was years before I knew it, but that son of a bitch got lucky with one of my bridesmaids. And over the years he was catting around all the time. Not just my friends, but my sister."

"Your sister?"

"Well, my half-sister, really. My daddy died when I was little, and my mama remarried, and that's where she came from." She told him more than he needed to know about her childhood, and he lay there with his eyes closed and let the words wash over him. He hoped there wasn't going to be a test, because he wasn't paying close attention. . . .

"So I decided to make up for lost time," she said.

He'd dozed off, and after she woke him they'd showered in separate bathrooms. Now they were dressed again, and he'd followed her into the kitchen, where she opened the refrigerator and seemed surprised to find it empty.

She closed it and turned to him and said, "When I meet someone I feel like sleeping with, well, I go ahead and do it. I mean, why wait?"

"Works for me," he said.

"The only thing I don't like to do," she said, "is mix business and pleasure. So I made sure not to commit myself until I knew you weren't going to buy this place. And you're not, are you?"

"How did you know?"

"A feeling I got, when I said how you should make an offer. Instead of trying to think how much to offer, you were looking for a way out—or at least that was what I picked up. Which was okay with me, because by then I was more interested in getting laid than in selling a house. I didn't have to tell you about a whole lot of tax advantages, and how easy it is to rent the place out during the time you spend somewhere else. It's all pretty persuasive, and I could give you that whole rap now, but you don't really want to hear it, do you?"

"I might be in the market in a little while," he said, "but you're right, I'm nowhere near ready to make an offer at the present time. I suppose it was wrong of me to drag you out here and waste your time, but—"

"Do you hear me complaining, David?"

"Well, I just wanted to see the place," he said. "So I exaggerated my interest somewhat. Whether or not I'll be interested in settling in here depends on the outcome of a couple of business matters, and it'll be a while before I know how they're going to turn out."

"Sounds interesting," she said.

"I wish I could talk about it, but you know how it is."

"You could tell me," she said, "but then you'd have to kill me. In that case, don't you say a word."

He ate dinner by himself in a Mexican restaurant that reminded him of another Mexican restaurant. He was lingering over a second cup of café con leche before he figured it out. Years ago work had taken him to Roseburg, Oregon, and before he got out of there he'd picked out a real estate agent and spent an afternoon driving around looking at houses for sale.

He hadn't gone to bed with the Oregon realtor, or even considered it, nor had he used her as a way to get information on an approach to his quarry. That man, whom the Witness Protection Program had imperfectly protected, had been all too easy to find, but Keller, who ordinarily knew well enough to keep his business and personal life separate, had somehow let himself befriend the poor bastard. Before he knew it he was having fantasies about moving to Roseburg himself, buying a house, getting a dog, settling down.

He'd looked at houses, but that was as far as he'd let it go. The night came when he got a grip on himself, and the next thing he got a grip on was the man who'd brought him there. He used a garrote, and what he got a grip on was on the guy's throat, and then it was time to go back to New York.

He remembered the Mexican café in Roseburg now. The food had been good, though he didn't suppose it was all that special, and he'd had a mild crush on the waitress, about as realistic as the whole idea of moving there. He thought of the man he'd killed, an accountant who'd become the proprietor of a quick-print shop.

You could learn the business in a couple of hours, the man had said of his new career. *You could buy the place and move in the same day,* Mitzi had said of the Lattimore house.

Patterns . . .

You could tell me, she'd said, thinking she was joking, *but then you'd have to kill me*. Oddly, in the languor that followed their lovemaking, he'd had the impulse to confide in her, to tell her what had brought him to Scottsdale.

Yeah, right.

He drove around for a while, then found his way back to his motel and surfed the TV channels without finding anything that caught his interest. He turned off the set and sat there in the dark.

He thought of calling Dot. There were things he could talk about with her, but others he couldn't, and anyway he didn't want to do any talking on a cell phone, not even an untraceable one.

He found himself thinking about the guy in Roseburg. He tried to picture him and couldn't. Early on he'd worked out a way to keep people from the past from flooding the present with their faces. You worked with their images in your mind, leached the color out of them, made the features grow dimmer, shrank the picture as if viewing it through the wrong end of a telescope. You made them grow smaller and darker and hazier until they disappeared, and if you did it correctly you forgot everything but the barest of facts about them. There was no emotional charge, no weight to them, and they became more and more difficult to recall to mind.

But now he'd bridged a gap and closed a circuit, and the man's face was there in his memory, the face of an aging chipmunk. Jesus, Keller thought, get out of my memory, will you? You've been dead for years. Leave me the hell alone.

If you were here, he told the face, I could talk to you. And you'd listen, because what the hell else could you do? You couldn't talk back, you couldn't judge me, you couldn't tell me to shut up. You're dead, so you couldn't say a goddam word.

He went outside, walked around for a while, came back in and sat on the edge of the bed. Very deliberately he set about getting rid of the man's face, washing it of color, pushing it farther and farther away, making it disappear. The process was more difficult than it had been in years, but it worked, finally, and the little man was gone to wherever the washed-out faces of dead people went. Wherever it was, Keller prayed he'd stay there.

He took a long hot shower and went to bed.

In the morning he found someplace new to have breakfast. He read the paper and had a second cup of coffee, then drove pointlessly around the perimeter of Sundowner Estates.

Back at the motel, he called Dot on his cell phone. "Here's what I've been able to come up with," he said. "I park where I can watch the entrance. Then, when some resident drives out, I follow them."

"Them?"

"Well, him or her, depending which it is. Or them, if there's more than one in the car. Sooner or later, they stop somewhere and get out of the car."

"And you take them out, and you keep doing this, and sooner or later it's the right guy."

"They get out of the car," he said, "and I hang around until nobody's watching, and I get in the trunk."

"The trunk of their car."

"If I wanted to get in the trunk of my own car," he said, "I could go do that right now. Yes, the trunk of their car."

"I get it," she said. "Their car morphs into the Trojan Chrysler. They sail back into the walled city, and you're in there, and hoping they'll open the trunk eventually and let you out."

"Car trunks have a release mechanism built in these days," he said. "So kidnap victims can escape."

"You're kidding," she said. "The auto makers added something for the benefit of the eight people a year who get stuffed into car trunks?"

"I think it's probably more than eight a year," he said, "and then there are the people, kids mostly, who get locked in accidentally. Anyway, it's no problem getting out."

"How about getting in? You real clever with auto locks?"

"That might be a problem," he admitted. "Does everybody lock their car nowadays?"

"I bet the ones who live in gated communities do. Not when they're home safe, but when they're out and about in a dangerous place like the suburbs of Phoenix. How crazy are you about this plan, Keller?"

"Not too," he admitted.

"Because how would you even know they were going back? Your luck, they're on their way to spend two weeks in Las Vegas."

"I didn't think of that."

"Of course you'd know right away," she said, "when you tried to get in the trunk and it was full of suitcases and copies of *Beat the Dealer*."

"It's not a great plan," he allowed, "but you wouldn't believe the security. The only other thing I can think of is to buy a place."

"Buy a house there, you mean. I don't think the budget would cover it."

"I could keep it as an investment," he said, "and rent it out when I wasn't using it."

"Which would be what, fifty-two weeks a year?"

"But if I could afford to do all that," he said, "I could also afford to tell the client to go roll his hoop, which I'm thinking I might have to go and do anyway."

"Because it's looking difficult."

"It's looking impossible," he said, "and then on top of everything else . . ."

"Yes? Keller? Where'd you go? Hello?"

"Never mind," he said. "I just figured out how to do it."

"As you can see," Mitzi Prentice said, "the view's nowhere near as nice as the Lattimore house. And there's just two bedrooms instead of three, and the furnishing's a little on the generic side. But compared to spending the next two weeks in a motel—"

"It's a whole lot more comfortable," he said.

"And more secure," she said, "just in case you've got your stamp collection with you."

"I don't," he said, "but a little security never hurt anybody. I'd like to take it."

"I don't blame you, it's a real good deal, and nice income for Mr. and Mrs. Sundstrom, who're in the Galapagos Islands looking at blue-footed boobies. That's where all the crap on their walls comes from. Not the Galapagos, but other places they go to on their travels."

"I was wondering."

"Well, they could tell you about each precious piece, but they're not here, and if they were then their place wouldn't be available, would it? We'll go to the office and fill out the paperwork, and then you can give me a check and I'll give you a set of keys and some ID to get you past the guard at the gate. And a pass to the clubhouse, and information on greens fees and all. I hope you'll have some time for golf."

"Oh, I should be able to fit in a few rounds."

"No telling what you'll be able to fit in," she said. "Speaking of which, let's fit in a quick stop at the Lattimore house before we start filling out lease agreements. And no, silly, I'm not trying to get you to buy that place. I just want you to take me into that bedroom again. I mean, you don't expect me to do it in Cynthia Sundstrom's bed, do you? With all those weird masks on the wall? It'd give me the jimjams for sure. I'd feel like primitive tribes were watching me."

The Sundstrom house was a good deal more comfortable than his motel, and he found he didn't mind being surrounded by souvenirs of the couple's travels. The second bedroom, which evidently served as Harvey Sundstrom's den, had a collection of edged weapons hanging on the walls, knives and daggers and what he supposed were battle-axes, and there was no end of carved masks and tapestries in the other rooms. Some of the masks looked godawful, he supposed, but they weren't the sort of things to give him the jimjams, whatever the jimjams might be, and he got in the habit of acknowledging one of them, a West African mask with teeth like tombstones and a lot of rope fringe for hair. He found himself giving it a nod when he passed it, even raising a hand in a salute.

Pretty soon, he thought, he'd be talking to it.

Because it was becoming clear to him that he felt the need to talk to someone. It was, he supposed, a need he'd had all his life, but for years he'd led an existence that didn't much lend itself to sharing confidences. He'd spent virtually all his adult life as a paid assassin, and it was no line of work for a man given to telling his business to strangers—or to friends, for that matter. You did what they paid you to do and you kept your mouth shut, and that was about it. You didn't talk about your work, and it got so you didn't talk about much of anything else, either. You could go to a sports bar and talk about the game with the fellow on the next barstool, you could gripe about the weather to the woman standing alongside you at the bus stop, you could complain about the mayor to the waitress at the corner coffee shop, but if you wanted a conversation with a little more substance to it, well, you were pretty much out of luck.

Once, a few years ago, he'd let someone talk him into going to a psychotherapist. He'd taken what struck him as reasonable precautions, paying cash, furnishing a false name and address, and essentially limiting disclosures to his childhood. It was productive, too, and he developed some useful insights, but in the end it went bad, with the therapist drawing some unwelcome inferences and eventually following Keller, and learning things he wasn't supposed to know about him. The man wanted to become a client himself, and of course Keller couldn't allow that, and made him a quarry instead. So much for therapy. So much for shared confidences.

Then, for some months after the therapist's exit, he'd had a dog. Not Soldier, the dog of his boyhood years, but Nelson, a fine Australian cattle dog. Nelson had turned out to be not only the perfect companion but the perfect confidante. You could tell him anything, secure in the knowledge that he'd keep it to himself, and it wasn't like talking to yourself or talking to the wall, because the dog was real and alive and gave every indication of paying close attention. There were times when he could swear Nelson understood every word.

He wasn't judgmental, either. You could tell him anything and he didn't love you any the less for it.

If only it had stayed that way, he thought. But it hadn't, and he supposed it was his own fault. He'd found someone to take care of Nelson when work took him out of town, and that was better than putting him in a kennel, but then he wound up falling for the dog walker, and she moved in, and he only really got to talk to Nelson when Andria was somewhere else. That wasn't too bad, and she was fun to have around, but then one day it was time for her to move on, and on she moved. He'd bought her no end of earrings during their time together, and she took the earrings along with her when she left, which was okay. But she also took Nelson, and there he was, right back where he started.

Another man might have gone right out and got himself another dog—and then, like as not, gone looking for a woman to walk it for him. Keller figured enough was enough. He hadn't replaced the therapist, and he hadn't replaced the dog, and, although women drifted in and out of his life, he hadn't replaced the girlfriend. He had, after all, lived alone for years, and it worked for him.

Most of the time, anyway.

"Now this is nice," Keller said. "The suburbs go on for a ways, but once you get past them you're out in the desert, and as long as you stay off the Interstate you've pretty much got the whole place to yourself. It's pleasant, isn't it?"

There was no answer from the passenger seat.

"I paid cash for the Sundstrom house," he went on. "Two weeks, a thousand dollars a week. That's more than a motel, but I can cook my own meals and save on restaurant charges. Except I like to go out for my meals. But I didn't drag you all the way out here to listen to me talk about stuff like that."

Again, his passenger made no response, but then he hadn't expected one.

"There's a lot I have to figure out," he said. "Like what I'm going to do with the rest of my life, for starters. I don't see how I can keep on doing what I've been doing all these years. If you think of it as killing people, taking lives, well, how could a person go on doing it year after year after year?

"But the thing is, see, you don't have to dwell on that aspect of the work. I mean, face it, that's what it is. These people are walking around, doing what they do, and then I come along, and whatever it is they've been doing, they don't get to do it anymore. Because they're dead, because I killed them."

He glanced over, looking for a reaction. Yeah, right.

"What happens," he said, "is you wind up thinking of each subject not as a person to be killed but as a problem to be solved. Here's this piece of work you have to do, and how do you get it done? How do you carry out the contract as expediently as possible, with the least stress all around?

"Now there are guys doing this," he went on, "who cope with it by making it personal. They find a reason to hate the guy they have to kill. They're mad at him, they're angry with him, because it's his fault that they've got to do this bad thing. If it weren't for him, they wouldn't be committing this sin. He's going to be the cause of them going to hell, the son of a bitch, so of course they're mad at him, of course they hate him, and that makes it easier for them to kill him, which is what they made up their minds to do in the first place.

"But that always struck me as silly. I don't know what's a sin and what isn't, or if one person deserves to go on living and another deserves to have his life ended. Sometimes I think about stuff like that, but as far as working it all out in my mind, well, I never seem to get anywhere.

"I could go on like this, but the thing is I'm okay with the moral aspects of it, if you want to call it that. I just think I'm getting a little old to be still at it, that's part of it, and the other's that the business has changed. It's the same in that there are still people who are willing to pay to have other people killed. You never have to worry about running out of clients. Sometimes business drops off for a while, but it always comes back again. Whether it's a guy like that Cuban in Miami, who must have had a hundred guys with a reason to want him dead, or this Egmont with his pot belly and his golf clubs, who you'd think would be unlikely to inspire strong feelings in anybody. All kinds of subjects, and all kinds of clients, and you never run out of either one."

The road curved, and he took the curve a little too fast, and had to reach over with his right hand to reposition his silent companion.

"You should be wearing your seat belt," he said. "Where was I? Oh, the way the business is changing. It's the world, really. Airport security, having to show ID everywhere you go. And gated communities, and all the rest of it. You think of Daniel Boone, who knew it was time to head west when he couldn't cut down a tree without giving some thought to which direction it was going to fall.

"I don't know, it seems to me that I'm just running off at the mouth, not making any sense. Well, that's okay. What do you care? Just so long as I take it easy on the curves so you don't wind up on the floor, you'll be perfectly willing to sit there and listen as long as I want to talk. Won't you?"

No response.

"If I played golf," he said, "I'd be out on the course every day, and I wouldn't have to burn up a tankful of gas driving around the desert. I'd spend all my time within the Sundowner walls, and I wouldn't have been walking around the mall, wouldn't have seen you in the display next to the cash register. A batch of different breeds on sale, and I'm not sure what you're supposed to be, but I guess you're some kind of terrier. They're good dogs, terriers. Feisty, lots of personality.

"I used to have an Australian cattle dog. I called him Nelson. Well, that was his name before I got him, and I didn't see any reason to change it. I don't think I'll give you a name. I mean, it's nutty enough, buying a stuffed animal, taking it for a ride and having a conversation with it. It's not as if you're going to answer to a name, or as if I'll relate to you on a deeper level if I hang a name on you. I mean, I may be crazy but I'm not stupid. I realize I'm talking to polyester and foam rubber, or whatever the hell you're made out of. Made in China, it says on the tag. That's another thing, everything's made in China or Indonesia or the Philippines, nothing's made in America anymore. It's not that I'm paranoid about it, it's not that I'm worried about all the jobs going overseas. What do I care, anyway? It's not affecting my work. As far as I know, nobody's flying in hired killers from Thailand and Korea to take jobs away from good homegrown American hit men.

"It's just that you have to wonder what people in this country are doing. If they're not making anything, if everything's imported from someplace else, what the hell do Americans do when they get to the office?"

He talked for a while more, then drove around some in silence, then resumed the one-sided conversation. Eventually he found his way back to Sundowner Estates, circling the compound and entering by the southwestern gate.

Hi, Mr. Miller. Hello, Harry. Hey, whatcha got there? Cute little fella, isn't he? A present for my sister's little girl, my niece. I'll ship it to her tomorrow.

The hell with that. Before he got to the guard shack, he reached into the back seat for a newspaper and spread it over the stuffed dog in the passenger seat.

In the clubhouse bar, Keller listened sympathetically as a fellow named Al went over his round of golf, stroke by stroke. "What kills me," Al said, "is that I just can't put it all together. Like on the seventh hole this afternoon, my drive's smack down the middle of the fairway, and my second shot with a three-iron is hole-high and just off the edge of the green on the right. I'm not in the bunker, I'm past it, and I've got a good lie maybe ten, twelve feet from the edge of the green."

"Nice," Keller said, his voice carefully neutral. If it wasn't nice, Al could assume he was being ironic.

"Very nice," Al agreed, "and I'm lying two, and all I have to do is run it up reasonably close and sink the putt for a par. I could use a wedge, but why screw around? It's easier to take this little chipping iron I carry and run it up close."

"Uh-huh."

"So I run it up close, all right, and it doesn't miss the cup by more than two inches, but I played it too strong, and it picks up speed and rolls past the pin and all the way off the green, and I wind up farther from the cup than when I started."

"Hell of a thing."

"So I chip again, and pass the hole again, though not quite as badly. And by the time I'm done hacking away with my goddam putter I'm three strokes over par with a seven. Takes me two strokes to cover four hundred and forty yards and five more strokes to manage the last fifty feet."

"Well, that's golf," Keller said.

"By God, you said a mouthful," Al said. "That's golf, all right.

How about another round of these, Dave, and then we'll get ourselves some dinner? There's a couple of guys you ought to meet."

He wound up at a table with four other fellows. Al and a man named Felix were residents of Sundowner Estates, while the other two men were Felix's guests, seasonal residents of Scottsdale who belonged to one of the other local country clubs. Felix told a long joke, involving a hapless golfer driven to suicide by a bad round of golf. For the punch line, Felix held his wrists together and said, "What time?" and everybody roared. They all ordered steaks and drank beer and talked about golf and politics and how screwed-up the stock market was these days, and Keller managed to keep up his end of the conversation without anybody seeming to notice that he didn't know what the hell he was talking about.

"So how'd you do out there today?" someone asked him, and Keller had his reply all ready.

"You know," he said thoughtfully, "it's a hell of a thing. You can hack away like a man trying to beat a ball to death with a stick, and then you hit one shot that's so sweet and true that it makes you feel good about the whole day."

He couldn't even remember when or where he'd heard that, but it evidently rang true with his dinner companions. They all nodded solemnly, and then someone changed the subject and said something disparaging about Democrats, and it was Keller's turn to nod in agreement.

Nothing to it.

"So we'll go out tomorrow morning," Al said to Felix. "Dave, if you want to join us . . ."

Keller pressed his wrists together, said, "What time?" When the laughter died down he said, "I wish I could, Al. I'm afraid tomorrow's out. Another time, though."

"You could take a lesson," Dot said. "Isn't there a club pro? Doesn't he give lessons?"

"There is," he said, "and I suppose he does, but why would I want to take one?"

"So you could get out there and play golf. Protective coloration and all."

"If anyone sees me swinging a golf club," he said, "with or without a lesson, they'll wonder what the hell I'm doing here. But this way they just figure I fit in a round earlier in the day. Anyway, I don't want to spend too much time around the clubhouse. Mostly I get the hell out of here and go for drives."

"On the driving range?"

"Out in the desert," she said.

"You just ride around and look at the cactus."

"There's a lot of it to look at," he said, "although they have a problem with poachers."

"You're kidding."

"No," he said, and explained how the cacti were protected, but criminals dug them up and sold them to florists.

"Cactus rustlers," Dot said. "That's the damnedest thing I ever heard of. I guess they have to be careful of the spines."

"I suppose so."

"Serve them right if they get stuck. You just drive around, huh?"

"And think things out."

"Well, that's nice. But you don't want to lose sight of the reason you moved in there in the first place."

He stayed away from the clubhouse the next day, and the day after. Then, on a Tuesday afternoon, he got in his car and drove around, staying within the friendly confines of Sundowner. He passed the Lattimore house and wondered if Mitzi Prentice had shown it to anyone lately. He drove past William Egmont's house, which looked to be pretty much the same model as the Sundstrom place. Egmont's Cadillac was parked in the carport, but the man owned his own golf cart, and Keller couldn't see it there. He'd probably motored over to the first tee on his cart, and might be out there now, taking big divots, slicing balls deep into the rough.

Keller went home, parked his Toyota in the Sundstrom carport. He'd worried, after taking the house for two weeks, that Mitzi would call all the time, or, worse, start turning up without calling first. But in fact he hadn't heard a word from her, for which he'd been deeply grateful, and now he found himself thinking about calling her, at work or at home, and figuring out a place to meet. Not at his place, because of the masks, and not at her place, because of her daughter, and—

That settled it. If he was starting to think like that, well, it was time he got on with it. Or the next thing you knew he'd be taking golf lessons, and buying the Lattimore house, and trading in the stuffed dog on a real one.

He went outside. The afternoon had already begun fading into early evening, and it seemed to Keller that the darkness came quicker here than it did in New York. That stood to reason, it was a good deal closer to the equator, and that would account for it. Someone had explained why to him once, and he'd understood it at the time, but now all that remained was the fact: the farther you were from the equator, the more extended twilight became.

In any event, the golfers were through for the day. He took a walk along the edge of the golf course, and passed Egmont's house. The car was still there, and the golf cart was not. He walked on for a while, then turned around and headed toward the house again, coming from the other direction, and saw someone gliding along on a motorized golf cart. Was it Egmont, on his way home? No, as the cart came closer he saw that the rider was thinner than Keller's quarry, and had a fuller head of hair. And the cart turned off before it reached Egmont's house, which pretty much cinched things.

Besides, he was soon to discover, Egmont had already returned. His cart was parked in the carport, alongside his car, and the bag of golf clubs was slung over the back of the cart. Something about that last touch reminded Keller of a song, though he couldn't pin down the song or figure out how it hooked up to the golf cart. Something mournful, something with bagpipes, but Keller couldn't put his finger on it.

There were lights on in Egmont's house. Was he alone? Had he brought someone home with him?

One easy way to find out. He walked up the path to the front door, poked the doorbell. He heard it ring, then didn't hear anything and considered ringing it again. First he tried the door, and found it locked, which was no great surprise, and then he heard footsteps, but just barely, as if someone was walking lightly on deep carpet. And then the door opened a few inches until the chain stopped it, and

William Wallis Egmont looked out at him, a puzzled expression on his face.

"Mr. Egmont?"

"Yes?"

"My name's Miller," he said. "David Miller. I'm staying just over the hill, I'm renting the Sundstrom house for a couple of weeks . . ."

"Oh, of course," Egmont said, visibly relaxing. "Of course, Mr. Miller. Someone was mentioning you just the other day. And I do believe I've seen you around the club. And out on the course, if I'm not mistaken."

It was a mistake Keller saw no need to correct. "You probably have," he said. "I'm out there every chance I get."

"As am I, sir. I played today and I expect to play tomorrow."

Keller pressed his wrists together, said, "What time?"

"Oh, very good," Egmont said. " 'What time?' That's a golfer for you, isn't it? Now how can I help you?"

"It's delicate," Keller said. "Do you suppose I could come in for a moment?"

"Well, I don't see why not," Egmont said, and slipped the chain lock to let him in.

The keypad for the burglar alarm was mounted on the wall, just to the right of the front door. Immediately adjacent to it was a sheet of paper headed HOW TO SET THE BURGLAR ALARM with the instructions hand-printed in block capitals large enough to be read easily by elderly eyes. Keller read the directions, followed them, and let himself out of Egmont's house. A few minutes later he was back in his own house—the Sundstrom house. He made himself a cup of coffee in the Sundstrom kitchen and sat with it in the Sundstrom living room, and while it cooled he let himself remember the last moments of William Wallis Egmont.

He practiced the exercises that were automatic for him by now, turning the images that came to mind from color to black and white, then watching them fade to gray, willing them farther and farther away so that they grew smaller and smaller until they were vanishing pinpoints, gray dots on a gray field, disappearing into the distance, swallowed up by the past.

When his coffee cup was empty he went into the Sundstrom bedroom and undressed, then showered in the Sundstrom bathroom, only to dry off with a Sundstrom towel. He went into the den, Harvey Sundstrom's den, and took a Fijian battle-axe from the wall. It was fashioned of black wood, and heavier than it looked, and its elaborate geometric shape suggested it would be of more use as wall decoration than weapon. But Keller worked out how to grip it and swing it, and took a few experimental whiffs with it, and he could see how the islanders would have found it useful.

He could have taken it with him to Egmont's house, and he let himself imagine it now, saw himself clutching the device in both hands and swinging around in a 360-degree arc, whipping the business end of the axe into Egmont's skull. He shook his head, returned the battle-axe to the wall, and resumed where he'd left off earlier, summoning up Egmont's image, reviewing the last moments of Egmont's life, and making it all gray and blurry, making it all smaller and smaller, making it all go away.

In the morning he went out for breakfast, returning in time to see an ambulance leaving Sundowner Estates through the east gate. The guard recognized Keller and waved him through, but he braked and rolled down the window to inquire about the ambulance. The guard shook his head soberly and reported the sad news.

He went home and called Dot. "Don't tell me," she said. "You've decided you can't do it."

"It's done."

"It's amazing how I can just sense these things," she said. "You figure it's psychic powers or old-fashioned feminine intuition? That was a rhetorical question, Keller. You don't have to answer it. I'd say I'll see you tomorrow, but I won't, will I?"

"It'll take me a while to get home."

"Well, no rush," she said. "Take your time, see the sights. You've got your clubs, haven't you?"

"My clubs?"

"Stop along the way, play a little golf. Enjoy yourself, Keller. You deserve it."

The day before his two-week rental was up, he walked over to the clubhouse, settled his account, and turned in his keys and ID card. He walked back to the Sundstrom house, where he put his suitcase in the trunk and the little stuffed dog in the passenger seat. Then he got behind the wheel and drove slowly around the golf course, leaving the compound by the east gate.

"It's a nice place," he told the dog. "I can see why people like it. Not just the golf and the weather and the security. You get the feeling nothing really bad could happen to you there. Even if you die, it's just part of the natural order of things."

He set cruise control and pointed the car toward Tucson, lowering the visor against the morning sun. It was, he thought, good weather for cruise control. Just the other day, he'd had NPR on the car radio, and listened as a man with a professionally mellow voice cautioned against using cruise control in wet weather. If the car were to hydroplane on the slick pavement, cruise control would think the wheels weren't turning fast enough, and would speed up the engine to compensate. And then, when the tires got their grip again, wham!

Keller couldn't recall the annual cost in lives from this phenomenon, but it was higher than you'd think. At the time all he did was resolve to make sure he took the car out of cruise control whenever he switched on the windshield wipers. Now, cruising east across the Arizona desert, he found himself wondering if there might be any practical application for this new knowledge. Accidental death was a useful tool, it had most recently claimed the life of William Wallis Egmont, but Keller couldn't see how cruise control in inclement weather could become part of his bag of tricks. Still, you never knew, and he let himself think about it.

In Tucson he stuck the dog in his suitcase before he turned in the car, then walked out into the heat and managed to locate his original car in long-term parking. He tossed his suitcase in the back seat and stuck the key in the ignition, wondering if the car would start. No problem if it wouldn't, all he'd have to do was talk to somebody at the Hertz counter, but suppose they'd just noticed him at the Avis counter, turning in another car. Would they notice something like that? You wouldn't think so, but airports were different these days. There were people standing around noticing everything.

He turned the key, and the engine turned over right away. The woman at the gate figured out what he owed and sounded apologetic when she named the figure. He found himself imagining what the charges would have added up to on other cars he'd left in long-term lots, cars he'd never returned to claim, cars with bodies in their trunks. Probably a lot of money, he decided, and nobody to pay it. He figured he could afford to pick up the tab for a change. He paid cash, took the receipt, and got back on the Interstate.

As he drove, he found himself figuring out just how he'd have handled it if the car hadn't started. "For God's sake," he said, "look at yourself, will you? Something could have happened but didn't, it's over and done with, and you're figuring out what you would have done, developing a coping strategy when there's nothing to cope with. What the hell's the matter with you?"

He thought about it. Then he said, "You want to know what's the matter with you? You're talking to yourself, that's what's the matter with you."

He stopped doing it. Twenty minutes down the road he pulled into a rest area, leaned over the seat back, opened his suitcase, and returned the dog to its position in the passenger seat.

"And away we go," he said.

In New Mexico he got off the Interstate and followed the signs to an Indian pueblo. A plump woman, her hair braided and her face expressionless, sat in a room with pots she had made herself. Keller picked out a little black pot with scalloped edges. She wrapped it carefully for him, using sheets of newspaper, and put the wrapped pot in a brown paper bag, and the paper bag into a plastic bag. Keller tucked the whole thing away in his suitcase and got back behind the wheel.

"Don't ask," he told the dog.

Just over the Colorado state line it started to rain. He drove through the rain for ten or twenty miles before he remembered the guy on NPR. He tapped the brake, which made the cruise control cut out, but just to make sure he used the switch, too.

"Close one," he told the dog.

In Kansas he took a state road north and visited a roadside attraction, a house that had once been a hideout of the Dalton boys. They were outlaws, he knew, contemporaries of the Jesse James and the Youngers. The place was tricked out as a mini museum, with memorabilia and news clippings, and there was an underground passage leading from the house to the barn in back, so that the brothers, when surprised by the law, could hurry through the tunnel and escape that way. He'd have liked to see the passage, but it was sealed off.

"Still," he told the woman attendant, "it's nice to know it's there."

If he was interested in the Daltons, she told him, there was another museum at the other end of the state. At Coffeyville, she said, where as he probably knew most of the Daltons were killed, trying to rob two banks in one day. He had in fact known that, but only because he'd just read it on the information card for one of the exhibits.

He stopped at a gas station, bought a state map, and figured out the route to Coffeyville. Halfway there he stopped for the night at a Red Roof Inn, had a pizza delivered, and ate it in front of the television set. He ran the cable channels until he found a western that looked promising, and damned if it didn't turn out to be about the Dalton boys. Not just the Daltons—Frank and Jesse James were in it, too, and Cole Younger and his brothers.

They seemed like real nice fellows, too, the kind of guys you wouldn't mind hanging out with. Not a sadist or pyromaniac in the lot, as far as he could tell. And did you think Jesse James wet the bed? Like hell he did.

In the morning he drove on to Coffeyville and paid the admission charge and took his time studying the exhibits. It was a pretty bold act, robbing two banks at once, but it might not have been the smartest move in the history of American crime. The local citizens were just waiting for them, and they riddled the brothers with bullets. Most of them were dead by the time the shooting stopped, or died of their wounds before long.

Emmett Dalton wound up with something like a dozen bullets in him, and went off to prison. But the story didn't end there. He recovered, and eventually got released, and wound up in Los Angeles, where he wrote films for the young motion picture industry and made a small fortune in real estate.

Keller spent a long time taking that in, and it gave him a lot to think about.

Most of the time he was quiet, but now and then he talked to the dog.

"Take soldiers," he said, on a stretch of 1-40 east of Des Moines. "They get drafted into the army, they go through basic training, and before you know it they're aiming at other soldiers and pulling the trigger. Maybe they have to force themselves the first couple of times, and maybe they have bad dreams early on, but then they get used to it, and before you know it they sort of enjoy it. It's not a sex thing, they don't get that kind of a thrill out of it, but it's sort of like hunting. Except you just pull the trigger and leave it at that. You don't have to track wounded soldiers to make sure they don't suffer. You don't have to dress your kill and pack it back to camp. You just pull the trigger and get on with your life.

"And these are ordinary kids," he went on. "Eighteen-year-old boys, drafted fresh out of high school. Or I guess it's volunteers now, they don't draft them anymore, but it amounts to the same thing. They're just ordinary American boys. They didn't grow up torturing animals or starting fires. Or wetting the bed.

"You know something? I still don't see what wetting the bed has to do with it."

Coming into New York on the George Washington Bridge, he said, "Well, they're not there."

The towers, he meant. And of course they weren't there, they were gone, and he knew that. He'd been down to the site enough times to know it wasn't trick photography, that the twin towers were in fact gone. But somehow he'd half expected to see them, half expected the whole thing to turn out to have been a dream. You couldn't make part of the skyline disappear, for God's sake.

He drove to the Hertz place, returned the car. He was walking away from the office with his suitcase in hand when an attendant rushed up, brandishing the little stuffed dog. "You forgot somethin'," the man said, smiling broadly.

"Oh, right," Keller said. "You got any kids?"

"Me?"

"Give it to your kid," Keller told him. "Or some other kid."

"You don't want him?"

He shook his head, kept walking. When he got home he showered and shaved and looked out the window. His window faced east, not south, and had never afforded a view of the towers, so it was the same as it had always been. And that's why he'd looked, to assure himself that everything was still there, that nothing had been taken away.

It looked okay to him. He picked up the phone and called Dot.

She was waiting for him on the porch, with the usual pitcher of iced tea. "You had me going," she said. "You didn't call and you didn't call and you didn't call. It took you the better part of a month to get home. What did you do, walk?"

"I didn't leave right away," he said. "I paid for two weeks."

"And you wanted to make sure you got your money's worth."

"I thought it'd be suspicious, leaving early. 'Oh, I remember that guy, he left four days early, right after Mr. Egmont died.' "

"And you thought it'd be safer to hang around the scene of a homicide?"

"Except it wasn't a homicide," he said. "The man came home after an afternoon at the golf course, locked his door, set the burglar alarm, got undressed and drew a hot bath. He got into the tub and lost consciousness and drowned."

"Most accidents happen in the home," Dot said. "Isn't that what they say? What did he do, hit his head?"

"He may have smacked it on the tile on the way down, after he lost his balance. Or maybe he had a little stroke. Hard to say."

"You undressed him and everything?"

He nodded. "Put him in the tub. He came to in the water, but I picked up his feet and held them in the air, and his head went under, and, well, that was that."

"Water in the lungs."

"Right."

"Death by drowning."

He nodded.

"You okay, Keller?"

"Me? Sure, I'm fine. Anyway, I figured I'd wait the four days, leave when my time was up."

"Just like Egmont."

"Huh?"

"He left when his time was up," she said. "Still, how long does it take to drive home from Phoenix? Four, five days?"

"I got sidetracked," he said, and told her about the Dalton boys.

"Two museums," she said. "Most people have never been to one Dalton boys museum, and you've been to two."

"Well, they robbed two banks at once."

"What's that got to do with it?"

"I don't know. Nothing, I guess. You ever hear of Nashville, Indiana?"

"I've heard of Nashville," she said, "and I've heard of Indiana, but I guess the answer to your questions is no. What have they got in Nashville, Indiana? The Grand Ole Hoosier Opry?"

"There's a John Dillinger museum there."

"Jesus, Keller. What were you taking, an outlaw's tour of the Midwest?"

"There was a flyer for the place in the museum in Coffeyville, and it wasn't that far out of my way. It was interesting. They had the fake gun he used to break out of prison. Or it may have been a replica. Either way, it was pretty interesting."

"I'll bet."

"They were folk heroes," he said. "Dillinger and Pretty Boy Floyd and Baby Face Nelson."

"And Bonnie and Clyde. Have those two got a museum?"

"Probably. They were heroes the same as the Daltons and Youngers and Jameses, but they weren't brothers. Back in the nineteenth century it was a family thing, but then that tradition died out."

"Kids today," Dot said. "What about Ma Barker? Wasn't that around the same time as Dillinger? And didn't she have a whole houseful of bank-robbing brats? Or was that just in the movies?"

"No, you're right," he said. "I forgot about Ma Barker."

"Well, let's forget her all over again, so you can get to the point."

He shook his head. "I'm not sure there is one. I just took my time getting back, that's all. I had some thinking to do."

"And?"

He reached for the pitcher, poured himself more iced tea. "Okay," he said. "Here's the thing. I can't do this anymore."

"I can't say I'm surprised."

"I was going to retire a while ago," he said. "Remember?"

"Vividly."

"At the time," he said, "I figured I could afford it. I had money put aside. Not a ton, but enough for a little bungalow somewhere in Florida."

"And you could get to Denny's in time for the early bird special, which helps keep food costs down."

"You said I needed a hobby, and that got me interested in stamp collecting again. And before I knew it I was spending serious money on stamps."

"And that was the end of your retirement fund."

"It cut into it," he agreed. "And it's kept me from saving money ever since then, because any extra money just goes into stamps."

She frowned. "I think I see where this is going," she said. "You can't keep on doing what you've been doing, but you can't retire, either."

"So I tried to think what else I could do," he said. "Emmett Dalton wound up in Hollywood, writing movies and dealing in real estate."

"You working on a script, Keller? Boning up for the realtor's exam?"

"I couldn't think of a single thing I could do," he said. "Oh, I suppose I could get some kind of minimum-wage job. But I'm used to living a certain way, and I'm used to not having to work many hours. Can you see me clerking in a 7-Eleven?"

"I couldn't even see you sticking up a 7-Eleven, Keller."

"It might be different if I were younger."

"I guess armed robbery is a young man's job."

"If I were just starting out," he said, "I could take some entry-level job and work my way up. But I'm too old for that now. Nobody would hire me in the first place, and the jobs I'm qualified for, well, I wouldn't want them."

"'Do you want fries with that?' You're right, Keller. Somehow it just doesn't sound like you."

"I started at the bottom once. I started coming around and the old man found things for me to do. 'Richie's gotta see a man, so why don't you ride along with him, keep him company.' Or go see this guy, tell him we're not happy with the way he's been acting. Or he used to send me to the store to pick up candy bars for him. What was that candy bar he used to like?"

"Mars bars."

"No, he switched to those, but early on it was something else. They were hard to find, only a few stores had them. I think he was the only person I ever met who liked them. What the hell was the name of them? It's on the tip of my tongue."

"Hell of a place for a candy bar."

"Powerhouse," he said. "Powerhouse candy bars."

"The dentist's best friend," she said. "I remember them now. I wonder if they still make them."

" 'Do me a favor, kid, see if they got any of my candy bars downtown.' Then one day it was do me a favor, here's a gun, go see this guy and give him two in the head. Out of the blue, more or less, except by then he probably knew I'd do it. And you know something? It never occurred to me not to. 'Here's a gun, do me a favor.' So I took the gun and did him a favor."

"Just like that?"

"Pretty much. I was used to doing what he told me, and I just did. And that let him know I was somebody who could do that kind of thing. Because not everybody can."

"But it didn't bother you."

"I've been thinking about this," he said. "Reflecting, I guess you'd call it. I didn't let it bother me."

"That thing you do, fading the color out of the image and pushing it off in the distance . . ."

"It was later that I taught myself to do that," he said. "Earlier, well, I guess you'd just call it denial. I told myself it didn't bother me and made myself believe it. And then there was this sense of accomplishment. Look what I did, see what a man I am. Bang, and he's dead and you're not, there's a certain amount of exhilaration that comes with it."

"Still?"

He shook his head. "There's the feeling that you've got the job done, that's all. If it was difficult, well, you've accomplished something. If there are other things you'd rather be doing, well, now you can go home and do them."

"Buy stamps, see a movie."

"Right."

"You just pretended it didn't bother you," she said, "and then one day it didn't."

"And it was easy to pretend, because it never bothered me all that much. But yes, I just kept on doing it, and then I didn't have to pretend. This place I stayed in Scottsdale, there were all these masks on the walls. Tribal stuff, I guess they were. And I thought about how I started out wearing a mask, and before long it wasn't a mask, it was my own face."

"I guess I follow you."

"It's just a way of looking at it," he said. "Anyway, how I got here's not the point. Where do I go from here? That's the question."

"You had a lot of time to think up an answer."

"Too much time."

"I guess, with all the stops in Nashville and Coffee Pot."

"Coffeyville."

"Whatever. What did you come up with, Keller?"

"Well," he said, and drew a breath. "One, I'm ready to stop doing this. The business is different, with the airline security and people living behind stockade fences. And I'm different. I'm older, and I've been doing this for too many years."

"Okay."

"Two, I can't retire. I need the money, and I don't have any other way to earn what I need to live on."

"I hope there's a three, Keller, because one and two don't leave you much room to swing."

"What I had to do," he said, "was figure out how much money I need."

"To retire on."

He nodded. "The figure I came up with," he said, "is a million dollars."

"A nice round sum."

"That's more than I had when I was thinking about retirement the last time. I think this is a more realistic figure. Invested right, I could probably get a return of around fifty thousand dollars a year."

"And you can live on that?"

"I don't want that much," he said. "I'm not thinking in terms of around-the-world cruises and expensive restaurants. I don't spend a lot on clothes, and when I buy something I wear it until it's worn out."

"Or even longer."

"If I had a million in cash," he said, "plus what I could get for the apartment, which is probably another half million."

"Where would you move?"

"I don't know. Someplace warm, I suppose."

"Sundowner Estates?"

"Too expensive. And I wouldn't care to be walled in, and I don't play golf."

"You might, just to have something to do."

He shook his head. "Some of those guys loved golf," he said, "but others, you had the feeling they had to keep selling themselves on the idea, telling each other how crazy they were about the game. 'What time?' "

"How's that?"

"It's the punch line of a joke. It's not important. No, I wouldn't want to live there. But there are these little towns in New Mexico north of Albuquerque, up in the high desert, and you could buy a shack there or just pick up a mobile home and find a place to park it."

"And you think you could stand it? Out in the boonies like that?"

"I don't know. The thing is, say I netted half a million from the apartment, plus the million I saved. Say five percent, comes to seventy-five thousand a year, and yes, I could live fine on that."

"And your apartment's worth half a million?"

"Something like that."

"So all you need is a million dollars, Keller. Now I'd lend it to you, but I'm a little short this month. What are you going to do, sell your stamps?"

"They're not worth anything like that. I don't know what I've spent on the collection, but it certainly doesn't come to a million dollars, and you can't get back what you put into them, anyway."

"I thought they were supposed to be a good investment."

"They're better than spending the money on caviar and champagne," he said, "because you get something back when you sell them, but dealers have to make a profit, too, and if you get half your money back you're doing well. Anyway, I wouldn't want to sell them."

"You want to keep them. And keep on collecting?"

"If I had seventy-five thousand a year coming in," he said, "and if I lived in some little town in the desert, I could afford to spend ten or fifteen thousand a year on stamps."

"I bet northern New Mexico's full of people doing just that."

"Maybe not," he said, "but I don't see why I couldn't do it."

"You could be the first, Keller. Now all you need is a million dollars."

"That's what I was thinking."

"Okay, I'll bite. How're you going to get it?"

"Well," he said, "that pretty much answers itself, doesn't it? I mean, there's only one thing I know how to do."

"I think I get it," Dot said. "You can't do this anymore, so you've got to do it with a vengeance. You have to depopulate half the country in order to get out of the business of killing people."

"When you put it that way . . ."

"Well, there's a certain irony operating, wouldn't you say? But there's a certain logic there, too. You want to grab every high-ticket job that comes along, so that you can salt away enough cash to get out of the business once and for all. You know what it reminds me of?"

"What?"

"Cops," she said. "Their pensions are based on what they make the last year they work, so they grab all the overtime they can get their hands on, and then when they retire they can live in style. Usually we sit back and pick and choose, and you take time off between jobs, but that's not what you want to do now, is it? You want to do a job, come home, catch your breath, then turn around and do another one."

"Right."

"Until you can cash in at an even million."

"That's the idea."

"Or maybe a few dollars more, to allow for inflation."

"Maybe."

"A little more iced tea, Keller?"

"No, I'm fine."

"Would you rather have coffee? I could make coffee."

"No thanks."

"You sure?"

"Positive."

"You took a lot of time in Scottsdale. Did he really look just like the man in Monopoly?"

"In the photo. Less so in real life."

"He didn't give you any trouble?"

He shook his head. "By the time he had a clue what was happening, it was pretty much over."

"He wasn't on his guard at all, then."

"No. I wonder why he got on somebody's list."

"An impatient heir would be my guess. Did it bother you much, Keller? Before, during, or after?"

He thought about it, shook his head.

"And then you took your time getting out of there."

"I thought it made sense to hang around a few days. One more day and I could have gone to the funeral."

"So you left the day they buried him?"

"Except they didn't," he said. "He had the same kind of funeral as Mr. Lattimore."

"Am I supposed to know who that is?"

"He had a house I could have bought. He was cremated, and after a nondenominational service his ashes were placed in the water hazard."

"Just a five-iron shot from his front door."

"Well," Keller said. "Anyway, yes, I took my time getting home."

"All those museums."

"I had to think it all through," he said. "Figuring out what I want to do with the rest of my life."

"Of which today is the first day, if I remember correctly. Let me make sure I've got this straight. You're done feeding rescue workers at Ground Zero, and you're done going to museums for dead outlaws, and you're ready to get out there and kill one for the Gipper. Is that about it?"

"It's close enough."

"Because I've been turning down jobs left and right, Keller, and what I want to do is get on the horn and spread the word that we're ready to do business. We're not holding any two-for-one sales, but we're very much in the game. Am I clear on that?" She got to her feet. "Which reminds me. Don't go away."

She came back with an envelope and dropped it on the table in front of him. "They paid up right away, and it took you so long to get home I was beginning to think of it as my money. What's this?"

"Something I picked up on the way home."

She opened the package, took the little black clay pot in her hands. "That's really nice," she said. "What is it, Indian?"

"From a pueblo in New Mexico."

"And it's for me?"

"I got the urge to buy it," he said, "and then afterward I wondered what I was going to do with it. And I thought maybe you'd like it."

"It would look nice on the mantel," she said. "Or it would be handy to keep paperclips in. But it'll have to be one or the other, because there's no point in keeping paperclips on the mantel. You said you got it in New Mexico? In the town you're figuring to wind up in?"

He shook his head. "It was a pueblo. I think you have to be an Indian."

"Well, they do nice work. I'm very pleased to have it."

"Glad you like it."

"And you take good care of that," she said, pushing the envelope toward him. "It's the first deposit in your retirement fund. Though I suppose you'll want to spend some of it on stamps."

Two days later he was working on his stamps when the phone rang. "I'm in the city," she said. "Right around the corner from you, as a matter of fact."

She told him the name of the restaurant, and he went there and found her in a booth at the back, eating an ice cream sundae. "When I was a kid," she said, "they had these at Wohler's drugstore for thirty-five cents. It was five cents extra if you wanted walnuts on top. I'd hate to tell you what they get for this beauty, and walnuts weren't part of the deal, either."

"Nothing's the way it used to be."

"You're right about that," she said, "and a philosophical observation like that is worth the trip. But it's not why I came in. Here's the waitress, Keller. You want one of these?"

He shook his head, ordered a cup of coffee. The waitress brought it, and when she was out of earshot Dot said, "I had a call this morning."

"Oh?"

"And I was going to call you, but it wasn't anything to discuss on the phone, and I didn't feel right about telling you to come out to White Plains because I was pretty sure you'd be wasting your time. So I figured I'd come in, and have an ice cream sundae while I'm at it. It's worth the trip, incidentally, even if they do charge the earth for it. You sure you don't want one?"

"Positive."

"I got a call," she said, "from a guy we've worked with before, a broker, very solid type. And there's some work to be done, a nice upscale piece of work, which would put a nice piece of change in your retirement fund and one in mine, too."

"What's the catch?"

"It's in Santa Barbara, California," she said, "and there's a very narrow window operating. You'd have to do it Wednesday or Thursday, which makes it impossible, because it would take longer than that for you to drive there even if you left right away and only stopped for gas. I mean, suppose you drove it in three days, which is ridiculous anyway. You'd be wiped out when you got there, and you'd get there when, Thursday afternoon at the earliest? Can't be done."

"No."

"So I'll tell them no," she said, "but I wanted to check with you first."

"Tell them we'll do it," he said.

"Really?"

"I'll fly out tomorrow morning. Or tonight, if I can get something."

"You weren't ever going to fly again."

"I know."

"And then a job comes along . . ."

"Not flying just doesn't seem that important," he said. "Don't ask me why."

"Actually," she said, "I have a theory."

"Oh?"

"When the Towers came down," she said, "it was very traumatic for you. Same as it was for everybody else. You had to adjust to a new reality, and that's not easy to do. Your whole world went tilt, and for a while there you stayed off airplanes, and you went downtown and fed the hungry, and you bided your time and tried to figure out a way to get along without doing your usual line of work."

"And?"

"And time passed," she said, "and things settled down, and you adjusted to the way the world is now. While you were at it, you realized what you'll have to do if you're going to be in a position to retire. You thought things through and came up with a plan."

"Well, sort of a plan."

"And a lot of things which seemed very important a while ago, like not flying with all this security and ID checks and all, turn out to be just an inconvenience and not something to make you change your life around. You'll get a second set of ID, or you'll use real ID and find some other way to cover your tracks. One way or another, you'll work it out."

"I suppose," he said. "Santa Barbara. That's between L.A. and San Francisco, isn't it?"

"Closer to L.A. They have their own airport."

He shook his head. "They can keep it," he said. "I'll fly to LAX. Or Burbank, that's even better, and I'll rent a car and drive up to Santa Barbara. Wednesday or Thursday, you said?" He pressed his wrists together. " 'What time?' "

"What time? What do you mean, what time? What's so funny, anyway?"

"Oh, it's a joke one of the golfers told in the clubhouse in Scottsdale. This golfer goes out and he has the worst round of his life. He loses balls in the rough, he can't get out of sand traps, he hits ball after ball into the water hazard. Nothing goes right for him. By the time he gets to the eighteenth green all he's got left is his putter, because he's broken every other club over his knee, and after he four-putts the final hole he breaks the putter, too, and sends it flying.

"He marches into the locker room, absolutely furious, and he unlocks his locker and takes out his razor and opens it up and gets the blade in his hand and slashes both his wrists. And he stands there, watching the blood flow, and someone calls to him over the bank of lockers. 'Hey, Joe,' the guy says, 'we're getting up a foursome for tomorrow morning. You interested?' "

"And the guy says"—Keller raised his hands to shoulder height, pressed his wrists together—" 'What time?' "

" 'What time?' "

"Right."

" 'What time?' " She shook her head. "I like it, Keller. And any old time you want'll be just fine."